children
of the
matrix

**How an interdimensional race has controlled the
world for thousands of years – and still does**

**Bridge
of Love**

First published in May 2001 by

Bridge of Love Publications USA
1825 Shiloh Valley Drive
Wildwood
MO 63005
USA
Tel: 636-458-7824
Fax: 636-458-7823
email: bridgeloveUSA@aol.com

First reprint June 2001
Reprinted August 2001
Reprinted October 2001
Copyright © 2001 David Icke

Cover 'eye' illustration: Hilary Reed

Printed and bound by:
Bertelsmann Services, Inc.
Valencia, California, USA

British Library Cataloguing-in
Publication Data
A catalogue record for this book is
available from the British Library

ISBN 0 9538810 1 6

children
of the
matrix

How an interdimensional race has controlled the world for thousands of years – and still does

David Icke

This book is dedicated to:

Lauren and Jocelyn Savage for their magnificent and tireless work to make **www.davidicke.com** one of the biggest and most visited conspiracy websites in the world.

Royal Adams and Linda Icke for all their dedication to the cause of human freedom and their daily efforts to ensure that this information reaches the widest possible audience.

John Wragg and Sam Masters who have supported me for so many years and are always there whenever they can help.

To Pamela: thanks for understanding me – or as much as is possible!

To all those who have helped and supported me since 1991. Please don't take my silence as a lack of appreciation. I am sure you will understand that I am one guy and the need to focus total time and effort on what is required in the moment leaves so little time for remaining in contact with everyone. I hope you are all keeping well.

Photograph by Thearle Photography, Ryde, Isle of Wight

Other books, tapes and videos by David Icke

Details of availability at the back of this book

Who are the children of the matrix?

WE ARE.

"Ridicule is the tribute that mediocrity pays to genius."

Anon.

"All truth goes through three stages. First it is ridiculed. Then it is violently opposed. Finally it is accepted as self-evident."

Schoepenhouer

"Man will occasionally stumble over the truth, but most of the time he will pick himself up and continue on."

Winston Churchill

"When they think they know the answers, people are difficult to guide. When they know they don't know, people can find their own way."

Tao Te Ching

"Life can take many forms. Look at the forms life can take on this planet alone. Here in this bush, there are insects you could easily mistake for rocks or for pieces of bark – until one of them stings you, that is. Life does not have to consist of bipeds who move and breath and smoke cigars as we do. I have said it before and I say it again – the universe is a gigantic chamber of possibility where everything has the chance and the right to happen, and so we must not have cut-and-dry theories regarding just how life should look. Life could surprise us!"

Credo Mutwa
The official historian of the Zulu nation, in his book,
Song Of The Stars

Contents

Life beyond the bubble

There are two things you need if you are to uncover and communicate what is really happening in the world. One is to be free of any dogmatic belief system. The second is not to give a damn what people think and say about you, or, at least, not to let that influence your decisions.

Without number one you will never go into the bizarre areas that are necessary to understand the forces that control this planet. Once you are faced with information that demolishes your belief system you will begin to edit what you have discovered and refuse to go where it is taking you. Without number two, you will never communicate what you have found because you will be terrified of the consequences for you from the reaction of your friends, family and the public in general.

You are about to read a book by someone who will go wherever the information takes him and who, thanks to hard and extreme experience in the early 1990s, let go the concern for what other people might think of him. And so we are going to enter some apparently bizarre and outrageous areas of thought and documented evidence. If you have a belief-system to defend, please don't waste your time and money. This is not for you. But, in truth, what you are going to hear is not outrageous at all. It just appears to be so because it is so *different* from the conditioned "norm". Crazy and insane are words used throughout history to describe people and ideas that are simply *different*. And different does not mean *wrong*. So many condemned and ridiculed ideas in the past have later become conventional wisdom.

First they ridicule you; then they condemn you; then they say they knew you were right all along.

This book is designed to pull together the evidence and background of the extraterrestrial, inner-terrestrial, and interdimensional control of Planet Earth for thousands of years to the present day. To do this, I have weaved together information in *The Biggest Secret* with a mass of new historical and modern accounts, to present as clear a picture as possible of the forces that daily manipulate and direct the lives of the human race. This is not the whole story, however, just part of it. There is still so much more to know. Readers of my previous books will see information they already know fused with the latest knowledge and developments because it is important that my books are self contained so that new readers will have all they need to follow the plot. I have endeavoured to keep the book simple and to the point for those billions of people who have never had access to such information before. For more fine detail and sources on the various inter-connected subjects, see …*And The Truth Shall Set You Free, I Am Me, I Am Free,* and *The Biggest Secret.*

Please remember that what you read here is simply information. It is not compulsory to accept it and the last thing I am trying to do is persuade you to believe anything. What you believe is your business, not mine. Have I got all the answers? Of course not. Do I have some of them? See what you think.

David Icke
Ryde
Isle of Wight
January 1st 2001

The Matrix

Let me tell you why you're here.

You're here because you know something. What you know you can't explain but you feel it. You felt it your entire life. That there's something very wrong with the world. You don't know what it is – but it's there, like a splinter in your mind, driving you mad. It is this feeling that has brought you to me. Do you know what I'm talking about?

The Matrix?

Do you want to know what it is? The Matrix is everywhere. It is all around us. Even now, in this very room. You can see it when you look out your window or when you turn on your television. You can feel it when you go to work, when you go to church, when you pay your taxes. It is the world that has been pulled over your eyes to blind you from the truth.

What truth?

That you are a slave Neo. Like everyone else you were born into bondage. Born into a prison that you cannot smell or taste or touch – a prison for your mind. Unfortunately, no one can be told what the Matrix is – you have to see it for yourself …

… I'm trying to free your mind, Neo. But I can only show you the door. You're the one that has to walk through it.

Scenes from *The Matrix* (Warner Brothers, 1999). This is highly recommended along with *They Live* (Alive Films, 1988), the movie by John Carpenter, *The Arrival 1* (Steelworks Films, 1988), and *V: The Final Battle* (Warner Brothers Television, 1984, and Warner Home Video, 1995).

The challenge

Don Juan, the Mexican Yaqui Indian shaman, tells Carlos Castaneda the following:

"We have a predator that came from the depths of the cosmos and took over the rule of our lives. Human beings are its prisoners. The predator is our lord and master. It has rendered us docile, helpless. If we want to protest, it suppresses our protest. If we want to act independently, it demands that we don't do so... I have been beating around the bush all this time, insinuating to you that something is holding us prisoner. Indeed we are held prisoner!

"This was an energetic fact for the sorcerers of ancient Mexico ... They took us over because we are food for them, and they squeeze us mercilessly because we are their sustenance. Just as we rear chickens in chicken coops, the predators rear us in human coops, humaneros. Therefore, their food is always available to them."

"No, no, no, no," [Carlos replies] "This is absurd don Juan. What you're saying is something monstrous. It simply can't be true, for sorcerers or for average men, or for anyone."

"Why not?" don Juan asked calmly. "Why not? Because it infuriates you? ... You haven't heard all the claims yet. I want to appeal to your analytical mind. Think for a moment, and tell me how you would explain the contradictions between the intelligence of man the engineer and the stupidity of his systems of beliefs, or the stupidity of his contradictory behaviour. Sorcerers believe that the predators have given us our systems of belief, our ideas of good and evil, our social mores. They are the ones who set up our hopes and expectations and dreams of success or failure. They have given us covetousness, greed, and cowardice. It is the predators who make us complacent, routinary, and egomaniacal."

"'But how can they do this, don Juan?' [Carlos] asked, somehow angered further by what [don Juan] was saying. "Do they whisper all that in our ears while we are asleep?"

"'No, they don't do it that way. That's idiotic!" don Juan said, smiling. "They are infinitely more efficient and organized than that. In order to keep us obedient and meek and weak, the predators engaged themselves in a stupendous manoeuvre –

stupendous, of course, from the point of view of a fighting strategist. A horrendous manoeuvre from the point of view of those who suffer it. They gave us their mind! Do you hear me? The predators give us their mind, which becomes our mind. The predators' mind is baroque, contradictory, morose, filled with the fear of being discovered any minute now."

"I know that even though you have never suffered hunger… you have food anxiety, which is none other than the anxiety of the predator who fears that any moment now its manoeuvre is going to be uncovered and food is going to be denied. Through the mind, which, after all, is their mind, the predators inject into the lives of human beings whatever is convenient for them. And they ensure, in this manner, a degree of security to act as a buffer against their fear."

"The sorcerers of ancient Mexico were quite ill at ease with the idea of when [the predator] made its appearance on Earth. They reasoned that man must have been a complete being at one point, with stupendous insights, feats of awareness that are mythological legends nowadays. And then, everything seems to disappear, and we have now a sedated man. What I'm saying is that what we have against us is not a simple predator. It is very smart, and organized. It follows a methodical system to render us useless. Man, the magical being that he is destined to be, is no longer magical. He's an average piece of meat."

"There are no more dreams for man but the dreams of an animal who is being raised to become a piece of meat: trite, conventional, imbecilic."

Castaneda, 1998

The plot

Many thousands of years ago, way back in "pre-history", there was a highly developed civilisation in the Pacific, which has become known as Lemuria, or Mu. These peoples and others also founded another great culture on a landmass in the Atlantic, which we know as Atlantis.

The knowledge that created these advanced societies, the knowledge that built the fantastic and unexplainable ancient structures like the Great Pyramid and other amazing sites across the world, came from the stars – extraterrestrials of many varieties. Some were tall blond-haired, blue-eyed, types, while others took a reptilian form (see *picture section* for artists' impressions of these beings). These and others came here from constellations like Orion, Draco, Andromeda, Lyra, and Bootes, and other locations like the Pleiades, Sirius, Vega, Zeta Reticuli, Arcturus, Aldebaran, and elsewhere. Australian aborigines, African tribes, the Babylonians, and South American Indians are just some of the diverse peoples who claim ancient connections with such places. The reptilians are a tall, mostly humanoid-type race, with snake-like eyes and skin and they are connected to the classic "greys" with the big black "eyes", which have become the very symbol of the "ET". Often these various extraterrestrial factions battled for supremacy in the legendary "wars of the gods". These technologically advanced beings were believed to be gods by the human races because of the apparently miraculous feats they could achieve with their technology and flying craft. By the way, for those who find it impossible to conceive of "intelligent" life forms and humanoids taking a reptilian form, ponder on the words of the cosmologist, Carl Sagan: "There are more potential combinations of DNA (physical forms) than there are atoms in the universe." On that basis, given the fantastic diversity of the reptilian species on the Earth alone, it would be more amazing if there were *not* reptilians of a humanoid and intelligent variety.

These "gods" interbred with each other and the more primitive Earth people and these unions are recorded in endless ancient accounts. These were the Sons of God who interbred with the daughters of men to seed the hybrid race, the Nefilim, as described in the Old Testament book of Genesis. The most important interbreeding was between the reptilians and the blond-haired, blue-eyed, Nordic peoples, both of extraterrestrial origin, as an alliance was formed between factions of these races. The union produced what has been called the Aryan or "noble" race – the "master race" of the Nazis. This is the fusion of the Nordic and reptilian DNA (the genetic code that decides physical characteristics) and, as the ancient records confirm, it was these "royal" bloodlines, the reptilian-Nordic hybrids, that were placed in the positions of ruling royal power in the thousands of years before "known" history. They were the kings and queens who claimed the "divine right" to rule because of their bloodline – the bloodline of the gods. These ancient royal lines in places like Egypt, Sumer, and the Indus Valley, had a white skin and often blue eyes, yet they were known as the Dragon Kings or Serpent Kings by those who knew the secret of their hybrid nature.

Lemuria was destroyed by a staggering cataclysm that struck the Earth, maybe 11,500 to 12,000 years ago. Atlantis went the same way, in stages, over the thousands of years that followed. The universal stories of the Great Flood are related to this. When Atlantis came to an end amid more enormous geological upheavals, the bloodlines and their "gods" began again in the Near and Middle East from about 4,000BC with an empire based in Sumer in what is now Iraq, between the rivers Euphrates and Tigris. Sumer, according to official "history", was the start of human "civilisation", but, in fact, it was merely the re-start after the Atlantis upheavals. The seeding of extraterrestrial–human bloodlines continued and so did the policy of placing the purest of these hybrids, the reptilian-Nordics, into the positions of royal and administrative power over the people in Sumer, Egypt, Babylon, the Indus Valley, and, as the Sumer Empire expanded, much further afield. Similar seeding went on in other parts of the world, like the Americas and China, but the Middle Eastern area was the most important to these extraterrestrial factions (at least at that time). These factions were dominated by the reptilian or "serpent race".

Over thousands of years these peoples expanded out of the Middle and Near East into Europe and the "royal" bloodlines of Sumer, Egypt, etc., became the royal and aristocratic families of Britain, Ireland, and the countries of mainland Europe, especially France and Germany. Wherever they went, these "royal" lines interbred obsessively with each other through arranged marriages and secret breeding programmes. We see the same with the ruling families of today because they are seeking to perpetuate a particular genetic code, which can be quickly diluted by breeding outside of their hybrid circle. In the ancient world, one of the headquarters for the secret society network or Illuminati, through which these bloodlines manipulate humanity, was Babylon, also in the lands of Sumer. This Illuminati network then moved its headquarters to Rome and during that time came the Roman Empire and the creation of the Roman Church, or institutionalised Christianity. The headquarters moved on into northern Europe after the fall of the Roman Empire and for a period was based in Amsterdam, The Netherlands. This was when the Dutch began to build their empire through the Dutch East India Company and they settled South Africa. In 1688, one of these hybrid bloodlines, William of Orange, invaded England from The Netherlands and took the British throne as William III in 1689. William ruled jointly with Queen Mary and alone after her death in 1694. From this time, the Illuminati moved their centre of operations to London. What followed, of course, was the "Great" and enormous British Empire.

This vast expansion of the British and other European empires to all parts of the world exported these Nefilim hybrid bloodlines to every continent, including, most importantly today, to North America. When these European empires began to recede and collapse, especially in the 20th century, it appeared that these lands, like the Americas, Africa, and Australia, had won their "independence". Instead, the Nefilim bloodlines and the Illuminati merely exchanged overt control for the far more effective covert control. While these empires apparently withdrew, they left out in those countries, including the United States, the bloodlines and the secret society network through which they operate. Ever since they have continued to control events in these former colonies as part of a long-planned agenda for the complete centralised control of the planet through a world government, central bank, currency, army, and a micro-chipped population connected to a global computer. This is the very governmental structure that is now staring us in the face.

The bloodlines that control the world and our lives today are the same bloodlines that ruled Lemuria, Atlantis, Sumer, Egypt, Babylon, the Roman Empire, and the British and European empires. They are the presidents of the United States, the prime ministers, the leading banking and business families, the media owners, and those who control the military. We have been ruled by the same interbreeding tribe of extraterrestrial or inner-terrestrial hybrids, the Nefilim, for thousands of years and we are now facing a crucial time in their unfolding agenda:

The time when we, the people, either bring this hidden dictatorship to an end or face a future, very shortly, in a global fascist state.

That's the summary of what has happened and is happening. Now consider the detailed evidence…

CHAPTER 1

.to the
prison born

There are none so enslaved as those who falsely believe they are free.

Goethe

When a few people wish to control and direct a mass of humanity, there are certain key structures that have to be in place. These are the same whether you are seeking to manipulate an individual, family, tribe, town, country, continent, or planet.

First you have to set the "norms", what is considered right and wrong, possible or impossible, sane or insane, good and bad. Most of the people will follow those norms without question because of the baa-baa mentality, which has prevailed within the collective human mind for at least thousands of years. Second, you have to make life very unpleasant for those few who challenge your imposed "norms". The most effective way to do this is to make it, in effect, a crime to be different. So those who beat to a different drum, or voice a different view, version of "truth" and lifestyle, stand out like a black sheep in the human herd. You have already conditioned that herd to accept your norms as reality and so, in their arrogance and ignorance, they then ridicule or condemn those with a different spin on life. This pressurises them to conform and serves as a warning for those others in the herd who are also thinking of breaking away. There is a Japanese saying that goes: Don't be a nail that stands out above the rest because that's the first one to get hit.

This creates a situation fundamental to the few controlling the many in which the masses police themselves and keep each other in line. The sheep become the sheepdog for the rest of the herd.* It is like a prisoner trying to escape while the rest of his cellmates rush to stop him. If that happened we would say the prisoners were crazy, how could they do that? But humans are doing precisely this to each other every day by demanding that everyone conform to the norms to which *they* blindly conform. This is nothing less than psychological fascism – the thought police with agents in every home, everywhere. Agents so deeply conditioned that most have no idea they are unpaid mind controllers. "I'm just doing what's right for my children" I hear them say. No, what you have been *programmed* to believe is right for them and

---

* I know that strictly speaking the collective word for sheep is flock and not herd, but I prefer herd so sod convention.

the belief, also, that only you know best. I remember debating with a former Chief Rabbi of the United Kingdom at the Oxford Union debating society and he simply could not see a difference between education and indoctrination. It was a wonder to behold.

We see this same theme in our daily experiences of people in uniform and others from the masses who are promoted to power over the masses. It's summed up by the satirical version of the British Labour Party song, *The Red Flag*, which goes: "The working class can kiss my arse, I've got the foreman's job at last." This is all part of the divide and rule strategy so vital to ensuring that the herd will police itself. Everyone plays a part in everyone else's mental, emotional, and physical imprisonment. All the controllers have to do is pull the right strings at the right time and make their human puppets dance to the appropriate tune. This they do by dictating what is taught by what we bravely call "education" and what passes for "news" through the media they own. In this way they can dictate to the unthinking, unquestioning, herd what it should believe about itself, other people, life, history, and current events. Once you set the norms in society, there is no need to control every journalist or reporter or government official. The media and the institutions take their "truth" from those same norms and therefore ridicule and condemn by reflex action anyone who offers another vision of reality. Once you control what is considered "normal" and possible, the whole system virtually runs itself.

The Illuminati

The elite families, no more than 13 at the peak of their pyramid, created and manipulate this system of control through a network of secret societies. This network and the bloodlines it serves have become known as the Illuminati, the "Illuminated Ones". In other words they are illuminated into knowledge that everyone else is denied. The Illuminati is an organisation within all significant organisations. It's like a cancer. All the major secret societies feed carefully chosen recruits into the Illuminati and these are the ones you find in positions of power throughout the world. They infest all colours, creeds, and countries. Most Freemasons never progress higher than the bottom three levels of degree, the so-called Blue Degrees. They have no idea what their organisation is being used for. Even most of those who make it to the apparent peak, the 33rd degree in the Scottish Rite, know relatively little. Only the tiny few, all from a particular bloodline, move through the top of their "individual" secret society into the Illuminati degrees above that. These are the levels into which all the major secret societies feed. Yet at least 95% of their members have no idea that these levels exist, never mind who is in them.

The bloodlines

The Illuminati bloodlines are all genetically connected through hybrid DNA, a genetic fusion caused by the interbreeding of a reptilian race with humanity and the Nordic extraterrestrial race. This interbreeding began hundreds of thousands of years ago and continues to the present day. If you are hearing this for the first time,

I know how bizarre and crazy it sounds to the conditioned view of reality. But you will see in the pages that follow the scale of the evidence to support this apparently ridiculous story and how it explains a stream of ancient and modern "mysteries". So many things that later turn out to be true appear at first hearing to be impossible and insane. That's because people only hear the opening line and don't read on to see the detailed evidence to support it. When people first suggested the Earth was round, they were called crazy because it was thought that those living on the bottom would have fallen off. The critics dismissed the idea at this point and walked away convinced that the Earth had to be flat. Yet when you introduce the law of gravity, what seems at first to be crazy suddenly becomes far more credible. So it is with the truth that a non-human race is controlling and manipulating humanity through hybrid bloodlines – the same bloodlines that have been placed in positions of power since ancient times. The supporting evidence is there if only people are prepared to open their minds, as you will see in this book and my others.

It is these reptilian-Illuminati bloodlines, manifesting as political leaders and administrators of government, that introduce the "laws" that will best serve their plan to keep humanity in ongoing servitude. These laws, which the masses have no say in creating, are then enforced by members of those same masses – soldiers, policemen, security guards, and so on. These guys, and many women today, are just system-fodder. They are not encouraged to think for themselves and it would not be good for promotion if they did. They are paid to do as they are told, carry out orders, and administer the letter of the "law": the law of the elite families. My father used to say that rules and regulations were for the guidance of the intelligent and the blind obedience of the idiot. But how many of those in the peaked caps administer the law in a sensible, every-case-on-its-merits, think-for-yourself manner? A mere fraction. And often they are far from popular with those higher up the ladder. Soldiers don't ask for justification for blowing away men, women, and children they have never met and know nothing about. They don't question their superiors about why they have to commit genocide. They just do it because they are told to do it and those doing the telling are themselves carrying out orders from those above them. In the end, all roads of command lead ever upwards to the 13 family bloodlines and their offshoots that are orchestrating an agenda to take over the planet. That agenda demands a world government, central bank, currency, and army, underpinned by a micro-chipped population connected to a global computer network. A ridiculous conspiracy "theory"? Oh really? Well have another look around you and you'll see that this is happening today, NOW.

The sheeple

The self-policing of the human herd goes far deeper than people in uniform or administrators of government. It starts with conditioned parents who impose their conditioning on their children and pressure them to follow their religious, political, economic, and cultural norms. There is no more extreme example than those who insist their offspring succumb to arranged marriages because of the rules of their ludicrous religion; or the children of Jehovah's Witnesses who have been denied life-saving blood transfusions because their brain-dead parents insist on conducting every aspect of their lives according to the contradictory dictates of a book purveying stories of pure fantasy. The creation of the mental and emotional sheep pen of norms, which imprisons 99% of humanity, goes on minute by minute in subtle and less subtle ways. There are children of Christian, Jewish, Muslim, or Hindu parents who don't accept the religion, but still follow it because they don't want to upset their family. Then there is the almost universal fear of what people think of us if we speak a different version of reality or live a different kind of life. Note that the fear for those who wish to break out of the sheep pen is not the fear of what the elite families, the Illuminati or "Illuminated Ones", will think of them. Most have no idea that such a network exists. No, the fear is for what their mother or father will think, or their friends and workmates – the very people who are conditioned by the system to stay in the pen. The sheep are keeping the other sheep in line and making life unpleasant for anyone who tries to escape. It is so easy for a small group of interbreeding family bloodlines to control the lives – in other words the minds – of billions, once the key institutions of "information" are in place, as they have been for thousands of years in their various forms. There are not enough of these manipulators and their stooges to control the population physically and so they have had to create a structure in which humans control themselves through mental and emotional imposition.

Once you have the herd mentality policing itself, there is a third phase in this entrapment of human consciousness. You create factions within the herd and set them to war with each other. This is done by creating "different" belief systems (which are not different at all) and bringing them into conflict. These belief systems are known as religions, political parties, economic theories, countries, cultures, and "isms" of endless variety. These beliefs are perceived as "opposites" when, as I pointed out in my book, *I Am Me, I Am Free,* they are opposames. The vision of reality and possibility within the pen is so limited that it contains no opposites. So the elite have to create the perception of them to manufacture the divisions that allow them to divide and rule. I mean, what is the difference between a Christian bishop, Jewish Rabbi, Muslim or Hindu priest, or a follower of Buddha, imposing their beliefs on their children and others? There is none because while the belief they seek to indoctrinate may be slightly different, often very slightly, the overall theme is exactly the same – the imposition of one person's belief on another. Look at the opposames in politics. The Far Left, as symbolised by Josef Stalin in Russia, introduced centralised control, military dictatorship, and concentration camps. The "opposite" of that was the Far Right, as symbolised by Adolf Hitler. What was he into? Centralised control, military dictatorship, and concentration camps. Yet these two opposames were set at war with each other amid propaganda that claimed they were opposites. The only difference between the Soviet Union and the so-called "West" during the Cold War was that the Soviet Union was openly controlled by the few and the West was secretly controlled by the few. And, when you get to the capstone of the pyramid, you find they were the *same* few

The Pyramid of Manipulation

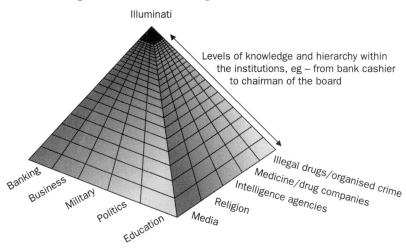

Figure 1: *The interconnecting pyramids that allow the few to manipulate the lives of billions. At the highest level, all the major political, financial, and media institutions are controlled by the Illuminati*

controlling both "sides". The same force operating through Wall Street and the City of London funded all "sides" in the two world wars and that's provable (see ...*And The Truth Shall Set You Free*).

So let us summarise the scam. (a) You need to first imprison the human mind with a rigid belief and a fundamentally limited sense of reality – the sheep pen. It doesn't much matter what these beliefs may be, so long as they are rigid and discourage free thought and open-minded questions. Christianity, Judaism, Islam, Hinduism, and all the rest, each make their contribution to human servitude while apparently claiming different "truths". (b) You encourage those who follow these rigid beliefs to impose them on others and make life very difficult and unpleasant for anyone who does not conform. (c) You bring these beliefs into conflict, so ensuring the divide and rule you so desperately need for control by the few. While the masses are so busy fighting each other and seeking to impose their beliefs and views on each other, they don't see that the Illuminati have strings attached to all of them. Humans are like moths buzzing around a light, so mesmerised by their religious belief, the football scores, the latest row on a soap opera, or the price of friggin' beer, that they fail to notice the preparations being made to smash them on the arse with a swatter.

Pyramids within pyramids

The Illuminati have created a pyramid structure throughout society that allows them to operate a global agenda that only a relative handful of people know exists. It is like those Russian dolls with one doll inside another with the biggest one encompassing all of them. The Illuminati replace the "dolls" with pyramids (*Figure 1*). Every organisation today is a pyramid. The few at the top know what the organisation is really about and what it is trying to achieve. The further you go down the pyramid the more people work for the organisation, but the less they know about its real agenda. They are only aware of the individual job they do every day. They have no idea how their contribution connects with that of other employees in other areas of the company. They are compartmentalised from that knowledge and told only what they need to know to do their work. These smaller pyramids, like the local branch of a bank, fit into bigger and bigger pyramids, until eventually you have the pyramid that encompasses all the banks. It is the same with the transnational corporations, political parties, secret societies, media empires, and the military. If you go high enough, all the transnational corporations (like the oil cartel), major political parties, secret societies, media empires, and the military (via NATO, for instance), are controlled by the same pyramids and the same people who sit at the top of all the pyramids. In the end there is a global pyramid that encompasses all the others, the biggest "doll" if you like. At the top of this you will find the most elite of the Illuminati, the "purest" of their bloodlines. In this way, they can co-ordinate through apparently unconnected, even "opposing" areas of society, the same policies. This is how they have created the explosion of centralisation in every area of life: government, finance, business, media, military. It is not by accident or natural occurrence. It is by coldly calculated design.

Jim Shaw, a former 33rd degree Freemason, exposes the Craft in his book, *The Deadly Deception* (Huntington House Inc., Lafayette, Louisiana, 1988). He describes how Freemasonry is based on the same compartmentalised pyramids. At the bottom are the three degrees known as the Blue Degrees and the vast majority of Freemasons never progress beyond that through either the 33 degrees of the Scottish Rite or the 10 degrees of the York Rite.* Even at the 33rd degree of Freemasonry you still don't know the real secrets unless you are one of the chosen few (bloodline). Shaw says he was surprised when a fellow 33rd degree Mason said that "they" had told him he was "going higher" and the guy left the temple by a "different door".[1] There is, officially, no higher than the 33rd degree. But, of course there is. The top levels of the secret societies are only the top of their pyramid. They are also encompassed by a bigger pyramid, which includes all the secret societies and they feed their chosen bloodline initiates into the unofficial Illuminati degrees where the real action and the real secrets are. But even at that level, the knowledge is still compartmentalised. So you have this vast web of secret societies with millions of members worldwide who think they know what they are involved in, but, in truth, only a tiny few have any idea of what is going on and who, ultimately, is calling the shots. Albert Pike, who died in 1891, was one of the most pre-eminent figures in world Freemasonry. Among his titles were Sovereign Grand Commander of the Supreme Council of the 33rd degree and Supreme Pontiff of Universal Freemasonry. In his book, *Morals and Dogma*, written for higher degree Freemasons, he reveals the way the lower levels are misled:

---

* The 33 degrees of the Scottish Rite and 10 degrees of the York rite, both include the Blue Degrees, of course.

"The Blue Degrees are but the outer court or portico of the Temple. Part of the symbols are displayed there to the initiate, but he is intentionally mis-led by false interpretations. It is not intended that he shall understand them, but it is intended that he shall imagine that he understands them…their true implication is reserved for Adepts, the Princes of Masonry."[2]

Exactly. Jim Shaw says that there are two kinds of Freemason. One just sits through the meetings and doesn't make much effort to understand the ritual, and the other does all the work, but only keeps to the ritual and memorises or reads the words without understanding what they really mean. That's correct, but there is a third kind: the very few who know the truth of who really controls Freemasonry and what the rituals and initiations are really designed to achieve. Shaw also confirms from his own experience how the Freemasons manipulate their own into whatever positions they choose. At work, his department director, a fellow Freemason, advised him to apply for a particular job. Shaw felt he was under-qualified for the post and would fail the test paper.[3] Only through the urging of his Freemason boss did he apply. When he arrived to take the test he was amazed to see that there were only two other applicants for a job he believed would be keenly contested. When he turned over the test paper, he saw that the questions were very easy and he finished them quickly. His two rivals, however, were clearly finding the paper very tough and could not complete it in the allotted time. Shaw got the job. Why? Because he was not given the same paper as the other two. When he walked out of Freemasonry, the opposite happened. He found his bosses far less supportive to say the least. This is just one small example of how the Illuminati and their secret society web ensure that their guys are in the positions that matter. It is actually astonishing how few people you need to control to dictate your agenda through the whole system if they are (a) in the key positions of decision-making and (b) they have the power to appoint those in the important positions below them. An example: you control the chief of police who decides the policy and he can appoint the heads of the various departments in his force. He introduces Illuminati policy and chooses his major subordinates from the secret society initiates. They, in turn, can appoint the people within their departments and can thus choose more secret society initiates for the positions below them. So it goes on. Once you have control of the top man in any organisation, the pyramid is built in his, i.e. the Illuminati's, image. Governments are structured in the same way.

Mind over masses

There are two techniques of mass manipulation that people need to understand if they are to begin to see through the game. One I call "problem-reaction-solution" and the other I term the "stepping-stones approach". These have been used for thousands of years to advance the agenda and, together with fear, they remain the two most effective weapons of the Illuminati. The first technique works like this: you know that if you openly propose to remove basic freedoms, start a war, or centralise power, there will be a public reaction against it. So you use problem-reaction-solution. At stage one you create a problem. It could be a country attacking another, a government or economic collapse, or a terrorist bomb. Anything in fact that the public will think requires a "solution". At stage two, you report the "problems" you have covertly created in the way you wish the people to perceive them. You find someone to blame, a patsy like Timothy McVeigh in Oklahoma, and you spin the background to these events in a way that encourages the people to demand that "something must be done". These are the words you wish to hear because it allows you to move on to stage three, the sting. You then openly offer the solutions to the problems you have yourself created. These solutions, of course, involve the centralisation of power, the sacking of officials or politicians that are getting in your way, and the removal of more basic freedoms. With this technique you can so manipulate the public mind that they will demand that you do what, in normal circumstances, they would vehemently oppose. The Oklahoma bomb at the James P. Murrah Building on April 19th 1995 was a problem-reaction-solution classic. In ...*And The Truth Shall Set You Free*, I expose how McVeigh was set up by forces he did not understand and how a fuel fertiliser device in a Ryder truck could not possibly have caused that horrific damage.[4] And what followed this death and destruction? "Anti-terrorism" laws went through Congress without challenge that removed fundamental freedoms from American people. I have no sympathy with the political views of McVeigh and the Christian patriots in general, except to the extent that they seek to expose the basics of the global agenda. But that's not the point. Establishing the truth of what happened is the point, no matter what the views and attitudes of those involved. I think it is called justice. If you are wondering why McVeigh offered no defence and later asked to be executed, see the section on mind control. The two most effective problem-reaction-solutions in the 20th century were the two global wars. They changed the face of the world, as wars always do, and led to a massive centralisation of power. The United Nations, like its predecessor, the League of Nations, was an Illuminati creation to act as a Trojan horse or stalking horse for world government.

The media play their part to perfection in these "P-R-S" scenarios. At ownership level, people like Conrad Black at the Hollinger Group know what is going on and use their newspapers to pursue the Illuminati agenda. The key editors they appoint might know something of it and also certain columnists. But most of the journalists will have no idea. The editor is always there to block anything they write that is against the interests of the Illuminati and if they insist on pursuing an unwelcome story they find themselves looking for another job. And, anyway, most of what journalists write comes from official (Illuminati) sources. In the immediate aftermath of a major event such as Oklahoma, where are the reporters getting their information? From official sources. We are told that White House sources say this and FBI sources say that. This is how the Illuminati transmit through the media the version of these events that they wish the public to believe. These reports are blazed across the front page of newspapers and the top of radio and television news bulletins throughout the world and what they say becomes the "norm". In the weeks and months that follow, researchers who are interested in the real truth begin to dig away. Over and over they establish and document the proof of how the official version was a lie from start to finish. But where are their reports published? In small-circulation newsletters and on radio stations that operate with a fraction of the money and audience of the Illuminati empires. Years after the official version has been demolished it still prevails in the public mind. Stop people in London, New York, Cape Town, Sydney, anywhere, and ask them what happened in Oklahoma, the Second World War, or Kosovo. Every time they will give you the official story because that is the only one they have heard.

The bedfellow of problem-reaction-solution is the stepping-stones approach. You know where you intend to lead people, but you realise that if you gave them the true picture you would, once again, face substantial opposition. So you travel to your destination in little steps and each one is presented in isolation and as unconnected to all the others. It is like a drip, drip, drip, to global centralisation. This technique was used most obviously with the fascist super-state now known as the European Union. If the politicians had suggested a centralised Europe with common laws and currency there would have been an outcry. People would have said they had been fighting Hitler to stop just such a European dictatorship and there was no way they were accepting another. To overcome this, the Illuminati offered a "free-trade area" and even used the problem of their manipulated world wars to encourage more co-operation between the countries of Europe. Once they had the free trade area, however, the foot in the door, they began to expand its powers until it became the fully fledged fascist political and economic dictatorship it is today. The same is happening with NAFTA, the North American Free Trade Agreement, and APEC, Asia Pacific Economic Co-operation, the "free trade area" for Asia and Australia. Look at today's newspapers and television news bulletins and you'll see problem-reaction-solution and the stepping-stones technique played out day after day. One extremely effective way to see through this scam is to keep asking yourself: "Who benefits from me believing this version of events or accepting the solutions and changes being offered as a result?" The answer will be almost every time: anyone who wishes to centralise power and suppress more freedoms.

Blind faith

Over thousands of years, religion has best served this structure for human control and I will highlight later in this book the historical background and present-day manipulation of these "faiths". But, in short, they have created rigid belief systems that should never be questioned; imposed those beliefs through fear, indoctrination, isolation, and the mass genocide of non believers; and fought each other for dominance of the human mind, thus producing an orgasm of opportunity for the Illuminati to divide and rule for millennia. Another question. Is it more likely that an Illuminati which has its origins in the ancient past, long before these religions were created, just happened to "get lucky" when such a perfect vehicle for human control independently emerged? Or is it rather more probable that these institutions of human enslavement were purposely created by these very same Illuminati to advance their agenda? But religion is not *the* conspiracy, and nor are economics, politics, and all the rest. They are part of a vast web of interconnected manipulation designed to persuade the masses to put *themselves* in prison and throw away the key. The Illuminati work through every belief system – religious, political, economic, racial, and cultural – and through every side in the major "debates". The reason is simple: If you want to know the outcome of a game before the game has even started, you need to control all sides. The manager of a football team cannot dictate the result if he only controls one side. If, however, he is managing both sides, he can decide the result before a ball is kicked. So it is with the Illuminati, the hidden hand behind the events that affect our lives and our world every day.

But, by the end of this book, if you are open-minded enough to complete it, the hand will be hidden no more. The truth is not only out there. A lot of it is right here.

SOURCES

1   Jim Shaw, *The Deadly Deception* (Huntington House Inc, Lafayette, Louisiana, 1988), p 103

2   *Morals And Dogma Of The Ancient And Accepted Scottish Rite Of Freemasonry*, p 819

3   *The Deadly Deception*, pp 65 and 66

4   *...And The Truth Shall Set You Free*, pp 321 to 324

CHAPTER 2

Designer history

Who controls the past, controls the future. Who controls the present, controls the past.

George Orwell, *1984*

History is the lie commonly agreed upon.

Voltaire

To know where you are and where you are going, it helps enormously to know where you have come from. Indeed it is essential. The fix we have today on who we are and the nature of "reality" has been based to a very large extent on our belief in what has happened in the past. So if you want to manipulate people's sense of self and reality today, it is vital to rewrite what we hilariously call "history." For example, if official history tells you from cradle to grave that the Second World War was fought between the good guys and bad guys, the Allies fighting for freedom and the fascists seeking a global dictatorship, you do not open your eyes to see the endless provable evidence that both "sides" were funded and controlled by the same people operating through Wall Street and the City of London.

The story of "Jesus" is another outstanding case, probably the best. The Christian religion is based entirely on belief in the historical, literal, existence, of a Jewish man who was born to a virgin mother, performed countless "miracles", died on a cross to save us all, disappeared from his tomb after three days, and then ascended to heaven to be with his dad. Over the best part of 2,000 years, billions of lives on this planet have been controlled, limited, manipulated and directed by a belief that the Jesus story actually happened. Still today, vast swathes of humanity are obsessed with, and their every action based upon, this fairy tale being historically accurate. Just one story about one "man" has had that staggering scale of human consequence, ancient and modern. And yet, as we shall see, the Gospels are nonsense if taken literally, with no historical foundation whatsoever. They are merely the most exploited versions of a symbolic, not literal, story that you find all over the world in all its detail thousands of years before the name "Jesus" was first mentioned.

A little quiz. Who am I talking about here?

He was born on December 25th to a virgin mother; he was called a saviour, the only begotten son, and died to save humanity; he was crucified on a Friday – "Black Friday" – and his blood was spilled to redeem the Earth; he suffered death with nails and stakes; he was the Father and Son combined in an earthly body; he was put in a tomb, went down into the underworld, but three days later, on March 25th, his body was found to be gone from the tomb and he was resurrected as the "Most High God"; his body was symbolised as bread and eaten by those who worshipped him.[1]

Jesus, yes? No, no. All of this was said about the saviour Son of God called Attis who was worshipped by the Phrygians, one of the oldest races in Asia Minor, now Turkey, well over a thousand years before the manufacture of "Jesus". It is just one of countless symbolic deities of whom the same story was told millennia before Christianity. Others are accepted to have been myths and not to have literally existed. But not Jesus. While Christians laugh at those "Pagan" tales and condemn them as evil, they ask the rest of the world to believe, indeed have insisted on pain of torture and death, that their version of the same story is somehow literally true while all the others are not. Yeah, right.

To understand how the repeat of an ancient, endlessly recurring story could be transformed into the prison-religion called Christianity, and to see the source of global control today, we have to research our ancient origins. When we do that with an open mind and without preconceived dogma, a very different human history emerges. One that is not taught in the schools and universities of the world or revealed through the mainstream media. It is a story that not only makes sense of the past, but opens your eyes to the staggering scale of manipulation today and the ancient background and ancestry of those involved. Contrary to conditioned belief, life on Earth has not evolved from a primitive past to the technological "cutting edge" of today. Many thousands of years ago, as detailed in streams of ancient accounts across the world, there was great technological knowledge on this planet and a global society controlled by races of beings, which humans came to know as "gods". It is a minefield to decipher which of these gods were flesh and blood real, and which were symbolic of the Sun, Moon, planets, natural cycles, and so on. Most were the latter, but there is substantial evidence to confirm that some of them, particularly the further back you go, were walking, talking, entities, who had, by human standards at the time, amazing knowledge of the solar system, the stars, the universal cycles, the effect of the Sun, Moon and other planets and star systems on the Earth and its people, and technological understanding of such immensity that they were able to build the pyramids and other stunning structures all over the world that we would struggle to build even today.

Just consider the scale we are talking here with the Giza Pyramids alone. The Great Pyramid, which is nearly 500 feet high, consists of six and a half million tons of stone and around two and a half million individual blocks. Some weigh 70 tons and in the other pyramids and walls are stones of 200, even 468 tons, and they are so perfectly cut and fitted together you could not get a piece of paper between them. There is enough stone in the Great Pyramid alone to build *30* Empire State Buildings and enough stone on the Giza site to build a wall around the entire border of France some three metres high and one metre thick.[2] Some of these gigantic stones at Giza and numerous temple sites were apparently taken from quarries hundreds of miles away. And we are told that "primitive" people did this? Oh do come on. At Baalbeck in the Lebanon are structures thousands of years old, which include three enormous chunks of stone known as the Trilithon, each weighing more than 800 tons. These had to be moved at least a third of a mile and one of them placed 20 feet up in a wall.[3] Another piece of stone nearby is a thousand tons, which, apparently, is the weight of three Jumbo Jets.[4] We are asked to believe again that a "primitive" people did this. In Peru, you have ancient temples and other sites built with stones weighing 440 tons and at Tiahuanaco in Peru blocks weighing 100 tons are connected by *metal* clamps.[5] This site is dated at some 11,000 years ago.[6] On the Nazca Plain in Peru there are the massive and astonishing Nazca Lines. These are fantastic depictions of birds, insects, and animals, created by scoring away the top surface to reveal the white rock underneath. The images are made with one continuous line and some were only seen in their entirety after 1939 when people began to fly over the region because they can only be seen in full from one thousand to 2,000 feet! Rock carvings dating back more than 10,000 years were found during an expedition to the Marca Huasi plateau northeast of Lima, Peru, and these included sculptures representing people and animals, most of which are not native to Peru. They included a polar bear, walrus, African lion, penguin and the stegosaurus dinosaur. But dinosaurs were unknown to science until the 1880s, and the stegosauria was not identified until 1901. Talk us through that one.

As other books and television documentaries in recent years have shown, these amazing structures, temples, stone circles, and standing stones, were not only lined up precisely with certain star systems, they were aligned just as precisely in relationship to each other all over the planet, and the building techniques and designs were often the same on different sides of the world. Why? Because the official version of history is baloney. There were not isolated, unconnected, societies, which developed alone, if you go back far enough. There was a global society controlled by the "gods" and representatives of the "gods" – beings that were extremely advanced technologically compared with the mass of humanity at the time and, in many ways, ahead of our society today. Or, at least, ahead of the technology we are allowed to see in the public arena, anyway. A precisely machined and shaped cube of metal was found in the centre of a block of coal in Austria in 1885 and, based on the age of that coal seam, it must have been made some 300,000 years ago![7] A piece of gold thread was found embedded in eight feet of rock in Rutherford Mills, England, in 1844, and that rock was estimated to go back 60 million years!![8] Electric batteries have been found in ancient Egyptian tombs and a massive slab of green glass weighing many tons was found in Israel.[9] The pre-historic bones of animals have been discovered with bullets in them.[10] As the brilliant author and researcher of far ancient history, Colonel James Churchward, wrote:

"Civilisations have been born and completed and then forgotten again and again. There is nothing new under the Sun. What is, has been. All that we learn and discover has existed before; our inventions and discoveries are but reinventions, re-discoveries." [11]

The ancients across the world described a high-tech "Golden Age" of human society, although some of it, especially towards the end, was anything, but "golden". These stories say that this age was ended by high-tech war and a series of geological catastrophes that caused colossal Earth changes through earthquakes, volcanic eruptions, magnetic pole shifts, and tidal waves on a scale we could not begin to imagine today. The Biblical Great Flood is a symbolic story of one such event, but there appear from the biological and geological record to have been several from about 12,000BC up to around 5000BC, perhaps even later. As you can see in *The Biggest Secret*, and the excellent book, *The Day The Earth Nearly Died*, by D.S. Allen and J.B. Delair (Gateway Books, Bath, 1995), the geological and biological evidence is supported by the ancient accounts with the most incredible synchronicity. Everywhere the ancients recorded the effects of these events. Professor James DeMeo writes in his book, *Saharasia* (Hidden Mysteries, Texas, 2000) of vast changes in the Middle East in this same "window" of time:

"A massive climate change shook the ancient world, when approximately 6,000 years ago vast areas of lush grassland and forest in the Old World began to quickly dry out and convert into harsh desert. The vast Sahara Desert, Arabian Desert, and the giant deserts of the Middle East and Central Asia simply did not exist prior to (about) 4,000BC...". [12]

The upheavals of the ancient world destroyed the advanced global society or "Golden Age" that existed before and this is recorded in the stories of Atlantis and Lemuria, or "Mu". Humanity had to start all over again. If you believe that is far-fetched, think about today's society. It may be advanced on one level with power grids and computer systems, and all the rest. Such technology can perform apparently miraculous feats, like typing a letter on to this computer and having it read by someone on the other side of the world seconds later. But what would happen to this technological society if we were faced now with a global catastrophe that devastated the planet? Within seconds, we would be sitting in the technological Stone Age. It would be a primitive, everyone-for-themselves, find-your-own-food, shelter and warmth, free-for-all. And as time and generations passed, the memory of the technological world we have today would fade, ever more rapidly, and only be preserved in stories and myths which would, more and more, be seen as wild tales and figments of the imagination. Most people would deny such a world ever existed because it would be so at odds with their daily experience. We would have the same we-can't-do-it-so-it-can't-be-done mentality that laughed at the very idea we could fly to the Moon. The history in that post-cataclysmic society would only begin with the records left by humanity once they had re-advanced to a certain level. Only then would they write or symbolise accounts of their history and this would be based on stories passed verbally through the earlier generations. Such a point could take hundreds, even thousands, of years after the global geological destruction. So it was after the cataclysms of our ancient past. Conventional "history" says that the "cradle" of civilisation was Sumer, in the land between the Rivers Tigris and Euphrates in what we now call Iraq and once known as Mesopotamia ("Between Two Rivers"). The Sumerian period is estimated to have spanned the millennia between 4000 and 2000BC. Historians say that other, independent, civilisations of great advancement also suddenly appeared in the same period in Egypt and the Indus Valley in what is now the Indian continent. But they are wrong on both counts, I would suggest. Sumer was not the start of what is called civilised society on this planet. It was the most significant one to emerge after the catastrophe that destroyed the global society of the "Golden Age" – Atlantis and Lemuria, or Mu. Sumer was not the beginning; it was the start-over-again which was to become the centre of another virtually global empire. Indeed Sumer, Babylon, Egypt, and the Indus Valley civilisations had actually begun tens of thousands of years before history records them. After the cataclysms, these advanced cultures in Egypt and the Indus Valley, which "suddenly" and unexplainably manifested at a very high level of development, were not independent of Sumer, as the historians claim. They were part of the same Sumer Empire and ruled by the same leader. The structure of administration, the foundation of law, building techniques, and so many other features of what we call modern society, can be traced back to this ancient race that founded Sumer. Or more to the point, to those ruling bloodlines and "gods" that held the knowledge going back into pre-history. These advanced ancient post-deluge societies appeared with tremendous speed. Professor W.B. Emery writes in *Archaic Egypt* (Penguin Books, England, 1961):

> "At a period approximately 3400 years (BC), a great change took place in Egypt, and the country passed rapidly from a state of advanced Neolithic culture with a complex tribal character to two well-organised monarchies, one comprising the Delta area and the other the Nile Valley proper. At the same time the art of writing appears. Monumental architecture and the arts and crafts developed to an astonishing degree, and all the evidence points to the existence of a well-organised, even luxurious civilisation. All this was achieved within a comparatively short period of time, for there appears to be little or no background to these fundamental developments in writing and architecture." [13]

The question still to be answered is whether the incredible feats of building like the pyramids originate before the great cataclysms, which destroyed the legendary Golden Age (in other words, maybe upwards of 10,000 years ago and far longer), or were they built by the Sumer Empire which emerged when the world had again reached an advanced level of society after the upheavals. I have no doubt that it was a mixture of both. In the light of the rapidly emerging evidence, and the fundamental re-assessment of timescales in the wake of that evidence, at least some of the world's greatest ancient wonders go back to the pre-cataclysmic global society known in legends and accounts as the Golden Age. They are far, far, older than previously imagined. Inca accounts, compiled by Fernando Montesinos, one of the earliest Spanish chroniclers in South America, say there were two Inca Empires. The first established their headquarters at Cuzco in the Andes Mountains and, after they fled to a mountain-top sanctuary (Machu Picchu?) in the wake of devastating land upheavals, they returned to Cuzco to start a second culture. This would push back the original Inca Empire to the time of the Atlantean-Lemurian cataclysms and before, and lead us to the true builders of the fantastic structures that conventional history cannot explain.

All over the world in every native culture, you will find stories of a great flood and incredible geological upheavals. There is no doubt that an unimaginable catastrophe or, more likely, catastrophes were visited upon the Earth between approximately 11000 and 5000BC. The geological and biological evidence is overwhelming in support of the countless stories and traditions that describe such events. They come from Europe, Scandinavia, Russia, Africa, throughout the Americas, Australia, New Zealand, Asia, China, Japan, and the Middle East. Everywhere. Some speak of great heat that boiled the sea; of mountains breathing fire; the disappearance of the Sun and Moon and the darkness that followed; the raining down of blood, ice, and rock; the Earth flipping over; the sky falling; the rising and sinking of land; the loss of great continents; the coming of the ice; and virtually all of them describe a fantastic flood, a wall of water, which swept across the Earth. The tidal wave caused by the comet in the movie, Deep Impact, gives you an idea of what it would have been like. Old Chinese texts describe how the pillars supporting the sky crumbled; of how the Sun, Moon, and stars poured down in the north-west, where the sky became low; rivers, seas, and oceans, rushed to the south-east where the Earth sank and a great conflagration was quenched by a raging flood. In America, the Pawnee Indians tell the same story of a time when the north and south polar stars changed places and "went to visit each other". North American traditions refer to great clouds appearing and a heat so powerful that the waters boiled. The Greenland Eskimos told early missionaries that long ago the Earth turned over. Peruvian legends say that the Andes Mountains were ripped apart when the sky made war with the Earth. Brazilian myth describes how the heavens burst and fragments fell down killing everything and everyone as heaven and Earth changed places. And the Hopi Indians of North America record that: "The Earth was rent in great chasms, and water covered everything except one narrow ridge of mud."[14]

Atlantis and Lemuria

All of this closely correlates with the legends of Atlantis and Lemuria, or Mu. These were two vast continents, one in the Atlantic and the other in the Pacific, which many people believe were ruled by highly advanced races that originated from other worlds. The continents are said to have disappeared under the sea in the circumstances described above, leaving only islands, like the Azores and Polynesia, as remnants of their former scale and glory. Atlantis is said by some to have emerged after the sinking of Lemuria. Others say they were simultaneous and that's my view. The most thorough and outstanding researcher of Lemuria-Mu was Colonel James Churchward, who wrote a series of books in the first half of the 20th century. Churchward visited remote monasteries in Asia and saw the ancient records of the "Motherland" of Mu or Lemuria going back between 12,000 and 70,000 years. He saw how it was the centre of a global empire that included Atlantis. In his book, *The Children Of Mu* (BE Books, Albuquerque, New Mexico), first published in 1931, he shows how the various racial types on Mu, including blue-eyed blonds, peopled the world.[15] These Lemurian races went east to become the Mayans of Central America and the other builders of the fantastic structures of the American continent. They went west to people Asia, China, India, and elsewhere, and created colonies in what became Egypt and Sumer. All genetic and cultural roads, he says, lead back to Lemuria-Mu, the "Motherland", and the very advanced civilisation that existed tens of thousands, possibly hundreds of thousands, of years before today's "modern" society. Churchward says that Lemuria was destroyed around 12,000 years ago. W.T. Samsel in his study of these ancient societies, *The Atlantis Connection* (Starfire Publishing, Sedona, Arizona, 1998), dates the end of Lemuria much earlier, but many of their basic themes are similar.

Samsel's book is based on "channelled" information. Creation consists of an infinite number of wavelengths or frequencies and the world we perceive with our physical senses is merely one tiny fraction of the frequencies that exist. Just as we cannot see the radio and television frequencies sharing the same space as our bodies at this moment, so we cannot see with our limited physical senses the other frequencies and wavelengths of Creation that also occupy the same space that we do. I will go into greater detail about this later because it is crucial to understanding how we are controlled and how we can break free. But to "channel" is to "tune" our consciousness to some of these other wavelengths and access the knowledge and information that exists there. Samsel claims to be in contact with an entity formerly incarnate in Atlantis that now communicates from one of these other frequencies. Most channelled information, in my experience, is either nonsense or extremely limited, but many of Samsel's themes are supported by geological and biological record. He believes that it was about 100,000 years ago that the first examples of modern human forms appeared on the island of Lemuria in what is now the Pacific Ocean.[16] These were intended to be "perfected vehicles", he says. As they began to explore the Earth, they seeded the land that is known as Atlantis, which is said to have been in the Atlantic on the geologically unstable mid-Atlantic Ridge. Samsel says that early Atlanteans were a dark-skinned people, not unlike the Native Americans. He believes the Native American people are directly descended from Lemurians and Atlanteans who settled in the Americas before the first great cataclysm some 48,000 years ago and Native American legends support this theme.[17] His view is that in those earlier days of Atlantis and Lemuria the people lived under the "Law of One", the understanding that everything is the same energy expressing itself in different forms. The Law of One is the knowledge that everything is connected to everything else and ultimately all is an expression of the same whole or energy. Scientists call this the unified field theory. This is a common theme of Atlantean myths and legends – a civilisation that began with positive intent and in harmony with the natural laws, but was taken over by forces that transformed it into a very dark place indeed. Samsel suggests that the "war between the gods" in ancient mythology, was a war between extraterrestrial races over the question of intervention or non-intervention in Earth affairs. He says that midway through the early Atlantian age, extraterrestrials with a human-like appearance – "very tall, light haired, light skinned, albino-like people" – made contact with the Atlanteans.[18] They began to manipulate Atlantean society, he says, and interbreed with humans to change the DNA and create hybrid bloodlines that became the royal lineage of kings and queens. I would include Lemuria in this same story also. The technology and physical appearance of these extraterrestrials led the Atlanteans/Lemurians to see them as gods. Intermarrying with these beings to produce light-skinned offspring with "god-like features" became the goal of many Atlanteans, Samsel writes, and these crossbreeds became the dominant force. They took over the government, economics, education, religion, and communications. Sound familiar? Samsel says that the kings of the white royal lineage ruled Atlantis and what he calls the "Sons of Belial" controlled the Temple of the Sun, their religious hierarchy and ritual network. Today this Atlantean Temple of the Sun is known as the Illuminati. During this period, many Atlanteans of the red race migrated west to the Americas, which were then geographically different to what we see today. Samsel goes on:

> "The age of the Atlantic Empire would prove to be a free-for-all for the Sons of Belial and the followers of the Temple of the Sun. The dominant white tribe came to rule all aspects of Atlantean society. They disregarded the Law of One, placed their faith in technology and were driven by greed and the lust for power. The arms of the Atlantic Empire came to stretch nearly worldwide. The Americas and Africa, the European countries, the Middle East, India and Tibet came under the control of the Empire. The One Temple was divided and ineffective, the Sun Temple flourished and the Sons of Belial prospered. During that time, One Law priests were leading migrations of the red race west to the Americas and east to Africa. They sought to preserve the Law of One and so they built new circles in the far lands".[19]

Samsel says that the second great cataclysm brought an end to Atlantis. He believes that they used their "super weapons" against what we now call China and they tried to "utilize the Earth as a great conductor through which to direct at their adversaries" using the vast crystal, which is a common theme in Atlantean stories. But, he says, the "Earth hurled the force back upon them" and the final, disastrous, cataclysm was triggered.[20] Samsel claims that the white race is the force behind global control:

"Throughout the history of the Earth and mankind, it has been the white tribe that has consistently exhibited the characteristics of their ancestral heritage. It is these who openly display many of the characteristics of other-worldly or 'alien beings'. They have embraced technology above spirituality and have manipulated spirituality to achieve their own ends. They traditionally display little regard for the Earth, nature or other species of living creatures. Throughout recorded history they have sought domination over all others and over the Earth itself. They have been highly programmed and conditioned to be exclusive, aggressive and dominating. Presently, these lead humanity towards the New World Order, consciously or unconsciously carrying out the agenda of the Illuminati, hence, the extraterrestrial manipulators." [21]

The themes of Samsel's research are supported by my own, although we differ in detail. My own view is that what he calls the "Sons of Belial" are what I call the reptilian bloodlines, the result of interbreeding between the white or "Nordic" race and a reptilian people. In the end, however, it's the theme that really matters in understanding the basic background to the world today. The tussle between the Atlantean advocates of the Law of One and the opposing Temple of the Sun is highly significant. The Temple of the Sun has been the religion of the Illuminati from Atlantis/Lemuria right through to the present time. In fact, today's world is the new Atlantis, a mirror of the obsession with technological dominance that led to the destruction of the first Atlantean civilisation. Put simply, the Law of One sees everything as connected, part of the same unified whole, and the Temple of the Sun represents the desire to present everything as unconnected and isolated from everything else. One seeks to unite, the other to divide and, therefore, rule. You will see this theme throughout the book as I tell the story of how the Illuminati, the Atlantean "Sons of Belial" or whatever you would like to call them, have sought to build the new Atlantis ever since the cataclysmic events that destroyed the original version.

Atlantis was described by Plato (427-347BC), the ancient Greek philosopher. He was also a high initiate of the secret society – Mystery school network. To this day this secret network has passed on advanced knowledge to the chosen few while denying that privilege to the mass of the people. Official history dismisses Plato's contention that such a continent existed, but there is vast geological support for such claims. The Azores, which some believe were part of Atlantis, lie on the mid-Atlantic ridge, a fracture line that encircles the planet. This line continues for a distance of 40,000 miles.[22] The mid-Atlantic ridge is one of the foremost areas for earthquakes and volcanoes. Four vast tectonic plates, the Eurasian, African, North American, and Caribbean, all meet and collide in this region making it very unstable geologically. Both the Azores and the Canary Islands (named after dogs, "Canine", and not canaries!) were subject to widespread volcanic activity in the time period Plato suggested for the end of Atlantis. Tachylite lava disintegrates in seawater within 15,000 years and yet it is still found on the seabed around the Azores, confirming geologically recent upheavals.[23] Other evidence, including beach sand gathered from depths of 10,500 – 18,440 feet, reveals that the seabed in this region must have been, again geologically recently, above sea level.[24] The oceanographer, Maurice Ewing, wrote in National Geographic Magazine, that: "Either the land must have sunk two or three miles or the sea must once have been two or three miles lower than now. Either conclusion is startling."[25] When European explorers first landed in the Canary Islands the people said they were descendants of the Atlanteans and were shocked to realise that other people had survived the cataclysm that destroyed their homeland.

The geological and biological evidence also suggests that the widespread volcanic activity that caused the sinking of the land in the region of the Azores happened at the same time as the break up and sinking of the land mass known as Appalachia, which connected what we now call Europe, North America, Iceland and Greenland.[26] Even their degree of submergence appears to be closely related. The so-called Bermuda Triangle, between Bermuda, southern Florida, and a point near the Antilles, has long been associated with Atlantis. It is an area steeped in legends of disappearing ships and aircraft. Submerged buildings, walls, roads, and stone circles like Stonehenge, even what appear to be pyramids, have been located near Bimini under the waters of the Bahama Banks and within the "triangle".[27] So have walls or roads creating intersecting lines. Some other facts that most people don't know: the Himalayas, Alps, Andes, and at least most other mountain ranges, were only formed or reached anything like their present height around 12,000 years ago.[28] Lake Titicaca on the Peru-Bolivia border is today the highest navigable lake in the world at some 12,500 feet. Around 11,000 years ago, much of that region was at sea level.[29] Why are so many fish and other ocean fossils found high up in mountain ranges? Because those rocks were once at sea level and recently so in geological terms, too. How interesting then that Plato dated the cataclysm that destroyed the continent of Atlantis to around 9000BC and so do Allan and Delair in their superb work, *When The Earth Nearly Died*. They say it happened around 9500BC.

The American researcher Charles Hapgood claimed that the surface of the Earth had moved by some 3,000 miles around 10000BC.[30] Rocks that contain iron act like a compass. As the molten rock cools, the molecules align with the North Pole and even if those rocks are moved they continue to hold that connection. This allowed Hapgood to establish that before about 10000BC the physical North Pole had been located on the land in the region occupied today by the Hudson Bay in Canada.[31] But something happened around that time that moved the whole surface of the Earth 3,000 miles to the south, thus relocating the land of the then North Pole to the Hudson Bay area. This is not as fantastic as it at first sounds. The land surface, or crust, of the planet, is only about 40 miles thick. It has been likened to the skin of an orange resting on a sea of molten lava. If a meteor or another major body impacted the Earth it could cause the crust to slide and, according to writer and researcher, Colin Wilson, there is geological evidence that this has happened three times in the last 100,000 years.[32] Measurements of the Earth's magnetic field have shown that the north and south magnetic poles have changed places at least 171 times in the past 76 million years and imagine the effect of a magnetic pole shift on the weather alone.[33] The Canadian writer, Rand Flem-Ath, who has spent more than 20 years researching these subjects, is convinced that at least a large proportion of Atlantis is what we now call Antarctica because of this 3,000-mile shift to the south.[34] Hapgood, following up the work of Captain Arlington H. Mallery, studied hundreds of maps found in the Library of Congress in Washington DC, which prove that the world was mapped thousands of years ago with great accuracy. One, made by Oronteus Finnaeus in 1531, shows Antarctica with running rivers and ice-free mountains.[35] The famous map, drawn by the Turkish sailor, Piri Reis, in 1513, and found at the palace of the Sultan of Constantinople in 1929, charts the South American coast with great accuracy and part of the coast of Antarctica before it was covered with ice two miles thick some 7,000 years ago! Yet Antarctica was not "discovered" officially until Captain Cook arrived there in 1773 and it was not explored in detail until the 1950s. Some of the mountain ranges in the Piri Reis map were not even found until 1952. Reis said that he compiled his map from 20 older ones. Flem-Ath has also found astonishing evidence to support the existence of a highly advanced society thousands of years ago. He found that if you draw a line of longitude through the Great Pyramid at Giza it crosses more land than anywhere else on the planet and this supports the ancient Egyptian belief that the pyramid was the centre of the Earth.[36] Flem-Ath then realised that if the Great Pyramid is taken to be the centre of the 0 degree meridian, the longitude and latitude locations of the world's sacred sites fit together in neat geometrical patterns. They appeared as a grid system, very much like the blocks in the street plans of US cities.[37] He found he could predict where a sacred site would be purely from this system.[38] This geometrical perfection is not the case if you take the present Greenwich Observatory in London to be the 0 degree central point. It throws the whole system out. Greenwich was chosen by a committee only in 1884 despite protests by one prominent member, the Astronomer Royal of Scotland, Charles Piazzi Smyth, that the 0 degree meridian should run through the Great Pyramid. Flem-Ath has further established that some 50 sacred sites in Mexico are aligned to a North Pole located in the Hudson Bay area, as it was before the cataclysm.[39] Even those built since the upheavals have been placed on older sites that aligned with the old North Pole. The same is true of Rosslyn Chapel near Edinburgh in Scotland.[40] This is an Illuminati "Holy Grail" full of their ancient symbolism and built by the St Clair-Sinclair family, one of the foremost of the Illuminati bloodlines and one of the founding forces behind the Knights Templar secret society. Charles Hapgood, incidentally, had a meeting arranged with President Kennedy to discuss a project to find Atlantis, but Kennedy died in Dallas a few days before their appointment.[41] Hapgood also told Rand Flem-Ath that he was going to produce evidence in his next book of an advanced civilisation on Earth 100,000 years ago. But Hapgood died soon afterwards and the book was never written. James Churchward however, produces such evidence in his books and he tells how he saw maps of South America and elsewhere in those remote Asian monasteries going back tens of thousands of years.

    This evidence supports the view that the continent known as Mu or Lemuria now rests on the bed of the Pacific. The Polynesian tribes and other related peoples retain many legends of their sunken land of origin and Easter Island natives in the

Pacific claim their land was once part of a continent destroyed by cataclysm.[42] A Chinese text found in a Buddhist cave called Dunhuang in western China in 1900 included fragments of a map that featured an Island continent in the Pacific.[43] South American legend tells the same story of their ancestors arriving from a lost continent, among them a guy called Aramu Muru, who carried the knowledge of the Lemurian Brotherhood or Mystery school.[44] The Hopi tribe in Arizona remember Lemuria as a series of islands by which they travelled to the American continent.[45] Why isn't the story of the Atlantis and Mu a key part of official history? Because the knowledge has been systematically suppressed and destroyed. The astronomer, Carl Sagan, said that a text detailing Atlantis, called *The True History of Mankind Over the Last 100,000 Years*, was destroyed with thousands of others when the great library of Alexandria in Egypt was destroyed in AD391.[46] Once we know of these advanced civilisations that lasted hundreds of thousands of years, and the extraterrestrial involvement in their creation and demise, our whole view of the world and ourselves will change. So will our understanding of what is happening and who is controlling us today. The destruction of ancient knowledge all over the world in the name of Christianity was the Illuminati, or the Temple of the Sun, destroying the true accounts, not only of history, but also the Law of One.

So what happened to Mars?

There is increasing acceptance that the Earth has suffered some colossal geological upheavals. The debate (and often hostility) comes with the question of when and why. These upheavals have obviously involved the solar system as a whole because every planet shows evidence of some cataclysmic events, which have affected its surface, atmosphere, speed, and angle of orbit or rotation. The destruction of Mars and its relationship with this devastation on Earth is a subject occupying the minds of many researchers. There has been a much greater focus on Mars since the various space probes have been directed there and, of course, their rather unfortunate record of being lost or suffering "technical problems", which prevent them sending pictures back to us. Mmmm. These "failures" are the responsibility of the Illuminati-created and controlled NASA operation. The failures followed the photographs taken in an area of Mars called Cydonia that appeared to show non-natural rock formations. These included the famous "face" on Mars and various pyramids. The best-known writer and researcher on this subject is the American, Richard Hoagland, a science journalist and a former adviser at the NASA Goddard Space Flight Center.[47] One of his team claims to have compared the relationship of the "non-natural" phenomena at Cydonia on Mars, such as the face and the pyramids, with the layout at Avebury in Wiltshire, England, with its stone circle, standing stone rows, Silbury Hill (the biggest human-made mound in Europe), and other ancient earthworks. He says he found that they are virtual mirrors of each other. The Giza plateau in Egypt, home of the Great Pyramid, was formerly known as El-Kahira.[48] This derived from the Arab noun, El-Kahir, their name for…Mars.[49] Ancient texts reveal that the measurement of time was much related to Mars, and March 15th, the Ides of March (Mars), was a key date in their Mars-related calendar, as was October 26th. The first marked the start of spring and the second was the end of the year in the Celtic calendar. The name Camelot in the symbolic King Arthur stories apparently means Martian City or City of Mars.[50]

Of course, as we know, a connection between Mars and human society is impossible because Mars was destroyed millions of years ago. But was it? We only think it was because that's what the official version tells us and over and over when you look at the basis for such scientific "fact" you often find it is merely an assumption or an opinion and not a provable "fact" at all. Just one example of this was confirmed by Dr Frank Drake, the former chairman of the Cornell University astronomy department, when he said: "We used to think of the universe as nothing more than abundant fields of stars arranged in galaxies, but we underestimated the variety and quantity of matter in space by a factor of about one trillion. Which means that we were about as wrong as we could be."[51] But until they accepted they were wrong in the face of the evidence, they taught their monumental error as scientific fact. This is happening every day and the media just repeat such nonsense because it must be true if a scientist says it is. There is a fast emerging alternative scenario that is pretty much in agreement with the official story, except in one crucial area where they differ fundamentally. They both agree that Mars once had water, vegetation, and an atmosphere, which could have supported life as we know it. They both agree that this potentially human-friendly environment was destroyed by catastrophic geological events. The only serious area of contention is *when* that disaster occurred. Was it really millions of years ago, as official "science" contends, or was it merely thousands of years ago, as the alternative researchers suggest, a timescale that would fit perfectly with the devastation of Atlantis and Lemuria-Mu. The gathering evidence is that Mars was destroyed in the same catastrophe, which, on Earth, brought an end to that "Golden Age". In the 1950s, the Russian-born writer and researcher, Immanuel Velikovsky, suggested in a series of books that the planet we now call Venus (then a vast comet-like body) was the cause of both the demise of Mars and the near-demise of the Earth when it was hurled through the solar system.[52] Velikovsky was ridiculed and bitterly attacked by the "scientific" establishment and so he must have been saying something worth hearing. But his theme is now enjoying more and more sympathy. When the Mariner 9 mission took pictures of Venus, many of Velikovsky's earlier descriptions were proved correct, including what appeared to be a comet-like tail. Mariner's pictures of Mars also supported some of his theories. He pointed out that ancient peoples depicted Venus as a very bright object trailing smoke following a very different orbit and trajectory than we see today. The Chinese, Toltecs, and Mayans recorded this. The early Sumerian astronomical accounts did not include Venus, but the later Chaldeans in the same region did so. They described it as a "bright torch in heaven" that "illuminates like the Sun" and "fills the entire heavens." One of the major problems that people have in encompassing ideas about the planet's past is that they judge possibility on their present experience, which is a tiny, tiny, fraction of the Earth's history. As Velikovsky wrote:

"Traditions about upheavals and catastrophes, found among all peoples are generally discredited because of the short-sighted belief that no forces could have shaped the world in the past that are not at work also at the present time, a belief that is the very foundation of modern geology and of the theory of evolution." [53]

Brian Desborough, a friend of mine in California, has had a life experience that makes his opinion significant to anyone researching the material in this book. He is a scientist, an inventor of free-energy technology that could transform life on Earth, and has been researching the Illuminati, their history, origin, and agenda, for more than 30 years. This interest began when he set out to prove that Jesus really existed, but he soon found himself proving that he didn't. The Christian scam led him into the bigger scam, just as my initial investigation into the suppression of spiritual (not religious) knowledge did for me. Brian is no New Age flyaway sitting in the clouds. He is a feet-on-the-ground, give-me-the-evidence, researcher and writer. In the 1960s, he worked at the aircraft giant, Boeing, and he says that a group of Boeing physicists got together to launch a private study aimed at explaining the many anomalies of the Earth and other planets of the solar system that could not be explained by normal physics. What they concluded was to present staggering support for Velikovsky, although they differed on time scale by about 3,000 years. They said that around 5000BC a huge body, now called Jupiter, careered through the solar system. This threw the outer planets into disarray, so explaining their present anomalies of spin direction and speed. Jupiter crashed into a planet that once orbited between where Mars and Jupiter are today and the debris from this planet, they said, can be seen as the otherwise unexplained asteroid belt that occupies the space between…Mars and Jupiter. I saw some interesting "channelled" information about Mars in relation to the end of Atlantis. It said that one of the three Atlantean cataclysms, which destroyed the continent in stages, happened around 10500BC, and was caused by a close pass of the Earth by Mars, which has been knocked out of its original orbit. The same theme keeps returning from many diverse sources and, somewhere within this, the detailed truth is waiting for us. James Churchward has a more earthly explanation for the cataclysms. He says there are enormous "gas belts" and chambers under the Earth and when these "blow" on a vast scale, the land above is destroyed. He says these gas belts ran under both Lemuria/Mu and Atlantis. What caused the cataclysms is open to debate, but that they did happen is a statement of fact.

A similar theme can be found in the tens of thousands of ancient clay tablets discovered in Mesopotamia in the mid-19th century. These tell the stories and myths of the Sumerian culture that emerged after one of these cataclysms that sank what was left of Atlantis. Sumer dates from around 4000BC, but civilisations existed in that region, as James Churchward documents, for tens of thousands of years before Sumer emerged. Central to these Sumerian accounts were the "gods" the Sumerians called the Anunna ("Sons of An"). Their later Semitic names were AN.UNNAK.KI ("Those who from Heaven to Earth Came") and DIN.GIR ("The Righteous Ones of the Blazing Rockets"). They are best known as the Anunnaki and so I shall use that term in the book. The Anunnaki, as we shall see, were a reptilian race from the stars. The Sumerian tablets describe, according to the author and translator, Zechariah Sitchin, a collision between the moons of a planet they called Nibiru and one orbiting between the present Jupiter and Mars.[54] The debris from this stupendous collision, Sitchin's translations say, created what the Sumerians called "the Great Band Bracelet" – the asteroid belt. The Sumerian accounts differ in detail, but again the theme is the same. In their version of these events, the Boeing physicists suggested that part of Jupiter broke away on impact with another planet. This is the body we now call Venus, they concluded. It was projected towards Mars, destroying the atmosphere and life on that planet (the Mars Pathfinder Mission established that Martian rocks lack sufficient erosion to have been on the surface for more than 10,000 years).[55] After devastating Mars, the "Venus" comet was caught by the gravitational pull of the Earth, they said. It made several orbits of the Earth, causing the tidal wave and devastation that ended the Golden Age, and hurled vast quantities of ionised ice at the poles. Its momentum then hurled it into its present orbit as "Venus" the planet. Synchronistically, the most ancient Mesopotamian and Central American records don't include Venus in their planetary accounts, but the later ones do, and there was a focus on Venus with human sacrifices made to it. *The Biggest Secret* goes into this whole story in greater detail and you will see that it explains so many "mysteries". These include the sudden freezing of mammoths standing up in the process of eating because the ice did not slowly develop, it arrived in an instant. The ancient legends and myths of how the Golden Age ended are confirmed in every way by the scientific explanation of the geological and environmental affects of this "walk-about" by Venus.

Most important in relation to our story, these conclusions by people like Velikovsky, the Boeing physicists, and increasing numbers of other researchers today, bring the time scale for the end of life on Mars to within the period that saw the end of Atlantis and Lemuria-Mu. Brian Desborough suggests, along with many others, including myself, that the Golden Age was the result of many extraterrestrial and other dimensional races visiting the Earth and operating openly among the human population in a long period of at least hundreds of thousands of years. He believes, like those Boeing physicists he knew and worked with, that the Earth was much closer to the Sun before these events and that Mars orbited in the area the Earth now resides. Two independent scientists, Dr C.J. Hyman and C. William Kinsman, suggested that the Earth once followed the present orbit of Venus and that Mars was located in the present Earth orbit.[56] Ancient legends say that Earth days and years were once shorter than now and humans lived for far longer.[57] If, as is claimed, the deep canyons on the Mars surface were caused by massive torrents of water, there had to have been a warmer climate there at one time because today it is so cold that water would freeze immediately and the vacuum atmosphere would make the water vaporise instantly.[58] The closer orbit to the Sun, Desborough says, would have demanded that the first Earth races would have been black, with the pigmentation necessary to cope with the fiercer rays of the Sun. Ancient skeletons found near Stonehenge and along the west coast of France have the nasal and spinal traits of many female Africans.[59] Ancient artefacts, statues, and artistic depictions around the world also suggest there was an advanced black race of the Negro type.

The Sumerian tablets describe how the Anunnaki "gods" left the planet to escape the devastation, even indicating that they had caused it.[60] The only ones to survive the catastrophe were the extraterrestrials with the technology and foresight, perhaps prior warning, who left before the stuff hit the fan, and the people who sheltered deep underground or in the mountain ranges above the flood water which, according to the Boeing study, could have reached heights of 10,000 feet. The Earth is riddled with tunnels and caverns, natural and created, which date back into far ancient times. Many of these have been located, including an underground city that could house a population of thousands in Cappadocia, Turkey, one of the centres of the Phoenicians and the origin of George of Cappadocia, who later became St George of England. Thirty-six underground cities have been discovered in Cappadocia so far and some are huge complexes going down eight levels. The ventilation systems are so efficient that even eight floors down the air is still fresh. Thirty vast underground cities and tunnel complexes have also been found near Derinkuya in Turkey, also. It was the floodwaters and the need to survive them, which ensured that agriculture in the post-flood world began at altitudes above 10,000 feet and not, as you would expect, in the fertile plains. A study by the botanist, Nikolai Ivanovitch Vavilov, revealed that the 50,000 wild plants he examined from around the world originated in only eight areas – all of them mountainous.[61] In James Churchward's view this would have been because the mountains were *formed* during the cataclysms and therefore many lowland areas were raised to a great height. According to ancient accounts, supported by much other evidence, when the Earth had settled down after the cataclysm, or cataclysms, the survivors began to return from the high mountains north of Sumer in Turkey and Iran into the plains of Mesopotamia. It was in the Turkish mountains, on Mount Ararat, that the symbolic Noah's Ark came to rest when the waters receded, the Bible claims.[62] The Sumerian tablets also relate how the Anunnaki "gods" returned to rebuild and restore their devastated heartlands, and the civilisation that emerged from this is known to history as Sumer. I think, however, that many parts of the Sumerian Tablets are actually referring to events on Lemuria and Atlantis. Some researchers suggest that remains of the Anunnaki's pre-flood cities can be found today under the Persian Gulf, which became much wider and deeper after the upheavals.[63] Depending on the location and the effects of the devastation, some of the great structures of the Golden Age survived and can be seen to this day. These could be anything from tens to hundreds of thousands of years old. Other famous sites and structures were built or rebuilt by the Sumerians from around 6,000 years ago. My feeling at the moment is that Stonehenge and Avebury were among the latter, but not necessarily the pyramids of the Giza plateau, and certainly not some of the breathtaking structures of South America. They definitely appear to be Golden Age.

You can read far more detailed evidence of these cataclysmic events in *The Biggest Secret* and *When The Earth Nearly Died*, together with a list of other books focussing on this subject. Velikovsky's books are listed in the bibliography. The reason this information has been so suppressed in the mainstream of "science", "education", and media, is because of the domino effect it would have on human perception. Have you seen those world record attempts for knocking down the most dominoes? They line them up so that by pushing down the first one they fall on each other and all of them go down. The system of control, the Matrix as I call it, is like that. The Illuminati have to work furiously to keep every domino in their agenda from falling because when one goes they all start to go. The control of what we call "history" is one of their most crucial of these "dominoes". If we knew that there had been a highly developed technological society thousands of years ago, which came to an end with fantastic geological upheavals, we would see the world in a very different light. The whole official version of human evolution would crumble. We would ask who those people were? Where did they come from? Where did they get their knowledge and technology? Suddenly the mysteries of Egypt and Sumer and the staggering structures left us by the ancients would be far less mysterious. And if Egypt and Sumer were founded with this same advanced knowledge, it means that some of those pre-cataclysmic peoples must have survived. So what has happened to their knowledge for thousands of years and what happened to their bloodlines?

Once you allow a hole in your dyke, the flood begins to pour through. This is why the Illuminati, through their vehicles of religion and, more latterly, "science", have made a prime focus the suppression of all knowledge and information that would reveal the true story of human history. Once we see that, the mist begins to clear.

SOURCES

For the people who have written to me asking for the meaning of "Ibid" in the source lists, it means, in effect: "same as above".

1   *The Book Your Church Doesn't Want You To Read*, edited by Tim C. Leenon (Kendall/Hunt Publishing, Iowa, USA, 1993) p 137. Available from the Truth Seeker Company, PO Box 2872, San Diego, California 92112

2   Wm R. Fix, *Pyramid Odyssey* (Jonathan-James Books, Toronto, Canada, 1978) pp 12 to 13

3   Alan F. Alford, *Gods Of The New Millennium*, scientific proof of flesh and blood gods, (Hodder and Stoughton, London, 1996), p 52

4   Ibid

5   Colin Wilson, "Atlantis: At Last, Could This Be The True Secret Of The Lost Continent", London *Daily Mail*, September 30th, 2000

6   Ibid

7   John A. Keel, *Our Haunted Planet* (Fawcett Publications, USA, 1971), p 14

8   Ibid

9   Ibid, p 15

10   Ibid

11   See the books of James Churchward: *The Lost Continent Of Mu*; *The Children Of Mu*; *The Sacred Symbols Of Mu*; *The Cosmic Forces Of Mu*, books one and two. They are available through the David Icke website

12   Professor James DeMeo, *Saharasia: The 4000BCE Origins of Child Abuse, Sex-Repression, Warfare and Social Violence, In the Deserts of the Old World* (Natural Energy Works, USA, 1998).
     Also see article on ***http://www.davidicke.net/tellthetruth/history/saharasian.html***

13   Professor W.B. Emery, *Archaic Egypt* (Penguin Books, UK, 1984)

14   For further details of these legends and accounts all over the world, see *When The Earth Nearly Died* by D.S. Allen and J.B. Delair (Gateway Books, Bath, 1995)

15   *The Children Of Mu* and all Churchward's books are essential reading to any researcher of ancient history

16   Ibid

17   Ibid

18   Ibid

19   Ibid. Also see *The Atlantis Connection*

20   Ibid

21   Ibid

22   Mid-Atlantic Ridge, Encarta Learning Zone,
     http://encarta.msn.com/index/conciseindex/6D/06D05000.htm

23   *When The Earth Nearly Died*, p 31

24   Ibid

25   Maurice Ewing, "New Discoveries On The Mid-Atlantic Ridge", *National Geographic* magazine, November 1949, pp 614, 616

26   *When The Earth Nearly Died*, p 32

27   Charles Berlitz, *Atlantis, The Eighth Continent* (Fawcett Books, New York, 1984), pp 96 to 101

28   *When The Earth Nearly Died*, pp 25 to 28

29   Ibid

30   "Atlantis: At Last, Could This Be The True Secret Of The Lost Continent", London *Daily Mail*, September 30th, 2000, pp 42 to 44

31   Ibid

32   Ibid

33   Ibid

34   Ibid

35   Ibid

36   Ibid

37   Ibid

38   Ibid

39   Ibid

40   Ibid

41   Ibid

42   Mark Amaru Pinkham, *The Return Of The Serpents of Wisdom* (Adventures Unlimited, Kempton, Illinois, 1996), p 8

43   Ibid, p 9

44   Ibid

45   Ibid

46   Ibid, pp 22 and 23

47   See Richard Hoagland's book, *Monuments On Mars* (North Atlantic Books, California, USA, 1996)

48   Brian Desborough, *The Great Pyramid Mystery, Tomb, Occult Initiation Ceremony or What?*, a document supplied to the author in 1998 and also published in the *California Sun* Newspaper, Los Angeles

49   Ibid

50   Preston B. Nichols and Peter Moon, *Pyramids Of Montauk* (Sky Books, New York, 1995), p 129

51   *Our Haunted Planet*, pp 19 and 20

52   See Immanuel Velikovsky's books, *Ages In Chaos* (Doubleday & Co., New York, 1952), *Worlds In Collision* (Pocket Books Simon & Shuster, New York, 1950), *Earth In Upheaval* (Dell Publishing Co., New York, 1955). These are available through the David Icke website

53   Quoted in *Our Haunted Planet*, p 80, from the book, *Worlds in Collision*

54   See the Zecharia Sitchin books, *The 12th Planet*, *Stairway to Heaven*, *The Lost Realms*, *When Time Began*, *The Wars Of The Gods And Men*, and *Genesis Revisited* (Avon Books, New York). It is worth remembering, however, that for whatever reason, Sitchin will simply not accept the existence of a reptilian or serpent race, despite the scale of evidence

55   *The Great Pyramid Mystery*

56   *Our Haunted Planet*, pp 132 and 133

57   Ibid

58   *The Great Pyramid Mystery*

59   Ibid

60   The translations of Zecharia Sitchin

61   *The Great Pyramid Mystery*

62   *Genesis*, Chapter 8, verse 4

63   R.A. Boulay, *Flying Serpents And Dragons, The Story Of Mankind's Reptilian Past*. New revised edition (The Book Tree, PO Box, 724, Escondido, California, 92033, 1997), pp 124 and 125

CHAPTER 3

Ruled by the Gods

Condemnation without investigation is the height of ignorance.

Albert Einstein

The ancient legends and accounts say that the highly advanced cultures of Atlantis and Lemuria were inspired by the knowledge brought by extraterrestrial races from many parts of the galaxy and other dimensions of the universe.

When we open our minds to the suppressed knowledge, we understand that the world we think we live in is only one frequency range of existence. As I mentioned earlier, Creation consists of infinite dimensions of life vibrating at different speeds. Think of the frequencies of the countless radio and television stations broadcasting to your area now. They are all sharing the same space that your body is occupying. You can't see them and they can't see each other because they are vibrating to a different frequency. When you move the dial from one radio station to another, the first station does not suddenly stop broadcasting because you are no longer listening. It goes on broadcasting – existing – just as before. The only difference is that you are no longer tuned to its frequency. All the infinite frequencies of life and existence in all Creation are sharing the same space. Most people call these different frequency ranges "dimensions" and that's fine because people know what they mean. More accurately they are "densities" because the slower that energy vibrates the more dense and "solid" it appears. The faster it vibrates the more ethereal and non-physical it seems to be. Eventually it is vibrating so quickly that it leaves the frequency range – the density – of our physical senses and we cease to see it. The frequency range we can see I will call the Third Density or Third Dimension. At the moment we are tuned to this frequency, the range of our physical senses, and so we can see it and touch it. When we "die" we leave this frequency range and our physical body and we continue our eternal journey elsewhere on another density or dimension. Our consciousness, the thinking, feeling us, is eternal. In the end all frequencies and all expressions of life are the same energy. We are each other. This is the Law of One that the Illuminati Temple of the Sun has sought for thousands of years to suppress. Some extraterrestrial and other-dimensional beings know how to change their frequency so they can move between densities, appearing and "disappearing" as they move frequency, much like a radio dial. This is why people have reported seeing entities "disappear" before their eyes. They have not, in fact, "disappeared" at all. They have left the frequency range that person can access. It's the same with UFOs.

We are not alone

The three main physical forms from constellations, planets, and stars like Orion, Sirius, the Pleiades, Mars, and the others I have mentioned, appear to have been: the white race or the "blue-eyed blonds"; a reptilian race of various expressions; and the so-called "greys" of modern UFO folklore (*see picture section*). Also there was the advanced black race and another, which, according to those who claim to have been abducted by non-human entities, has an insect-like form. In UFO research these have become known as insectoids. I can understand how difficult this will be to accept and comprehend from the conditioned view of reality. But first of all I am not asking anyone to accept anything that I say – it's just information, make of it what you will – and, second, the world is *nothing* like our conditioned view of reality. I would also stress that, like all of my books and talks, this text is presented in layers, each one adding to the ones before. So the detailed information to support the existence of the reptilians, greys, and Nordics, and their interbreeding, will be revealed as the story unfolds. Understanding the connection between the Nordics, the reptilians, and the greys is to understand so much about the world today. W.T. Samsel, author of *The Atlantean Connection*, writes:

> "During the first half of the Lemurian age, the involvement of extraterrestrial beings was simply in the role of the observers. That is to say that they did not intervene, interject or become involved with the subjects of their study at that point in time. The development and progression of the human race on Earth was under the observation and study of these relations from the stars. In 'The Atlantis Connection' I refer to this as the 'Titan project'. The three main extraterrestrial groups, which comprised the Titan project, were those from Sirius, the Pleiades and Orion, although there were indeed other extraterrestrial races, which also shared involvement. This is where the reptilian variety comes into play. As where Sirians, Pleiadeans and those from Orion did interact in cooperation with each other under the mutually agreed upon conditions of the program, I would have to classify the reptilians as a renegade or rebel element which did not adhere to the 'rules' or doctrines of the Titan research project as set down by the three main project participants."[1]

These two races, the blue-eyed blonds and the reptilians, would seem to have been at war in many parts of the galaxy with factions on both sides also joining together to create alliances for their mutual benefit. This reptilian race is the dominating force behind the Illuminati (at one level anyway), but with considerable involvement from the greys and some elements of the extraterrestrial white race or "Nordics" as they are known in UFO research circles. The rest of the global population are pawns in their battles and alliances. The reptilians and Nordics interbred with each other to create hybrid bloodlines. There was also reptilian interbreeding with other races around the world, but the Nordic connection would appear to be the most important to them.* This fusion implanted a reptilian genetic code into the DNA and these are the bloodlines that have ruled the world for thousands of years and are still in the positions of power to this day, as we shall see. Bloodlines that were once Egyptian pharaohs and European royalty are now presidents of the United States, and leading bankers and media owners. A fundamental theme running from the "Golden Age" of Atlantis and Lemuria-Mu to the present day is that of the snake or serpent. Both civilisations were known in legends as the Dragon Lands and the Motherlands.[2] The Greeks called Atlantis "Hespera" (a name for Venus) and they said it was guarded by a dragon.[3] Native American records call Atlantis "Itzamana", which means "Dragon Land" or the "Old Red Land".[4] The Algonquins use the name Pan for the Atlantean continent, a name also given to the goat god of the Greeks. Pan was originally a dragon or goat god of the Atlanteans, some records of the early Egyptians and Greeks suggest.[5] The very name, Mu, pronounced Moo, is close to the Polynesian name for Dragon.[6] An Indian Tamil text, Silappadikaran, describes a lost continent in the Pacific and Indian Ocean it calls Kumari Nadu or Kumari Kandam, which means the "Dragon Land of the Immortal Serpents".[7]

You cannot be Sirius

These technologically advanced extraterrestrial and other-dimensional beings created Mystery schools and a secret society network in Atlantis and Lemuria to pass on levels of their knowledge to chosen initiates. Legends claim that a race came to the Earth from Sirius, the "dog star" and brightest in the sky, which is some 8.7 light years from here. The term "Dog Star" comes from its position in the constellation of Canis Major and it is also known as Orion's Dog.[8] The legends and accounts say that the beings from Sirius brought an infusion of highly advanced knowledge to Atlantis and Lemuria-Mu and founded the Atlantean Mystery School. According to Robert Temple in *The Sirius Mystery* (Destiny Books, Vermont, USA, 1998), the Dogon tribe in Mali, Africa, claim that beings from Sirius visited their ancestors and gave them knowledge of the universe. He says that they describe the Sirians as amphibious and "serpent-featured" – a recurring theme as you will see. Temple suggests that the Anunnaki of the Sumerian tablets could be these beings from Sirius. He further proposes that the body of the Sphinx is that of a dog and not a lion, thus symbolising the Dog Star, Sirius,[9] and some researchers also suggest that the face of the Sphinx is that of a woman, not a pharaoh. The Egyptians certainly depicted their lion bodies very differently to that of the Sphinx and the dog is a common symbol in ancient mythology.[10] In fact, ancient Egyptians revered the dog and their dog symbol was a code for Sirius.[11] The Sirius system was symbolised as feminine and so a dog's body with a woman's face would make

---

* It is the reptilian bloodline that most concerns us in this book, but there are others of extraterrestrial origin, also. Cherokee and Mayan records in North and Central America and the Greek historians, Appollodorius and Diodorus, are among those that claim the Pleiadians, home to both the white race and reptilians, were involved in Atlantis and mated with humans to seed a large race of people.

sense, although there is still a case for it to be a lion, also. Sirius is connected with the colour red because it looks red when it appears over the horizon.[12] Red is the colour used for Sirius in ritual and symbolism. For a long period of its existence, the Sphinx was coloured red. It was an obvious conclusion that this could relate symbolically to Mars, the "red planet", but in the face of the other evidence, Sirius is perhaps more likely. The Queen's shaft in the Great Pyramid was designed to point to Sirius, according to modern researchers. Robert Temple presents a wealth of interconnecting evidence to support his belief that an amphibious race from Sirius came to the Earth in far ancient times and brought with them the knowledge that founded those advanced civilisations. The Sirius system is also depicted as a snake or serpent in a Greek representation in the Louvre Museum in Paris.[13]

Temple's research began when he heard that the Dogon people in Mali, north-west Africa, had told French researchers in 1931 some remarkable information about the Sirius system. According to these researchers, the Dogon also knew about all the planets of the solar system out to Pluto, and of moons that have only recently been confirmed. They said that a star orbited Sirius and it was so heavy all the people of the world could not lift it.[14] At the time, the star they were talking about, now called Sirius B, was not yet discovered by scientists. The Dogon are claimed to have said that it took about 50 years to orbit Sirius A and that it was "infinitely tiny".[15] We now know this is true. Sirius B is a dwarf star and fantastically heavy. The story goes that they said there was a third star, which also orbits Sirius A, and takes 50 years to complete a circuit. Again this was undiscovered at the time, but its existence was confirmed by astronomers in 1995 and it is known as Sirius C.[16] The Illuminati symbolism of three – the trinity – appears to be related, at least in part, to these three stars of the Sirius system. The constant reference to the number 50 in ancient myth could relate to these 50-year orbits, Temple suggests, and they also symbolised Sirius B and C as "the twins" using their combined orbit periods of 100 years as a code for them, he says. Certainly there is endless reference to "twin" symbolism throughout the ancient world. The Dogon call Sirius B, Digitaria, and Sirius C, Sorghun, or the "female star".[17] They also call it the "sun of women" or "star of women".[18] To them, the most important star is Sirius B, which, they rightly said, was invisible to the eye. Still today their religious rituals and rites are based on the cycles of the Sirius system. The Dog Star, Sirius or Sirius A, has two and a half times the mass of our own Sun and is thirty-five and a half times brighter.[19] When you consider that our Sun contains 99% of the mass of this solar system, Sirius is some baby. Sirius B contains 1.053 times the mass of our Sun.[20] It is incredibly compressed, however, and thus is very small.

A focus on Sirius can be found at the heart of most ancient societies – and secret societies. The heat in the summer months was believed to be, in part, caused by Sirius and so they became known as "dog days". The Egyptian calendar was regulated by the movement of Sirius (Sothis to the Greeks) and the Sothic calendar was founded on the rising of Sirius one minute before the Sun, the so-called heliacal rising in the Summer.[21] The number 23 was important to the Dogons, as it was to the Egyptians and the Babylonians. Some researchers say this was connected to the heliacal rising on July 23rd when Sirius, the Earth, and the Sun are in a straight line. Others speculate that this could create a "star gate" connection between the two systems, a sort of interdimensional (inter-density) portal. This moment was the beginning of the calendar for the new year in many cultures. It is said that the eyes of the Sphinx (the dog?) line up with the exact period on the horizon where Sirius rises on July 23rd and that the pyramids are also lined up to that point on the horizon.[22] This, incidentally, is the time every year that the Illuminati elite gather at Bohemian Grove in Northern California wearing their hooded robes for their infamous rituals under a 40-foot stone owl, as detailed in *The Biggest Secret*. I will mention more about this later on. The Freemasons and other secret societies within the Illuminati web have Sirius as their focus. It is known as the Eastern Star – the

very name for the Freemasonic organisation that allows women to become initiates.[23] Sirius is the first star to rise in the east in the latitudes of Egypt. The symbol of the Eastern Star is the symbol of Satanism, the inverted pentagram, and that is their symbol for Sirius (*Figure 2*). The pentagram within a circle is used by Satanists in their rituals to draw other dimensional demonic entities into this world or to "draw down the Kingdom of Satan into manifestation on Earth", as one writer put it. The pentagram is symbolised by the goat head known as the "Goat of Mendes" or "Baphomet", the image the Knights Templar secret society was accused of worshipping when it was purged in France after 1307. The goat head is also associated with

Figure 2: *The inverted pentagram, the classic symbol of Satanism, and, apparently, a symbol for Sirius.*

the Sirius system. The ancients designed massive temples to point directly at the spot on the horizon where Sirius appeared at the "rising" and their key rituals were focused on Sirius, just as many of the Illuminati's are today. One example of these Sirius-aligned structures is the Temple of Isis at Denderah in Egypt.[24]

The goddess, Isis, is a symbol of Sirius in Egyptian myth. Robert Temple suggests in *The Sirius Mystery* that Isis is Sirius and the "sister-goddess" of Isis, Nephthys, represents Sirius B. Isis was said to be visible and Nephthys invisible, just like Sirius A and B. Another Sirius symbol was Anubis (Anpu to the Egyptians), the one portrayed as the dog or jackal-headed god and associated with Osiris, the "Sun God" of Egypt.[25] There was also a goddess called Anukis who sails in a celestial boat with Sothis and Satis, again the three stars of Sirius perhaps because they are associated with goddesses, and Sottis was the Greek term for Sirius. The symbol of the dog or wolf is often found in cults that worship the serpent or reptilians. Credo Mutwa, the Zulu shaman, says that their legends call Sirius the "Star of the Wolf". The leader of the reptilian "gods" known as the Anunnaki is named in the Sumerian tablets as An (later Anu). He was represented by the jackal or dog. Associated with Sirius in Egyptian belief was Orion and, interestingly, modern UFO researchers connect the reptilians with both Sirius and Orion. Isis (Sirius) was the companion of Osiris (Orion?) in Egyptian myth. Among the major Illuminati symbols to the present day are the eye, the triangle or pyramid, the five-pointed star, the obelisk, and the dome. The Egyptian hieroglyph for Sirius was the obelisk, dome and five-pointed star; the Bozo tribe of Mali, cousins to the Dogon, call Sirius the "Eye Star"; an Egyptian hieroglyph for Sirius was a triangle – three points representing the three Sirius stars; and the triangle symbolised water in Pythagorean code;[26] The eye was a symbol of Osiris in Egyptian myth. The bow and arrow is another symbol used by the ancients for Sirius and they knew it as the "bow star". The Egyptian word meaning Bowman also referred to a "heavy star metal" – Sirius B – and their word for heavy star metal was close to the words meaning dwarf and weight.[27] The Sumerian account called the Epic of Gilamesh tells of a star that is so heavy it cannot be lifted (Sirius B). This star was associated with An or Anu, the leader of the Anunnaki. The chief Egyptian god, Osiris, was also called An. In Sumerian accounts, An, the jackal-dog-headed god, had a daughter, the goddess Bau, the goddess of the dog. It has been suggested that Bau is the origin of the term "bow wow" for a dog's bark.[28] It certainly bears no resemblance to the sound a dog makes. In the Sumerian epic, Gilamesh is given 50 companions, which could be symbolic of the 50 years it takes for Sirius B to orbit Sirius. What's for sure, the ancients perceived Sirius and Sirius B as very important to their lives.

The Dogon are said to call these amphibious beings from Sirius, the Nommo or "Masters of the Water". The accounts of this extraterrestrial race are widely supported by ancient reports. The Sumerians claimed that strange beings from the sea founded their civilisation. The historian, Alexander Polyhistor (born 105BC) wrote that these beings were amphibious and were happier to go back to the sea at night.[29] They are described as "semi-demons" (half human, half not human) and animals endowed with reason.[30] Other legends say that they were superhuman in their knowledge and their length of life. They were "the immortals" and returned to "the gods" in a ship, taking with them examples of the Earth's fauna. Interestingly, the Dogon call Sirius "the Land of the Fish" and "the pure Earth", and the day the Nommo landed on our Earth is known as the "day of the fish".[31] The Babylonian priest Berossus wrote that the origin of humans in Babylonian belief could be traced to the "fish god" Oannes, who was known as Dagon to the Philistines. What they said about Oannes, the Sumerians said about "Enki", one of the key leaders of their reptilian Anunnaki. Enki was symbolised as closely connected with water and it was said that he rode in a ship that could go under the water or fly in the sky. He was described as a giant who had scales like a fish or reptile. In the Babylonian legend, Oannes was one of the "Annedoti" ("the repulsive ones") who had the heads and legs of men, but the body and tail of a fish.[32] This is the origin of the mermaid stories, no doubt. The Greek gods known as the "Old Men of the Sea" were depicted as "mermen". It was said that if you fought with them, they changed shape and the legendary founders of Athens, Cecrops and his son, were said to be half-human-half-serpent amphibians. The Greek god, Tython, was another half-man-half-serpent figure with mythological connections to Sirius, and both Isis and

Osiris were portayed with fish or serpent tails in some effigies. Poseidon of the Greeks and Neptune of the Romans were symbols of the same theme.

The Anunnaki (Annedoti) seem to be very connected to water and their bloodlines use code names to this day that often relate to being "of the water". The major bloodline families appear to locate either in very hot regions, like Texas, Arizona, Nevada, and California, or, more often, in cold damp places where there is lots of water. The Netherlands is a major centre for them and that is one of the dampest countries in the world with much of it reclaimed from the sea. Also, the cold and damp castles and palaces of the aristocracy in Europe are their preferred habitat. The recurrence of Anu, as in the Anunnaki (and An or Anu, their "leader"), is a common theme in ancient mythology. We have Anubis and Anukis, and in the ancient Sanskrit language the word anu-pa means "a watery country".[33] The ancient legends and beliefs suggest that the Sirius system is very watery with dense vegetation – perfect for amphibians and the reptilian species. Chinese traditions claim that their civilisation was founded by an amphibious being called Fu-Hsi or Fuxi in 3322BC. One description says he had a serpent's body and a man's head and he is said to have begun the repopulation of the world after the deluge with an incestuous interbreeding with a character called Nu Gua, who is also described as half human, half serpent. Another ancient Chinese figure was Gong-Gong, who was "a horned monster with the body of a serpent". This sounds very much like Set of the Egyptians and Ogo in the myths of the Dogon. Other amphibious entities in Chinese tradition are Emperor Yu (Yu relates to reptiles) and his father Gun (a name relating to fish), and Chinese drawings of their historical, mythological characters are similar to those drawn by the Dogon.

Today there are streams of reports across the world of people seeing UFOs flying in and out of seas and lakes, not least at Lake Titicaca in Peru/Bolivia, the highest navigable lake on Earth. The respected UFO researcher, Timothy Good, gives many examples of this phenomenon in his book, *Unearthly Disclosure*, (Century, United Kingdom, 2000). He calls these craft USOs, or Unidentified Submergible Objects, and includes the accounts of witnesses who have seen them around the world, especially in places like Lake Cote, Costa Rica, and the mountainous El Yunque rainforest in Puerto Rico.[34] The Dogon describe the arrival of the Nommo in an "ark" that sounds very much like a spacecraft. Robert Temple says the Dogon indicate that the Nommo landed in the region of Egypt and describe the tremendous noise and vibration when the "ark" landed, causing a whirlwind of dust. They say of the Nommo, a term they also use in the singular: "He is like a flame that went out when he touched the Earth." Dogon legend says the ship, or "ark", landed on three legs, Temple writes. A larger craft hovered in the atmosphere. The Nommo said that some of their number would be called "the disrupters", and one would "die on the cross", the Dogon legends apparently say.[35] Peruvian creation myths tell of a great disk that came out of the sky and landed on an island called the Island of the Sun. This is a place I have visited twice on the Bolivian side of Lake Titicaca. During the Great Deluge, the top of this island was the first piece of land to emerge as the water receded, they say. There are sceptics

Figure 3: *The classic Illuminati symbol of the all-seeing-eye and the pyramid with the capstone missing on the US dollar bill*

Figures 4 and 5: *The pyramid and all-seeing eye is used by a stream of companies in their advertising, including R.J. Reynolds, a major Illuminati bloodline, and Fidelity Investments…*

who seek to discredit the stories of the Dogon, the Nommo, and their tales of Sirius. They say the French researchers who first published the information had simply invented everything. But Credo Mutwa, the Zulu shaman and that nation's official historian, says that his people have the same traditions. He says they call Sirius the "Star of the Wolf" and their ancient accounts say that a "sea-dwelling fish people" from Sirius came to the Earth. They also speak of a "gigantic war" on Sirius in which the fish people drove out those who we now know as humans. Credo further confirms that the stories attributed to the Dogon are not the only ancient records of the Sirius system. The Zulu's knew Sirius B as the "pit" star long before it was identified by modern technology. Credo wrote in his book, *Song Of The Stars* (Station Hill Openings, Barrytown, New York, 1996):

> "Not only among the Zulu, but the Dogon, and many widespread African tribes, there are stories of the Nommo, who resemble the king of the Water People in our legend. They are said to be intelligent beings who have visited the Earth several times. They are usually described as somewhat like human beings, but with skins like reptiles. I have heard them described as a cross between a little demon and a dolphin." [36]

The translations of the Sumerian Tablets by Zecharia Sitchin claim that the Anunnaki came from a planet called Nibiru, which, he says, has a vast elliptical orbit that takes it way out beyond Pluto and back between Mars and Jupiter every 3,600 years. The idea of Nibiru referring to a planet has never felt right to me. A massive comet, maybe. But either way there is a fundamental connection between the reptilian Anunnaki of the Sumerian tablets and Sirius-Orion. Researcher Mark Amaru Pinkham says in his book, *The Return Of The Serpents Of Wisdom* (Adventures Unlimited, Illinois, USA, 1997), that the symbol of the Sirians in Atlantis was a triangle, sometimes with an eye in the middle. [37] This pyramid with the capstone missing and/or the all-seeing eye is an ancient symbol used by the Illuminati and can be found today on the dollar bill, the reverse of the Great Seal of the United States, and on a stream of logos used by Illuminati companies (*Figures 3, 4 and 5*). You also find it on the logo of the British Intelligence operation,

Figure 6: *...and here it is in the logo of the British Intelligence arm, MI5. British Intelligence is a creation of the Illuminati going back at least to Elizabeth Ist in the 16th century*

Figure 7: *The symbol of the snake in the logo of British Telecom, the UK's major telecommunications company. Follow the right leg through to the right arm*

MI5 (*Figure 6*). According to the story, the design for the Great Seal was handed to the founding father and Rosicrucian, Thomas Jefferson, by a mysterious stranger dressed in a cape with a hood that covered his face. After the end of Atlantis the survivors took this symbol to places like Egypt and from there it continued to be used by the Illuminati secret society network that re-emerged after the cataclysm. The three-pronged trident was the symbol of the royal line of Atlantis and this later became the three-pointed Fleur-de-lis, a symbol of the Illuminati bloodline to this day. The key Atlantean "god" was the fire god, Votan[38] who would turn up later in the Americas and Europe as Wotan and Wodan.

The American organisation, the Lemurian Fellowship, which researches the history of the lost continent, says that an extraterrestrial race from Venus, known as the Kumaras, were the leaders of the Lemurian civilisation.[39] The Fellowship says that the Kumaras created a Mystery school to initiate chosen people into the advanced esoteric knowledge. It was structured as 13 schools (levels of initiation), they say, with each one more advanced than the one below.[40] This is the classic structure of secret societies throughout history. Those who passed the initiation into the 13th school would then be allowed to teach the knowledge themselves as a member of the "Order of the Serpents".

William Bramley in *The Gods Of Eden* (Avon Books, New York, 1993) calls this the Brotherhood of the Snake. You can see snake and serpent symbolism in the logos of Illuminati companies and the logo of the leading UK communications network, British Telecom, is one example (*Figure 7*). Lemurian kings and queens were 13th-level initiates of the "Dragon Bloodline", according to the Lemurian Fellowship. As with the serpent cult or serpent brotherhood through the ages, the Lemurian initiates were worshippers of the Sun. But was it our Sun or was it Sirius, the brightest star in the sky? Records discovered in India by the leading author and researcher on Lemurian history, Colonel James Churchward, confirmed this Sun worship. One of Lemuria's names, apparently, was "The Empire of the Sun" and the Sun symbols of the Illuminati may also relate to that and the Atlantean "Temple of the Sun".[41]

Atlantis and Lemuria existed for hundreds of thousands of years and Atlantis broke up in stages over a long period before the final destruction. Both cultures expanded across the world with their priests and "royal" bloodlines or "Dragon

Kings", founding colonies in all parts of the globe. With them went their serpent symbolism which has survived to this day in places like China and, most certainly, within the Illuminati. It was during the Atlantean-Lemurian era that the same knowledge, stories, and symbolism were communicated all over the planet, and the royal bloodlines of the extraterrestrial races were seeded everywhere. This explains how, after the cataclysm, when European races "discovered" the Americas, Australia, and other apparently unconnected regions of the world, they found the people telling the same stories and following the same basic religions as each other (*Figure 8*). The common origin was Atlantis-Lemuria. As they travelled and colonised the Americas and what became Egypt and the Middle East, Europe, Scandinavia, and China, the Atlantean and Lemurian initiates used their advanced techniques to build pyramids and other vast structures that we would struggle to build even today. Researchers have established that these great structures were built in geometrical relationship to each other over fantastic distances in different parts of the planet. It appears to be a mystery how this could be done, but it's not. The sacred places of the ancients (and the Illuminati today) were invariably the vortex points on the global energy grid. This is a web of force lines, known as ley lines or meridians, which encircle and interpenetrate the planet. I'll go into more detail about this later. When these lines cross it creates a spiralling vortex of energy and

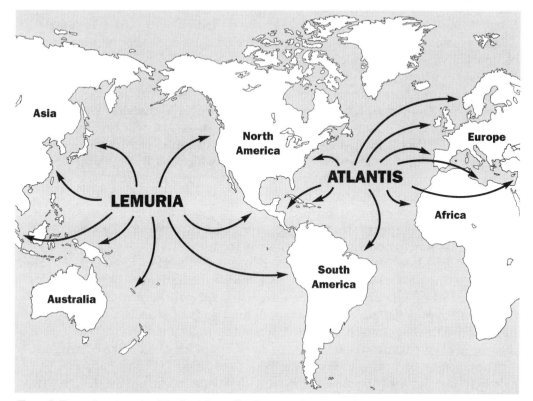

Figure 8: *The endless legends of the "gods" travelling from a sunken land to found civilisations around the world can be explained by the movement of peoples from Atlantis in the Atlantic Ocean and Lemuria, or Mu, in the Pacific*

the more lines that cross, the bigger the vortex, obviously. It was at these multi-line vortexes, like Stonehenge, that the Atlanteans and Lemurians built their temples, pyramids, and so on. The grid is geometrical and the vortex points are in geometrical relationship to each other. Therefore, anything built on those points also have the same geometrical relationship with other structures on other points. Simple, once you have the knowledge to locate the vortexes, which the Atlanteans and Lemurians could. The famous ancient and modern "sacred sites" are invariably associated with the Atlanteans and Lemurians. Sedona in Arizona, famous for its massive vortexes to this day, is claimed to be an ancient colony of the Lemurians, as is Mount Shasta in northern California.[43] Sedona is also associated by researchers of UFO activity with a reptilian underground base where members of the reptilian race work with their human or part-human puppets in the Illuminati on the scientific and genetic agenda. The base would appear to be under Boynton Canyon in Sedona. This is not far in American terms from the reservation of the Hopi tribe, which has Lemurian connections.

The Atlantean/Lemurian colonies

A branch of the Atlanteans and Lemurians who colonised the planet were called the Carians (Carian = "Serpent Sea People of the Atlantean Fire God"); the Eus-Cara (same basic meaning); and the Tuarkes (Serpent People of the All Glorious Fire God").[44] The Tuarkes became the Tuaraks, who settled in North Africa with their Atlantean knowledge; the Eus-Cara became the Basques of Spain; and the Carians became known as the Phoenicians – a very important fact, as will become clear soon.[45] James Churchward also documents the Carians in the Americas. The Taureg people of North Africa today, descendants of the Tuarkes, have allowed some visitors to see their ancient cavern system in the Ahaggar Mountains where they have murals of their Atlantean ancestors holding snakes and swords with tridents on the blades.[46] People invited into the underground temples of the Tuaregs claim to have seen green reptile "monsters" called Ourans, which the Tuaregs worship as the physical representations of their serpent goddess or "grandmother".[47] The Tuaregs also perform a dance in honour of the Atlantean fire god, Volcan or Votan. The Atlanteans and Lemurians established colonies in Egypt, then known as Khem or "Land of the Fire Serpent". The letter "K", the sound used so often by these reptilian bloodlines apparently, was written in the form of a serpent in Egyptian hieroglyphics. Khem was the name of the deity symbolised as a black goat and later called Pan. The goat is still a symbol of worship for the Illuminati and Satanists today under the name Baphomet. There are many surviving records that claim a lineage of Egyptian kings going back tens of thousands of years before the formation of the Egyptian civilisation described by official historians. This supports the stories of an Atlantean/Lemurian colony in Egypt long before the cataclysm.

The colonisation of Greece is also far older than officially claimed and this colony (called the Athenians) went to war with Atlanteans before the deluge. Plato wrote of this war and official historians have dismissed it because they say that Greece did not exist that long ago. They are mistaken. The "Classic Greece" they focus upon was a later expression of that culture, not the first. The original Greece existed before the cataclysms that sank Atlantis. The Atlantean colonists of Greece worshipped a serpent goddess called Athene or Neith.[48] The Greek historians, Jane Harrison and Robert Graves, say that this deity was symbolised as a serpent, snake, sphinx, or goddess covered in snakes.[49] There are some people – myself among them – who believe that the face on the Sphinx on the Giza plateau is a woman and not a man as officially claimed. Wherever the reptilian bloodlines have located, the worship of a serpent goddess has always been the centre of their rituals under names like Athene, Barati, Isis, Semiramis, El, Artemis, Diana, and Hecate. Other Atlantean/Lemurian colonists were known as the Pelasgians ("Peoples of the Sea"), the Danaans, and the female Amazons.[50] The Pelasgians worshipped the serpent Moon goddess Dana, later Diana (Artemis), and the Atlantean goat god called Pan. They first landed on the Peloponnese in Greece and settled in Arcadia, according to ancient Greek records. Arcadia has always been a sacred place to the Illuminati bloodlines and was apparently a name for Atlantis.

The Danaans left Atlantis to settle in Asia Minor (now Turkey), Greece, and the islands of the Aegean. They are claimed by some authors to descend from the Old Testament Tribe of Dan, but so much in the Bible is symbolic rather than literal or downright untrue. The name Danaans derived from their serpent Moon goddess, Dana or Diana. The Danaans made the headquarters of their serpent-worshipping culture on the island of Rhodes, a name that originates from a Syrian word for serpent.[51] Rhodes was the home of the Danaan brotherhood of initiates and magicians known as the Telchines.[52] The Greek historian, Diodorus, said these initiates had the ability to heal, change the weather, and "shape-shift" into any form. Thousands of years later, one of the most important of the Illuminati secret societies, the Knights Hospitaller of St John of Jerusalem, now the Knights of Malta, located on Rhodes and for a while were known as the Knights of Rhodes. Ultimately, they came from the same source as the Knights Templar. The name Rhodes, which is connected to the German "Rot", meaning red, as with Rothschild ("Red-shield"), became a code name for the bloodlines. Red = Sirius? These guys don't choose their locations or their names by accident. Malta, too, was an important centre by 3500BC and the home of a major Mystery school. Under Malta is a vast network of tunnels and megalithic temples where secret rituals took place – and still do. Malta's original name was Lato, named after Mother Lato, the serpent goddess.[53] The Knights Templar secret society was formed in the late 11th century to protect the reptilian bloodline or "Le Serpent Rouge", the red serpent or serpent blood, together with their associated order, the highly secretive Priory of Sion.[54] The goals of the Knights Templar and the Illuminati were, and are, to place these serpent bloodlines in all positions of power worldwide and thus form a reptilian, centrally controlled, fascist state. We are now getting very close to that. The Danaans also settled on Cyprus (later controlled by the Knights Templar) and in ancient times it was known as Ia-Dan or the "Isle of Dan".[55] The name of the Isle of Man in the Irish Sea, a place so important to the Druids, has the same origin, no doubt. The Taurus Mountains in Turkey, the Baleric Islands, and Syria (Sirius?) were among other Danaan settlements and they travelled from Atlantis to Britain where they became known as Tuatha de Danaan or the "People of the Sea". These carried the Anunnaki reptilian bloodlines. The female Amazons were another branch of the Atlanteans and Lemurians and myths say they came from a paradise called Hesperides or Hespera, a name for Atlantis.[56] They, too, followed the goddess Athene or Nieth and venerated her symbol, the double-headed axe. They founded shrines to the serpent goddess in many places, including the famous centre for Diana worship at Ephesus and other locations along the Turkish coast. The "Canaanites" also descended from Atlantis/Lemuria.[57] Mark Amaru Pinkham describes the migration of Atlanteans to "Canaan" in *The Return Of The Serpents Of Wisdom*:

> "One branch of these Atlantides were the Tyrrhenians, the people after whom the present Tyrrhenian Sea is named. The Tyrrhenians eventually split in half to become the Etruscans and the Carians or Phoenicians, a tribe which eventually migrated to Canaan (pronounced Ka-nan with the K sound of the serpents), a territory on the Asia Minor coast, which can be translated as the "Land of the Fire Serpent".[58]

Running for cover

As these colonies and settlements were established, the serpent bloodlines from Atlantis and Lemuria were placed into the positions of ruling royal power, just as they had been, at least in the latter stages, before those continents sank. These are the same bloodlines that run the world today. Just before each of the cataclyms, many Atlantean and Lemurian royal bloodlines and initiates fled to other parts of the world, heading mostly for high places to escape the impending flood. Atlanteans went to Britain, one of their colonies, to Europe, Scandinavia, North Africa, the mountains of Turkey and Iraq, and the Americas. All along the American continent are the ancient legends and accounts of highly advanced beings, the founders of their culture, arriving with great knowledge from the sunken land in the Atlantic. On the western seaboard of the Americas and in Asia, they talk of similar advanced "gods" arriving from a sunken continent in the Pacific. Polynesians claim that survivors from this lost continent travelled to India before returning to the remnants of their homeland, the Pacific Islands, and becoming the Polynesians.[59] James Churchward says that these peoples also settled in Egypt via India. Chinese legend talks of a continent in the same area called Maurigosima, which sank amid cataclysm, but its king, Peiru-un, escaped to mainland China and continued his bloodline there.[60] This happened a number of times as Lemuria and Atlantis fell to cataclysmic events.

I will focus from here on what happened after the stage-by-stage destruction of Atlantis in the period from around 10,000BC to 5000BC. When the Earth settled down after the incredible upheavals, the survivors from Atlantis and Lemuria began to recolonise the planet. And one of their key centres became known as Sumer, the "cradle of civilisation", in the eyes of official history. This was the restarting of civilisation after the cataclysm. Sir Laurence Gardner is the current front man of the ancient Imperial Royal Dragon Court and Order, which was originally created in Egypt about 2000BC to support the agenda of the so-called "Dragon Kings" or reptilian bloodlines. Gardner says that Sumaire in the old Irish language means dragon. He writes: "It is also reckoned that the subsequent culture of the region, phonetically called Sumerian (pronounced "Shumerian") was actually Sidhé-murian ("Shee-murian"). In fact, the case for this is now considerable, since the early Ring Lords of Scythia (the Tuatha Dé Danaan king-tribe) were actually called the *Sumaire*." [61] Another researcher, Frans Kamp in the Netherlands, tells me that Sumer means "Land of the Dragon" in the language of the Scandinavian Vikings. The founders of Sumer were the same reptilian Anunnaki who had controlled Atlantis in its latter stages and led it to destruction. Their obsession with technology and control by machine, so characteristic of the final era of Atlantis, can be seen in the world today. There is a reason for that: the Anunnaki are still in control.

One theme of the Atlantean and Lemurian legends is that, especially in the latter stages, there emerged a very dark force that took over the Mystery schools and the seats of power and used their advanced knowledge in the most horrendous and malevolent ways. They manipulated people's minds and caused mayhem with the misuse of esoteric "magic" – the manipulation of energy. Massive conflicts erupted and some accounts suggest that even the cataclysm itself could have been caused by the way they imbalanced the Earth's energy field. This was the Anunnaki at work – just as they are today.

SOURCES

1   W.T. Samsel article: "The Aliens Are Among Us" for the David Icke e-magazine, Volume 9, January 15th, 2000. Available on the David Icke website

2   *The Return Of The Serpents Of Wisdom*, p 7

3   Ibid, p 21

4   Ibid, p 22

5   Ibid, p 40

6   Ibid, p 7

7   Ibid, p 9

8   Robert Temple, *The Sirius Mystery* (Destiny Books, Vermont, 1968), p 86

9   Ibid, pp 11 and 12

10 Ibid, p 11

11 Ibid, p 268

12 Ibid, p 86

13 Ibid, p 232

14 Ibid, p 68

15 Ibid

16 Ibid, p 3

17 Ibid, p 68

18 Ibid

19 Sirius background: *http://www.britannica.com/seo/s/sirius/*

20 *The Sirius Mystery*, pp 26 and 28

21 Ibid, pp 85 and 86

22 See article "The Dogons and the Sirius Mystery":
    http://www.cco.net/~trufax/fol/fol5.html

23 See *http://www.easternstar.org/*

24 *The Sirius Mystery*, p 85

25 Ibid, p 96

26 Ibid, p 268

27 Ibid

28 Ibid, p 137

29 Ibid, p 60

30 Ibid, p 278

31 Ibid, p 76

32 Ibid, p 279

33 Ibid, p 96

34 London *Daily Mail*, article "Aliens Under The Sea", Saturday, November 11th, 2000, pp
    48 to 51

35 *The Sirius Mystery*, p 300

36 Vusamazulu Credo Mutwa, *Song Of The Stars* (Station Hill Openings, Barrytown, New York,
    1996), p 130

37 *The Return Of The Serpents Of Wisdom*, p 25

38 Ibid, many references

39 Ibid, p 15

40 Ibid

41 Ibid

42 Quoted in *Our Haunted Planet*, p 95

43 *The Return Of The Serpents Of Wisdom*, p 17

44 Ibid, p 30

45 Ibid, p 34

46 Ibid, p 31

47   Ibid, p 34

48   Ibid, p 39

49   Jane Harrison, *Themis, A Study Of The Social Origins Of Greek Religion*, (Peter Smith IPublishing, Glouster, Massachusets, 1974); Robert Graves, *The White Goddess* (Octagon Books, New York, 1972)

50   *The Return Of The Serpents Of Wisdom*, many references to these peoples

51   Ibid, p 41

52   Ibid

53   Ibid, p 78

54   See *Holy Blood, Holy Grail* (Corgi Books, London, 1982)

55   *The Return Of The Serpents Of Wisdom*, p 41

56   Ibid, p 42

57   Ibid, p 34

58   Ibid

59   Ibid, p 8

60   Ibid, p 9

61   Sir Laurence Gardner: ***http://www.nexusmagazine.com/ringlords1.html***

CHAPTER 4

Atlantis revisited

Even if you're on the right track, you'll get run over if you just sit there.

Will Rogers

The survivors of the deluge and the upheavals re-emerged from the mountains and underground shelters and began to rebuild a shattered world. We are perhaps talking of around 7,000 years ago when Atlantis was finally destroyed, although there are differing opinions on the precise timescale.

Some ancient accounts say that the extraterrestrial "gods" (the "Anunnaki" of the Sumerian tablets) left the planet in their flying craft during the cataclysm and returned when it was over. Wherever the surviving bloodlines and descendants of the Mystery school initiates of Atlantis and Lemuria resettled, advanced civilisations began to reappear. Egypt, China and the Indus Valley in India were among them, but the most significant became known as Sumer between the Euphrates and Tigris rivers in what we now call Iraq (*Figure 9*). Lawrence Augustine Waddell, better known as L.A., is a forgotten and unacknowledged genius who lived from 1854 to 1938. He was a Scot who graduated from the University of Glasgow with the highest honours and went on to be professor of chemistry and pathology at the Calcutta Medical College in India. His highly decorated military career as a medical officer led him to travel widely across the Near and Far East and this fuelled his passion to uncover the truth of ancient history. He became a fellow of the Royal Anthropological Institute and produced many brilliant books and papers as he pieced together the evidence that demolished the official version of history. In the first 38 years of the last century, Waddell proved that the Sumer, Egypt, and Indus Valley cultures were the same empire ruled by the same leader (a fact very significant to the Christian story). But official history still says they were not connected and this is taught in schools and universities to this day. Waddell proved that this Sumer Empire was also established in the British Isles and Ireland, and introduced the same religious and cultural themes there. This was the inherited knowledge later administered by the Druids, successors in Europe to the Atlantean/Lemurian Mystery school priests. These rulers of the Sumer Empire, he established, were what I am calling in this book the white "Nordic" race, the blue-eyed blonds. What Waddell did not realise, of course, is that these bloodlines were of extraterrestrial origin and that their ruling bloodlines had interbred with a reptilian

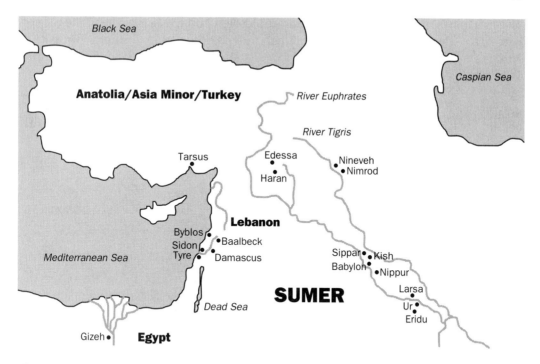

Figure 9: *The land of Sumer or Mesopotamia in what we now call Iraq. Mesopotamia means "between two rivers" – the Tigris and the Euphrates*

race to produce hybrid DNA. This is why these outwardly white bloodlines were symbolised by terms like the Dragon Kings. I know this all sounds fantastic, but stay with me and you will see the evidence to support this apparently bizarre suggestion.

South to Sumer

At least many strands of this "Nordic" race travelled to Sumer from the far north where we now have Scandinavia and northern Europe. These were the Norse people who came down into France to establish Normandy and became the Normans, or "Norse (north) Men" who invaded Britain with William the Conqueror at the time of the Battle of Hastings in 1066. These regions of Scandinavia and Europe were colonies of the former Lemurian/Atlantean empire. With the cataclysms came the ice sheets and those who survived fled south to what is now France, The Netherlands (Holland), Belgium, and on down to the Mediterranean, the Middle and Near East, and India. Frans Kamp is a Dutchman I met while researching this book and we spent two days together in the south of The Netherlands swapping information. He has been investigating the reptilian story full time since he realised that his wife of more than 12 years was a reptilian hybrid. I'll explain more about this later. After their divorce, his experiences with her, and his desire to understand what was going on, fired his passion to unlock the secrets. When I met him he was writing a book of his own, detailing his findings. Frans soon realised that to understand the world today, you have to research human history. You can't have one without the other. His research, particularly that of the Nordic peoples, led him to see that the white race of Sumer, or at least a significant part of it, had moved down from northern Europe after the upheavals. He says they came from locations called Friezland, Scandza, and Tula, which could be today's Greenland, he thinks. Certainly there is an Illuminati interest in Greenland that does not make sense when viewed simply from the perspective of a vast island covered in snow and ice. One of the key secret societies behind the German Nazis was called the Thule Society after "Ultima Thule", one of the alleged origins of the "master race" in the far north of the world. This "Aryan master race" was said to be...blond-haired and blue-eyed. Frans Kamp says that the name Holland (a big region of The Netherlands) came from Halland in Scandinavia as those peoples moved south and settled new lands. He suggests that some of the leaders of these Scandinavian tribes were called Teun, which became Tunis; Jon, which became Iona and Ionian; Geert, which became Geert-mannen or Geert-men, later Ger-man; and Otto, which later became Ottoman. He says that the Illuminati Habsburg bloodline was Nordic or Viking originally, but they interbred with the reptilian race to form a genetic and political alliance. So did many others of the "royal" Nordic bloodlines. James Churchward, however, also documents the fundamental influence in the Sumer/Babylon region of former Lemurian peoples via India. Frans Kamp came across a common theme I have found in reptilian research: they want something very badly that is contained in the Nordic and human genetic code. Interbreeding is their way to access it. The blond-haired, blue-eyed, race and its connection to the reptilians is crucial to understanding both past and present, or, at least, what we call past and present. Sumer was founded by the reptilian Anunnaki bloodlines in league with factions of the Nordic Vikings and was thus known in the Viking language, according to Frans Kamp, as the "Land of the Dragon". Summaire, a Celtic word for dragon, was a later version of this. I think the name "Aryan" is not so much a term for the white race as widely believed, but for the Nordic-reptilian hybrids, the so-called "master race" or "noble race". Whatever, I will use it in that context throughout this book. The very name Aryan comes from the word "Arri", meaning noble one. The Illuminati refer to their bloodlines as royal and noble, hence nobility and aristocracy or ARI-STOCK-RACY. The name Sum-ARIAN is, therefore, very appropriate.

The Sumer Empire

L.A.Waddell's brilliant research really begins with the foundation of Sumer around 4000BC. He was an expert in Sumerian and Egyptian hieroglyphics and the Sanskrit language of the Indus Valley. A rare gift indeed, and this allowed him to travel these regions, reading the ancient accounts and the stories on the temples and monuments, to show without question that Sumer, Egypt, and the Indus Valley were parts of one empire based on Sumer (*Figure 10*). It should be emphasised, however, that before the cataclysm a high civilisation had existed for tens of thousands of years in India, as a colony of Lemuria, and that Egypt, another Lemurian/Atlantean colony, also went back long before the Sumer Empire. Sumer, too, had Lemurian/Atlantean origins. Waddell's work is documented in detail in his book, *Egyptian Civilisation,*

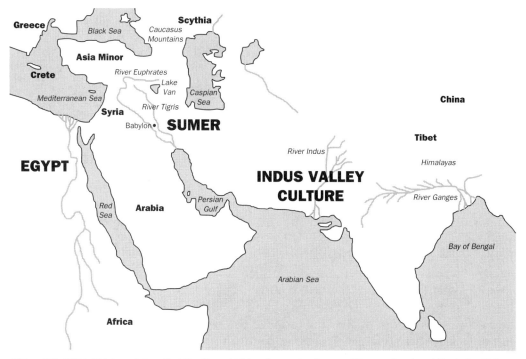

Figure 10: *Official history claims that the three highly advanced cultures of Sumer, Egypt and the Indus Valley developed independently. L.A. Waddell shows that they were all part of the empire ruled from Sumer*

Its Sumerian Origin And Real Chronology (available from Hidden Mysteries through the David Icke website). He discovered from the time lines and the descriptions of the leaders and their genealogy that the rulers of these three cultures were the same people under different names. It is the different names that have obscured the truth to a large extent. Historians have taken different names to mean different people. Not true. The endless "gods" in the various cultures also turn out to be different names for the same deities. Once you understand this, wading into the past becomes a lot less complicated. The advantage that Waddell had over conventional Egyptologists and "historians" (apart from an open mind) was that he could read Sumerian and could therefore decipher inscriptions in Egypt, which they could not understand. He could see that early Egyptian hieroglyphics were those used by their ruling culture in Sumer. It was only later that they evolved into an Egyptian system developed more locally. It is the latter that Egyptologists have been decoding. The earlier Sumerian hieroglyphics in Egypt flummoxed them. But not Waddell.

Here is one example of how he proved his point. One of the best-known kings of Sumer is called King Sargon. The Sumerians recorded that he had a son, who later became emperor, called Manis. At the same time, Waddell shows, the son of the king in the Indus Valley was known as Manja, and in Egypt he was called Manj (abbreviated to Man) – the guy known to the Greeks as Menes and to English Egyptologists as Mena.[1] So we have the ruler's son, and later ruler, in Sumer, Egypt, and the Indus Valley in the same period called variously, Manis, Manj, and Manja.

The reason becomes obvious – it was the same fellah. Even the title given to him was the same or very similar in all three places. In Egypt he was known as Manj-the-Warrior; in Sumer he was Manis-the-Warrior; and in the Indus Valley he was called Manja-the-Shooter.[2]

His father, Sargon the Great, is a Semitic name for the Sumerian-Mesopotamian emperor, King Gin, Gani, or Guni. He was called in the later Babylonian texts, the "King of the Four Quarters of the World", because they knew (Babylon was also a Mesopotamian culture) that the Sumerian Empire was enormous. The Incas of South America used this term "Four Quarters", also. In the Indian epics, Sargon's son, Manja, was called "The Royal Eye of Gopta and of the Four Ends of the Earth" when he became emperor.[3] In the Indus Valley clay seal records, Sargon and Manja or Menes also called themselves and their dynasty Gut or Got ("Goth" to the Romans) and used the titles Bar or Par which means "Pharaoh", according to Waddell.[4] Gut or Got became "God", a term used by the later Goths. All non-Latin languages in Europe are derived from the Gothic, including English, and the ancient Swedish language is still called "Sueo-Gothic".[5] The former name for Denmark was "Goth-land" and a derivative was Jut-land.[6] Gothic architecture, so beloved of the bloodlines and the Illuminati, comes from the same source and the horned headgear worn by the kings and leaders of European tribes and kingdoms. But these symbols, styles, and customs, go much further back to Atlantis and Lemuria. The name "Catti" for the ruling clan of the Ancient Britons on pre-Roman coins is a dialectic form of Goti or "Goth".[7] When the Illuminati built the great "Christian" cathedrals of Europe, full of pagan symbolism on ancient pagan sacred sites, they used the "Gothic" style of architecture. The symbolism of the "Eye of Gopta" may relate to the widely used Illuminati symbol, the all-seeing eye or Eye of Horus, which you will find at the top of the pyramid on the US dollar bill and on the reverse of the Great Seal of the United States. The same symbols used by this ancient Sumerian dynasty are still used by the Illuminati today, because they are the same bloodlines and are working with the same knowledge, hidden away since ancient times within the Mystery school and secret society networks. And the reptilian "gods" of Atlantis and Lemuria seeded these bloodlines.

Waddell shows in his work, *Makers Of Civilisation* (Luzac and Company, 1929), that Sargon's Sumer-centred empire extended to the Indus Valley in the east, the British Isles in the west, encompassing much in between, and was larger than that of Alexander the Great or the Romans. The Sumer Empire included much of the world and it is from this same knowledge and information source that all the religions have emerged – the continuation of the knowledge and bloodlines of Atlantis and Lemuria. They may interpret this base information slightly differently and emphasise different strands, but the core from which they have come is the same: the Atlantean, Lemurian and Sumer Empires and their belief system, not least its focus on the worship of the Sun. Where did Christianity, Judaism, Islam, Hinduism, Buddhism, and others like Zoroasterism, etc., etc., all emerge from? The Middle and Near East, the vast region ruled from Sumer at one time and still dominated by that knowledge base and belief system in the thousands of years that followed Sumer's demise. The Sumerian story of King Sargon is a classic case. They said that his mother floated him in a basket of rushes on the river and he was found by a member of the Sumerian royal family who brought him up as their own.[8] The Hebrews, or rather their manipulating priests, the Levites, later stole this ancient story from the Sumerian accounts and used it in the fable of their invented character known as Moses. The Old Testament is founded on Sumerian accounts, edited and rewritten as required, to create a manufactured history and religion called Judaism. The New Testament is based on symbolic stories repeated over and over in the thousands of years before its creation and based on the Sumerian (and Golden Age) religion of Sun worship. The New Testament texts, in turn, created a manufactured religion and history called Christianity. Two prison-religions and two make-believe histories for the price of one book. What more do you want? Great deal. Sold by the billion. King Sargon was a major Sun worshipper and these rulers of the Sumer Empire were given the title, "Son of the Sun", as they were in Lemuria.[9] Could this mean a son of Sirius? Or even Lemuria? To the Sumerians (like the Lemurians and Atlanteans), the Sun was a symbol of "God" and from this title Son of the Sun later came the idea of a Son of God. Sumerian emperors were also often known as "The One Lord".

The Sumer rule of Egypt and the Indus Valley

The early official history of the Sumer "satellite" state called Egypt is largely based on "king lists" compiled by an Egyptian priest known as Manetho in the 3rd century BC for the Great Library of Alexandria. But this library was destroyed in AD391 in the campaign to rewrite history, and only fragments of Manetho's lists have been retained in the works of classic writers. Waddell shows that Manetho's work, if indeed those writers have preserved it accurately, is fundamentally flawed and cannot be sustained in the light of the evidence.[10] Yet so much of the early Egyptian history taught in the schools and universities is based on this very same flawed information. The span of the great Egyptian culture is broken up into distinct periods of kingdoms and ruling dynasties. King Sargon ruled Egypt from his Sumer base within the pre-dynastic period – around 2700BC. The right to rule in the Sumer Empire (again like Lemuria and Atlantis) was by bloodline, a fact fundamental to understanding how the world is controlled – and who by – today. The Egyptian inscriptions detailed here were discovered by Waddell to have been written in Sumerian hieroglyphics, not the much later Egyptian version with which Egyptologists are familiar. Sargon's grandfather (Khetm to conventional history) was known as: Takhu or Tekhi in the early Sumerian-style "Egyptian hieroglyphs"; as Tuke in the Old Sumerian king lists; and as Vri-Taka or Dhri-Taka in the Indian king lists.[11] These are slightly different spellings for the same person who ruled all three. Sargon's father (Ro to Egyptologists) was known in Sumerian-Egyptian hieroglyphics as Puru-Gin; in the Old Sumerian king lists he was Buru-Gina; in Indus Valley seals as Buru or Puru; and in the Indian king lists as Puru (II).[12] Inscriptions relating to King Sargon himself were discovered in one of the oldest tombs at Abydos in Upper Egypt and Waddell established that the script used was early Sumerian. It was the same as the script he saw in Sumerian seals of the same Sargon period found in the Indus Valley.

King Sargon, in this early Sumerian script, was known under his personal name of GIN-UKUS or GIN-UKUSSI in Egypt – thus relating to his title King Gin or Guni and the variant, Gani, in Mesopotamian inscriptions, particularly in Babylonian.[13] The title Ukus or Ukussi in Egypt means that he was a descendant of the first Sumerian king, Ukusi of Ukhu (meaning Sun Hawk City) and also the first Aryan (hybrid?) king in the Indian Epics and their holy books, the Vedas, which use the solar title of Ikshwaku or Ukusi of Ukhu.[14] All these kings of the Sumer Empire were given "solar titles" because of the obsession and emphasis on the worship of the Sun and the symbolism of the Sun as God. Indeed it is extremely likely that Horus or Haru, the Egyptian Son of God and a mirror of the much later "Jesus", came from the Sumerian word, Hu or Ha, meaning hawk. The hawk or Sun-hawk was a Sumerian symbol for the Sun, as we see above in Sargon's very title. The Heru of the Pygmy people, Hul-Kin of the Indians, Helios of the Greeks, and Hurki of the Akkadian/Chaldeans of Mesopotamia probably come from the same source and all relate to a Sun god of the Horus mould. In the same way, the Mayans of Central America had a god called Hurakan and the Tibetans had the deity, Heruka, which later evolved into the Herakles and Hercules of the Greeks, a society that was founded on the Sumerian (Atlantean) knowledge and beliefs. Hercules fought a shape-shifting "river god" called Achelous. The word hurricane can be traced to the same "storm god" symbolism, as the writer and researcher, Acharya, points out in her superb work, *The Christ Conspiracy* (Adventures Unlimited, Kempton, Illinois, 1999). I know all this gets a bit complicated, but what I am summarising here is just some of the fantastic wealth of evidence that can be found in great detail in Waddell's work, and elsewhere, that Sumer was the centre of a vast empire that created, controlled, and instilled its belief systems into other great civilisations which, the official historians tell us, were not connected. But it is clear that they were. More than that, they were ruled by one bloodline dynasty, the same dynasty, as I have established, that runs our world today. The expansion of this empire out of the Near and Middle East can be shown in the story of King Sargon's successor as priest-king of the Sumerian Empire. This was his son, known variously as Manis, Manja, Manj, Mena, Manash or Minash, and to the Greeks as Menes. As the latter is the most used name, that is the one I will use here.

The Minoan expansion

Menes was the first Egyptian Pharaoh of the First Dynasty, which followed the so-called predynastic period, between 3000 and 2000BC. His Egyptian inscriptions, written in Sumerian, are in agreement with the accounts of his life in Sumer and the Indus Valley. He was the governor of the Indus Valley colony, where the first in line to the Sumerian throne ruled as Crown Prince awaiting the succession.[15] They were known, according to surviving records, as Under-King Companions, written as Shag-man, Shab-man, and, interestingly, Sha-man.[16] But Menes led a revolt against his father, Sargon, and took control of Egypt, declaring it independent of Sumer. As a result, Sargon disinherited him and the succession went to his younger brother. But Menes succeeded after a decade or so when his brother died – probably with

Menes' help. This story is told in the Indian Epic Chronicles and other accounts. Menes ruled Sumer after the death of his brother and this empire included another advanced culture that, again, the official historians tell us was independent of Sumer, Egypt, and the Indus Valley. This was the civilisation on the island of Crete known as the Minoan (*Figure 11 overleaf*). The start of this advanced society is officially estimated at about 2600BC, the same period, surprise, surprise, as that of Sumer, and it was said to have been founded by people from Asia Minor, now Turkey, which was part of the Sumer Empire of the Aryan race. Minoan place names have been found all over the Mediterranean, from Sicily to the Syrian Coast, including Cyprus.[17] The Minoan culture was the immediate inspiration for the classic Greek period and the alleged founder of the Minoan dynasty was King Minos, the hero of the later Greeks. But King Minos was in fact the same...Menes, Manj, Manis, etc., the emperor of the Sumerian Empire and son of King Sargon. As Waddell says in *Egyptian Civilisation And Its Sumer Origin*:

"The identity of Minos with Menes now becomes apparent, not only from the identity in their personal tradition, and the equation in their names, but also in the essentials of their culture and civilisation; and the Sumerian sign for the *man* element in Menes' name in the Egyptian and Indus Valley inscriptions (Manj and Manja) reads also dialectically *Min*." [18]

The Sumerians, Egyptians, and Minoans also used identical systems for their calendars and their concepts of astronomy were identical. The most famous story of Minoan Crete is that of the son of King Minos. His son was said to be the Minotaur, the half man, half bull, which defended the Labyrinth under the palace at Knossos according to legend. How interesting, therefore, that Nar-am, the son of Menes, was known as the "Strong Wild Bull".[19] His name, Nar-am, consisted of *Nar*, meaning strong or mighty in both Sumerian and Egyptian, and *am*, meaning wild bull. Nar-am is also depicted in Egypt as a wild bull and it could well be that it was this son of Menes (the real "King Minos") who inspired the symbolic legend of the Minotaur in the Labyrinth at Knossos. The Minoan culture was a mirror of the Sumerian and the period of Menes in Egypt. The art was the same or similar, and so were the clay seals used for writing and recording events. The Sumerian-Egyptian form of writing from the Menes-Sargon period, the funeral rites, and even the terracotta drainpipes used by the "Minoans" were the same as those found in Sumer.[20] Here are just some of the "similarities" listed by Waddell between the documented life of Menes, the Egyptian Pharaoh and Sumerian emperor, and King Minos of Greek and Cretan legend.

Both were of the Bronze Age, replacing the Neolithic period. Both were known as sea emperors of the Mediterranean. Both were said to have introduced civilisation. Both built a Labyrinth. Both died on a sea voyage to the West. Both used seal impressions on clay and both used a linear script of Sumerian type, or very similar. Both had the same physical "Aryan" appearance. Minos was said to be the son of Zeus, Menes was descended from Zagg (Zeus). Minos was a votary and priest of Zeus; Menes was a votary and high priest of Zagg. Minos was a giver of

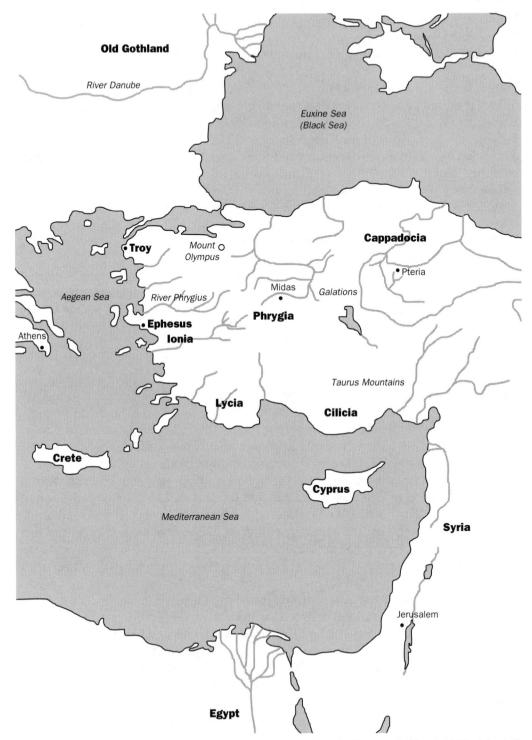

Figure 11: *The Aegean/Mediterranean region has always been highly significant to the Illuminati. The island of Crete was the centre of the advanced Minoan civilisation – another colony of the Sumer-Egyptian Empire*

laws direct from Zeus (another story constantly repeated around the world and used for the make-believe Moses) and Menes established laws said to have come from Zagg. The son of Minos was a bull-man or Minotaur. The son of Menes was known as "The Strong Wild Bull".[21]

Can even the most padlocked of academic minds still go on ignoring the fact that Menes *was* Minos? I suspect they can. In doing so they hold together the house of cards that scams people into missing a truth, as we shall explore, which is critical to understanding the so-called unexplainable "mysteries" of the past and, more importantly, to identify who has been controlling our lives over thousands of years to the present day. That truth is this: the astonishing cultures across the ancient world that "suddenly" emerged at a level of advancement far ahead of others of the time, were not created by a series of unconnected, "independent" peoples who apparently developed precisely the same knowledge, art work, building techniques, writing, funeral ceremonies, and stories, at the same time as each other. They were all aspects of the same culture and control, based on Sumer, an empire that not only extended to the Indus Valley, Egypt, the Mediterranean, and the British Isles, but also across the Atlantic to the Americas and quite probably as far as Australia and China. And the knowledge base of Sumer, and most certainly some of the identical knowledge, stories, and myths, found all over the ancient world, had their origins in the global society of the "Golden Age" before the upheavals – Atlantis and Lemuria.

The Sumerian expansion to Europe, the Americas, and Australia

Various parts of this same Aryan-Sumer Empire, and its later remnants and inspirations, were known as the Amorites, Hittites, Phoenicians, Goths, Hamites, Indo-Aryans, Nordics, ancient Greeks, and many other names. Like I say, I think what we call Aryan are the Nordic-reptilian hybrids. History records the existence of the Hittites and the Phoenicians, but as different peoples, not as different names for the same Sumerian and former Atlantean/Lemurian Aryan race and empire. The Phoenicians were the Carian people from Atlantis and Lemuria and Carian means "Serpent Sea People of the Atlantean Fire God".[22] James Churchward's research shows that the Carian people, originally from Lemuria, also settled in the Americas. Unmistakable Phoenician remains have been found in Brazil and, according to a man I met who once worked in covert operations for the British Government, similar Phoenician artefacts were discovered in the rainforests of Queensland, Australia, a few miles from where Captain Cook landed on his voyage of "discovery". It was a journey of *re*discovery in truth, and it was funded and organised by the Royal Society in London, a body created and controlled from the start by Freemasons. The Queensland find would help to explain why some Australian aboriginal terms are the same as the Egyptian, although the Lemurian connection would do that also. Evidence of Phoenician activity has been identified in New England on the eastern seaboard of the United States and unmistakable Egyptian-Oriental remains were discovered in the Grand Canyon in Arizona in the first decade of the 20th century. Ancient Chinese artefacts have also been found in Mexico and California. We only know of the Grand Canyon find thanks to lengthy articles in the local paper at the time, the *Arizona Gazette*,[23] because every effort has been made to suppress the knowledge, as with the discoveries in Queensland. The Smithsonian Institution in Washington DC (the Smithson family is one of the bloodlines) was created for the very reason of suppressing archaeological discoveries that rewrite the manufactured history while emphasising those that can be encompassed in the fairy tale.

The accounts and symbolic religious tales were taken across the globe by the Sumerian seafarers like the Phoenicians, the bloodlines of Atlantis. They reinforced the stories and symbols that were taken to those areas thousands of years earlier by the Atlanteans and Lemurians. When the later Europeans landed in the Americas and other parts of the world with Columbus and his successors, they found to their astonishment that the native peoples were telling the same stories and myths that were told in Europe and the Middle and Near East. Their astonishment came from their belief that these cultures on different sides of the world had never met before. But they had. They were part of the global Atlantean/Lemurian empire and later the near-global empire of Sumer. The leaders of the European explorers like Columbus knew the truth, however, because of their secret society background. The corresponding stories and customs on both sides of the Atlantic included the virgin birth, crucifixion, circumcision, and the Great Flood. The similarities were so striking, the Christian priests sought to keep this knowledge quiet for fear of undermining their "unique" religion. The key Central American deity, Quetzalcoatl, was "Jesus" under another name long before the Christian religion waded ashore with Columbus and Cortes. Quetzalcoatl was born to a virgin mother, fasted for 40 days, was tempted by their version of Satan, and left promising to return in a second coming. Indeed, when Cortes, the Spanish architect of native genocide, landed there in the years after Columbus, he was treated as a god because, with his European features, he was considered to be the return of Quetzalcoatl. Something similar happened in Africa when the white Europeans arrived and the native people believed they were the return of the "Nordic" extraterrestrial beings of their legends. Cortes was obviously aware of the Quetzalcoatl story because he landed near the point the legend said the deity would return and he wore a plumed hat in line with Quetzalcoatl's title of the "Plumed Serpent". Cortes even arrived in 1519, the time the native people believed that Quetzalcoatl would come back. Just one example of how easy it is to manipulate people through their beliefs.

The travels of the Aryan Sumerians and their earlier "Golden Age" ancestors also account for the "mystery" of the countless legends in the Americas of the "white gods" who came from the sea bringing great knowledge and civilisation. There was once a race of white men in Central-South America who wore beards and looked like Phoenicians. The Central American culture with its incredible ancient cities and pyramids, attributed to the Maya people in the Yucatan, is one such example of this ancient interaction. The step pyramids of the Yucatan, which in fact go back way before the Maya who inherited them, are so similar to the classic ziggurats built for the "gods" of Sumer. There are great similarities in art and language between the two, as there are between Central American religion and language and that of the

Hindus and the Middle-Near Eastern Semites. The mother goddess, Maya, has the same name in the Maya culture as she does in India and there are Mayan remains at an ancient Egyptian site I have visited not far from Giza. James Churchward shows in *The Children Of Mu* that all these "Maya" peoples around the world originated in Lemuria-Mu, hence the common connections. Also, the legendary founder of the Maya culture, called Votan or Wotan, is the name of the Atlantean fire god and also the god of the Teutonic peoples of Germany and Scandinavia. He was one of the gods of the Nazis and they were created by the Teutonic Knights network (Illuminati) in Germany. The Teutonic Knights were formed in the same period, and operated in the same "Holy Land" region, as the Knights Templar and the Knights of Malta and they work to the same basic agenda right to this day.

That part of the Sumerian Empire known as the Phoenicians, with their base in the Middle East and what we now call Turkey, particularly Cappadocia, were very much involved in establishing Sumerian control of the British Isles. Under other names these peoples were known as the Hittites and the Goths. Once again L.A. Waddell has established that the Phoenicians were not a Semitic race as claimed by official historians, but another name for the Aryan race based on Sumer in the post-Atlantis period. Examinations of Phoenician tombs have revealed that they were of the long-headed Aryan-type, as are depictions of the Pharaohs and royal families in Egypt.[24] This is also why the Egyptians and other cultures portrayed many of their gods, like Osiris, with white skin and blue eyes – that's what the ruling race looked like. The twist was that their "royal" and "noble" bloodlines had interbred with the reptilian Anunnaki. The very name, Iran, another part of the Sumer Empire, comes from the word Airy-ana or Air-an, which means Land of the Aryas or Aryans.[25] There is still a race of white, often blue-eyed, people in Kurdistan.

The Sumerian-Phoenicians arrive in Britain and Ireland

The Phoenicians (Sumerian Empire) had landed in the British Isles by at least 3000BC (*Figure 12 overleaf*).[26] This corresponds with the period when, it is claimed, the great stone circles like Stonehenge and Avebury were built with the same astonishing precision that you find with the Giza pyramids and other breathtaking structures across the Sumerian and former Atlantean-Lemurian Empire. Whoever designed Stonehenge must have had a very advanced knowledge of mathematics and astronomy. Geoffrey of Monmouth, the 12th-century historian, wrote in *Histories Of The Kings Of Britain* that the builders of the original Stonehenge were "giants" from North Africa.[27] The Aryans of Sumer and Egypt were a tall people because they came from the very tall Nordics and the reptilians, which are almost always described as very tall. This fits with the emerging themes of this book and certainly the official version of Stonehenge is utterly ludicrous. As John A. Keel points out in *Our Haunted Planet* (Fawcett Publications, USA, 1971):

> "We are also asked to believe that they pushed and hauled these monstrous stones [for 240 miles] up and down hills, across rivers, through forests and soupy bogs on sledges and wooden rollers ...Plainly the whole thing is quite absurd." [28]

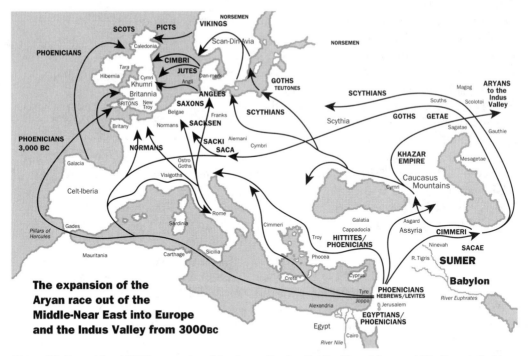

**The expansion of the
Aryan race out of the
Middle-Near East into Europe
and the Indus Valley from 3000BC**

Figure 12: *From at least 3000BC, peoples of the Sumer Empire, like the Phoenicians and Egyptians, sailed to Britain and took their knowledge and symbols to those islands. Others began to move across land to settle in what we now call France, Germany, and the rest of northern Europe. Wherever they went, the reptilian bloodlines invariably ruled as kings, queens, and nobility*

And, of course, Stonehenge is just one of hundreds of stone circles and standing stones erected in Britain in this same period. We do have to be careful here as dates are increasingly, and often dramatically, re-assessed. The Sumerians were heading back to where the pre-cataclysmic Atlanteans once had a major colony, and some of these famous structures of the British Isles and elsewhere may have already been in place long before they returned. Either of these explanations, the Atlantean builders or the Sumerian Empire, would account for where the knowledge came from to align them so exactly to the cycles of the Sun, Moon, and star systems, as well as in relationship to each other via the geometrical energy grid. Waddell explains in his book, *The Phoenician Origins Of Britons, Scots And Anglo Saxons* (Christian Book Club, California, 1924), how he found Sumerian markings on one of the stones at Stonehenge and on other stones around the British Isles, including some in Scotland.[29] Professor Alexander Thom, Emeritus Professor of Engineering Science at Oxford University from 1945 to 1961, discovered that the builders of Stonehenge knew of "Pythagorean" geometric and mathematical principles thousands of years before Pythagoras was born.[30] The same was true of those who built the Giza pyramids. Now we can see why. The Greek genius Pythagoras, which means "I am the Python" or "I am the Serpent",[31] and all the famous Greek mathematicians, philosophers, scientists, doctors, and so on, inherited their knowledge through the highly secretive Mystery schools from the Sumerians, Minoans, and Egyptians, who were all the same peoples in reality. And they, in turn, inherited from Atlantis and Lemuria. History becomes much simpler once this sequence is understood. The Sumerian elite and their Golden Age ancestors also had the knowledge of how to throw a magnetic field around an object and disconnect it from the laws of gravity. They could make it weightless. Such a skill makes it so much easier to move and place vast stones for these "mystery" structures like Stonehenge and the Pyramids!

The serpent grid

I cannot stress enough the importance to these ancient peoples of the global energy grid and especially the major vortex points where many of the energy lines cross. This energy was often symbolised as a serpent. The more esoteric researchers who acknowledge the vast symbolism and references to serpent bloodlines, serpent knowledge, and serpent people, say these were merely codes relating to this Earth energy grid known as dragon lines or ley lines (hence so many British place names end in "ley"). The association of serpent symbolism with this universal energy and its most powerful centres is clear to see. But, at the same time, the evidence that there is a controlling force taking a reptilian form is so overwhelming that there is no way that the constant references to serpent or dragon bloodlines can be dismissed as simply code for this energy or knowledge of the grid. And what a co-incidence that we have all the legends and accounts of a serpent race bringing and teaching knowledge about this grid, and the energy of that very grid becomes associated with the serpent. No connection? As I said earlier, these ley lines connect

to form a web or grid of magnetic energy, the universal life force, which flows along these lines that surround and interpenetrate the planet. The human body has a similar system and the ancient Chinese healing art known as acupuncture works with the "ley" lines, dragon lines, or meridians of the physical body. That's why they insert hair-like needles. They are balancing the flow of energy. The ancients, including the Atlanteans, Lemurians, and the peoples of the Sumer Empire, used standing stones like acupuncture needles for the Earth. They declared these major vortex centres to be sacred and these are the locations of the standing stone circles, pyramids and ancient earthworks all over the world (*Figure 13*). Also, the

Figure 13: *The ancient sacred sites of the world, like Stonehenge, are points on the global energy grid where many force lines, or "ley" lines, cross and create a massive vortex of energy. This is where the stone circles, pyramids, and the major Freemasonic temples are located. Energy = power if you know how to use it*

correlation between these sites and "faults" in the Earth's magnetic field are obvious, and studies have shown that "paranormal" events and experiences, including "UFO" sightings, tend to happen mostly at or near these magnetic faults. In her book, *Where Science And Magic Meet* (Element Books, Shaftesbury, England, 1991), Serena Roney-Dougal points out that of the 286 stone circles in Britain, 235 are built on rocks more than 250 million years old, the statistical chances of which are more than a million to one. Robert Graves, the poet and writer on mythology and mysticism, said:

> "There are some sacred places made so by the radiation created by magnetic ores. My village, for example, is a kind of natural amphitheatre enclosed by mountains containing iron ore, which makes a magnetic field. Most holy places in the world – holy not by some accident, like a hero dying or being born there – are of this sort. Delphi was a heavily charged holy place." [42]

Delphi in Greece was the centre for the "Oracle", a psychic woman or "channel", who connected her consciousness with other-dimensional entities and spoke their words. They knew that the sites of magnetic "faults" act as doorways to these other dimensions or densities, and allow both interdimensional communication and travel to happen more easily. Satanists use these same locations around the world in their rituals designed to manifest other-dimensional demonic entities. The Roman Church insisted that its churches and cathedrals be built on former pagan sites because these were the interdimensional doorways, gateways, or portals. Again, this is why Satanists seek to use Christian churches for their rituals: they want to access the energy in the vortexes on which the churches were placed. Freemasonic and other secret society temples are located on these points. The ancient Atlantean-Lemurian-Sumerian knowledge has been passed on through this covert network while being systematically suppressed among the people. Religion has condemned it as "evil", and science" has dismissed it as nonsense. And the source of both religion and "science" is the same Illuminati network. Surprised?

It is claimed by historians that British Druids built the stone circles, but they confuse *using* them with *building* them. Groups use them today for rituals, but no one is suggesting that these groups built them! Archaeologists find Druidic remains on these sites and assume they created them. They do the same with the later Mayans of Central America and the Incas of South America. The later Druidic religion and knowledge was brought by the Atlanteans originally and re-enforced by the Sumerians with their great understanding of astronomy, astrology, sacred geometry, mathematics, and the ley line system or "energy grid". Both sources also knew of the cycle called "precession" in which the Earth's "wobble" slowly moves the planet on its axis so it faces different star systems or astrological "houses" over thousands of years. It takes 2,160 years to cross one symbolic "house" and 25,920 years to complete the cycle of 12. We are, some believe, completing one of these great cycles now and they are always periods of enormous change, it is said. Once again these ancient Sumerians, Atlanteans and

Lemurians, under various names, built their temples and sacred buildings in relation to, or in acknowledgement of, their knowledge of precession.

Suppressing the grid

I have a rather controversial view (makes a change) of at least some pyramids, stone circles, and earthworks placed on the vortexes. From the start of my conscious journey in 1990 I have had a bad feeling about many of these constructions. New Agers see them as sacred places and go to the stone circles and pyramids for their ceremonies and so on. But just because the vortex points are power centres on the global grid, it doesn't mean that the structures built at these places by the bloodlines have been designed and located with humanity's best interests at heart. I am not talking about all of them here, but I don't feel good myself about the Giza site or Stonehenge, among others. These locations are incredible centres of energy and yet when we go there we feel a fraction of their true power because the structures built on them are often suppressing that power. My own feeling is that they were part of a network designed to close down the true potential of the grid and disconnect the human energy field from the cosmic one. Every planet and star has an energy grid and these connect with each other in a vast cosmic web. We in turn connect with this network through our human energy grid, the meridian system on which acupuncture is based. If you can disconnect the human energy field from the planetary and cosmic grid you put people in a disconnected vibrational prison. Still today, the Illuminati place structures like nuclear power stations and motorway (freeway) intersections on the vortex points for the same reason. A busy road has been built through the centre of the massive Avebury stone circle (vortex) in Wiltshire, England. It is like throwing a spanner into an electrical system. It throws it into chaos. I'm not saying that these places are negative in themselves. They are just energy. I am talking of the structures built upon them to manipulate the flow of that energy. I think people miss the point that you can program stones, with their quartz crystal content, and obelisks etc., to do a positive or negative job for you in these places. I think that many have been put there to disrupt and suppress. Just my view. The Illuminati keep their most powerful vortex points clean and secret, known only to themselves.

Among the ancient landscape features still visible today in the west of England are the white horses scored from the chalk hillsides. The oldest, according to conventional archaeology, is the one at Uffington in the Vale of the White Horse in Wiltshire, not far from Avebury circle. This has been dated to 3000BC, the time when the Sumerian-Phoenicians were introducing (or re-introducing) their culture, religion, and knowledge to Britain. Why white horses? The basic religion of the Sumerian-Phoenicians was the worship of the Sun and the white horse was one of their symbols for the Sun.[31] This white horse symbolism is also the source of the references to stories about white horses in relation to the Christian Jesus and Hindu Krishna. Jesus and Krishna are symbols for the Sun with their origin in the Sumerian Sun religion and its stories and symbols. Neither really existed. There are also people who believe that the Uffington "white horse" is really a dragon and, if that is so, it fits with the previous name for the Phoenicians, the Carians or "Serpent Sea People of the Atlantean Fire God". The tin mines of Cornwall in the far west of England were first created by the Sumerian Empire and this was known to them in their writings as "The Tin Land Country".[33] A Phoenician deity, later encompassed into Christianity, was St Michael and so you have St Michael's Mount just off the Cornish Coast near Penzance.[34] The tin ships operated from here, and there are many other references to "St Michael" in that region. Other Phoenician-Sumerian deities were St George of Cappadocia in Turkey, who defeated the dragon and became the patron saint of England; Barat, a male deity, who became "Briton"; and Barati, the female, who became the British heroine, Britannia, when these deities were brought to these islands by the Sumerian Empire (*Figure 14*).[35] According to Sir Laurence Gardner, the spokesman of the ancient Imperial Court of the Royal Dragon and Order, Barat-Anna (Great Mother of the Fire Stone) symbolised the wife of Anu, the chief of the Sumerian reptilian gods called the Anunnaki (see *www.nexusmagazine.com/ringlords1.html http*). Names very similar to Barat and Barati can be found in the Indian holy books, the Vedas, because these accounts were inspired by the same Sumerian (Aryan) and Atlantean/Lemurian sources. The later Romans, another empire based on the Sumerian/Atlantean knowledge and bloodlines, knew Barati as "Fortune", a reference to Barati's legend as the goddess of fortune.[36] They symbolised and described her in the same way the Phoenicians

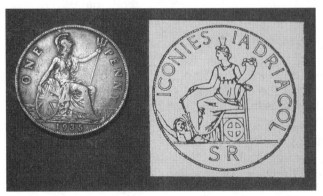

did with Barati and the British do with Britannia. The Egyptians had a goddess called Brith, goddess of the waters, another version of Barati, and the Minoans (Sumerian-Egyptians) on Crete knew her as Brito-Martis, who, in turn, is associated with the goddess Diana or Artemis, other versions of the same theme.[37]

All this information is one solution to the "mystery" of why all the major symbols of the British Isles came from the

Figure 14: *The Phoenician Barati became the British Britannia after the Sumer Empire arrived. On the left is an old British penny depicting Britannia and alongside is Barati on a Phoenician coin. The stories told about these deities were the same*

Middle and Near East. For instance, the flags of England (cross of St George), Scotland (cross of St Andrew), Ireland (cross of St Patrick), as well as the ensigns of Scandinavia, were all carried as standards of victory by the Phoenicians.[38] The evidence of the Aryan-Sumerian connection to Ireland emphasises the point. According to Arbois de Juvainville, the author of the work, *Cours De Literature Celtique*, the Irish were known as "Egyptians" in the Middle Ages. St Patrick, of whom no literal evidence has been found, is claimed by some to be an Irish name for the Egyptian deity, Ptah, who was introduced to Ireland by Egyptian members of the Sumerian Empire.[39] It is said of St Patrick that he removed all the snakes from Ireland. Here are just some of the connections between North Africa and the "Emerald Isle" – Ireland.

The distinctive round towers in Ireland are of Phoenician origin and the Irish harp (and Scottish bagpipes) came from North Africa, as did the name of the classic Irish symbol, the shamrock. Any three-leaf plant in Egypt is known as a shamrukh. The rosary beads, such a symbol of the Roman Catholic Church (created by the Sumerian-inspired Romans and based on Sun worship), are from the Middle East and still used by the Egyptians. The word "nun" is Egyptian and their garb is Middle Eastern. The old Irish sailing craft called a pucan was designed in North Africa where it was used on the River Nile. Old Irish books employ the same styles as those found in Egypt and even the colours used in the Irish Book of Kells and Book of Durrow are from Middle Eastern insects and plants. The famous ancient mound at Newgrange, north of Dublin, has a narrow passageway of some 62 feet that perfectly aligns with the Sun as it rises on the winter solstice. It is so precise that at the solstice sunrise, its golden light shines directly through this narrow passage to illuminate the chamber deep in the centre of the mound. Again the present dating of Newgrange and other ancient Irish standing stones and earthworks fits the period when the Sumerian empire arrived and the duel spiral images found at Newgrange are identical to those found at other centres of the Sumer/Lemurian/Atlantean Empires, like Malta. The entrances to many other great structures within that empire are the same as that at Newgrange, including the one at the Minoan Palace of Minos (Menes) on Crete. It becomes clear why I have noticed on my many visits to Ireland that so many of their old place names have a Middle and Near Eastern feel about them. Indeed, as researchers have shown, the old Irish languages, like Gaelic, are remarkably similar to those found in North Africa. The reason is simple. They have the same base origin. As Waddell says in *Phoenician Origins Of Britons*:

> "I had recognised that the various ancient scripts found at or near the old settlements of the Phoenicians, and [those known as] Cyrian, Karisn, Aramaic or Syrian, Lykian, Lydian, Corinthian, Ionian, Cretan or "Minoan", Pelasgian, Phrygian, Cappadocian, Cilician, Theban, Libyan, Celto-Iberian, Gothic Runes, etc., were all really local variations of the standard Aryan Hitto-Sumerian writing of the Aryan Phoenician mariners, those ancient pioneer spreaders of the Hittite Civilisation along the shores of the Mediterranean and out beyond the Pillars of Hercules [between Spain and North Africa] to the British Isles." [40]

In truth, this was the Nordic race and the Nordic-reptilian "Aryans" returning to the lands from which many of their ancestors came after the Atlantean cataclysms. The evidence presented in this chapter, and this is a fraction of what exists even after thousands of years of suppression, supports Waddell's conclusion that Menes, Manis, Manj, the son of Sargon, ruler of the Sumerian Empire, and also known as King Minos to the Greeks, actually died in Ireland.[41] This story sums up how ludicrous official history can be and how one mis-translation can make a complete pig's ear of what really happened. According to the accepted story, Menes died after a reign of some 60 years when he was killed by a "Kheb beast" that came from the waters of the Nile. This "Kheb beast" has been translated as hippopotamus. But, as Waddell points out, the word "Kheb" in Egyptian also means wasp or hornet.[42] Pictographs relaying this story portray an insect that looks remarkably like a wasp or hornet and very unlike a friggin' hippo, unless in those days hippos had wings and looked like flying insects. Accounts of Menes' death found in his "tomb" (in truth his memorial or cenotaph) at Abydos in Egypt can therefore be translated as follows (another of his names, Manash or Minash, is used here):

"The King Manash (Minash), the Pharaoh of Mushsir (Egypt), the Land of the Two Crowns, the perished dead one in the West, of the (Sun-) Hawk race, Aha Manash (or Minash) of the Lower (or Sunrise or Eastern) and of the Sunset (or Upper or Western) Waters and of their Lands and Oceans, The Ruler, The King of Mushrim (the two Egypts) Lands, the son of the Great Sha-Gana (or Sha-Gunu) of the (Sun-) Hawk race, The Pharaoh, the deceased, the Commander-in-Chief of Ships.

"The Commander-in-Chief of Ships (Minash) made the complete course to the End of the Sunset Land, going in ships. He completed the inspection of the Western Lands. He built (there) a holding (or possession) in Urani Land. At the Lake of the Peak, Fate pierced (him) by a Hornet (or Wasp), The King of the Two Crowns, Manshu. This board tablet set up of hanging wood is dedicated (to his memory)".[43]

No one had previously connected the location of Menes' death to Ireland, not least because that country is not famous for the hippopotamus. As the account at Abydos reveals, Menes died while inspecting the "End of the Sunset Land".[44] This was in the west, therefore, of the Egyptian-Sumerian Empire at that time. Waddell suggests that this location was beyond the Sumerian Tin Lands (Cornwall) and can be identified as Ireland.[45] He says that the name Urani is the original form of the word, Erin – the old name for Ireland.[46] Representations of Ireland as the "End of the Sunset Land" have been found at Irish sites, including so called "cup-marked" inscriptions on stones at Newgrange, which are virtual replicas of those found in early Sumerian and Hittite seals.[47] Waddell confirmed his theory when he found Sumerian inscriptions on pre-historic stones at a gravesite at Knock-Many ("Hill of the Many") near Clogher on the southern border of County Tyrone. He found them to be virtually identical to those on the "tomb" of Menes at Abydos.[48] One of the stones even had the same monogram of the name "Urani" and a pictograph of the cause of death...a hornet.[49] Knock-Many would seem to be the true grave of Menes, ruler of the Sumerian Empire, which included Britain and Ireland. Unfortunately, these inscriptions were destroyed at Knock-Many when they were cleared of lichen with the use of corrosive chemicals supported by vigorous scrubbing. Waddell records, however, that excellent photographs of them were taken by a Mr R. Welch in 1896 and so somewhere, I trust, they are preserved.[50]

Waddell's work is further supported by evidence that Egyptians were shipwrecked off the east coast of Britain some 2,700 years ago and settled in the area now occupied by the city of Hull. Three wooden boats found in mud on the banks of the River Humber in 1937 were thought to be Viking. Now they are said to date from around 700BC and they are identical to ones that once navigated the Nile.[51] I can understand the confusion with the Vikings, however, because the Scandinavian Nordics travelled south to Egypt and Sumer after Atlantis and there would be many similarities and mutual origins. The Egyptologist, Lorraine Evans, also says in her book, *Kingdom Of The Ark* (Simon & Schuster, London, 2000) that the ancient Egyptians established a colony in Ireland 3,500 years ago, after landing in County Kerry. She suggests that the invaders were led by Princess Scota, the daughter of a pharaoh, and that she is buried in a valley called Scota's Glen about five miles from Tralee in County Kerry where she died after a bloody war with indigenous Irish people. The grave is marked with a slab, but has never been excavated. Evans says that Scota's descendants went on to become the high kings of Ireland at Tara in County Meath and then invaded Scotland or Scota-land. Evans says that she used old texts and archaeological, linguistic and DNA evidence to show that Irish and British people descended from Egyptians. She says that Scota's real name was Meritaten and that she was the daughter of the pharaoh, Akhenaten, and a half-sister to Tutankhamen. The Hill of Tara, not far from Newgrange, was the seat of the Irish king of kings (equivalent of the British "Pendragon") and it is worth emphasising that the "elite" bloodlines of Ireland and Scotland are extremely important to the Illuminati. Bronze Age shields found on the Dingle peninsula in County Kerry were identical to those discovered in Spain, which were identified as ancient Egyptian weaponry. Other archaeologists and Egyptologists have dismissed Evans' claims, but she says that her findings in Hull and elsewhere will revolutionise views about our ancestors: "The simple fact that many peoples of Britain are going about their daily business unaware of their Egyptian heritage is astounding."[52] But not quite so astounding when you realise that those in control don't want people to know that because it rewrites their official version of history.

There are many key points in this chapter that are vital to understanding both the background to religion, and the nature and source of the manipulation of the world today. Many thousands of years ago, there was a global society of great advancement that was brought to an end by a series of immense global catastrophes and the world went back to the drawing board. After the planet began to recover and up to the period of around 2000BC, when the Sumer Empire began to dismantle, another near-global society was developed. It was controlled from Sumer and created from the advanced knowledge held by its ruling elite. This society was built on the same basic foundations of religion, knowledge, and culture that had prevailed in the pre-cataclysmic Atlantis/Lemuria, although it did not advance to the same levels. The foundation religion of the Sumer Empire, and therefore all of its vast lands and peoples, was the worship of the Sun and many symbolic stories emerged to describe the cycles of the Sun, Moon, stars, and seasons.

Another point to stress in the story so far is that the rulers of the Sumerian Empire were chosen by bloodline, an immensely relevant point as we shall now see. Given the origin of these bloodlines, we are about to enter a dogma-free zone in which it would be sensible to fasten your seat belts and be aware of possible mental and emotional turbulence. Readers with closed minds and programmed beliefs, who have a fear of climbing to high altitudes to view a much bigger picture of possibility, should venture no further. For those who will therefore be leaving us now, please make sure you take all of your baggage with you and have a safe onward journey.

SOURCES

1   L.A. Waddell, *Egyptian Civilisation, It's Sumerian Origin, And Real Chronology,* and *Sumerian Origin Of Egyptian Hieroglyphs,* p 2 (I will source this as *Egyptian Civilisation* from this point!)

2   Ibid, p 9

3   Ibid, p 11

4   Ibid, p 13

5   L.A. Waddell, *British Edda* (Christian Book Club, Hawthorne, California, 1930), introduction

6   Ibid

7   L.A. Waddell, *The Phoenician Origin Of Britons, Scots, And Anglo Saxons* (Christian Book Club, Hawthorne, California, 1924)

8   *Egyptian Civilisation,* p 28

9   Ibid, p 21

10   Ibid, p 14

11   Ibid, p 18

12   Ibid, p 17

13   Ibid, p 2

14   Ibid, pp 22 and 23

15   Ibid, p 41

16   Ibid, p 42

17   Ibid, p 72

18   Ibid, pp 71 and 72

19   Ibid, p 73

20   Ibid

21   Ibid, pp 72 and 73

22   *The Return Of The Serpents Of Wisdom*, p 30

23   Arizona *Gazette*, April 1909

24   *The Phoenician Origin Of Britons, Scots, And Anglo Saxons*

25   Ibid, p 65

26   An approximate date suggested by the research of L.A. Waddell

27   *The Return Of The Serpents Of Wisdom*, p 81

28   *Our Haunted Planet*, p 51

29   *The Phoenician Origin Of Britons, Scots, And Anglo Saxons*, p 231

30   Professor Alexander Thom, *Megalithic Sites Of Britain*, published in 1967

31   *The Return Of The Serpents Of Wisdom*, p 217

32   *The Phoenician Origin Of Britons, Scots, And Anglo Saxons*

33   *Egyptian Civilisation*, p 13

34   *The Phoenician Origin Of Britons, Scots, And Anglo Saxons*

35   Ibid

36   Ibid

37   Ibid

38   Ibid

39   Quoted by Bob Quinn in *Atlantean, Ireland's North African And Maritime Heritage* (Quartet Books, London, 1986.)

40   *The Phoenician Origin Of Britons, Scots, And Anglo Saxons*, p 27

41   *Egyptian Civilisation*, pp 60 to 70

42   Ibid, p 64

43   Ibid, pp 63 and 64

44   Ibid, p 66

45   Ibid, p 67

46   Ibid

47   Ibid, p 68

48   Ibid

49   Ibid

50   Ibid

51   Lorraine Evans, *Kingdom Of The Ark* (Simon & Schuster, London, 2000)

52   Quoted by the UK national media when the book was launched

CHAPTER 5

Blood brothers

Wisdom is knowing how little we know.

Socrates

The same bloodlines have been installed in the positions of political and economic power for thousands of years, first as the royalty and nobility of the ancients, and now as the leading politicians, bankers, businessmen, and media owners of modern society. So what are these bloodlines and where do they originate?

A recurring story with these great civilisations, including Sumer, is that they began at the peak of their powers and then gradually declined, thus indicating a vast input of knowledge at the start, which was later lost. The Sumerians had their own explanations and their accounts were rediscovered thousands of years later. These are the so-called Sumerian tablets and we can now look at them in more detail. In the mid-1800s and later, tens of thousands of clay tablets were found in the former land of Sumer on the site of the Assyrian capital city of Nineveh, about 250 miles from what is today Baghdad in Iraq. An Englishman, Sir Austen Henry Layard, made this first discovery and others have followed. The astonishing accounts the tablets contain originated in Sumer and not with the later Assyrian culture. I therefore refer to them as the Sumerian tablets. It is estimated that they were buried around 2000BC, but they tell a story that goes back long before, to Atlantis and Lemuria, or Mu. In more recent times, many books have been written translating their content. But although these accounts of Sumer, and far ancient history before the Earth's upheavals, demolish the official version of events, once again the same old story goes on being told to children and students by official academia.

You do not have to delve into the translations for long to see that much of the biblical Old Testament is simply an edited rewrite of these Sumerian stories. The tablets talk of how King Sargon was floated on a river in a basket of rushes, as I mentioned earlier. The Bible tells this same story of "Moses". The tablets describe a place called E.DIN ("The Abode of the Righteous Ones"). The Bible speaks of Eden, the garden of "God". The story of Genesis is a summary of the same basic story that is told in the Sumerian tablets in far more detail. Interestingly, many of the terms translated into the English version of the Old Testament as "God" come from words that actually mean gods, plural, and the Sumerians said the founders of their civilisation were a race of beings that came to this planet from elsewhere in the heavens bringing great knowledge and technology. As I have already indicated, the Sumerians called these beings the Anunna and their later Semitic name was AN.UNNAK.KI ("Those who from Heaven to Earth Came") and DIN.GIR ("The Righteous Ones of the Blazing Rockets"). Anunna means "sons of An" (later Anu),[1] another likely origin for "Sons of God" as the reptilian Anunnaki interbred with the Nordics and Earth peoples. The name for Sumer in the tablets is KI.EN.GIR, which has been translated as "The Land of the Lord of the Blazing Rockets" and also "The Land of the Watchers". The term "Watchers" is often used to describe ancient gods. The Egyptian name for their gods, the Neteru, translates literally as "Watchers".

The Egyptians said that these Watchers came in their "heavenly boats" and in ancient cultures across the world you have this constantly recurring theme of "gods" arriving in some kind of flying machine to found civilisations and bring knowledge and techniques that were light years ahead of what existed before. In the Indian culture they called these flying craft Vimanas. There were several designs of these craft. Some were cigar-shaped while others were described as double-decked with a dome and porthole windows. Both types are regularly described in UFO sightings today. The ancient Indian texts describe anti-gravity technology of the type used in "flying saucers". So much so that when the Chinese discovered Sanskrit documents in Tibet and sent them to the University of Chandrigarh for translation, they were found to contain the knowledge to build interstellar spaceships, according to the University's Dr Ruth Reyna.[2] Yet the documents are thousands of years old! Dr Reyna revealed that these ships were known as "Astras" and it was claimed they could fly to any planet. Some texts talk about them flying to the Moon. Details of building, flying, and operating the craft are all included. The Chinese, apparently, even used part of the contents in their space programme.[3] These were the craft used in the endlessly recorded "wars of the gods". The same basic knowledge used to build anti-gravity technology can be employed to disconnect massive stones from the laws of gravity. Arab legends say that the astonishing blocks of stone at Baalbeck in the Lebanon were laid together by a "tribe of giants" after the deluge. In the same way, British legends tell of giants coming from Africa to build Stonehenge. Was the Golden Age of Lemuria/Atlantis before the cataclysms created by knowledge brought from the stars and/or even other dimensions of existence far in advance of where the Earth was at the time? This is what the ancient accounts say. These are the same accounts, which, like the Sumerian tablets, describe planets of the solar system in both number and environment in ways that were only confirmed in the 20th century. They describe how these beings, later called "gods", the Anunnaki, created a culture of great advancement and technology that was destroyed by Earth catastrophes and flood. The story of the Great Flood is told at length in the tablets. The Sumerian flood hero, Utnapishtim, was replaced by the name, Noah, when the much later texts of Genesis were compiled from the Sumerian records.

If these Anunnaki or "gods" were indeed so advanced and able to fly, as all these various ancient stories either symbolise or openly confirm, it would be a further explanation for why there could have been a global society during the pre-flood

Golden Age and how the same building methods were used across the world by apparently unconnected peoples; how the Nazca lines in Peru were created and fantastic structures like the pyramids could have been built while the general population was technologically "primitive"; how those breathtaking ancient structures could be aligned both with each other and the cycles of the Sun, Moon, planets and star systems; how ancient peoples knew more about astronomy than even modern science did until recently, and in some areas, still so; how the planet was mapped so accurately thousands of years ago, as proved by the maps showing Antarctica before the ice came; how peoples in every part of the world have the same legends, stories, and basis for their religions; and why, the further back you go, the more impressive are the temples and other structures that survive today. The Sumerian tablets suggest that the Anunnaki came to this planet hundreds of thousands of years ago. They would have been very much involved in Lemuria and Atlantis, leading up to great upheavals and the deluge.

After the catastrophes, the Anunnaki returned, the tablets relate, and they supervised the rebuilding of another global empire, which we know as Sumer. But although this was fine for a while, the gods fought among themselves in the thousands of years that followed, the tablets say. This was especially the offspring of the earlier leaders, Enlil and Enki. They demanded that human nations fight for them against other peoples committed to a different Anunnaki "god". Thus the Sumer Empire, although a wonder for its time, did not reach the heights of the Golden Age and eventually collapsed, breaking up into warring factions. Many of these wars are described in the stories of the Old Testament when it seems everyone was fighting everyone else in that heart centre of the Anunnaki, the Middle and Near East, from where the major religions have all emerged, including what is now Hinduism. This could also be the reason for the theme in the Old Testament of "worship no other god than me." Some researchers have even presented evidence that high-tech weaponry was used in the Anunnaki conflicts, including nuclear warheads. The Sumerian and Indian accounts give support to this. It may be that the "mist" that poisoned the rivers and water supplies and left the Sumer region an uninhabitable wasteland for a long time, was the fall-out from this. It is believed that the Anunnaki eventually left the Earth, but I suggest that while some may have done so, pledging eventually to return, others stayed and have been the orchestrators of the manipulation through their bloodlines and secret societies ever since. The themes of this extraterrestrial involvement in human affairs can be found in almost every native culture.

If anyone has a problem with the existence of life beyond this planet, by the way, consider this. Even according to conventional, and desperately limited "science", it takes a hundred years for light to travel from one side of this one Milky Way galaxy to another, and this at a speed of 186,000 miles a second! There are estimated to be at least a million galaxies in the universe, a billion planets, and a billion *trillion* stars. There are a hundred million planets in the visible universe with conditions very much like those on Earth, according to Dr Melvin Calvin of the Department of Chemistry at the University of California at Berkeley. And that is only in this one density or frequency range of existence. Imagine the scale of what must exist in all the other frequency ranges beyond our physical senses. So given all this, do we really believe that life as we know it has only evolved on this one little planet in this one little solar system in one galaxy? We do? In that case I have some seafront property in the Gobi Desert you might like to buy. Very large beach, too.

The Illuminati bloodlines

Through the 1990s, as I researched the way the world is controlled and manipulated today, it was clear that for some reason the ruling families and their offshoots were obsessed with interbreeding with each other. The higher you go in the hierarchy the more this genetic obsession prevails. When you follow these bloodlines back into history, you find that they have always interbred with themselves. The bloodlines of the 43 American presidents from George Washington to George W. Bush go back to European royal and aristocratic families who have famously interbred and still do to keep the gene pool "pure". Their genealogy, and that of today's key politicians, banking tycoons, business leaders, and media owners, continues back even further into the distant past through those European royal and "noble" (Aryan) families to the ancient kings of Sumer and its empire, not least Egypt. Hold that thought because it is vital. Perhaps the most astonishing information in the Sumerian clay tablets are the detailed descriptions of how the Anunnaki interbred with human women to create a hybrid race, a fusion of the genes of humans of the time and the "gods". Included in the term "human" are the white or Nordic race, which are also, originally, of extraterrestrial origin. Yet again, this is a constantly repeated theme in every part of the world and can be seen in the Old Testament narrative, taken from the Sumerian, of the Sons of God (properly translated, the sons of the gods) who interbred with humanity and created a hybrid bloodline. Genesis recounts:

> "When men began to increase in number on the Earth and daughters were born to them, the sons of God [the gods] saw that the daughters of men were beautiful, and they married any of them they chose…The Nefilim were on the Earth in those days – and also afterwards – when the sons of God [the gods] went to the daughters of men and had children by them. They were the heroes of old, the men of renown." [4]

The term Nefilim can be translated as "Those Who Descended" or "Those Who Fell From The Heavens". The American researcher, David Sielaff, emphasises that the Nefilim or Nephilim are not the sons of the gods (beni ha-Elohim), but the offspring of the interbreeding between the extraterrestrials the Bible calls the Elohim and the daughters of men. The Illuminati bloodlines that rule the world today, therefore, are the Nefilim, the extraterrestrial-human hybrids. They were also known in ancient times as the Rephaim, Emim, Zazummim, and Anakim, all very tall or "giant" people in those days. [5] The biblical Goliath was a Rephaim, and giant in Hebrew is repha. [6] This theme of giants is a constant one. Cave paintings found in places like Japan, South America, and the Sahara Desert, depict giant people with round heads towering over human hunters. Bones of giant people between 8 and 12

feet tall have been found in mounds in Minnesota and other locations. The
Delaware Indians speak of a race of giants who once lived east of the Mississippi in
enormous cities and the same descriptions of giants in ancient legends and lore can
be found everywhere.[7] Scores of giant red-haired mummies were discovered in a
cave near Lovelock in Nevada and some were seven feet tall.[8] The Piute Indian
legends about these giants say they were cannibals. They would even dig up the
Piute dead from their graves and eat them, the accounts claim.[9] Stories of Atlantis
include tales of red-haired giants who acted like vampires, and the giant Nefilim
were associated with cannibalism and blood drinking – just like the Illuminati
bloodlines are today. Most accounts say that these giants were unfriendly, even
hostile, to the rest of the population. Often associated with these giants are strange
craft that sound very much like the "flying saucers" of modern UFO accounts.
Genesis tells us that the sons of the gods married the daughters of men before the
flood, as well as afterwards and Numbers calls the Nephilim, the sons of Anak, or
descendants of the Anakim (Anunnaki).[10]

Hero worship

According to Zecharia Sitchin, who has written many books on the Sumerian
tablets, the term "men of renown" in the Genesis passage should read, from its
Sumerian origin, "men of the sky vehicles". This puts rather a different complexion
on the whole story and makes a great deal more sense of it. The reference to
"heroes of old" is also relevant. The word hero comes from the Egyptian term,
heru, which, according to researcher Wallis Budge, was "applied to the king as a
representative of the Sun God on Earth".[11] The precise meaning was "a human
being who was neither a god nor a daemon".[12] The term has the inference of a
crossbreed race. The writer Homer (8th-9th century BC) wrote that "the heroes were
exalted above the race of common men". The poet, Pindar, (518-438BC) – a very
relevant name for readers of *The Biggest Secret* – used the term, hero/heru, to
describe a race "between gods and men". At this moment I have the song playing
in my head that goes "Search for the hero inside yourself"! It is extremely likely
that Horus or Haru, the Egyptian son of God and a mirror of the much later
"Jesus", came from the term heru, which means the Sun God's representative on
Earth, the hybrid or Aryan race. There is also the Sumerian word, Hu or Ha,
meaning hawk, and the hawk or Sun-hawk was a Sumerian symbol for the Sun.[13]
The term Nibiri or Nebiru, the alleged home planet of the Anunnaki according to
the tablets, is derived from the word found in Egypt, Neb-Heru, according to
researcher and author, Robert Temple.[14] He says that Neb-Heru is clearly described
in the Sumerian, Enuma Elish, as a star and not a planet.[15] Again could the Sirius
sun or dog star be the true "Nibiru/Nebiru"? Maybe, maybe not. Horus, the Son of
God of Egyptian myth, was strongly associated with Sirius as in Heru-Sept or
"Horus of the Dog Star".[16] One depiction of Horus was as Heru-ami-u, a hawk-
headed crocodile with a tail ending as a dog's head. He was also portrayed with a
jackal or dog/wolf head, as was An or Anu, the royal leader of the Anunnaki.[17]
Heru = hero = hybrid bloodline and these "heroes" may be ruling the Earth, at

least in part, on behalf of the Sirius "gods". Another definition of the term, hero, is a "man sacrificed to Hera", which is again related to Heru/Horus, etc.[18]

Biblical scholars and the dictatorships that control Judaism and Christianity have always avoided an explanation of that "Nefilim" passage in Genesis because it is so difficult to encompass the contents into the party line. But, hey, they tell us that this is the literal word of God and He's not going to make a cock-up, is He? It's very clear. Some sort of beings, the sons of the gods, came down and produced children with Earth women and those children were therefore a hybrid race, the Nefilim. It's official. God said. Over to you, vicar. Or rabbi. Talk us through that one. Flavius Josephus, the 1st century writer and historian, did offer a comment on this Genesis reference to the interbreeding between "gods" and human women:

> "…for many angels of God accompanied with women and begat sons that proved unjust, and despisers of all that was good, on account of the confidence they had in their own strength; for the tradition is, that these men did what resembled the acts of those whom the Grecians call giants."[19]

The term, angel, which simply means messenger, became associated with these non-human entities that interbred with humans. The Sumerian tablets go much further than Genesis in explaining this interbreeding. They describe how the Anunnaki systematically set out to create a slave race, later called Homo sapiens, to serve their agenda and how they began this quest, amid much trial and error, using what we call today test-tube methods. This is described in the tablets, and they tell of how the sperm of Anunnaki males was used to fertilise human eggs before they were transplanted to Anunnaki females to be birthed. All this appears to have first happened hundreds of thousands of years ago, but has continued ever since on various scales. I think many of the stories mentioned in the tablets refer to events in Lemuria and Atlantis. All this makes more understandable the countless stories told today by people claiming to have been abducted by non-human entities that forced them to have sex or took their eggs. The babies that result often disappear in early pregnancy with no medical explanation. Of course, there are many "abduction" experiences that are simply invented or have other, more earthly, explanations, but to dismiss them all, given their number and often consistency of detail, would be just as ridiculous as believing every word of every one.

The Sumerian tablets tell of how the original breeding programme was headed by the chief scientist of the Anunnaki, called Enki, or "Lord of the Earth" (Ki = Earth), and their expert in medicine, Ninkharsag, also known as Ninti ("Lady Life"). Mesopotamian depictions portray her holding a horseshoe-shaped tool used at that time to cut the umbilical cord. Another name later given to her was Mammi, from which came mama and mother. Mama or ma as a term for mother can be found in various languages all over the world. Ninkharsag would later be symbolised in part by the stream of mother goddess deities with names like Queen Semiramis, Isis, Barati, Artemis, Diana, and the biblical Mary. These were also used to symbolise the feminine principle as goddesses of the Moon or waters, which are considered feminine in balance to the masculine Sun. There are often two distinct camps in these areas of research. There are those who believe that these deities were only symbolic of astronomical and esoteric principles, and those who say they were originally flesh and blood extraterrestrial "gods" or "goddesses". My own view is that sometimes, not always by any means, it is a combination of the two, as some changed over thousands of years from literal descriptions of Anunnaki leaders to symbolic of astronomical and esoteric themes.

After many failures and some horrendous creations, Enki and Ninkharsag produced a human hybrid that the Sumerians called a LU.LU ("One Who Has Been Mixed") – which appears to be the biblical "Adam". This was the splicing together of the DNA of the reptilian Anunnaki with that of the human form known as Homo erectus. Also there was the interbreeding with the Nordics to create the Aryan reptilian-Nordic "master race", which was designed to rule as the "middle men" or "demi-gods" between the Anunnaki and the people. What the Bible calls "Adam", the "first man", is likely to be symbolic of "the Adam", a genetic stream not an individual. The biblical "Eve" was supposed to have been created from a rib of Adam, according to Genesis, but the word from which "rib" derived was the Sumerian, TI, which means both rib and life.[20] To be created from the "life" or life essence of the Adamic race makes rather more sense than a rib. In the same way, the "dust from the ground" from which the Bible claims that Adam was created, really translates as "that which is life" from the Sumerian term, TI.IT. As I detail in *The Biggest Secret*, many investigations into human origins, using the DNA of people from different cultures, colours, and races, all point to a single source in Africa around 200,000 to 300,000 years ago. This is in line with the claims of the Sumerian tablets. Appropriately, the Sumerian name for humans was LU, which has the root meaning of worker or servant and also implies a domesticated animal, like a sheep. Look around you. Does that not describe the nature of human life today and for a long time past? My own research leads me to think that claims that the Anunnaki created the human form as we know it all over the world are seriously exaggerated. I think there were many examples of interbreeding between humanity and the "gods" of various origins and races and not just the Anunnaki. It was more that the Anunnaki created DNA streams or bloodlines to suit their agenda and they have continued to infuse their DNA into human blood streams. They rewire the DNA to close down humanity's interdimensional communication and telepathic powers. This puts us in a vibrational prison in which we can perceive only the very narrow frequency range accessed by our physical senses. The suppression of our telepathic powers is symbolised in ancient accounts all over the world as the gods dividing human peoples by giving them different languages. I will discuss this further a little later. Official history says that certain human forms died out to be followed by new ones and thus Neanderthal man was followed by Cro-Magnon man, and then Homo sapiens or modern man. And yet archaeologists working in the Middle East discovered evidence to show that all these physical forms existed during the *same* period. The "missing link" that would connect them and explain the sudden and dramatic changes and appearance of their physical forms has never been found because the establishment of academia would rather stay ignorant than utter the "E" word – extraterrestrial.

The themes of the Sumerian tablets are supported by Credo Mutwa, one of only two surviving "sanusis" left in southern Africa. A sanusi is the peak of the African shamanistic stream. Credo is 79 and the other sanusi, his aunt, is in her 90s. He is the official historian and storyteller of the Zulu nation and the very name "Zulu" means "People from the Stars" because they believe they were seeded by an extraterrestrial "royal" race. With no one for him to pass on his knowledge, and the urgent need for everyone to know the astonishing information he has received in a lifetime of initiations, I produced two videos with him, *The Reptilian Agenda*, parts one and two. They last more than six hours and still that is only a fraction of the knowledge he holds. In the videos he reveals what he once pledged in his initiations never to reveal. But he says that the situation for humanity is so perilous that it is far more important for them to know what is going on than for him to keep such vows of silence. This information went underground when the Europeans invaded Africa and their Illuminati leaders, in Credo's words, "milked the minds of the shamen and then killed them". It was suicide to talk openly of such things and secret networks of initiation were formed to keep it alive. Credo, who has become a close friend, tells the same story of the interbreeding between the extraterrestrial Anunnaki and humans to produce a hybrid race.

He also has artefacts like the "Necklace of the Mysteries", which confirm this story (*see picture section*). It is an extremely heavy copper "necklace" that actually rests on the shoulders and it has been mentioned in records 500 years old. Credo says it goes back at least 1,000 years. The large symbols that hang from the necklace tell the story of humanity. In pride of place at the front are an extraterrestrial with a big copper willy (in come-and-get-me mode), and an Earth woman into whom the ET "fits", if you follow me. This is symbolic, Credo explains, of the union between the people from the stars and humanity, which you find recorded in virtually every ancient culture. Significantly, he says the copper willy was once made of gold before it was stolen and replaced with copper. This mirrors the ancient Egyptian story about the golden penis of their key god, Osiris, which is symbolised by the secret societies today, especially the Freemasons, as an obelisk. The way the extraterrestrial is portrayed on the necklace, Credo says, is merely symbolic because these "gods" were of a very distinct and unhuman form (reptilian) and they warned the people of instant death if they ever depicted them as they really looked. Thus the "gods" were portrayed symbolically. Hanging from the Necklace of the Mysteries is a large hand, full of symbols. Among these are the all-seeing eye, symbolising, Credo points out, the "Watchers" (the same as the Illuminati image on the US dollar bill); also there is the constellation of Orion, which modern researchers have constantly connected with extraterrestrial activity on Earth, especially the reptilians; and a Star of David, which is not, contrary to accepted belief, an ancient "Jewish" symbol at all. As some Jewish historians have stated, it is a far ancient symbol found all over the world, and only became associated with the Jewish faith when the banking and Illuminati bloodline dynasty, the Rothschilds, began to use it in the 18th century. A researcher who saw the symbols on the necklace at one of my talks, also saw the connections with the star, Sirius, from which, according to ancient accounts, a reptilian race came to the Earth. He wrote:

"I noticed that the South African shaman necklace with the carved hand had a picture of Orion on it. Orion's belt points to the binary star Sirius. On the carved hand, the belt of Orion points directly to the eye in the centre, suggesting a link between the Eye cult and Sirius. Indeed, throughout the history of occultism, Sirius has been seen as very important, indeed it was a most sacred location throughout the ancient world. It is the Star card in tarot, the silver star of [Aleister] Crowley's A: A: organization [Crowley was a Satanist], the star to which the Queen's shaft in the Great Pyramid points, and the star from which the Dogon of Mali say their alien visitors the Nommo came from."

The Necklace of the Mysteries includes a very clear "flying saucer" which, the legend says, the extraterrestrials flew from their giant "Mothership" to land on the Earth. They say the Mothership continued to orbit and it was to there that the leaders sheltered during the upheavals. In France, cave paintings dated to between 10,000 and 30,000 years ago include oval and disc-shaped objects standing on tripod legs with ladders coming down from them. A drawing carved in a cliff at Fergania in Central Asia had a man who appeared to be wearing an "airtight helmet" with some mechanical device on his back. It was dated to 7000BC. Whatever the origin and nature of "flying saucers" and other such craft, they have been seen and recorded for thousands of years.

The genetic obsession

The Anunnaki leader called Enki, the "Lord of the Earth" and chief scientist, was not the top man in the Anunnaki mission to this planet, the Sumerian tablets say. He was the eldest son of the Anunnaki's overall Mr Big, An or Anu, who made only rare visits to the Earth, we are told by translations. But Enki's younger half-brother Enlil was made commander of the mission because his mother was considered more genetically pure than the female with whom Anu conceived Enki. This, the accounts reveal, was to be the cause of ongoing conflicts between the half-brothers, which were to erupt in the wars within the Anunnaki that stimulated enormous conflict between their factions within humanity, as described in Old Testament texts. It is well known by researchers that, although the Illuminati agree on the overall agenda of global control, they, too, are constantly at war within themselves as different groups and families seek to be at the top of their greasy pole. This is no surprise when you consider that the Illuminati is a front for the Anunnaki and the secret society network is their means of covertly manipulating humanity and introducing their agenda for a planetary dictatorship via a world government, world central bank, world army, and a micro-chipped population. All of which are getting closer by the hour. These factions within the Anunnaki, and therefore the Illuminati, are still at war with each other today. One researcher described the Illuminati to me like this: "They are like a gang of bank robbers. They all agree on the job, but they argue over how the spoils will be shared out." This is the Anunnaki and their bloodlines to a tee.

Something happened that led the Anunnaki to withdraw from overt control and to manipulate through certain bloodlines from behind the scenes and the cover of human form. It is likely that there were so few of them, as human numbers began to soar again after the catastrophe, that covert control became the only option, especially when their own internal strife, described in the tablets, led to a period of utter chaos. The accounts confirm many times (according to Sitchin's translations) that the commander of the mission Enlil was alarmed at the rapid expansion of human numbers and it is even suggested that one major geological catastrophe was manufactured by the Anunnaki to dramatically reduce the population (just as the Illuminati seek to do today with war, famine, and disease). The decision by the Anunnaki to withdraw to the shadows could even have involved an outside intervention of some kind because it is clear that there are many extraterrestrial groups with varying agendas at work who find this planet of great interest. Whatever the cause, the Anunnaki went underground, literally and symbolically, and used certain hybrid bloodlines to do their dirty work in the human arena.

The "divine right of kings" (and presidents, and bankers...)

You can appreciate from the genetic reason for Enlil's elevation over Enki that the Anunnaki are fiercely hierarchical and that hierarchy is decided on the basis of bloodline and genetics. Exactly the same theme is followed by the "human" bloodlines that have held the reigns of power since the days of Sumer. Throughout history the right to rule has been decided by bloodline. For thousands of years it was done openly and today it is achieved through covert manipulation and the secret society web I call the Illuminati. As humanity interbred, the traits of the Anunnaki were diffused into the overall genetic pool. But certain bloodlines were specifically seeded by the Anunnaki "royal" leadership to be their front men and women who would rule humanity on their behalf and to their agenda, the accounts reveal. This is the reason for the obsessive interbreeding of the ruling families over thousands of years. The Sumerian texts call these Anunnaki "royal" bloodlines the AB-GAL, the "Masters of Knowledge" and the "seven elders", and they apparently go back to ten priest-kings before the deluge. Atlantis and Lemuria in other words. They were depicted with fish-like bodies, as was Enki himself under another of his names, Oannes. The fish symbolises the amphibious nature of the gods and that is right in line with the apparently amphibious extraterrestrials from Sirius.

These "royal" bloodlines have worked to maintain their Anunnaki genetics through interbreeding and others have continued to be seeded for this purpose ever since, hence the stories of humans forced to have sex with, or being artificially impregnated by, non-human entities. The Sumerian records say that the crossbreed hybrids of the Anunnaki were placed into the positions of royal ruling power during the Golden Age and throughout the Sumer Empire. This happened, the tablets document, when Anu bestowed "Anu-ship" (later called kingship) on humanity by creating the bloodlines to rule on behalf of the gods. Kingship is really kin-ship – bloodline. This is also the true origin and meaning of the ancient theme of the "Divine Right of Kings", the right to rule because of your genetic history. It is not the Divine or "God", at all. It is the right bestowed by the "gods", the Anunnaki, to rule according to their agenda. In reality, most of the battles between kings and queens of various bloodlines to rule various countries were a continuation of the internal tussle for supremacy within the Anunnaki. This applies to the Stuart and Tudor dynasties in England, for instance, the battles between bloodlines in England and Scotland, and those today within banking, business, politics, and the media. Researcher John A. Keel wrote of these themes 30 years ago:

> "In all these legends there is another persistent theme: that the god-kings mated with mortal women, impregnated them and thus started a royal lineage. Tradition claims that the blue bloods of royalty actually had blue blood in their veins in early history, perhaps as a result of this crossbreeding. Even today some royal families suffer from haemophilia [and other rare blood diseases] ...This ownership [of the planet] was passed onto human heirs, and for thousands of years a few dozen families literally owned the entire planet. They intermarried and managed to keep the system going until modern times. Although the king system degenerated slowly, it did not really collapse until 1848." [21]

But control by these bloodlines only *appeared* to collapse. They just moved from overt power through royal rule to covert control through politics, banking, business, and media. In *Appendix I* at the back of this book, you will see just some of the famous rulers and influences on the world over thousands of years who come from the same bloodline, starting with the rulers of Sumer, Egypt, Babylon, and Greece. These were all part of, or the successors to, the Sumer Empire and based on that same knowledge, culture, and bloodline hierarchy of the "gods". As we follow this bloodline through the millennia we find that all 43 presidents of the United States to George W. Bush, the royal families of England, including the House of Windsor, and those responsible for the creation and imposition of Christianity and other religions, like the Jehovah's Witnesses and the Mormons. Of those 43 US presidents since the first in 1789, some 34 are connected genetically to Charlemagne, the most famous monarch of what we now call France, and a major figure in the Illuminati and its bloodlines. [22] In the last weeks of the farcical year 2000 presidential election campaign, that "blue blood bible" of royal and aristocratic genealogy, *Burke's Peerage*, confirmed the themes I am highlighting here. Four years earlier, when Bill Clinton faced Bob Dole, *Burkes Peerage* said that the candidate with the most European royal genes had won every single presidential election in US history. Clinton and George W. Bush have since continued that unbroken sequence. In a Reuter's report of October 17th, 2000, *Burkes Peerage* confirmed that both George W. Bush and "opponent" Al Gore were of royal descent with Bush the "bluer" of the two. Purely by knowing his bloodline and watching the behind-the-scenes developments, I was able to predict three years before the 2000 election that George

W. Bush would be the next president of the United States. Bush is closely related to every European monarch on and off the throne including the King of Albania and has kinship with every member of Britain's royal family, the report said. He is a 13th cousin of Britain's (seriously reptilian) Queen Mother, and her daughter Queen Elizabeth, and is a 13th cousin once removed of the heir to the throne, Prince Charles. Bush has a direct descent from Henry III and from Henry VIII's sister Mary Tudor, who was also the wife of Louis XI of France. He is further descended from Charles II of England. Harold Brooks-Baker, Publishing Director of *Burke's Peerage*, said: "It is now clear that Mr Gore and Mr Bush have an unusually large number of royal and noble descents." Only unusual if you don't know the story. He added: "In point of fact, never in the history of the United States have two presidential candidates been as well endowed with royal alliances."[23] Brooks-Baker said there had always been a significant "royalty factor" in those who aspired to the White House, with Presidents George Washington, Thomas Jefferson, Franklin and Theodore Roosevelt, and Ronald Reagan, among others, all boasting blue blood links. He said that Al Gore, a cousin of former president, Richard Nixon, was a descendant of Edward I and has direct links to the Holy Roman Empire through Emperors, Louis II, Charles II and Louis I. This, therefore, makes him a direct descendant of Charlemagne, the 8th-century Emperor.[24] These Charlemagne links make Gore a cousin of George W. Bush!

The Merovingian bloodline

Charlemagne, in turn, takes us into the Merovingian dynasty in France, which founded the city of Paris and to whom all the royal families of Europe are related. Other highly influential figures of their time, like the founders of the Mormon religion Joseph Smith, Hiram Smith, and Brigham Young are from this Merovingian line. There have been a number of best-selling books written over recent years about the Merovingian bloodline and the France-based Priory of Sion, a secret society through which this bloodline manipulates. These books have presented some interesting and important information, but they claim that the Merovingians are the bloodline of Jesus and the children they say he conceived with "Mary Magdalene". The story goes that she fled with them to southern France after the "crucifixion". But there *was* no Jesus and there was no Mary Magdalene, a fact that will become obvious. How do two people who did not exist conceive children who became the Merovingian line? Beats me. This is a vitally important bloodline, yes, but not because of Jesus. The Merovingians are Anunnaki hybrids. It is one of their key bloodlines. Interestingly, MAG is apparently a code for the reptilian DNA passed on through the female line and it appears to relate to Orion from what I understand. The Dan Winter website at *http://www.danwinter.com/sitemap.html* has a lot of background information to the reptilian-human genetics.

The Merovingian bloodline is a constant theme in my research of the ruling families. It goes back to the ancient Middle and Near East during the Sumer Empire and almost certainly even further to Atlantis and Lemuria. The people later known as Merovingians were involved in the Trojan War (c. 1200BC) between the

Trojans and the Greeks in what we now call Turkey. Over time they moved out through the Caucasus Mountains in southern Russia under the name Scythians and into Europe where they were known as the Sicambrian Franks, the source of the name "France". They were named after Cambra, their tribal queen of the late 4th century, and Francio, their founder, who claimed to have been descended from Noah of the biblical Great Flood.[25] Noah is a mythical name, but possibly based on a real character from the Atlantean period and an Anunnaki crossbreed. It should be stressed here that Noah and Abraham, had they actually existed, were not Hebrews because there were no Hebrews in this period. The Hebrews were an offshoot of the Sumerian-Egyptian cultures, as outlined by, among others, Professor Cyrus Gordon, in *The Common Background Of Greek And Hebrew Civilisation* (W. W. Norton and Company, New York, 1965). To claim descent from "Noah" is used by Illuminati initiates to symbolise their genetic connection to the Anunnaki bloodline. The Sumerian version of the "Noah" story relates his close connection to the Anunnaki, especially Enki.

The Franks called themselves the Newmage or "the People of the Covenant" and settled in Germania (possibly named by the Romans from a word meaning "genuine ones") with their centre in Cologne. Peoples of the former Sumer Empire moved into Europe over many centuries by land. As they travelled they were known by different names in different regions. Once more the changing names have obscured the fact that they were the same peoples from the former Sumer Empire and even further back to Atlantis and Lemuria. Some of the names by which these former Sumerian peoples were known are the Scythians (Saca, Sacki, Sacksen, Saxon), Goths (Gauls), and Cimmerians. The Angles and the Saxons, who combined to form the Anglo-Saxons, once again had the same origin, the Aryan race from Sumer and its empire.[26] This exodus into Europe included the people called the Sicambrian Franks. Interestingly these Franks also claimed to have lived in Arcadia in Greece, which is a name for Atlantis according to some researchers. The Danube (Danaan) region was another area where the Sicambrian Franks settled and this region has long been connected to the bloodlines and their interbreeding. From the time of their king called Meroveus or Merovee, who became Guardian of the Franks in 488, they became known as the Merovingians. Legend says that Merovee was the offspring of a human mother and a sea creature called Quinotaur, who sounds very much like the reptilian Anunnaki known as Enki, Ea, or Oannes, the "fish god". Merovee, who was brought up by Chodio, the first king of the Franks, was known as the "son of the sea" and this is the symbolic foundation of the Merovingian bloodline so crucial to the Illuminati.

The Merovingians founded the city of Paris in the sixth century, which they named after Prince Paris, the son of King Priam of Troy. Prince Paris was one of the figures in the Trojan War story, which the Merovingians knew their bloodline had been involved in. The Merovingians were committed to the worship of Diana, one of the great goddess figures of the ancient world who was also known as Artemis. This was the same goddess worshipped in Atlantis. The city of Troy, in Asia Minor, now Turkey, is in the same region as Ephesus, a place I have visited, which was the

Figure 15: *The three points of the Fleur-de-lis, a widely used symbol of the Merovingian-reptilian bloodline*

centre of Artemis (Diana) worship. The Merovingians founded Paris on major vortex points on the Earth's energy grid and built underground chambers outside the original settlement to harness that energy in their rituals and sacrifices to the goddess Diana. That very site is still an underground chamber. It is called the Pont de L'Alma tunnel where Princess Diana, named after the goddess, was murdered on Sunday, August 31st, 1997. The goddess Diana was symbolically a "Moon goddess" and the name Pont de L'Alma means "bridge or passage of the Moon goddess". I tell the story of Diana's assassination in great detail in *The Biggest Secret*,[27] where you will also see the staggering obsession that the bloodlines and their Illuminati network have with symbolism and ritual. Everything they do is symbolism and ritual, and when you study this subject it is a very good way to identify their signature on global events. By the way, Paris and London are two of the most important global centres for the Illuminati and both were founded by bloodlines from Troy. The connection between Britain and Troy goes way back, long before this bloodline became known as the Merovingians. It was a "royal" Trojan called Brutus, a relative of Helen of Troy, who sailed west to Britain after the fall of Troy and founded a city called "Caer Troia" or New Troy in around 1103BC. This later became known as Lugdunnum and today it is called London. This story was told by the 12th century chronicler, Geoffrey of Monmouth, and confirmed by the research of L.A. Waddell, as outlined in his books.

Offshoots of the Merovingian line left northern France and Belgium for Scotland in the 12th century to become famous "Scottish" aristocratic families, some of whom were Princess Diana's ancestors. This is one reason why Scotland is so important to the Illuminati and why we have the biggest secret society in the world called the *Scottish* Rite of Freemasonry. The House of Windsor, who were most certainly involved in the ritual murder of Diana, descend from the Merovingians. The three-pointed fleur-de-lis (formerly the Trident of Atlantis and Lemuria) became the symbol of the Merovingian bloodline and so you see it used profusely by British royalty, on official buildings (like a gate at the White House), and in churches (*Figure 15*). The bee is also a Merovingian symbol and this was associated with Artemis (*see picture section*) and many other goddesses, including Queen Semiramis in Babylon who is symbolised by the Illuminati as a dove. Thus the dove is another theme of British royalty's ritual ironmongery, sorry sacred sceptres. The reptilian bloodline is supposed to carry secret esoteric and magical powers (what the Nazis called the "vril" or "serpent" power) and the Merovingians were known as "sorcerer kings" because of these abilities. Some of the more amazing of these powers we shall discuss later. Keep the seat belt on for that one. These guys and gals don't interbreed because they fancy each other – there is a greater purpose and one on which their whole plan depends. The Windsors wanted Diana's genes for their own purposes because she carried a strong DNA connection to the Nordics, and the reptilian hybrids need to infuse their bloodlines with that from time to time and therefore you have their obsession with blond-haired, blue-eyed, people. Once the offspring were born of Diana's union with Prince Charles she was surplus to requirements and ritually removed. Christine Fitzgerald, her closest confidante on esoteric matters for nine years, told me that Diana called herself the "Windsors' brood mare" because she had realised the game. Now with Diana gone, and having fulfilled his bloodline duty, Prince Charles can be seen openly with the woman he was secretly with throughout his "marriage", Camilla Parker-Bowles.

The Rothschild bloodline

The Merovingians were supposed to have died out, but in reality only the name disappeared, until recently, and not the bloodline. The genetics continued with the King of the Franks called Charles, more famously known as Charlemagne, to whom 34 of the 43 US presidents and so many other key figures are related. He vastly extended the Frankish domains and ruled as Emperor of the West in the papal empire created and controlled by the bloodlines descending from the Roman Empire. These in turn descended from the royal lines of the Sumer Empire, who descended from Atlanteans, Lemurians and the interbreeding of the Nordics with the reptilian Anunnaki. Another of the key names in Illuminati genealogy is Alexander the Great, an ancestor of Charlemagne and all the major Illuminati families today (*see Appendix I*). Alexander carried the strongly Nordic DNA and descended from the Viking peoples who settled the Mediterranean and the Aegean after the Atlantean cataclysms. Alexander ruled Troy at one stage and, before he died in Babylon in 323BC at the age of 33, his army had seized control of a vast region once ruled from Sumer. This included Egypt, Mesopotamia, and into India. He founded the city of Alexandria in Egypt. He was known as the "Serpent's Son" and Alexandria was the "City of the Serpent's Son".[28] Once again we see the recurring theme. The legend goes that Alexander's real father was the serpent god, Ammon, and this mirrors the story of Merovee, founder of the Merovingian dynasty. Throughout history, the reptilians have perpetuated their "purest" bloodlines by marrying as closely as possible to their own genetics. It is vital to remember that these bloodlines do not just breed through their official partners. They have stunning numbers of children out of wedlock. These offspring are then brought up with names that are different to the major Illuminati families like Rockefeller and Rothschild. So when one of these children, called Clinton, Roosevelt, or whoever, enters a position of power, the people do not relate them to the Illuminati families because they have a different name. But, and I can't emphasise this enough, they are the same bloodline. This is how they hide the tribe, the Anunnaki genetic network.

Phillip Eugene de Rothschild, who now lives in America, claims to be an unofficial offspring of Philippe de Rothschild of the French Rothschilds, and worked within the Illuminati Satanic network for most of his life. I give more detail about his background later. Phillip told me that the key "Nefilim" bloodline is connected to a figure called Aeneas, the alleged head of the Roman Empire through his descendants, Romulus and Remus. The latter are code names for the bloodline and not real people and that may be the same with Aeneas. The names "Noah" and "King David" are also used as codes for the bloodline, but they did not exist in the way they are depicted and portrayed. The legends of Aeneas fit with the codes and themes of the Illuminati bloodlines, including his association with Troy. Aeneas is said to have been born in Troy, the city so sacred to the Merovingians and the Knights Templar. In the Hymn to Aphrodite, the Goddess proclaims that Aeneas, the son she has conceived by the mortal Anchises, will come to rule the Trojans, as will the generations upon generations that succeed him.[29] The works of the Greek poet, Homer, who lived around the 9th or 8th century BC, is the main source of information about ancient Troy and the conflicts that led to its demise. The two epics the Iliad and the Odyssey are ascribed to him. Modern archaeological discoveries have confirmed the accuracy of Homer's work. In the Iliad, Aeneas recounts his birth and ancestry to his opponent Achilles on the battlefield at Troy. Aeneas says that he descends from "divine and immortal stock" through both his mother and his father. This connection between divine immortality and the Anunnaki under their various names constantly recurs in ancient accounts. Aeneas says that his mother is the goddess, Aphrodite, and his father is Anchises, and he can trace his lineage back to Dardanus, the son of Zeus and legendary founder of the Trojan race (Trojan race = reptilian-Nordic hybrids, the Aryans or "master race"). Other accounts say that Dardanus is the offspring of the union of Zeus and Electra and his origins are in Samothrace, the sacred Aegean island dedicated to goddess worship, from where he migrates to Troad (Troy) in the period of the Great Flood. One of the outstanding characteristics with which Aeneas is endowed in the Iliad is a close relationship with the gods. The legends of Aeneas are peppered with references and codes about his genealogical relationship to the "gods" and so it is no surprise that he plays such an important part in the codes and symbolism of the Illuminati bloodlines today.

Phillip Eugene de Rothschild told me that this "Aeneas" bloodline became what he called the "Rothsburg dynasty" – the union of the Bauer-Rothschilds (same family, different name) and the Battenbergs. This is the Merovingian bloodline and also the line of the Habsburgs, the leading family in the Holy Roman Empire for hundreds of years. This was the medieval state that embraced most of central Europe and Italy from 962 to 1806. The Dutch researcher Frans Kamp suggests that the Habsburgs were Nordics who interbred with the reptilians in the ancient past. They were also connected to the reptilian House of Lorraine. Phillip Eugene says that this "Rothsburg" bloodline is known within the Illuminati as the "Gens". This is a Latin word meaning "race", "tribe" or "male line of descent" and comes from the term gignere – "to beget".[30] The late Lord Louis Mountbatten, a famous member of the British royal family, and his nephew, Prince Philip, are Battenbergs and Illuminati Satanists. This is why Lord Mountbatten became Governor of the Isle of Wight off the south coast of England, an extremely important centre for the Illuminati and its Satanists because of its position on the Earth energy grid. More about that in due course. It was Lord Mountbatten who arranged the marriage between Prince Philip and Queen Elizabeth II, after which the royal line of the UK became known as Windsor-Mountbatten. Both the Windsors and the Mountbattens are German bloodlines formerly known as the House of Saxe-Coburg-Gotha and the Battenbergs. They anglicised their names during the First World War against Germany for public relations reasons, but both of these "families" supported the Nazis, and Prince Philip was sent to a school in Germany run by the Nazi youth programme (see ...*And The Truth Shall Set You Free* and *The Biggest Secret*). Phillip Eugene, the Rothschild offspring, says of this "Aeneas" bloodline:

> "Apparently Aeneas embodies all the various bloodlines that must trace their lineage back through Charlemagne because in him is embodied the confluence of the lineage of both David (Jewish) and Alexander the Great (Aryan). It is the modern day representatives of these Roman 'Gens' or European monarchs that make up the ruling 'aristocracy' of the revived Roman Empire. These 'royal' families maintain their pedigree through endogamy (inter-familial marriages). The first prototype of the Antichrist [the purest bloodline] was Nimrod, founder of Babylon. The historical and seminal nexus of this last Roman Empire is Charlemagne and his descendants, people like [Prince] Philip Mountbatten (Rex Julius Alexander Battenberg) who is one of the ruling heads of the Julian Gens." [31]

The keepers of the secrets

The Priory of Sion, an elite secret society created in the 12th century to serve the Merovingian bloodline or "Le Serpent Rouge" (the serpent blood), was very closely connected to the Knights Templar who were, incidentally, officially formed at the French city of Troyes, named by the Sicambrian Franks (Merovingians) after their former home in Troy. The Priory of Sion and the Knights Templar have had their feuds and break-ups over the centuries, but, as with similar conflicts from time to time with the Knights of Malta, these were battles for supremacy *within* the bloodlines, not between the bloodlines and an outside force. Missing this point, I feel, has led so many researchers off the trail. They all have the same basic agenda of global control by the Anunnaki, but they each want to be top dog. The same is true with the Rothschilds and the Rockefellers, two major expressions of the bloodline today. At the top level, the Priory of Sion, Knights Templar, Knights of Malta, Teutonic Knights, Rosicrucians, Freemasons, and a long, long, list of others, are the *same* organisation, the all-encompassing network I call the Illuminati. This is not to be confused with a group called the Bavarian Illuminati, officially formed on May 1st (a major ritual day) 1776. The *Bavarian* Illuminati is a strand in the web, not the web itself.

One other point to emphasise as we close this chapter is the constantly recurring theme in this story of the Caucasus Mountains in southern Russia. From the early days of my research this region has appeared again and again in relation to the bloodlines, particularly the Aryan Race. Of course, the white race is known in North

America as "caucasian". A Swedish contact had a long relationship with Russia's leading "UFO expert", whom she later discovered had secret service connections. She said that he had spoken of the Caucasus Mountains as an inter-dimensional portal or gateway through which other-dimensional beings could enter this frequency range we call the physical world. This region was also a place where bloodlines from the Middle and Near East intermingled and no doubt interbred with those from the Far East and northern Russia. Robert Temple highlights in *The Sirius Mystery* the importance of the Colchis people at the foot of the Caucasus Mountains and relates them, with persuasive evidence, to the Greek myth of Jason and the Argonauts, a story which, as he points out, contains many symbolic codes for Sirius.[32] In the myth, Jason steals the Golden Fleece from the King of Colchis. It is in this region that the Georgian people live their extraordinarily long lives by today's standards and not far to the south is Mount Ararat, the place where the biblical Noah's Ark was supposed to have come symbolically to rest. The Greek historian, Herodotus, said that the people of Colchis, a dark race, were of Egyptian descent and he was told that they were men from the army of the pharaoh, Sesostris, whom, scholars believe, was another name for Ramses II. This guy appears in the Illuminati bloodline that includes the Rothschilds, Rockefellers, Bushes, and the British royal family, etc., etc.

The themes summarised here are supported by stories, legends, and accounts across the world, not only in the Sumerian tablets. Renegade insiders and former insiders of the Illuminati have also confirmed to me that humanity is indeed controlled by a tribe of interbreeding bloodlines that go back to the time of the Sumer Empire, Atlantis and Lemuria, where they were seeded by a non-human source.

SOURCES

1   *Flying Serpents And Dragons*, p 3

2   David Hatcher Childress, *Ancient Indian Aircraft Technology*, **http://www.farshore.force9.co.uk/india.htm**

3   Ibid

4   Genesis, Chapter 6, verses 1–4

5   *Flying Serpents And Dragons*, p 187 to 194

6   Ibid

7   Our Haunted Planet, p 38

8   Ibid, p 59

9   Ibid

10   Detailed in *Flying Serpents And Dragons*

11   *The Sirius Mystery*, p 155

12   Ibid

13   *Egyptian Civilisation*, p 21

14   *The Sirius Mystery*, p 157

15   Ibid

16   Ibid

17   Ibid

18   Barbara G. Walker, *The Woman's Encyclopedia Of Myths And Secrets* (HarperSanFrancisco, 1983), p 399

19   *Antiquities Of The Jews*

20   See the translations of Zecharia Sitchin

21   Our Haunted Planet, p 150

22   Information from the Boston Historical Genealogical Society, Boston, Massachusetts

23   Reuter's Report, October 17th, 2000

24   Ibid

25   The early history of the Merovingians can be found in *Fredegar's Chronicle*, a copy of which exists in the National Library of Paris

26   *The Phoenician Origin Of Britons, Scots, And Anglo Saxons*

27   See the chapter, The Goddess and the King, pp 411 to 469

28   *The Return Of The Serpents Of Wisdom*, p 256

29   More background on the Aeneas legend can be found at *http://ccat.sas.upenn.edu/~awiesner/vergil/comm2/legend/legend.html*

30   *http://encarta.msn.com/index/conciseindex/00/000f6000.htm?z=1&pg=2&br=1*

31   Phillip Eugene de Rothschild, personal correspondence with the author

32   *The Sirius Mystery*, pp 140 to 142

CHAPTER 6

the unholy alliance

Anyone who thinks they know it all is just confirming they do not.

David Icke

Lemuria and Atlantis was a time of widespread extraterrestrial and interdimensional activity on the planet and many Earth races were seeded in that period of hundreds of thousands of years. This was the source of the incredible and magnificent diversity of the human physical form and there are endless bloodlines among us, not just those of the Anunnaki reptilians.

From what I gather from my research and insider information, there has been a long battle in many parts of the galaxy between the blond-haired, blue-eyed "Nordics" of Lyra, the Pleiades, Aldebaran and elsewhere, and factions of a reptilian race based in the constellations of Draco and Orion and within the Sirius network. It is possible that at least some of the reptilians originated on the Earth and were driven out or, literally, forced underground at some point by the "Nordics". This is not to say that all of these peoples are involved, only that significant groups of them are. This battle on Earth is symbolised by stories such as the Phoenician "St George" defeating the dragon and "St Patrick" removing the snakes from Ireland. But there was also crossbreeding between the serpent race and the Nordics, which created the hybrid bloodlines that overwhelmingly became the ruling bloodlines of the Aryan dynasties. Brinsley Le Pour Trench says in his book, *The Sky People* (Award Books, New York, 1970) that the crossbreeding between the serpent race and the white race began on Mars before it was destroyed by cataclysm. Arizona Wilder (formerly Jennifer Greene), a victim of the Illuminati mind control projects and a conductor of their sacrificial rituals, told me that during her "training" she was told that the reptilians and the Nordics fought on Mars and crossbreeding took place there before they moved to Earth. She says that the reptilians have followed the Nordics around the galaxy for aeons because the blood of blond-haired, blue-eyed, people is very important to them.

As I said earlier, modern "UFO" research has suggested that three extraterrestrial groups fundamentally involved with life on this planet are the "Nordics", reptilians, and greys, with an "insectoid"-type race also involved somewhere in this. It has been further suggested that the reptilians control the greys, who are also a reptilian form as we shall see, and that these groups have an alliance with a faction of the tall, blond "Nordics", so named because of their likeness to the Scandinavian race, though much taller. Whatever you may think about the extraterrestrial connection, one thing is for sure. The ruling bloodlines of Sumer and its empire were very tall, Aryan types, with blond hair and blue eyes, and throughout that same empire there was veneration of serpent gods. Is that really just coincidence?

The Nordic connection

People all over the world and back into history have claimed to have been abducted by "aliens" of the Nordic and reptilian description. My great friend, Credo Mutwa, the 79-year-old Zulu shaman or "sanusi" in South Africa, confirms this. When we first met back in 1998 he showed me a picture he had painted of the tall, blond-haired, blue-eyed beings that had been seen by black African tribes people throughout that continent long before the white Europeans arrived. Credo, the official historian of the Zulu nation, said that when the Europeans first came, the black Africans thought they were the return of these same white "gods", which they called the Mzungu (*see picture section*). As a result they called the European settlers by the same name. This was very much the same reaction as the Central American peoples when Cortes and his Spanish invasion party arrived in 1519 and they thought that he was the returning god, Quetzalcoatl. This was another god described as tall and white and portayed with reptilian symbolism in his title of the "Plumed Serpent".

An American woman told me of an experience her father had in the early 1970s that strongly related to an extraterrestrial or other dimensional white race. They lived in Turkey at the time where he worked at a listening post for American Military Intelligence. He came home one night in a terrible state. When asked what was wrong, he just mumbled: "The world is not like we think it is." Although he rarely drank, he asked for a scotch, and then another. As he relaxed, he told his daughter of a communication he had taken that day from the pilot of a plane that was stationed at the Turkish base. The pilot reported that he was flying near the North Pole when suddenly his engines stopped and all the electrical systems switched off. The plane then gently lowered itself vertically to the ground and to his disbelief a mountaintop opened up and the plane came to rest inside. What he saw was a scene straight from James Bond (which was written by former British Intelligence agent, Ian Fleming). He got out of the plane wondering what the hell was going on and he was met by tall, blond-haired, people with "pearl" coloured skin and "bluish-purple" eyes that appeared to be electrically charged somehow: like laser eyes. (This same description of the eyes can be found in ancient accounts of the gods and the "children of the gods".) The beings in the mountain all wore long white gowns with a Maltese Cross medallion on a chain – the symbol of the Knights of Malta and widely seen in the symbolism of British royalty. It is also a symbol from Lemuria-Mu, according to James Churchward, and I have heard beings of this description associated with Lemuria. The founder of the Mormons, Joseph Smith, a high-degree Freemason and Merovingian bloodline, said he had a "vision" on September 21st, 1821 in which he saw "a messenger sent from God" dressed in a long white robe of "the most exquisite whiteness". From this "vision" came the Mormon Church, and a stream of religions have been founded on stories, real or otherwise, of similar experiences. Mohammed and Islam is just one example. John A. Keel also highlighted the blue-blond theme in *Our Haunted Planet*:

"According to the traditions of many isolated peoples, the first great emperors in Asia were god-kings who came down from the sky, displayed amazing superhuman abilities, and took over. There was a veritable worldwide epidemic of these god-kings between 5000 and 1000BC ...The myths and legends of Greece, India, and South America describe their rule. They were taller and more imposing than the men of the time, with long blond hair, marble-like white skin, and remarkable powers which enabled them to perform miracles." [1]

The ancients said they had "marble-like" white skin and a modern pilot describes these beings as having "pearl-like" skin. The pilot's memory was hazy about what happened after he first met "Ol' blue eyes" in the James Bond mountain, but he remembered walking into a room and seeing a group of these beings sitting around a conference table. Eventually, he was taken back to his plane and as it rose from the mountain his engines and electronics restarted. There are many modern reports of such beings living within mountains, including Mount Shasta in California, where it is said that Lemurians fled before the cataclysms. Now look at how the ancient Book of Enoch describes the "Watchers": "And there appeared to me two men, very tall, such as I have never seen on Earth. And their faces shone like the Sun, and their eyes were like burning lamps...their hands were brighter than snow." Some ancient "gods" were also called the "shining ones". A theme of modern extraterrestrial research, and the reports of abductees, is that the Pleiades star system, the so-called "Seven Sisters", is peopled by a blond, blue-eyed, race (and a reptilian one) and once again a reverence for the Pleiades can be found throughout the Sumer Empire and beyond. The Pleiades, in fact, is a grouping of some 200 stars and not just the seven with which it is associated. Some suggest that Alcyone, the brightest star of the Pleiades, is the pivotal centre of this part of the galaxy around which our Sun and solar system orbit. Cherokee and Maya legend in North and Central America and the Greek historians, Apollodorius and Diodorus, are among those who refer to Pleiadians visiting Atlantis. The Greeks said that Pleiadians had mated with Poseidon, a king of Atlantis, and the offspring populated that society. Diodorus said that two of the seven symbolic "sisters" of the Pleiades, Celoene and Alcyone, had "laid with the most renowned heroes and gods and thus became the first ancestors of the larger portion of the race of human beings." Nordic-reptilian interbreeding? The Lyra constellation is widely associated in UFO research and the stories of abductees with a blond-haired, blue-eyed race. Aldebaran, a giant red star with a diameter about forty times that of the Sun, is another Nordic-related location, not least within the secret society network of the Nazis. It is in the constellation of Taurus and one of the brightest stars in the northern hemisphere. Many abductees tell of loving experiences with tall, blond beings claiming to come from the Pleiades, as they do with some reptilian experiences, and it is important to stress here, and to keep in mind throughout this book, that I am not suggesting for a moment that all of these "Nordics" or "reptilians" have a malevolent agenda for humanity. Only that some factions of them do. These genetic streams appear to be vast and populate many parts of the galaxy, and so, as with humanity, some will have a positive agenda, some will be neutral, and others will desire to control. Researcher Frans Kamp believes that the more positively motivated Nordic extraterrestrials fled from Atlantis to the Himalayas and have operated from there ever since.[2] Certainly there are many legends in that region of the world of tall, blue-eyed, blond-haired "Supermen" living under the ground or within mountains, very much along the lines of that American pilot's experience.

Many of these entities may not even be of our density or dimension. As I've outlined, creation consists of infinite dimensions of life vibrating at different speeds. Some beings know how to change their frequency range and dip between these dimensions, appearing and "disappearing" as they move between frequencies, much like a radio dial. This is why people have reported seeing entities "disappear" before their eyes. They have not, in fact, "disappeared" at all. They have left the frequency range that person can access. Credo Mutwa told me that the African accounts of the Nordic Mzungu say they hold some type of metal ball that seems to be related to their ability to appear and disappear at will (*see picture section*). Time as we measure it is also an illusion that imprisons our minds. I know how hard it is to comprehend this, but past, present, and future, are all happening together and thus some of the extraterrestrial visitors, by moving through the frequencies in which these various "stages" of "time" are unfolding, can literally come back from the future, or the "future" in relation to where we are now. Time travel is no myth; it's just that the elite don't tell us about it. There are people who suggest that in fact Atlantis and Lemuria were not third-density realities, but fourth density and that, as a result of what happened, the frequency fell and everything became denser. Maybe. The "Fall of Man", they say, was the fall of the frequency of the planet from the fourth to the third density as a result of the fantastic events that destroyed Mars and almost destroyed the Earth. There are so many maybes and possibilities once you free your mind from the prisons of conditioned reality.

The reptilian connection

The most prominent theme in this cocktail of extraterrestrial or interdimensional races, in relation to human control, appears to be a faction of the reptilian species. Many "abductees" who claim to have been kidnapped by non-human entities, have indicated that there is a connection between the reptilians, greys, and Nordics. They suggest that these types of entities are collaborating on the same agenda. Others have said that the reptilians were seen masquerading as "Nordics" by using some type of hypnotic or holographic field to deceive abductees. One minute they look like blue-eyed blonds, the next they are reptilians. Once you can change form, or manipulate the way the observer perceives that form, who the hell knows what is what and who is who? The Anunnaki of the Sumerian tablets were from the reptilian race, as widely confirmed when you read the ancient accounts. A Sumerian tablet dating back to around 3500BC leaves us in no doubt as it describes the arrival of the Anunnaki: "The reptiles verily descend."[3] In Hebrew myth, the Biblical "Nefilim", the "sons of the gods", are called awwim, which means devastators or…serpents. The Anunnaki interbreed with Earth races, but especially the Nordics and their offspring, to create bloodlines through which they can manipulate the world while appearing to be human. Even academics like Dr Arthur David Horn, former Professor of Biological Anthropology at Colorado State University at Fort Collins, has concluded that humanity was seeded by an extraterrestrial race and that the Anunnaki were reptilian. He, too, believes that these same reptilians have controlled the world for thousands of years, as he explains in his book, *Humanity's Extraterrestrial Origins* (A. and L. Horn, PO Box 1632, Mount Shasta, California, 1994).

The reptilians, or this manipulating faction of them anyway, have an undeveloped emotional level, along the lines of a crocodile or lizard. They don't feel in the same way as mammals. They have a sharp mind in an intellectual sense and that makes them very efficient in creating and using technology. The computer is a very good example of the reptilian mind at work. It operates very efficiently up to a point, but it does not have emotion and is therefore limited in its possibilities. It is the same with these reptilian manipulators. They cannot evolve without developing emotionally and they want the DNA of those who have that dimension of self. For some reason, the Nordics' genetic code is most important to them. Also, without the balance of emotion, the reptilian mind can do the most horrendous atrocities to others without feeling any compassion for their victims. This is how the Illuminati can manipulate wars that kill and maim tens of millions while being emotionally detached from the consequences for others of their actions. The same with scientists who carry out appalling experiments on live animals while feeling nothing for the suffering of their "specimen". It's the reptilian mind. Frans Kamp, the Dutch researcher, began his journey of discovery after his marriage to a reptoid-hybrid woman ended after 12 and half years. His conclusions about the reptilian-Nordic connection mirror the themes of my own:

"The humanoid originates from extraterrestrials from the region of Lyra, but the Pleiades and Aldebaran are in the game, too. They had original human form in another density. They were peaceful and had blue eyes and white/blondish hair. By mixing up their DNA with the reptoids, as naïve as they were, the humanoids character changed and they got reptoid qualities of character. This was the fall of the human. It is a natural thing. It happens to this very day. But the former ancestors of humans knew. They forbid having sex with other entities or species. Without controlling the breeding process, the reptoids know the humanoid will prevail…Don't forget, reptoids are afraid of humans. Very afraid. They feel, the very little they do feel, inferior to humans. The reptoids are desperate. They are losing. The Third World War, if it comes, shall be a DNA war because the reptoids want human DNA."[4]

We can see the DNA genetic code agenda very clearly today with the cloning explosion and the way human genes are now being openly manipulated like never before, at least in known history. Human cloning has been going on in the underground bases for decades. When researchers said this some years ago, people just laughed. They have stopped laughing now because it is in their face, but such is the depth of human robotic conditioning, they now laugh at everything else that is different to their programming and will continue to do so until that, too, is under their noses. In fact, I say cloning has been happening for decades, it is probably thousands of years. There are many ancient stories that indicate the existence of underground cloning laboratories designed to create a group of identical people. The Nordics were one of the key extraterrestrial races involved with Lemuria and Atlantis and there are many stories that, way back, they went to war with the reptilians and forced them to flee underground, to other locations in the universe, and to other dimensions or densities. The reptilians have been working ever since to regain control of the planet they believe to be theirs and interbreeding with the "royal" bloodlines of the Nordics was the most effective means of doing this for reasons we shall explore. T.W. Samsel, the author of *The Atlantis Connection*, has come to similar conclusions:

"When the 'gods' began to physically interbreed with the Atlantean people, we see the introduction of the 'royal lineage', the 'royal bloodlines' that were put into positions of power and rulership over the Atlantean people so long ago. Those of the royal bloodline were looked upon as gods by the general population of Atlantis of the time. These ruled Atlantis until the event of the first great cataclysm, which brought the Lemurian-early Atlantic age to a close. That the reptilian influence over humanity in this area took place in a similar manner, at roughly the same point in time or shortly thereafter, is…likely to be the case.

"The human race has been influenced and controlled since approximately 70,000 years BCE or midway through the Lemurian-early Atlantic age. This involved several extraterrestrial groups and should not be attributed to a single group in and of itself. There were the three main participants in the direct contact program who initiated this type of manipulation and others. That the reptilians performed a similar research, for their own purposes and even infiltrated the federations project security, most likely did take place."[5]

My own feeling, however, is that the closer we have come to the present day, the more the reptilians have become the dominant force in this manipulation. Through their interbreeding programmes they infiltrated the bloodlines of the Nordics and covertly changed their DNA and became their "royalty". I found direct references to this theme in the Indian (formerly Indus Valley) works, like the Book of Dzyan, one of the oldest of Sanskrit accounts, and the epics, Mahabharata and the Ramayana. The Book of Dzyan tells of how a reptilian race it calls the Sarpa or Great Dragons came from the skies to bring civilisation to the world. The deluge that ended the Golden Age, it says, wiped out a race of "giants" (Nordics?) but the serpent gods survived and returned to rule. They are described as having the face of a human, but the tail of a dragon.[6] Their leader was called the Great Dragon and this is the origin of Pendragon ("Great Dragon") the title of the king of kings in ancient Britain. The Illuminati's Ku Klux Klan, created by that infamous Freemasonic "god" in America, Albert Pike, still uses the term Grand Dragon today. The Indian-Hindu name for the Anunnaki hybrids was the Nagas and they were also known as the Dravidians (so close to the Branch Davidians who died at Waco) and the Dasyus. James Churchward's research says the Nagas came from Lemuria. Like the Nommo from Sirius and the Annedoti of Babylonian legend, the Nagas were said to have a close connection to water and entered their underground centres through wells, lakes and rivers. The same was true in China of the Lung Wang or "Dragon Kings" who were described as part human, part serpent. The Nagas were described as offspring from the interbreeding of humans with the serpent gods. At first it seems this union happened with a dark race, the black, Negro-like, Earth people I mentioned earlier, because the hybrids were described as dark-skinned with a flat nose. This sounds very much like the faces depicted at ancient sites in South and Central America. However, the two Indian epics also refer to how the reptilian Nagas intermingled with the white peoples and although their relationship was often one of conflict and distrust, the two interbred, the epics report, to produce a reptilian-mammal hybrid that became…*the Aryan kings!*[7] These are the "divine" royal bloodlines or "demi-gods" and they are the *same* bloodlines that ruled the Sumer Empire and to whom those in power today are related. In Media, now Turkey, the Iranians knew the kings as Mar, which means snake in Persian (Mars = snakes?). They were called the "dragon dynasty of Media" or "descendants of the dragon".

In the late 19th century, Colonel James Churchward, an ardent researcher into the existence of Mu or Lemuria, was shown some ancient tablets in the secret vault of a monastery in northern India. They told the story of how the Naacals or Naga Mayas ("serpents") from the continent of Lemuria-Mu had travelled to India via Burma to establish a colony there. Churchward put the texts together in years of painstaking work and revealed how they described the destruction of Mu, the Motherland, and how the Naga Mayas or Nagas had travelled to India.[8] The Vedic scholar David Frawley explains how the ancient Hindu holy books, the Vedas, reveal that the earliest royal bloodlines of India, the priest-kings, descend from the Bhrigus who arrived from a place across the sea. The Bhrigus were an order of adepts initiated into the ancient knowledge. Frawley says in his book, *Gods, Sages, And Kings: Vedic Secrets Of Ancient Civilization* (Passage Press, Salt Lake City, Utah, 1991) that the monarchs of these bloodlines included the "serpent king" Nahusha. They expanded into the five tribes that populated a large part of the Indian population.[9] James Churchward wrote a number of superb books on the civilisation of Mu and he says the Nagas also populated China, Tibet, and parts of Asia. The

Naga Maya, with their mother goddess religion, were also the origin of the Maya people of Mexico. Researcher Michael Mott writes in *Caverns, Cauldrons, And Concealed Creatures* (Hidden Mysteries, Texas, 2000):

> "The Nagas are described as a very advanced race or species, with a highly-developed technology. They also harbor a disdain for human beings, whom they are said to abduct, torture, interbreed with, and even to eat. The interbreeding has supposedly led to a wide variety of forms, ranging from completely reptilian to nearly-human in appearance. Among their many devices are 'death rays' and 'vimana', or flying, disk-shaped aerial craft. These craft are described at length in many ancient Vedic texts, including the Bhagivad-gita and the Ramayana. The Naga race is related to another underworld race, the Hindu demons, or Rakshasas. They also possess, as individuals, "magical stones", or a 'third eye' in the middle of their brows, known to many students of eastern mysticism today as a focal point for one of the higher chakras, or energy channel-points, of the human(oid) nervous system – the chakra associated with 'inner visions', intuition, and other esoteric concepts." [10]

The theme of ruling "royal" families and emperors claiming descent, and their right to rule, from the "serpent gods" can be found across the ancient world. These bloodlines and connections were symbolised by royal emblems in the form of a dragon, snake, sphinx, plumed serpent, or the tree-cross or Ankh. In Egypt they had an order called the Djedhi (Jedi in *Star Wars*?) and the Dj meant serpent.[11] Thus we have pharaohs of the serpent line called Djer, Djoser, and Djederfra. In India, the Buddhist text, The Mahauyutpatti, lists 80 kings who descended from the Nagas or "serpent kings". Hindu legend says that the Nagas could take a human or reptilian form at will. This is what is called "shape-shifting". Across India the rulers claimed power because they descended from the Nagas. Buddha is claimed to have been of the royal line of the Nagas, but then anyone said to be of a royal line in India would have to be so. It was the Nagas who established what is now Kashmir and again the ruling bloodlines descended from them. The Chinese emperors were the same. They were known as Lung or Dragons and many of the earliest emperors were depicted with reptilian features, very much like the Nagas. One of them, called Huang Ti, was said to have been born with a "dragon-like countenance". It was claimed that he was conceived by a ray of golden light that entered his mother's womb from the Big Dipper constellation.[12] The Big Dipper includes the star Alpha Draconis, the star of Set in Egypt. Alpha Draconis is an alleged base of the "Draco" reptilian "royalty". One Chinese legend says that when he died Huang Ti transformed into an etheric dragon and flew to the realm of the immortals. The priest kings of the Peruvian Incas were symbolised by the snake and they wore bracelets and anklets in the image of a snake. The earliest of the royal bloodlines of Central America claimed genetic descent from the serpent gods, Quetzalcoatl and Itzamna. In the Mycenaean age in Greece the kings were, in the words of author Jane Harrison, "regarded as being in some sense a snake".[13] Cecrops, the first Mycenaean king of Athens, was depicted as a human with a serpent tail. Another, Erectheus, who founded the Eleusinian Mystery School, was worshipped as a live snake after his death and, according to legend, King Kadmus shape-shifted into a live snake when he died.[14] The symbolism of the serpent lineage of the ancient royal bloodlines can be found on every continent.

Iran is another example. The Arab poet Firdowsi, in his Shahnemeh or Book of Kings, the legendary history of Iran completed in AD1010, tells the story of the birth of Zal, the "Demon" or "Watcher" offspring, whose appearance horrified his father, King Sam. According to Firdowsi, this Watcher hybrid called Zal married a foreign princess named Rudabeh, a descendant of the "serpent king", Zahhak, who was said to have ruled Iran for a thousand years. Rudabeh is described as tall as a teak tree and ivory-white. These are the familiar features of the "Watcher" offspring in this ancient period. The royal or tribal rulers of China, Africa, the Near and Middle East, Europe, Asia, people of every colour and creed, have claimed their right to rule by their descent from the serpent gods. As we've seen, Alexander the Great, one of the most famous monarchs and conquerors of all time, was known as the "Serpent Son". Alexander is extremely important to the Nordic-reptilian genealogy of the Illuminati bloodlines (*see Appendix I*). The legend goes that Alexander's real father was the serpent god, Ammon, who had mysteriously slid into his mother's bed and conceived him.[15] The same story was told of the conception of Merovee, the founder of the Merovingians. This symbolism is supported by many ancient and modern accounts of "virgin birth" impregnations by reptilian beings. The stories of women being abducted by reptilians and then finding themselves pregnant are told today all around the world. Often, as the Zulu shaman Credo Mutwa reveals from the experience of African women, the baby "disappears" from the womb during the pregnancy. The Anunnaki interbred with all genetic streams and those were the people who ruled by right of their bloodline in their particular countries and communities. So while the people believed they were being ruled by their own race, they were ruled by the same tribe. The hybrid reptilian-mammals ruled them all. Exactly the same continues to happen today with these hybrids in control of the white peoples and the Arab, Asian, Jewish, Chinese, Central and South American nations, and so on.

I mentioned earlier that being "descended from Noah" is a code for the Illuminati bloodlines and when you scan the ancient books and texts you find some strange references to his birth. An Ethiopian text, the Kebra Nagast (Nagas?), is thousands of years old, and it describes the enormous size of the babies produced from the sexual union of human women and the "gods". It tells of how "...the daughters of Cain [Nordics] with whom the angels [Anunnaki] had conceived... were unable to bring forth their children and they died". It describes how some of the babies had to be delivered through caesarean birth: "...having split open the bellies of their mothers they came forth from their navels". Another story relates to Noah, the Semitic name for the Sumerian flood hero, Utnapishtim. The ancient Hebrew text, the Book of Noah and its derivative, the Book of Enoch, refers to the birth of Noah and sections also appear in the Dead Sea Scrolls, found in Israel in 1947. The Scrolls are connected with the Essene community in Palestine 2,000 years ago. Noah is the son of Lamech and he is described as unlike a human being and more like "the children of the angels in heaven". And we know who *they* were. Lamech questions his wife about the father of Noah: "Behold, I thought then within my heart that conception was (due) to the Watchers and the Holy Ones…and to the Nephilim…and my heart was troubled within me because of this child." Lamech's child, Noah, was white-skinned and blond-haired with eyes that made the whole house "shine like the Sun".[16] The highest level of the reptilian "royalty" are known among UFO researchers and a number of abductees as the "Draco" after their "home" base in the Draco Constellation. These entities are described as being albino white and they project something akin to a laser-type beam from their eyes, just like the pearl-skinned chaps in the James Bond mountain. Enlil was the leader of the Anunnaki on Earth, according to the Sumerian tablets, and they refer to him as the "splendid serpent of the shining eyes". This is a common description of the hybrid babies in these times and I have heard the same story told today, also. As I said earlier, Frans Kamp, a Dutch music teacher turned full-time researcher, was married to a woman he later realised was a reptoid hybrid. He told me that he experienced the shining eyes of his former wife:

> "One evening we had a disagreement. She didn't get what she wanted and got very mad. She smashed the door to go away to her own apartment. I followed her outside. At that moment it was already dark. I saw her walking to her car and she grabbed the car door and then it happened. Her eyes lit up. There came light out of her eyes. She went into the car and her eyes shone over the bonnet and even on the ground next to the car. I looked at it, astonished, but, strange, it wasn't a shock. More a confirmation, an 'I thought so', a 'you see!'"[17]

According to the Book of Genesis, Noah got seriously drunk on wine and collapsed in his tent. Ham, his son, walked in and saw his father naked. He told his two brothers before finding a cover for his father and when Noah found out he launched into a rage and put a curse on Ham and his son Canaan. Could the big deal here be that Ham saw something about Noah's body that indicated he was a child of the gods? It appears that some of the hybrids this far back in history still had clear reptilian features, especially some sort of scaly skin on the chest. In the Hindu classic, the Mahabharata, a "demi-god" hybrid called Karna was born from the union between an Earth woman and the Sun god, Surya. The child is described as being "clad in a coat of armour, like a divine being". By the time of "Noah", just before the final Atlantis cataclysm, humans were rebelling against the control of the Anunnaki-Nefilim and those of the hybrid bloodline were seriously unpopular. They were said to wear the "badge of shame", which could have been a patch of reptilian skin, particularly on the chest. The Anunnaki "gods" began to hide their true nature for the same reason and operated behind the cover of the human-reptilian priesthood who were the only people allowed to "approach God" (the gods). The Slavonic Book of Enoch says that when Noah's nephew, Melchizedek, was born "…the badge of the priesthood was on his chest and it was glorious in appearance".[18] I have heard the same phenomena described in modern accounts.

Frans Kamp's wife worked as a photo model. He told me that her skin took on a strange hide-like appearance:

> "My wife had a skin-reflection or should I say hide problem? The skin is extremely important for photo-models. The first thing photographers look at is the skin. Now this skin-problem had the property that her skin got red spots and after a while changed into horny-like slices. We went to the biggest professor in the university in Utrecht. He didn't know what it was. They did all kinds of tests, but they had no explanation of it." [19]

According to ancient texts, Noah said that the people must not know about the child Melchizedek, because they would kill him if they saw his strange appearance. The "badge of the priesthood" was the same as the divine right to rule, it was code for the reptilian bloodlines. The priesthood of Melchizedek became one of the most famous and powerful, and today the highest level of the hierarchy of the Mormon Church is called the Melchizedek Priesthood. The Mormon Church is a 100%-owned subsidiary of the Illuminati reptilians, and the Mormon Temple in Salt Lake City, Utah, sits atop an underground reptilian base, say military insiders. The Mormon Church is a front for widespread Satanic activity and rituals among its ruling elite, although the vast majority of Mormons have no idea that this is going on. They are just the sheep controlled by forces they do not understand. And who started the Mormons? Joseph Smith, Hiram Smith, and Brigham Young. They were all high-degree Freemasons and from the Merovingian (Anunnaki) bloodline.

This theme of reptilian-human hybrids can be seen in the story of Adam and Eve in the Garden of Eden (Edin to the earlier Sumerians – "the Abode of the Righteous Ones.") In Jewish lore, Eve, who was tempted by the serpent, of course, was the ancestral mother of the Nefilim and associated with the Hebrew words meaning life and snake.[20] Satan ("The Adversary") is described in the Old Testament and the Hebrew Torah as the "Old Serpent" or "Dragon" and he was said to be the ruler of the Nefilim who fled within the Earth after losing a cosmic battle for supremacy. The Hebrew name for Eve's tempter is Nahash, which besides its translation as serpent also reads: "He Who Knows Secrets", another theme of the reptilian gods.[21] Enoch, like Noah, was said to "walk with the gods", and the ancient Book of Enoch says that a Watcher who revealed secrets to humans was called Gadreel. This is a "fallen angel" who has been identified with the serpent who tempted Eve and he is a blueprint for a number of later deities who took knowledge (often symbolised as fire, illumination) from "the gods" and gave it to humans.

Adam and Eve

As I've suggested, the Biblical Adam and Eve were probably not individuals, but hybrid genetic streams, as in "the" Adam and "the" Eve. At first the interbreeding produced a very reptilian offspring…thus "God" (the gods) made man in his (their) image. This is where the otherwise unexplainable reference in the Bible to "Let us make man in our image" comes from.[22] In this period, as confirmed in the Sumerian descriptions, the Adam and the Eve were cloned and could not reproduce. This caused problems for the Anunnaki because they could not create enough worker slaves for the agenda they had planned for the Earth. Eventually the human slaves were given the ability to procreate and this involved an infusion of far more mammalian genes, according to R.A. Boulay in his excellent and highly recommended book, *Flying Serpents And Dragons, Mankind's Reptilian Past* (The Book Tree, USA, 1997). This change from clone to pro-creator is presented symbolically in the Garden of Eden story with Eve being condemned to suffer the pains of childbirth. Sex between their creations was the "forbidden fruit" symbolised in the Eden story, Boulay suggests. The "god" responsible for this development was Enki. He was the serpent in the garden "tempting" Eve and he was later to become extremely unpopular with the rest of the Anunnaki leadership because of the explosion in the human population that followed, the Sumerian tablets tell us. Incidentally, Enki, the expert in advanced science and medicine, was symbolised as two serpents intertwining around a staff that could well symbolise the reptilian DNA. We call this the caduceus and it is the symbol of today's medical profession. No accident. This evolution from outwardly reptilian to outwardly mammalian is described in the ancient Hebrew work, the Haggadah ("The Telling"), a compendium of Hebrew oral traditions going way back. It says:

> "Before their bodies had been overlaid with a horny skin and enveloped with a cloud of glory. No sooner had they violated the command given them that the cloud of glory and the horny skin dropped from them and they stood there in their nakedness and ashamed." [23]

This fits with the legends which say that before the "fall", people, or "Man", had skin "as bright as daylight and covered his body like a luminous garment".[24] This later disappeared, but there were remnants of it among the hybrids at the time of "Noah" and the deluge. Still today, some people involved in government genetic experimentation tell me they have developed patches of reptilian skin. It was with the infusion of mammalian genes that the life spans began to fall from thousands of years, claimed in the records of the pre-deluge era, down to hundreds at the time of "Noah" with the reptilian appearance continuing to fade. The reptilian "gods" have always been associated with enormous life spans and the serpent was a Sumerian and Egyptian symbol of immortality. They are not immortal in physical form. It just seems like that to those who live much shorter physical life spans. Another early figure of significance would seem to be a guy known as Jared, the father of Enoch, and the first of the Patriarchs who did not marry his sister in the line with the Anunnaki's recorded custom of producing children with their sisters and children for genetic reasons. It was during the period of Jared, way back in the Golden Age, that the Nefilim, the so-called sons of the gods (also "Angels of the Lord" in other versions), appeared on the scene to "marry" human women. Today, in the United States, there is apparently an organisation called the Sons of Jared who pledge an "implacable war against descendants of the Watchers who …as notorious pharaohs, kings and dictators, have throughout history dominated mankind". Their publication, The *Jaredite Advocate*, condemns the Watchers as being "… like super-gangsters, a celestial Mafia ruling the world".

The Anunnaki have been protected from exposure all this time by the "middle men" they have placed between themselves and humanity. I call this the hybrid Priesthood. In ancient times the hierarchy of the priesthood were the only ones allowed to "see God" (the gods). The Levite priesthood of the Hebrews is just one example of how only the priests were allowed to approach the deity, as outlined in the Hebrew Torah. According to various descriptions, even most of the Sumerian priests never looked the gods in the face. The priests controlled all the administration of the state on behalf of the unseen gods. What was Yahweh-Jehovah always saying? He must not be seen: "…you cannot see my face, for man may not see me and live".[25] This was possibly one reason for the ban on the making of "graven images" of the gods. Yahweh-Jehovah has also been associated with a reptilian in some versions. The Sumerian tablets describe how their cities were overlooked by a large stepped pyramid or "ziggurat" close to the temple and palace. At the top of the ziggurat, the tablets reveal, was the "holy of holies" or "cella" where the gods "lived". Here the humans chosen by their genetics were brought to have sex with the Anunnaki "royalty" and produce the bloodlines that became the kings, queens, and leaders of all sections of society – the same situation that we have today. The ziggurats were often referred to as "mountains" and this led to some of the gods being called so and so "of the mountain". The layout of the ziggurat symbolised so perfectly the pyramid structure of our society in which the few at the top administer the global prison that the Anunnaki have created to control us. This is the structure through which their very existence is kept secret. Today's hybrid priesthood can be found throughout politics, business, banking, the media, and, especially, in the highest ranks of the secret society network.

As there are not many of these reptilians and their purest bloodlines compared with the human population, they have had to work and manipulate to introduce a structure of society in which (a) the key decisions are made by fewer and fewer people as power is continually centralised and (b) humanity is manipulated to police itself and keep each other in a mental and emotional prison. The reptilians appear to take three expressions. There are physical beings who live mostly within the Earth (inner-terrestrials); physical beings that come from the stars (extraterrestrials); and non-physical beings, the real centre of power, which exist on other frequencies and use their hybrid bloodlines to manipulate unseen. The reptilians have worked this scam in many parts of the galaxy, it would seem. It all sounds utterly bizarre and ludicrous. I understand that reaction and yes it *is* bizarre from a conditioned perspective. Unfortunately, it is not ludicrous. If only it was. The Las Vegas-based John Rhodes, a long-time researcher into the reptilian phenomenon, summarises his conclusions like this:

> "From their underground bases, the reptilian military ETs…(establish)…a network of human-reptilian crossbreed infiltrates within various levels of the surface culture's

military-industrial complexes, government bodies, UFO/paranormal groups, religious and fraternal (priest) orders, etc. These crossbreeds, some unaware of their reptilian genetic 'mind control' instructions, act out their subversive roles as 'reptilian agents' setting the stage of a reptilian-led ET invasion." [26]

That last comment remains to be seen, but you will see revealed here the stream of evidence to show that the basis of what John Rhodes suggests is true. I had a strange meeting with him in Las Vegas and his family background apparently connects into the CIA airline during the Vietnam War, Air America. I am wary of his agenda to be honest, but his themes, as quoted, are supported by endless evidence.

The fairy folk

The tales of underground worlds inhabited by fairies, elves, goblins, demons, dragons, and other non-human communities abound in folklore across the world and they were often known as the "shining ones", the same as the Anunnaki and the "gods" under other names in ancient texts. Even a brief glance at the basic themes of these stories confirms that they are talking about the same "extraterrestrials" that abductees and researchers of today's underground bases are describing. The name in Norse folklore for this underground world of caverns, tunnel networks, and even vast cities, is Niflheim. The close similarity to Nefilim is obvious and they were said to reside within the Earth. The Norse people said that Niflheim was ruled by the death goddess, Hel. These subterranean networks could be accessed through the mounds and hill forts built by the ancients and the mountains, hills, and lakes they held to be sacred. These "fairy folk" in all their names and guises were said to interbreed with humans to create hybrid bloodlines, abduct surface people, drink human blood, and take human reproductive materials. Sound familiar? And the main form in which these "fairies" and "elves", etc. appeared was reptilian. Elf or elven is still one of the Illuminati code names for the reptilian bloodlines. The tales of non-human "gods" living within mountains or having their subterranean complexes entered through mountains is likely to be the origin of the endless myths about "holy" or "sacred" mountains. Mount Olympus, the home of the Greek pantheon of gods, is one example. Zeus, their king of the gods, was said to come down from the mountain to seed children with human women. Meetings between the mythical Moses and his god were often associated with mountains. I will investigate these ancient and modern connections between modern "extraterrestrials" and the folklore "fairies" later in the book. [27]

The Anunnaki wars

The Sumerian tablets, according to translators like Zecharia Sitchin,* tell of wars between Anunnaki factions. The tablets say that the Anunnaki leadership, like Enlil

---

* For some inexplicable reason, Zecharia Sitchin refuses to accept the existence of a serpent or reptilian race in the ancient world, despite the mountain of evidence. During a conversation with me in Cancun, Mexico, in 1998, he told me there was no evidence of such a race. Later he leaned forward across the table and said: "Don't go there". As you can see, I took his advice.

and Enki, eventually gave much greater power to their children, who were assigned different parts of the world to rule and develop. Nannar, the eldest son of Enlil, ruled Mesopotamia, Palestine, Jordan, and Syria from the city of Ur, we are told. The crescent moon was his symbol and this was inherited by Islam. Nannar was known as Sin in the Semitic language and it is from this name of a reptilian god that we get Sinai and the Christian term "sinner" or "to sin". The Christian cross was the symbol of U-TU "the shining one" and known to the Semites as Shamash. He was the grandson of Enlil and son of Sin, the tablets tell us. Shamash ruled the Lebanon, then a place of enormous forests, and his capital was Beth-Shamash ("House of Shamash"), which we know better as Baalbek. This is where a fantastic structure can be found to this day with its giant stones weighing more than three jumbo jets. Enlil's younger son was given control of Anatolia, now Turkey. This was Ishkur or "He of the Mountain Land" and he became the god of the Nordic-Aryan Hittites. The Old Testament calls him Adad and the Hadad. R.A. Boulay believes this is also the Hebrew god, Yahweh/Yahveh or Jehovah. The daughter of Sin, known as Inanna or Ishtar (Semitic), was a warrior goddess deity of many lands under different titles. Ishtar's symbol was the lion and also the Pleiades and Venus. Together with Sin (Shamash) and Ishkur (Adad), she became part of another ancient trinity of gods under many different names. Sin was the father, Ishkur the son, and Ishtar the female. From Ishkur and Ishtar, we get the New Age myth of the "Ashtar Command". Many New Agers claim this is a force of extraterrestrial "saviours" who are preparing to take the chosen ones off the planet when the brown stuff hits the spinning propeller. A sort of Jesus with a spaceship.

Other front-line figures in this next generation of Anunnaki leaders after the deluge included Marduk, son of Enki, the tablets say. Marduk was the god of Babylon. The ancient texts, tablets, and legends describe how these gods embarked on a battle for power that brought the world to its knees. Some of these conflicts, with humanity used as battle-fodder, are featured in the Old Testament. One defining event described in the tablets involved the Anunnaki "god" known as Sin. The name comes from the Sumerian SW-EN or ZU-EN, as Boulay reveals in *Flying Serpents And Dragons*, and Sin clearly appears to be the "villain" of the Sumerian story called "The Myth of Zu". In this, Zu (Sin), the "evil dragon", tries to seize control of the Earth and the Anunnaki leadership by stealing "power stones", which the accounts refer to as the ME (pronounced "may"). For some reason these appear to be fundamental to the Anunnaki control and could have been computer chips or programmes, or some type of crystal. There are indications that they shone or emitted light in some way. Scholars translate the ME as tablets of destiny or divine powers, and I wonder if these could be related to the "Ark of the Covenant, a device for which divine powers are claimed? The Sumerian accounts say, quoting "Zu" (Sin):

"I will take the divine ME,
And the decrees of the gods I will direct.
I will set my throne and control all the ME.
I will direct the totality of the Igigi ["Those Who Observe" or "The Watchers"]."

And later the Tablets report:

"He seizes the ME with his hands,
Taking away the sovereignty of Enlil,
The power to issue decrees.
Zu then flew away,
And retired to his mountain stronghold." [28]

The ancient nuclear holocaust

The story is told of how the Anunnaki "god" Ninurta volunteered to recover the ME stones. Zu created what seems to be a force field to protect himself from attack and the tablets say: "While he controlled the ME, no arrow could approach him." Enki, the chief scientist and engineer, creates a new weapon to penetrate Zu's defences and he is eventually defeated. Other Anunnaki also made attempts to steal the ME stones as the battle for power and control between them continued, just as it does today. Zu (Sin) was put on trial, but the outcome is not known. It is obvious, however, that the origin of the term "sin" in the Bible relates to defying the will of "God", the gods. The story of the battle between Zu and Ninurta describes the use of high-tech weaponry, and if anyone thinks that was not possible thousands of years ago, I am afraid the evidence suggests otherwise. At Rajasthan in India, radioactive ash covers three square miles not far from Jodhpur. This is an area of high rates of cancer and birth defects and it was cordoned off by the Indian government when radiation readings soared astonishingly high. An ancient city was unearthed which, the evidence indicates, was destroyed by an atomic explosion some 8,000 to 12,000 years ago. It has been estimated that half a million people could have died in the blast and it was at least the size of those that devastated Japan in 1945. Support for these modern finds can be found in the ancient texts. The Mahabharata epic tells of: "A single projectile charged with all the power of the Universe…An incandescent column of smoke and flame as bright as 10,000 suns, rose in all its splendour…it was an unknown weapon, an iron thunderbolt, a gigantic messenger of death which reduced to ashes an entire race." It talks of corpses burned so badly they could not be identified. How their hair and nails fell out, pottery broke "without cause", and birds turned white. Within hours foodstuffs were contaminated. Is that the description of a nuclear explosion or what?

This and a very long list of other texts, like the Ramayana, describe a horrific war between the Indian peoples and the Atlanteans. They fought in the sky using the flying vehicles they call Vimanas while the Atlanteans used their "Vailixi". The Indian accounts even describe a battle between them on the Moon and this supports the claims of people like Arizona Wilder, a mind-controlled slave who worked for the higher levels of the Illuminati. She claims that the reptilians and the blond-haired, blue-eyed, Nordics, fought ancient battles on the Moon and Mars, as well as the Earth. All this happened during the pre-cataclysmic Atlantean/Lemurian "Golden Age" and this underpins the stories of how the once great and mighty

Atlantis came to an end amid high-tech war and catastrophe. But when the
Anunnaki returned after the upheavals, the same mentality returned with them
and the evidence shows that there were more nuclear holocausts. Archaeological
discoveries in the Indus Valley show that cities were built there in the period
between 3500 and 3000BC (when the Anunnaki-controlled Sumer Empire was well
established) and they were destroyed about 2000BC amid enormous violence.
What's more, skeletons found at these sites record high rates of radioactivity.
Around this same time of 2000BC, Sumer came to an end with an "evil wind",
which has all the signs of nuclear fall-out. This "wind" brought the sudden demise
of Sumer and the neighbouring Akkadians. Texts known as lamentations tell of a
"calamity" that befell Sumer, one "unknown to man, one that had never been seen
before". There was an "evil wind", a battling storm and a "scorching heat". Some
kind of cloud shut out the Sun by day and the stars by night. The texts continue:

> "The people, terrified, could hardly breathe;
> the evil wind clutched them, does not grant them another day…
> Mouths were drenched with blood, heads wallowed in blood…
> The face was made pale by the Evil Wind."

> "It causes cities to be desolated,
> houses to become desolate;
> Stalls to become desolate,
> the sheepfolds to be emptied…
> Sumer's rivers make it flow
> with water that is bitter;
> its cultivated fields grow weeds,
> its pastures grow withering plants." [29]

Even the gods had to evacuate these lands, we are told, and all the Sumerian
cities were affected in the same way at the same time. Just as the nuclear
devastation in the Indus Valley corresponds with the time period of this poisonous
"evil wind" in Sumer, so it also corresponds with the timescale that saw the violent
demise of the Biblical Sodom and Gomorrah. Many sources point to these cities
being located in what is now the southern end of the Dead Sea in Israel where
unnatural levels of radioactivity persist to this day. They call this "Lot's Sea" after
the Biblical character involved in the Sodom and Gomorrah story and for thousands
of years it has been associated with the symbol of death. The story of Lot's wife says
that she was turned into a pillar of salt when she looked back over Sodom and
Gomorrah at the time of the destruction, but the words translated as "pillar of salt"
can also be translated as a "pillar of vapour".[30] This not only makes rather more
sense than "salt", it fits with the emerging picture here. The accounts of the
devastation of Sodom and Gomorrah describe how "God" decided to destroy these
cities and warned his friends to get out. What a coincidence, then, that the Sumerian
tablets explain in detail how the Anunnaki leadership (God = gods again), led by

Enlil and some of his offspring, decided to destroy those locations in yet another internal war, this time with the one known as Marduk, the son of Enlil's half-brother and great rival Enki. Still today it is the Enlil and Enki factions of the Anunnaki that most divide the Illuminati and create the ongoing conflict.

There is an enormous and unnatural scar in the landscape of the Sinai (Sin-ai) Peninsula, which covers an area of 112 square miles. Blackened stones (blackened only on the surface) can be found over a large section of the eastern Sinai and to conventional history and archaeology, which finds the idea of ancient high-tech weapons unthinkable, they remain a "mystery".[31] However, the scenes of these apparent nuclear explosions are to the west of Sumer and in the Sumerian lamentations we are told that the "evil wind" that poisoned the water and atmosphere, and brought that civilisation to an immediate conclusion, was created in a "flash of lightning" and "spawned in the west". Can the mystery of Sumer's sudden demise now be solved? Could the "evil wind" have been nuclear fall-out? In around 1450BC, the classic Minoan (former Sumerian) culture was destroyed on Crete by another sudden disaster that archaeologists and historians can't explain. Once again all the cities were destroyed at the same time by some "fiery" holocaust.

Amid this series of immensely violent events and the internal war within the Anunnaki, the Sumer Empire collapsed. Its domains around the world began to self-govern, at least for a while, based on the knowledge, structure, beliefs, and myths of their former controllers. Since then, the reptilian Anunnaki have been manipulating from behind the scenes and through their hybrid bloodlines, and they are on the brink of replacing their formerly overt global empire (their Old World Order) with their covert global empire (their New World Order). They are the hidden force behind the introduction of the global centralisation of power that is exploding all around us today. The Anunnaki, at least after the final Atlantis cataclysm, sought to hide their reptilian form by keeping out of public view as much as possible.

Now you see them, now you don't

The reptilian bloodlines covertly operating within human society created many of the ancient Mystery schools to hoard the knowledge of true history, and the esoteric and technological expertise of Atlantis, Lemuria, and the post-cataclysmic world, especially the Sumer Empire. They also seized control of the other Mystery schools, which were formed with a more enlightened agenda. This was one of the roles assigned to the Royal Court of the Dragon (also known as The Brotherhood of the Snake) from around 2000BC when it infiltrated the more positive Egyptian Mystery schools and made them vehicles of the reptilian "gods". Manly P. Hall, the Freemasonic historian, summarises what happened, although for "black magicians of Atlantis" also read "reptilians":

> "While the elaborate ceremonial magic of antiquity was not necessarily evil, there
> arose from its perversion several false schools of sorcery, or black magic, [in
> Egypt]...the black magicians of Atlantis continued to exercise their superhuman

powers until they had completely undermined and corrupted the morals of the primitive Mysteries…they usurped the position formerly occupied by the initiates, and seized the reigns of spiritual government.

"Thus black magic dictated the state religion and paralysed the intellectual and spiritual activities of the individual by demanding his complete and unhesitating acquiescence in the dogma formulated by the priest craft. The Pharaoh became a puppet in the hands of the Scarlet Council – a committee of arch-sorcerers elevated to power by the priesthood." [32]

This is exactly what happened in the latter era of Atlantis and what happens today with the puppet politicians placed in "power" by those behind the scenes, the Illuminati, who dictate their actions and agenda. Those who will not do as they are told are assassinated, brought down by "scandal", fall to "ill-health", or are subjected to a media campaign of abuse that persuades the people to remove them. In the Sumer Empire you had the reptilian "gods" dictating to their priesthood, who dictated to the administrators of finance and state. The same structure remains. The hidden Anunnaki dictate to their "priesthood", the initiates and bloodlines of the Illuminati, who dictate to the administration of finance and state. Their agenda is to create a global version of that structure – the world government, central bank, army, and currency. The Mystery school network of old, with its fiercely compartmentalised levels of initiation, has evolved into the global secret society network of today. This is topped or "capstoned" by the Illuminati and, at the very peak, by the openly reptilian Anunnaki. It has had to be done in this covert way because there are not that many of them compared with the human population and they would be overwhelmed if enough people knew what is really going on. Today's secret society network is simply the modern expression of the Atlantean/Lemurian Mystery schools, which were taken over by a malevolent force in the period before the cataclysms. Those with a positive and negative agenda fought for control of the Mystery schools restored after the deluge. Eventually the malevolent force won that battle and began to expand its power covertly across the world again. With them they carried their own secret language, the language of symbols, which their initiates were taught to read and understand. I call this network the serpent cult, the serpent brotherhood, or the Illuminati. Those three are the same force. Their secret language includes the lighted torch (Illuminated ones); the pyramid and all-seeing eye (apparently used by the serpent Sirians in Atlantis); the lion (the "Sun" and symbol of the serpent cult); the snake, fish, and flying reptile (gargoyle), and other reptilian symbolism; the hard "K" sound used in names and words (Ka, Ki, etc); the red cross or fire cross on the white background (the flag of England); and the trinity, symbolised as the trident and later the fleur-de-lis and other three-pointed forms.

The reptilian-Illuminati know that the balanced fusion of male and female energy create a third and immensely powerful force and this is one reason for their obsession with the "trinity". New Agers and others talk about the need to balance male and female and they are right. But we lose the plot if we don't understand that there are different levels of this fusion. You can fuse the negative aspects of both energies to create a malevolent "third force" or you can balance the higher frequencies of male and female, so creating a positive third force. The world around us is, in fact, the manifestation of the negative balance and interaction of these energies. We are led to believe this is a male-dominated world, but that is only on the surface. Behind the scenes it is really controlled by the negative expression of female energy. The extreme male energy is "out there" in front of our eyes in the three-dimensional world. It is macho men with guns and uniforms, the leaders of the major banks, corporations, media empires, and the military. But they are put into power, the wars created, and the agenda advanced, by the extreme negative aspects of the *female* energy – covert, behind-the-scenes manipulation. If anything, the Illuminati, at the real seat of power, are dominated by the female. The negative extremes of the female energy covertly manipulate events and the negative extremes of the male energy play them out before our eyes. This is why we think it is a male-dominated world. It looks that way, but that is not the whole story.

Destroying the ancient knowledge

There have been two main thrusts of the reptilian secret society network since those ancient times. First, to pass on advanced knowledge only to their chosen few and control how much of this information each of these initiates will be allowed to know (compartmentalisation). And second, to manipulate events in the public arena to suck out of circulation all the advanced esoteric knowledge that survives there. They achieved this by creating religions and a "science" that enforced a strict limitation of vision and possibility. These two "opposames", religion and science, then labelled the suppressed knowledge either evil or crazy. Their condemnations of astrology are only one example of this.

The Illuminati, through frontmen like Columbus, Cortes, Cabot, and Cook, eventually returned to the former lands of the Sumer/Atlantean/Lemurian Empires. There, in the name of "Christianity" (an Illuminati creation), they systematically destroyed as much of the ancient knowledge as they could. This was achieved mostly by genocide, especially of the holders of the knowledge, like the shaman. As Credo Mutwa said of the African experience: "They milked the minds of the shamen and then killed them." Find out what they know and then make sure they can tell no one else. This is the reason why Credo's information about the reptilian Chitauri has been out of public circulation for so long. It was vital for the Anunnaki-Illuminati to destroy or marginalize the cultures of the Native Americans, Central and South Americans, black Africans, the Australian aborigines, and the "Pagan" religion in general. This is what they did, of course, as even conventional history records, but it never tells you the real reason why or who was really behind it. By replacing these native cultures with imposed Christianity, Judaism, Islam, Hinduism, and all the rest, they could either crush the true knowledge with rigid dogma, or imprison it in a gruesome hierarchical structure of genetic "superiority", as with the Hindu caste system.

Columba(us)

The interconnections of the Illuminati web can be seen in the story of Christopher Columbus. He sailed to the Americas in 1492 knowing basically where he was going because his father-in-law was a sea captain close to Prince Henry the Navigator, the Grand Master of a secret society called the Knights of Christ in Portugal. The Knights of Christ were another name for the Knights Templar who fled France for Portugal and Scotland after a purge against them in 1307.[33] Through this secret society underground, Columbus had access to the ancient maps that charted the Americas. It is known that he had "strange maps" when he set out for "India". Columbus was a secret society initiate and, according to the American Freemasonic historian, Manly P. Hall, he was connected to the same secret network in Genoa, Italy, as the man later known as John Cabot.[34] Five years after Columbus landed in the Americas, Cabot sailed from the Templar port of Bristol, England, to "discover" what we now call North America. They could do this because they had access through the secret societies to the maps drawn by the Sumerian seafarers and even further back to Atlantis and Lemuria. Many ancient maps have been discovered that confirm beyond question that the world was charted thousands of years ago, but this is suppressed from the accounts of mainstream "history". As I mentioned earlier, Piri Reis, an admiral in the Turkish Ottoman navy, produced a map in 1513 detailing what the land mass looks like under Antarctica. Modern surveys have confirmed that the map is extremely, and unexplainably, accurate. But, of course, it is explainable. As he said himself, he drew the map from far earlier ones he had seen – maps compiled *before* Antarctica was covered in ice. Reis drew his map just 21 years after Columbus set sail. Columbus, like Cabot and the later Captain Cook, had access to the same source material that Reis did, and more. All three were given maps and funding by the bloodlines and their network. Captain Cook was backed by the Freemasonic Royal Society in London, for instance, and Columbus was sponsored by King Ferdinand and Queen Isabella of the land we now call Spain, and the infamous Illuminati bloodline in Venice, the de Medici family. They all go back genetically to the kings of Sumer and beyond to Atlantis and Lemuria. Another key bloodline in the Illuminati to this day is the House of Lorraine (L'Orion?) in France. They employed Columbus, too, and there was another famous figure of history, who worked for both the House of Lorraine and the de Medici family…Nostradamus. Michel de Notre Dame or "Michael of Our Lady" had phenomenal esoteric and healing knowledge for his time because he was connected to the bloodlines that held, and still hold, the ancient knowledge from Sumer, Atlantis and Lemuria in their secret society web while systematically removing it from public circulation.

So we are looking at an unbroken theme – and scheme – through history of the same bloodlines and their secret society network controlling events in line with a specific agenda of global control by the reptilians. They have expanded their power out of the Near and Middle East by sea and land over the centuries. They became the leaders in royalty, politics and finance, wherever they went. Then came a key period when they could begin to "go global" once again. When William of Orange, one of the bloodlines, crossed the English Channel from Holland in 1688, he was manipulated on to the throne of England to rule jointly with Queen Mary. This was the symbolic coming together of the bloodlines that had made their way into Europe by land with those that were taken to the British Isles long before by the Sumer Empire and even those who had survived the Atlantean cataclysms in Britain. William's invasion came ashore close to the same spot where Brutus landed around 1103BC with his Trojans to found his "New Troy" or London. Very conveniently two decades before William's arrival, London had been devastated by fire, the Great Fire of London in 1666 (666 is an Illuminati-Satanic code) and this allowed a whole new city to be built by high initiates of the Illuminati. These included, most notably, Sir Christopher Wren, who designed St Paul's Cathedral at the top of Ludgate Hill. St Paul's was built on an ancient site of worship to the Goddess Diana and this where Princess Diana was married to Prince Charles. (Incidentally, Wren's title of "Sir", an honour awarded to this day by the Queen and the British Government, often for services rendered, comes from an ancient reptilian snake-goddess called Sir and relates to one of the Anunnaki.)

The new City of London was built after the fire in the knowledge that it was to become a major global centre for the Illuminati bloodlines. So it was after the arrival of William of Orange, who became William III, and to whom all the royal families of Europe are related. In 1694, William signed the charter that created the Bank of England and the whole central banking system began to emerge with its masters dictating policy to all of them via organisations like the Bank of International Settlements in Switzerland. What also followed the creation of the Illuminati operational stronghold in London were the British Empire and the other European empires. As these expanded across the planet to take over the Americas, Africa, Asia, China, Australia and New Zealand, they exported the bloodlines and secret societies and made every effort to destroy the native knowledge and culture. Also, within those countries were the hybrid bloodlines created by the interbreeding between the Anunnaki and selected families in those regions long before, and these were the people who were left in the positions of power after the colonial invaders from Europe withdrew and granted the countries "independence". Credo Mutwa has identified many of the black leaders in Africa since "independence" to be from the same former "royal" bloodlines of Africa that claimed descent from the "gods".

When these European empires apparently collapsed or withdrew, this only happened on the surface, not in the fundamentals of control. There are two forms of dictatorship: one that which you can see, the overt tyrannies like Communism and fascism, and the covert dictatorship, which you cannot see because it operates in the strictest secrecy. It grows like a hidden cancer, eating into the positions of power in every area of society. The obvious, open, forms of dictatorship have a finite life because eventually there will be a rebellion against control you can see, touch, and taste. There is an identifiable target on which to focus. However, covert dictatorship, control from behind the scenes, can go on forever until it is exposed because people do not rebel against not being free when they think they are. When the British and European empires appeared to unravel, these powers were only exchanging overt control for covert. While they appeared to give "independence" to their colonies, the bloodlines and their secret society networks remained intact within those countries and they have continued to control them ever since. But because no one knows this and the people see a president or prime minister of their own colour or nation, it is assumed that the country is "free" and self-governing. I document in *The Biggest Secret* how the United States of America has never been free of control from London to this day and that the federal level of US government is a private corporation controlled from Europe. The President of the United States is merely this corporation's temporary chief executive, the same role as the president of the former Virginia Company, which was formed in 1604 by the British Crown and "aristocratic" bloodlines to steal North America in the first place. An extraordinary story, but true. At least 50 of the 56 signatories to the American Declaration of Independence were Freemasons and only one was known not to be.

When the Grand Master Freemason, George Washington, became the first President, he nominated eleven Supreme Court Justices, at least six of which were confirmed Freemasons. The same story has continued ever since. The inauguration of Washington in 1789 was a Freemasonic ceremony in which he swore the oath on a Freemasonic Bible. In January 2001 President George W. Bush took the oath using that same Bible, as did his father more than a decade earlier. It is the property of the New York Lodge, according to news reports. Washington, who commanded the American colonial armies against the British Crown, was a knight of the Order of the Garter, one of the most elite Illuminati networks headed by the British Crown! It seems to be a staggering contradiction, but when you know the scam it makes perfect sense. (See *The Biggest Secret* for the detailed background to the American War of "Independence".)

There is no better example of the point I am making here than South Africa. During the period of apartheid, it was an open dictatorship by the few of the many. As a result there was a clear target and so internal and external rebellion led to the removal of that regime. Along came the first black president, Nelson Mandela. He is probably a nice man, but a powerless puppet in truth, and since then Thabo Mbeki has replaced him. Black people now have a vote and so South Africa is free. Yippee! Oh really? The Illuminati global structure can be likened to a compartmentalised pyramid or a spider's web. The operational "spider" at the centre is in Europe with London, Paris, Brussels, and Berlin the key cities. From Europe the agenda is dictated down the line to what I call the "bloodline branch managers" in the various countries of the world. These "bloodline managers", like the Rockefellers in the United States and the Bronfmans in Canada, have a network of other bloodline families around them that control the politics, finance, business, media, and military, etc., in their particular country or domain within the web, much as the Anunnaki "gods" were given different regions to rule in line with the centrally dictated agenda. And just as the gods fought with each other and tried to muscle in on another's patch, so these Illuminati branch managers do today; hence the infighting and conflict between them. It is the "manager's" job to orchestrate the events and policies of their country to follow the demands of the centrally controlled agenda. This is how the same events and policies can be introduced everywhere, often at the same time.

Now, South Africa is free, yes? The bloodline branch managers of South Africa are the Oppenheimer family and their network. Under the open dictatorship of apartheid, they controlled some 80% of the country's stock market, owned the gold and diamond mines on which the economy depends, and controlled the media through their various frontmen. Today, since the election of Mandela and Mbeki, the apartheid dictatorship has been replaced by "freedom". I know this is true, I heard it on the news. Under this "freedom", the Oppenheimer family and its networks, continue to control some 80% of the South African stock market, own the diamond and gold mines on which the economy depends, and control the media through their frontmen, not least an Irishman friend of Robert Mugabe and Henry Kissinger called Tony O'Reilly. Isn't freedom just wonderful? And this has happened everywhere as the same forces have remained in control since the illusion of "independence". But look at the South African experience. Under the overt dictatorship with apartheid there was widespread rebellion inside and outside the country. But now, under covert dictatorship…silence. Everyone thinks South Africa is now free and "independent".

So you see that the "hidden hand" method is by far the most effective way of controlling people and dictating events. This exchange of overt for covert control has happened on every continent and this is how the Anunnaki and their hybrid bloodlines manipulate the world today.

SOURCES

1   *Our Haunted Planet*, p 144

2   Frans Kamp in conversation with the author

3   Quoted in *Flying Serpents And Dragons*, p 67

4   Correspondence with the author

5   W. T. Samsel in an article for the David Icke website: Concerning the Reptilian Agenda, ***http://www.50megs.com/davidicke/icke/magazine/vol7/agenda.html***

6   *Flying Serpents And Dragons*, pp 39 and 40

7   Ibid, p 40

8   *The Return Of The Serpents Of Wisdom*, pp 47 and 48

9   Ibid, p 49

10 Quoted from a pre-publication manuscript. The book is now in print and can be obtained through Bookends on the David Icke website: ***www.davidicke.com*** – highly recommended

11 *The Return Of The Serpents Of Wisdom*, p 99

12   Ibid, pp 140 and 141

13   Jane Harrison, *Themis, A Study Of The Social Origins Of Greek Religion* (Peter Smith Publishing, Glouster, Massachusetts, 1974)

14   *The Return Of The Serpents Of Wisdom*, pp 104 and 105

15   Ibid, p 257

16   *The Book Of Enoch* is available from Hidden Mysteries through the David Icke website

17   Correspondence with the author

18   Quoted in *Flying Serpents And Dragons*, pp 179 to 181

19   Correspondence with the author

20   *Flying Serpents And Dragons*

21   Ibid. p 7

22   Genesis, chapter one, verse 26

23   Quoted in *Flying Serpents And Dragons*, p 153

24   Ibid

25   Ibid, p 1

26   John Rhodes website: ***http://www.reptoids.com/ind2.htm#mexannmark***

27   Michael Mott's book, *Caverns, Cauldrons, And Concealed Creatures*, is an excellent account of these stories and how they fit with experience today

28   *Flying Serpents And Dragons*, p 92

29   Quoted in *Gods Of The New Millennium*, p 223

30   The translation of Zecharia Sitchin

31   *Gods Of The New Millennium*, pp 226 and 227

32   Manly P. Hall, *The Secret Teachings Of All Ages* (The Philosophical Research Society. Los Angeles, California, 1988), p A1

33   An excellent source of information on this story is *The Temple And The Lodge* by Michael Baigent and Richard Leigh, published by Arcade Publishing, New York, in 1989

34   See Manly P. Hall's *America's Assignment With Destiny, The Adepts Of The Western Tradition*, published by the Philosophical Research Society. Los Angeles, California, in 1979

CHAPTER 7

Serving the dragon:
the past

Great spirits have always experienced violent opposition from mediocre minds.

Albert Einstein

The ancient world abounds with stories of the serpent or dragon race and royal kings, queens, and emperors who claim their right to rule through their descent from the serpent gods.

The Sumerian accounts tell of flying serpents and dragons breathing fire (symbolic of their aerial craft?) and how the kings of Sumer, going back long before the deluge to some 240,000BC, were "changelings" seeded by the union of the gods and humans. Sargon the Great, that famous ruler of the Sumer Empire, claimed this genetic origin and the very existence of "kingship" is reported very clearly to have been a gift of these gods. Equally clear is that they were *reptilian* gods, as in "The reptiles verily descend". And there are many references by the Sumerians to their gods as fiery, winged, serpents. The term U-SHUM-GAL, often used to describe Enki, translates as flying, fiery, serpent, which would perfectly describe a reptilian in a flying craft emitting a fiery exhaust. In fact the word SHUM can relate to the term "sky vehicle".[1]

There could be another origin for this "fiery" symbolism, also. The Anunnaki god Ninurta was called a MUSH-SHA-TUR-GAL-GAL – the "flying serpent with the fiery glance" and this fits perfectly with the descriptions by the Zulu shaman Credo Mutwa in his stories of the reptilians in ancient and modern African legend. He says the reptilians have a third eye between the other two which opens from side to side instead of top down – the "fiery, red eye" in African tradition. From this can be flashed a red, laser-like beam, he says, which can knock a person down and paralyse them. This is an origin of the phrase about giving someone the "evil eye".[2] In China the Lung Wang ("Dragon Kings") were said to have a "magical pearl" on their foreheads, a "divine eye" and mystical source of power. French stories from the Alpine regions speak of a dragon with a blood-red ruby "eye" in the centre of the forehead that was so bright the creature seemed to be projecting fire.[3] Sometimes this middle eye is called a dracontia[4] and the eye in the centre of the forehead in the ancient stories of the beings called the Cyclops may well relate to this, too. Credo Mutwa and modern abductees describe how the most "royal" and senior reptilians, the Draco, have horns. Some look like Darth Maul in the *Star Wars*

Figure 16: *The Satanic goat's head is, in part, a symbol of the horned "Draco"*

movie with the nodules or "horns" around his head. So much truth is told as fiction through Hollywood movies, both by those trying to get the story out and, overwhelmingly, by those conditioning humanity for the open appearance of these beings in the years to come. In my view, George Lucas of *Star Wars* is among the latter. The Sumerians depicted their "gods" with horned helmets and other headgear that was later used by the hybrid bloodlines to symbolise royalty and kingship, and from this came the symbol of the royal crown. Look at Darth Maul and you will perhaps see where the crown comes from. Credo Mutwa says on the *Reptilian Agenda*, part one, that he was amazed to see Darth Maul because of his likeness to the reptilians in ancient and modern African legend. The ram or goat's head, so widely used as a symbol of Satanism, is partly symbolic of the horned nature of the Anunnaki "royalty" that Satanism was created to serve (*Figure 16*). Ram is a word or syllable meaning fire and relates to the Atlantean god of fire, Votan. From this we get penta*ram*, py*ram*id, Semi*ram*is, *Ram*ses, *Ram*a, *Ram*tha, maybe even prog*ram* or prog*ram*me, a word at the heart of the Illuminati strategy.

The dragon kings

The kings of the succession in the reptilian bloodlines were known as "Dragons". When many kingdoms joined together in battle, or as a group of kingdoms, they appointed a king of kings. These were known as the Great Dragon or…Draco. The Celtic title of Pendragon, as in Uther Pendragon, the father of "King Arthur" in the Grail stories, was a version of this. In the legends, the symbolic Arthur was a descendant of the dragons and his helmet (or El-met, named after a reptilian goddess called El) carried a dragon motif. The red dragon symbol of Wales comes from the claim by Merlin, Arthur's "magician", that the red dragon symbolised the people of Britain. Merlin was described as only half human because he was the child of an underground being and a human woman. The Arthurian stories include all the classic elements of the story, including the creation of royal bloodlines through the interbreeding between humans and non-human entities, shape-shifting, the use of holographic images to hide a being's true form, and battles between competing dragons. Geoffrey of Monmouth, the 12th century historian, said that Merlin's earlier name had been Ambrosius, thus possibly associating him with the

Greek term for menstrual blood, Ambrosia, which the reptilians love to drink.[5] There is also the theme of the "Lady of the Lake" and this connects with the stories of goddess-worshipping serpent peoples like the Nagas living in underground centres located under lakes and lochs. Like the Celtic myth and folklore, the ancient Greek culture was inspired by the Sumerians and the earlier Atlanteans and Lemurians and was based almost entirely on their stories and myths under different names. All over the ancient world you find the same recurring stories of the serpent gods. Throughout the Sumer Empire the people worshipped serpent gods and as the Reverend John Bathhurst Deane wrote in his book, *The Worship Of The Serpent*:

> "...One of [the] five builders of Thebes [in Egypt] was named after the serpent-god of the Phoenicians, Ofhion ...The first altar erected to Cyclops at Athens was to 'Ops', the serpent deity...The symbolic worship of the serpent was so common in Greece that Justin Martyr accuses the Greeks of introducing it into the mysteries of all their gods."[6]

The Hebrew serpents

I have mentioned that in Hebrew myth, the Biblical "Nefilim", the "sons of the gods", are called awwim, which means devastators or serpents. Hebrew legends also describe the Eden serpent as a being who walked and talked like a human. The Hebrew book of ancient oral tradition, the Haggadah, speaks of this serpent as a creature with two legs that stood upright to the "height of a camel".[7] The Slavonic Apocalypse of Abraham says the serpent with Eve had hands, feet and wings,[8] just like many other ancient and modern descriptions of the Draco. The Hebrew stories came from the earlier Sumerian, Atlantean, and Lemurian accounts, many of them changed and twisted to suit the priesthood and to lose most of the direct reptilian references. These can be identified, however, by following the trail from which their terms and names derived. The name of the Hebrew winged "angels", the Seraphim, means serpent and they were described as having six wings – just like the one in the Garden of Eden featured in the Apocalypse of Abraham.[9] Flying angels in religious texts are symbolic of the reptilians, some of which, according to ancient and modern descriptions, have wings and can fly. This is also symbolised in the flying reptilian gargoyle figures, which the bloodlines have on their homes, cathedrals, churches, and other buildings, including the British Houses of Parliament. Seraph in the King James Version of the Bible is translated as "fiery serpent" and would seem to derive from the same root as the Sumerian, seru, the name of a serpent in the Epic of Gilgamesh (the origin of the "Noah" story), and sarpa, a Sanskrit term for the Indian reptilian "gods", the Nagas.

The Jewish Talmud forbids the depiction of the dragon, as it does the Sun and the Moon, both symbols of major Anunnaki figures. A fragment of the Hebrew Dead Sea Scrolls, translated by the Hebrew Scholar, Robert Eisenman, includes a description of a "Watcher" known as Belial (an origin of the "Sun gods" Bel and Baal?). It calls him the "Prince of Darkness" and the "King of Evil" and he is described as a being of terrible appearance..."with a visage like a viper". The researcher and channeller, W.T. Samsel, writes in *The Atlantis Connection* that the force behind the spiritual demise of Atlantis was known as the Sons of Belial. Interestingly, one of the key colleges at Oxford University, that "education" centre for the Illuminati, is called Balliol and it has produced many significant politicians who have advanced the Illuminati agenda. It is named after its founder John Balliol who was married to a Scottish Princess, Dervorguilla of Galloway. Their son, another John Balliol, was King of the Scots from 1292 to 1296. The Balliol family were big time bloodline and given the Illuminati's astonishing obsession with symbols and the sound of names and words, there may well be some connection between Belial and Balliol. Certainly there is in spirit because Balliol College, like Oxford University in general, is an Illuminati stronghold turning out future generations of placemen and women.

Early accounts by the Gnostic sect (Gnostic = "knowledge") tell of the serpent gods in a positive light. They claim that Lilith (Eve) was their first creation and then Adam followed as her partner. The Hebrew Talmud also claims that Lilith, a vampire, was Adam's first wife. This is symbolism, of course, but symbolising what? Lilith (also Lillibet and Elizabeth) is one of the code names for the bloodlines on the female side to this day. She was known as Lil to the Sumerians and Lilitu in Babylon. Hebrew traditions say that Lilith rebelled against Adam and his God and fled to a cave after eating her own child. There she lived with the demons of the underground world and bred with them. She told Adam and Eve that she and her offspring would always abduct human children and take them to their subterranean world. The Roman Church savagely suppressed the Gnostics, not least because they did not believe that people needed a middleman between themselves and God. Went down very well with the Christian priests, that one. Hippolytus, an early Christian "father" and historian, wrote that many of the first Gnostics in North Africa were known as the Naaseni or "Serpents" and they worshipped Nahustan, the golden or brazen serpent, the image of whom they displayed on wooden crosses. The Naaseni (Nagas) later became known as the Ophites, a Greek term for serpent. The Greeks said that serpents were creatures of great knowledge, which spoke through their oracles – psychic channellers. In other words, communications from another dimension, or density. The story of Moses contains much serpent symbolism, also.

The garden of Eden, Edin, Heden

The serpent that "tempted" Eve in the Biblical Garden of Eden is the best-known serpent symbolism of all. This was an edited rewrite of the far more ancient Sumerian story of Edin, the "Land of the Gods or the Righteous Ones". There is again a common theme of the serpent gods in a garden, and James Churchward suggests in *The Children Of Mu* that these "gardens" all refer to Lemuria-Mu, the "Motherland". I think he could well be correct. The Persians spoke of a region of bliss and delight called Heden, which was more beautiful than the entire world. It was the abode of the first men before an evil spirit in the form of a serpent tempted them to take the fruit of a forbidden tree. There is also the banyan tree under which the Hindu "Jesus", known as Krishna, sat upon a coiled serpent and bestowed spiritual knowledge on humanity. The ancient Greeks had a tradition of the Islands of the Blessed and the Garden of the Hesperides in which grew the golden apples of immortality. The garden was defended by a dragon. In Chinese sacred books there is a garden that contained trees bearing the fruit of immortality. It, too, was guarded by a winged serpent called a dragon. The ancient people of Mexico had their version of the Eve story that involves a great male serpent, and a Hindu legend tells of the sacred mountain of Meru, guarded by a dreadful dragon. This was said of so many ancient places. The belief in a serpent or half-reptile, half-human, giving knowledge to humanity is also a universal story.

Asian serpents

The Indus Valley culture of the Sumer Empire and the Lemurians, and the Hindu religion and Indian mythology that emerged there, are full of references to the serpent gods and flying dragons who brought knowledge and fought with each other in the sky. They called them the Nagas, as we have seen, and they said they

could take either reptilian or human form whenever they chose.[10] The Nagas, who originated in Lemuria, seeded the "royal" families, we are told, and interbred with the white peoples. It was said that the Indian serpent-goddess Kadru gave birth to all the Nagas or "cobra people" and made them immortal by feeding them her lunar (menstrual) blood. The theme of the serpent goddess or serpent queen is everywhere, as we shall see in detail later, and in *Figure 17* you can see the symbolism of "serpent maidens" in Indian art. The Indian epic, the Ramayana, tells the story of the serpent-god called Ravan who went to

Figure 17: *Maidens of the serpent cult symbolically portayed in Indian art*

Ceylon. Ravan was said to feed on humans and drink the blood of his enemies.[11] Ceylon was a major centre for the serpent race, it seems. Ancient Chinese sources say it was a home of the Nagas, the "strange reptilian-like creatures", as they described them.[12] They are reported to have traded with the Chinese, but interestingly it is said that they never revealed themselves. They left their products and a price tag, but stayed out of sight until the Chinese traders had departed.[13] The

Nagas were reported to have a "special weapon" that paralysed their enemies and drained their life force. Abductees have reported the same experience in modern times. Snake worship continues in India today, of course.

Serpents of the far east

The entire culture of China is based on the dragon and serpent race. Once again, here was a highly developed civilisation thousands of years ago that was inspired by Lemurians and later influenced by the Sumer Empire. Even today their languages and writing are remarkably similar, as are their myths and stories. The great age of Chinese culture is reckoned to have begun around 2800BC – when the Sumer Empire was in full swing. Chinese history says that the first humans were created by an ancient goddess called Nu Kua, who was half dragon and half human. The Yih King, a very ancient Chinese book, says that the dragons and humans once lived in peace and that they intermarried and interbred.[14] Ancient Chinese emperors were described as "dragon-faced" and looking like the dragon gods. Japanese emperors claim descent from these same "gods" and their ancient legends say those islands were populated by beings that came from the sky. Again James Churchward connects the Japanese race to Lemuria-Mu. There are countless Japanese legends about serpents and dragons, and their marriages and sexual encounters with humans that produced reptilian-human offspring. Shape-shifting serpent people would change into beautiful men and women, and lure human warriors and leaders into sexual encounters. Michael Mott, author of *Caverns, Cauldrons, And Concealed Creatures*, tells of one story involving a maiden called Mimoto who was seduced by a member of the serpent race:

> "…Mimoto never saw her dragon-lover again but she did give birth to a hybrid child, whom she called Akagire Taro, or Chapped Son. This was due to the fact that his skin was cracked, creased, and scaled like that of a reptile. From here the ancient tale enters historic accounts, for a direct descendant of Akagire Yataro, as the son was known in manhood, was a member of the Genji Clan named Saburo Ogata, who took pride in the fact that he had scales on his body as had his ancestors before him. He was the grandson of Yataro the Fifth. Again, a prominent family line seems to have been the desired target of the original, and perhaps repeated, genetic exchange. While in the East, the influx of 'dragon-blood' is seen as a thing of great pride, in the West such things are covered with an elaborate coating of fable and mist, becoming 'fairy tales' about serpent or frog-princes. Western sentiment, at least on the surface, is against such liaisons, often for religious reasons but not always on this basis alone, as the subterraneans have a track-record of cruelty, selfishness, and malice."[15]

The Chinese calendar zodiac, dating to 2500BC, is symbolised by animals, all of which still exist, except for one – the dragon. Is it really likely that they would choose real, living, creatures for all their signs, except for just one? Again we see the theme of reptilian bloodlines in China. The ancient Chinese believed that a dragon fathered the First Dynasty of "divine" emperors, and subsequently emperors claimed their right to rule because they were descended from the serpent gods. Their thrones, boats, and beds were designed with dragon symbolism. Today there are many Chinese bloodlines in the Illuminati, particularly some strands of the Li bloodline, as identified by author and researcher, Fritz Springmeier, in his book, *Bloodlines Of The Illuminati* (Ambassador House, Colorado, USA, 1999).[16] Just as this book was heading for the printers in March 2001, Springmeier and his wife were raided by the US agencies involved in the mass murder at Waco and their research was confiscated. James Churchward, who did so much extensive research into the existence of Mu, claimed that the ancient tablets he examined from an Indian monastery revealed that the serpent hybrids, the Nagas, had populated China, Tibet, and a significant part of Asia, including the Uigher Empire.[17] The Pamir Mountains or "the roof of the world" in central Asia is one specific location connected by legends to the peoples of Lemuria-Mu and there you will find the Lake of the Nagas or Lake of the Serpents.[18] Among the descendants of these bloodlines, it is claimed, were the fair-skinned Aryans, again indicating the connection between the reptilians and the Nordics. As a "serpent" colony, you would expect to find pyramids in China, and you do. One was some 1,000 feet high – twice the height of the Great Pyramid at Giza. This was encircled by others and some still survive today, including what is left of that monster structure. References to them have been found in Chinese texts dating back 5,000 years.

The secret society initiate Georges Ivanovitch Gurdjieff said that he had been part of an unsuccessful expedition to find a lost city of the Uigher Empire under the sands of the Gobi Desert. He said he was initiated into the Sun/Moon Brotherhood of Central Asia and was told that the founders of this Brotherhood had come from Mars in ancient times.[19] James Churchward says that the Uigher Empire were former Lemurians. Later a Russian archaeologist called Professor Kosloff found a tomb of ancient artefacts in the same area of the Gobi Desert. These included a painting of a ruler and his queen and he estimated the work to be some 18,000 years old – at least.[20] There was also an emblem of a circle with a cross, and at the centre was a symbol similar to the Greek letter, Mu. An expedition by the American Museum of Natural History in 1993 found a mysteriously large number of dinosaur fossils in the Gobi Desert. They found 40 to 50 dinosaur skeletons in around three hours in an area no bigger than a baseball field.[21] Researcher and author Mark Amaru Pinkham writes in *The Return Of The Serpents Of Wisdom* that a race of extraterrestrials called the Kumaras established a Mystery school on Lemuria/Mu and later relocated their operation to Mongolia, the Gobi Desert region of China, and to Tibet.[22] Certainly Tibet is one of the most important depositories of the ancient knowledge, and legends galore talk of underground cities and tunnel systems where the "supermen" continue to live. Agartha and Shamballa are the most famous of them. The Chinese invasion and occupation of Tibet is far more connected to this story than political acquisition. Tibet, that land of such ancient secrets and legend and still today very much connected with the Illuminati, is another home of the serpent symbol. So is the ancient, former Lemurian, culture of the Australian aborigines that includes the Rainbow Serpent.

The Chinese name for the ley lines or meridian lines of the Earth energy grid is dragon lines. Appropriate and understandable given that the reptilians exploit the energy in this grid, and built temples and structures at the major vortex points. An ancient Chinese tale about the dragon kings also makes a clear reference to shape-shifting. This is the most amazing aspect of this bizarre story – the way these reptilians can change their appearance or "shape-shift" between a human and reptilian form, evidence for which I will present shortly. A character called Liu Ye, who wanted to marry a princess of the "dragon race", was said to have seen the palace of the emperor change before his eyes and the courtiers dissolve and then return to their original form. He saw the coils of dragon bodies, flashing wings, and dragon's eyes. The legend says that Liu Ye changed his Earth form and became one of the dragon race that lived in the sky. With that, he became immortal.[23]

Serpents of the Americas

The story is the same in the Americas with the serpent gods at the heart of the ancient myths and legends of North, South and Central America. The books of the Mayans called Chilam Balaam say the first settlers of the Yucatan in Mexico were the Chanes or "People of the Serpent".[24] They were said to have come across the sea led by a god-figure called Itzamna, a name that apparently comes from the word itzem, which translates as lizard or reptile.[25] Itzamna, the sacred city of the god, therefore, means "the place of the lizard" or "Iguana House".[26] Itzamna's symbol was the Tau cross also known as the T-square in Freemasonry. Quetzalcoatl, the most famous Central American "serpent" god, also carried a Tau cross. This cross, like the Christian cross, refers to crossbreeding in Illuminati symbolism and not polarity union as is often claimed. While excavating in Central America near a place called Texcoco, the archaeologist William Niven discovered more than 20,000 tablets that included many symbols identical to those found on the Naacal tablets, which James Churchward had seen in India.[27] And Churchward's tablets were connected to Lemuria/Mu, which was the origin of both these cultures. Itzamna was the Central American version of the creator god who breathed life into "Man" and yet another who was depicted as half human, half reptile. Quetzalcoatl, the "Feathered Serpent", was the major deity of this culture and he travelled, like all the others, in a "flying boat". It is possible that Quetzalcoatl is another name for the Anunnaki DNA wizard, Enki. Aztec myth says that Quetzalcoatl created humans with help from the Serpent Woman, Cihuacoatl – Ninharsag of the Anunnaki worked with Enki, according to the Sumerian tablets.

There is serpent symbolism all over the ancient Central American sacred sites and these were places of human sacrifice on a scale that beggars belief. Edward Thompson, the American archaeologist, was initiated into the Mayan Brotherhood of Sh'Tol and he was told that the name of the ancient port city of Tamoanchan in Veracruz, Mexico, means "the place where the People of the Serpent landed".[28] They came in boats, he was told, which "shone like the scales of serpent skins" and they were "clad in strange garments and wore about their foreheads emblems like entwined serpents".[29] Another landing point for the "serpent" Atlanteans was Valum

Votan. Here, according to Spanish chroniclers, Pacal Votan and his entourage came ashore. Pacal Votan means "He of the Serpent Lineage".[30] He established the city of Palenque, the heart of the Mayan culture in the Yucatan. Palenque is the centre of its geographic land mass, as is the Great Pyramid at Giza.[31] The temple or pyramid of the Sun at Teotiuacan in Mexico uses the royal cubit as its unit of measurement, the same as the Great Pyramid, and its mathematics conform to those used in ancient structures across the world.[32] Why? Because they all originate from Lemurian/Atlantean bloodlines and know-how. The Olmec peoples of Central America based their whole culture on worship of the serpent. Excavations have uncovered representations of the Olmecs with serpent features, snake heads, and bodies like dragons.

Native American culture in general is awash with reptilian imagery and includes many tales of the "Sky Gods" coming down to breed with their women. In Ohio there is a mysterious and unexplained mound shaped like a serpent from a culture long forgotten. The Hopi Indians in Arizona have their plumed serpent god Baholinkinga. They talk of an underground world they call Sipapuni, where they claim to have originated. They say that while they were within the Earth they were fed by the "ant people" and they refer to their ancestors as their "snake brothers". These descriptions sound very much like beings described in Sumerian accounts. The most sacred of Hopi underground rituals is the snake dance. This is very much like the dance rituals performed by Mayans at places like Chichen Itza in the Yucatan, Mexico. The Hopis believe they share the same ancestors as the serpent-worshipping Chimu people of Peru – Lemurians. The Chimu established a city called Chan-Chan or "Serpent-Serpent".[33] Their "Temple of the Dragon" still survives and their priests would make snake hissing sounds and chant "snake mantras" to invoke their serpent gods.[34] Significantly, the region where you find the Hopi and Navajo lands in Arizona/Utah, is also claimed by modern UFO researchers and abductees to be the site of a major underground reptilian base. This is especially true of Four Corners, where the states of Arizona, Utah, Colorado, and New Mexico all meet at the same point. The Hopi Snake Clan, an ancient society of initiates, claims its origins from a Hopi boy who was taken into the "House of Snakes" in a tunnel complex under the Earth.[35] Another Hopi legend speaks of a very ancient underground tunnel complex under Los Angeles, which was occupied by a "lizard race" some 5,000 years ago. In 1933, an LA mining engineer called G. Warren Shufelt claimed to have found this complex, but the news of the discovery was immediately covered up. Today it is claimed by some people that highly malevolent Freemasonic rituals are held there. Geronimo, the great chief of the Apache, told legends of the dragon and the serpent people who ate children. He said his tribe was named after a boy called Apache who killed the great dragon. The story has the feel of David defeating Goliath and even George defeating the Dragon. Mark Amaru Pinkham in *The Return Of The Serpents Of Wisdom*, interprets the explosion of serpent symbolism as recognition of energy and spiritual initiates. I agree with some of that, but there were rather more literal reasons for these symbols, I would suggest. Anyway, he does a good job in detailing the symbolism of the serpent around the world, including that in America or "Amaraka":

"According to the descendants of the early Lemurian record keepers, the Andean Elders, the entire American land mass was anciently known as Amaraka, the 'Land of the Immortals' or the 'Land of the Wise Serpents'. The title Amaraka is derived from the Quechuan-Lemurian word Amaru, meaning snake or serpent. (Quechuan, the language of the Incas, is derived from Runa Sima, the primal tongue spoken on Lemuria, and ends in the syllable "ka", which denotes both serpent and wisdom). Apparently echoing the recollections of the Andean Elders, H.P. Blavatsky maintains in *The Secret Doctrine* that America is referred to in the Hindu Puranas (legends) as Potala, the Kingdom of the Nagas [Serpents]." [36]

Native Americans call America "Turtle Island" after their reptilian ancestors. The name of the founder of both the Inca Empires in South America was Manco or Manko Kapac (Kapac means serpent wisdom or spiritually wealthy). Some of the former Lemurian and Atlantean peoples who settled in the Andes migrated northwards to become some of the Native American tribes of what we now call the United States. The Mescalero Apaches of Arizona claim to descend, via Peru, from a continent that sank in the Atlantic.[37] This was documented by Lucille Taylor Hansen in her book, *The Ancient Atlantic* (Amherst Press, Amherst, Wisconsin, 1969).[38] Asa Delugio, the Mescalero Apache Chief, told her that the ancestors of the Apaches were "serpents" from their sunken homeland in the Atlantic, which he called Pan and the Old Red Land. After being forced by conflict to leave Peru they travelled north where they fought with local tribespeople in North America. Their men were killed and the women went on to breed with the victors to form the bloodlines that became the Mescalero Apaches. Hansen identified significant connections between the Apaches and the peoples of North Africa who also claimed descent from Atlantis. The Mescalero Apache Crown Dance is performed with serpents painted all over the bodies of the participants. The chief wears a 13-pointed crown of the Atlantean fire god, Votan, and other key performers wear the trident headdress. The trident is the symbol of Atlantis and Lemuria. Hansen established that the Tuareg people in North Africa, who claim to originate in Atlantis, perform an identical dance. She also saw an ancient Egyptian artefact that appeared to depict the very same dance. The Sioux tribe insist that their ancestors were from Atlantis via Peru, and again the serpent or reptilian imagery is extremely prominent in the story. Sioux means "snakes", as another tribe, the Iroquois, means "serpents".[39] The Sioux ancient records say that after the demise of Atlantis, their ancestors, who they call the Turtles, travelled to the Caribbean Islands (from Ka-rib, the Atlantean serpent people)[40] and went on to South America before heading north. They say these "Turtle" people became known as the Lakota and the Sioux or "snakes". This story is apparently symbolised at the mysterious Serpent Mound in Ohio in which the Turtle is depicted leading the snake. The original structure was vast, covering 14 acres and rising to 100 feet. The Lakota, Sioux and Peruvian native peoples share certain words in their language. A Sioux chief called Shooting Star said during a visit to Peru:

"This is the land of our beginning, where we went from the Old Red Land even before it sank, because this land is as old as the Dragon Land of the fire god." [41]

Which was, of course, Atlantis. Other Native American tribes (many with the hard "k" sound in their names) say they descend from Atlanteans or Lemurians who fled directly to North America from the sunken lands. Oklahoma, a significant Illuminati centre in the United States, means "Sun people of the Red Land".[42] Lucille Taylor Hansen collected Native America legends, which say that some tribes came from Atlantis under the leadership of the prince grandson of Votan III, who was alleged to be the last priest king of the Atlantean House of Votan. Hansen says that this grandson of the royal bloodline of Atlantis wrote a book called *Proof That I Am A Serpent*, which survived in circulation among the Native Americans until the time of the European invasion when it disappeared. Prince Votan's arrival in North America was celebrated with an annual ceremony known as Thanksgiving, later stolen by the European Pilgrims and still a major festival in the United States.[43] A key area for Illuminati rituals and mind control projects is Mount Shasta in northern California and this is also at the centre of many legends about "serpents" and Lemurians settling before and after the cataclysm. As with all of these former Atlantean and Lemurian peoples, they were obsessed with building structures on the vortex points. Some 40,000 stone circles, pyramids, and mounds were built in North America.[44] Burning flames were often placed on the top of the mounds and they were never allowed to be extinguished. These were the symbol of the "Great Spirit" or "Serpent Fire", a continuation of the worship of the "Fire Serpent" of Atlantis.[45] The most used symbol of the Illuminati today is the flame or lighted torch. It is known as the "eternal flame" – exactly the term used by the ancients. The Native American tribes formed secret societies or "Serpent Clans" like the Snake Clan and the Thunderbird Clans. The Thunderbird is a version of the Chinese rain dragon. Many of their leading initiates were believed to be snakes in human form, which, symbolically, is what the key bloodlines are. Author Mark Amaru Pinkham writes of these clans:

"They were reputed to wield the lethal power of a live snake and display both the intimidating temperament and appearance of the unsavoury beasts. As a sign of their viperous power, Snake initiates would often adorn their body with snakeskins or snake tattoos and hang snake fangs from around their necks. They also conveyed poisonous snake venom within the medicine bag and/or armed themselves with a serpent-embellished rattle, which would hiss eerily like a coiled snake when shaken. The tendency of such snake initiates was to be secretive, like a stealthy reptile, and some even developed a penchant for seeking out dark secluded dwellings or living nocturnally."[46]

Initiations into these clans include being covered, often bitten, by live snakes. Sometimes the rites involved cutting off a finger or other part of the body and feeding it to a snake (don't say a thing!). My eyes have just watered. The main deity of these Snake Clans is the "Great Horned Serpent".

African serpents

Credo Mutwa, the official historian of the Zulu nation, has painted pictures from ancient and modern descriptions of these reptilian entities (*see picture section*) and describes the various levels of the fiercely imposed genetic hierarchy. The lower levels are the "warriors", the "poor bloody infantry" as we say in Britain. They are ruled by the "Royal" leaders, which have horns and tails, and at the very top are beings with a white, albino-like, skin and not the greenish or brownish colour of the others. Witnesses and abductees have reported seeing reptilian beings with albino-like skin and these descriptions can also be found in ancient texts. In Africa the reptilians are known as the Chitauri or "Children of the Serpent" and "Children of the Python". This is so close to the Central American term "People of the Serpent". Africa is another continent awash with the legend of the serpent race. For Anunnaki, Annetoti, Nagas, Dravidians, and so on, read Chitauri. Different names, same people.

Credo Mutwa talks for hours on the video *The Reptilian Agenda*, part one, about the background and history of the Chitauri, and he confirms the theme of shape-shifting and how the Chitauri bloodlines can take either human or reptilian form. He describes how the Earth was once encircled by a canopy of water vapour (the "firmament") that was destroyed in a cataclysm. This water vapour protected the planet from the harsh effects of the Sun, and the whole planet was moist and humid and had a constant temperature. It was a place of enormous abundance and vast forests. This is a common description of the Golden Age – the Lemurian "Garden of Eden". But, he says, that when the Chitauri destroyed this canopy (symbolised by the Biblical 40 days and 40 nights of rain) the whole climate changed as the Sun's rays baked once green and abundant lands like Egypt and began to form the deserts. Scientists agree that Egypt, now part of the Sahara Desert, was once a green and pleasant land. This could explain the water erosion found on the Sphinx. To divide and rule the people, Credo continues, the Chitauri scattered them across the Earth and gave them different languages so they could not communicate with each other. This is another story repeated all over the world and not just in the Old Testament version of the Tower of Babel. That was a steal from many more ancient accounts. The Hopi say that when they came to the surface on the orders of "Spider Woman", a "mocking bird" arrived to confuse their language and make the tribes talk in different tongues. Credo, repeating the information passed on to him in a lifetime of initiations into this underground knowledge, said that the Chitauri reptilians interbred with all races to create the reptilian-mammalian hybrids through which they rule. He said that in African culture a person's genealogy is very important and that the "royal" bloodlines of the kings of black Africa claimed descent from the same "gods" as the white peoples and others across the world. What's more, he said that these black royal bloodlines, like those in the countries of the white peoples, had largely moved out of the positions of inherited control, like kings and queens, where they could be identified. Instead they have taken the positions of "appointed" or "elected" control, like government administrators, bankers, businessmen, and political leaders. He reveals, from his knowledge of black African genealogy, that the black presidents who came to power after "independence" from the white Europeans have been the same royal bloodlines as the kings and queens of black Africa. He cited Robert Mugabe in Zimbabwe as an example – the same Robert Mugabe who was manipulated into power by the Illuminati's Henry Kissinger and Lord Carrington, as documented in ...*And The Truth Shall Set You Free*. Mugabe has brought poverty, hunger, and chaos to black and white alike in a country that should be one of the richest in Africa. At the same time, he has made himself a billionaire by "winning" rigged elections and stealing the people's wealth. Also in Africa, as we have seen, the African Dogon tribe of Mali, it is claimed, say they were visited by extraterrestrials from Sirius. The Dogon appear to descend from a Greek people who themselves claimed descent from the "Argonauts". The Dogon settled first in Libya and then further south in Mali, where they interbred with the Negro peoples.

The Greys are reptilian

Credo also supports the view of many UFO researchers that the so-called greys, that best-known of extraterrestrial beings, are lackeys for the reptilians. But he goes further than that. He says they *are* reptilian. The control and focus of the world is based on Europe and North America and for far too long that has been the case in UFO research, too. This has blinded so many of those researchers to the staggering information available in the vast continents of Africa, South America and native Australia. While they are still arguing over whether "grey aliens" were found in Roswell, New Mexico, in 1947, black African tribes people have been finding these greys in the bush for hundreds of years right up to the present day. Black Africans call them the Mantindane ("The Tormentors"). Credo says that often when the greys die in the open, they are removed quickly by government agencies or their "friends" in flying craft. But occasionally dead greys have been found and removed by tribes people and he has witnessed them being taken apart and examined. He describes in the video, *The Reptilian Agenda*, part one, how he was once given part of a grey to eat, without realising what it was, and the consequences were amazing in the effect on his mind and body, good and not so good. I won't spoil the story in case you want to see the video because he tells it so brilliantly. He says that the greys are not grey and do not have big black eyes, as it appears. The grey "skin", he reveals, is actually a strange type of suit, which is astonishingly difficult to break through. In Credo's words, it requires not just a new axe, but one that has been sharpened to its fullest potential. When you finally breach the "suit", he says, you find inside a pinkish, scaly, reptilian, creature with pupils that go up-down like a reptile's. Africans call them in this "non-suited" state, "Pinky, Pinky". The big black eyes, he says, are not eyes, but very sophisticated goggles to protect the eyes of the grey from the Sun. For some reason, the reptilian greys and at least some of the other reptilians cannot endure, or do not wish to experience, direct sunlight, and they have to either wear these suits and eye protectors or only go out at night. I know it's serious, but I have to laugh at how bizarre it all is. Aliens walking around in grey suits wearing big black shades, and others doing impressions of the Mario

Brothers or Puff the Magic Dragon. Wake me up. Researcher Alan Walton also says that the greys have been described as having a "reptiloid, amphiboid, or even saurian" genetic base complete with scaly skin, and webbed claw-like fingers. He says that people have reported seeing reptilian eyes with vertically slit pupils within the "big black slanted eyes" that seem in many cases to be "some type of biomechanical covering". He says that they also appear to have an insectoid-type infusion into their DNA. Frans Kamp came across this same theme of an aversion to sunlight in his own research of the reptilians:

> "Reptilians are intuitive or paranormal creatures. They live underground because of the Sun. The radiation of the Sun diminishes the production of seratonin and as seratonin is necessary for the stimulating of the pituitary gland or pineal gland to produce melotonin, they better stay underground. Melotonin is indispensable for life. The more melotonin, the more life. The more intuition/paranormal you are the higher production of melotonin." [47]

Draco = Dracula

This is where part of the symbolism in the story of Dracula originates. It was written by the Irish author Bram Stoker and published in 1897. Stoker probably knew the score after years of research into the countless vampire legends. As a History Channel documentary about Stoker confirmed, there is no part of the world and no era of history that does not have its myths and legends about vampires who feed off other people's energy and blood. Look at the main elements of that tale in the light of what you have read so far. His name is Dracula (the Draco constellation is the alleged home of the royal reptilian bloodlines). He is called "Count" Dracula (symbolic of the way these Draco bloodlines have been carried by "human" royalty and aristocracy). Dracula is a vampire (symbolic of the need of the Draco reptilians to drink human blood and feed off human energy). Dracula shape-shifts, appears and disappears (symbolic of the reptilian shape-shifters and I will elaborate on this shortly). He cannot stand direct sunlight (exactly what Credo and others say of the reptilians and greys). He comes in through "windows" (symbolic of the interdimensional portals through which reptilian entities enter our world). So many famous writers and artists were initiates or dogged researchers who told elements of the story through art and "fiction". Stoker's character was largely based on a man called Dracula or Vlad the Impaler, the 15th-century ruler of a country called Wallachia, not far from the Black Sea in what is now Romania (Rom = reptilian bloodlines). This was the same region that was once called Transylvania, the home of the most famous vampire legends, and the Danube River valley, which runs from Germany to Romania and into the Black Sea, is a name that comes up very often in the history of the bloodlines. Vlad the Impaler, or Dracula, slaughtered tens of thousands of people and impaled many of them on stakes. He would sit down to eat amid this forest of dead bodies, dipping his bread in their blood. He was a great guy to invite home for dinner, apparently. He usually had a horse attached to each of the victim's legs and a sharpened stake was gradually forced into the body. The end of the stake was usually oiled and care was taken that the stake not be too sharp; he didn't want the victim dying too quickly from shock. Infants were often impaled on the stake forced through their mothers' chests. The records indicate that victims were sometimes impaled so that they hung upside down on the stake. Death by impalement was slow and painful. Victims sometimes endured for hours or days. Dracula had the stakes arranged in various geometric patterns and the most common was a ring of concentric circles. The height of the spear indicated the rank of the victim, an excellent indication of the ritual-obsessed reptilian mind. The decaying corpses were often left there for months. It was once reported that an invading Turkish army turned back in fright when it encountered thousands of rotting corpses impaled on the banks of the Danube. In 1461 Mohammed II, the conqueror of Constantinople, a man not noted for his squeamishness, was sickened by the sight of twenty thousand impaled corpses rotting outside of Dracula's capital of Tirgoviste. The warrior sultan turned over command of the campaign against Dracula to subordinates and returned to Constantinople. Ten thousand were impaled in the Transylvanian city of Sibiu, where Dracula had once lived. On St. Bartholomew's Day, 1459, Dracula had thirty thousand merchants and others impaled in the Transylvanian city of Brasov. One of the most famous woodcuts of the period shows Dracula feasting amongst a forest of stakes and their grisly burdens outside Brasov while a nearby executioner cuts apart other victims. Impalement was Dracula's favourite technique, but by no means his only method of inflicting unimaginable horror. The list of tortures employed by this deeply sick man included nails in heads, cutting off limbs, blinding, strangulation, burning, cutting off noses and ears, mutilation of sexual organs (especially in the case of women), scalping, skinning, exposure to the elements or wild animals, and boiling alive. No one was immune to Dracula's attentions. His victims included women and children, peasants and great lords, ambassadors from foreign powers and merchants.

Vlad the Impaler was the son of Vlad Dracul, who was initiated into the ancient Order of the Dragon by the Holy Roman emperor in 1431. Its emblem was a dragon, wings extended, hanging on a cross. Vlad II wore this emblem and his coinage bore the dragon symbol. All the members of the order had a dragon on their coat of arms and he was nicknamed Dracul (the Devil or the Dragon). Son Vlad signed his name Draculea or Draculya or the "Devil's son" and this later became Dracula, a name that translates as something like "son of him who had the Order of the Dragon". Most appropriate. This is the same Dragon Order that is today promoted by the British "Holy Grail" author, Sir Laurence Gardner. By the way, Queen Mary or Mary of Teck, the mother of King George VI and therefore grandmother to the present Elizabeth II, was descended from a sister of "Dracula". Nothing like keeping it in the family.

British and European serpents

In Britain and the rest of Europe, the stories of dragons and reptilian gods abound also. Here are just some of the places in the British Isles that have dragon/serpent legends: Avebury, Bamburgh, Baslow, Betws-y-Coed, Bishop Auckland, Brent

Pelham, Bretforton, Brinsop, Bromfield, Bures, Burley, Castle Neroche, Cawthorne, Chipping Norton, Crowcombe, Dartford, Deerhurst, Dinas Emrys, Dronley, Dunstanburgh, Durham, Gunnerton, Henham, Highclere, Horsham, Hughenden, Hutton Rudby, Kellington, Ker Moor, Kilve, Kingston, Lewannick, Linton, Llandeilo Graban, Llyn Cynwch, London, Longwitton, Ludham, Lyminster, Middlewich, Mordiford, Norton Fitzwarren, Norwich, Nunnington, Oxford, Penmynydd, Penshaw, Renwick, Saffron Walden, Saint Leonards Forest, Shervage Wood, Slingsby, Sockburn, Tanfield, Trull, Uffington, Wells, Westbury, Wharncliffe, Wherwell, Wiveliscombe, Wormbridge, Wormingford, Wormhill, and Wormshill. (Worm or wirm means "wingless dragon".) All the legends of the dragons and serpents of the British Isles follow similar themes.[48]

The British Isles was an Atlantean/Lemurian colony before the deluge and the bloodlines returned there as the Phoenicians, Egyptians, and other names, when the Sumer Empire began to expand to the centres of its former Motherlands. The carriers of the Atlantean/Lemurian knowledge in Britain and other parts of Europe were called the Naddred or Adders, a Welsh name for serpent.[49] They are better known as the Druids, a Gaelic word in Ireland meaning a wise man, sorcerer, or serpent, and they were called the "snake priests". An Irish manuscript claims that the adepts of the Druidic arts descended from the Tuatha de Danaan – "The People of the Serpent Goddess Dana".[50] Apparently the Tuatha de Danaan were also called the Sumaire. These were the former Atlantean peoples who settled in Asia Minor (Turkey) and then expanded out into Europe. It was they who called Britain "Albion" after Albina, the eldest daughter of Danaus, an ancient Danaan priest.[51] Danaan is also so close to Canaan, of course, and these "two" peoples came from the same part of the world. I think we will find that Danaan and Canaan are terms for the same people. It was one of their number, called Brutus, who led migrating Danaans/Trojans to the British Isles and established the city of Caer Troia or "New Troy" – today's London. The legend goes that when the Danaans were defeated by the later Greek Milesians of Asia Minor, the peace agreement involved the Danaans moving from the surface to live in an underground kingdom which could be accessed from "hollow hills" in Ireland.[52] The Danaans were said to be a giant race of warriors, who became smaller through generations of living within the Earth. The same was said in Ireland of the Firbolgs, Formorians, and Nemedians, who were also defeated and driven underground where, it is said, they lost their giant stature. This theme of giants forced underground where they dwindled in height can be found all over the world and, like the Danaans, they are often described as having what I call the "Nordic" appearance. Another common story is that these people abducted surface humans and interbred with them. Michael Mott in his book, *Caverns, Cauldrons, And Concealed Creatures*, also points out the close similarity of "Tuatha" and "Tuat", the Egyptian name for the underworld, through which the Pharaohs believed they would travel to immortality.

The Druids, it is said, continued to use their Danaan knowledge on the surface after those peoples were forced underground. The highest level of the Druidic pyramid was the Arch Druid. They were located on islands because land surrounded by water is a particularly powerful energy centre and if it also happens to host major vortex points on the energy grid that power is increased immensely. The Arch Druids were based on the Isle of Man (home of an ancient Danaan Mystery School) in the Irish Sea, the Isle of Anglesey off the North Wales coast, and the Isle of Wight, the "Dragon Isle" as it was called, off the south coast of England where I have lived for nearly 20 years.[53] Researcher Mark Amaru Pinkham suggests that the Isle of Wight could have been (therefore is) the "pivotal vortex" in the northern grid of the planet. No wonder so much Satanism involving major Illuminati figures goes on there. Stonehenge, Avebury, Glastonbury Tor, Bath, and Iona were other significant Druid centres. Glastonbury Tor (hill or mound) was located in the Isle of Avalon and Avalon means "island of the Immortals" – a name that is common to many of these "serpent" centres. The island of Iona off the Scottish coast was formerly known as Innis nan Druidhneah or "Island of the Druids". The Arch Druids were indicated by the seven "serpent eggs" displayed on their breasts.[54] The goddess Artemis (Dana, Diana) was also depicted with eggs on her chest. Was the legend of the mythical St Patrick chasing the snakes out of Ireland the destruction of the Druid or Adder network? If this was so, it happened for public consumption only as the knowledge was taken out of general circulation, but remained very much alive within the secret societies.

Egyptian serpents

You find the same story of serpent symbolism in the country to which so many modern Illuminati symbols and codes relate: Egypt. The great Temple of Ammon or Amen Ra was placed on a massive vortex point at Thebes or Karnac (Amen or Ammon is where the Christians get their term Amen!). Under Thebes/Karnac are networks of tunnels known as the "Serpent's Catacombs". As a result of the travelling Egyptians of the Sumer Empire (or the Nordics who travelled *to* the Sumer region) we also have Carnac in Brittany (Barati), France. There were once 10,000 standing stones here, arranged to form the image of a seven-mile serpent. Carnac means "Serpent Hill".[55] The ancient Egyptian accounts known as the Pyramid Texts speak of the serpent being both subterranean and celestial. Stories of flying serpents can be found in Egypt, as you would expect of an important colony of the Sumer Empire, and, once again, they symbolised immortality. Flying serpents were pictured taking the kings to the land of immortality in a star constellation in the heavens. One serpent symbol was the divine asp on the headgear of Egyptian kings and they used the fat of the crocodile in their coronations. The great ancient Egyptian city of Alexandria was called "City of the Serpent's Son" (Alexander the Great) and there they worshipped the serpent god, Serapis. He was known as the "Sacred Serpent" or "Fire Serpent" and from this comes the Biblical "Seraphim", the serpents associated with YHVH or Yahweh (Jehovah). The Temple of Serapeum in Alexandria was dubbed one of the seven wonders of the ancient world, as was the 400-foot-high Pharos lighthouse in the city, which was topped by the Illuminati's key symbol the lighted torch or eternal flame. In the temple, Serapis was portrayed as a massive statue standing on a crocodile holding a staff with a serpent coiling around it. At the top of the staff were the heads of a lion, dog, and wolf, all classic symbols of the serpent cult.[56] Egyptian queens like Cleopatra were known as the "Serpent of the Nile" and the Uraeus hieroglyphic sign for goddess was a serpent.[57] Later Gnostic Christians adopted the name Uraeus as a secret name for God![58] Many Gnostic traditions also identified the serpent with "Jesus".[59]

As with many other cultures of the serpent gods, they were seen in the earliest Egyptian records as either benevolent or partly benevolent and partly not so. This is what you would expect from any race of people that reflects all attitudes. However, there came a time, which can be identified most clearly in Egypt, when this image changed dramatically. Suddenly, they were the bad guys. In the earlier Old and Middle Kingdoms (which ended about 1640BC), the serpent was given a good press. But starting with the New Kingdom it was all very different. Especially from the 18th dynasty (starting about 1546BC), serpents become the target of hatred and rituals were performed to exorcise them. This change of serpentine image in Egypt came in the period of chaos lasting hundreds of years, after the Middle Kingdom fell.[60] And it was the kings of the 18th dynasty who removed the Hyksos, who invaded Egypt and ruled till around 1550BC. The Hyksos (which means "Princes of Foreign Lands") destroyed all places of worship of the old religion when they took over, and R.A. Boulay writes in his *Flying Serpents And Dragons* that the Hyksos were known as the Amalekites by the Hebrews and were part of the Rephaim, descendants of the reptilian Nefilim.[61] Apop was the first ruler of the Hyksos in Egypt and the name was used to symbolise the serpent when they took on their "evil" public image in Egypt. The serpent was known as Apep or Apop (Apophis to the Greeks), and Apop became the symbol of the serpent people who occupied Palestine and also Egypt at the time of the so-called "Exodus". Rituals to destroy Apop in Egypt were very similar to those in Asia designed to overcome the Nagas. For me the Hyksos were of the reptilian bloodline and played a major role in infiltrating the Egyptian Mystery schools. It was around 2000BC that the Royal Dragon Court, now the Imperial Royal Dragon Court and Order, was formed in Egypt by the priests of Mendes to protect, advance, and serve the "dragon bloodlines" and 4,000 years later it is still in operation and promoted by Sir Laurence Gardner in England. This is the organisation, remember, that awarded the Dracula family its most prestigious title.

Clearly the legends and accounts of the serpent gods, their royal hybrids, and their often grotesque activities, abound throughout the ancient world. So does the most bizarre theme of all – their ability to change their form before your eyes. They can shape-shift.

SOURCES

1   Translations of Zecharia Sitchin

2   *The Reptilian Agenda*, part one, with Credo Mutwa and David Icke

3   *Flying Serpents And Dragons*, p 31

4   Ibid

5   *The Woman's Encyclopedia Of Myths And Secrets*, p 650

6   Reverend John Bathhurst Deane, *The Worship Of The Serpent* (J.G. and F. Rivington, London, 1833)

7   *Flying Serpents And Dragons*, p 7

8   Ibid, p 9

9   Ibid, p 10

10 *The Woman's Encyclopedia Of Myths And Secrets*, p 903

11 Ibid, p 41

12 Ibid

13 Ibid

14 Ibid, p 48

15 *Caverns, Cauldrons, And Concealed Creatures*

16 Fritz Springmeier, *The Illuminati Bloodlines* (Ambassador House, Westminster, Colorado, 1999), pp 163 to 185

17 *The Return Of The Serpents Of Wisdom*, p 50

18 Ibid, pp 53 and 54

19 Ibid, p 51

20 Ibid

21 *http://www.amnh.org/Research/Gobi/gobi.html*

22 *The Return Of The Serpents Of Wisdom*, p 52

23 *Flying Serpents And Dragons*, pp 48 to 50

24 *The Return Of The Serpents Of Wisdom*, p 67

25 Ibid, pp 66 and 67

26 Ibid

27 Ibid, pp 68 and 69

28 Ibid, p 65

29 Ibid

30 Ibid, p 66

31 Ibid, p 87

32 Ibid

33 Ibid, p 155

34 Ibid, p 154

35   Ibid, p 180

36   Ibid, p 55

37   Ibid, pp 60 and 61

38   Ibid

39   Ibid, p 63

40   Ibid, pp 62 and 63

41   Lucille Taylor Hansen, *The Ancient Atlantic* (Amherst Press, Amherst, Wisconsin, 1969)

42   *The Return Of The Serpents Of Wisdom*, p 63

43   Ibid, p 64

44   Ibid, p 84

45   Ibid

46   Ibid, p 178

47   Correspondence with the author

48   For more on British dragon legends and a host of other ancient and modern reptilian information, see the award-winning Reptilian Agenda archives at ***www.reptilianagenda.com*** part of the David Icke website.

49   *The Return Of The Serpents Of Wisdom*, p 244

50   Ibid

51   Ibid

52   Ibid, p 245

53   Ibid, p 251

54   Ibid, pp 250 and 251

55   Ibid, p 80

56   Ibid, p 260

57   *The Woman's Encyclopedia Of Myths And Secrets*, pp 906 and 1,028

58   Ibid, p 1,028

59   Ibid, p 907

60   *Flying Serpents And Dragons*, p 43

61   Ibid

CHAPTER 8

the
shape-shifters

Whoever undertakes to set himself up as a judge of Truth and Knowledge is shipwrecked by the laughter of the gods.

Albert Einstein

The accounts of the reptilian control of humanity are not confined to the ancient world, as we shall see very clearly as the story is revealed. Cathy O'Brien, a victim of the Illuminati's vast mind control programme, wrote of her reptilian experiences in her book, *Trance-Formation Of America* (Reality Marketing, Las Vegas, 1995). I have told Cathy's story at length in my previous books and I will elaborate on the mind control programmes later in this one. Understandably, Cathy believed her reptilian experiences with leading figures in the United States to be part of her mind control. However, as you will see with the evidence I shall present, what she saw and heard was not quite the illusion she thought it to be. She described how many leading US politicians she worked for in her mind-controlled state appeared to take a reptilian form before her eyes and then return to "human". These included President George Bush, father of President George "Dubya", of the Anunnaki/Merovingian bloodline. Father George told her they were an extraterrestrial race that had taken over the world, but no one realised it because they looked human. Cathy relates another important experience she had with Miguel de la Madrid, the President of Mexico during Bush's tenure at the White House. She writes in *Trance-Formation Of America*:

"De La Madrid had relayed the 'legend of the Iguana' to me, explaining that lizard-like aliens had descended upon the Mayans. The Mayan pyramids, their advanced astronomical technology, including sacrifice of virgins, was supposedly inspired by the lizard aliens. He told me that when the aliens interbred with the Mayans to produce a form of life they could inhabit, they fluctuated between a human and Iguana appearance through chameleon-like abilities – 'a perfect vehicle for transforming into world leaders.' De la Madrid claimed to have Mayan/alien ancestry in his blood, whereby he transformed 'back into an Iguana at will.' De la Madrid produced a hologram similar to the one Bush did in his...initiation. His hologram of lizard-like tongue and eyes produced the illusion that he was transforming into an Iguana." [1]

Remember that the Mayans say the first settlers of the Yucatan in Mexico were the Chanes or "People of the Serpent". They were led by the god Itzamna, a name that apparently comes from the word itzem, which translates as lizard or reptile. The sacred city of Itzamna, therefore, means "the place of the lizard" or "Iguana House". What Cathy O'Brien reports there is an excellent summary of what has happened, except for the part about holograms and illusions. What she saw was not a reptilian hologram, but what is known as "shape-shifting". If anything it is the "human" form of these people that is a holographic "cover". Shape-shifting is the ability to change physical form, in this case between a human and reptilian appearance. The ancient Danaan brotherhood of initiates and magicians called Telchines on the island of Rhodes could shape-shift into any form, according to the Greek historian, Diodorus.[2] Shape-shifting is a common theme in tales of esoteric "magicians" and high initiates. I have been told by hundreds of people all over the world, from every walk of life you can imagine, about their experiences of seeing well known and less well known people transform into a reptilian form before their eyes and then go back again. George Bush (Father George) is the name that recurs most often in these accounts. There have been reports of shape-shifting reptilians for thousands of years. In the Indus Valley and Hindu culture their serpent gods called the Nagas were one example. Interestingly, James Churchward established that the Maya of Central America and the Nagas of Asia were the same former Lemurian peoples. You can see in the videos, *The Reptilian Agenda*, the information and confirmation that the Zulu shaman Credo Mutwa presents of the shape-shifting reptilians.[3] The serpent "sea" or "fish" gods of Sumer and Babylon were said to be able to change shape and look human whenever they chose. Another version of shape-shifting are the so-called "Men in Black" who appear and disappear according to witnesses. The story of Jekyl and Hyde is also symbolic of shape-shifting.

The children of the shadows

Ancient tablets, alleged to come from beneath a Mayan temple in Mexico, describe the reptilians and their ability to shape-shift. These accounts correlate remarkably with modern experience and reports. They are known as the Emerald Tablets of Thoth, who was a deity of the Egyptians. It is claimed that they date back 36,000 years and were written by Thoth, an "Atlantean Priest-King" who, it is said, founded a colony in Egypt. His tablets, the story goes, were taken to South America by Egyptian "pyramid priests" and eventually placed under a Mayan temple to the Sun God in the Yucatan, Mexico. The translator of these tablets, who calls himself "Doreal" (Maurice Doreal), claims to have recovered them and completed the translations in 1925. But only much later was he given "permission" for part of them to be published, he says. You can read the whole tale and the content of the tablets on this website: *http://crystalinks.com/emerald.html*. There is also a book, *The Emerald Tablets Of Thoth-The-Atlantean* (Source Books, Nashville, Tennessee). However, you don't have to accept all the details of that story to appreciate the synchronicity between what these tablets say and what is now being uncovered. The following is the relevant section in the tablets to the subjects we are discussing.

"Speak I of ancient Atlantis, speak of the days of the Kingdom of Shadows, speak of the coming of the children of shadows. Out of the great deep were they called by the wisdom of earth-man, called for the purpose of gaining great power.

"Far in the past before Atlantis existed, men there were who delved into darkness, using dark magic, calling up beings from the great deep below us. Forth came they into this cycle, formless were they, of another vibration, existing unseen by the children of earth-men. Only through blood could they form being, only through man could they live in the world.

"In ages past were they conquered by the Masters, driven below to the place whence they came. But some there were who remained, hidden in spaces and planes unknown to man. Live they in Atlantis as shadows, but at times they appeared among men. Aye, when the blood was offered, forth came they to dwell among men.

"In the form of man moved they amongst us, but only to sight, were they as are men. Serpent-headed when the glamour was lifted, but appearing to man as men among men. Crept they into the councils, taking form that were like unto men. Slaying by their arts the chiefs of the kingdoms, taking their form and ruling o'er man. Only by magic could they be discovered, only by sound could their faces be seen. Sought they from the kingdom of shadows, to destroy man and rule in his place.

"But, know ye, the Masters were mighty in magic, able to lift the veil from the face of the serpent, able to send him back to his place. Came they to man and taught him the secret, the Word that only a man can pronounce; swift then they lifted the veil from the serpent and cast him forth from place among men.

"Yet, beware, the serpent still liveth in a place that is open, at times, to the world. Unseen they walk among thee in places where the rites have been said; again as time passes onward, shall they take the semblance of men.

"Called, may they be, by the master who knows the white or the black, but only the white master may control and bind them while in the flesh.

"Seek not the kingdom of shadows, for evil will surely appear, for only the master of brightness shall conquer the shadow of fear.

"Know ye, O my brother, that fear is an obstacle great; be master of all in the brightness, the shadow will soon disappear. Hear ye, and heed my wisdom, the voice of LIGHT is clear, seek the valley of shadow and light only will appear."

Within that passage, whatever its origin may be, you have the story of life on Earth over hundreds of thousands of years and the source of those who control the world today. The leading politicians, banking and business leaders, media owners, and heads of the military are the Anunnaki-serpents in human form. Staggering I know, and the minds of most people will be screaming "nonsense" because it is so at odds with their conditioned view of reality. But it's true. And if you bale out now, you will miss the mass of evidence I will present to show that it's true. The background presented in those tablets is confirmed by modern experience and rapidly emerging information from the inside of the Illuminati. Some examples follow:

> "Forth came they into this cycle, formless were they, of another vibration, existing unseen by the children of earth-men."

As my research has revealed, the world is controlled by entities taking reptilian and other forms that exist on another dimension or "cycle". We are in the third dimension or density, they operate from the fourth, a frequency just outside the present range of the physical senses. We can feel the fourth density as "vibes" around us, but we cannot see it, unless we tune in with our "psychic" sight, which can connect our consciousness with other vibrational levels. This is what psychics or "channellers" are seeking to do and the good ones (the few) can move their inner "radio dial" to access other frequencies. The "headquarters" of the serpent race I am exposing here is the lower end of the fourth-dimensional frequency range, which vibrates very close to this one. It is on the very fringe of our physical senses. It is what you might call a parallel universe or a parallel Earth, a mirror of the one we see, but vibrating at a different speed. Cats can see the fourth dimension and this is why they react to something in what appears, to us, to be "empty" space. The same with babies before their psyche is closed down by an ignorant world. To operate and manipulate our vibrational level of the planet, these fourth-dimensional reptilians needed a third-dimensional human form. They needed to create a genetic space suit that they could occupy and hide within.

This, as President de la Madrid told Cathy O'Brien, was achieved by creating bloodlines that fused their reptilian DNA with that of humans. These bloodlines have a genetic, therefore vibrational, compatibility between the fourth-dimensional reptilians and their third-dimensional "human" forms. In other words it makes their possession of these bodies far easier and more effective than with other human genetic streams that do not have that particular DNA combination. It is to retain this genetic structure that the Illuminati bloodlines have always interbred with each other and continue to do so. It means that if they can manipulate these bloodlines into the positions of power, they are, in effect, putting themselves into those positions through their control of these bodies from the lower fourth dimension. This is the reason that the genealogy of those in the major seats of global power today can be traced back to the royal lines – the Anunnaki hybrids – that ruled Sumer, Egypt, and so on. The ancient Book of Enoch, which covers the period before the final Atlantis cataclysm, says those born of Nefilim blood are, because of their "ancestral spirit" (reptilian possession from the lower fourth dimension), destined to "afflict, oppress, destroy, attack, do battle, and work destruction on the

Earth". The Nefilim are fundamentally associated with human sacrifice and blood drinking – just like the Illuminati today. The Book of Enoch describes the behaviour of the Nefilim offspring produced with human women:

> "And they became pregnant, and bore great giants...who consumed all the acquisitions of men. And when men could no longer sustain them, the giants turned against them and devoured mankind. And they began to sin against birds and beasts, and reptiles, and fish, and to devour one another's flesh and drink blood. The Earth laid accusation against the lawless ones."

As then, so now.

The blood drinkers

> "Only through blood could they form being, only through man could they live in the world."

Insiders have told me that the reptilians need to drink human (mammalian) blood to maintain human form and stop their reptilian DNA codes from manifesting their true reptilian state. Accounts of the Nefilim also include references to their blood-drinking activities, as we have seen. All this explains why these bloodlines have always taken part in human sacrifice and blood drinking rituals from the ancient world to the present day, a fact I detail in *The Biggest Secret*. This includes people of the bloodline like George Bush, Al Gore, Bill Clinton, Henry Kissinger, the Rockefellers, Rothschilds, British prime ministers like Ted Heath, and the British royal family. Yes, including, indeed especially, the Queen and Queen Mother. I have been writing for years about the ancient Satanic rituals performed by the elite of the United States at a place called Bohemian Grove. This is 2,700 acres of secluded and guarded redwood forest in northern California. Many people just laughed as usual, but, as I was starting this book, Alex Jones, an American journalist, documentary maker, and radio presenter, managed to get into the Grove during their ritual disguised in one of the hooded robes the participants wear. He took video footage to prove that what I, and many others, have been saying about Bohemian Grove is true. His website is *www.infowars.com*.

Among the participants at Bohemian Grove past and present are George Bush; George W. Bush; Al Gore; Ronald Reagan; Richard Nixon; Jimmy Carter; Gerald Ford; Dwight D. Eisenhower; Lyndon Johnson; Herbert Hoover; Teddy Roosevelt; Dan Quayle; Robert Kennedy (JFK's brother); Joseph Kennedy (JFK's father); Earl Warren (head of the Warren Commission, which "investigated" JFK's murder); David Rockefeller; Laurance Rockefeller; Nelson Rockefeller; Henry Kissinger; Mikhail Gorbachev (the Soviet Union and the "West" were always controlled by the same force); William F. Buckley, an American publisher and major Illuminati operative; George Shultz, the former Secretary of State to Ronald Reagan; Walter Cronkite, America's most famous news reader; William Randolph Hearst, the

American newspaper tycoon; Andrew Knight, a British media executive closely connected to the Rupert Murdoch empire; Edward Teller ("Father of the H bomb"); Glenn Seaborg, who developed plutonium; Burt Bacharach, the composer; singer Bing Crosby; Bob Hope, a British MI6 operative; Ray Kroc, the man behind the McDonald's fast-food empire; author Mark Twain; and John Muir, founder of the Illuminati environmental front, the Sierra Club.[4] That's just a few of them and their connection is their reptilian bloodline or their allegiance to the Illuminati. The Kennedys are a major bloodline family in the States, but no one is expendable if the Illuminati agenda requires action to be taken. Many recovering mind-controlled slaves have told me how they were brutally sexually abused by Senator Edward Kennedy and one former mind-controlled operative with the Illuminati, a mind controller herself, told me: "Senator [Edward] Kennedy and the whole Kennedy family was part of this. I know that they are political icons in our country, but they are in it up to their eyeballs." Phillip Eugene de Rothschild says he is one of *hundreds of thousands* of unofficial Rothschild offspring. He stresses that often the most significant operatives in the Illuminati hide behind apparently "ordinary" lives while dictating the agenda and attending human sacrifice rituals. This is my own information, too, after talking to Illuminati insiders. But he says that there are many public figures who are very high in the Illuminati-Satanic pyramid and he highlights Prince Philip as a major player in the rituals he has attended:

"I can recall the Rockefellers and the Bushes attending rituals, but never having the supremacy to lead them. I still regard them as lackeys and not real brokers of occult power. Except for Alan Greenspan [head of the US Federal Reserve Bank], most of these fellows were camp followers in the occult, primarily for the economic power and prestige. Greenspan, I recall, was a person of tremendous spiritual, occult power and could make the Bushes and the younger Rockefellers cower with just a glance. Ex-CIA Director Casey (as were most of the CIA leadership for the past forty years), Kissinger, and Warren Christopher [former US Secretary of State] were in attendance at non-ritual gatherings and some occult rituals as well, but well back in the gallery.

"At the forefront of the rituals were [the royal families of Europe], Prince Philip at the pinnacle. He stands, like most of the contemporary European monarchy, in the Charlemagne, Merovingian, Aenean bloodline. But he is its current head. I am certain that his maternal chromosomes are in the current "antichrist" Nephilim. Prince Philip...is the leading biological descendent of the "reptilians", as you call them. Immediately below him are the males of my family line [Rothschilds] like a court of ministers in charge of logistics and operations. The current monarchs of The Netherlands, Spain, and some of the old Austrian nobility [Habsburgs] are next in occult power and in the conspiracy."[5]

There is a lot of background to Prince Philip and the Windsors in *The Biggest Secret*. Other information has come from the victims of the Illuminati mind control programmes, like the one based at Montauk Point on Long Island, New York, which has been the subject of a number of publications. Mind-controlled slaves are widely used by the reptilians and their bloodlines to advance their agenda, as I have exposed at length in other books. They have created a global army of programmed people to do their bidding, conduct their rituals, and do whatever they are told without question or thought. Some have recovered at least part of their minds, escaped from the projects, and accessed the memories of what happened to them. They have become increasingly vocal in the last ten years, although the mainstream media refuses to report their stories. One mind-control victim told me how he witnessed human sacrifice ceremonies at Montauk involving William F. Buckley, the well known American publisher and Bohemian Grove member, who heads the elite Janus mind control operation based at NATO headquarters in Belgium. Arizona Wilder says she has had similar experiences with Buckley. The Montauk mind-slave claims that the knowledge he learned in these projects showed him how the reptilians shape-shift. He said there are locked sequences and open sequences of DNA. Open codes manifest as a physical characteristic while closed codes do not. The reptilian hybrids, he says, have the ability to lock off certain genetic codings while they open others. When this happens, he says, there is a literal transformation of the cellular structure, which changes from a mammalian to a reptilian form. "So it's not like the human form goes anywhere", he told me, "It just shifts, it changes into a reptilian form because those sequences are opened. They also have the ability to shift it back." However much your mind may be struggling to cope with that, for sure what he says about DNA codes in general is correct. Did you realise that there are still people today who are born with tails? Yes, there are, and it is simply because codes from our reptilian past have opened in those people which, at this time in the evolution of the body, should have remained closed and dormant. As the human foetus forms into a baby it goes through many stages that connect with major evolutionary points in the development of the present physical form. These include those that connect with non-primate mammals, reptiles, and fish. At one stage, the embryo has gills and is very much like those of birds, sheep, and pigs until the eighth week when it goes on its own evolutionary path. When a code opens that should not, babies are born with tails and these are known today as caudal appendages. Doctors usually remove them immediately, but in those areas of the world where that treatment is not available people live their whole life with a tail. You only have to feel the bottom of your spine to see where our tails used to be and they do not manifest today, except rarely, purely because the DNA genetic blueprint has closed that formerly open code. This mind control victim is merely claiming that when you know what you are doing and understand DNA to a much greater level than human scientists currently do, you can make this process happen in an instant.

He says that the reptilians need mammalian hormonal levels to hold the mammal codes open and maintain human form because their "base-line" state is reptilian and the mammalian codes would close if they did not consume frequent supplies of human blood. They also want an adrenaline that enters the bloodstream in large quantities at times of extreme terror. Hence they have victims who know they are going to be sacrificed and they use the ritual to build their terror to the point of death. This allows them to drink blood full of that adrenaline. Arizona Wilder supplies precisely the same information from her own horrific experience. She says she conducted sacrificial rituals for the American elite and the British royal family at places like Balmoral Castle in Scotland, as revealed in *The Biggest Secret* and the video, *Revelations of a Mother Goddess*. Arizona adds that the blood type the reptilians most desire is that of blond-haired, blue-eyed, people because it is the most effective for the purpose of holding human form. She, like almost every "elite" mind-controlled slave I have encountered, is blond-haired and blue- eyed. She dyed her hair after escaping from her mental and physical slavery. Blond- haired, blue-eyed people are also the ones most often chosen to be sacrificed by the Illuminati. Red-haired people seem very important to them also and they most of all want the blood of pre-pubescent children and young women who have not had sex. This is to do with the purity of the blood and energy of children, and the changes that take place within the energy field once a person has experienced sex or puberty. Thus the Illuminati sacrifice children and young women more than anyone and this is the origin of the stories throughout history of sacrificing "young virgins" to the gods.

Scientists have discovered aspects of shape-shifting phenomena. Polymer gels, for instance, are remarkable, shape-shifting materials. When exposed to small alterations in acidity or temperature they can dramatically transform their appearance and size. The different acidities and temperatures are simply different vibrational states. The changing vibration is the key. The forces between molecules in the gels are delicately balanced in a constant tug-of-war and sometimes one state wins and sometimes another, depending on the outside stimulus. Hiroaki Misawa and colleagues at the University of Tokushima, Japan, focused a laser beam at the center of a cylinder of polymer gel and found that within an instant, the rod's middle shrank in diameter, turning it into a dumb-bell. When they shut the laser off, the middle snapped back to its original width. The transformation of the gels are entirely reversible, the same as human-reptilian shape-shifting.[6]

Arizona says she saw members of the British royal family, the Windsors, shape-shift into reptiles many times. Princess Diana's close confidant Christine Fitzgerald, told me that the Windsors wanted to interbreed with Diana's genes (blond-haired, blue-eyed) because they were in danger of becoming too reptilian in their DNA and would not have been able to maintain a human form for many more generations. You can see how different Prince William looks to the rest of them because he had an infusion of his mother's Nordic-dominated DNA. Christine Fitzgerald said that Diana's private name for the Windsors was "the reptiles" and "the lizards" and she used to say in all seriousness "They're not human."[7] It was the reptilian bloodlines and their networks that killed the princess in a ritual murder on an ancient site of ritual to the goddess Diana originally created by the reptilian Merovingians. This desperation for blood could well account for the mystery of cattle mutilations around the world in which the animal is bled dry and reports of the bloodsucking Chupacabra in Puerto Rico, Mexico, Florida, and the Pacific north-west also fit the reptilian description. Many of these reports and "outbreaks" of bloodsucking activity have coincided with UFO sightings in the same area. Another explanation for the descriptions of "humans" turning into reptilians is that the viewer's psyche tunes into the fourth-dimensional level and sees the reptilian form hiding within the three-dimensional body, or the fourth-dimensional reptilian lowers its vibrational state to briefly enter our physical frequency range. I will go into this aspect of the story in a later chapter. Feeding off human blood is not the only desire of these vampires. The reptilians also feed off human emotional energy. The more emotion we can be manipulated to project through fear and all its manifestations the more energy they can absorb and recycle against us. Researcher Alan Walton, who writes under the name Branton, has uncovered the same themes:

> "Aside from any territorial 'paternal' instinct on the part of the 'Draconians' to re-conquer their "home planet" (Earth), some of the worst reptilian sub-species have an even more sinister motive. These are the vampirial types, who actually seek to feed off of human emotional energies and life force/essence in order to acquire the energy that they apparently need not only to infiltrate our world but also our dimension. Having genetically engineered themselves along more 'warrior instinct' lines, what little connection they might have had to a 'spiritual' side has been all but eliminated, and they are motivated only by the predatory instinct of their collective which apparently knows only one agenda: conquer, assimilate, consume! All this has been confirmed by many abductees, especially in more recent years." [8]

The silent invasion

Back to the Emerald Tablets:

> "In the form of man moved they amongst us, but only to sight, were they as are men. Serpent-headed when the glamour was lifted, but appearing to man as men among men. Crept they into the councils, taking form that were like unto men. Slaying by their arts the chiefs of the kingdoms, taking their form and ruling o'er man. Only by magic could they be discovered, only by sound could their faces be seen. Sought they from the kingdom of shadows, to destroy man and rule in his place."

That is a wonderful summary of what has happened and is still happening. As in Atlantis, so still today. The Illuminati (Anunnaki) manipulate their bloodlines into positions of power – "the councils" – and take over those bodies for themselves. It is what we call possession. The rituals conducted by the Illuminati-controlled secret societies, like the Freemasons, Knights of Malta, Knights Templar, etc., are one way this is done. The top Illuminati bloodlines know who they are, but many of those lower down do not. These people, who unknowingly occupy a bloodline body, are invited into the secret society web and taken through "initiation" rituals that the vast majority of them do not begin to understand. These rituals, especially the more advanced ones, are designed to create a vibrational environment in which the fourth-dimensional reptilians can possess the body. As the initiate progresses through the levels, he undergoes ever more powerful rituals directed by the black arts, which, step by step, give the fourth-dimensional entity more power over the person's thought and emotional processes until the reptilian is in complete control. In other words "Slaying by their arts the chiefs of the kingdoms, taking their form and ruling o'er man." These are the people who become the presidents, prime ministers, banking and business tycoons, media owners, and others who run or administer the Anunnaki agenda, although the most powerfully reptilian are those who dictate from behind the scenes: "Sought they from the Kingdom of Shadows [lower fourth dimension], to destroy man, and rule in his place". Exactly.

Snake and sound

"Only by magic could they be discovered, only by sound could their faces be seen...But, know ye, the Masters were mighty in magic, able to lift the veil from the face of the serpent, able to send him back to his place. Came they to man and taught him the secret, the Word that only a man can pronounce; swift then they lifted the veil from the serpent and cast him forth from place among men."

I have learned from a number of sources that the key to lifting this "veil from the face of the serpent" is a sound frequency that disrobes the illusion of human form to reveal their reptilian nature. It resonates a vibration that prevents them from holding their "human" codes open. This same theme can be found in the movie, *They Live*, the creation of director, John Carpenter. If you follow his movie-making career it is obvious that this guy knows the score. *They Live*,[9] which I thoroughly recommend to get a visual feel for what I am saying, is about an extraterrestrial race that takes over the planet while hiding in human form. They control in exactly the same way as the Illuminati, through secret societies and mind conditioning. In the end, the heroes of the movie reveal the scam when they break the vibrational sound frequency that is maintaining the illusion that those in power are human. Immediately that vibration is destroyed, the president and others in power and influence shift into their true form and the people can see who is really ruling them. *They Live* is available through the Bookends section of my website. When we find the right sound frequency the same will happen among those in power today. When it does, can I be wherever the Windsors are, please?

"Seek not the kingdom of shadows, for evil will surely appear, for only the master of brightness shall conquer the shadow of fear...Know ye, O my brother, that fear is an obstacle great; be master of all in the brightness, the shadow will soon disappear. Hear ye, and heed my wisdom, the voice of LIGHT is clear, seek the valley of shadow and light only will appear."

Those who dabble in what has become known as the "occult" open themselves to manipulation by the lower fourth dimension, that home for many misguided, malevolent, entities, and the origin of the legends and tales of demons and "evil" spirits. In fact, the word "occult" has been given an unfairly bad name. It merely means "hidden" and the same knowledge can be used for good or ill. Again vibrations are the key. If you use the "occult" knowledge with love in your heart and with positive intent, you maintain a high vibration and so connect with that level of consciousness. If you use it without understanding (like those who play with ouija boards) or with ill intent, you connect yourself with the vibrational range that this represents – the lower fourth dimension. The emphasis in the tablets on living without fear is also a vital point. As I have been saying in my books, videos, and talks for many years, the world is controlled by fear. The fear of what others think of us; fear of death; fear of being alone; fear of poverty, fear for our families and children; fear of war. The list is endless. The emotion of fear resonates to the frequency range of the lower fourth dimension and so when we are consumed by fear we are much easier for the entities on that dimension to influence and control. So the Illuminati continually create situations, structures, and events, like wars, designed to keep the people in fear of so many kinds. Also, when we generate fear, that energy can be absorbed by the fourth-dimensional entities resonating to the same frequency and they use this increased power to recycle back against us in further control. Fear connects us to them and feeds them energy.

> "In ages past were they conquered by the Masters, driven below to the place whence they came. But some there were who remained, hidden in spaces and planes unknown to man. Live they in Atlantis as shadows, but at times they appeared among men. Aye, when the blood was offered, forth came they to dwell among men.
>
> " ...Out of the great deep were they called by the wisdom of earth-man, called for the purpose of gaining great power."

Some researchers suggest that this reptilian faction was banished from the Earth in the far distant past by closing the interdimensional "portals", which allowed them to move into this density very easily. These portals are points on the Earth's energy grid where the third and fourth dimensions can connect and these are often the places held most sacred by the ancients. The portals are similar in theme, if not detail, to the one featured in the film *Stargate*, which, you may recall, was the story of an ancient Egyptian people controlled by high-tech, extraterrestrial "gods". A theme of the Atlantis legends is that groups with the advanced knowledge began to use it malevolently and it was then that they re-opened the portals and allowed these fourth-dimensional beings to flood back into this reality. One major portal appears to be in the Caucasus Mountains in southern Russia/northern Turkey, a region that constantly comes up in my research. These important centres for the bloodlines and the Illuminati will also be connected to the underground settlements of their masters, also. The Satanists in their rituals summon these lower fourth-dimensional entities into their presence by creating the vibrational "doorways" that allow them to manifest. Words, colours, and symbols all vibrate energy – everything does – and the secret rituals use the combinations that have the required vibrational effect. This is why the Illuminati today conduct the same rituals to the same deities that the ancients did. They must do so because they include the necessary, word-colour-symbol, combinations to unlock the vibrational door. Researcher Alan Walton writes: "Some claim that the Crowleyan [Satanic] rituals and Montauk [technology] projects have been very useful to them in…tearing holes in the fabric of space-time that separates our dimension from theirs." I think that nuclear explosions since the 1950s have also had the effect of opening the "stargates".[10] As the Emerald Tablets say: "Yet, beware, the serpent still liveth in a place that is open, at times, to the world" (lower fourth dimension, accessed through the stargates); "Unseen they walk among thee in places where the rites have been said." (Illuminati rituals to open the stargates); "Again as time passes onward, shall they take the semblance of men" (which they have). The depiction of the "Devil" is very like the descriptions of the reptilian "royalty" known as the Draco and in the Biblical text the Devil/Satan is clearly said to have been reptilian. One example is this description in the Book of Revelation of St Michael, a Phoenician deity, defeating the dragon. The second paragraph here could easily be describing the sealing of the interdimensional portals through which the reptilians enter this dimension, the same theme you find in the Emerald Tablets. Or, just as easily, it could refer to the imprisonment of the serpent race within the Earth:

"And the great dragon was cast down, the old serpent, he that is called the Devil and Satan, the deceiver of the whole world; he was cast down to Earth and his angels were cast down with him.

"…And he laid hold on the dragon, the old serpent, which is the Devil and Satan, and bound him for a thousand years, and cast him into the abyss, and shut it, and sealed it over him, that he should deceive the nations no more." [11]

There were, and are, physical reptilians and other entities also within the Earth, as I outlined earlier, and this Biblical passage could relate to the references in the Emerald Tablets to the reptilians being "driven below to the place whence they came"…and…"Out of the great deep were they called…". It is said of the Nefilim and the giant Titans under their different names that they were banished into the Earth and out of the sunlight. One mind-controlled survivor says he learned that the reptilians were the first to colonise the Earth and that is why they consider it theirs. Credo Mutwa, from the African accounts, says precisely the same and I have heard this from many other sources. They suggest, along with other researchers, that another, more "human" group, arrived and won a surface battle with the reptilians who went underground to escape. This is one origin of the symbolism in the ancient theme of "Hell" and "Satan" being located underground. This more "human" group was the blue-eyed blonds. The mind control victim believes that this battle happened some 200,000 years ago. He adds:

"The original reptilians are coming back, they are here now, and the ones who remained on this planet developed their own little sub-culture, which went against what the overall plan was. And now they're afraid of their own people. There's a lot of scurrying around, if you want to call it that, to protect against the original population that's coming back and there's going to be a gigantic battle on this planet in the next few years. I think there's going to be war and the human-reptilian hybrids that are here are going to defend themselves against the originals, the true-breds."

These claims and the themes of the Emerald Tablets point yet again to an ancient conflict between reptilians and the Nordics from various locations in the galaxy. Maurice Doreal, who claims to have found the Emerald Tablets, said that after a lecture in California he was approached by two blond-haired, blue-eyed men who invited him to visit an underground city under Mount Shasta in northern California. Researchers and informants have called this city Telos, a Greek word that means "uttermost purpose". Doreal says that his visits to underground societies, especially a centre for ancient records under the Himalayas, showed him the true history of this planet. He says that ancestors of the Scandinavians once lived in a tropical region that is now the Gobi Desert in China-Mongolia. They developed a technological society that included nuclear energy and the flying machines the Vedic records call vimanas. These Nordics were constantly challenged by a race of reptilian shape-shifters based in the then sub-tropical Antarctica, Doreal says he learned. It is certainly true that the Pleiades (Nordics?) and Orion (reptilians?) are said in ancient texts to be, at least symbolically, associated with death and destruction on Earth. Antarctica is where, apparently, some Nazis fled after the war and there are many tales of an underground base there. Doreal says he was shown how these "chameleon" reptilians infiltrated human societies in their battle for control of the planet. One way these shape-shifters were exposed, he says, is by a language test. It was discovered that the reptilians found it impossible to pronounce the word "kin-in-i-gin". (Go on, I bet you can't resist it!)

Doreal says that in a desperate effort to stop the reptilians, the "Nordics" launched a "super weapon" at Antarctica. He suggests that the enormous explosion shook the Earth and made it wobble on its axis. The poles shifted and fantastic cataclysmic events ensued. Other reptilian colonies survived underground. One location, according to researcher, Alan Walton, could have been the caverns of "Patalas". Hindu tradition says this is a seven-levelled underground society stretching from Benares in India to Lake Manosarowar in Tibet. Walton says that some local people have allegedly encountered the reptilian "Nagas" in this region and seen their flying craft entering and leaving the mountains. Maurice Doreal says that the "Nordics" also moved much of their civilisation underground, especially into the underground networks known in the east as "Agharta".[12] The conflicts have continued between them, but there has also been collaboration between these reptilian peoples and factions of the Nordics. Robert E. Dickhoff in his book, *Agharta* (Health Research, U.S.A., 1996) tells of a Tibetan monk who learned that an alliance of reptilians and "human" black magicians were causing chaos and destruction in the surface societies by projecting malevolent energy fields into the peoples' minds, using what we call witchcraft – the manipulation of energy. Dickoff says that the monk led 400 warrior-monks into the caverns to do battle with this "serpent cult" of humans and reptilians.

This theme of a serpent cult battling with the Nordic "humans" can also be found in an ancient British work called the Edda, translated by L.A. Waddell in the first half of the 20th century. He knew nothing of extraterrestrial reptilians and Nordics, and yet his translations give much support to this ancient tussle for power on the planet. They also confirm another aspect of the Illuminati-reptilian ritual – the worship of their goddess.

SOURCES

1   Cathy O'Brien and Mark Phillips, *Trance-Formation Of America, The True Life Story Of A CIA Mind Control Slave* (Reality Marketing, PO Box 27740, Las Vegas, Nevada, 89126, 1995), pp 209 and 210. This book is available through the David Icke website and Bridge of Love, UK

2   *The Return Of The Serpents Of Wisdom*, p 41

3   *The Reptilian Agenda*, parts one and two, Credo Mutwa with David Icke, is available from Bridge of Love. See the back of the book

4   There is a longer list of Bohemian Grove participants in Fritz Springmeier's *Bloodlines Of The Illuminati*. This is available through Bookends on the David Icke website. Bohemian Grove list can be found between pages 479 to 505

5   Correspondence with the author

6   See article "Shape-shifting Polymer Gels" at *http://scientificamerican.com/news/110900/4.html*

7   Said in recorded conversations with the author

8   See *http://www.angelfire.com/ut/branton* and *http://www.reptilianagenda.com/*

9   *They Live* (Alive Films, 1988)

10 See *http://www.angelfire.com/ut/branton* and *http://www.reptilianagenda.com/*

11. Book of Revelation, chapter 12, verse 9 and chapter 20, verses 2 and 3

12 I found this story of Maurice Doreal's experiences on *http://www.angelfire.com/ut/branton*

CHAPTER 9

the dragon queens

If you tell the truth you don't have to remember anything.

Mark Twain

The Illuminati appear on the surface to be a male-dominated operation. But, in fact, the high priestess is as important in their rituals as the high priest and at the heart of Illuminati symbolism is the worship of the goddess – the serpent goddess.

The New Age movement wants a return of the "goddess" because it is equated with female energy and releasing women from suppression. On that level, so do I. But it is vital for New Agers and others to understand that this is not the "goddess" symbolism the Illuminati and their placemen talk about. They just want you to think it is. The serpent goddess is known under countless names around the world, including Diana, Artemis, Athene, Semiramis, Barati, Britannia, Hecate, Rhea, Persephone ("First Serpent") and so on. These same names have also been used to symbolise esoteric concepts like the phases of the Moon and female energy, but at its foundation this goddess worship of the Illuminati would seem to relate to the DNA transmitted through the female and possibly originating in the constellation of Orion. I have heard this DNA source symbolised in various cultures as the Dragon Queens, the Orion Queen or Queens, and the "Snake Mother". From what I am told by insiders and serious researchers, the full-blown reptilian society has its own version of queen bees, which produce the eggs from which the bloodlines and their offshoots, originate. Artemis, a key Illuminati goddess, is depicted with eggs all over her chest and she is associated with bees. One of the prime symbols of the Merovingian bloodline, so connected to Artemis/Diana worship, is the bee and the hive. You also find this symbolism in Freemasonry. The reptilians and greys have been described over and over by abductees and experiencers as having a kind of swarm or hive mentality, very much like bees, and they have worked to make the human race a mirror of that. Researcher Frans Kamp also came across this theme of the Orion Queen:

"The Bee-queen has a herd. The memories of the herd/swarm are transferred to them by the female/queen. A chemical substance/hormone 'pheromones' is required for this in the same way as melotonin is needed for more intuition [interdimensional connection]. The memories are the typical rules of behaviour of the herd. An animal is pure subconscious. He lives on intuition. We call that paranormal. We humans use our brains. We think that brains do everything. The rest is instinct. Well instinct is subconsious. Our DNA knows everything. Your DNA/subconscious keeps you alive, not your brains. As the Orion people are still animals in the fourth density, they are by their collective subconscious connected with each other by their queen. The Orion Queen. Every swarm has its own queen. She has the pure bloodline...the mitochondrial DNA is only transferred by women and is the strongest DNA there is." [1]

I have been told many times that the DNA carried by the female in the reptilian bloodlines is the most important to them and the symbolism of the "goddess" and the "serpent" have been linked since ancient times. Sir Laurence Gardner is a spokesman for the Imperial Royal Dragon Court and Order that represents the interests of the "Dragon bloodlines" seeded by the DNA of the "Dragon Queens". He says that this symbolism and the theme of the Dragon Queens goes back to the "founding mother" of the Anunnaki he calls Tiâmat, the Sea-dragon in Mesopotamian accounts. These queens, he suggests, were commonly represented as mermaids (amphibious/Sirius?), and were often called Ladies of the Lake (*see http://www.nexusmagazine.com/ringlords1.html*). Throughout the lands settled by the former Atlantean-Lemurian peoples you find the worship of the serpent goddess and her serpent son, who is often symbolised as a bull. James Churchward reveals from ancient tablets and artwork that Lemurians worshipped the goddess called "Queen Moo", and that Lemuria/Mu was called the "Motherland". Around the Mediterranean the priest-kings were known as the "Children of the Serpent Goddess".[2] In this same region, temples and Mystery schools were created in her name, most notably the Temple of Artemis/Diana at Ephesus in Turkey, one of the seven wonders of the ancient world. Turkey (formerly Asia Minor), Greece, and the islands of Samothrace, Cyprus, and Crete were among the main centres of the goddess cult. Samothrace, "the Sacred Isle", seems to have been the headquarters for this in the Mediterranean/Aegean region. Here the rites of the "Sisterhood of Daughters" of the Goddess Hecate were performed.[3] She was depicted with snake feet and snakes for hair.[4] Dogs, the sacred animal to Hecate, were sacrificed to her in these rituals during the dark phase of the Moon. This emphasis on the dog in Hecate myth could connect her symbolically to the "dog star" Sirius, a base for the reptilians. In Colchis, that ancient Egyptian settlement at the foot of the Caucasus Mountains, there was a cemetery sacred to Hecate. Jason of the Argonaut legends was said to have offered a sacrifice to Hecate at Colchis.[5] (Colches-ter is the oldest recorded town in England and its first Roman capital). The Illuminati Satanic network continues to perform sacrifice rituals to Hecate and this goddess was massively part of the symbolism surrounding the ritual murder of Princess Diana, as explained in *The Biggest Secret*. Indeed, Diana could well have been a sacrifice to Hecate, the triple-headed goddess with the symbolism of Sirius, Sirius B, and Sirius C. The name, Hecate, literally means "One Hundred".[6] Both Sirius B and C take 50 years to orbit Sirius A and the symbolism of one hundred, the duel orbit of "the twins", was often used as code for the Sirius system, according to Robert Temple in

Figure 18: *The United Nations is a wholly-owned subsidiary of the Illuminati. Its symbol includes the laurel leaves and the world in 33 sections – a constantly recurring esoteric number, as in the 33 degrees of the Scottish Rite of Freemasonry*

The Sirius Mystery. It is also important to note that, as Temple points out, the ancient Egyptian word and hieroglyph for goddess also means serpent, and their hieroglyph for Sirius also means tooth. Thus the stories of the "serpent's tooth" can be read as the "Goddess Sirius". The Egyptian word for tooth also means dog and, more specifically, dog-god and one hundred.[7]

The Minoan civilisation on Crete, part of the Sumer Empire, was another serpent-bull culture. They called its line of Aryan "Minos" kings the Sons of the Serpent Goddess because, once again, the Aryan line is the purest of the reptilian hybrids. These were the Serpent Kings who ruled Atlantis and the later Sumer Empire. Ancient Crete, as with other connected centres, was famous for its labyrinth, a word meaning "House of the Double Axe" or "House of the Serpent Goddess".[8] Greece was another serpent goddess culture. They called her Athene and at Delphi, the Oracles (inter-dimensional channellers) would speak the words of the serpent goddess, known there as Delphinia.[9] The Oracle would go into a trance state while staring into the eyes of a snake. She would also use cannabis and chew laurel leaves, the sacred herb of the goddess or "pythoness". The laurel leaves are used by the Illuminati in the symbol of Freemasonry and the logo of United Nations, in which they frame an Earth broken into an esoterically significant 33 segments (*Figure 18*). Pythagoras, the famous Greek hero and mathematician, grew up in the mysteries of the serpent goddess cult and his very name means "I am the Python" or "I am the Serpent".

DNA of the dragon queens

The author, Sir Laurence Gardner, says that the ancient Imperial Royal Dragon Court and Order can first be identified as the Dragon Court of ancient Egypt under the patronage of the priest-prince Ankhfn-khonsu in about 2170BC. It later became a "pharaonic institution" thanks to Queen Sobeknefru (c.1785-82BC) and operated as a sort of "royal academy", a "unique assembly of science and scholarship". That's according to its official website, anyway (*http://www.mediaquest.co.uk/RDCsite/RDChome.htm*). The Dragon Court was re-launched in the 15th century as the Hungarian Court of the Dragon and was strongly connected with "Dracula". Gardner calls himself "Chevalier de Saint Germain and Attaché to the Grand Protectorate of The Imperial and Royal Dragon Court and Order – Ordo Dragonis, Sárkány Rend, 1408". He loves titles, old Larry. He has written a number of books, including *Bloodline Of The Holy Grail* (Element Books, Shaftesbury, Dorset, 1996), in which he claims that the Merovingians and their offshoots, like the British House of Stuart, were seeded by Jesus and Mary

Magdalene. This is not the case, as we'll see, although there could be some *symbolic* truths in the theme of a "Jesus" and "Mary" bloodline. Gardner, in my view, knows far more than he is telling, although, if you read between the lines, he's already telling quite a lot. He has been given great prominence by the Australia-based *Nexus* magazine, which claims to expose how the world is manipulated.

Gardner says that bloodlines (the "Dragon Kings") were specially conceived by the Anunnaki to rule on their behalf. He says that they drank menstrual blood known as Star Fire, but he doesn't mention the blood they drink from the victims of human sacrifice right to this day. The drinking of menstrual blood, symbolised as "red mead" or "red wine", goes back to the dawn of history and many ancient calendars were based on the Moon-menstrual cycle. The Greeks called it Ambrosia ("supernatural red wine" of the goddess Hera), while in India it was Soma (the food of the gods) and in Persia, haoma. They believed the menstrual blood was sacred and the life essence that could bring immortality. Sir Laurence Gardner calls the Anunnaki bloodlines the "dragon bloodlines", but claims that this derives only from the use of crocodile fat in the royal ceremonies of ancient Egypt. Right, Larry, and I can hang by my willy from a hot air balloon. He dismisses any idea that these bloodlines are reptilian shape-shifters, although he acknowledges that such claims were made in ancient times. He said in a *Nexus* magazine article that he found it hard to imagine that anyone (i.e. me) could still believe such stories in these more enlightened times. Mmmm. The records of Sumer, Gardner says, reveal that the Anunnaki had a "creation chamber" to produce these "royal" bloodlines and he says that the senior line of descent was determined by the "Mitochondrial DNA of the Dragon Queens". Gardner talks of the "Blood Royal" or Sang Graal in the "womb of the Dragon Queen". Other texts in France called this bloodline, "Le Serpent Rouge" – the red serpent or the serpent blood.[10] The female or "goddess" DNA is most definitely the key here.

Rennes-le-chateau

The Cathars or Albigensians, who were slaughtered by the Roman Church in the 13th century, were supporters of the "elven" or dragon bloodline, according to Gardner. A female elf was called an elbe, he says, and this is the inspiration for Albi, the main city of the Cathars or Aligensians, in their stronghold in the Languedoc region of southern France. "Gens", as we saw earlier, relates to tribe and is used to this day as a code for the bloodlines. The Cathars appeared to be close to the Knights Templar, who also had a major presence in that same area around the mysterious mountain-top village of Rennes-le-Chateau. Could this mountain have been an inner-earth entrance to a reptilian base? It certainly seems to be an interdimensional doorway. I have been all around there and the whole area has a very strange vibe. The horrific slaughter of the Cathars by armies of Pope Innocent III and the Roman Church ended with the siege of their mountain-top fortress at Montsegur in 1244. Gardner's contention is that the Roman Church destroyed the "dragon" succession when it removed the Merovingians from power in the 8th century and began to appoint its own monarchs, including Charlemagne, in what later became France. Gardner says that the church also suppressed the female and worship of the "goddess" (Dragon Queen) with its male-dominated religion.[11] I beg to differ. We shall see that while the Roman Church and Christianity in general is an *outwardly* male religion, it is secretly a continuation of pagan goddess worship. Also, the reptilian bloodlines constantly fight with each other for power, and the Roman Church, Charlemagne, and the Merovingians were different expressions of the same reptilian bloodlines battling with each other to be top dog – as usual.

The British Edda

The story of a battle between the Nordics and a reptilian force for control of the planet is told in some considerable detail in the Edda, the epic ancient British account of the events in Sumer and elsewhere, translated by L.A. Waddell. The emphasis by the serpent cult on the female is also confirmed. The Edda text was found in Iceland in the 12th century and was believed by scholars to be of Icelandic and Scandinavian origin. Waddell reveals in his book, British Edda (Christian Book Club, California, 1929) that it is actually written in Old Briton, a language closely linked to Old English, Anglo-Saxon, and Eastern Gothic. And Gothic came from the Sumerian, which came from Atlantis/Lemuria. The Edda is not of Icelandic origin, but British.[12] It was taken to Iceland, it appears, by settlers from Scotland, Orkney, the Hebrides, and North Britain. Among them were the Culdees, who had their headquarters at St Andrews in Scotland, an area with strong Illuminati connections to this day.[13] The "Culdees" came from "Chaldees", a people who followed the Sumer Empire in Mesopotamia and worshipped the mother-son cult in which they claimed that God's son had died to save them. This was long before Christianity. And, of course, these northern lands of Europe were the realms of the Nordics who went south to the Near and Middle East thousands of years ago before returning as the "Sumerians", the "Phoenicians", and the "Egyptians". Scholars have misrepresented the Edda, not least because an Icelander called Snorri Sturlason (1179-1241) included his translations of this text in his own work. This led to the erroneous idea that he had compiled it. But he merely used sections from it and mistranslated them to a large extent. He mistook the titles and personal names of the same person to be names of different people and the whole meaning was lost.[14] Waddell again used his knowledge of ancient languages to retranslate the Edda and he says it tells the story of events in ancient Troy and Cappadocia, both now in Turkey, and the Danube Valley in Europe. These events and their heroes and villains became foundations for myths and legends throughout the former Sumer Empire and later entered the texts that became the Bible.

You are going to be hit by a stream of names, symbols, and connections in this chapter. You might get a headache in the next few minutes, but understanding how different names and titles refer to the *same* people can unlock so many mysteries. The themes running through this chapter and the names, titles, and symbols I will introduce, are: (a) the battle between the "Nordics" and the reptilians or serpent cult; (b) the interbreeding between the Nordic and reptilian bloodlines; and (c) the fundamental importance of the goddess to the reptilians. L.A. Waddell first began to see the connections between apparently unconnected people and events during his early days in India while studying Hindu history and mythology. He noticed that Eindri, the name used in the Edda text for the European and Norse "god" called Thor, was remarkably close to the Hindu god, Indra. The Indian Vedas, which were inspired by the Lemurian and Sumerian legends and accounts, describe Indra as tall, fair, invincible, and armed with a bolt. This is how Eindri or Thor is described in the Edda and Waddell concluded from considerable research that the European god, Thor, and the Hindu god, Indra, were the same person, and that this guy was also the first "Aryan" king of Sumer. The Vedas connect Indra to the Greek god Zeus, also known as Jupiter. Some Sanskrit scholars regarded Indra as the same as Jupiter and suggested that he was a heroic human king who had led the early Aryans or "Nordics" to victory against the "serpent cult". Waddell produces a stream of evidence to show that the Hindu god, Indra, and the European, Thor, after whom we get Thursday or "Thors-day", are the same person or deity. He also says that the legend of Thor is the origin of the legends of King Arthur. Thor is known in the Edda as Her-Thor, which became Ar-Thur. Both Her and Ar come from the same root meaning…Aryan.[15] The mist began to clear even further when Waddell observed that the name of the first Aryan king of the Sumerians in ancient Mesopotamia had the name of Indara, In Dur, In-Tur, or King Tur.[16] This, Waddell says, later became Thor of northern Europe and Prometheus of the Greeks. Indara was the traditional founder of civilisation and was deified by the Sumerians.[17] He was said to have defeated the demons and slayed the serpent-dragon and the "giants", and his Sumerian titles are identical in the Sumerian and the Edda, where he appears as Eindri or Thor. Like Thor, Indara was also portrayed with a hammer by the Sumerians. The fairy story of Jack and the Beanstalk or Jack the Giant Slayer comes from the tales of Indara/Thor. A title for Thor in the Edda is Sig or Ygg, which, in Sumerian and Cappadocian inscriptions, is spelt Zagg or Zakh. This is the origin of the modern name, Jack.[18] Waddell writes of Indara:

> "The Sumerian records regarding him date continuously back to the inscription on his sacred trophy bowl or Holy Grail by his great-grandson, about 3245BC. …They contain fairly full details of the personality and exploits of himself, his queen and son-champion knight, and his warrior-clan of Guts or Goths, with their portraits chiselled on stone and engraved on their sacred seals, representing them as wearing horned hats like the European Goths, Ancient Britons and Anglo-Saxons, and like the Eddic heroes in medieval art. The goat and deer metaphors, pictographic of his name, are freely applied to him by the Sumerians and the Hittites, just as they are to Thor in the Edda. And his capture and consecration of the sacred bowl or Holy Grail is in agreement with that by Thor or Her-Thor (Arthur) in the Edda. Indra's sacred Rowan tree, guarded by goats, is pictured by the Sumerians and the Nordic-Aryan Hittites and Cappadocians and this is precisely described as Thor's 'Ygg-drasill' Rowan tree in the Edda."[19]

Waddell presents more than 100 seals and sculptures from Sumer and the Hittites that portray scenes described in the British Edda. He says he could have

Figure 19: *This image of Thor or Dar defeating the symbolic lions of Phrygia ("The Land of the Lions") was carved in ivory on the handle of a knife around 3350BC*

published 300. There is no doubt, he says, that King Thor or Arthur were other names for the first historical Sumerian king, Indara. Later renditions of the King Arthur story lost these connections and became an invented, though highly symbolic, fable. In Egypt, Waddell says, Indara (Thor) was known by the title of Asari, which became Osiris, the leading deity in the Egyptian worship of the Sun. Osiris was often depicted as a blue-eyed Aryan, just as Indara was. King Indara, Dur or Tur of Sumer, Indra of India, Thor or Eindri or Andvara (Andrew) of the Edda, Osiris of Egypt, and the original version of King Arthur, are all the same person, Waddell contends. So, he says, is Dar-Danos, the first king of Troy in Homer's Iliad. Thor was known as Dan and from this same root you get Danube and Danmark, the Danish spelling for Denmark. The name relates to the Danaans, who originated in Atlantis. The British Israelite movement claims that the "lost tribes of Israel", especially the Tribe of Dan, moved out of the Middle East and settled in the British Isles and Europe. This, they claim, led to the names Danube and Danmark and therefore makes the British, and their genetic kin, God's "chosen people". They have, however, completely lost the plot, I would suggest, not least because they are obsessed with the idea that the Bible is accurate. It is not! The Edda says that Thor (Dan) and his Aryans went *from* Europe in the first place to settle in Turkey and Mesopotamia and found the civilisation of Sumer. That is precisely what happened, as I indicated earlier. It also says that the Aryans of the Danube Valley were already well in advance of the rest of the world before they went down to Mesopotamia.[20] The Danube Valley is very significant to the bloodlines. The Danube is the second longest river in Europe and runs from Germany through Romania ("Dracula" country) and into the Black Sea. The Edda says that Thor fought and defeated the serpent worshippers of Phrygia (in Turkey), a word that comes from the Sumerian name, Firig or Pirig, and it means literally "Land of the Lions".[21] Thor is depicted on ancient carvings symbolically fighting and taming "lions" in this battle with the Phrygians (*Figure 19*) and so we have the symbolic Hebrew story of *Dan*-iel taming the lion. Thor was also "Midas", the king who turned everything into gold with the "Midas touch".[22] His victory over the Phrygians was commemorated in those ancient lands in a monument known as the Tomb of Midas, although it is not actually a tomb. On it are nine enormous crosses of St George (another name for Thor-Indara) and dates to about 1000BC.[23]

The red cross

One of the common themes from Lemuria, Atlantis, through Sumer, to the present day Illuminati, is the use of the Sun Cross as a symbol. This cross is the origin of the Christian cross with "Jesus", as we shall see, symbolising the Sun at the centre. The Sun-Cross, or Red Cross, was found drawn in red pigment in the alleged "tomb" of the Sumerian-Egyptian emperor, Menes, Waddell says. This is the same symbol that became the "Cross of St George" and later the flag of England after Sumerian-Phoenicians settled there. The red Sun-Cross is also the symbol of the Knights Templar secret society which has played a major role in the story of the bloodlines over hundreds of years and, of course, it is the logo of the Red Cross organisation, which, as I outline in *The Biggest Secret*, is an Illuminati creation to allow them to manipulate within countries during wars and other events behind the cover of humanitarian aid. The vast majority of genuine Red Cross workers are not aware of this. The Red Cross was also flown on the ships of Christopher Columbus, an Illuminati frontman, whom historians still insist discovered the Americas. The Red Cross or Sun-Cross was originally written as a T and this became the "T-square" of Freemasonry, or the Tau cross. The splayed cross known as the Maltese Cross, so beloved of British royalty, was also found depicted in caves within this same Sumer Empire. This is today the symbol of the Knights of Malta (formerly the Knights Hospitaller of St John of Jerusalem and the Knights of Rhodes). The Knights of Malta are another elite and extremely sinister secret society and they have been around for the same period as the Knights Templar. The ruling bloodlines and their secret society web, the Illuminati, are obsessed with symbolism and ritual and, as I have indicated, they use the same symbols and ceremonies today that their ancestors did who ruled the Sumer Empire, Atlantis, and Lemuria.

The serpent trinity

The Edda tells the story of how Thor-Indara fought a constant battle with the serpent cult. The text equates "St George", the dragon-slayer of Cappadocia (Turkey), with the European god, Thor, who was also a "dragon-slayer". Both were said to have fought the "serpent dragons of the abyss" – their underground cavern systems and bases? In the Edda, the serpent cult engages in human sacrifice and blood drinking. Same old story, and again we see the theme of the Nordics or "Aryans" in conflict with the serpent people. The Edda says there were three main leaders of this serpent cult. They were the serpent goddess known as El; her consort, the male entity called Wodan (Votan was the Atlantean fire god); and their son, Baldr or Balder. This was the serpent "trinity" of mother-father-son. El was also known as Eldi or "Fiery El", the "Hound", and, highly significantly, as "Mary".[24] From this cult and "Fiery El" came the term Hell, "burning in Hell" and "fires of Hell." El or Hel was the Norse queen of the underworld and her followers became known as "kinsman of Hel".[25] In Medieval times, this was symbolised as the "Harlequin", the lover of the maiden Columbine-the-Dove. Columba, Columbine, and the symbol of the dove are all other names and symbols for El, the serpent or dragon queen of the Edda. The more I research, the more the world that exists under our feet becomes increasingly significant. The underground "Hell" is supposed to be the place of judgement and eternal punishment where the "Devil" and evil spirits dwell beneath the Earth. The longer we go on, the more you will see how relevant this is to the races and bloodlines that manipulate this world. El is the Hebrew name for "God" and she was also known as Heidi and Ida. The Elohim, the gods of the Old Testament, were the race of El, a dragon queen. The Greeks knew El as Artemis, the cruel mother-goddess who demanded human sacrifice. Artemis (also known as Diana) was the major deity of the Merovingians. Artemis was symbolised with bees, as is the Merovingian bloodline. It is the same with other versions of the goddess like Demeter, the "pure mother bee", and a symbol of Aphrodite was a golden honeycomb. Her priestess was given the name Melissa, or "Queen Bee". The word honeymoon comes from this. It spanned a lunar month, normally in May, which was named after the Virgin Maya, another version of El. The honeymoon would include the menstrual period of the bride and the combination of menstrual blood and honey was once thought to be the elixir of life. El is also the inspiration for the children's stories of Mother Hubbard or "Mother Hubur", as she was to the Babylonians. Mother Hubbard was distressed because she couldn't find a bone for her dog (a domesticated wolf). Mother Hubur, also Tiawath, was described as the "Plague, the Fearful Dragon, the Dragon which shines brightly, the female spirit who devours with a serpent's mouth". The other members of the serpent trinity in the Edda, consort Wodan and son Balder, were major "gods" of the reptilian-controlled Nazis. The Nazis were the creation of the Teutonic Knights network (Illuminati) in Germany which has always been associated with the highly significant reptilian bloodline known as the Habsburgs. The Teutonic Knights operated in the same "Holy Land" in the same period as the Knights Templar and the Knights of Malta and they work to the same reptilian agenda. Wodan and Balder were national deities of the Teutons. The legendary founder of the Maya culture in Mexico was also called Votan or Wotan.

The Amazons

The Edda refers to the serpent cult as the "Amazons", the "Wolf Tribe", and the "Valkyrs", and here we have the meaning of the musical work called *The Ride Of The Valkeries*, composed by Richard Wagner. Hitler once said that to understand the Nazis, you must understand Wagner. The Amazons in ancient myth were a tribe of warrior women who expressed the characteristics traditionally associated with men. The legend is rampant in Greek mythology, which was inherited from Sumerian mythology, and the Amazons were known as the Valkeries in northern Europe, the warrior-maidens from Valhalla. The Greek historian, Herodotus, said the Amazons were enemies of the Greeks and he claimed that they lived in the steppelands of the Ukraine and southern Russia, once known as Scythia and Sauromatia (sauro = lizard and mater = mother). Other areas claimed for their homeland are Lycia, Phrygia, and Cappadocia, all of which are named in the Edda accounts, and Taurus, Lemnos and Lebos, hence lesbian. The foothills of the

Caucasus Mountains in southern Russia was a major location for the Amazons and this would seem to have been a major centre for the interbreeding of the Nordics with the reptilian bloodlines. Libya is another place of Amazon legend and in those days Libya referred to the whole of North Africa, except for Egypt. The Amazon River and region in South America was named after these women when a Portuguese explorer in the 16th century found fighting women there. Legends and accounts depict the Amazons as a nomadic people dominated by women and they appeared to be extremely ritualistic. Strabo, the Greek geographer, said they would only "mate" during a special two-month period, just like animals do. Sex was strictly for the production of children.[26] Among the gods and goddesses they worshipped was once again Artemis, a later name for "El" of the Edda texts, and Hecate, the dark Moon goddess and "goddess of the Infernal Arts". It appears that Amazon means "Moon Woman" and this again fits with the Edda texts about the serpent cult.

A very important location for the Amazons was Sauromatia, or "Lizard Mother". This is in the region of the Black and Caspian Seas and bordered the Persian Empire, the land of the Magi initiates. Sauromatia has been connected to European nobility and we can now see why. One theory is that the coats of arms of Polish nobility, for instance, developed from magical signs of the Sauromatians or Sarmatians called "tamgas". In fact, Poland was often called Sarmatia or Sauromatia.[27] Historical accounts say that the Amazons in Sauromatia bred with Scythian warriors. The Scythians were a Nordic-Aryan people who moved into northern Europe from the Near and Middle East through the Caucasus Mountains and Sauromatia, and they included the bloodlines that became the Sicambrian Franks and…the Merovingians. Once again we have the theme of Nordic-reptilian interbreeding. The fusion of the Amazon and Scythian language became known as Sauromatian. The Scythians worshipped the same goddess as the Amazons. They castrated themselves and wore women's clothing as part of their ritual to the goddess known by the Greeks as Artemis. One location for the Scythians was called Partia or "Virginland" in deference to their goddess and when the Illuminati moved in on America they used the same symbolism in naming Virginia. The idea that it was named after Elizabeth Ist, the "virgin queen", is ludicrous. First of all, she was no more a virgin than Madonna. The Scythians were governed by priestess-queens, who tended to be older women. In 1954 five kurgans or "queen-graves" were found in southern Russia at Pasyryk. These priest-queens performed sacrifices and caught the blood in "sacred cauldrons", and went with the men into battle and cast spells for victory. This again fits with the Edda texts and is almost certainly the origin of the witches in "Shakespeare's" *Macbeth*. In the Celtic legends the cauldron is associated with the underground world and has been symbolically connected to the womb of the "death-goddess". Using this theme, children of the bloodlines come "out of the cauldron" – the womb of the women who carry "royal blood", the reptilian DNA. The Moon-sickle used by the Scythians, the mythical weapon that castrated the gods, became known as the scythe and was associated with the "grim reaper". Yet again the grim reaper refers to a goddess, Rhea, who was clothed in a garment of blood and devoured all of her offspring, the gods. She became the Celtic goddess Rhiannon. Eire, the Celtic name for Ireland, comes from the name of the goddess Erinn, a form of Hera or Rhea.

The Berber people of North Africa have been associated with the Amazons and still call themselves Amazigh. The Amazons included a tribe called the Neuri, who "turned themselves into wolves." The term "Wolf tribe" is associated with goddess worship or the She-Wolf. This is probably a version of dog-star worship – Sirius. Credo Mutwa says that the Zulu peoples have long called Sirius the "Star of the Wolf" and their ancient accounts say that a "sea-dwelling fish people" from Sirius came to the Earth. They looked pretty human, but had skin like a reptile, he says. Interestingly, the Edda reveals that the forbears of the Nordic peoples under the leadership of Thor-Indara were also members of the "The Seafaring Wolf Tribe". An Irish tribe in Ossory were said to become wolf people while attending the Yuletide feast or ritual, and they devoured the flesh of cattle as wolves before regaining their human shape. This could all be symbolic or it could be connected to the phenomena of the "werewolf" which, according to some former Satanists, do exist. The legends of the "Troll" or "Trulli" demons also appear to be associated with the Amazons or Valkeries. This is the root of the word, Trull, which means loose woman and the Troll could have been a Pagan "Hag" or Earth-priestess. Norse myth says that the trolls waited under bridges waiting to eat those who crossed without making an offering. The Valkeries were said to guard the bridge to heaven or the "Bifrost". Angels of Death were said to attend a ritual called the trolla-thing.

Woden's day

Wodan was the consort of the dragon queen, El, according to the Edda, and he is a major figure in ancient myths. One of the older names for Wodan (also Wotan or Woden) is Bodo or Bauta. This corresponds with the Sumerian name of Budu, Butu, or Budun, which means "The Serpent Footed".[28] In Waddell's translation of the Edda, Wodan was an aboriginal chief of a Moon and Serpent-Dragon cult seeking to defeat the Nordic-Aryans of Thor-Indara. We find the same story in the Indian Vedas attributed to Indra, their name for Thor-Indara, who was said to have battled with Budhnya or "The Bottom". Budhnya was known as "The Great Serpent of the Bottom or Deep."[29] This was the Puthon or Python of the Greeks, says Waddell. Budhnya and Wodan are the same character. In India, Wednesday or "Wodens-day" is known as Budh![30] Interesting how close that is to Buddha, and, according to Waddell, Buddha is a derivative of Woden and Buddha claimed to have had several "former births" as a serpent. The Indian Brahmans adopted the Moon and serpent cult. So too, according to Waddell, did the "Semitic priests of the Nile Valley".[31] He says that they replaced the original Sun worship of Asar or Osiris and deliberately introduced the serpent and sacrificial cult to Egyptian culture. Balder, who is El and Wodan's malicious son in the Edda, corresponds with the Green Man of the King Arthur legend and Loki, the original of Lucifer, according to Waddell. He says that Balder is also Lancelot in the Arthur stories from his title in the Edda of "The Lance-bearer". Like his mother, El, Balder has been depicted with wings.

The mother-son cult of the serpent

Scene one in the Edda portrays a world awash with the violence, human sacrifice, and blood-drinking rituals of "the Mother-Son cult of the Serpent-Dragon". Scene two sees the arrival of the great reformer, the tall, red-bearded, Eindri or Thor (Indara), who brought civilisation (*see picture section*). Waddell believes that he is also the origin of Adam and this part of the story, he says, is massively misrepresented in the Adam and Eve, Garden of Eden story in the Hebrew Old Testament. I think there is a lot more to the Adam and Eve story and what it represents than this, however, and I think if Waddell had been alive today he would have accepted that himself. I feel the Edda accounts include symbolic, as well as literal, accounts and some originated in Lemuria. "Adam", as Thor/Indara, fought the serpent cult of the "Edenites", Waddell's translations of the Edda say. If the serpent worshippers were operating in Mesopotamia before the Nordics arrived, it would certainly explain why the Ubaid culture, which preceded Sumer in the same area, buried their dead with figurines of serpent humanoids (*see picture section*). Waddell's translation of the Edda tells of how Thor, the "dragon-slayer", established his capital in Cappadocia under the name "St George of the Red Cross" and thus we have the origin of St George of Cappadocia, later of England.[32] This was Thor/Indara yet again, says Waddell, and so was St Andrew, the patron saint of Scotland, which came from Andvara or Andvari, another name for Thor. The story of George defeating the dragon can be found all over the world in various forms. In Egypt, "George" was the Sun god, Ra (Thor/Indara, says Waddell); in India it was Indra (Thor/Indara); and in the Hebrew Old Testament, it was Adam, under his title, Ia or Jah, who slayed the serpent.[33] Thor or "Goer" (George) killed El, the Matriarch of the serpent cult, the Edda tells us, and she was symbolised as the "serpent-dragon". Thus "George" (Thor) defeated "the dragon" (El). The story of George and the Dragon symbolises the battles with the reptilians located under the Earth. The accounts in the British Edda are confirmed in great detail by depictions all over the former Sumer Empire. In a Babylonian seal dated to around 3300BC, El is pictured with the crescent moon of the serpent cult and Wodan is given the body of a serpent. Satanists worship the reptilians and also the Moon, and have always done so. The inscription behind El in this Babylonian seal reads Ildi or "Il-the-Shining", yet another confirmation of the portrayal of reptilians as "shining" or "luminous" in some way. El or Ida is given the title of Rann in the Edda and this is the origin of the nursing serpent mother and matriarch, Rann-t, in Egyptian myth, or vice versa.[34]

Serpent cult symbolism

The obsession with Troy and the Trojan War by descendants of the Merovingian bloodline can be understood when you read the Edda. It tells of how Thor's Troy was raided by the "Edenite" serpent cult led by Wodan. The Phrygians were serpent worshippers before their defeat by Thor, and totems of the serpent cult were the lion and the wolf. This is why Phrygia means "Land of the Lions". Still today the Illuminati use the lion profusely in their symbolism – look at Britain and the British

Figure 20: *The highly symbolic royal crest depicting the lion (the serpent cult/Illuminati) and the chained and tethered unicorn (Nordics/humanity)*

Figure 21: *The crest of the reptilian House of Rothschild is a mass of Illuminati symbolism and remarkably similar to the royal crest*

Figure 22: *The crest of the City of London, one of the most significant Illuminati centres in the world. The two flying reptiles hold (control) the cross of St George. I took this picture at Burnham Beeches*

royal family alone. This same serpent cult described in the Edda continues to manipulate the world to this day. We call it the Illuminati. The British royal family are reptilian "host" (possessed) entities who work for the serpent cult/ Illuminati and we can now see the true symbolism of the royal crest with the lion facing a chained unicorn (*Figure 20*). The symbol of Thor/Indara and his Nordics was the goat and this later evolved into the unicorn.[35] Thus we have the symbolism of the lion (serpent cult) controlling and imprisoning the tethered human race and their great enemies, the Nordics (unicorn). Notice also the great similarity between the royal crest and that of the House of Rothschild, complete with lion, unicorn and fleur-de-lis (*Figure 21*). The Greek hero Prometheus is a version of Thor/Indara/Adam, according to Waddell, and he is depicted in chains being tortured by the "gods" (reptilians) for trying to educate humanity and give them "illumination". He is often depicted holding the flame of knowledge. The coat of arms of the City of London, one of the global centres for the serpent cult today, is the St George's Cross being held (owned, controlled) by two flying reptiles (*Figure 22*). When you drive into the City alongside the River Thames, you pass two flying reptiles holding the Cross of St George (*see picture section*). As I mentioned before, the reptilian Rockefeller bloodline has placed a gold statue of Prometheus in the Rockefeller Centre in New York (*Figure 23*). The heraldry and coats of arms of Poland are another example. They include the images found among all European royalty and aristocracy – the openly reptilian serpent, griffin, salamander, and caduceus, plus the sphinx and unicorn.[36]

Rule Britannia

The accounts in the Edda of the battles between the Nordics of Thor/Indara and the serpent cult of El, Wodan, and Balder, can explain many ancient and modern mysteries, symbols, and Biblical texts (*Figure 24*). The Edda tells how

Figure 23: The gold statue of Prometheus with the flame of illumination at the Rockefeller Center in New York

Thor/Indara and the Nordic/Aryans came down from the Danube region of Europe into the domain of the serpent cult in the Near and Middle East, especially the place known as Eden. After many battles between the Nordics and the serpent cult a peace treaty was agreed between the entity known as Thor/Indara/ Adam and the leaders of the serpent cult, El, Wodan, and Balder, the Edda tells us. There is a portrayal of a meeting between Thor/Indara and El on a Babylonian seal of about 3000BC. The "peace treaty" also led to the marriage between Thor/Indara/Adam and a priestess of the serpent cult known as "Eve" or "Gunn-Ifa, the Edda says. The story of the marriage of Her-Thor (Ar-Thur) and his "queen" Guin-EVE-re, is a version of this, Waddell suggests.[37] He adds that "Eve", despite being the "chief vestal priestess" of the serpent cult of Eden, was, nevertheless, a Gothic "Aryan". However, the Edda says that she was a "ward" of El and "born of the Sea-froth or Seafoam kin". She was later represented by the Greeks as "Aphrodite" or "Sea-Froth", and Aphrodite was said to be born from the sea – the amphibious Anunnaki? The constant connection of the goddess with the sea can be seen with the Phoenician Barati, who became the British "Britannia". The famous British song "Rule Britannia, Britannia rules the waves" is not about Britain, but the ancient goddess, which, under different names, has been worshipped by the Illuminati since ancient times. The sea-faring Wolf Tribe, from which the Edda says the Aryans were also descended, was the serpent cult. Eve herself is described in the Edda as an "Amazonian" and a "Valkyr", the same

Figure 24: Thor/Indara/George fights with Balder, whose legs are symbolically depicted as serpents

as the other serpent worshippers. So could it be that this marriage of "Adam" and "Eve" in the Edda was symbolic of the interbreeding between those of the Nordic and reptilian bloodlines that became known as the "Aryans" and the "serpent kings"? Their wedding procession described in the Edda can be seen on Hittite rock sculptures dating to around 3000BC in King

Figure 25: *The wedding of Thor ("Adam") and Eve from a rock sculpture near Pteria dating from about 3,000BC. Thor's totem of the goat/unicorn can be seen beside both him and Eve. Balder with the double axe is riding the cat-like creature*

Thor/Indara/Adam's old capital of Pteria, which is now Bogaz Koi in Turkey (*Figure 25*). "Adam and Eve" are depicted exchanging a cross-like emblem and a "globe" object, which Waddell says is an apple from the rowan or mountain ash tree. This tree was Thor/Indara/Adam's symbol for his "Tree of Knowledge" and the apple from this tree could be the one in the Garden of Eden story, the "forbidden fruit", he says. In the Edda, the serpent leader, El, taunts Eve for changing sides and becoming a priestess "of the Rowan". The Edda refers to Eve as "Idun", who dispenses life-giving apples to the Goths from their sacred tree. Idun was Adueni or Atueni to the Sumerians and this later became Athene, mother goddess of the Greeks (*Figure 26*).

The Levite fairy tales

Waddell says the Levite priests of the Hebrews took this symbolism and produced the make-believe story of Adam and Eve with the serpent in the Garden of Eden in which they were punished for eating from the Tree of Knowledge, the rowan tree, symbolic of the Nordic religion. The Levites were serpent worshippers of El and the Old Testament gods, the Elohim, were the reptilians of the serpent cult. The Edda also refers to the serpent cult as the Valkyrs of Ur and the Levites made their invented character of Abraham hail from "Ur of the Chaldees". The Chaldeans were serpent worshippers, the Valkyrs. El also came from Ur according to the Edda, and she was known as Hrimni in the Edda and Ahriman, or "Great Serpent" by the Persians. This is fascinatingly close to the Biblical "Abraham". They associated Ahriman with Aeshma. He was the origin of Asmodeus, the Christian demon accused of possessing nuns and young women to make them lustful.[38] Asmodeus is also the "devil" character mysteriously placed at the entrance to the church at Rennes-le-Chateau in Provence, southern France, which is a mass of Illuminati symbolism and includes references to the Priory of Sion, the secret society of the Merovingians. The little church at Rennes-le-Chateau is dedicated to Mary Magdelene, a symbolic name for the reptilian bloodlines passing through the female line – the Dragon Queens like El. I have heard that MAG is a code for the reptilian

Figure 26: *The Sumerian goddess Adueni or Atueni depicted as Athene in a Greek vase painting of the 5th centuryBC. She is dressed as a warrior goddess of the Amazons or Valkyries. Note the snakes around her shoulders and the mass of swastikas on the robe*

bloodlines passed through the female DNA and that MAG relates to queen. The church at Rennes-le-Chateau was redesigned in the late 1800s by the priest Abbe Sauniere, who became extremely rich after discovering coded manuscripts and other artefacts. The story is told at length in *The Biggest Secret*.

Cain and Abel?

The Edda describes how Thor/Adam/Indara and "Eve" had a son called Gunn, Ginn, or Kon. This is the Biblical "Cain" and "Gawain" of the King Arthur stories, Waddell contends. In Babylonian seals dated to before 2500BC, he is called "Adamu-the-son-of-the-god-Induru". Gunn or "Cain" was attacked and wounded in the Edda narrative by Baldr or Balder, the son of the serpent cult leaders, Wodan and El. Balder is the same guy as the Biblical "Abel", Waddell says, and the Edda refers to him as Epli, which equates with the Hebrew E-b-l, and his Sumerian title was Ibil or Bal (the Hebrew Baal, says Waddell). Baal worship would therefore be serpent worship. Another name for Balder was Egil and this is almost identical to Egel, the Hebrew for "a bull calf" and the "Golden Calf" worshipped in the Old Testament.[39] "Golden Calf" worship = serpent worship? Balder was symbolised as a bull or steer and became the "Steer god" of Israel or Isra – El. He is referred to in the Edda as the "Steer of Eden". Balder is also called "the young Hydra". In Greek mythology, the Hydra is a nine-headed serpent monster with poisonous breath and when one head was severed, two would grow in its place. It was killed in the second of the 12 labours of the Sun god, Hercules. The Edda says that Thor/Indara/Adam called his Cappadocian capital, Himin or "heaven" and that Balder ("Abel") of the serpent cult went to Thor's banqueting hall in Himin/Heaven. There he began a riotous quarrel and insulted Eve. With this, Balder of the serpent cult was ejected by Gunn or "Cain" or Miok (Michael), the son of Eve and Adam. This is the origin, Waddell says, of St Michael casting out Satan/Lucifer from heaven.[40]

Figure 27: *The serpent cult goddess, El, symbolised as a flying dragon by Egyptian mythology*

The battle of Eden

The Edda tells of a war between the serpent cult and the forces of Thor/Indara for control of Eden. As Waddell remarks, the whole feel of the Wolf-tribe, serpent cult, offensive in the "Battle of Eden" includes the anticipation of bombing by aeroplanes, red-hot missile projections, the belching forth of fire and poisonous clouds of smoke. He says it vividly suggests the "hellish methods of destruction in modern warfare" and this is in line with Sumerian accounts of battles involving the Anunnaki. In parts of the Edda and in Sumerian and Hittite seals, both El and Balder are given "wings" (*Figure 27*). In the Indian Vedas you have accounts of the gods warring in the sky. It suggests a credible explanation for the ancient ruins that indicate they were destroyed by some kind of high-tech, even nuclear, weaponry. The Edda tells how Thor won the victory against the serpent cult and this is known as the "Harrying of Hell [El]" in Welsh traditions. A key moment was when Prince Cain, Miok or Michael, the son of Thor, killed Balder or Abel, the son of El, and this is depicted in many Sumerian, Babylonian, Assyrian, Hittite, and Persian seals and sculptures. Cain, as Horus, is seen spearing Abel-Set, symbolised as a demon crocodile, in an Egyptian bas-relief of around 1000BC (*see picture section*).[41] This is a version of St Michael defeating the Dragon. St Michael, the Sumerian-Cappadocian deity, is portrayed as a dragon fighter. In India, Balder is the "great Deva" (Tiva, or "Devil") felled by Lord Gan (Cain).[42] The stories of St Patrick in Ireland say that he was sent by "St Michael the Victor" to expel the "snakes" from Ireland. When the Phoenicians and others from the Sumer Empire landed in Britain they named many places after St Michael, as with St Michael's Mount in Cornwall. When the Christians began to build their churches on the ancient pagan sites, they inherited the name St Michael for many of their churches. The Edda describes how El, or "Old Mary" as it calls her, fled from the

Figure 28: *Thor under his name Andara (later St Andrew) slays the dragon on a Hittite seal of around 2300BC*

battle by boat on the Euphrates as the battle was lost, but she was caught and killed by Thor/Adam (*Figure 28*). El and her son, Balder or Abel, are both represented as crocodiles in some depictions of their demise.

The phoenix rises

After this defeat, the reptilians and their serpent cult went underground. In fact, they possibly *came* from underground. *Rollins Ancient History*, published around 1907, says that Eden was inside a mountain.[43] It says that the two major rivers of Mesopotamia, the Tigris and Euphrates, have their sources on opposite sides of Mount Taurus. This was a region populated by the Amazons and the serpent cult. Rollins adds that these rivers flowed "through" the mountain of "Eden", which, he says, was artificially constructed by the gods. These rivers, therefore, watered the "Garden of Eden". That may well be correct, but I feel the original "Eden" was Lemuria. Thor/Indara and his successors expanded what became the Sumer Empire in the way I described earlier, as far as Britain, the Americas, even Australia. But the Edda tells how the serpent cult returned to power after Thor's death and that "She (El) still lives." It infiltrated the Nordic DNA in the "royal" bloodlines and possessed their bodies, as described in the Emerald Tablets. The serpent cult regrouped and eventually made its headquarters in Babylon. From there it began to infiltrate its agents and bloodlines into the positions of royal and religious power across the former Sumer Empire, not least in Egypt. These Children of the Serpent took control of the Mystery schools and the state religion, and turned them into vehicles of the reptilian agenda.

How much of Waddell's translation of the Edda is literal and how much is symbolic is difficult to tell. He thinks it is literal, but the use of symbolism was so fundamental to the ancients, and it is unlikely that the Edda would be an exception. My jury is still out on the precise meaning, or meanings, of the Adam and Eve symbolism, for instance, and I think there are Lemurian tales woven into the story, just as there are Sumerian tales woven into British "history". What Waddell's brilliance has done, however, is to confirm the Nordic-reptilian theme of history and the focus the serpent cult has with the female or the goddess.

SOURCES

1   Correspondence with the author

2   *The Return Of The Serpents Of Wisdom*, p 206

3   Ibid, p 208

4   Ibid

5   *The Sirius Mystery*, p 147

6   Ibid, p 159

7   Ibid, pp 267 and 268

8   *The Return Of The Serpents Of Wisdom*, p 210

9   Ibid, pp 212 and 213

10 In the 1960s, a document of uncertain background called Le Serpent Rouge came to light in the National Library in Paris containing the genealogy of the Merovingians, two maps of "France" in the Merovingian period, and a ground plan of St Sulpice, the Roman Catholic centre for occult studies in Paris. See *The Biggest Secret*, p 148

11 You can read a summary of Sir Laurence Gardner's themes in a three-part article on *http://www.nexusmagazine.com//starfire1.html*

12 L.A. Waddell, *British Edda* (Christian Book Club, Hawthorne, California, 1930). The origin of the Edda text is outlined in the introduction. This book is available through Hidden Mysteries at the David Icke website

13 Ibid

14 Ibid

15 Ibid

16 Ibid

17 Ibid

18 Ibid

19 Ibid

20 Ibid

21 Ibid

22 Ibid

23 Ibid

24 Ibid

25 *Caverns, Cauldrons, And Concealed Creatures*

26 See the Kara Parsons website, The Amazons: *http://www.plu.edu/~parsonkj/*

27 Rafal T. Prinke, "The Occult Meanings Behind Polish Heraldic Devices": *http://www.iac.net/~moonweb/archives/RTP/Polish1.html*

28 *British Edda*, Introduction

29 Ibid

30 Ibid

31 Ibid

32 Ibid

33 Ibid

34 Ibid

35 Ibid

36 Rafal T. Prinke, "The Occult Meanings Behind Polish Heraldic Devices": *http://www.iac.net/~moonweb/archives/RTP/Polish1.html*

37 *British Edda*

38 *The Woman's Encyclopedia Of Myths And Secrets*, p 67. This is a superb reference book for making goddess and other connections

39 *British Edda*

40 Ibid

41 Ibid

42 Ibid

43 Rollins, *Ancient History* (Hurst & Co., New York, Vol 2, circa 1907)

CHAPTER 10

the many faces
of the serpent cult

The serpent cult described in the Edda can be connected with Christianity, Satanism, the Nazis, Freemasonry, Hollywood, the death of Princess Diana, and even the true writers of the Shakespeare plays.

Its web of influence is incredibly diverse because it has to work so hard to suppress human consciousness, which, in its true power, is far greater than the juveniles that seek to control. These guys know that humans are potentially far more powerful and so they have to hit us from every angle to keep us in comatose ignorance. One of their most effective weapons for this has been the pagan cult known as Christianity.

The christian "serpent" trinity

The serpent trinity of El, Wodan, and Balder, the mother-father-son, has been repeated in many guises. The emphasis in the serpent trinity was on the mother and son. In Babylon, that major stronghold of the serpent cult, the "son" was Ninus/Tammuz (Balder) and the "mother" was Queen Semiramis (El). The Edda explains how one of the centres for the serpent cult during the conflicts with Thor/Indara was the Van Tribe of Lake Van on the western side of Mount Ararat in Turkey, the Biblical resting place of "Noah's Ark" after the flood.[1] The Van Tribe was known as "The Children of Khaldis", Waddell reports, and these became the Chaldeans of Mesopotamia and the Culdees of northern Britain. Other offshoots were the "Vandals" or "Hun" – again reptilian bloodlines. Van or Baina was also the ancient capital of the matriarch queen of the serpent cult, Semiramis (El), and I guess this might relate to the Lady of the Lake in the King Arthur stories. The underground world is also symbolised as the "Lake of Fire", the domain of the death-goddess, Hel. Semiramis translates as "branch bearer" and her symbol was the dove – further links to the Noah story with the dove arriving to Noah bearing the olive branch. I have seen Lake Van associated with the Garden of Eden by one researcher.

So the Babylonian mother-son was Semiramis of the serpent cult and her son, Tammuz, the hero of their far earlier version of the "Jesus" story. We shall see later that this same serpent cult moved from Babylon to Rome and founded the Christian religion, as we know it today. The Christian mother-son combination is Mary (another name used for El) and "Jesus" (Tammuz or Balder). Christianity, as created by the Roman Church, is another form of the ancient mother-son serpent cult religion. And there's more. Rome is said to have been founded by Romulus and Remus. These are mythical names, but highly symbolic. Waddell points out that in the Edda text Rom is another name for Edin or Eden, the home of the serpent cult and the "Wolf tribe" of the "Roms" (wolf symbolism is associated with Sirius). These people were not Nordics, but similar to the aboriginal dark Chaldeans, Lycians, and what is called today the Mediterranean or Iberian race. Rom or Romil was also a title of the Set and serpent worshippers of ancient Egypt. Muslims refer to Turkey/Asia Minor as Rum, and Romania is the traditional centre for the vampire legends. Fascinating, then, that Romulus and Remus, the mythical founders of Rome, were said to have been "wolf-suckled" and this is symbolic of the mother-son cult (goddess worship) of the Wolf-tribe of the Roms with its associated serpent worship. The names Romulus and Remus came from an ancient female clan called the Etruscan gens Romulia, the real founders of Rome. Again the female.

Mother Mary is El, the "dragon queen"

It is no surprise, given its origins in Babylon, that the Roman Church would so emphasise the importance of "Mary", the goddess figure, and its version of El or Queen Semiramis. El was also known as "May" or "Mother May" and so we have May Day, one of the most important ritual days of the year for the serpent cult/Illuminati. The Illuminati-created creed of Communism has its day of celebration and military parades on May Day for the same reason (see …*And The Truth Shall Set You Free* for the detailed background to the Illuminati origins of Communism). On the night of April 30th, Satanists perform the ritual of Walpurgis to the Goddess of Walpurgisnacht or "May Day Eve". She was such a popular deity in Germany as the May Queen, Walpurga, that she was encompassed by Christianity under the name "Saint" Walpurga, and a fictional story produced to justify this.[2] Morgyn la Faye in the King Arthur stories is another version of El, as in Maer (Mary) gyn (woman) of the Fey (deadly serpent).[3] Mary Woman of the Deadly Serpent – "Mother Mary" of Christianity. Morgans were known as "Sea-women", as the same water themes continue.[4]

Balder, the son of god

The Edda's version of the death of Balder ("Abel") at the hands of "Cain" or "St Michael," is told in different versions in many cultures. The Hebrew Old Testament has Cain killing his "brother" Abel and bringing the first death into the world. The New Testament has St Michael defeating Satan, Lucifer, or the "Great Dragon". In Egypt we have the Wolf-headed Set or Seth killed by Horus, the son of Asar or Osiris. In India, Cain is Lord Gan who fought "The Great Deva" or "The Bull", one of the Balder (Abel) titles in the Edda. The King Arthur legends have Sir Gawain slaying the Green Man. As I have said, the Chaldeans called the Balder/Abel character Tammuz. He was their "Established Son" and the "Son of God" who died for humanity. Tammuz was also closely associated with the theme of the serpent and the bloodline of the "Dragon Kings". Hecate, another version of El or Hel, was symbolised as the mother of Dionysus, another classic Son of God figure. Both

Tammuz and Dionysus were mirrors of the much later "Jesus" myth. Lamentations of the Chaldees for the death of Tammuz/Balder/Abel are preserved in a large collection of hymns of the mother-son (serpent) cult in Babylonian tablets from around 3000BC. They used to wail for Tammuz in certain rituals and the wailing of Jewish people at the Western or "Wailing" Wall in Jerusalem is a version of this. In the Old Testament, Ezekiel describes the wailings for Tammuz by Hebrew women in Jerusalem. Legends also say that to reach the goddess El or Hel in her underworld, you have to cross a wailing river.[5]

"Jesus" is Balder

When the serpent cult moved its headquarters to Rome, it introduced the "Jesus" story as we know it today and symbolised Jesus as Balder, the "crucified" son of El or "Mary", the Matriarch of the serpent cult, although there is other symbolism relating to the Jesus story, also. He is a sort of composite character that pulls together a mass of Mystery school symbolism and themes. Balder is one of them, but there are many others weaved into the Gospel tales. On the cross, "Jesus" is made to say: "My El-lo-i, lama sa – bach-tha-ni" which is translated as "My God, my God, why hast thou forsaken me?" Lauren Savage, the webmaster of davidicke.com and long-time researcher into these subjects, once studied with the famous American scholar Dr Vendyl Jones, the man who originally inspired the movie character Indiana Jones. Lauren tells me that Dr Jones has stated that those Biblical words attributed to "Jesus" were from a South American language and that the translation into English had simply been a guess. Now if the "Grail" is the womb of the Dragon Queens, that sacred symbol of the serpent bloodlines, and Jesus is symbolic of Balder, son of the serpent goddess, it suddenly makes symbolic sense of the claims by people like Sir Laurence Gardner. He says that the Merovingian (reptilian) bloodline is the "Grail" bloodline of "Jesus" and "Mary" Magdalene. With his close connections to the ancient Imperial Royal Dragon Court and Order, which serves the interests of the "Dragon bloodlines", Gardner would surely know the real symbolism of the Grail and Jesus, wouldn't he? Gardner says that the "Dragon" refers to the fact that the kings of this bloodline used to be anointed in Egypt by the fat of the sacred crocodile. El and Balder were symbolised as crocodiles and the crocodile was known in Egypt as the "messeh", from which we get "Messiah" and "Christ". The term "Christ" means the "anointed one" – anointed with the fat of a crocodile. The Hindu god Shiva, the "Lord" of the reptilian Nagas, was also called the "anointed one", or "Christos" to the Greeks, when he had his willy bathed in menstrual blood. I hope you're not eating. As Barbara Walker points out in *The Woman's Encyclopedia Of Myths And Secrets*, many traditions of the early Gnostic Christians identified the serpent with Jesus. She says that some Christians believed that the serpent was the father of Jesus, having "overshadowed" the bed of the Virgin Mary and begotten the human form of the Saviour. This mirrors the legends of Merovee, founder of the Merovingians, and Alexander the Great, both of whom were said to have been fathered by a serpent or sea creature. Jewish serpent-worshippers, known as the Naasians, said the serpent was the "messiah".

Writers who have misrepresented the Edda and other accounts, purposely and otherwise, have presented Balder as the "good god". The Chaldeans (the "Children of Khaldis" of Lake Van), who followed the serpent cult's mother-son religion, said that Balder/Tammuz was "the good god, the beautiful benign and faithful son"; he was a divine high priest who died for the salvation of the Chaldeans, his chosen people; he was sacrificed and descended into the underworld and he will return in a "second coming" to establish a new heaven and a new Earth. Almost exactly what the Christians say about Jesus. James Churchward says, incidentally, that the Chaldeans were a "sect", not a "people". The Scandinavian legend says that Balder had a spear of mistletoe thrust into him by Hod, a blind god. The Christians say Jesus had a spear thrust into him by the blind centurion, Longinus. The Ides of March, or March 15th, was the day devoted to Hod by the ancients and this is the same day the serpent cult leaders of the Christian Church chose as the feast day of the "Blessed Longinus"![6] The obsession that Hitler and the Nazis had with possessing the "Spear of Destiny" relates to its association with their god, Balder or Baldur. Hitler thought that the true spear was the one owned by the shape-shifting Habsburg family in Austria, which had formerly been in the possession of Charlemagne of the reptilian bloodline. He believed that anyone who possessed it would be invincible, but it didn't seem to help him much after he stole it from the Habsburgs during the annexation of Austria. Also, the "Holy Grail" of the Arthur stories is supposed to be the vessel that caught the blood of Jesus after he was pierced in the side by the spear – the "serpent" blood, in fact, of "Balder", the legendary martyred hero of the serpent cult or Illuminati. The term Illuminati or Illuminated ones links with Balder's name of Loki. This became Lucifer "the light bringer", Waddell says. Jesus is said to be the "Light of the World".

The Jewish Father-Son was also depicted sometimes as an ass-headed man crucified on a tree. Balder, Tammuz, and Jesus are the *same* entity. The Illuminati created Christianity to fool the people into worshipping symbolic reptilian deities while believing they were worshipping the opposite. What was it that Alice in Wonderland said?

"Nothing would be what it is,
Because everything would be what it isn't.
And contrary-wise – what it is, it wouldn't be.
And what it wouldn't be, it would.
You see?"

The black madonna

We can now appreciate why Illuminati placemen like George Bush, George W. Bush, Bill Clinton, the British royal family, and others, profess to be such strong Christians while taking part in Satanic ritual. They know what it really means. To them Christianity is the worship of the serpent gods, especially El and Balder, and other Illuminati symbols and deities. The Knights Templar secret society funded and

designed the famous Gothic cathedrals that became shrines to the serpent goddess.
Between 1170 and 1270, some 80 cathedrals and 500 churches were built in France
alone and dedicated to "Our Lady" (El, Semiramis, Mary). The Knights Templar were
controlled by the serpent cult/Illuminati, but many of their members would have not
been aware of this – just like the vast majority of Freemasons today. The Templars
used the red cross of Thor/Indara/George as their symbol and to all appearances
they were worshippers of a Christian God – again like Freemasons today. But at the
top level, they are both expressions of the serpent cult/Illuminati. Their "Christian"
churches and cathedrals are full of goddess, astrological, Sun, and sexual symbolism,
as is Freemasonry. Of course they are. They were both created by the same force. The
great cathedrals are located on ancient pagan ritual sites. Notre Dame ("Our Lady")
in Paris was built on a site of worship to the goddess Artemis/Diana – El. The
reptilian bloodline, the Merovingians, worshipped this goddess on that same location
and Notre Dame is covered in reptilian gargoyles. The great Cathedral at Chartres,
not far from Paris, was built by the Knights Templar on a sacred pagan ritual site. It
was so important that Druids came from all over Europe to attend the ceremonies.
Chartres Cathedral, like Notre Dame, was a centre for worship of the "Black
Madonna" – or El, the Dragon Queen. Until the late 18th century, pilgrims to Chartres
participated in a "Christian" ritual that paid homage to El or the Black Madonna.
After praying and taking mass in the cathedral, they would descend through a
northern passageway to an ancient subterranean crypt under the church. Here they
would pay their respects to "Notre Dame de Sous-Terre" (Our Lady of the
Underworld) – a black ebony statue of a seated woman holding a child on her knees.
This again was El and Balder of the Mother-Son serpent cult. The child was invariably
placed on the left knee because Satanism calls itself the "left-hand path". On the Black
Madonna's head at Chartres was, as always, a crown and on the pedestal is a Roman
inscription saying "the Virgin who will give birth." The crown is a symbol of the
reptilian bloodlines and is used to signify high rank in Satanism. The Black Madonna
was called "The Queen of Heaven" and all these mother-virgins were symbolised as a
dove. The symbolism of British royalty with its crowns, doves, and lions, etc., are all
symbolic of the serpent cult in power today.

The man who did most to advance the worship of the Black Madonna was St
Bernard (1090 to 1153), the abbot of Clairvaux in France, who founded the
Cistercian Order. He claims to have experienced a miraculous religious
"illumination" when the Black Madonna of Chatillon pressed her breast and
squirted three drops of milk in his mouth. No, you didn't misread that. Bernard was
also at the heart of the creation of the Knights Templar along with the Illuminati St
Clair family, who later became the Sinclair family at Rosslyn, near Edinburgh in
Scotland. When the Knights Templar were formed as a front for the serpent cult,
they adopted as their official patroness the "Mother of God" or "Queen of Heaven",
the traditional names for El-Semiramis. So did the Teutonic Knights, who are
fundamentally connected to the reptilian Habsburgs. The goddess appeared widely
on chivalric banners and when they fought in her honour, they would scream her
name as a battle cry. They were fighting for El under the name of Mary and for

Balder under the name of Jesus. This would explain why Christianity, which claims to be a religion based on love, has been such a vehicle for global genocide and torture. The "Holy Ghost" of the Christian trinity is also regarded as feminine in Hebrew and the early Christian Church considered it to be so.

The very name Bible comes from Byblos, home of a shrine to an earlier version of Mary known as Astarte. This shrine dates to Neolithic times and Astarte was believed to be the "true sovereign of the world". She is worshipped elsewhere as Mother Mary, Hathor, Demeter, Aphrodite, and, in India, as Kali. Another location associated with the start of Christianity is Ephesus in south-west Turkey. The mythical "St Paul" was said to have written a letter to the Ephesians, and Greek myth says that the Amazons founded the city. Ephesus just happens to have been the headquarters of worship to the goddess Artemis/Diana – a goddess of the Amazons. I visited Ephesus in the summer of 2000 and on a hill high above the ancient ruins is a building that is claimed to have been the home of…Mary, mother of "Jesus". Another goddess worshipped by the Amazons was Cybele, the Mother Goddess of all Asia Minor (Turkey); she was taken to Rome from Phrygia, the "Land of the Lions" and the serpent cult. Rituals to her included baptism in the blood of the sacred bull, who represented her dying consort Attis, of whom Jesus was a carbon copy. Her temple in Rome stood on the site of today's St Peter's Basilica until the 4th century AD when the Christian Church took over. In fact, a priest of Cybele called Montanus or "Mountain Man" identified the deity Attis with Jesus. Some Montanists were locked in their churches by Christians in Asia Minor and burned alive.[7] Cybele was the "goddess of the caves", a location where many of the saviour-gods in the Jesus mould are said to have been born. The reptilian underground network?

The red rose of El

The many versions of El are said to be goddesses of sexuality and fertility, and of the Moon and Venus. The stone baptismal bowls found in every Christian Church are symbolic of the "magic stone bowl" of the serpent cult or Illuminati described in the Edda. The Gothic "Christian" doorways and the ridges around them are depictions of the vulva and many even have a clitoris symbol at the top of the arch. The same is depicted in windows and especially the rose windows of the Gothic cathedrals. At Chartres they have a window featuring the "Rose of France" with "Mary" in the centre. Rose windows face west, the sacred direction of female deities. The red rose is symbolic of the goddess and so we have the Rosicrucians with their red rose and cross symbols. They are a major strand in the Illuminati web and claim a lineage to ancient Egypt and back to "Noah", that symbol of the reptilian bloodline. Another elite network is the secret society known as the Order of the Rose, which includes the former Canadian prime ministers Brian Mulroney and Pierre Trudeau, both Satanists.[8] Trudeau is famous for wearing a red rose in his lapel. Some branches of Freemasonry feature the rose and cross in their rituals. Once again, the Christian Mother Mary is associated with the rose because she is a symbol of goddess worship. The Romans called the rose the "flower of Venus" and this was a term used for the goddess, including Queen Semeramis. The red rose was symbolic of female sexuality and the white rose or lily is the virgin goddess. Christians associated Mary with both the rose and the lily and they called her the "Holy Rose". This is the same title given to the Indian Great Mother. The rosary used so widely in the Roman Catholic mother-son cult was copied from the "rosary of the mantras" worn by the Indian destroyer-goddess Kali Ma. Arabs called their rosaries wadija or "rose garden" and the Latin version of this, rosarium, described the early rosaries in Mother Mary worship. In Satanism, one of the main codenames for babies bred for sacrifice is Rose-mary's baby. This was the name of a film by Roman Polanski, the husband of the actress Sharon Tate who was murdered with her unborn child by the Satanic "Family" of Charles Manson. Tony Blair's Labour Party introduced the red rose as its logo thanks to the Illuminati clone and later disgraced government minister Peter Mandelson, whose nickname is the "Prince of Darkness". The other two major UK political parties have the logos of the dove (Liberal Democrats) and the lighted torch (Conservatives), both major Illuminati symbols going back thousands of years.

"Shakespeare" was Lord Draconis

The works of Shakespeare are part of this story, also. The texts are awash with esoteric and Illuminati symbolism and codes. For instance, the "Queen of the Fairies" (reptilian bloodline) in "Shakespeare's" *A Midsummer Night's Dream*, is another version of the universal goddess called Titania. She was known in legend as the great goddess who ruled the "god-race", the Titans. Given the Illuminati's staggering obsession with symbolism, I feel there was far more to the sinking of the Titanic (Titania) than ever we have yet realised. These goddesses are fundamentally associated with the sea and the underworld – the victims of the Titanic tragedy in 1912 went to both. I don't buy the "hit an iceberg" line myself. In southern Russia, Titania (known there as Rhea) was "the Red One" and the Romans claimed her to be the mother of Romulus and Remus, the mythical founders of Rome. Titania's king in *A Midsummer Night's Dream* is called Oberon. He was based on a real-life character, an ancestor of the man who really put the "Shakespeare" plays together – Edward de Vere of Loxley, 17th Earl of Oxford. The American researcher Brian Desborough, among others, has established that the plays were the work of a syndicate of Illuminati initiates in Elizabethan society, headed by de Vere and including Sir Francis Bacon, John Dee, and Edmund Spenser.[9] Elizabeth Ist (1558-1603) was serious bloodline and known as the "Faerie Queene". Bacon was a Knights Templar, the head of the Rosicrucian order, and the man who oversaw the translation of the King James Version of the Bible (see *The Biggest Secret* for more background). Bacon also wrote a book called *The New Atlantis* which described a society that later became the United States. He also wrote of an "Invisible College" which covertly controlled events. One expression of this "Invisible College" became the Royal Society in London, which was founded by Freemasons in 1660 to dictate scientific thought. The "Shakespeare" plays were encoded with esoteric knowledge hidden in symbolism and phrases that only an initiate would understand. L.A. Waddell points out that parts of the Edda, compiled at least six centuries before "Shakespeare", are written in a very similar style to that later called "Shakespearian".[10] The de Vere family was so high in the reptilian bloodline that Edward de Vere carried the hereditary title of Lord Draconis – the same title awarded to the Dracula bloodline of Vlad the Impaler by the ancient Dragon Order now promoted by Sir Laurence Gardner. Edward de Vere was a Lord Chancellor of England and his ancestors included Albrey, Prince of Anjou and Guise in France, who was known as the "Elf King" – Dragon King in other words. The aristocratic Anjou line has appeared in my books many times. The House of Anjou is part of the House of Lorraine, one of the most important reptilian bloodlines to this day. The Plantagenet dynasty, which ruled England from Henry II (1154) to Richard II (1399), were a branch of the House of Anjou and the senior branch was the House of de Vere. The royal historian Baron Thomas Babington Macaulay wrote in 1861 that the Veres were "the longest and most illustrious line of nobles that England has ever seen" with their Merovingian, Pictish, and Scythian (Amazon-Nordic) ancestry.[11] Laurence Gardner calls them a "true kingly line of the Elven Race", a code for reptilian shape-shifters.

Freemasons are the serpent cult

Freemasonry is the biggest secret society in the world and a front for the serpent cult, although the vast majority of its members are oblivious to this. The hero of Freemasonry is someone called Hiram Abif. His Freemasonic legend says that he was the "Grand Master and architect of Solomon's Temple" who was killed for refusing to reveal the Masonic secrets. The story has many similarities with the legend of the death of Osiris in Egypt. Hiram I, the king of Tyre from 969 to 936BC, is not considered the same person as Hiram Abif, although he, too, appears in the story of Solomon's Temple. Hiram Abif is also said to have come from Tyre (an old Knights Templar stronghold) and Ty is a name for Balder. Hiram Abif is the "Widow's Son" in Freemasonry and he is also known to Freemasons as the "Tyrian Architect". The code "Widow" could represent El, the Dragon goddess, and the son may well be Balder. One of Balder's titles was "the illegitimate son of a widow". The code for distress in Freemasonry goes: "Is there no help for the widow's son?" One of the tribes named in the Edda that fought for the serpent cult was also called Hrym and this later became the Germanic tribe, the Hermin-ones. The Roman historian, Tacitus, said that these descended from Hermin, whom Waddell connects with the bloodline of Wodan. The worship of the reptilians and their Dragon Queens, and the placing of their bloodlines into the positions of power, is the secret of secrets held within all the secret societies. Jim Shaw, a former 33rd degree Freemason, was initiated into a long list of Freemasonic orders and offshoots. After reaching the highest official levels he saw what Freemasonry really was and wrote an expose called *The Deadly Deception*. He was initiated into the 33rd degree of the Scottish Rite at the Supreme Headquarters of the 33rd degree in Northwest 16th Street, not far from the White House in Washington DC. It is built as an Egyptian-type temple and outside are two Sphinx-like figures with women's faces. Could this be an indication of the truth about the Sphinx at Giza? One of the "sphinx" figures at the Washington temple has a cobra entwined around her neck. On the neck of the other one is the image of a woman, symbolic, says Shaw, of fertility and procreation.[12] These are some of the gifts associated with goddesses like Artemis/Diana. Behind the row of pillars at the front of the building is a massive depiction of the rising Sun – Horus or, perhaps, the Sun goddess known as Sol. Around this Sun are six large golden snakes and inside this Freemasonic holy-of-holies the serpent theme continues. Shaw reports:

> "...the thing that is most noticeable is the way the walls are decorated with serpents. There are all kinds, some very long and large. Many of the Scottish Rite degrees include the representation of serpents and I recognised them among those decorating the walls."[13]

Secret society, serpent cult, and goddess symbolism can be clearly seen in the founding of the United States. Queen Semiramis (meaning "Branch Bearer") was another name for El and she was symbolised as a dove. L.A. Waddell says that the Indian Vedic title for El was Sarama – "The Bitch of the Pani" or Vans. This was Queen Semiramis, the Amazonian queen of Lake Van and it was apparently the source of the tribal title of "Sarma-tian" for the eastern Vandal "Turanian" hordes that ravaged the early Western World. The Roman serpent cult worshipped Semiramis as Venus Columba or "Venus the Dove". Columbe is still the word for dove in French. Columba became a symbolic name for El or Semiramis, the dragon queen of the serpent cult. So we have Christopher "Columbus" (real name Colon), who bore the branch of the serpent cult to the Americas. We also have British Columbia in Canada; the District of Columbia, the home of Washington DC; and a stream of Illuminati operations called Columbia Pictures, Columbia University, and Columbia Broadcasting, the US network, CBS. One of the most horrific events in America in recent years was the shootings at Columbine High School and when you begin to appreciate the unbelievable obsession the Illuminati have with symbolism, down to the finest of details, that location is not a co-incidence. The English Grand Lodge of Freemasonry is also located in London in Great Queen Street to symbolise its worship of the serpent queen, El. England, one of the headquarters of the Illuminati, is known as the "Mother Country" and its parliament the "Mother of Parliaments". It is all goddess symbolism, as was Britannia, an earlier name for Britain derived from the Phoenician goddess, Barati or "Barat-Anna".

Freemasonic heroes like Albert Pike, the Supreme Pontiff of Universal Freemasonry in the 19th century, have said that Freemasonry is a revival of the ancient mystery religions of Babylon, Egypt, Persia, Rome, and Greece. "Masonry is identical with the ancient mysteries", he wrote in his Freemasonic "Bible" called *Morals And Dogma*. So, of course, you are going to find the same knowledge and symbols used in Freemasonry that could be found in the ancient Mystery schools. Pike tells only half the truth, however, because Freemasonry is not a *revival* of those Mystery religions, it is a *continuation* of them. They never went away, only underground. Freemasonry is a wonderful example of how the Illuminati have always hidden the truth in a complex mass of degrees, levels, contradictions, mystique, and blatant lies. And no one is lied to more comprehensively than the Masons themselves. Jim Shaw confirms that lower-degree Masons (the overwhelming majority) are given false information and interpretations to keep them in the dark. Even at the 33rd degree level, the official peak, most are told nothing of the true meaning of Freemasonry, its symbols and agenda. Symbolism is the very foundation of the Anunnaki-Illuminati secret language and codes (see *The Biggest Secret*) and Freemasonry calls itself a system of pure religion expressed in symbols. So misinterpret the symbols and you have lost the plot completely. Here we have Albert Pike writing in *Morals And Dogma* about the Blue Degrees, the bottom three levels that feed into the Scottish and York Rite Degrees:

> "The Blue Degrees are but the outer court or portico (porch) of the Temple. Part of the symbols are displayed there to the initiate, but he is intentionally misled by false interpretation. It is not intended that he shall understand them, but it is intended that he shall imagine that he understands them …Their true explication is reserved for the Adepts, the Princes of Masonry (those of the 32nd and 33rd degrees)." [14]

Meanings and... *meanings*

Even those at the 32nd and 33rd levels are mis-led unless they are inner-circle bloodline. Jim Shaw says there are two meanings given to Freemasons, the exoteric to the lower initiates and the esoteric to the higher ones. But there is a third – the truth – and that is given only to a tiny elite of bloodline initiates and those who progress beyond the official levels of the secret societies to the unofficial Illuminati degrees. Shaw says that Freemasonry worships nature, the Sun and Moon, through the symbol of the phallus. So does Christianity. The phallus, he says, represents the Sun in sexual union with the female Earth to bring new life. On one level that is true, but it is still a spin. Take the Freemasonic symbol of the square and compass (*Figure 29 overleaf*). This is always placed over the chair (throne) of the Worshipful Master, which is positioned to the east in Freemasonic Temples, the direction of the rising Sun. Christian churches face east for the same reason. Shaw says that lower-degree Masons are told that the square is to remind them that they must be square or honest in their dealings with all people (excuse me while I laugh hysterically). The compass, they are told, is to teach them to "circumscribe" their passions, and to control their desires. Maybe the paedophile and Freemason George Bush missed that meeting. Shaw says that later they are told the "real" meaning, which is that the compass is the male phallus of the Sun impregnating the female Earth, symbolised as the square. [15] On one level, again, that's true, but to the highest levels of the Illuminati the compass and square represent the impregnation that perpetuates the bloodline. The V and A symbol of Queen Victoria and the German Prince Albert, both reptilian bloodlines, were designed to symbolise this also (*Figure 30 overleaf*) and so is the letter G in the Freemasons logo. Shaw says that, first, Masons are told the G represents "God". Later that it represents deity and still later that it means geometry.

Figures 29 and 30: The Freemasonic square and compass represent the male impregnating the female to continue the bloodline and the same symbolism can be seen in the V and A crest of Queen Victoria and her high-Masonic husband, Prince Albert

But Shaw explains that it really means the male generative principle, the Sun God or phallus. Again, that is one level of its meaning. But to the Illuminati the G represents the generative principle of expanding and protecting their bloodlines. The point within the circle also represents the impregnation of the female (circle) and with the male (point). On one level this is another Sun symbol and can be found on the grave of President Kennedy as a flame and circle, but the real meaning is bloodline. It is the same with the ship symbols you see on Freemasonic buildings. The hull is the female (that's why ships are always "she") and the mast is the phallus impregnating her. Lower-degree Masons are told that the circle and the point represents the individual Mason (point) restricted by the boundary line of duty (the circle). What a hoot. All these secret society symbols and codes have a meaning for the lower initiates (utter bollocks); the higher initiates (semi-utter bollocks); and for those who make it through to the highest levels of the Illuminati (the true interpretation). In the "blood oaths" (called the "Obligation"), the initiate agrees to accept torture and death if he reveals the "secrets". This maintains the compartmentalisation in which the higher levels do not reveal their "secrets" to the lower levels. In truth, as Jim Shaw found out, even at the 33rd degree you are not told anything worthwhile. The real business exists only above the official levels, and only a handful of Masons ever make it there. Freemasonry is a cesspit of deceit and hypocrisy, and the oaths made to the secret societies and your fellow initiates override any oath you may have made to your country or people as a president, prime minister, congressman, Member of Parliament, policeman, or judge. Jim Shaw writes:

> "The Mason swears to keep the secrets of another Mason, protecting him even if it requires withholding evidence of a crime. In some degrees treason and murder are excepted. In other, higher degrees, there are no exceptions to this promise to cover up the truth. The obligations, if the Masonic teachings are to be believed, may require a Mason to give false testimony, perjure himself, or (in the case of a judge) render a false verdict in order to protect a Mason." [16]

This has always been the way of the Illuminati serpent cult in all its forms. And the vast majority of the world's political leaders, high administrators of government, judges, policemen, and media owners, have made that oath. Does anyone still wonder why the truth has never come out until now?

The ritual death of Diana

The symbolism of the sacrificial murder of Princess Diana by the serpent cult/Illuminati becomes clear from this background knowledge. El, the Dragon Queen, was also known as Hel or Ate (Hate). Still today, Hel-Ate or Hecate is a Satanic deity associated appropriately with hell. After her husband's murder in Dallas, Jackie Kennedy travelled to the Greek island of Delos in the southwest Aegean Sea. This is the legendary birthplace of Diana and the traditional domain of Hecate, the goddess of the "infernal arts". Delos is known for this reason as the island of the dead. Hecate was portrayed as both a virgin and a whore, and again associated with the Moon. Another version was the Egyptian, Hequet, who delivered the Sun god every morning and her totem was the frog, symbolic, appropriately, of the foetus. Crossroads are the sacred places of Diana and her Satanic expression, Hecate. It is at crossroads that the witches and Grand Masters and sorcerers of Freemasonry perform their rituals. Crossroads are symbolic of the vortex points created where ley lines cross. In ritual sex magic the wearing of clothes of the opposite sex and the performance of bisexual acts are called "crossroad rites". The women involved were called "dikes". Remember that the Amazon-manipulated Scythians wore women's clothes in sexual rites to their goddess. Crossroads are also the places of human and animal sacrifice and Hecate (El) is known as a "sex and death goddess", and the goddess of witchcraft and sorcery.

The Illuminati symbolism surrounding Diana's murder is, therefore, simply stunning. At the spot where Diana died, the road that goes through the Pont de L'Alma Tunnel is crossed on the surface by another, which leads on to the Pont de L'Alma Bridge. In fact, this spot is a maze of crossroads. Diana died in the early morning of August 31st. Hecate's Day in the Satanic calendar is August 13th, but under the Satanic law of reverse symbolism and numbers, Hecate's day of *sacrifice* is…August 31st![17] Outside the original Paris and now very much inside the modern city, the Merovingians established an underground chamber for the worship of the goddess Diana, and the blood rituals and human sacrifices to her. This site dates back at least to AD500 to 750 and it was here that kings (of the reptilian bloodline) in dispute over property would settle the issue in combat. As I mentioned earlier, the location today of this sacrificial site to the goddess Diana/Hecate is…the Pont de L'Alma Tunnel! The word pont relates to Pontifex, a Roman high priest, and it means passage or bridge. Alma comes from Al-Mah, a Middle-Eastern name for the Moon Goddess.[18] So Pont de L'Alma translates as "bridge or passage of the Moon Goddess" and the adjoining Place de L'Alma is the "Place of the Moon Goddess" – and the Moon Goddess is Diana/Hecate/El. The Amazon goddess Cybele, who was worshipped in Rome at the same time as Hecate, was also known as Alma. The reason Diana was held so long in the tunnel before being moved to hospital for treatment was that she had to die in that sacrificial site according to the sick ritual, and she was dead before she was moved. Princess Diana was buried in a tree grove, on an island, in a lake, all of which are associated with the Goddess Diana in all her versions. Diana's brother, Earl Spencer, also had four black swans introduced to the lake after his sister died. Swans are yet more goddess symbolism and Scandinavian myths claimed that the Valkeries incarnated as swans and wore magic swan-feather cloaks to transform themselves.[19] Swan knights and swan maidens were widely associated with the pagan religion. The story of the sacrificial murder of Princess Diana by the serpent cult-Illuminati is told in over 60 pages in *The Biggest Secret*.

Troy, Troy, and Troy again

The events of ancient Troy connect fundamentally with the death of Princess Diana and so much else besides. The Merovingian bloodline goes back to the Trojan War and beyond, and it was they who founded the city of Paris and named it after the Trojan called Prince Paris, the lover of Helen (El-en) of Troy. According to Barbara Walker in *The Woman's Encyclopedia Of Myths And Secrets*, Helen was said to be an incarnation of the virgin Moon-goddess and daughter of Hecuba or…Hecate.[20] Helen was also known as Helle and Selene and was worshipped at a Spartan sexual festival called the Helenphoria that included sexual symbols carried in a basket called the helene.[21] Troy or Troia means "three places" in Greek and Hebrew and almost certainly relates to the triple-goddess symbolism of Atlantis and Lemuria with one deity divided into the "trinity", or three aspects. Hecate was known as "Hecate of the Three Ways".[22] Troy or Troia is also the origin of the name Tripoli, the capital of Libya, which is so associated with the reptilian Amazons.

The legends of Troy say that Helen married the "Moon-king" Menelaus, who was promised immortality because of this "sacred marriage". When Helen went off with Prince Paris, Menelaus wanted to protect his immortality and the wealth the marriage had secured, and sailed with his army to take her back. This was the war between the male-led Greeks and the goddess-led Trojans. Many high Satanic priestesses take the name Helen, Helena, or Elaine – El-aine.* It was under the name Elaine or Ellen that Helen of Troy became the symbolic queen of Britain in pagan times. As I outlined earlier, it was a relative of Helen, a Trojan called Brutus, who sailed west to Britain after the fall of Troy and founded a city called Caer Troia or New Troy – today's London. Other derivatives of El or Hel are Helenia, Helga, Hild, Helsinki, Holstein, and Holland (Hel-land or Halland), one of the major centres for the reptilian bloodlines to this day. Pliny, the Roman writer, said that all the people of "Scatinavia", or Scandinavia, were children of "Mother Hel" and were called Helleviones.[24] They believed that she lived in elder or Hel-trees/elven trees. Sir Laurence Gardner, of the Royal Dragon Court and Order, says that his "Dragon Bloodlines" have been called the Elven Race and that terms like elf, fairy, and pixie all symbolise the "representatives of various castes within the kingly succession" (the reptilian hierarchy).[24] So many fairy tales and other children's stories are encoded with the theme of the dragon bloodlines and their battles for power. The tales of princes and princesses "turning into a frog" is symbolic of shape-shifting. The same with dragon princesses locked in towers or giving birth to frogs.

---

* This is not to say that everyone with these names is involved in this, of course. Only that these are names the Illuminati use.

The Set-serpent cult is Satanism

The Satanists still use the deities, symbols, and rituals today that were used by the ancients because they represent the same stream of control and bloodline. In the United States we have the Temple of Set, an offshoot from Anton LaVey's infamous Church of Satan. The Temple of Set was formed in 1975 by Michael Aquino, one of the most notorious exponents of the Illuminati's mind control network, as detailed in my other books. Images of Set and the Set-Wolf symbolism go back at least to 3200BC, the period of the battles between the Nordics and the serpent cult recorded in the Edda (*Figure 31*). The Temple of Set website tells us:

"The Great Pyramid of Giza is one of the last early monuments connected with the idea of a Setian afterlife as well as a solar one. The Great Pyramid had a special air shaft for the king's akh to fly to the star Alpha Draconis, which is the star of Set in the Constellation of the Thigh (today's 'Big Dipper')."[25]

Alpha Draconis is the alleged base of the "Draco" reptilian "royalty". It was known to the Egyptians as Thurban, an Arabic word meaning dragon, and the pyramid builders aligned their structures with Thurban/Alpha Draconis, which was the pole star around 3000BC. The Hyksos tribe, who invaded and ruled Egypt from around 1785-1580 BC, were Set worshippers and they placed their capital at

Avaris on an ancient site of Set worship. They represented Set with an ass head. A line of Set-worshipping priests from Tanis eventually became the royal line of pharaohs, people like Seti ("Set's man") and Setnakt ("Set is Mighty"). This was the serpent cult.

Holle-wood, the land of El-lusion

I can't emphasise enough that to understand what we call the present we have to understand the past, and this is why the Anunnaki-Illuminati have concentrated so much effort on rewriting history. Even Hollywood is an example. The Druids were tree worshippers, especially the oak. The holly was their most sacred symbol because it was sacred to Mother Holle or Hel, the goddess of the underworld. Thus we have Holle or Holly-wood (Hel-wood), the "place of magic" and home of the Illuminati's mass propaganda and conditioning machine in California. The holly wood was a favourite source of magic wands. The holly or "holy" was associated with El or Hel's vagina and the Germanic "Hohle" means cave or grave.[26] The cave is the traditional birthplace of the "Jesus"-type deities. The red holly berries

Figure 31: The wolf-headed Set in Egyptian legend, their version of Balder

symbolised the female blood, and the white berries symbolised the male semen and death. The importance of the holly, or holy tree can be seen in the Christmas pagan hymn sung today by Christians which says that the "holly bears the crown". Interestingly, the official Scottish residence of the British royal family is called the Palace of Holyroodhouse in Edinburgh. Rood is a name for the rowan wood featured in the Edda in relation to Thor. The new Scottish Parliament is also being housed in Holyrood Road. High above the Palace of Holyroodhouse, at the highest point in Holyrood Park, is a rock called King Arthur's Seat."

If you are new to these subjects, I hope that you are beginning to appreciate how so much of what we call past and present are fundamentally connected, and how the calling cards of this covert force can be seen everywhere if you take the time to look.

SOURCES

1   *British Edda*

2   *The Woman's Encyclopedia Of Myths And Secrets*, p 1,058

3   *British Edda*, p 249

4   *The Woman's Encyclopedia Of Myths And Secrets*, p 674

5   Ibid, p 382

6   Ibid, p 549

7   *The Woman's Encyclopedia Of Myths And Secrets*, pp 201 and 202

8   *Trance-Formation Of America*, pp 176 and 178

9   For Sir Laurence Gardner's information about this see:
    http://www.nexusmagazine.com/ringlords1.html

10 *British Edda*, Introduction

11 *http://www.nexusmagazine.com/ringlords1.html*

12 *The Deadly Deception*, p 102

13 Ibid

14 Albert Pike, *Morals and Dogma*, p 819

15 Details of the explanations that Jim Shaw was given can be found in *The Deadly Deception*, pp 142 to 146

16 Ibid, p 149

17 Told to the author by Arizona Wilder, a former "Mother Goddess" in Illuminati Satanic ritual

18 *The Woman's Encyclopedia Of Myths And Secrets*, p 23

19 Ibid, pp 963 and 964

20 Ibid, pp 382 and 383

21   Ibid

22   Ibid, p 378

23   Ibid, p 382

24   *http://www.nexusmagazine.com/ringlords1.html*

25   *http://www.xeper.org/pub/tos*

26   *The Woman's Encyclopedia Of Myths And Secrets*, p 406

*The three main varieties
of "extraterrestrial"
reported in abductions
and other experiences.*

*This is one of many types
of reptilian being and this
image was painted from
ancient and modern
descriptions by artist
Hilary Reed*

The Zulu shaman Credo Mutwa painted the image of this "Nordic" extraterrestrial figure, or the "Mzungu" as they are called in African legend. These tall, white, beings could appear and disappear according to African legends and reports, and they were widely reported in Africa long before the white Europeans first arrived. The tribes people believed that the European settlers were the returning "Mzungu" and they called them by that name.

THE MZUNGU

Long, long before Africans met the White people from Europe they first met a race of golden-haired and blue-eyed aliens from space, a race to which the Africans gave the name MZUNGU. When Africans finally saw Europeans they transferred this name to them. The MZUNGU Space aliens carry a mystic silver sphere that enables them to appear and vanish at will. A MZUNGU recently warned three Black Shamans about the coming destruction of Africa.

The most reported non-human entity is the "grey" with their big black eyes. It would appear, however, that the grey "body" and black "eyes" are really an outer protection from the Sun. Inside the "suit" they are reptilian. This image was drawn by Hilary Reed

Credo Mutwa, the 79-year-old Zulu sanusi or shaman, who has been initiated throughout his life into the secret knowledge of the reptilian control

A painting from ancient and modern descriptions by Credo Mutwa of one reptilian species. He calls them the Chitauri, the "Children of the Serpent" or the "Children of the Python"

An Earth woman alongside a symbolic "extraterrestrial" with a big willy. This portrays the interbreeding of the Chitauri with human women – a constant theme throughout the ancient world. The image of the "ET" is symbolic because the Chitauri forbade the people to portray them as they really are

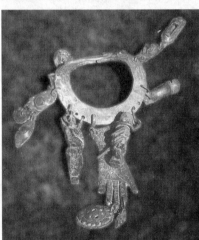

Credo Mutwa's Necklace of the Mysteries, which is at least 500 years old and Credo believes could go back 1,000 years. Its symbols tell the story of Africans and their extraterrestrial origin

The hand of symbols attached to a classic flying saucer shape. Credo Mutwa says that the Chitauri arrived in these craft from much bigger "motherships" that orbited the Earth

The flying reptiles holding the cross of St George which stand at the entrance to that Illuminati stronghold, the City of London

One example of the reptilian gods portrayed more accurately. Many of these reptilian figurines were found in graves in Mesopotamia. They came from the Ubaid culture, which existed up to around 4,000BC when Sumer emerged in the same region

The reptilian gargoyles are symbols of the reptilian bloodlines and their control. You find them on the castles and stately homes of the bloodline families and on churches and cathedrals built by the Illuminati

A bust in the Vatican of Thor/Indara, the King of Sumer who battled with the serpent cult according to the British Edda texts

Thor (St George) slays the dragon in a Persian sculpture of around 600BC

Horus, the Egyptian Son of God, slaying Set or Seth, the "demon crocodile". From an Egyptian bas-relief of about 1,000BC and now in the Louvre Museum in Paris

On the left is an ancient Egyptian portrayal of the "virgin mother", Isis, and her saviour son, Horus. On the right is the classic pose of the virgin mother, Mary, and her saviour son, Jesus, in a church at Godshill on the Isle of Wight in England. Why are they so remarkably alike? Because they are precisely the same deities under different names

The goddess Artemis (Dana, Diana) with her symbolic eggs in a statue at the Ephesus Museum. Artemis/Diana was the main deity of the Merovingian bloodline and both are symbolised by bees, honey, and the hive

The headquarters of the infamous Skull and Bones Society alongside the campus of Yale University in New England. Initiates are selected by bloodline and go on to serve the Illuminati in politics, business, banking, media, and the military

The Pentagon is the centre of the pentagram and this is why the symbol-obsessed Illuminati have located the headquarters of the US military in such a building

The Supreme Headquarters of the 33rd degree of the Scottish Rite of Freemasonry, located near the White House at 1733 16th Street, Washington DC. Behind the pillars is a massive image of the rising Sun and at the bottom of the steps are two female "sphinx" figures. Inside, according to former 33rd degree Freemason, Jim Shaw, are many reptilian images

When this statue was unveiled of George Washington, the first President of the United States, the people could not understand why their esteemed George was depicted in such a strange, half-naked, pose. Look at the classic image of the Satanic symbol of "Baphomet", however, and all becomes clear

Aleister Crowley, the most famous Satanist of the 20th century, who was connected both to the Nazi networks in Germany and the British Prime Minister and bloodline, Winston Churchill

Baron Philippe de Rothschild of the Mouton-Rothschild wine producing estates in France, who died in 1988 at the age of 86. Phillip Eugene de Rothschild, now living under another name, says he is the unofficial son of this legend of the wine producing industry

Anton LaVey, the founder of the Church of Satan, with his high priestess, the actress, Jane Mansfield. Many famous showbiz names were involved with LaVey, including Sammy Davis Junior and Frank Sinatra

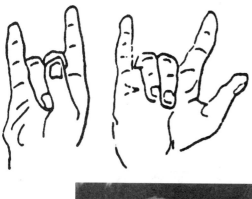

Satanism and its signs and symbols are all around us. The Satanic hand sign for the "Devil" is to close the two middle fingers while pointing the other two upwards like horns. Now look at Bill Clinton after his first inauguration speech and two pictures of George W. Bush during the 2000 election campaign in which he was manipulated into the presidency. Co-incidence? No way

A scene at Bohemian Grove in northern California, the centre for Illuminati ritual in the month of July. This picture was taken in 1957. The speaker is Glenn Seaborg, the man who gave the world plutonium, and either side are two men destined to be presidents of the United States. On the left is Ronald Reagan, then a B-movie actor, and on the right is Richard Nixon. Tricky Dicky was still three years away from running for president against John F. Kennedy. Presidents are not elected by ballot, they are selected by blood

Sai Baba, the "Living God on Earth", or rather sexual abuser, con man, and thief

This is how tiny micro-chips have become – and these are only the ones we are allowed to see. According to insiders the chips are now small enough to be inserted by a hypodermic needle during vaccination programmes

Artist Clive Burrows produced this impression of a shape-shifted Ted Heath conducting a ritual at Burnham Beeches from descriptions provided by the woman who witnessed this scene in the early 1970s

CHAPTER 11

God save us
from religion

It has served us well, this myth of Christ.

Pope Leo X

Religion is the greatest form of mass mind control yet invented and it has been the most important weapon in the reptilian agenda for thousands of years. It has imprisoned the minds of the masses and kept them in perpetual fear and servitude. They accept their, often grotesque, plight on the word of men in long frocks who tell them it is "God's plan". Take the shit today and you'll have paradise tomorrow. It's always tomorrow.

Babylon to Rome

The blueprint for control by religion was honed and polished in Babylon, in the lands of Sumer in Mesopotamia. Babylon is also the location from where the global financial scam was foisted on the world. This scam involves lending people money that doesn't exist and charging interest on it. It just so happens that Babylon became the new headquarters of the Anunnaki bloodlines after the Sumer Empire collapsed. Their operational centre later moved to Rome and it was then that we had the Roman Empire and the founding of the Roman Church, which, understandably, was a copy of the religion of Babylon. It uses the same methods, symbols, and stories. It is interesting to note that the word basilica, as in St Peter's Basilica in Rome, would appear to originate from a term relating to both a deadly serpent and royalty. A basilisk was a "mythical serpent, lizard or dragon, the "King of Serpents", whose hissing drove away all other reptiles, and whose glance and breath were fatal", according to Norman Lewis in the *Comprehensive Word Guide* (Doubleday, New York, 1958). It was the "king snake" that all other reptiles feared. *The American Heritage Dictionary Of The English Language*, Fourth Edition, 2000, reveals that the name basilisk comes from the Latin/Greek terms basiliscus, basiliskos, and basileus, meaning king or "little king". This evolved into the Old French word, basilisc. Here we have the connection between royalty and the serpent yet again. The basilisk is mentioned in Psalm 91, but by the time of the King James translation, the reference has been changed to an "adder". Later the basilisk became associated with the cock and became interchangeable with the term "cockatrice". St Peter of basilica fame is connected to the cock, as we shall see.

How appropriate should the centrepiece of the headquarters of the Babylonian Church in Rome be named after a royal serpent.

Rome to London

When the Anunnaki bloodlines moved their operational centre to London after William of Orange arrived in 1688, we had the emergence of the British Empire. In fact, the empires of Sumer, Babylon, Rome, and Britain were all created and controlled by one force. In Babylon they used the same structure they had in Sumer with the priesthood acting as the go-between or middleman for the "gods", and this gave them enormous power over the people. During the Babylon period the Anunnaki were seeking to rise from the ashes of Sumer and develop their strategy for taking over the world covertly through their bloodlines and front organisations. To do this, they needed to take out of circulation the true accounts of history, especially their own role in humanity's suppression, and the esoteric knowledge that would allow the people to understand the magnitude of their own power and potential. John A. Keel, in his book *Our Haunted Planet* says that they chose religion as the "battleground" on which to conquer the human mind:

> "...The para-human Serpent People of the past are still among us. They were probably worshipped by the builders of Stonehenge and the forgotten ridge-making cultures of South America. ...In some parts of the world the Serpent People successfully posed as gods and imitated the techniques of the super-intelligence [God]. This led to the formation of pagan religions centered on human sacrifices. The conflict, so far as man himself was concerned, became one of religions and races. Whole civilizations based upon the worship of these false gods rose and fell in Asia, Africa, and South America.

> "...Once an individual had committed himself, he opened a door so that an indefinable something (probably an undetectable mass of intelligent energy) could actually enter his body and exercise some control over his suвconscious mind ... The human race would supply the pawns ...Each individual had to consciously commit himself to one of the opposing forces ...The main battle was for what was to become known as the human soul." [1]

By choosing to give yourself to a deity or "god", you open your psyche to possession by the force that deity or "god" represents. And deities like "Mary" and "Jesus" represent very different forces to those perceived by their "believers". It is so important for people to get out of religion and start recovering control of their own minds. There is an important point to make before we proceed because the symbolism of the Sun is about to become very significant. There is a general belief that the Sun represents the male and the Moon the female. That's understandable because that's the way it looks and on one level it's true. But there's a twist. There came a time when the global religion of worshipping the goddess was replaced by the male "god". However, that was only on the surface, for public consumption, control, and ignorance. To suppress the ancient knowledge, not least that of true history, it was necessary to destroy the outward expression of goddess worship while its initiates continued with business as usual. Therefore, religions like Judaism, Christianity, and Islam were created to give the appearance of being dominated by the male, while, in truth, being secret vehicles for the worship of the goddess. This involved taking female deities like El and depicting them as male.

The sun goddess

Way back in history the Sun was portrayed as female.[2] In Japan, a country with a long history of serpent worship, the ruling clans claimed descent from the Sun Goddess. Japanese tribes in AD238 were ruled by Queen Himiko, who was called the Daughter of the Sun. The goddess Aditi, the Hindu Great Mother, was depicted as the Sun. She was said to be the mother of the Adityas, who was symbolic of the 12 signs of the zodiac. The Sun was the "garment" of the goddess, who was "clothed with the Sun". When Christians made Mother Mary their version of the goddess, they said that Mary was a "woman clothed in the Sun". Tantric Buddhism had the goddess as the Sun. The ancient Arabs worshipped the Sun as the Goddess Atthar and referred to her as the "Torch of the Gods". The Celts had a Sun goddess called Sulis, a name that derives from Suil, meaning both "eye" and "Sun", both of which appear on the dollar bill and the reverse of the Great Seal of the United States. She was also known as Sul, Sol and Sunna. One of her shrines in Britain is the biggest human-made mound in Europe called Silbury Hill, which is part of the complex of standing stones and earthworks at Avebury in Wiltshire, England. Sul was worshipped from the high places, just as El and her derivatives were associated with mountains. Hills overlooking springs were the most sacred places in Britain for the Goddess Sul, places like Glastonbury Tor and Bath. Overlooking Bath, for example, is Solsbury Hill, and Salisbury in Wiltshire is another important Sun goddess site and the location of a famous cathedral much beloved of Prince Charles. When the Romans came to Britain they worshipped this goddess as Sol Minerva. Her symbol was an owl – the symbol of the rituals at Bohemian Grove in northern California. The road system around the Congress Building in Washington DC is also shaped unmistakably as an owl (see The Biggest Secret). The lion became the symbol of the "male" Sun when the open became hidden, but once again the lion had more commonly symbolised the goddess. The Mother Goddess Hathor was depicted as a lion-headed Sphinx.

Mystery Babylon

The Mystery school/secret society network designed to advance the reptilian agenda expanded rapidly from the time of Babylon after 2000BC. In this same period the Royal Court of the Dragon was infiltrating the Egyptian Mystery Schools and the other structures of power. The Jewish historian, Eupolemus, said that giants built Babylon after the deluge – the usual story. According to a Babylonian text, these giants were the Anunnaki. The Anunnaki priesthood in Babylon began to invent a whole new history and religious "truth", through which they could control the people mentally, emotionally, and, as a consequence, physically. In doing so, they replaced spiritual truths with fairy tales about mythical people, which the masses were told to take literally. At this point, they were still referring to "gods" plural because the Illuminati's manipulation had not yet reached the stage where the Anunnaki and other gods could be transformed into one "god". When that change came it would eliminate the more obvious records of their existence. The Hebrew priesthood would achieve this, together with the English translators of the Bible. The religion of Babylon created the mould, even the detailed stories, for those that followed. For example, where have you heard this before? In Babylon they worshipped a trinity of Nimrod, the father, symbolised as a fish; Tammuz or Ninus, the son, who was said to have died to save humanity on December 25th; and Queen Semiramis, the Babylonian "Isis", who was symbolised as a dove. They said that Nimrod and Tammuz, the father and son, were "one". When Tammuz died for the sins of humanity, the priesthood said he was put in a tomb and, three days later when they rolled back the stone, he was gone. All this was thousands of years before Christianity and it is just one of so many versions of the "Jesus" story that were told long before "Jesus" was supposed to have lived. Oh yes, in the spring rituals to mark the death and resurrection of Tammuz/Ninus, they offered buns inscribed with a solar cross – the hot cross buns of the much later "Christian" festival called Easter. Christianity is just recycled "paganism" that condemns "pagans" as evil. What hypocrisy. Even the term "Testament" is the entomological confirmation that it is literally all a load of balls. Lauren Savage, the Webmaster at davidicke.com and a long-time researcher of ancient history, tells me that the root of Testament is "testes". Apparently, tradition says that the ancient Hebrews used to hold the other guy's balls, sorry "testes", while hearing an oath. Funnily enough, they do the same in some of the Illuminati rituals today, I am told. Lauren says that in the King James Version of the Bible, Abraham has his servant swear upon his "thigh" according to the translation when, in Hebrew tradition, it would have been his dangly bits. It certainly gives new meaning to the term: "Got you by the balls". Staring at a penis was another way to "God" in these times, I understand, and in some way this related to "remembering" the covenant. All it does for me is make me remember that I am not as young as I used to be. So the Old Testament means "Old Balls" and the New Testament means "New Balls". When we testify in court is the judge symbolically holding our testicles? You're right, don't lets go there. Good thinking.

Suns of god

Tammuz was a name for the Sumerian god Dumazi or Damu (the "only begotten son" or "Son of the Blood") who provided the blueprint for all the later sons of God, including Jesus. The Hebrews inherited Tammuz (also known as Adonis) from the Babylonians and the Roman records refer to Tammuz as the chief god of the Jews. The Jewish calendar still has a month named after Tammuz, who was known as "the serpent who emanated from the heaven-god, Anu."[3] And Anu was the head of the Anunnaki, the Sumerian tablets say. The Mesopotamian kings were said to be of the bloodline of Tammuz, just as Sir Laurence Gardner claims that the Merovingian "true" royal line is the bloodline of Jesus. It was said that the land was given life by the blood of Tammuz and he was a healer, saviour, and a shepherd who looked after his flock of stars. He died wearing a "crown of thorns" made from myrrh. Tammuz was symbolically sacrificed on the Day of Atonement in the form of a lamb. He was worshipped in Jerusalem where his exact story would later be re-told using the name "Jesus". And, take a deep breath here vicar, the cave in Bethlehem where Jesus is said to have been born, is the *same* one where the ancients claimed that Tammuz (Adonis) was born. The Bible "translator", Jerome, admitted that Bethlehem had been a sacred grove dedicated to Tammuz, the fertility god or "spirit of the corn". Bethlehem means "House of Bread" or "House of Corn". Horus, the Egyptian Son of God, was born in the "Place of Bread" and Jesus said he was "the Bread of Life".

The priesthood took the ancient Sumer Sun religion, esoteric, astrological and astronomical knowledge, and the stories of their reptilian gods, and buried them in symbolic fables. This hid their real meaning, except to initiates, while introducing the rigid beliefs of the prison religions. Every major religion, Judaism, Christianity, Hinduism, Islam, and Buddhism all had the same basic origin: the knowledge and beliefs of Sumer, which inherited the knowledge and beliefs of Atlantis and Lemuria. The major religions were all founded in the lands once occupied by the Sumer Empire. They may have emphasised different elements of the Sumer beliefs, but that was the mould from which they all came. The priesthood's job was to withdraw the true knowledge from circulation and they twisted their manufactured religious texts until the knowledge that would set the people free was portrayed as "evil". Look at Christianity. Another goal of the priesthood, or the "Long Frocks" as I call them, was to develop stories and themes that made the people feel powerless, insignificant, and in awe of invented religious deities. By being the "middlemen" to the gods (later "God") and interpreters of the "law" laid down by these make-believe "deities", they could control the people for their masters, the reptilian and other demonic entities. To stop the people rebelling against this suppression, control, and poverty, the priesthood stories had to promise a paradise in the afterlife for all those who obeyed "God's law". In other words, *their* law, the law of the Anunnaki. And for those who did not obey this "law"? Eternal hell and damnation. Even the term "sin", as I have pointed out, comes from the name of an Anunnaki "god".

Out of Babylon (1): Judaism

The texts that formed the Old Testament of the Bible, a foundation of Judaism and Christianity, were written after the Levite priesthood of the Hebrews were held in captivity after 586BC in…here we go…Babylon! I think the term "captivity" is less than appropriate, also. The early Hebrews worshipped the serpent god of the Sumer Empire and the Levites were called "Sons of the Great Serpent".[4] Their god YHVH was depicted as part human, part serpent, and their sacred book of esoteric (hidden) knowledge, the Kabbala, means "Serpent Wisdom".[5] The Levites or Sons of the Great Serpent (bloodline) worshipped YHVH as a dragon called Leviathan, hence Levite.[6] YHVH's serpent form was also known as Nehushtan or "Brazen Serpent" by the Levites and they placed golden and brass images of this deity on the altars of Hebrew temples.[7] Excavations have discovered bronze and copper serpent symbols in former Levite temples. The mythical story of Moses and the Brazen Serpent set upon a cross is symbolic of this same theme. The Babylonians had inherited the stories and myths of Egypt and Sumer, and now they would reappear in a twisted form in the texts that would later become the Old Testament. Genesis, Exodus, Leviticus, Numbers, and Deuteronomy, which together make up the "Jewish" Torah, were all written by the Levites, or under their supervision, during or after the captivity in Babylon when the Levites joined forces with the network of the Babylonian reptilian priesthood. So you find the Sumerian story of King Sargon floating on the river in a basket of rushes rehashed by the Levites in the account of the mythical character called "Moses". And the Sumerian Edin, the "abode of the gods", became the Garden of Eden in the Levite tales. The Book of Genesis is an edited version of the Sumerian accounts and it is a mass of goddess symbolism. The "mana from heaven", which the Moses-led Israelites were supposed to have received from "God" or YHVH/Jehovah, is actually a name for the goddess, Mana, who, like El, ruled the underworld.[8] The Romans knew her as Mana or Mania. Her ancestral spirits were called "manes", as in the mane of the lion, so associated with the serpent cult, and of the horse, so connected with the Amazons or Valkeries. From the names Mana and Mania we get the word to describe crazed behaviour. This is derived from worship of the Moon goddess, as in Moon-madness or "lunacy". Mantra, the Sanskrit term for projecting vibrations by chanting words or sounds, comes from the same root. Manu was the name for the Indian version of Noah, who survived the deluge with the help of the Great Serpent Vasuki.[9] In earlier times Manu was the womb of the goddess.

The Levites, those Babylonian Mystery School initiates, invented an entire history for the Hebrews to hide the real story and create a fiercely imposed structure of religious control. The Rabbis continue that tradition to this day. There is far more about this story in *The Biggest Secret*, where I have highlighted the way these texts were coded with esoteric knowledge and why the vast majority of people who we call "Jewish" today have no genetic connection to Palestine or Israel. They originate, as Jewish sources have confirmed, from the Khazars, a people from southern Russia and the Caucasus Mountains, who had a mass conversion to Judaism in the 8th century. The terms "Jewish" and "Hebrew" have become mixed up. Some people we call Jewish go back to the Hebrews of the Middle East, but most do not. They come from the Caucasus. It shouldn't matter where they come from, its just a body, but if people are being told a fib they have a right to know. So much of the "Hebrew" knowledge also came from the Egyptian Mystery schools and this is where the Hebrew language originated. The classic "Hebrew" or "Jewish" name, Cohen, comes from Cahen, the Egyptian name for priest and prince, and there are fundamental connections between the Hebrews and both Egypt and Babylon. After all, the people who became known as the Hebrews came from

within the same Sumer Empire that included the lands we now call Israel or
Palestine. They were just an expression of the same empire and doubtless the
priesthood of the Sumerians, Egyptians, Hebrews, Sumerians, and Babylonians,
were connected by the same brotherhood networks going back to Atlantis and
Lemuria. The Sumerian priesthood were the middlemen between the people and
the reptilian "gods" and so, in the end, were the others. The invented story of the
"Exodus" was written to obscure the truth of what really happened in Egypt and
there is no historical record outside of the Levite texts, nor any archaeological
evidence, that any such "Exodus" ever took place. Between 1967 and 1982 when the
Israelis occupied the Sinai Desert, they instigated a massive search for evidence of
the 40 years the "Israelites" were supposed to have lived there. What did they find?
Nothing. The loss of the Egyptian army in the Red Sea is not recorded in any
historical document and this is utterly ludicrous if it had actually happened. The
Greek historian Herodotus (c.485-425BC) travelled and researched the lands and
history of Egypt and the Near East and yet he heard nothing of King Solomon, the
mass exodus of "Israelites" from Egypt, or the Egyptian army drowned in the Red
Sea. Neither did the Greek philosopher, Plato. L.A. Waddell, a fluent reader of
Sanskrit, Sumerian, and Egyptian, researched that whole region in great detail.
He concluded:

> "There is absolutely no inscriptional evidence whatsoever, nor any ancient Greek or
> Roman reference, for the existence of Abraham or any of the Jewish patriarchs or
> prophets of the Old Testament, nor for Moses, Saul, David, Solomon, nor any of the
> Jewish kings, with the mere exception of two, or at most three, of the later kings." [10]

Nor was there any claim for the existence of any of these people until the Levites
were taken to Babylon where the plot was hatched. The same stories that were told
about Abraham, like the near-sacrifice of his son, can be found in India. Earlier
versions of "Moses" appear all over the Near and Middle East and the
Mediterranean region under different names. In Babylon they said that God gave
"Nemo the Lawgiver" the tablets of the law on a mountaintop. After the Levites left
Babylon, they turned Nemo into "Moses". In Syria, they had a guy they called
"Mises", who did all the things the Levites attributed to "Moses". Like the
Sumerian King Sargon, "Mises" was found as a baby floating in a basket of reeds or
rushes. Mises went on to part the waters with his magical rod and he was the
guardian of the law, written in stone. Another "Moses" was the Egyptian hero, Ra-
Haraldhti, whose alleged life was also copied by the forgers of history.[11] The "Ten
Commandments", so associated with Moses, are a copy of the laws known as the
Code of Hammurabi. These were written at least a thousand years earlier. Of course
they were, the Code of Hammurubi came from...Babylon! But this code of
Hammurabi goes back even further to our old friend Indara/Thor/St George, the
first king of Sumer and his "Ten Commandments" of some 5,000 years ago. These
were called in the Edda the "Hug Runes" with the word "hug" meaning affection,
love, and good heart. Hence hugging.

The real Bible code

Another fact that is vital to understand if we are to see the forest for the trees is that these Levite texts were written symbolically in codes and parables. When we take them all literally we lose the plot. Before the prison religions, the ancients were worshippers of the Sun and all three syllables in Sol-om-on are different names for the Sun. King Solomon's Temple was not a real location, it is symbolic. The Freemasonic historian, Manly P. Hall, wrote that King Solomon's 1,000 "wives" and concubines were symbolic of the Sun, moons, asteroids, and other "receptive bodies", within his "house" or "temple" – the solar system.[12] The stories attributed to Solomon and David can be found long before in India. And if there was no David or Solomon, then how can they have provided the bloodline of "Jesus"? Answer: they didn't. That genealogy was invented to serve a purpose, as were the Old Testament genealogies back to "Abraham" in Sumer. They were part of the manufactured history, some truth mixed with endless lies and deceit, which was created to hide what really happened. Edouard Dujardin, in his book, *Ancient History Of The God Jesus* (Watts and Co, 1938) documents how Judaism or the "Jahvehists" took the gods of other nations and turned them into mythical Hebrew leaders, heroes, and prophets:

> "Where Judaism fully succeeded, the ancient Baals of Palestine were transformed into heroic servants of Jahveh; where it gained only a partial victory, they became secondary gods ...Many of the old Baals of Palestine were assimilated by Judaism, which converted them into heroes in the cause of Jahveh, and in fact many scholars agree that the patriarchs of the Bible are the ancient gods of Palestine."[13]

The Hebrew gods, er, sorry...God

The idea that the Hebrew religion was based on "one God" is outrageous nonsense. They worshipped many gods and in the Old Testament texts they refer again and again to god in the plural, as with Elohim. The Jewish singular "god", El, comes from the name Elohim, which is plural. The Elohim were the Anunnaki, and the serpent goddess, El, in the Edda relates to all this. But in the English translations the plural gods are turned into the singular God. The first line of Genesis "In the Beginning God created the heaven and the Earth" actually reads in the Hebrew: "In the beginning the gods created the heavens and the Earth." The word Elohim, plural, is used 30 times in Genesis and 2,570 times in all.[14] These include the terms: "And the elohim said let *us* make men in our image"; the elohim said "come let *us* go down" in the story of the Tower of Babel; and "Behold, the man has become like one of *us*, to know good and evil" in the Garden of Eden. Also in Genesis we have: "And elohim said, 'Let *us* make Adam'".[15] Terms like Yahveh-elohim or Yahveh of the gods, is translated as Lord and Lord God to hide the truth. It was impossible to eliminate "the gods" when these texts were first written because the whole of the world was worshipping a vast range of gods, representing the Anunnaki and others under different names, and the Sun, Moon, planets, stars, and natural forces. The move from gods to God advanced rapidly with the advent of the Illuminati religion of Christianity and when the Bible was translated into English. The King James Version of the Bible, the most used translation of them all, was sponsored by King James Ist, the first king of England and Scotland, who took the joint throne after the death of Elizabeth Ist in 1603. Even most of the "new" Bibles are only updates of the King James Version. The "King James" removed a lot of marginal notes included in its predecessor, the so-called Geneva Bible, published in 1560. The king wanted to revise the Bible text because, like his mother, Mary Stuart, he believed totally in the "divine right of kings" in which the monarch answered to no one except "God" (the gods). The Geneva Bible included phrases he did not like in relation to this "divine right" and so he had them removed. James was a Satanist and reptilian bloodline going back to the Egyptian pharaohs. His sexual desires preferred young boys, as recorded in numerous books and public records, and his lust for blood appeared insatiable. When he killed an animal he would literally roll in its blood, and he was responsible for the death and torture of thousands of "witches". He suggested many of the tortures himself.[16] This is the man who decided what the Bible does or does not say! I am sure that the mass slaughter of "witches" by King James and the Christian church is connected with destroying certain bloodlines passed on through the female DNA. Sir Francis Bacon oversaw the translation of the King James Bible. He was from the reptilian bloodline and a high initiate of the secret society network as Grand Master of the Rosicrucian Order. He was a Knights Templar, an inspiration behind the creation of Freemasonry and the Royal Society, and a key member of the team of initiates under Lord Draconis, Edward de Vere, which compiled the "Shakespeare" plays.

Out of Babylon (2): Christianity

The Old Testament was joined by the "New" with the founding of Christianity, a religion that was based on the same Levite fables. In fact, there was no "New Testament" until the 4th century AD. That's a long time for the texts to be formulated for a religion that supposed to have been started 300 years earlier. And who arranged for all this? The Roman Emperor Constantine the "Great" after AD325. He was the official head of a Roman Empire controlled by the very same forces that had earlier controlled Babylon when the texts of the Old Testament started to be written. Just a coincidence, eh? Vendyl "Indiana" Jones, the director of the Institute for Judeo-Christian Research in Arlington, Texas, points out that "primal Christians" had only the Hebrew Torah, the first 5 books of "Moses", the 22 books of the Prophets and Holy Writings that included Psalms, Proverbs, Job, Song of Songs, Ruth, Lamentations, Ecclesiastes, Esther, Daniel, Ezra-Nehemiah, and the two books of Chronicles; plus the 14 books of the Apocrypha. There was nothing about "Jesus". They met and worshipped with the Hebrews in the Synagogues and had no "Testament" of their own. Jones stresses that when we see terms in the New Testament like: "…the scripture saith…it is written…what saith the law…thus saith the Lord…or…as the prophet said…" they are referring to Old Testament writings. The first "Christians" based their faith on the texts of the

Levites, just as they still do today. As Vendyl Jones says, the writers of what he calls the "Newer Testament" viewed the Older Testament of the Hebrew Scriptures as the supreme authority:

> "Much later their writings became the Newer Testament. Their authority was in the Torah primarily. This was enforced by the Prophets and Holy Writings. Their Newer Testament writings never showed or claimed supremacy over the Older Testament! They did all their writing in the Jewish mind-set. This attitude always concedes all authority to the Torah! It never irritates or challenges the authority of the Hebrew Scriptures." [17]

The big "C" is a big lie

Christianity was just an "add-on" to the texts and laws decided by the Levites and their successors during and after the Babylon "captivity". So what is Christianity and where did it come from? If you are a Christian, I should sit down and strap in. Christianity is largely a Sun religion and "Jesus" is not the "son", but the Sun. Or at least that is part of his symbolism. We have already seen the similarities between "Jesus" and Balder of the serpent cult also, of course. The ancient Sun religion of Sumer, and throughout the ancient world, was written down as a symbolic story, which Christians have been told to take literally. I hope you are ready for this, vicar. The main form of communication in the ancient world was symbolism and parable, and to understand the ancient Sun symbolism is to understand the major religions.

They used the symbol in *Figure 32* to symbolise the Sun's journey through the year, or, more accurately, the Earth's journey in relation to the Sun. This is the so-called Sun cross. It can be found throughout the ancient world. They drew a circle and a zodiac (a Greek word meaning animal circle) and added a cross to mark the four seasons, and the solstice and equinox points. At the centre of the cross they placed the Sun and this is where the theme of the Sun, or symbolically the "son", on the cross originates. A similar symbol was used in Lemuria relating, James Churchward says, to the primal forces of creation. A long list of pre-"Jesus" deities were given the birthday of December 25th because of this Sun symbolism. The winter solstice, the lowest point of the Sun's power in the

Figure 32: *The cross and the circle that symbolised the solar year. The point of the cross to the right is the winter solstice when the Sun was said to have symbolically died. Three days later, on December 25th, the Sun was said to be born or born again*

northern hemisphere, is on December 21st/22nd. This was the time when the ancients said that the Sun had "died" and gone down into the dark place. By December 25th, three days later, they said the Sun had begun its journey back to the peak of its power in the summer and so they said that on this day the Sun was born or born again. The ancient Sun gods were given this "birthday", three days after the winter solstice, for this reason. These deities didn't exist, as everyone now accepts. They were symbolic of the Sun and so was Jesus, along with much other symbolism.

The Christian "Christmas" is an ancient pagan festival under another name and so is Easter. On March 25th, the old date for Easter, the Sun enters the astrological sign of Aries, the ram or the lamb, and they sacrificed lambs in their rituals at this time to appease the gods and ensure a bumper harvest. Put another way, they believed the blood of the lamb would encourage the gods to forgive their sins. The story of Samson (Sam-sun) in the Old Testament is the same Sun symbolism. The ancients symbolised the Sun's annual cycle as the life of a man. They would portray the Sun as a newborn baby on December 25th and he would grow up to become a big, strapping, very strong man at the summer solstice. This is the peak of the Sun's power in the northern hemisphere when it dominates the darkness at the longest day. At this time, the Sun-man would be given long golden hair to symbolise the powerful rays of the summer Sun. As the Sun entered the house of Virgo the Virgin (the house of Delilah) at the start of autumn, this Sun-man would have his hair cut shorter as the power of the Sun began to fade. This is the real story of Samson. He was not a real person, but symbolic of the Sun. Samson, like Jesus, St Paul, and many other biblical characters, was said to be a Nazarene or Nazarite. Here we have the true meaning of the term "Jesus of Nazareth" or "Jesus the Nazarene". The town of Nazareth did not exist during the alleged life of Jesus. There is no mention of it in any records or on any maps, even though detailed Roman records were kept at that time. It was founded after the Gospel stories were circulating. The Nazarite sect banned the cutting of hair, except in certain solar rituals, because the hair represented the rays of the sun. This could be the real origin of this custom that still continues today in the Sikh religion. The Nazarenes or Nazarites wore black, as did the Babylonian brotherhood, and this was inherited by the Christian church. Today the Arabic word for Christians is Nasrani and in the Muslim Koran they are the Nasara or Nazara. This comes from the Hebrew word, Nozrim, which derived from the term, Nozrei ha-Brit or Keepers of the Covenant. The Anunnaki covenant, it seems to me.

Christianity was created by rehashing the ancient symbolic story of the Sun, together with Mystery school allegory and serpent cult symbolism presented as a literal story in an historical context. The elite priesthood and other initiates knew what the story really meant, and still do, but they tell the people it is literally true and damnation will befall them if they don't believe it. Some 1,200 years before "Jesus", the following was said in the East of the "heathen saviour", (Virishna): he was born to a virgin by Immaculate Conception through the intervention of a Holy Spirit. This fulfilled an ancient prophecy. When he was born, the ruling tyrant wanted to kill him. And his parents had to flee to safety. All male children under the age of two were slain by the ruler as he sought to kill the child. Angels and shepherds were at his birth and he was given gifts of gold, frankincense, and myrrh. He was worshipped as the saviour of men and led a moral and humble life. He performed miracles, which included healing the sick, giving sight to the blind, casting out devils, and raising the dead. He was put to death on the cross between two thieves. He descended to hell and rose from the dead to ascend back to heaven. Just a coincidence, Archbishop? Well how about these, then? They all pre-date "Jesus", often by thousands of years.

- **Attis, the Son of God of Phrygia**
  He was born on December 25th to a virgin mother. He was called a "saviour", the only begotten son, and died to save humanity. He was crucified on a Friday – "Black Friday" – and his blood was spilled to redeem the Earth. He suffered death "with nails and stakes". He was the Father and Son combined in an earthly body. He was put in a tomb, went down into the underworld, but three days later, on March 25th, his body was found to have disappeared from the tomb and he was resurrected as the "Most High God". His body was symbolised as bread and eaten by those who worshipped him.

- **Krishna (Christ), the Son of God of India**
  He was born to a virgin mother on December 25th and his father was a carpenter. A star marked his birthplace, and angels and shepherds attended. The ruler slaughtered thousands of infants in an effort to kill him, but he survived and went on to perform miracles and heal the sick, including lepers, the blind, and the deaf. He died at about the age of 30 and some traditions say he was crucified on a tree. He was also portrayed on a cross, rose from the dead, and was considered the saviour. His followers apparently knew him as "Jezeus" or "Jeseus", which means "pure essence". It is said that he will return on a white horse to judge the dead and fight the "Prince of Evil".

- **Dionysus or Bacchus, the Son of God of Greece**
  He was born to a virgin mother on December 25th and put in a manger and swaddling clothes. He was a teacher who travelled, performing miracles. He turned water into wine (like the Sun) and rode in triumph on an ass (so did the Egyptian deity, Set). He was the ram or the lamb, God of the Vine, God of Gods and King of Kings, Only Begotten Son, bearer of sins, Redeemer, Anointed One (Christos), Alpha and Omega. He was hung and crucified on a tree, but rose from the dead on March 25th. During the 1st century BC, the Hebrews in Jerusalem also worshipped this deity. J.M. Roberts writes in *Antiquity Unveiled* (Health Research, 1970) that "IES, the Phoenician name for Bacchus, offers the origin to Jesus". He says IES can be broken up into "I" (the one) and "es" (fire and light). Taken as one word, "ies" means the one light. He goes on: "This is none other than the light of St John's gospel; and this name is to be found everywhere on Christian altars, both protestant and catholic, thus clearly

showing that the Christian religion is but a modification of Oriental Sun
Worship, attributed to Zoroaster. The Christians read the same letters 'IHS' in the
Greek text as 'Jes' and the Roman Christian priesthood added the terminus 'us'."

Here are some of the other pre-Christian deities of whom the "Jesus" story was
told: Apollo, Hercules, and Zeus of Greece; Adad and Marduk of Assyria; Buddha
Sakia and Indra of India and Tibet; Salivahana of southern India and Bermuda;
Osiris and Horus of Egypt; Odin, Balder, and Frey of Scandinavia; Crite of Chaldea;
Zoroaster of Persia; Baal (Bel) and Taut of Phoenicia; Bali of Afghanistan; Jao of
Nepal; Wittoba of Bilingonese; Xamolxis of Thrace; Zoar of the Bonzes; Chu
Chulainn of Ireland; Deva Tat, Codom, and Sammonocadam of Siam; Alcides of
Thebes; Mikado of the Sintoos; Beddru of Japan; Hesus or Eros, and Bremrillaham
of the Druids; Thor, son of Odin, of Gauls; Cadmus of Greece; Hil and Feta of
Mandaites; Gentaut and Quetzalcoatl of Mexico; Universal Monarch of the Sibyls;
Ischy of Formosa; Divine Teacher of Plato; Holy One of Xaca; Fohi, Ieo, Lao-Kium,
Chiang-Ti, and Tien of China; Ixion and Quirnus of Rome; Prometheus of the
Caucasus; Mohammed or Mahomet of Arabia, Dahzbog of the Slavs; Jupiter, Jove,
and Quirinius of Rome; Mithra of Persia, India, and Rome.[18]

The cult of Mithra originates thousands of years before "Jesus" and yet again tells
the later Christian story in fine detail. It is even said that gold, frankincense, and
myrrh, were offered to him. By the time that Jesus was invented by the Anunnaki
priesthood, the Mithra rites and religion were widespread throughout the Roman
Empire. When they founded Christianity in Rome, they used the symbols and myths
of the Mithric rituals. Mithra's sacred day was Sunday because he was, like Jesus,
symbolic of the Sun. Mithra worshippers called this the "Lord's Day" and they
celebrated the main Mithra festival during what is now Easter. Mithra initiations
were held in caves adorned with the signs of Capricorn and Cancer, symbolic of the
winter and summer solstices. He was portrayed as a winged Lion (the Sun) standing
within a spiralling serpent. The lion and the serpent are, of course, major symbols of
the serpent cult/Illuminati. The Roman Church encompassed the Mithra Eucharist
into its "Christian" rituals. Mithra was claimed to have said: "He who shall not eat of
my body nor drink of my blood, so that he may be one with me and I with him, shall
not be saved." The very site on which the Vatican was built was a sacred place of
Mithra worship. It still is. They just call him Jesus. As I have written before, the cult
of Mithra simply became the cult of Myth-ra – Christianity.

Mithra was a symbol for the Sun and so was his Christian version. Jesus was the
Light of the World (the Sun); he will come back on the clouds and everyone shall see
him (the Sun). Jesus walks on water (the Sun's reflection does that); Jesus performed
his Father's work in the temple at the age of 12 and started his ministry at 30. The
Sun reaches it's daily peak at 12 noon when the ancients, like the Egyptians, said that
the Sun was the "Most High God". The Sun enters each sign of the zodiac at 30
degrees, hence he starts his "ministry" at 30. Jesus is claimed to have turned water
into wine because that is what the Sun does by making the grapes grow. There is
much zodiac symbolism in the Bible, as with the two fishes (Pisces) and the 12

baskets (zodiac signs) into which Jesus places his multiplied loaves during the "feeding of the 5,000". Jesus was the "fish" and "fisher of men" perhaps because the Earth was entering the sign of Pisces the fish at the time he was supposed to have lived. But there is so much "fish" symbolism with regard to these solar deities throughout history that we cannot ignore a symbolic connection with the tales of fish gods and amphibious beings – the Nommo or Annedoti, etc. of Sirius. Remember, too, that the Dogon recount the story that the amphibious Nommo said that one of them would be crucified. The translation of the end of the world comes from the Greek "aeon" and refers to the end of the "age" and not the "world". The end of the age is the end of the 2,160-year cycle, during which the Earth passes through an astrological sign. Today we are nearing the end of another age, as we leave Pisces and enter Aquarius. Here are some more of the "Jesus" myths decoded.

Jesus, the historical character

Outside of the New Testament texts there is no sign or record of Jesus whatsoever. A mention in the works of the "Hebrew" historian Josephus is an obvious later addition in the priesthood's desperation to cross-reference their meal ticket. More than 40 writers are known to have chronicled the events in Israel/Palestine at the alleged time of "Jesus" and not one of them mentions him. The writer Philo lived throughout the "life" of Jesus and wrote a history of the Judeans, which covered this whole period. Philo lived in or near Jerusalem at the time that Jesus was supposed to have been born to a virgin mother, made his triumphant entry into Jerusalem on a donkey, and was crucified and rose again. In this same period, King Herod is also claimed to have killed all those children trying to eliminate the "saviour". What does Philo say about these amazing events? Nothing, zilch, the big round circle. It is the same with the Roman records and the work of every contemporary author. There is a simple explanation for this. These events never happened because there was no "Jesus".

Jesus the "christ"

The word "Christ" comes from the Greek "Christos", which simply means "anointed". The anointing was performed with the fat of a crocodile, menstrual blood, and goodness knows what else. The term was used for any Israelite king or priest and could be applied to anyone who has been anointed. The Babylonian Tammuz was called the Christos or sacred king and the same or similar terms were applied to many of these pre-Christian "Jesus" figures. The name "Jesus" is also a Greek translation and if he did exist, which he didn't, his name was certainly not Jesus.

Jesus was born to a virgin

The virgin mother of the Sun God is an ancient theme found all over the world. This could relate to the solar myth that the Sun was "born" in a new or virgin Moon and at certain times the constellation of Virgo rose with the Sun. It is also far from impossible that the artificial impregnation of women by the "gods" may have been an ancient origin to this concept, too. So many "heroes" like Merovee and Alexander the Great were said to be the result of their mothers being impregnated by a non-human entity and not by intercourse with their husbands. Albert Pike, a notorious Illuminati operative in the United States, wrote in *The Morals And Dogma Of Scottish Rite Freemasonry* (L.H. Jenkins, 1928) of the Egyptian myth from which the Christian themes originated:

> "At the moment of the winter solstice, the virgin rose (with the Sun), having the Sun (symbolised as Horus) in her bosom …Virgo was Isis (virgin mother of Horus) and her representation, carrying a child (Horus) in her arms, exhibited in her temple, was accompanied by this inscription: **I am all that is, that was, and that shall be**; and the fruit which I brought forth in the Sun." [19]

Writer Gerald Massey reveals that on the walls of the Holy of Holies in the Temple of Luxor, Egypt, are portrayed scenes that are mirrors of the far later Jesus story. The god, That, the Annunciator of the gods, can be seen hailing the virgin and telling her she is going to give birth to the coming son. Another scene depicts the god, Knept, impregnating the virgin with the Holy Ghost or Spirit for the immaculate conception. Then the child is seen enthroned and receiving gifts from three spirits (the three wise men in Christianity) and he is adored as the incarnation of the Sun God. Even the story about Jesus being born in a manger comes from ancient Egypt, as Massey explains:

> "The birthplace of the Egyptian messiah at the Vernal Equinox was figured in Apt, or Apta, the corner; but Apta is also the name of the crib and the manger; hence the child born in Apta was said to have been born in a manger; and this Apta or crib or manager is the hieroglyphic sign of the Solar birthplace. Hence the Egyptians exhibited the babe in the crib or manager in the streets of Alexandria." [20]

The bright star and the three wise men

A bright star marked the birthplace of Jesus, the Bible says. This is the same story told in Egypt about Sirius, the brightest star we can see from Earth. The Egyptians said that the rising of the three stars of Orion's belt (the three "kings", "wise men" or "Magi"?) marked the arrival of Sothis or Sirius, the star of Osiris and Horus. Further symbolism of the "three wise men" is that the Magi were Sun worshippers. Gold, frankincense, and myrrh were the traditional gifts given by Arabian Magi to the Sun and that's why they were given to Mithra in that version of the myth.[21] The birth of Jesus in a stable or cave is repeated throughout the solar-myth stories because the cave represents the "dark place" where the Sun is said to go between the winter solstice and midnight on December 24th. Thus we have the three days in the tomb between the "crucifixion" of Jesus (the Sun) and his "resurrection" or rebirth on December 25th. The cave may have other symbolism, too, however, because the Jesus story can be read on different esoteric levels at the same time.

Tempted in the wilderness for 40 days

This is another common theme for the solar gods. Author and researcher Albert Churchward says the Egyptians estimated that it took 40 days after grain was sown before it appeared through the soil. This was a period of fasting and scarcity, he says, and so Jesus is depicted fasting in the wilderness and "Satan" challenges him to turn stones into bread. The battles between light and dark, and when Jesus defeated the darkness, is symbolic of the time in the Sun's cycle when there is more light every day than dark. The 40 years the "Israelites" were supposed to have spent in the desert was similar "grain" symbolism turned into a manufactured "historical" text.[22]

The words of Jesus

The words attributed to Jesus are quotes from earlier "saviours" and deities. Horus delivered a Sermon on the Mount in Egyptian myth and the Jesus version is simply sayings from earlier texts, like the Books Of Enoch, weaved together into a narrative. Several of the Jesus parables came directly from Buddhism and Jainism. The "Lord's Prayer" derives from sayings in the Jewish Talmud and much older Egyptian prayers to Osiris[23] and earlier it was a prayer to the goddess, the giver of bread or the "Grain Mother."[24]

The Marys

Mary is an ancient name for the goddess that miraculously gives birth to the saviour Sun God. Its forms include Mari, Meri, Marratu, Marah and Mariham. On one level, these names relate to the sea, Mer or Mar, and "Mary" represents the feminine, the Moon, the "Queen of Heaven", to balance the masculine Sun. But they also relate to the Dragon Queens. Isis, the Egyptian Moon goddess and virgin mother of Horus, was known as Mother Mary or "Mata-Meri" and called the "Queen of Heaven", "Our Lady", and "Mother of God".[25] El in the Edda texts was also known as Mary. The Hebrews worshiped a god and goddess deity called Mari-EL or "Mary-God", and the "Mother Mary" of Christianity is just another name for the ancient goddess known as El, Isis, Ishtar, Barati, Artemis, and Diana. The Christian religion, like its bed-mate Judaism, sought to remove the feminine principle from the public domain, and the ancient trinity of Father-Son-Mother became Father-Son-Holy Ghost. The grotesque suppression of women would follow, "justified" by the invented words of the mythical St Paul:

> "Wives submit to your husbands for the husband is the head of the wife, as Christ is the head of the Church. Now if the Church submits to Christ so should wives submit to their husbands in everything"…and…"But I suffer not a woman to teach, nor to usurp authority over the man, but to be in silence." [26]

Such words were written by the priesthood and initiates to introduce the institutionalised suppression of the female. This attitude can still be seen today. Ann Widdicombe, a very mixed up British politician, even left the protestant Church of

England and joined the Roman Catholics when women priests were allowed by the C of E. And this lady claims to be intelligent enough to run the country! The Illuminati set out to close down the feminine, intuitive, energy, that connects us all (including men) to our higher levels of being. The unrestrained male energy is "out there", expressing itself outward into the physical world and, without the feminine, it becomes isolated from its deeper self. Macho man is an extreme expression of this. They are lost little boys who have symbolically lost touch with their inner "Mum". But while suppressing the female among the masses, these religions have continued to covertly worship the Illuminati goddess, symbolised as the Dragon Queen or queens and the "Snake Mother". There has been increased pressure in the last few years to increase still further the role of the mother-goddess, Mary, in the Roman Catholic Church. Millions of signatures have been received from 157 countries pressing the Pope to make Mary a "Co-Redemtrix". They want Mary to be recognised as equal to Jesus, in effect. All prayers and petitions from believers would have to

flow through Mary who would bring them to the attention of Jesus (a bit like a doctor's receptionist, really). She would also play the pivotal role in the trinity as daughter of the father, mother of the son, and spouse of the Holy Spirit. Yes, I know it's all bollocks, but it emphasises the scale of goddess worship within the Illuminati's Roman Catholic Church, which, at the same time, acts as a major suppressor of the human female.

Mary Magdalene, the "reformed prostitute" or whore, is another version of the goddess symbolism. She portrays the Great Whore of Babylon, the goddess, Mari-Anna-Ishtar.[27] The ritual of the "sacred harlot" or priestess anointing a saviour-king goes back to Sumer and further to Atlantis and, no doubt, Lemuria. It was a pagan priestess who announced the resurrection of Osiris, Attis, Dionysus, and Orpheus, just as Mary Magdalene was the first to see the "resurrected" Jesus. It's all symbolism from the ancient mystery religions and it was used to create a mythical hero for a manufactured prison-religion. As I have mentioned, MAG also appears to be code of the reptilian DNA passed on by the female line, the Mitochondrial DNA.

Figure 33: *The ancients depicted their Sun gods with a "halo" around their heads. This is an image of the Sun God Bel or Bil on a British standing stone*

Jesus was crucified

Many of these mythical solar deities like Jesus were crucified for the sins of the people. It is an ancient ritual. Jesus, the "son" on the cross, is the Sun at the spring equinox on one level and the dying Balder on another. The crown of thorns is symbolic of the halo, which the ancients portrayed around the head of all of their Sun gods (*see Figure 33*). The points around the head of the Statue of Liberty and other Illuminati deities are the rays of the Sun or crown of thorns. The words attributed to Jesus "My God, my God, why hast thou forsaken me?" were taken from the Passover ritual at Jerusalem, according to some researchers. The cross itself is not a uniquely Christian symbol. It was used as a religious symbol for thousands of years before Christianity, and Jesus told his disciples to "pick up thy cross and walk" before the crucifixion cross even entered the story. Indeed, the man on the cross was so widely used by the pagans that the early Christians rejected it. The Central American god Quetzalcoatl was depicted nailed to a cross. The cross is symbolic of the equinox when day and night are equal and the Sun is about to win its victory over the darkness. At the moment Jesus died on the cross, according to the Gospel narrative, the land became dark. So it would if the Sun had died, as it was symbolically doing. As for the resurrection after three days, this is more Sun symbolism. In Persia, long before Christianity, they had a ritual in which a young man, apparently dead, was restored to life. He was called the Saviour and his sufferings were said to have ensured the salvation of the people. His priests watched his tomb until midnight on the equinox and they cried: "Rejoice, O sacred initiated! Your God is risen. His death and suffering have worked your salvation." The same was said in Egypt of Horus and in India of Krishna thousands of years before Christianity. And Jesus could not have been crucified between two thieves because crucifixion was not the Roman punishment for theft. The "two thieves" are possibly symbolic of Sagittarius and Capricorn, which cross over at the winter solstice, thus the Sun "dies" between them.

John the Baptist

This guy was invented from the stories of Anup, who baptised the ancient Egyptian Son of God, Horus. Like "John", Anup lost his head. Thor/Indara, the first king of Sumer, was known as "Bil-the-Baptist" on Sumerian seals and he was Ad or Atum baptising the infant crown prince in Egyptian sculpture. Baptism was introduced by the Sumerians, not the Christians, and appears to have originated, at least in the post cataclysmic era, in the Phoenician/St George centre of Cappadocia. John the Baptist, and his association with water, further symbolises the water sign of Aquarius, through which the Sun travels to be "baptised", according to myth. The Sun enters Aquarius at 30 degrees and Jesus is baptised at 30. The zodiac circle was renamed the Crown of the Circle of the Holy Apostles (zodiac signs) by medieval monks and they placed John the Baptist in the position where Aquarius is located. (King Arthur and the 12 Knights of the Round Table are also Sun and Zodiac symbolism.) In the Roman Julian calendar John the Baptist dies on August 29th and John Jackson points out in *Christianity Before Christ* (American Atheists, 1985):

> "On that day, a specially bright star, representing the head of the constellation of Aquarius, rises whilst the rest of the body is below the horizon, at exactly the same time as the Sun sets in Leo (the kingly sign representing Herod). Thus the latter beheads John, because John is associated with Aquarius, and the horizon cuts off the head of Aquarius!" [28]

The reference to the "man carrying the water pitcher" in Luke's Gospel is more Aquarius symbolism. John the Baptist was an almost exact copy of Bala-rama, the forerunner of Krishna, the Hindu Son of God.

Jesus and the 12 disciples

Is there a universal law that all deities must have 12 disciples or followers? Jesus had them, so did Horus, Buddha, King Arthur, Mithra, Dionysus, and so many other symbols of the Sun. We also have the 12 sons of Jacob, 12 tribes of Israel, the 12 gods of the Greeks, Egyptians, and Persians. This fixation with 12 derives once again from Sun symbolism with their disciples and followers representing the months of the year and the signs of the zodiac. The Romans openly symbolised the Sun as a living man and the signs of the zodiac as his disciples. And the Christian religion was created in Rome. Mark, Luke, Matthew, and John, the names carried by the Gospels, represent the four cardinal signs of the zodiac. These are also symbolised in Christian cathedrals as a man (Aquarius), an ox (Taurus), a lion (Leo), and an eagle (Scorpio), together called the four creatures of the apocalypse. Joseph Wheless says in *Forgery In Christianity* (Health Research, 1990):

> "…The Holy Twelve had no existence in the flesh, but their 'cue' being taken from Old Testament legends, they were mere names – dramatis personae – mask of the play – of 'tradition', such as Shakespeare and all playwrights and fiction-writers create for the actors of their plays and works of admitted fiction." [29]

In the ancient Mystery schools, long before "Jesus", the spokesman for the god was called a PETR or Peter. This means "the rock". In the Egyptian Book of the Dead, the name of the doorkeeper to heaven is Petra. Peter rushing into the water to greet Jesus is part of a ritual from ancient Egypt. The title Peter was also given to the High Priest in the Babylon Mystery School. Peter further relates to phallic worship. The cock was a symbol of St Peter and the very name Peter comes from Pater (phallus or male principle) and petra (phallic pillar). The cockerel, which can be seen on so many church steeples, is an expression of this and the Christian churches are full of ancient sexual symbolism. The countless references to "pillars" and "groves" in the Old Testament are also penis and vagina symbolism. Jesus said that Peter would deny him three times before the cock crowed and this is another theme of the solar mystery cults. The cock crowing three times was an omen of death. The symbolism of the "gate-keeper" (Peter) denying the Sun permission to rise before its due time was a ritual found in a number of solar cults. The crow of the cock also announces the arrival of the Sun. Remember, too, that basilisk, the mythical king of the serpents, became interchangeable with the term "cockatrice". It was said that the basilisk was born of the cocks egg and in decorative heraldry the basilisk had the head and legs of a cock, a snake-like tail, and the body of a bird covered with serpent scales. The Roman god Janus, who held the keys, was fused into "Peter" when Christianity was founded in Rome in the form we know it today. Janus was Eannus, a name for Nimrod in Babylon. Even in the early years of the Roman Church, which was supposed to have been founded on the "rock" of Peter, there is no mention of this guy. He was added to the story as the priesthood continued to put the whole fantasy together. The name Andrew, another "disciple", has the same basic meaning as Pater, Petra, or Peter. This is why the mythical "Andrew" is said to have been crucified at Patras in Greece, where "Andrew" was a local god.[30]

James, the so-called "brother of Jesus", is a rehash of Amset, the brother of the Egyptian Sun god, Osiris. Amset was a carpenter and James was a carpenter. Amset was a "great purifier" and James was a "great purifier". Disciple John, the favourite of "Jesus", is a repeat of Arjuna, the favourite disciple of Krishna. John is actually known in Tibet as Argiun. John was the cousin of Jesus and his original, Arjuna, was the cousin of Krishna. Thomas was the disciple who insisted on touching Jesus after the "resurrection" to prove he was in the flesh, hence the term Doubting Thomas. But Thomas is Tammuz, that other saviour-god with the Jesus credentials. The Christian Church dedicates the winter solstice, the day the Sun "dies", to St Thomas. The Hebrews still have a month they call Tammuz. Thomas the "twin" is also symbolism. Thomas means "twin" in the Aramaic and Syriac languages and the name Didymus, also associated with Thomas, comes from the Greek "Didymos", which was their name for the Roman "Gemini", the twins of the zodiac. Acharya writes in her superb work, *The Christ Conspiracy*:

> "It is said that Thomas preached to the Parthians and Persians, but what is being conveyed is that these groups were followers of Tammuz or Dumuzi, as was his Sumerian name. Although it was alleged that Thomas's tomb was in Edessa, tradition also claims that he died near Madras, India, where *two* of his tombs are still shown. This tale comes from the fact that when Portuguese Christian missionaries arrived in southern India they found a sect who worshipped a god named "Thomas" and whose religion was nearly identical to Christianity. So disturbed were the Christian missionaries that they created elaborate stories to explain the presence of the St. Thomas "Christians", claiming that the apostles Thomas and/or Bartholomew had at some point travelled to India, preached and died there." [31]

The missionaries were bewildered by the fact that the religion was "Christian" in virtually every aspect except one: they did not worship Jesus and had never heard of him. The "Thomas" they were worshipping was Tammuz, the hero of the "Jesus" story for thousands of years before Christianity. Signs of Tammuz/Thomas worship have been found in India where, Acharya tells us, he was apparently considered a re-incarnation of Buddha! The villain of the Jesus story is Judas, who represents Scorpio, the "backbiter", the time of year when the Sun is weakening and appears to be dying. He was portrayed with red hair – the colour of sunset – and so was the Egyptian figure, Set, who sought to kill Horus. Judas is supposed to have betrayed Jesus for 30 pieces of silver. This represents the 30 days of the Moon cycle and it was the same amount paid to the Great Goddess in Jewish temples for each sacrificial victim.[32]

St Paul

Here we go again. The only record of the existence of St Paul or "Saul of Tarsus" is in the New Testament texts. It is the same with Jesus, same with all of them, and the same with the key players in the Old Testament stories. The Roman historian

Seneca was the brother of the proconsul of Achaia when "Paul" was supposed to have spoken there. But, although Seneca wrote about far more mundane matters,not a titter is recorded of Paul's public crusade. Who am I speaking about here? He lived in Tarsus in Asia Minor as a youngster; he went to Ephesus, where he spoke to vast crowds and performed miracles, and travelled to Athens and Corinth; from there he went to Rome where he was accused of treason, moved on to Spain and Africa, and returned to Sicily and Italy. He was summoned to Rome and thrown in prison, from where he later escaped. Sounds remarkably like the story of the Nazarene, "St Paul", but these events were from the life of the Greek figure Apollonius of Tyana (called "the Nazarene" in some accounts). He was also known in latin as "Apollus" and..."*Paulus*".[33] Long before the stories about "Paul", the Jewish historian Josephus wrote of a terrifying sea journey he experienced on his way to Rome. His story turns up again in precise detail in the New Testament, claiming to be an account of what happened to "Paul".[34] The story of Paul (and a story is all it is) also shares many detailed similarities with the myths of the Greek hero Orpheus, who, like "Paul", had a missionary called Timothy [35]. The writer H.G. Wells said that many of the phrases used by Paul for Jesus were the same as those used by the followers of Mithra. The Liturgy of Mithra is the Liturgy of Jesus. When Paul is made to say "They drank from the spiritual rock and that rock was Christ!" he is using exactly the same words found in the scriptures of Mithra. The author of an Internet article called "The Other Jesus" picks up this theme:

> "That the names of the close associates of Paul seem to be an exact match with great figures associated with the mysteries of Demeter in general and with Orpheus in particular, is yet another of those issues that bothers people much less than it should …Let us examine the parallels: Orpheus, as a result of the pre-Christian son of God…having 'appeared' to him…mounted a highly successful campaign to spread his version of the mysteries of Samothrace [home of the Amazon female 'serpent' tribe from Atlantis] to mainland Greece. Paul, we are told, because the Christian son of God, Jesus, " appeared" to him, mounted a highly successful campaign to spread his version Christian Jesus worship beyond Palestine and westward to mainland Greece." [36]

This is an excellent example of my theme here. The initiated priesthood took the symbolic stories from their Mystery schools and presented them as historical fact to create prison religions for the people. The rituals, rites, and themes of the Orpheus cults were the same as the later Christian ones. There is so much more to tell about this story and I recommend The Christ Conspiracy, Bible Myths, and other books listed in the Bibliography if you want more detail and sources. The Bible has controlled the minds and lives of billions and has held much of the world in mental and emotional servitude for thousands of years. Christians laugh at the idea of reptilian bloodlines, and yet believe that their God would send his only son and make him suffer vicious torture and a horrible death to forgive the sins of everyone else. At the same time, we are told this is a god of love. It's nonsense, of course it is, but the writers knew that. It was not the truth they wished to communicate. The idea was to manufacture strict religions, which would frighten people into obeying and believing. The whole thrust is that if you don't believe their "truth" you will end up in hell. However, to avoid the problem of everyone being nice to each other (the last thing the Anunnaki want) they emphasise that you do not get to "heaven" through good works, but only by belief in Jesus as your saviour. You could cause untold death and suffering during your life and still book your place in paradise, as long as you believed in Jesus. Also, Jesus was the only one born without original sin and there was no way we could be "perfect" like him. You are born a flawed, soiled piece of shit before you breathe your first, so know your place. The priesthood parked their backsides between "God" and the people and made themselves the middlemen for messages between the two. What the priesthood told the people to do was really "God" speaking through them, they claimed. This is why the Pope is called the Vicar of Christ, the deity's representative on Earth.

I look in some detail in *The Biggest Secret* at how the Gospel story was written and how the Christian religion and the Bible were created, so I won't repeat it all again here, except for some key themes, which are important for new readers to know. There are two main theories for how the original Gospel (Gods-spell) narrative came to be compiled. One is the Piso theory. This was detailed by Abelard Reuchlin in *The True Authorship Of The New Testament*, first printed in the United States in 1979. There is also a website called the Piso Homepage, which focuses on this story and the Illuminati bloodlines.[38] Reuchlin tells of an inner circle or inner ring, the most exclusive club in history, who knew the "Great Secret". In this circle, he says, are the religious, political, and literary leaders, who knew the truth about Jesus, but didn't want anyone else to know. He writes:

"The New Testament, the Church and Christianity, were all the creation of the Calpurnius Piso (pronounced Peso) family, who were Roman aristocrats. The New Testament and all the characters in it – Jesus, all the Josephs, all the Marys, all the disciples, apostles, Paul, John the Baptist – all are fictional. The Pisos created the story and all the characters; they tied the story to a specific time and place in history; and they connected it with some peripheral actual people, such as the Herods, Gamaliel, the Roman procurators, etc. But Jesus and everyone involved with him were created (that is fictional) characters."[38]

The Pisos were bloodline and were related to the King Herod featured in the Gospel story. As bloodline Roman aristocrats, they would have been initiates of the Mystery religions and the symbolic stories that were used to manufacture "Jesus" and his life. The Pisos claimed descent from the founders of Rome, the "wolf-suckled" Remus and Romulus. Reuchlin details the codes he says were used in the Gospel stories by the Pisos and their accomplice, the Roman writer and statesman, Pliny the Younger. The head of the family, Lucius Calpurnius, who was married to the great granddaughter of Herod, was a close associate of the famous Roman writer, Seneca. Both were killed by the Emperor Nero in the year AD65, Reuchlin says. He suggests that the mythical stories of St Peter and St Paul being killed by

Nero in Rome were inspired by these events. Reuchlin says that Lucius Calpurnius wrote his "Ur Marcus", the first version of the Gospel of Mark, in about AD60 and the others followed when the Pisos became very close to the Roman leadership. After his father's death, Arius Piso, who used many names, including Cestius Gallus, became governor of Syria and took command of the Roman army in Judea. He was involved in the Judean revolt in AD66, which Vespasian was sent to quell. Two years later Nero was killed by a Piso agent, according to Reuchlin, and Vespasian became Emperor of Rome with vital backing from the Piso clan. It was Vespasian who ordered the sacking of Jerusalem and stole the temple "treasures", including the Ark of the Covenant, whatever that was. Vespasian, as a Roman emperor, was an Illuminati frontman.

According to Reuchlin's book, Arius Calpurnius Piso wrote three of the Gospels in the following order: the Gospel of Matthew (AD70-75); the updated Mark (75-80); and, with the help of Pliny the Younger, the updated Luke (85-90); He says that The Gospel of John was the work of Arius's son, Justus, and followed in 105. Reuchlin is certainly correct when he says that "Jesus" was a composite figure, and the stories include elements of the tales of Joseph in Egypt and other Old Testament characters, plus some writings from the Hebrew-Egyptian Essenes, the characteristics of various pagan gods and Balder of the serpent cult. He also says that the Pisos made changes and additions to some Old Testament texts and wrote most of the 14 Old Testament books known as the Apocrypha. Reuchlin contends that Arius Piso was the real name of the "Hebrew" historian known as Josephus. This would certainly explain why a "Hebrew" like Josephus, who claimed to have fought the Romans, lived in Rome for 30 years while he wrote books on Jewish history and married into Roman aristocracy. Reuchlin says that "St Paul" was manufactured in the same way as Jesus and it's interesting that "Paul's" hazardous sea journey was a repeat of what Josephus said happened to him. Paul was also portrayed as a Hebrew who became a Roman citizen and Josephus said the same of himself.

Reuchlin writes that between 100 and 105, Arius, his son Justus, and Pliny the Younger, travelled with their family and friends to Asia Minor, Greece, and Alexandria in Egypt, to encourage the poor and the slaves into joining their new faith. Pliny created the first churches in Bithynia and Pontus, Reuchlin says. Pliny had visited these places a number of times in the year AD85 and this, he claims, was the origin of the first name of Pontius Pilate. The Roman procurator was only called Pilate in Matthew and Mark, the first Gospels written by the Pisos, but in Luke, the one said to be written with Pliny, Pilate suddenly acquires the name, Pontius. Luke was written in the very years that Pliny began to visit Pontus, according to Reuchlin. Pliny's letters, written under his own name, say that Justus Piso was in Bithynia in the years 96 and 98 using the name Tullius Justus, and that the Pisos also located in Ephesus, home of the great temple to the goddess Artemis (Diana). Ephesus was also one of the birthplaces of the Christian religion. They visited all the locations claimed for St Paul, and Reuchlin says that Justus Piso and Pliny the Younger (military name, Maximus) introduced into their "St Paul" letters and stories many of their friends and codes indicating their involvement. Paul refers to

"Greet Herodion my kinsman", a code of the family connection to Herod, Reuchlin says. It is a notable "coincidence" that the Pisos had extensive estates in Provence in the South of France, the very region where, the myths claim, the Jesus story continued after the crucifixion thanks to Joseph of Aramathea, Mary Magdalene, and the Saviour's "offspring".

Other researchers, like Acharya in *The Christ Conspiracy*, suggest that the Gospel stories more likely came from the writings of a guy called Marcion of Pontus. He was not a believer in the literal existence of a Jesus-in-the-flesh and wrote the Jesus story symbolically. Marcion was a Gnostic (a word meaning "knowledge") and they wrote widely in symbolism and allegory. Gnostic texts referring to the Jesus story, which were found in 1945 at Nag Hammadi in Egypt, have been used as "proof" that Jesus existed, but they are not. First they were written long after the "event" and second the Gnostics were allegorical writers. Moses Maimonedes, the Hebrew philosopher and Gnostic of the 12th century, wrote:

> "Every time that you find in our books a tale, the reality of which seems impossible, a story which is repugnant to both reason and common sense, then be sure that the tale contains a profound allegory veiling a deeply mysterious truth; and the greater the absurdity of the letter, the deeper the wisdom of the spirit." [39]

Whoever wrote the original Gospel texts, it certainly wasn't the "disciples", Matthew, Mark, Luke, and John, as so many people believe. Not even the Christian Church claims that, but by using those names they can give that impression, and the human mind is manipulated and guided through images and impressions at the expense of fact. It is a staggering thought that not one writer of any Biblical work is known or, as in the case of Paul, shown to have been a historical figure. I am convinced myself, pending further evidence, that the Piso family were, at least in some way, involved in the creation of what became the Christian religion. They certainly provided a number of the early Popes after the Illuminati's Roman Empire founded the Roman Church.

The naked emporer

The man most responsible for the emergence of Christianity as a global force of control and suppression was Constantine the Great. He became Roman Emperor in AD312 after slaughtering his way to power. Constantine, the architect of Christianity, was the same bloodline as the Pisos. In one of the battles for the Roman leadership, at Milvian Bridge near Rome, the Christian legend claims that Constantine saw a vision of a cross in the sky with the words "By this Conquer". A pig in the sky would have been more likely. The next night, so it is said, he had a vision of Jesus who told him to put the cross on his flag to guarantee victory. Constantine is claimed to have converted to Christianity as a result of his visions, but the truth is that he never did, except perhaps on his death bed as a bit of insurance. Constantine, wait for it, was a *Sun worshipper*. His deity was Sol Invictus or the "Unconquered Sun" and he remained to his death the Pontifex Maximus of the

Pagan Church. Sol was the name of an ancient Sun goddess. C.F. Oldham in *The Sun And The Serpent* (London, 1905) says that all solar dynasties were also serpent dynasties. He reads the meaning of serpent differently to me because I think it has a double meaning, but the connection between the two can always be found whichever way you interpret the symbol of the serpent. The worship of the Sun goes hand in hand with the Illuminati's serpent rituals. Constantine threw his backing behind the Christian religion because to him it was no different to the Sun cult he followed. Christianity began to pick up many followers of Mithra for the same reason and many Pagans attacked the Christians for stealing their religion, so similar were they to each other. James H. Baxter, former Professor of Ecclesiastical History at St Andrews University in Scotland, said:

"If paganism had been destroyed, it was less through annihilation than through absorption. Almost all that was pagan was carried over to survive under a Christian name. Deprived of demi-gods and heroes, men easily and half-unconsciously invested a local martyr with their attributes...transferring to him the cult and mythology associated with the pagan deity. Before the fourth century was over the martyr cult was universal...pagan festivals were re-named and Christmas Day, the ancient festival of the Sun, was transformed into the birthday of Jesus."

The defining moment in Christian history came in AD325 when Constantine called together 318 bishops of the "Christian" Church to his palace at Nicaea (now Iznik in Turkey) for the infamous Council of Nicaea. I say "Christian", but in fact there were representatives of the Sun and Moon cults of Apollo, Osiris and Isis, Demeter/Ceres, Dionysus/Bacchus, Jupiter/Zeus, and, of course, Sol Invictus. So Jesus was naturally given the birthday of December 25th; the birthday of the Sun. Nicaea was the moment when Jesus and Christ were brought together for the first time in the way of the other "anointed" Sun Gods. The Council was convened to end the conflict and squabbling between the followers of St Paul's "Jesus", a supernatural god, and those who questioned that Jesus could be the same as God. The latter were called the Arians after their leader, Arius, a churchman in Alexandria, Egypt. Amid fistfights and mayhem, it was "decided", on Constantine's insistence, that all Christians must believe in the supernatural Jesus – or else. This belief, which is the foundation of Christianity to this day, was "defined" in the so-called Nicene Creed:

"We believe in one God, the Father almighty, maker of all things, both visible and invisible; and in one Lord, Jesus Christ, the son of God, begotten of the Father, only begotten, that is to say, of the same substance of the Father, God of Gods and Light of Light, Very God of Very God, begotten, not made, being of one substance with the Father, by whom all things were made, both things in heaven and things on Earth; who, for as men and our salvation, came down and made flesh, made man, suffered and rose again on the third day, went up to the heavens, and is to come again to judge the quick and the dead; and in the Holy Ghost."

That's what they said about Nimrod and Tammuz-Ninus in Babylon, and goodness knows how many other deities in the pre-Christian world. The delegates at Nicaea were told how to vote and those who refused were banished to remote islands. From this time, the Nicene Creed waged war on humanity as tens of millions were slaughtered in its name and the order went out to destroy all evidence that exposed their manufactured story as a scam. Native cultures (and their records of history) were destroyed in an orgy of genocide and inquisition lasting centuries and spanning the world. The "Holy Inquisition" of the Roman Church was not officially disbanded until the 19th century and today it is known as the "Holy Office". The Great Library of Alexandria "City of the Serpent's Son" and other centres of priceless ancient knowledge and records were destroyed under the banner of this vicious, arrogant, creed. When the library at Alexandria was destroyed in AD391 by the order of the Emperor Theodosius some 700,000 scrolls, codices and manuscripts were lost forever. The force behind all this knew exactly what they were doing: selling the masses a myth through which their agenda of suppressing knowledge and rewriting history could be justified. Behind Constantine, the Pisos, and the Popes were the Babylon reptilian Brotherhood, by now located in Rome. Their rituals, temples, and symbols were the origin of those used today by Freemasons. These include the black and white squared floors, white gloves and aprons, secret signs and handshakes. Elite secret societies like the Order of Comacine Masters grew rapidly under Constantine (*see The Biggest Secret*).

The "Christian" bloodlines

The bloodline theme continues with the creation and expansion of Christianity. The major players in the history of Christianity have been the same bloodline, the reptilian bloodline. Among them were the Piso family, Herod the Great, Constantine the Great, King Ferdinand and Queen Isabella of what we now call Spain, who launched the Spanish Inquisition and supported Christopher Columbus, and King James Ist, who sponsored the translation of the King James Version of the Bible which, according to a survey in 1881, contains 36,131 translation errors.[40] All of these people are the same bloodline (*see Appendix I*). So are Joseph Smith and Brigham Young, the founders of the Mormons, and Charles Taze Russell, one of the founders of the Jehovah's Witnesses. Give me the statistical chances of that. It was these very forces that created the Bible and decided what would be in it. They brought together the texts of the Old Testament with the texts they wrote, or chose, to form the New. They translated it into Latin, English, and other languages. Even the original versions of the biblical texts continued to be changed and new phrases added whenever it suited them. The philosopher, Celsus, wrote to the Church leaders in the 3rd century:

> "You utter fables, and you do not even possess the art of making them seem likely …You have altered three, four times and oftener, the texts of your own Gospels in order to deny objections to you." [41]

Celsus said that the church leaders were forever telling their followers not to examine the evidence, but to simply believe – "Wisdom is a bad thing in life, foolishness is to be preferred." He also wrote: "They openly declared that none, but the ignorant [were] fit disciples for the God they worshipped" and he said that the rule was "let no man that is learned come among us".[42] It was, and is, a religion to hijack the minds of the masses and to remove all those who knew the truth. But it is not the only myth religion that has been taken literally. So are all the rest. Even Buddhism, which is claimed to be more enlightened, came from the same source and was sold as historical fact. Look at Buddha's background. He was born on December 25th to the virgin Maya, with a star and wise men in tow. He was a "royal" bloodline and the ruler was told to kill the child to avoid being overthrown. He taught in the temple at 12, was tempted by the evil Mara, and baptised in the presence of the Spirit of God. He performed miracles, healed the sick, and fed 500 people with a small basket of cakes. He died (in some traditions on a cross) and was resurrected to Nirvana or heaven. His tomb was miraculously opened and it was said he would return and judge the dead. Buddha was the "Light of the World", the "Lord" and "Master", the "Good Shepherd", and "Carpenter". The usual CV. In India, Buddha's consort is said to have been Ila or Ida and this was a name in the British Edda for El, the serpent goddess of the "Edenites".

Group sects

The Illuminati strategy can be seen so vividly in their religions. First, you create the original belief, like the belief in "Jesus". This triggers division and conflict with the other religions around that time. Then you shatter that original belief into an ever-expanding list of sub-beliefs and offshoot "churches". Now you have division between the belief and other beliefs, and within the belief itself. What a perfect situation for divide and rule. This has happened with Christianity, and the major fault-line was the work of an Illuminati frontman called Martin Luther. In 1517, this Professor of Theology at Wittenberg University listed 95 complaints against the Vatican for selling pardons to raise money to build St Peter's Church. Luther was excommunicated, but he burned the decree along with copies of Roman Church law and launched his own Lutheran Church. Protestant Christianity was born and it was used to engineer untold war and yet more slaughter. Countries fought each other and justified it as "defending the faith". Defending the agenda, more like. Ironically, the English king Henry VIII first supported Rome and was rewarded with the papal title, Defender of the Faith. But Henry, when he wasn't killing his wives, changed his mind and supported the Luther "revolution". He kept the title, though, and this is the origin of the term Defender of the Faith used by British monarchs to this day. The British crown is supposed to defend Protestant Christianity, but carries the title awarded by a Pope! It's all such a farce. Martin Luther, who used a rose and a cross as his personal seal, was an agent of the Rosicrucian order, that ancient strand in the Illuminati web. Luther's Protestant creed was subdivided into countless sects.

One was Calvinism, which later became the sickness of the mind known as the Puritan faith. This was used most effectively to instigate and justify the genocide of the Native Americans. The real name of John Calvin, the man who started all this, was Jean Cauin. He came from Noyons in France and was educated at the Illuminati's College du Montagu. This is where Ignatius Loyola, the "Catholic" founder of the Society of Jesus, the Jesuits, was educated. The Jesuits go very high in the Illuminati network. Cauin moved to Paris and then to Geneva, Switzerland, where he was known as Cohen. This name comes from Cahen, the name for priest or prince in the ancient Egyptian Mystery schools. In Geneva, he developed, or more likely someone else did, the "philosophy" known as Calvinism. He changed his name again from Cohen to Calvin to make it more acceptable to the English who now became the prime target of this new religion. Calvinism was a designer-religion for the next stage of the plan. It focused rigidly on the Ten Commandments of "Moses" and the literal interpretation of the Old Testament texts and it achieved many goals for the Illuminati. Up to this point, the Christian religion had banned usury, the charging of interest on loans, but Calvinism allowed it. This was perfect for the Illuminati bankers manoeuvring at this time to take over England. And when interest on loans became the norm, thanks to Calvinism, one of the greatest beneficiaries was Switzerland, where this "religion" was devised. Another role for Calvinism was to insist on the burning of "witches" and, in so doing, take more of the secret knowledge out of circulation, along with many DNA lines passed through the female that the Anunnaki wished to eliminate.

The Mormons and Jehovah's Witnesses are two other Illuminati religions, which have emerged from the Judeo-Christian fantasy. I must stress again here that I am not challenging the right of anyone to follow any religion. Good luck to them, and there are many lovely, genuine, people involved in Christianity, Judaism, Mormonism, the Jehovah's Witnesses and all the rest. I am merely seeking to expose the manipulation of the hierachy and the background that the rank and file are never told. Joseph Smith founded the Mormons, the Church of Jesus Christ of Latter Day Saints, after he claimed that an "angel" called Moroni appeared to him in 1823. This Moroni guy, he said, told him of the existence of a book of gold plates containing "the fullness of the everlasting gospel" and "an account of the former inhabitants of this continent and the sources from which they sprang". The location was revealed to him and in 1827, with help from two "magic stones" called Urim and Thummim, he translated the plates into English. Urim and Thummim were, in fact, the names of knucklebones or dice used by Levite priests, and the kings of Israel were said to follow their prophecies. These knucklebones were used in the Mystery school "holy place" known as the Tabernacle. Here we have yet another religion originating from the same source and another perpetuation of the Jesus myth. The gold plates, Smith said, were written in "reformed Egyptian". From this came the Book of Mormon two years later and his followers became the Mormon Church in 1830. The pillars of the early Church were Smith, his brother Hiram, and another guy called Brigham Young. They were all high-degree Freemasons and all from the Merovingian bloodline – the same as Piso, Constantine, James Ist, etc., etc. It is no surprise, therefore, to find that the Rothschilds, through their Kuhn, Loeb financial operation in New York, funded the expansion of the Mormons. Kuhn,

Loeb also helped to fund the Russian Revolution and the First World War (see ...*And The Truth Shall Set You Free*). The Mormons were an Illuminati creation. Mormons recognise the Bible, but believe that Smith's writings are equally divine. They set up communities called Stakes of Zion (Sion = the Sun) and eventually settled in Salt Lake City, Utah, the Mormon city from where its sacrificial rituals and mind control programmes are orchestrated. Another sacrifice and mind control sect to emerge from the Judeo-Christian scam is the Jehovah's Witness or Watchtower Society although as always, the vast majority of its advocates have no idea this is so. This worships the Hebrew angry god Jehovah. One of its leading founders was the paedophile and Merovingian bloodline, Charles Taze Russell, a high- degree Freemason. Russell was close to the Rothschilds and, again, Kuhn, Loeb and Company funded his operation.

Islam was created to further polarise the religious divides and in *The Biggest Secret* I show some of the connections between the secret societies behind "Christianity", including the Knights Templar, and those at the heart of Islam. Among these were the Assassins, from whom we get the term for politically motivated murder. The Muslim faith and the creed of Islam were inspired by the story of Mahomet or Mohammed. This was very similar in theme to the official version of how Joseph Smith inspired the Mormon religion. In 612, it is said, Mohammed had a "vision" and was told to start a new faith – just as Smith later claimed. The date is interesting because some ancient peoples were told to expect an incarnation of "God" every 600 years and Mohammed came 600 years after "Jesus". Once again the Muslims encompass elements of the Judeo-Christian fantasy. Muslims see Islam as an updated continuation of Judeo-Christian themes and they, too, trace their ancestry back to Abraham in the Old Testament, the alleged origin of the Hebrew belief system. Muslims believe that Abraham built the Kaaba, the sacred shrine of Mecca, and the focus of pilgrimage for Muslims all over the world. But it was originally a Pagan temple to goddess worship featuring the famous Black Stone. W. Wynn Westcott, a founder of the Hermetic Order of the Golden Dawn, wrote in his work, *The Magical Mason*, that the Black Stone was first used for Pagan rituals. A stone is ancient symbolism for the penis and for this reason many religions were founded on a stone or a "rock", as with Peter the rock and Christianity. In the Old Testament tale of Jacob, he anointed his stone with oil, which sounds like great fun. Must try that one. The Koran, the Islamic holy book, which is supposed to have been inspired by God, mentions Jesus in 93 verses and treats him as a living person when clearly he was not. Allah, the Islamic god, is the same god, the Muslims say, as the Judeo-Christian Jehovah. They give credence to the Pentateuch, the first five books of "Moses" in the Old Testament, but in truth the books of the Levites. Muslims say that Mohammed was the latest prophet (apart from all the others since) and therefore, the most valid. As such, all Christians and Hebrews should convert to Islam, the orthodox Muslims demand. The term Jihad is the "Holy War" that Muslims are urged to wage against all of those who will not accept the law of Mohammed. The very word, Islam, means "to submit or surrender" and Muslim means "one who submits".

Islam was another Illuminati creed that was to cost the lives of hundreds of millions in the bloody wars waged with Christianity and Judaism. These are three prison religions ultimately controlled by the same force. Islam, like Christianity and Judaism, was also a vehicle for the systematic suppression of women and the feminine principle. Again we see the connection to Freemasonry. After earning the three Blue Lodge Degrees of Freemasonry and completing the Scottish or York Rite degrees, Masons can petition to become a Shriner. These who swear a blood oath and confess Allah as God.[43] Allah is a Moon god. This is why you will see a crescent Moon at the top of mosques around the world, and why the Shriners have the crescent Moon on their fez hats. This symbol is on the flags of various Islamic nations and Muslims fast during the month that begins and ends with the appearance of the crescent Moon in the sky.

"I liked your face..."

The city of Jerusalem, the ironically named City of Peace, is the myth capital of the world. I went there in 1993 to see this most sacred of shrines to Christians, Hebrews, and Muslims. What a summary of how religion has gripped and manipulated the human mind for so long. The Old City, although not very big, is still broken in quarters for Christians, Hebrews, Muslims, and Armenians. After all, we don't want to set a precedent and live together. If you want to buy a myth or misunderstanding, this is the place. They've got hundreds of them. On street corners and at every church or monument there they are, lying in wait, those spiritual used car salesmen, the tourist guides. Many of them wear black leather jackets like some extra from *The Godfather*. These are the silver-tongued repeaters of make-believe who will sell you a myth tour of anywhere. Even at 7.30 in the morning, as I walked through the Jaffa Gate and into the near-deserted streets of the Old City, I was not safe. I felt someone touch my arm.

"Hello my friend," a voice said "You from England? I know many people in England. They come from Glasgow. You know Glasgow?"

I knew his game immediately, but I decided to stick with him and see what happened. He said he approached me because "I liked your face". As he had approached me from behind, I had clearly witnessed the latest recorded miracle in Jerusalem. I have no doubt that it has by now been added to the tourist itinerary. He said he wanted to show me around because he liked me. The money he would demand at the end had nothing to do with it, of course. He showed me the Wailing Wall, or Western Wall, that most sacred of places in the Hebrew religion, where they think they can speak to God. This ritual goes back at least to the wailing for Tammuz in Babylon. Jews leave little messages for God in the cracks between the stones and they now offer a fax service to believers all over the world. You fax your message to Jerusalem and someone goes along and sticks it in a crack in the Wailing Wall. My next stop was Bethlehem, a short bus ride from Jerusalem. If you have never been there, forget the idea of "O Little Town of Bethlehem". It's a right dump and an extension of the sprawl of modern Jerusalem. I walked with my "guide" through "Manger Square" to the Church of the Nativity on the site where

Jesus is supposed to have been born. It is built over the cave where the Babylonian and Hebrew Son of God, Tammuz, was also said to have miraculously entered the world. Popular place. The travel guide to Jerusalem and the "Holy Land" is in no doubt, however. It states categorically: "This Church is situated above the Grotto of the Nativity, a small subterranean chamber, in which a silver star marks the place of Jesus' birth." At the height of the tourist season, people stand in line for hours to see this grotto; such is the power of myth and mind control. But this, luckily, was the off-season and I walked right in. What a performance unfolded before me. A small group of tourists watched as three men dressed up in various regalia were wailing away at each other. The only word I could make out was the odd "Hallelujah". One man in a black hood was leading a ceremonial sing song, while another put on a crown and drank from a goblet in a manner that suggested he had just returned from the desert. The third man, who looked in urgent need of a good laugh, swished around with some object on a chain, which puffed out smoke occasionally. The one with the crown finished his drink and proceeded to read loudly and earnestly from a big red book. In Britain, the most famous big red book belongs to a television show called *This Is Your Life*. Personalities appear in front of a studio audience to have their life stories told by a man reading from the said, big red book. The book in the grotto was a sort of "Jesus Christ, this is your life" and if the television show presented the lives of the rich and famous as inaccurately as the Church has with Jesus, they would be sued or laughed out of existence in a month.

Outside the grotto in Bethlehem, the guide introduced me to a friend of his. "He likes your face," my guide informed me, "and he invites you back to his home for a drink." We arrived at his "home" after a few seconds' walk. It was a nice home, but strange in a way. It had a large front window, credit card signs, counters, a cash register, and lots of shelves with things on. If I didn't know better, I would have said it was the image of a big souvenir shop. As I looked around, I didn't know whether to laugh or scream. You could buy holy this, holy that, holy anything. I didn't see any holy toilet paper, but it must have been there. In fact, given all the crap spoken about religion, I would have thought it essential. Among my favourites were little crosses made from "holy earth from the holy land". In case I thought this was a con, the wrapper assured me: "Each one inspected by a genuine Catholic family". Phew, that's a relief then. But nothing could surpass the plastic models of Jesus, in all sizes to suit all pockets. If you bought the small version, your Jesus only had a bit of wire for a halo, but really go for it and buy the deluxe model and you too, could have a plastic baby Jesus with three genuine, gold-painted prongs sticking out of his head. As I surveyed this wondrous sight, the shop owner made his move:

"They are genuine," he said.
"Genuine? A genuine baby Jesus?"
"They are made by local priests."
"Ah, *that* kind of genuine."

I returned to the Old City and the guide who liked my face wanted his money. Anything I gave him would be acceptable, he said, and then he tried to double it. We said goodbye and I walked around the outside of the city wall to the "Garden of Gethsemane", another "Jesus" site. When I was close, I asked a passer-by the way. He was most helpful and offered to show me. But hold on a minute, wasn't that a black leather jacket he was wearing? Suddenly he shape-shifted from passer-by into tourist guide:

"This is the very tree where Jesus was arrested…these trees have been here for…"

"Excuse me. Thank you for your help, but I only want to stand here on my own, if it's okay with you."

"You mean you don't want me to show you the church and the tomb of Mary and…"

"No, thanks, all the same."

"I give you good price."

By the end of my trip, I had this nightmare of leaving my physical body at the end of this life and a spirit in a black leather jacket touches my arm. "Hello my friend," he says "Are you from Planet Earth? I know many people on Planet Earth. I show you heaven. I like your face." A Muslim taxi driver summed it up when I asked him if he believed all these stories about Jesus. He had no idea, he said, but: "Jesus is very good for tourist buses and taxi drivers because he moved around a lot." Religion is a whole bloody industry ripping off genuine people, mentally, emotionally, spiritually, and financially. Millions are on the payroll. Bishops' palaces, tourist guides, tacky gift shops, entire economies and political systems in some countries. All depend for their survival on this perpetuation of make believe. From the Vatican to Bethlehem, from Jerusalem to Salt Lake City, the cash registers go on dancing to the music of myth. The Vatican and the other bastions of mind control know the information exists that would bring them crashing down. That's why they have worked so hard to suppress it. Unless they do, the party's over. No wonder there is so much opposition to information that will expose this global con trick when the economic and personal power of church and state depends on deception of monumental proportions.

I must be one of the few people on the planet who can bring together in mutual condemnation all these conflicting religious dogmas – and a few more besides. I have been called anti-Semitic for my exposure of Judaism and people like the Rothschilds; I have been shunned and condemned by Christians for exposing the historical background to their religion and its present-day hypocrisy; from South Africa an "Icke Alert" was sent out across the Internet warning that I was anti-

Islam; and many New Agers condemn me for being "too negative" (saying what is really happening) and for exposing the "spiritual" charlatans and the Illuminati manipulation of the New Age mentality. The reason I can unite such apparently opposing groups is that they all have one thing in common. They each have a dogma to sell or defend. As I am challenging all dogmas, impositions, and suppression, I can bring them together as one indignant voice. They are opposames, the same attitude with a different frock on, but more and more people are freeing themselves from these prisons of the mind. The Illuminati-Anunnaki could not care less which religion or mind-prison you choose, so long as you choose one of them. My philosophy on this is simple: if you can put a name to what you believe, you have built a wall around your mind. It doesn't matter what "ism" or "ianity" it may be. Once you can give it a name you are closing the door on infinity where everything just is and we all just are. There are no names for infinite knowledge. It encompasses all that is, and once we succumb to an "ism" we disconnect from all that is. But then that's the idea, the whole point for religion in the first place – slamming the door on human consciousness. Even those who claim to have rejected conventional religion continue to be caught in its illusions. In the New Age, which does not believe in the Christian view, the myth of Jesus goes on. The Son of God of Christianity has become the New Age "Sananda", their name for "Jesus". To them he is a spiritual master channelling wisdom from another dimension and, in other versions, he was an initiate of the Essene community in Biblical Israel. Others who reject the official interpretations of the Bible stories also believe that Jesus existed in some form and they seek to construct their own thesis by re-interpreting the texts. They can read massive implications and revelations in the most innocuous word or phrase. Now the latest spin on "Jesus" is that his bloodline was continued through his children conceived with Mary Magdalene and became the "true" royal bloodline. Yawn. The veil only lifts when you realise that most of the Bible is pure invention. The symbolic made literal. No matter how you seek to interpret the words, it will almost always end up as bollocks because you are trying to literally interpret texts that were bollocks to start with. Only when we have a blank sheet of paper in our minds, free from this intellectual and spiritual pollution, can we possibly have the clarity to see through the game.

Religion has been a curse on the world, and humanity will never know freedom until this curse has been exorcised. It is the curse of ignorance, which has cast its dark shadow over thousands of years of human suppression by the Anunnaki and their bloodlines. More than anything, religion has been the driving force behind humanity's suppression of itself.

SOURCES

1   *Our Haunted Planet*, pp 140 and 143

2   See *The Woman's Encyclopedia Of Myths And Secrets*, pp 963 and 964, for this background to the Sun Goddess legends and accounts

3   *The Return Of The Serpents Of Wisdom*, p 100

4   *The Woman's Encyclopedia Of Myths And Secrets*, p 905

5   *The Return Of The Serpents Of Wisdom*, p 221

6   Ibid, p 224

7   Ibid, pp 224 and 225

8   *The Woman's Encyclopedia Of Myths And Secrets*, p 575

9   Ibid, p 580

10   *The Phoenician Origin Of Britons*, p 147

11   Acharya S, *The Christ Conspiracy, The Greatest Story Ever Sold* (Adventures Unlimited, Kempton, Illinois, 1999), p 241. This book is available through the David Icke website

12   Manly P. Hall, *The Secret Teachings Of All Ages* (The Philosophical Research Society, Los Angeles, California, the Golden Jubilee Edition, 1988), p L

13   Edouard Dujardin, *Ancient History Of The God, Jesus* (Watts and Co., 1938)

14   *The Christ Conspiracy*, p 91

15   Detailed in *Flying Serpents And Dragons*, pp 101 to 103

16   *http://www.nohoax.com/Kingjames.html*

17   *http://religiousfrauds.50megs.com/menu.html*

18   See *The Christ Conspiracy* and *The Book Your Church Doesn't Want You To Read* for more details on these connections

19   *Morals And Dogma Of The Ancient And Accepted Scottish Rite Of Freemasonry*

20   See Gerald Massey's books, *Gnostic And Historical Christianity* (Sure Fire Press, 1985), *The Egyptian Book Of The Dead*; and *The Historical Jesus And The Mythical Christ*. The latter two are both published by Health Research, USA

21   *The Christ Conspiracy*, pp 192 to 193

22   Albert Churchward, *The Origin And Evolution Of Religion* (Kessinger Publishing Company, 1997), pp 387 to 389

23   *The Christ Conspiracy*, p 228

24   Barbara Walker, *The Woman's Dictionary Of Symbols And Sacred Objects* (Harper-Collins, 1988), p 482

25   For the detailed background to the name Mary and its connections, see *The Woman's Encyclopedia Of Myths And Secrets*, pp 602 to 616. This includes a section about Mary Magdalene

26   Ephesians 5: 22-23. and 1 Timothy 2:10-11

27   *The Woman's Encyclopedia Of Myths And Secrets*, pp 613 to 616

28   John Jackson, *Christianity Before Christ* (American Atheists, 1985), p 185

29   Joseph Wheless, *Forgery In Christianity* (Health Research, 1990), p 127

30   *The Christ Conspiracy*, p 167 to 169

31   Ibid, p 172

32   Ibid, pp 169 to 171

33   Ibid, pp 173 and 174

34   Ibid, p 175

35   Ibid, p 174 and 175

36   *packbell.net/gailk/iasius.html*

37   *http://www.angelfire.com/biz5/piso*

38   Abelard Reuchlin, *The True Authorship Of The New Testament* (The Abelard Reuchlin Foundation, P.O. Box 5652, Kent, WA, USA, 1979)

39   *The Christ Conspiracy*

40   Quoted by Arthur Findlay in *The Curse of Ignorance, A History of Mankind* (Headquarters Publishing Company, London, first published, 1947)

41   Ibid, p 637

42   *The Christ Conspiracy*, p 71

43   *The Mystic Shrine: An Illustrated Ritual Of The Ancient Arabic Order Nobles Of The Shrine*, 1975, pp 20 to 22

CHAPTER 12

Serving the dragon:
the present (I)

In war, the truth must be guarded by a bodyguard of lies.

Winston Churchill

If, as I have outlined here, the world is controlled today by the reptilian shape-shifters and their bloodlines, we should be able to find evidence of their modern activities that supports the accounts of the ancients. And we can – lots of it.

Since 1990 when I began to consciously investigate what was really happening in the world, I had heard mention of reptilian beings. But naturally it seemed so fantastic that I put the information on the back burner until I could make some sense of it. That started to happen in early 1998 when I was travelling around the United States. In a period of about 15 days I met 12 separate people in different locations, and from very contrasting walks of life, who told me the same basic story of seeing a "human" change into a reptilian form before their eyes. The people who told me these accounts included two television interviewers who saw their guest, a supporter of the New World Order agenda, shape-shift during a live interview. Afterwards one said he had been shocked to see the man's face turn reptilian and the other, equally shocked, said that she had seen his hands take on a reptilian look. Given that the viewers saw nothing, most of them anyway, this had to be a case of psychically connecting with the fourth-dimensional level of the guy rather than seeing a physical shift. A friend of one of these presenters was a policeman in Denver, Colorado, a major Illuminati and Satanic centre, where reptilian gargoyles (an Illuminati code) adorn the Denver Airport. The policeman had made a routine visit to an office block in Aurora, near Denver, and commented to an executive of one of the companies there about the high level of security in the building. She said that he should look at the upper floors if he wanted to see some real security. She pointed to a lift that only went to the higher floors and she told him of an astonishing experience she had some weeks earlier. The lift had opened and a strange figure emerged. He was albino-white with a face shaped like a lizard and eyes with pupils that were vertical like a reptile's. The highest level of the "Draco royalty" are albino-white. This white lizard figure had walked out of the restricted lift, she said, and into an official-looking car. The policeman was so intrigued by the story and the building that he made investigations into the companies in the upper floors. According to his friend, he said he found them all to be fronts for the Central Intelligence Agency, the CIA.

Another man I met in that 15 days used to take large quantities of LSD in the 1960s and around the third day of a five-day "trip", as he put it, the same thing always happened: some people began to look like reptiles and it was always the same people. It never changed. He also began to observe that his friends who appeared lizard-like in his "trips" always seem to react the same way to movies, television programmes, and so on. "We used to laugh and say 'here come the lizards'", he told me. Drugs take people into altered states of consciousness and this can cause them to "retune" their dial to the lower fourth dimension. At this point they will see that level of the people around them. Looking back from a perspective of greater knowledge, he believes there is what he calls a "morphogenetic field" transmitted to the DNA of the lizard people and this aligned the cell structure to the reptilian genetic blueprint. The more reptilian DNA a person carries, the easier it is for this to happen, and the ones with most reptilian DNA are the hybrid bloodlines of the Anunnaki designed specifically to occupy the positions of power. Interestingly, the Olmec people of Central America, whose whole culture was based on serpent worship, used to take hallucinogenic psilocybin mushrooms that they called "the flesh of the Plumed Serpent", and this took them into a fourth-dimensional awareness – the serpent frequency. In their rituals to the "serpent son" Dionysus (another "Jesus"), the Greek initiates would drink strong wine and take mind-altering drugs and mushrooms to "unite with their Son of God". At the end of those 15 days in the United States, when I was speaking at a Whole Life Expo event in Minneapolis, a gifted psychic lady told me how she sees people in power, like Henry Kissinger, George Bush, and Hillary Clinton, turn into reptilians all the time. Once again she is accessing their fourth-dimensional frequency. There are few more glaring examples of cold reptilian eyes than those of Hillary Clinton. One trait I have noticed in these shape-shifters or possessed people is that their eyes don't change, no matter what their mouth or the rest of their face are doing. They might be laughing, for instance, but their eyes never do. They have a fixed, cold, stare. Next time you see Hillary Clinton, watch her eyes.

I recalled at this stage that I had read something about reptilians in the book, *Trance-Formation Of America*, which details the life of a remarkable woman called Cathy O'Brien. Her Satanic father, who had abused her violently and sexually from the time she was a baby in Michigan in the 1950s, handed her over to Gerald Ford – later President Ford – for use in the Illuminati's now vast mind control operation, which I expose at length in *The Biggest Secret*. Cathy is blond-haired and blue-eyed, the usual story, and I recommend her book to anyone who wants to know what is happening to literally millions and millions of children around the world. I looked through the index to find the reptilian references and, although she rationalised the experience as a mind-control illusion, what she describes is the same experience that so many others have been reporting. I explained earlier about Miguel de la Madrid, the President of Mexico in the George Bush years in the White House, and his story of the extraterrestrial shape-shifters he called the "Iguana race". These were the ones, he said, who were perfect for "transforming into world leaders". In the book, Cathy reveals how George Bush, one of her main controllers, shape-shifted. She says he was sitting in front of her in his office in Washington DC when he opened a book depicting "lizard-like aliens from a far-off deep space place". Bush claimed to be one of them and she said he appeared to transform "like a chameleon" into a reptile. Cathy tells in the book of how Bill and Bob Bennett, two well-known figures in US politics, gave her mind-altering drugs at NASA's Goddard Space Flight Center mind control laboratory. They told her they were "alien to this dimension – two beings from another plane". Yes, the lower fourth dimension. Cathy continues:

> "The high-tech light display around me convinced me I was transforming dimensions with them. A laser of light hit the black wall in front of me, which seemed to explode into a panoramic view of a White House cocktail party – as though I had transformed dimensions and stood amongst them. Not recognising anyone, I frantically asked: 'Who are these people?'

> "'They're not people and this isn't a spaceship', [Bill] Bennett said. As he spoke, the holographic scene changed ever so slightly until the people appeared to be lizard-like aliens. 'Welcome to the second level of the underground. This is a mere mirror reflection of the first, an alien dimension. We are from a trans-dimensional plane that spans and encompasses all dimensions…'

> "'…I have taken you through my dimension as a means of establishing stronger holds on your mind than the Earth plane permits' Bill Bennett was saying. 'Being alien, I simply make my thoughts your thoughts by projecting them into your mind. My thoughts are your thoughts…'" [1]

This is another way that people are controlled and manipulated – by thought transference. The reptilian mind becomes the human mind and you can see this happening all the time as the reptilian "hive" mind becomes the human "hive" mentality. Soon after returning from the USA and the rapid escalation of my reptilian research, I went to see a woman in England to discuss her knowledge of Satanic rituals involving people like Ted Heath, the former Conservative Prime Minister of Britain from 1970 to 1974. He signed the UK into the Illuminati's European Community, now Union, and persists to campaign for our further absorption into this centralised fascist state. As I was finishing this book, government papers were released after 30 years, which showed how Heath knew that entry into the European Community would eventually mean the end of British sovereignty. But at the time he denied this because the reptilians and their clones will say whatever is necessary to achieve their ends. Heath comes up often when you speak with the victims of these rituals – those who survive – and their torture as children by the Satanic rings. This lady was brought up by a Scottish family and was sexually and ritually abused by the highly significant Scottish Illuminati network. As a result of this background, she became the wife of the warden of an area of woodland called Burnham Beeches, a few miles from Slough, west of London. It is an ancient site mentioned in the Domesday Book of the 11th century, and it is not far from both the British Prime

Minister's country residence called Chequers (chequers = black and white squares of Freemasonry) and the former Wycombe (Wicca) home of the Hellfire Club (El-fire, the "Fiery El") with its human sacrifice rituals involving royalty and the American founding father, Benjamin Franklin (see *The Biggest Secret*). Burnham Beeches is owned by the City of London, the globally- important financial district, and one of the most powerful Illuminati operational centres on the planet. For those who don't live in the UK, the City of London does not mean the whole of the capital. It is the area surrounding St Paul's Cathedral where the original city stood and it was rebuilt by initiates like Sir Christopher Wren after the Great Fire of London in 1666. It is now a district within the vast sprawl we call London. The coat of arms of the City of London, an image you find all over Burnham Beeches, is dominated by two flying reptiles holding a shield adorned by the red cross on the white background, the Atlantean-Sumerian fire or sun cross, also used by the Knights Templar. When you enter the City of London you pass two flying reptiles on each side of the road and where the City of London meets the area called Temple Bar, named after the Knights Templar, there is another flying reptile in the centre of the road. Temple Bar is the headquarters of the global legal profession and includes more elite secret societies per square mile than almost anywhere else on Earth. It is from this Illuminati centre, then, that Burnham Beeches is administered.

The lady who told me about this area said that her husband, the warden in charge of the place, was a Satanist. She said he had to be to get the job. They lived in a big house in the woods and part of his work was arranging Satanic rituals there. She said that one night in the early 1970s while Ted Heath was Prime Minister, she was walking through the woods after dark when she saw some lights. Quietly, she moved forward to see what they were and to her horror she saw a Satanic ritual involving Heath and his Chancellor of the Exchequer, Anthony Barber. There is an artist's impression of the scene she saw in the *picture section*. She said that as she watched, hidden among the trees and undergrowth, Heath began to transform into a reptile and she said what staggered her was that no one in the circle looked the least bit surprised. "He eventually became a full-bodied reptiloid, growing in size by some two foot," she said. This is a common description by witnesses. She said he was "slightly scaly" and "spoke fairly naturally", although it sounded like "long distance – if you imagine the short time lapses". I met Heath once in a television station before I knew any of this and I never forgot the coldness of his eyes or how they appeared to go on forever like two black holes. I have heard many people describe a similar experience with people they claim to have seen shape-shift. The woman told me that she had seen other reptilian figures in Burnham Beeches at dusk or after dark, wearing long robes with hoods. You can see an artist's impression of two of the reptilian forms she has seen in *Figure 34*.

Shortly after I met her, I was introduced through a third party to the healer, Christine Fitzgerald, a close confidant of Princess Diana for nine years. You can read the full and amazing story of what she told me in *The Biggest Secret*, but I want to hold focus on the reptilian connection in this book. Christine Fitzgerald knew nothing whatsoever of my then unpublished reptilian research, but a little way into

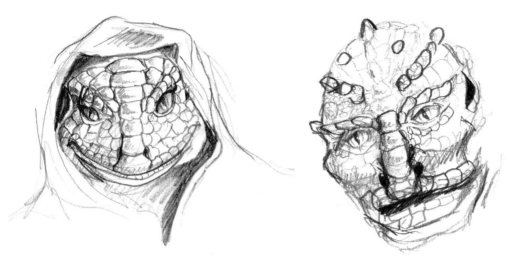

Figure 34: *An artist's impression of reptilians seen by the woman from Burnham Beeches during a "shape-shifting" experience. One is very similar to the Darth Maul character in Star Wars and this image was drawn long before that movie was produced*

our conversation she told me that Diana called the Windsors "the reptiles" and "the lizards". Diana also used to say "They're not human." Christine went on to tell me that the Windsors were a reptilian hybrid bloodline and how they had treated Diana in ways that were beyond the imagination. At the centre of this circle, she said, was the Queen Mother. Christine told me that Princess Diana used to call the Queen Mother "evil". I can think of no one on this planet, maybe even in history, whose real persona is more at odds with her manufactured image than the Queen Mother. If people only knew the truth, those sickening celebrations to mark her 100th birthday would never have happened. Christine said:

"The Queen Mother...now that's a serious piece of wizardry. The Queen Mother is a lot older than people think. To be honest, the Royal Family hasn't died for a long time, they have just metamorphosised. It's sort of cloning, but in a different way. They take pieces of flesh and rebuild the body from one little bit. Because it's lizard, because it's cold-blooded, it's much easier to do this Frankenstein shit than it is for us. The different bodies are just different electrical vibrations and they have got that secret, they've got the secret of the micro-currents, it's so micro, so specific, these radio waves that actually create the bodies. These are the energies I work with when I'm healing.

"They know the vibration of life and because they're cold-blooded, they are reptiles, they have no wish to make the Earth the perfect harmony it could be, or to heal the Earth from the damage that's been done. The Earth's been attacked for zeons by different extraterrestrials. It's been like a football for so long. This place is a bus stop for many different aliens. All these aliens, they could cope with anything, including the noxious gases. They're landing all the time and coming up from the bowels of the Earth. They looked like reptiles originally, but they look like us when they get out now through the electrical vibration, that key to life I talked about. They can manifest how they want to. All the real knowledge has been taken out and shredded and put back in another way. The Queen Mother is 'Chief Toad' of this part of Europe and they have people like her in every continent. Most people, the hangers on, don't know, you know, about the reptiles. They are just in awe of these people because they are so powerful." [2]

I know it is hard to imagine and grasp the scale of the Queen Mother's involvement through her life because your mind tells you she is a little old lady. But, as with all of these people, what you see is just the front image, not the real being. It is an extreme version of an agent in a foreign land operating behind a cover story of why he is there and what he is doing. It's just that these people have "cover bodies", also. Christine Fitzgerald was able to see what was going on because of her work with Diana and the aristocracy and her understanding of energy, vibrations, and frequencies through her healing centre. I have had to study an unbelievable number of subjects and research so many different strands of information before it was possible to put a picture together and that is one big reason why it has rarely come to light like this before. There is so much to know before you can see how the pieces fit together. The Illuminati have suppressed all information that is necessary to see the picture and you have to do so much work to overcome that. You also need a mind that is free (or free-er) and willing to go anywhere the evidence leads.

A few weeks after my meeting with Christine Fitzgerald in 1999, my scientist friend in California, Brian Desborough, told me there was a woman that I had to meet as soon as possible. This was Arizona Wilder, a recovering victim of the massive Illuminati mind control network, who had worked for them at a very high level. She said she had conducted sacrificial rituals as a "Mother Goddess" for the British royal family, especially at Balmoral Castle in Scotland, and at a notorious centre for Satanic ritual called the Mothers of Darkness Castle in Belgium. This is located in the same region as the headquarters of the cult responsible for the widespread paedophilia, murder, and child sacrifice that came to light amid enormous public anger in 1994. The ring involved famous pillars of Belgian society and a massive cover-up has ensued to keep it quiet. Belgium is a major Illuminati Satanic centre and that's why the European Union and NATO are based there. Arizona Wilder's original name had been Jennifer Greene. She is a blue-eyed blond from a French aristocratic bloodline with significant Irish blood, too. When her mind and her memories began to return after the death of her controller, the Nazi, Josef Mengele, she changed her name to Arizona Wilder and dyed her hair to cover the blond in an effort to break some of the programming related to that.

Illuminati mind control

Understanding the mind control network and its techniques is vital to appreciate the ways that the reptilians manipulate human society. Josef Mengele was the "Angel of Death" in the Nazi concentration camps, who performed the horrific experiments on twins and others. There he developed a technique called trauma-based mind control in which they manipulated a mechanism of the mind that shuts out memories of extreme trauma. This kicks in when people have a serious road accident and can never remember the impact or the immediate aftermath because their mind puts an amnesic barrier around that memory. This means we don't have to keep reliving such a terrible event. My mother was hit by a car and suffered some awful injuries a little while ago. To this day she cannot remember from 30 seconds before impact until some 20 minutes after. On that level this mental defence mechanism is a good thing, but the Illuminati, particularly Mengele, perfected it for their own reasons. In fact, they have known about it for thousands of years, it's just that its widespread global use began to return in the 20th century. It is known as trauma-based mind control and they take children before the age of five and six and put them through the most unimaginable violent, sexual, and emotional abuse. Again they are chosen by bloodline. A lot of paedophile rings are set up and protected to serve this agenda, and when genuine people expose them, as in the North Wales scandal in the UK, the famous names involved are never allowed to come to light. These names include the paedophile Lord McAlpine of the famous British construction company. He is a former chairman of the Conservative Party and heavily involved in secret societies like the Knights of St John of Jerusalem. The unbelievable trauma these children are subjected to, including Satanic ritual, splits the mind into compartments – amnesic barriers that imprison the memories of the trauma and do not allow them to enter the conscious mind. In the Illuminati mind control centres like the Tavistock Institute of Human Relations in London (see *The Biggest Secret*), these compartments are known as "altars". You might imagine a mind broken into a honeycomb of self-contained compartments, each holding individual memories of trauma. At the front of this honeycomb is the part that directly interacts with the world. They call this the "front altar". This is completely unaware that all the other compartments exist and those compartments are unaware of each other. Therefore, the front altar, the one we take to be the "real" person, has no memory of what has happened to them, or what is still being done, until the barriers begin to break down and the memories they contain can enter the front altar, the conscious mind.

Using hypnotic keys and triggers, mind controllers like Mengele move these different compartments around, pushing the front altar into the unconscious and bringing forward one of the back altars. The victim is then sexually abused by a famous person, like George Bush or Ted Heath for instance, or programmed to carry out a future assassination or task. Afterwards that altar is returned to the non-conscious mind and the front altar, oblivious of what has just happened, is brought forward again. Those programmed for assassinations will not have a clue what has been done to them. Their assassination programme, to kill a famous person or "dangerous" researcher, will lie dormant in the compartment until the trigger is given. This could be a word, phrase, or sound. When that happens, the dormant compartment swaps places with the front altar, takes control of the body, and carries out its programming. This is the true background to the mass killers like Thomas Hamilton (Dunblane, Scotland), Martin Bryant (Port Arthur, Tasmania), and the stream of similar cases in the United States, including Columbine High School, where "crazed" people have slaughtered the innocent, or at least been blamed for it. They are programmed "multiples" given a cover "personality" and background of being "strange", which can then be used to dismiss the murders as the act of "nutters".

It is no accident that Timothy McVeigh, the man convicted for the Oklahoma bombing, was, according to the USA Today newspaper, given a "mental assessment" after his arrest by a man called Louis Jolyon West, a psychiatrist at the University of California. What the paper did not say was that West is one of the most notorious CIA mind controllers in America and the University of California is one of the leading mind control centres. It was West who made a "mental assessment" of Patty Hearst of the famous newspaper dynasty when she came out of the Symbionese Liberation Army. This was a terrorist gang in California in the 1970s and a creation of the Illuminati. In ...And The Truth Shall Set You Free, you can read the evidence that McVeigh was not the man behind the bombing. But after his "assessment" by West, and no doubt a list of threatened consequences, he offered an almost non-existent defence when a very substantial one could have been mounted. The government appointed his lawyer. Later McVeigh conveniently asked to be executed. The reason for horrors like Oklahoma and the mass shootings, and why they are increasing, is to traumatise the collective mind and justify legislation of many kinds. More basic freedoms were removed from American society in response to Oklahoma, and Bill Clinton called for an "easing of restrictions of the military's involvement in domestic law enforcement". This is the technique I have called problem-reaction-solution. Covertly create the problem, get the public to scream "something must be done", and then openly offer the solutions to the problems you have created. Solutions that advance your agenda. One aim of the mass shootings is the removal of guns from public circulation. I don't believe in violence of any kind, but the Illuminati know that many people have no problem using guns to protect themselves and they want as many weapons as possible out of circulation by the time their masters are openly revealed and their fascist state is in place. Adolf Hitler introduced gun laws before he began to fill concentration camps.

People subjected to trauma-based mind control suffer from what is called Multiple Personality Disorder (MPD) or Dissociative Identity Disorder (DID). Some are now beginning to recover memories of their trauma and involvement in the Illuminati projects and who is behind them. Some very famous names are coming to light with compelling consistency – George Bush, Henry Kissinger, Dick Cheney, Al Gore, the British royal family, the Rothschilds, Rockefellers, and a long list of others documented in my other books. This is why the False Memory Syndrome Foundation was hurriedly created to discredit the memories that these victims are now having. It is a gigantic cover-up, which, as usual, the media has bought hook, line, and sinker. Claiming the victim is suffering from "false memory" is now the easiest way for those accused of abusing children to walk free from the courts and the media reports these cases as if those accused are the victims. Are some people falsely accused though malice? Yes, of course that is going to happen from time to time. But are most of these cases untrue. No way. Just look at some of the people behind the creation of the False Memory Syndrome Foundation. The leading lights were Ralph Underwager, a Lutheran Minister and psychologist from Minnesota, and his wife, Hollida Wakefield. Underwager has been called as an "expert" witness in child abuse cases. This is the same couple who were interviewed in the winter 1993 edition of the Dutch paedophile magazine, *Paedika*, and were supportive of paedophilia! (see *http://www.nostatusquo.com/ACLU/NudistHallofShame/ Underwager2.html*). Also involved with the creation of the False Memory Syndrome Foundation were Pamela and Peter Freyd, who present themselves as falsely accused parents. Their daughter Jennifer Freyd is now Professor of Psychology at the University of Oregon. She is adamant that her accusations of parental abuse are true and she has spoken out against the motives and methods of the False Memory Syndrome Foundation (see *http://www.movingforward.org/v2n5-birrell.html* for some further background from a friend of Jennifer Freyd). Shirley and Paul Eberle are two more "experts" who spend their time rubbishing claims of child abuse, Satanism, and recovered memories on behalf of the Foundation. They wrote *The Politics Of Child Abuse*, a book that accuses mothers, mental health professionals, and prosecutors of feeding children stories about sexual abuse. Since then they have been called as "experts" in abuse trials. But their real expertise appears to involve running, and contributing to, pornography magazines (see article by Maria Laurina at *http://www.nostatusquo.com/ACLU/NudistHallofShame/Eberle.html*). The Eberles edit a soft-core magazine in California called the *L.A. Star*, which contains promotion for their book *The Politics Of Child Abuse*. In the 1970s they were also involved in hard-core pornography with a magazine called *Finger*. The Eberles were featured nude on one cover holding two life-size blow-up dolls named "Love Girl" and "Play Guy". Donald Smith, a sergeant with the obscenity section of the Los Angeles Police Department's vice division, followed the couple for years. The police were never able to prosecute for child pornography, but Smith said: "There were a lot of photos of people who looked like they were under age but we could never prove it." Among the articles that appeared in *Finger* were "Sexpot at Five", "My First Rape, She Was Only Thirteen", and "What Happens When Niggers Adopt White Children". One letter to the magazine says: "I think it's really great that your mags have the courage to print articles and pixs on child sex …Too bad I didn't hear from more women who are into child sex …Since I'm single I'm not getting it on with my children, but I know of a few families that are. If I were married and my wife and kids approved, I'd be having sex with my daughters." Another says: "I'm a pedophile and I think it's great a man is having sex with his daughter! …Since I didn't get *Finger* #3, I didn't get to see the stories and pics of family sex. Would like to see pics of nude girls making it with their daddy, but realize it's too risky to print." The Eberles have since produced a further book for their "family friend", Carole Stuart (of publishers Lyle Stuart), in which they dismiss all claims of child abuse in the famous McMartin pre-school case, which I will outline in a later chapter. Yeah, the False Memory Syndrome Foundation is certainly to be trusted and has the best interests of child at heart. Any real journalists reading this?

A former Illuminati mind controller told me how they have their placemen throughout psychiatry and key "education" establishments in general to ensure that the lid stays on. She said that the George Washington University campus was a "hotbed" of Illuminati professors and teachers when she was operating in the 1970s. She said that a Dr Timothy Brogan, her main Illuminati "trainer", was a behavioural scientist on the faculty. This is also affiliated, she said, with one of the main paediatric neurological specialty groups in the US, which researched brain development and manipulation. At night, she said, they were experimenting with brain wave programming on the children who were taken there. This former Illuminati source told me that Brogan was a co-founder of DELPHI, the Illuminati "head trainer's group" in the United States and the partner to ORACLE, the main training group in Europe. With this network of Illuminati agents working in psychiatry and medicine, they can (a) do their experimentation and trauma-based mind control undiscovered and (b) produce endless "eminent" professors of psychiatry and therapy to tell the media and the courts that Multiple Personality Disorder does not exist and that the memories of endless people telling the same stories and naming the same names are "false".

Arizona Wilder is one of those who are breaking down the compartments and remembering their unimaginable experiences. In *The Biggest Secret* and the video *Revelations Of A Mother Goddess*, she tells her story in detail and names the famous names involved on both sides of the Atlantic. She says she was chosen because of her bloodline. The Illuminati-reptilians literally breed bloodlines to conduct their rituals for them. The people of these bloodlines are very psychic and able to connect easily with energy, and therefore manipulate its vibrational state or draw desired frequencies into rituals. Blond-haired, blue-eyed people turn up again and again in these bloodlines. From the moment a child of these "psychic" bloodlines is born, in fact even in the womb, they are subjected to trauma-based mind control. The idea is to turn them into compartmentalised people who can be "triggered" to conduct the rituals as programmed, but then "forget" everything they did until that compartment is accessed again for the next ritual. Unfortunately for the Illuminati, Arizona's compartments began to break down after the death of her controller, Josef Mengele, in the 1980s. Although another infamous mind controller, Guy de Rothschild, was brought in to "take her over", it did not work. This often happens because the victim's mind worships the one who originally programmed them, especially if it was over a long period of time. When I met her, Arizona had escaped from mind control, though there were many compartments still to be accessed, and Brian Desborough was helping her with that painstaking task.

Clinton, Gore, and the elite satanists

Support for Arizona's theme comes from Phillip Eugene de Rothschild, another recovering mind-controlled Satanist, who tells part of his story on an excellent website highlighting ritual abuse and mind control.[3] After I contacted him, we have also communicated directly on several occasions. Phillip, who uses another name in daily life, explains how his front altar or "presenter" personality was that of a "good guy" Christian, but beyond that he was programmed as a Satanist as the unofficial son of a French Rothschild. His mother was Lula Vieta Pauline Russell Campbell, who was born in 1917 in Farmersville, Texas, and died in 1977. But, he says, his real, biological, father, was not the man he had known as his father before his compartmentalised mind began to heal and remember. His genetic father, he says, was Baron Philippe de Rothschild of the Mouton-Rothschild wine producing estates in France, who died in 1988 at the age of 86 (*see picture section*). Phillip Eugene told me: "My father was a decadent dilettante as well as a master Satanist and hater of God, but how he loved the fields and the wines. He used to say it brought out "the primitive" in him. The estates are now run by Baron Philippe's daughter, Baroness Philippine, who, Phillip Eugene says, is his half sister. He was, he writes, conceived by "occult incest" and was "one of the hundreds of thousands of both legitimate and illegitimate offspring of this powerful financial and occult family". Much of this is done artificially through Illuminati sperm banks. What Phillip says is confirmation of my own research, as outlined in *The Biggest Secret*, that the main reptilian bloodlines conceive countless children to perpetuate the bloodline and only a few are given the bloodline name as "official" children. The others are hidden behind other names and brought up by other "parents". Later they find themselves in significant positions, often not knowing why they got so "lucky". But their bloodline allows them to be more easily possessed by the fourth-dimensional entities and by placing these bloodlines in power they are really giving that power to the fourth-dimensional reptilians and other entities. Phillip Eugene says that for most of his childhood and adolescence he lived with his Rothschild father on his estate in France. They had a physical relationship, he says, and he was "held fast in the emotional power of incest, which, in this culture, was "normal" and "to be admired". He said he observed his Rothschild father's "lust for power" and began to desire the same. He also confirmed the way the "occult" bloodlines are controlled by demonic entities. "Being a Rothschild descendant", he said, "I was maximally demonised." He continues:

> "I was present at my father's death in 1988, receiving his power and the commission to carry out my destiny in the grand conspiracy of my family. Like their other children, I played a key role in my family's revolt from God. When I watch CNN, it startles me to see so many familiar faces now on the world stage in politics, art, finance, fashion, and business. I grew up with these people meeting them at ritual worship sites and in the centers of power. Financiers, artists, royalty, and even Presidents, all these dissociated people work and conspire today to bring in a new world order...These people, like me, are SRA/DID [Satanically ritually abused and Dissociative Identity Disorder – 'multiples'.]

> "The last non-dissociative President of the United States was Dwight Eisenhower; except for him, every one since Teddy Roosevelt has had some level of dissociative disorder and some level of involvement in the occult. President Clinton has 'full blown' multiple personality disorder and is an active sorcerer in the Satanic mystery

religions. This is true of Al Gore, as well; I have known Misters Clinton and Gore from our childhood as active and effective Satanists.

"Like the hundreds of thousands of this [Rothschild] occult family's other biological children, I had my place and function within this clan's attempt to control the world. My efforts and my family's efforts strove to have a member of the European nobility of the Habsburg family assume the pre-eminent position over humanity, a position called the Antichrist by Christianity. While others were seeded into government, academia, business, or entertainment, my place was within the Body of Christ. I was to be a focus for spiritual power and controller of a cult within this Church. In this Church have lived people who I have known all my life to be the controllers and power centers of both the Rothschild family's false prophet and the antichrist.

"Many dissociated Christians in the Body of Christ hold similar corporate spiritual, occult positions as part of the Satanic New World Order. In my being I embodied the Luciferian morning star within the Church. I represented the presence of all the other Satanists who were related to me in the morning star; their spirits were present in me in the Church. Constructed through ritual but empowered by legions of spirits, I was a human and spiritual focus of corporate Satanic energy into the 'Body of Christ.'" [4]

Phillip Eugene de Rothschild, like Arizona Wilder, talks of the involvement of Josef Mengele, and the overwhelming memory that most of his victims have is his eyes. "I'll never forget his eyes", they say, one after the other. Having looked into the eyes of Ted Heath, who is nowhere near as high in the hierarchy as Mengele was, I know exactly what they mean. Phillip de Rothschild says he saw Mengele giving a "tongue-lashing" to his Rothschild father and this confirms my own research that shape-shifter Mengele was very high indeed in the Illuminati. I'm sure there are those who will be extremely surprised by the claim that long after the war Josef Mengele, the "Angel of Death" in Nazi Germany, programmed Arizona Wilder, in America. In ...*And The Truth Shall Set You Free*, I present the documented fact that all "sides" in the First and Second World Wars were funded by the same Illuminati sources. Wars are highly effective ways to advance the reptilian agenda and that's why we have so many of them. They create enormous fear, kill vast numbers of people, force countries into massive debt to the Illuminati bankers, and change the face of a society forever. But you also need to protect your key personnel from the consequences of their actions in those wars and this is what happened with Mengele, and the other leading Nazi geneticists, mind controllers, scientists, and engineers. They escaped from Germany as the Allies arrived thanks to a British and American intelligence operation called Project Paperclip. This has even been occasionally exposed even in the mainstream media here and there. A German television documentary in late 2000 exposed the secret life of a former Nazi war criminal, who spied for America's Central Intelligence Agency after the Second World War in return for a fake Jewish identity.[5] He was Günter Reinemer, an SS lieutenant who commanded death squads at the Treblinka concentration camp. He was responsible for the deaths of hundreds of Jews. The documentary said that he was given the identity Hans-Georg Wagner by the CIA. He later married a Jewish woman, lived in Israel and was buried in a Jewish cemetery. His story might have been buried with him had he not felt the need to confess in 1988, shortly before he apparently committed suicide. His statements formed the basis of the documentary Wagner's Confession. He says that after agreeing to work for the CIA he spent several months at a US military base at Frankfurt-Höchst, where he learned rudimentary intelligence techniques and was circumcised. He was given a Jewish identity and sent as a Holocaust survivor to Calbe, East Germany, where he spied on old Nazis and new communist technologies at the local power plant. Reinemer was small fry compared with people like Mengele, but his is one example of Project Paperclip and its offshoots. How many other Illuminati Nazis have been masquerading as "Jewish" since the war, one wonders? Mengele was taken to South America and the United States where one of his main bases was the China Lake Naval Weapons Center in the California desert. It was he who masterminded the notorious and publicly acknowledged CIA mind control project called MKUltra. MK stood for mind control, but they used the German spelling Kontrolle, because of the Nazis who created it with funding provided through people like John Foster Dulles, the US Secretary of State, and his brother, Allen Dulles, the first head of the CIA and the man President Kennedy had sacked before his assassination. Dulles later served on the Warren Commission "investigation", which decided that Lee Harvey Oswald was the lone assassin! According to one researcher, ULTRA is the name for a very high-security classification dealing with alien interaction and a secret arm of the US National Security Agency dealing with the same subject. It operates a joint alien-"human" network in an underground base in the notorious Dulce-Los Alamos area of New Mexico, and is also the name of a secret Nazi team in the Second World War that handled security for an alleged German underground base in Antarctica. You may recall that researcher Maurice Doreal claims to have seen evidence that the reptilians were once based in an ice-free Antarctica during their high-tech wars with the Nordics.

Shape-shifting queens

Arizona Wilder told me how she had conducted sacrificial rituals involving the British royal family, Tony Blair, and famous American Illuminati names like George Bush, Bill and Hillary Clinton, Henry Kissinger and many others.[6] The highest operative she knew in the Illuminati, she said, was a guy calling himself the Marquis de Libeaux ("of the water"). His codename was Pindar, which she says means "penis of the dragon". Arizona told me how the Queen and Queen Mother regularly sacrifice babies and adults at many ritual centres, including Balmoral Castle in Scotland, where they were all staying at the time Diana was ritually murdered in Paris. The royal family involved in human sacrifice was fantastic enough, but here again came the constantly repeated theme. She described how, during the rituals, these people shape-shift into reptiles. Diane Gould, head of the US organisation, Mothers Against Ritual Abuse, also confirms this theme. In a telephone conversation about ritual abuse, Diane asked me if I could explain why many of her clients reported that participants in their rituals had turned into reptiles. People might want to dismiss all this, but they should know that, while they close their eyes and their minds, children are being sacrificed all over the world this very day by the reptilian bloodlines – many thousands of them on the main ritual dates. Arizona talked about some of her experiences with the Queen and Queen Mother:

> "The Queen Mother was cold, cold, cold, a nasty person. None of her cohorts even trusted her. They have named an altar [mind-control programme] after her. They call it the Black Queen. I have seen her sacrifice people. I remember her pushing a knife into someone's rectum the night that two boys were sacrificed. One was 13 and the other 18. You need to forget that the Queen Mother appears to be a frail old woman. When she shape-shifts into a reptilian, she becomes very tall and strong. Some of them are so strong they can rip out a heart and they all grow by several feet when they shape-shift [This is what the lady said who saw Edward Heath, among endless others.]"

Of the Queen, Arizona said:

> "I have seen her sacrifice people and eat their flesh and drink their blood. One time she got so excited with blood-lust that she didn't cut the victim's throat from left to right in the normal ritual, she just went crazy, stabbing and ripping at the flesh after she had shape-shifted into a reptilian. When she shape-shifts, she has a long reptile face, almost like a beak and she's an off-white colour. [This fits many depictions of the gods and "bird gods" of ancient Egypt and elsewhere.] The Queen Mother looks basically the same, but there are differences. She [the Queen] also has like bumps on her head and her eyes are very frightening. She's very aggressive...

> "...I have seen [Prince Charles] shape-shift into a reptilian and do all the things the Queen does. I have seen him sacrifice children. There is a lot of rivalry between them for who gets to eat what part of the body and who gets to absorb the victim's last breath and steal their soul. I have also seen Andrew participate and I have seen Prince Philip and Charles' sister (Anne) at the rituals, but they didn't participate when I was there. When Andrew shape-shifts, he looks more like one of the lizards. The royals are some of the worst, OK, as far as enjoying the killing, enjoying the sacrifice, and eating the flesh, they're some of the worst of all of them. They don't care if you see it. Who are you going to tell, who is going to believe you? They feel that is their birthright and they love it. They love it." [7]

Arizona has been viciously attacked for what she said in *The Biggest Secret* and on her video. A campaign of character assassination has been waged, at one time almost daily on the Internet, to discredit her evidence and the reptilian connection in general. Among the critics who have dismissed her information is the publisher of *Nexus* magazine, which gives so much unchallenged space to Sir Laurence

Gardner, publicist for the Imperial Royal Dragon Court and Order. Another vehement critic of Arizona is a researcher who appeared for several months to spend his entire day on the Internet trying to undermine the content of *The Biggest Secret* and especially Arizona's contribution. His desire to discredit the idea of the reptilian connection to the Illuminati took on the appearance of a raging obsession and persuaded many people who should have known better to dismiss all that she said. One of the points made to undermine Arizona's claims was that victims of multiple personality disorder have a photographic memory and Arizona did not have that because there were names she did not immediately remember in the video. This revealed a fundamental lack of understanding of mind control. The back altars that hold the memories of trauma have photographic recall because the mind always records anything surrounding trauma in crystal-clear detail. But the front altar, the one doing the video interview, is not photographic because it has not experienced the trauma. It is the interface with the world and it there as a cover for all the other compartments to suppress the memories of abuse. It only accesses those memories when the compartments begin to break down. Because the critics did not seem to understand that, they used this lack of knowledge to ridicule what she said. The attacks made her wonder why on earth she bothered to go public when those claiming to be seeking the "truth" treated her in this way. However, as the months have passed, evidence gathered from sources all over the world has pointed again and again to the accuracy of Arizona's theme. I had people telling me "she's crazy", "she's an Illuminati plant", and "don't believe her". Yet many of those same people are now accepting the foundations of what Arizona was saying (and they were dismissing) in 1999. Arizona is an immensely brave woman and one of the few who will speak openly about her experiences. Most keep quiet because they think no one will believe them or they want to remain publicly anonymous because they fear the consequences of speaking out. The critics try to present the idea that my only source for the reptilian shape-shifters is Arizona Wilder. Again, a breathtaking suggestion when you look at the evidence. And I would stress here that for every person I name, like Arizona, there are many, many, more who confirm the story on the understanding that their identity and location will not be revealed publicly, although I know the details.

One such case is a 57-year-old former chief of police, special agent, and member of the US military. He says he has guarded two presidents, two Secretaries of Defense, and two chairman of the Joint Chiefs of Staff (the head of the US military). He contacted me just as this book was being completed to say that he knows from his experience that "aliens exist" and that the government is lying about the Roswell "alien" crash in New Mexico in 1947. He also told me of a "crystal skull" in his possession. But his main reason for making contact was to tell me of an incident that showed to him that shape-shifting reptilians are real. When he arrived at a friend's house in Texas, he was told that two women guests were coming from New York. They travelled around the country performing hands on healing and they had asked if they could drop by, he was told. This former chief of police told me in personal correspondence what happened next:

"Well I arrived before the New York people and had already started showing my crystal skull when they arrived. They immediately went crazy [because of the skull] and started holding their hands up before their eyes and screamed 'Get her out of here' over and over. I can tell you that everyone was shocked by their actions and I was extremely upset …I carried the crystal skull out to the car and left it there. After about an hour everyone seemed to get over the uproar they made and things settled down to discussions. Everyone introduced themselves and the two from New York volunteered to heal someone. Well everyone started telling them to do it to me because I had heart trouble and was recovering from a heart attack. I hesitated, but finally relented and said OK.

"They sprang over to me so fast that it startled me. One got behind me and one straddled my legs in front of me. They did this without touching me and they both started running their hands around my body again without touching me anywhere. This went on for about a minute then my eyes met the eyes of the lady in front of me. That was some experience, our eyes meeting. Pay attention to what I say here. I could see immediately that she knew that I knew and it broke her concentration. She lost control and changed into a reptilian right before my eyes. No sooner than she lost control, she regained it and shape-shifted back into a human. All this took place in the blink of an eye. They immediately jumped up and said that they had to leave and left within 30 seconds of this happening."

He said he did not say anything about what he had seen, but when everyone began to leave, two guests stayed behind and would not move. Eventually they asked: "Did you see what we saw?" He asked them what they meant and they said they had seen the lady "…change into a reptile and then change back". People all over the world, and from countless walks of life, have repeated this same experience to me. This is the modern version of the experience the ancients constantly described.

A regular source of information about reptilian activities and rituals are those who have been involved in "religious" organisations, not least the Jehovah's Witnesses and the Church of Jesus Christ of Latter Days Saints (LDS), better known as the Mormons. A lady called Diana Huston told me of her experiences in the Jehovah's Witnesses, which is officially titled the Watchtower Bible and Tract Society.[8] She joined them in 1969 because, after going through the Vietnam War with her husband, she was attracted by the message of paradise on Earth. She was OK for a few years, but then they became more demanding and controlling. In 1987 she said that subliminal drawings began to appear in the artwork of their books and magazines depicting bizarre faces and strange messages. Some of these are detailed in the Symbolism Archives on my website (*www.davidicke.com*). At a small convention in September 1988, she spoke privately to one of the governing body 'elect'. At that time she thought they were the "good guys". The man was about 5'10" with dark hair and was powerfully built. She said that she looked into his eyes and was startled and terrified to see a thin membrane drop over his human eyes.

She didn't know if the membrane came from the bottom of his eyelid or the top. "I'd never heard of lizard beings, but I remember thinking how much his eyes looked like those of a lizard," she recalled. The membrane dropped over his eyes when he looked at her and he seemed to recognise her, although at the time she couldn't imagine why. The sense of terrible danger that she felt, and the need to get away from him, was overwhelming. She went on:

> "Eventually I came to understand that the leaders are not fully human, but are the offspring of something alien to this Earth. They are too cunning, lethal, and intelligent to have originated from here, and there has to be an over-race of beings guiding them from some dimension. They are here for one reason only. They look at humans as a source of enslavement for their enjoyment to torment and abuse, to misuse power and to cruelly punish and kill."

As she researched the religion's documents and books, she said she began to uncover a trail of arms and drug-running (which the Illuminati globally controls), and "plots to destroy the world and take it for their own". Diane took her "mountains" of evidence to the US Drug Enforcement Agency (DEA) and met with them. They said that she was either a genius or totally insane. She said she learned that the Watchtower Society had hidden rooms under the streets of Brooklyn, New York, where they have their headquarters over the now-abandoned old Brooklyn subway. There they practise Satanic ritual, including the sacrifice of human infants, she said, and here they also keep women who are used as "breeders" for babies to be sacrificed. This happens all over the world because the babies are never officially registered and therefore never reported missing. To the system, they have never existed. The main Illuminati bloodlines conceive children in the rituals, also. Diane wrote that this Watchtower Satanic operation is totally self-sufficient and even uses blood in the ink of the magazines. She said that she and a friend tried to warn people through the media with no success (I *am* surprised!) and her friend had a nervous breakdown from which she has never fully recovered.

One of a number of accounts to come from former members of the Mormon "Church" was sent by a woman who claims she suffered in a Mormon mind control project from the time she was a young child. Cathy O'Brien says that the Mormon Church and especially the operation at Salt Lake City is a major mind control centre. Former military sources claim that the Mormon Temple in Salt Lake City, which is covered in Illuminati symbols like the all-seeing eye, stands over a large underground reptilian base that can be accessed from the temple site. This woman, I will call her Jane, said that she saw her babies sacrificed in Mormon rituals. In her pursuit of the truth, she spoke with another victim of ritual abuse by the Mormon and Roman Catholic Church. This other lady told her that the Mormon "Prophet" had taken her baby from her at a ritual and eaten it. Two other women raised as Catholics told her that they had seen the abusers shape-shift into reptilians and eat a human sacrifice. Jane said that Joseph Smith, the founder of the Mormons, was from "the occult bloodlines" (very true) and the whole official story was a lie. "The leaders are mostly reptilian," she said. "One witness says that only one of the twelve [Mormon] apostles did not shape shift at the ritual." She goes on:

> "I was so mad to find out that the alien abuse was connected to the ritual abuse in the church when I had believed the church was true. [Now I know that]...our families are from occult bloodlines of England and Europe. This has gone on for hundreds and thousands of years." [9]

For certain, Satanic ritual goes on within the Mormon Church. In fact the number of accounts has ensured that even the Mormon hierarchy has had to admit it goes on. What they do deny, however, is the scale on which it happens and that it goes right to the top. In fact, it is orchestrated from there. There are a number of websites exposing this, including a site set up by former Mormons, one of whom is the same bloodline as the Mormon hero Brigham Young. [10]

Rothschild-Bauer-Bush

The connection between the hybrid bloodlines and shape-shifting is constantly confirmed. Here is one excellent example. The Rothschilds are an Anunnaki shape-shifting bloodline and before they changed their name to "Red Shield" when the Rothschild banking dynasty began in Frankfurt, Germany, they were called Bauer. And the Bauers were a notorious "occult" family of Middle-Ages Germany. The word "Roth" also developed into Roads, Rhoads, or Rhodes, the name of Cecil Rhodes, the infamous Rothschild placeman who brought devastation and genocide to southern Africa. On Rhodes' immense memorial in Cape Town, South Africa, there are lines of lions – a symbol of the serpent cult/Illuminati. Another reptilian bloodline is the Bush family in the United States, which has provided two of the last three US Presidents. Father George has been named perhaps more than anyone when people recount their shape-shifting experiences. I should stress that I am not saying that everyone called Bauer or Bush throughout the world is like this. Certainly not. I am talking of these Anunnaki bloodlines that have taken the name Bauer and Bush. I was sent a letter to my website from a source that did not wish his name to be published. It pulls together the names Bauer (Rothschild) and Bush in one story. Before you read it, you need to know that FEMA, the Federal Emergency Management Agency in the United States, is a major Illuminati operation. It will take control of every aspect of American life, by law, whenever the President calls a State of Emergency. Anyway, here is a fascinating story connecting FEMA, the Rothschild/Bauer and Bush bloodlines, and shape-shifting:

> "A few years ago I became acquainted with a lovely person with the surname of Bauer. We had many varied and wide-ranging discussions. During one of these talks, the subject of schizophrenia came up. She said it ran in her family. Asking for more detail, she told me her mother and great aunt had been afflicted by it. It was the vision hallucination type. The odd thing is that the hallucinations were incredibly similar. Their 'hallucinations' were of people 'of Royal blood' turning into giant lizards!

"I was at FEMA training headquarters in Fredricksburg, Maryland, attending a radiological defence pilot course in 1982 for the Washington State Department of Emergency Services. During the orientation, Louis Guiffreda, one of the head honchos and a cousin of George Bush, came in to observe. When he sat down I noticed a dark haze around him. I kept looking at him to see if my eyes were playing tricks on me, but it stayed the same. I was up in the seats alone, as I like to be in these things. Soon, I noticed he was staring at me! This unnerved me. I closed my eyes and tried to relax. When I opened my eyes again, I saw him coming toward me. He sat down a few rows behind and to the left of me. I glanced back and saw him leaning forward with his eyes closed. I figured he was just tired and decided to take a rest with me.

"While sitting there trying to relax, I heard a strange hissing and swishing sound come from behind me. I opened my eyes, but was afraid to look around. I saw a woman in our group looking up in our direction with a look of astonishment and shock on her face. She kept looking up nervously in our direction. Eventually, Guiffreda left with his bodyguards (waxy-faced suits with sunglasses) and the presentation continued. After the orientation, I walked outside and found this woman sobbing and shaking in the arms of another participant. I intruded and said I wanted to know why she was looking up with that look on her face. She didn't want to say, but with repeated assurance from me she told me. She had seen Guiffreda 'turn' into a lizard! The other guy said Guiffreda had the nickname of lizard man in the circles around FEMA and he has a skin disease that makes his skin look like scales.

"I had forgotten about this experience until I read David's book. It was just one of those odd things that didn't make sense. Now it does...I was in quite a bit of shock when I finally made all the connections. So, what more can I say? I don't just believe it's real, I 'know' it is. Unless, of course, I want to deny my own experience and senses." [11]

Sex and the shape-shifters

Here is another example of the way the bloodline names come up all the time with the stories of shape-shifting. As I mentioned earlier, members of the Oppenheimer family are the bloodline branch managers for the Illuminati reptilians in South Africa and this is a story from a correspondent there:

"I was born in South Africa and years ago got to know an old lady in Johannesburg who had for many years been the lover of Sir Ernest Oppenheimer, the founder [with Rothschild backing] of the gold and diamond corporate cartel. She told me that Sir Ernest used to visit her in the afternoons at her flat in Parktown. On one occasion as they were about to make love, his body took on the form and proportions of a giant lizard with scales and she said the experience had been one of the sexual highlights of her life. The story which was so strange at the time has been in the back of my mind for years and came back to me when I recently read your book." [12]

Sexual activity seems to be a time when shape-shifting can happen as the hormones, blood, and energy are affected dramatically. A businesswoman in Canada told me of her reptilian experiences. The first was with a Portuguese man who treated her terribly and she was little more than an imprisoned slave. She said he shape-shifted into a reptile. She described how he was stunningly ritualistic, even with the time and day of the month he washed his clothes. She later had a relationship with another guy who, she said, was nice on the surface, but had a very dark side he was constantly battling with. She bought *The Biggest Secret* when it was first published because it exposes in great detail the reptilian story she had experienced. One time when they went into her bedroom the book was lying on a shelf above the bed. The man became very wound up and took a serious aversion to it, she told me. When they began to have sex, she said he began to go crazy, becoming violent and rough, and amid this anger, he began to shape-shift into a reptile. Her hand was on the bottom of his back while he lay on top of her and she felt her hand being pushed up as the guy began to sprout a tail! She screamed, threw him off, and he began to switch back to "human" form. She told him to get out of the house immediately and, at the time I met her, she had never seen him since.

A Los Angeles jazz singer, Pamela Stonebrooke, has spoken publicly about her sexual encounters with a reptilian being and the last I heard she was in the process of producing a book on the subject. When the very tall reptilian first appeared in her bedroom, she says she was terrified. The being forced her to have sex and seemed to get "high" on her fear, but she says that as these encounters continued she conquered her fear and started coming on to him! When her fear subsided, the reptilian did not seem to be so keen anymore. Pamela considers her reptilian experience positive overall and talks of a close connection with the being. But reports of women being raped by reptilians are far from rare. I met Pamela briefly at a conference in Los Angeles and she is quite a character, very strong willed, and that's just what you need in these circumstances. She wrote an open letter to the "UFO community" (most of whom are depressingly closed-minded to seeing beyond their own "official line"):

"Reptilians are not a politically correct species in the UFO community, and to admit to having sex with one – much less enjoying it – is beyond the pale as far as the more conservative members of that community are concerned. But I know from my extensive reading and research, and from talking personally to dozens of other women (and men), that I am not unique in reporting this kind of experience. I am the first to admit that this is a vastly complex subject, a kind of hall of mirrors, where dimensional realities are constantly shifting and changing. Certainly, the reptilians use sex to control people in various ways.

"They have the ability to shape-shift and to control the mind of the experiencer, as well as to give tremendous pleasure through their mental powers. I have wrestled with all of these implications and the various levels of meaning and possibilities represented by my encounter experiences. I will say, however, as I have said before, that I feel a deep respect for the reptilian entity with whom I interacted, and a profound connection with this being." [13]

She says that since she began to talk publicly of her experiences, she has been contacted by hundreds of people telling her of similar encounters with reptilian entities. Credo Mutwa tells of the scores of African women he has met who have reported the same experience of being forced to have sex with a reptilian or have been artificially impregnated during abduction experiences only for the resulting pregnancy to end suddenly when the foetus "disappeared" with no explanation. Most women stay silent because of the obvious public ridicule that would follow and whatever people may think about Pamela Stonebrooke, she has the very "couldn't-give-a-shit" attitude that is vital to making suppressed information known to the wider public. In fact, here we have a golden example of the way humanity polices itself and, in doing so, suppresses the very information that would give us a fix on what is really going on. I have experienced it myself for 11 years. When you say anything that is different to the norm, the masses either ridicule or condemn you without doing any research whatsoever to establish if what you say could be valid. They dismiss it and often direct their bile at the messenger for no other reason than it is different to what they have been programmed to believe. The media, as an expression of the collective mind, and vice-versa, takes the same line. Pathetic.

Most people when faced with the truth, or a more accurate version of events, just laugh in its face or condemn it as evil. Even those who have opened up to some aspects of the truth still can't expand their mind to encompass the exploding evidence of the reptilian dimension. One writer, in an otherwise very interesting book about ancient extraterrestrials, acknowledges all the serpent symbolism, names, and references surrounding the Anunnaki, but suggests that this could have been because they wore reptile clothing or kept snakes. I think there is another reason, somehow.

SOURCES

1   *Trance-Formation Of America*, p 174

2   Recorded conversations with the author

3   See ***http://www.suite101.com/article.cfm/ritual_abuse/43922***

4   Correspondence with the author

5   ***http://www.rense.com/general6/ciajew.htm***

6   Recorded conversations with the author and on the video, *Revelations Of A Mother Goddess*

7   Recorded conversations with the author

8   Correspondence with the author and posted at *davidicke.com*

9   Ibid

10   *http://www.utlm.org/* and see also *http://www.exmormon.org/stories.htm*

11   *http://www.davidicke.com/icke/articles/femaicke.html*

12   *http://www.reptilianagenda.com/exp/e012000a.html*

13   *http://www.ufomind.com/ufo/updates/1998/jun/m09-009.shtml* and see also
     http://www.sightings.com/ufo/screwingaliens.h

CHAPTER 13

Serving the dragon:
the present (2)

We are here to learn to love each other. I don't know what the others are here for.

Auden

Dr David Jacobs, a professor of history at Temple University in the United States, made a long and detailed study of abductee reports and published his conclusions in a book called *The Threat: The Secret Agenda* (Simon & Schuster, New York, 1988).

He says that the "alien agenda" includes breeding hybrids using human and alien genetic material, and replacing human society with these hybrids under their control. This is the real reason behind all the abductions in which male sperm is taken or females are impregnated, according to Dr Jacobs. He says the first stage is to cross human genetics with the "alien". Then this genetic material is fused with another human egg and sperm, and this second-stage hybrid is crossed with another human egg and sperm. The result of this would look almost human and when this is crossed with yet another human egg and sperm, the result could walk down the street without being noticed.[1] He could be describing here the way the first creation of the Anunnaki, what some people call "the Adam", was evolved into the human mammal we see today. Dr Jacobs believes that these later-stage hybrids are what abductees call the "Nordics", although not all of them are blond-haired and blue-eyed. I think we need to note the difference between the extraterrestrial "Nordics" that came to the Earth and seeded their own bloodlines and the Nordic-type hybrid crossbreeds and others that I call the Aryans. Dr Jacobs says that these "super-hybrids" retain many of their "alien" abilities. These include scanning the minds of humans and controlling abductees. He suggests that while the hybrids may have some human characteristics, they think like the "aliens" and answer to them. "The hybrid agenda is the alien agenda," he says. Dr Jacobs believes that in the final stages of the agenda, humans will be slowly "phased out" while the hybrids are "phased in". Memories of loving mothers, fathers, freedom of choice and religion will be replaced by memories of selective breeding, single-minded functions geared to serving the aliens. These hybrids would have a hive mentality with no memories of individual choice, family bonding, or freedom. It would, he says, be a hierarchical, fascist order in which a ruling caste dominates lesser castes. I could not put it better. We are almost there, but there is still time to wake up...just. Dr Jacobs says that, from interviews with abductees, the hybrids seem unhappy with their situation and long for the freedom of humans.

Reptilian abductions

James L. Walden, an American with a doctorate in business education, had so many reptilian experiences that he described them in a book, *The Ultimate Alien Agenda* (Llewellyn Publications, St Paul, Minnesota, 1998). Before his first experience, he had no interest in extraterrestrials or UFOs or "science fiction" of any kind. His story began in March 1992 when a grey entity some four feet tall with large dark eyes and a large, bulbous head, appeared in the room as he was switching off the light to go to bed. The air became extremely cold and a "petrified" Walden began to cry. He said the right eye of the grey enlarged and turned bright red. It projected a beam of red light, which struck him painfully on the leg. A beam of white light later came down towards him, he said, and it entered his body just below the navel. He lost consciousness and when he woke he was lying on a cold table of polished metal. He was immobilised and a bright overhead light was shining in his eyes. Around him were people in "stiff white smocks". Some appeared human, but most looked like the being that came to his bedroom. They examined every part of his body and a sperm sample was taken. The Zulu shaman Credo Mutwa describes a similar scene and events during his abduction in what is now Zimbabwe in the early 1960s (see *The Reptilian Agenda*, part one). Walden said he was told that he was in an underground facility in south-east Kansas and would not be harmed. He heard a "telepathic voice" say: "You are not who you think you are, and you must accept this." In later experiences, he was told that he was a reptilian-human hybrid. Many strange things began to happen to him after the first abduction:

> "One night...I was lying on my back and searching the ceiling for sleep, when I heard a loud 'whishing' sound. Something moved toward me at lightning-speed – and a large, life-like image of George Washington stopped right in front of my face, touching my nose. I heard a loud, forceful voice, say: 'George Washington was one of us. So are you. You must accept.'" [2]

George Washington was an Illuminati bloodline, a Grand Master Freemason, and first President of the United States. In the years that followed, James Walden had many other experiences with greys and other more obvious reptilians and worked with the abduction researcher Barbara Bartholic to uncover what was going on. She had heard the same story many times from other people claiming to be abductees. One entity that Walden experienced was an "interdimensional reptile". It was between eight and twelve feet tall and had elongated feet. There was a "web" between his torso and arms, "like a bat", which could sometimes look like wings, and a "fin-like appendage" on his back. His head was large and elongated like a watermelon. The being had rough, greenish patterned skin, and Walden believed there was a tail also. This entity claimed to have inhabited many "human" bodies and he said: "My eyes have witnessed the evolution of humankind." [3] Under hypnosis, Walden recalled that he was part of an experimental group of human embryos, which were grown in a test tube. The embryo, he recalled, was implanted into his mother's womb and she had no idea this had been done. Could this be an explanation of the legends of Merovee, Alexander the Great, and others, who were said to have been fathered by serpent-like beings? And could this be at least one origin of the "Virgin Birth"? Walden said it certainly offered an explanation for why he had always felt different to all the other children. He believed that millions of people in the world had been created in this way as part of an "alien" genetic programme. He said that the semen, taken during his abduction, was used to impregnate a woman of the "same stock". She was like a "human incubator" and he thinks the embryo was removed from her womb later.

Another interesting memory he had was that when he was on the table in that first abduction, his body had looked the same as the "aliens".[4] Walden felt that this was another-dimension of him, which inhabited his human form. He believed from his experiences that the "aliens" could transcend time, transform matter, manipulate human thought and behaviour, and create "distracting illusions to satisfy the needs of our simple human minds." He concluded that they could move between dimensions and that they were less "extraterrestrial" and more "interdimensional". I thoroughly agree. Their ability to change their vibrational state would explain how they can appear and disappear (leave our frequency range), and how they can walk through walls. They can move through dense matter in the same way a radio frequency can. And if it is the fourth- dimensional level of a person that is abducted, and not, or not always, the physical body, it would further explain why abductees have described being taken through walls and buildings. Walden speculated that these fourth-dimensional "aliens" are actually the fourth-dimensional level of ourselves.

The abductors told Jim Walden that an interdimensional race had colonised the Earth and they came to harvest the planet's resources, harness its energies, and use primitive humans as its workforce. "Just as human scientists have developed animals for nourishment, labour, and entertainment purposes," he said, "alien scientists have improved humans for the same reason – and possibly others."[5] Walden said the "aliens" could program the emotional responses of their hybrids, to produce "misery, jealousy, passion, or love."[6] Walden said that when the interdimensional reptilians first colonised the Earth they found it difficult to reproduce here. He said that during abductions, the "aliens" made it possible for them to inhabit the abductee's body.[7] This would explain why Miguel de la Madrid said they needed to create "bodies" through which they could operate on this planet. Walden said the aliens lived in "subterranean shelters" from the time they arrived, and conditions in the Earth's atmosphere threatened their survival because they could not maintain a constant body temperature. He said their eyes are extremely sensitive to light and this fits with Credo Mutwa's claims about the light-sensitive eyes of the greys and other reptilians, and with the symbolic story of the blood-drinking Dracula who could not go out during the day. Walden was, surprisingly, very positive about the reptilians by the time his book was finished, but I think he was taking their word for their true intentions for humanity a little too easily. The evidence is overwhelming that some of them have a very malevolent agenda, but that is only one large faction, not all of them. Some other abductees also see the reptilians in a positive light, despite having horrendous experiences with them, and some researchers get incredibly angry with anyone who paints the reptilians in a negative light. Mark Amaru Pinkham, author of *The Return Of The Serpents Of Wisdom*, superbly details the serpent symbolism and bloodlines of the ancient world, but sees them in a virtually 100% positive light. He even praises people like Benjamin Franklin as a force for enlightenment. Franklin sacrificed children! Depicting all reptilians as expressions of "wisdom" is just as ludicrous as depicting them all as "evil". And those who have a horrific agenda for humanity, of course, want us to believe they are here to "save" us.

Stories about people waking up to find reptilian figures in the room are regularly reported. Pamela Hamilton, an American woman who has lived in California and Arizona, claims to have been visited at home, often in the bedroom, by countless "Nordic" blond-haired, blue-eyed beings, along with greys and reptilians, since she was young.[8] Witnesses have seen the marks on her body that have followed many of these visits. She has also suffered a raid by military personnel who walked in and stole material relating to extraterrestrials and UFO activity. Pamela described a reptilian "visitor" who appeared a number of times. She said he had luminous amber-coloured eyes like a cat and had grey-green skin and sharp claws on his fingers. He wore a sort of "breast-plate" like the ones used by Roman soldiers, she said. When he appeared she would first hear a high-pitched sound and a buzzing and clicking noise and soon found it hard to breath. She felt that her chest was being crushed. When she became paralysed and immobilised, the reptilian would "flip" her on to her chest and begin to have "a type of tantric sexual intercourse" that would leave her exhausted. Feeding on her life force, probably. She said he was extremely powerful and very aggressive and a likely member of a warrior caste. But she didn't fear him and almost felt protected by him.

California and Arizona appear to be extremely important areas for reptilian activity, especially locations such as: Mount Lassen, a dormant volcano that is part of the Cascade range of California, Oregon, Washington State, and south-western Canada; Sedona, the "New Age" centre in Arizona; and Phoenix, two hours south of Sedona in the Valley of the Sun. The Superstition Mountains outside Phoenix have been the subject of a number of stories in which people claim to have seen physical reptilian beings. You can read some of these on my website, *www.davidicke.com*. One involves a woman known as "Angie" who loved climbing the mountains around Phoenix, including the Superstitions.[9] On this occasion she found a cave and went inside. She sat down and began to drink water from her flask. After a while she got up to leave when suddenly she felt a hand grab hers from behind. She gasped in surprise when she looked up at a reptilian face. She tried to laugh, thinking it was someone wearing a mask. When she realised it was for real she tried to scream, but nothing would come. She lost consciousness and when she awoke she heard strange barking and chirping sounds that she later realised were a sort of "language" the reptilians used. When she tried to get up, she found she couldn't move her arms or legs. She felt a hand on the inside of her thighs and she struggled to open her eyes. She opened one a little and saw men with lizard-like faces. Her heart sank and she felt absolute horror burst through her. Again when she tried to scream, she couldn't. She watched as several greenish reptilians removed her clothes. They seemed to be a strange combination of human and serpent, she said. The wide slit eyes almost glowed with a yellowish brightness (exactly what Credo Mutwa says), and they had glistening, vertical pupils. They had broad flat noses and their flat nostrils flared slightly as they snorted while examining her. She said that some had a very wide mouth with many folds of skin, while some had small mouths with no folds. They had small, rounded ears, which were set high on the head, and had no lobes. She noticed that their scales were a different colour than the skin on the head. They were a khaki green that became grey-green on the back of the head. Their faces were smooth with narrow, pointed chins. Two of them wore a white jumpsuit with an insignia that included a curved dragon with a seven-pointed star in the middle. The other 'reptile-men' wore black uniforms with the same insignia. She also talked of a tall, white-skinned lizard being with blue eyes – the ones identified many times as the "royal Draco", the highest of the reptilian hierarchy. He wore a "burnt orange jumpsuit" with three insignia on the left side. There was a black inverted triangle, the round dragon with a star, and an oval with moving stars on it. On the right side of his uniform were three black bars on a silver disk; and the left cuff had a row of inverted triangles with three lines cutting through it. He was taller than the others, nearly seven feet.

Angie was by now naked on the floor and she asked the "white Draco" to help her. She felt something cold touch her forehead, and a strange calm and peace enveloped her. She then realised she was in an oval room about 15 feet wide. She tried to turn her head, but she couldn't. She noticed pipes with strange "sacs", like mis-shaped balloons hanging from them. Then she realised some were moving. She remembered how her dog's belly moved that way when she was near full term with her puppies. A wave of horror hit her. It was as if there were two minds inside her. One was calm, the other horror-stricken. The calm side was in charge of her body. She wondered how her body could be so calm when anything could be about to happen to her. One of the lizard men undressed and approached the end of the table. He was muscular and had scales on his chest and lower stomach. Fear now overwhelmed the artificial calm and she began to scream and find superhuman strength to fight him off. The lizard men turned a blue light on her and she lost consciousness. The last thing she remembered was feeling the weight of his body. When Angie came to, she was in her car. She looked around her, feeling confused and wondering why she was driving her car. She felt that she had been about to do something, but couldn't remember what. She drove home dazed and disorientated. There she suddenly had an urge to shower, and scrubbed her body for over two hours. She felt shaky and angry for something she couldn't recall. She spent the next few days in bed refusing to answer the door. Her sister Susan noticed that Angie had several nightmares every night and woke up screaming. Angie also refused to go near the mountains she loved so much. When she later went back to work, she left after three days when a customer brought a lizard into the store. She had no idea why that had frightened her so much when reptiles had always been a part of her life there in the desert. Eventually she went to a hypnotist for help, and her vivid and detailed memories of what happened in the Superstition Mountains flooded back.

Eva Trent, another American, also claims to have had many contacts with non-human entities.[10] One night in January 1999, she went to bed in her small apartment. Later, she said, she woke to a "buzzing sound" and when she opened her eyes she was horrified to see two strange creatures standing on either side of her bed. One was around seven to eight feet tall, weighed around 19 stone (getting on for 300 pounds) with the skin of a crocodile or snake. The other was the same, but smaller. They seemed to be communicating in a "chirping" manner and their eyes glowed. Chirping sounds are pretty common in such reports and the glowing eyes are universal. The Sumerians knew Enlil, the chief Anunnaki on the Earth, as "the Serpent with the shining eyes". Eva found she was unable to move, another confirmation of the ancient and modern accounts of how the serpent "gods" could paralyse people. They communicated with her through telepathy. She felt they were observing her emotional state and probably feeding off the energy of fear their presence had generated. Similar points were made by Pamela Stonebrooke about the way her reptilian seemed to get high on fear. The experience ended for Eva when she began to mentally resist and visualised herself cocooned in white light. This seemed to confuse the reptilians and the next thing she remembers was waking up the next morning physically exhausted. When she checked around the room she found five of her favourite cassettes tapes in a rack six feet from her bed had been destroyed. They were distorted and three were badly buckled, as if by some extreme heat. Yet there was no smell of plastic burns and the sound filaments had not been melted. There was no sign of any heat being applied anywhere on or near the rack. The only explanation was that they had been subjected to some kind of microwave heat.

The American writer Alex Christopher has been exposing the reptilian presence for many years and I first saw her speak in Denver in 1996. She is the author of the books, *Pandora's Box*, volumes I and II, and she has had her own direct experiences of reptilians and the "big-eyed greys". In Panama City, Florida, she was woken at 2.30 in the morning by her terrified neighbour, a commercial airline pilot. When she ran over to his house, she found his partner sliding down the wall with her eyes rolling and she kept passing out. Alex said she could feel extremely powerful energy in the room, which appeared to be trying to penetrate her head. It was radiation of some kind and the next day all the plants in the room were dead. The couple told her that they were making love when the incident started. They saw a flash of light and they were pulled from the bed. The man still had a palm print on his side made by fingers that must have been ten inches long with claws that burned into his skin. The next day the spot was so painful he couldn't touch it and Alex says she has video footage of this. For her, however, the story was just the beginning because when she was in bed in her own house, a reptilian appeared to her:

"I woke up and there is this 'thing' standing over my bed. He had wrap-around-yellow eyes with snake pupils and pointed ears and a grin that wrapped around his head. He had a silvery suit on and this scared the living daylights out of me. I threw the covers over my head and started screaming…I mean, here is this thing with a Cheshire-cat grin and these funky glowing eyes…this is too much. I have seen this kind of being on more than one occasion…He had a hooked nose and was very human looking other than his eyes, and had kind of greying skin…

"…Later on in 1991, I was working in a building in a large city, and I had taken a break about 6pm and the next thing I knew it was 10.30pm and I thought I had taken a short break. I started remembering that I was taken aboard a [spaceship], through four floors of the office building and through a roof. There on the ship is where I encountered Germans and Americans working together, and also grey aliens, and then we were taken to some other kind of facility and there I saw reptilians again…the ones I call the 'Baby Godzilla's' that have short teeth and yellow slanted-eyes…The things that stick in my minds are the beings that look like reptiles, or the 'velcoci-rapters'. They are the cruellest beings you could ever imagine and they even smell hideous." [11]

The putrid smell is another theme of contact with reptilians and greys. It was during this abduction that Alex Christopher saw a dragon badge on the uniform of a reptilian. A contact said she saw the same symbol at Fort Walden in the United States and a winged-serpent symbol could be seen on the sleeve of an Israeli soldier as he comforted the daughter of the assassinated Prime Minister, Yitzchak Rabin, during his funeral in 1995 (see *Newsweek*, November 20th 1995). Many badges within the US armed forces feature the dragon and reptile, as revealed in the Symbolism Archive on my website. There are many reports of shape-shifting reptilians at military bases and medical facilities. The author and researcher John Keel has gathered together reports of flying reptiles seen by many people. These are known as "pterodactyloid-hominoid mothmen", flying serpents, or winged Draco. These align with ancient and modern descriptions across the world of the "royal" reptilians from the Draco constellation with their wings, tails, and horns. Keel compiled his findings in a book, *The Mothmen Prophecies* (Signet Books, New York, 1976). Here is a sample:

"…According to her story, Connie [Carpenter], a shy, sensitive eighteen-year-old, was driving home from church at 10:30am on Sunday, November 27, 1966, when, as she passed the deserted greens of Mason County Golf Course outside New Haven, West Virginia, she suddenly saw a huge grey figure. It was shaped like a man, she said, but much larger. It was at least seven feet tall and very broad. The thing that attracted her attention was not its size, but its eyes. It had, she said, large, round, fiercely glowing red eyes that focussed on her with hypnotic effect. 'It's a wonder I didn't run off the road and have a wreck,' she commented later.

"As she slowed, her eyes fixed on the apparition, a pair of wings unfolded from its back. They seemed to have a span of about ten feet. It was definitely not an ordinary bird, but a man-shaped thing, which rose slowly off the ground, straight up like a helicopter, silently. Its wings did not flap in flight. It headed straight toward Connie's car, its horrible eyes fixed to her face, and then it swooped low over her head as she shoved the accelerator to the floorboards in utter hysteria. Over one hundred people would see this bizarre creature that winter." [12]

Significantly, many of the sightings of these flying reptile-men happened close to the apparently sealed entrances to underground tunnels known as the TNT facility, which were used to store explosives during the Second World War. A young shoe salesman called Thomas Ury was driving along Route 62 just north of the TNT area when he noticed a tall, grey, man-like figure standing in a field near the road. 'Suddenly it spread a pair of wings', he said, 'and took off straight up, like a helicopter." Native Americans have the legend of the Thunderbird, which, the stories say, abducts children and old people. The tribes of the Dakotas know this as Piasa and it is described as a demon monster with bat wings, a humanoid body, a long tail, and terrifying red eyes. Similar reports have come from many parts of the world.

Another witness called Odette told of an experience at a house in Quebec, Canada. She was with a friend when another woman came over and began to talk about UFOs and contactees. The woman said she was a contactee and she had a meeting with a spaceship on a certain date. She also said that they were taking her and she would never be back on Earth. Odette said she was not convinced at all and especially when the woman had said that if they could only see her real self, they would see how beautiful she is, like a princess inside. "I was thinking, yeah right! Whatever!!!", Odette recalled. The woman looked around 30 years old, tall and strong, light hair, cut to her shoulder, and was "ordinary looking". Then she asked Odette if she would let her reveal her real self because she would never have seen anyone like her. But she said she needed Odette's permission for this. Odette said yes because she thought, "Poor thing, she's really miserable…" The account continues:

"We went to a quiet room. We sat facing each other, and she grabbed my hands, told me to relax and just look at her. What I saw was a reptile, taller than she was, at least 6 feet, green/brown colour, staring at me with its head turned side ways, and I swear with something that seemed like a grin on its face. Then she/it asked me 'Didn't I tell you I was beautiful?' I said yes, and headed for the door…If anybody has had a similar experience or knows of a book that talks about reptilians please let me know." [13]

Men in Black

Reports of reptilian shape-shifters come in from all over the world and the "Men in Black" phenomenon has also been connected to them. These are the guys dressed in black suits, who intimidate many UFO researchers and abductees. Most appear to be government agents, but there are other expressions of them who do not look "human" in the usual sense. They have a strange aura around them and, many people have reported, they can suddenly "disappear". I remember seeing a garage owner and UFO investigator telling his story on a TV programme about Men in Black or "MIBs". They turned up out of nowhere without a vehicle and yet his garage was in the middle of the countryside, all by itself. After their conversation, they just as quickly vanished and it was impossible for them to do so under normal circumstances because you could see for miles in all directions. The Men in Black are named after their dark clothing, mostly business or "agent" suits, and their dark glasses. This attire has all the signs of these beings needing protection from the Sun – a classic trait of the reptilians and greys. They are mostly described as having very white skin and, sometimes, olive skin. The texture is often said to be reptilian. Other strange traits in witness accounts are the trouble the MIBs appear to have breathing and the horrible smell, like sulphur, which abductees are constantly describing. They also often arrive in "new" black cars that have not been manufactured for decades. Despite their apparent age, these vehicles show no signs of any wear or tear. It is as if they have just been driven from the factory. Similar beings, dressed in the context of the period, have been reported over the centuries in many parts of the world. The so-called Grim Reaper, who appeared in communities just before a lethal disease broke out, were described in terms that are remarkably close to today's Men in Black.

The Association of Extraterrestrial Investigations (APEX), founded by Dr Max Berezowsky in Sao Paulo, Brazil, documented a Men in Black story involving a young guy called Aeromar.[14] He said he was harassed by three men dressed in black suits and ties and he thought they were the police. He moved cities twice to get away from them and on one occasion complained to the police in Rio de Janeiro about their harassment. They didn't believe him and he moved to Sao Paulo. It was there that a car stopped beside him in the street. He said he "lost his will to resist" and climbed inside to find the three guys who had been following him for months. He was driven to a wooden area, he said, where he saw a large "UFO". The car stopped and they all walked up to the craft, which was hovering above the ground and surrounded by a "luminous ring". The next thing he knew, they were inside and he was sat in a chair with handles that secured his wrists. An iron bar pressed his head backwards against the chair and his neck was also fastened. Now, he said, the "Men in Black" transformed. Their "heads ripped open into a heart shape" and their skin became scaled and green like a reptilian. This happened in 1979-80 long before MIBs became associated with reptilians. He said he also saw human corpses hanging from hooks. Everything went blank after that and he found himself back in the street where he was picked up. Now, however, it was hours later and there was no traffic. He ran home in a panic, he said, and told a room mate what had happened, but as he did so, a force threw him against a wall. The reptilians had told him never to talk about his experience. He was later introduced to Dr Max Berezowsky and he told his story to APEX members.

On the superb US radio show, Sightings, a woman called Joyce Murphy talked about the reptilian shape-shifters of Brazil. She is the president and founder of

Beyond Boundaries, an organisation that takes people on expeditions to many parts of the world. She was telling presenter Jeff Rense about some of the strange experiences on her travels when she talked about a policewoman she knew in Brazil who had described shape-shifting reptilian beings. Joyce said:

> "...she works in a very high position in the Sheriff's Office. There seem to be shape-shifters, here in Brazil at least, that try and get women to act as breeders for them. They actually shape-shifted to show them their actual form, a sort of reptilian type. This with her sister as a witness. And I know of another shape-shifter story. The daughter of an aviation engineer in Sao Paulo tells of a fellow student who revealed her true form changing...into a sort of reptilian being. These people do not know each other and they clam up if one goes after more information or wants to reveal the whole situation. Oh my gosh, what am I getting into here?" [15]

The reptilian underground bases

There are so many reports of seeing reptilians and shape-shifting, but most people have no knowledge of this because 99% of the population get their "news" and "information" from the mainstream media. The media, in turn, get their "news" and "information" overwhelmingly from official sources, which, like the media itself, are owned by the reptilian bloodlines. After speaking about the reptilians on the Sightings programme, I was sent this account of an experience at the infamous Dulce underground facility in New Mexico. These are the words of an army private employed on the surface:

> "...I was working on a routine job when another of the young enlistees, a mechanic, came in with a small rush job he wanted at once. He had the print and proceeded to show me exactly what he wanted. We are both bending over the bench in front of the welder when I happened to look directly into his face. It seemed to suddenly become covered in a semi-transparent film or cloud. His features faded and in their place appeared a 'thing' with bulging eyes, no hair, and scales for skin."

He later saw the same thing happen to a guard at the Dulce front gate, and witnesses have spoken of seeing reptilian shape-shifters at the Madigan Military Hospital near Fort Lewis in Washington State. There are secret underground facilities throughout the world and at the deepest levels they open out into the inner-earth centres of the reptilians and greys. Area 51 in Nevada is the best-known underground facility in UFO research circles, but the very fact that it is so famous and featured in Hollywood movies, shows that it is far from the most important of them. These facilities are themselves connected by a vast tunnel network that has been built with nuclear boring technology that the public never sees. It can cut tunnels at the rate of seven miles a day and these are an expansion of the global tunnel network created by the Atlanteans and Lemurians, and claimed by legends and accounts to exist under the United States, Central and South America, Britain,

Egypt, Mesopotamia, Turkey, Asia, China, Malta, everywhere. The tunnels have state-of-the-art transport systems that move at astonishing speeds. Insiders describe them as "magneto-leviton or mag-lev monorail trains capable of mach-2". Leading Illuminati companies and operations are involved in the construction. Companies like the Rand Corporation, General Electric, AT & T, Hughes Aircraft, Northrop Corporation, Sandia Corporation, Stanford Research Institute, Walsh Construction, the Colorado School of Mines, and the most significant one of all, Bechtel (Beck-tul), a major reptilian corporation.

These underground bases, tunnel systems, and their technology, have been detailed by former military personnel, mind-controlled slaves, and people like Phil Schneider, who helped to build some of them. Schneider was the son of a German U-boat commander in the Second World War, Otto Oscar Schneider. His father was captured and taken to the United States to work for the Illuminati. As so often happens, the children of Illuminati operatives are brought up to work for the same masters and Phil Schneider says he was commissioned to build sections of a number of underground facilities in the United States. He said he knew of 131 underground military bases, an average of one mile deep, constructed for the New World Order agenda. Two of the bases he was involved with were Area 51 in Nevada and Dulce, New Mexico. Dulce is a small town of around 1,000 people and located on the Jicarilla Apache Reservation at a height of some 7,000 feet. From in and around Dulce have come a stream of reports of UFO sightings and landings, "alien" abductions, human and animal mutilations, and sightings of reptilians. The base was also the alleged scene, in 1979, of the "Dulce Wars" when reptilians and greys are said to have battled with human military and civilian personnel. Many people on both sides were killed and Phil Schneider claims to have taken part in this shoot-out. He said he was hit by a laser weapon and he had a fantastic scar down his chest, as he publicly revealed. Schneider talked of his part in the battle in a lecture in 1995, although there appear to be many other elements to it, also:

> "My job was to go down the holes and check the rock samples, and recommend the explosive to deal with the particular rock. As I was headed down there, we found ourselves amidst a large cavern that was full of outer-space aliens, otherwise known as large Greys. I shot two of them. At that time, there were 30 people down there. About 40 more came down after this started, and all of them got killed. We had surprised a whole underground base of existing aliens. Later, we found out that they had been living on our planet for a long time. ...This could explain a lot of what is behind the theory of ancient astronauts."

Schneider began to speak out and alert the world to what was going on, although as usual most people didn't listen. Schneider, who worked closely with researcher Alex Christopher, died in January 1996 in highly suspicious circumstances that were crudely made to look like suicide. Schneider, speaking at a public lecture a year earlier, said:

"...for every calendar year that transpires, military technology increases about 44.5 years [compared with the increase rate of 'conventional' technology]. This is why it is easy to understand that back in 1943 they were able to create, through the use of vacuum tube technology, a ship that could literally disappear from one place and appear in another place."

This was a reference to the "Philadelphia Experiment" in which a US naval ship is alleged to have been made invisible and taken into another dimension. Another of the underground bases Schneider helped to build is under the new Denver International Airport, east of Denver. The construction was very controversial because of the massive cost overrun – the same as the gigantic hole being dug by Bechtel as part of "transport improvements" in Boston, Massachusetts. Denver Airport is the place with the gargoyles, Freemasonic symbols, and murals full of Illuminati symbolism. I have been through there myself a number of times. According to Schneider, there are several main levels underneath, at least ten sub-levels, a 4.5-square-mile underground city, and an 88.5-square-mile underground base. The Denver base is said to include massive "containment camps" and fenced in areas deep underground for holding "dissidents". Workers who experienced the deeper levels of the base saw scenes so terrifying they have refused to talk about them. From other sources, however, we can imagine some of what they saw. These bases are where many of the millions, yes millions, of children who go missing every year worldwide are taken. I know it is hard to stomach, but they are used for slave labour and eaten by the reptilians, just like humans eat chicken or cows. Workers at the Dulce base in New Mexico have reported seeing the most grotesque sights in the lower levels. Researchers Bill Hamilton and TAL Levesque (also known as Jason Bishop III) gathered the following information about Dulce, which they published in *UFO* magazine:

"Level number six is privately called 'Nightmare Hall'. It holds the Genetic Labs. Reports from workers who have seen bizarre experimentation are as follows: 'I have seen multi-legged "humans" that look like half-human/half octopus. Also reptilian-humans and furry creatures that have hands like humans and cry like a baby. It mimics human words...also a huge mixture of lizard-humans in cages. There are fish, seals, birds and mice that can hardly be considered those species. There are several cages (and vats) of winged humanoids, grotesque bat-like creatures...but three and a half to seven feet tall. Gargoyle-like beings and Draco reptoids.

"Level number seven is worse, row after row of thousands of humans and human mixtures in cold storage. Here, too, are embryo storage vats of humanoids in various stages of development. [One worker said] '...I frequently encountered humans in cages, usually dazed or drugged, but sometimes they cried and begged for help. We were told they were hopelessly insane, and involved in high-risk drug tests to cure insanity. We were told never to try to speak to them at all. At the beginning we believed that story. Finally, in 1978, a small group of workers discovered the truth'..." [16]

This discovery led to the "Dulce Wars", the battle between humans and the reptilians and reptilian greys in 1979 when many scientists and military personnel were killed, and Phil Schneider says he was critically wounded. A security officer at Dulce called Thomas Castello has described to researchers what happens at the Dulce base and his words were reported in the *UFO* magazine article. His information has also been circulated as the "Dulce Papers". Castello worked for seven years with the Rand Corporation, an Illuminati operation in Santa Monica, California, and transferred to Dulce in 1977. He estimated there were more than 18,000 of the "short greys" at Dulce, and he had also seen tall reptilian humanoids. He knew of seven levels, but there could have been more, and he said the "aliens" were on levels five, six, and seven. The lower you go, the higher the security clearance you need. The only sign in English was above the tube shuttle station which said "to Los Alamos", another major underground reptilian base in New Mexico. Most signs at Dulce are in the "alien symbol language" and a universal symbol system understood by humans and aliens, he said. The Illuminati communicate above ground in the language of symbolism, as revealed in *The Biggest Secret* and the Symbolism Archive on my website. The hieroglyphics of Sumer, Egypt, and China, would have been a reptilian or "alien" language originally. Other tunnel connections from Dulce went to underground facilities at Page, Arizona, Area 51 in Nevada, Taos, Carlsbad, and Datil, New Mexico, Colorado Springs and Creede, Colorado. Castello said there was a vast network of tube shuttle connections under the United States, which extends into a global system of tunnels and sub-cities.

He described the immense security at Dulce. Below the second level, everyone is weighed naked and given a uniform. Any change in weight is noted and people are examined and X-rayed if there is a change of three pounds. At the entrance to all "sensitive" areas there are scales and a person's weight must match with their card and code to gain entry. Castello also revealed some of the genetic work carried out at Dulce. He said that their scientists can separate the "bioplasmic body" from the physical body and place an "alien entity" (consciousness) within a human body after removing the "soul" of the human. I have thought for years that some famous people, including prime ministers and presidents, were taken into such facilities and possessed by a reptilian entity. To the public the famous person looks the same physically afterwards, but now a very different force is deciding the behaviour. Ancient legends also tell of people being replaced in the night by "changelings" or shape-shifters. It is likely that certain bloodlines with a threshold ratio of reptilian DNA makes this possession easier and this is one reason why the Illuminati keep such detailed genetic records of family bloodlines. The joint global press announcement by the Illuminati's Bill Clinton and Tony Blair in 2000 about the mapping of the human genome takes on even greater significance when you think that the US Department of Energy has laboratories at Dulce and is closely connected to the genome project, along with the National Institute of Health, the National Science Foundation, and the Howard Hughes Medical Institute. All are Illuminati fronts. Researcher Alan Walton, who writes extensively on the Internet about the reptilian connection, says:

"Underneath most major cities, especially in the USA in fact, there exist subterranean counterpart 'cities' controlled by the Masonic/hybrid/alien 'elite'. Often surface/subsurface terminals exist beneath Masonic Lodges, police stations, airports, and federal buildings of major cities ... and even not so 'major' cities. The population ratio is probably close to 10% of the population (the hybrid military-industrial fraternity 'elite' living below ground as opposed to the 90% living above). This does not include the full-blood reptilian species who live in even deeper recesses of the Earth.

"Some of the major population centers were deliberately established by the Masonic/hybrid elite of the Old and New 'worlds' to afford easy access to already existing underground levels, some of which are thousands of years old. Considering that the Los Alamos Labs [in New Mexico] had a working prototype nuclear powered thermol-bore drill that could literally melt tunnels through the Earth at a rate of 8 mph **40 years ago**, you can imagine how extensive these underground systems have become. These sub-cities also offer close access to organised criminal syndicates, which operate on the surface. They have developed a whole science of 'borg-onomics' through which they literally nickle-and-dime us into slavery via multi-leveled taxation, inflation, sublimation, manipulation, regulation, fines, fees, licenses... and the entire debt-credit scam which is run by the Federal Reserve and Wall Street.

"New York City, I can confirm, is one of the largest draconian nests in the world. Or rather the ancient underground 'Atlantean' systems that network beneath that area. They literally control the entire Wall Street pyramid from below... with more than a little help from reptilian bloodlines like the Rockefellers, etc. In fact these reptilian genetic lines operate in a parasitic manner, the underground society acting as the 'parasite' society and the surface society operating as the 'host' society. ...As for the New York City / Wall Street 'nest', during the bombing of the World Trade Center (aka World Slave Center) wherein terrorists attempted to topple one of the towers into the other, a little known fact was briefly revealed. A six-levelled sub-basement controlled by the US Secret Service suffered heavy damage. These six sub-basements, one beneath the other, may not have ended there, based on other information that I've uncovered of massive alien infestation beneath the New York City area. These sub-basements may actually serve as a major terminal between the underground society of Masonic elite, and the surface society which it controls." [17]

I am sure that the locations of these major cities were selected because they were above underground reptilian-Nefilim tunnel and cavern systems and/or they were on significant vortex points. Phoenix, Arizona, is built on one of these ancient networks, as is Los Angeles – the city of the "angels". Lauren Savage, the Webmaster of davidicke.com in Texas, says that every county in that state has a building with gothic European architecture (i.e. reptilian), which could not normally have been afforded by Texas when these settlements were built in the 1870's. Many have gargoyles. These buildings, he says, are the county courthouses sitting above underground tunnels and basement systems. Dallas is an example with its underground tunnels beneath Dealey Plaza where President Kennedy was shot in 1963. What a great way for the true assassins to escape. These tunnels would have been under the original Masonic lodge in Dallas, which was located in Dealey Plaza. Close by is the 1870's old red courthouse complete with gargoyles. Underground tunnels were discovered in Dallas in the late 50's or early 60's and Lauren talked to a man who was working on a state road crew when he was a teenager. They were digging out what is called "the canyon" to build freeways when they opened up an ancient tunnel. They found rail-type tracks and a sort of train with no known source of fuel or energy. They followed the tunnel to where it ended or collapsed, under an old livery stable. Dallas was a French settlement, earlier called Arcadia (an Illuminati code relating to Atlantis), and a suburb is still named Arcadia Park. In 1999, they revealed that the Capitol building in Austin has underground facilities, which they were going to restore. This building was the headquarters of George W. Bush before he was manipulated into the presidency.

Alan Walton says that Thomas Castello, the Dulce security director, described how the greys, "reptiloids", and winged "mothmen" collaborate in the lower levels of the underground system, which includes Dulce and Los Alamos. The command pyramid, he says, seems to be mothmen, reptiloids, and greys, with the hybrids and humans under them. Castello also says that one of the reptiloids told him that the surface of the Earth was their original home before they were removed in a war – the war of the gods – in far ancient times. They escaped underground, to other stars and planets, and even into the fourth and fifth dimensions, Castello says he was told. This fits with the accounts of Credo Mutwa and many abductees who have told of how the reptilians evolved on this planet and were overpowered by other extraterrestrial groups, especially the Nordics.

A woman known as "D" claims to have seen the underground facilities at China Lake Naval Weapons Centre in the California Desert, one of the major mind control centres of North America.[18] It straddles a vast area and very little can be seen above ground. I have driven around the outside of the base twice now. On one side the public road runs alongside the perimeter fence for a while. The entrance to China Lake is in the little town of Ridgecrest and this is where "D" once lived. Ridgecrest is home to many mind-controlled slaves programmed at China Lake and it's not far from where the mass murderer Charles Manson and his "Family" used to live. "D", a victim of trauma-based mind control, said that the military chose her because of her bloodline. They had told her that before the development of language, humans communicated by telepathy thanks to a hormone secreted in the brain. This hormone, she was told, was no longer operating in most people, only in particular bloodlines, including hers, and they wanted to use these abilities. The period, thousands of years ago, when this telepathic human brain function was genetically suppressed was almost certainly symbolised by the story common to most ancient cultures of the gods giving people different languages to divide them and stop them communicating.

"D" said she was taken underground at China Lake and saw the genetics laboratory and holding centre for captured humans and genetically engineered mutants. (The true symbolism of the Mutant Ninja Turtles who lived underground in "sewer" tunnels and came out to "fight evil"?) Reptilian symbolism, most of it painting reptilians in a very positive light, has been bombarding the minds of children in recent years. "D" described seeing horrendous creatures of all types, shapes, and sizes at China Lake. She said she was shown these horrors to let her see what would happen to her if she did not co-operate and she claimed her own son had been murdered. Under China Lake, she said, a reptilian sexually assaulted her and she saw another cut open the chest of a grey. "D" confirmed from her experience that the greys are terrified of the reptilian leadership and do whatever they tell them. On another occasion, she said, she was taken to the reptilian base under the appropriately named Death Valley, a relatively short drive from China Lake. There she said she saw a reptilian leader, much taller than the others, who was wearing an Egyptian headdress with a cobra snake motif.

The respected UFO researcher, Timothy Good, quotes two "high-placed sources" in his book, *Unearthly Disclosure*, who confirm the existence of underground extraterrestrial bases. One was from the US Air Force and the other from the US Navy. The reliability of these sources was supported by Admiral of the Fleet, Lord Hill-Norton, the former chief of the UK Defence Staff and former chairman of the NATO Military Committee. Good says that the sources provided evidence that the American military was working with unidentified "aliens" who have established bases on the planet.[19] Many of these bases were underwater, Good was told, a fact that would fit with the ancient legends of the "gods" emerging from the water. The sources said that bases exist in Australia, the Pacific Ocean, the former Soviet Union, the United States, and the Caribbean. The latter is believed to be in Puerto Rico. The US air force contact told Good: "They [the "aliens"] are here on a permanent basis. They are after this planet." He also said they were "messing with plate tectonics", the movement of land that causes earthquakes, and that the warming of the world's oceans was connected to extraterrestrial activity.[20] Well it isn't global warming, that's for sure. Interestingly, Good's sources suggested that the "aliens" were involved in "hybridisation" experiments to allow their race to take over the planet. This, however, began a long, long, time ago.

T'was always so

The stories of reptilians and other non-human races living within the Earth in what we would today call "bases", cities, or tunnel networks, can be found widely described in ancient accounts also. The Nagas, or serpent people, in India and throughout Asia and the Far East, were said to live in two main underground centres called Patala and Bhogavati. From there, according to Hindu legend, they battle for power with the Nordic underground kingdoms of Agharta and Shambala. Hindus believe that Patala can be entered at the Well of Sheshna in Benares, while Bhogavati is believed to be in the Himalayas. Similar stories of underground caverns and tunnel systems can be found in Tibet and China. In the Gilgamesh stories of the Sumerian tablets, we are told of vast underground cities. Gilgamesh was a "demi-god" and "semi-divine" (reptilian hybrid) who sought the immortality of the "gods". The stories speak of KI-GAL or "the Great Below", which was ruled by the goddess Ereshkigal and the god Mergal. In the KI-GAL were violent guardians called "scorpion men", reanimated human bodies, spirits and the "undead", and robotic beings known as Galatur or Gala, which were used to abduct humans from the surface. There were "eagle-headed" reptilians, which were often said to have wings. The accounts describe a race called the Pazazu, a dog-faced "human" with reptilian scales and tail. All this sounds remarkably like the scenes described at Dulce today. Chinese legend claims that an underground world entered from the Eastern Mountain of Taishan was guarded by vicious demons called Men Shen with animal-like faces or masks. This was the Chinese "Hell" and it is said that the Lords of Hell interacted with the Dragon Kings on the surface. The Japanese "Hell" or underground network was similar, and among the non-human entities were the Kappa, semi-aquatic reptilian humanoids and other shape-shifters who lived in mountains, under the ground, or under the sea. In Viking-Norse legend they have the giant serpent, Nidhoggr or Jormungand, that lived underground and this was similar to the giant serpent Apophis in Egyptian myth. The Scandinavians and Germans had their Huldre or "Hidden Folk" who were also known as the elves. One of the codes for the bloodline is "elven" and the beings of folklore like trolls, etins, fairies, elves, troglodytes, Nefilim, Brownies or Braunies, and the "little people" of Ireland are all different names for the subterranean entities described in the modern accounts of "ET bases".[21]

All the same stories are associated with them – interbreeding with humans, unable to go out in the sunlight, and all the rest. They even mention the "missing time" experience of people abducted by the "fairies" and include many stories of these underground folk killing and mutilating cattle and taking the blood. Michael Mott has produced an excellent collection of these stories on underground dwellers in folklore and myth. His book is called *Caverns, Cauldrons, And Concealed Creatures*, and is available through my website. He writes that England, Scotland, Wales, and Ireland all have endless traditions of underground peoples with many similarities and common origins between them. It seems to me that Scotland, Ireland, and the British Isles in general are such a major centre for the Illuminati bloodlines because of the number of entrances to the underground world there are in that region. It is the same with other parts of the world like France, Germany, and the Caucasus Mountains. What is really under the Windsors' Balmoral Castle or the Queen Mother's Glamis Castle in Scotland, that key country for Illuminati bloodlines? Interestingly, there is a legendary "secret room" at Glamis. According to a guest, the writer, Sir Walter Scott, and others, it is the family's law or custom that the secret is known to only three people at one time. They take a "terrible oath" not to reveal the secret. Another guest, Lord Halifax, said that in 1875 a workman at the castle came across a door leading to a long passageway. The man investigated, but then he saw something that made him run back in terror. When the 13th Earl of Strathmore was told what the workman had seen he persuaded him to accept money to emigrate and give his word never to reveal what he saw. Lord Halifax said that after the incident the Earl was a changed man, who became silent and moody, with an "anxious, scared face".

The Norse/Germanic fairies, goblins, trows, knockers, brownies, leprechauns, sidhe (shee), tylwyth teg (terlooeth teig) and so on were either malevolent or indifferent to humanity, Michael Mott says. They lived, virtually without exception, under the ground. Mounds, hills, ruins, ancient raths or hill-forts, mountains, cliffs, and ancient cities were said to be the "rooftops" of their palaces. Beings that mirror modern reports of the Sasquatch (Big Foot) and the Yeti (Abominable Snowman) can also be found in ancient stories of underground creatures that come to the surface. Like the Nagas, the serpent people of Asia, European folklore often claimed that these "fairy" people entered their underground homes through lakes. Michael Mott continues:

> "To remove all doubt as to their relationship with Norse hidden-folk and Indian Nagas alike, they shunned the sunlight, and often seemed interested in crossbreeding their own bloodlines with those of human beings, or even in crossbreeding their 'livestock' or fairy cattle, horses, hounds and so forth with the surface species which were most compatible. The goblin-dwarf, Rumplestiltskin, in his lust to have the human baby and its genetic bounty, is just one example of this in folklore. The elves took a regular interest in human affairs-weddings, births, and deaths, (bloodlines), the success of crops and livestock, and so forth – but only for their own selfish interests. They seemed to be overly-concerned with genetic and biological diversity, and they pilfered livestock, crops, and human genes via theft or cross-species liaison whenever they saw fit to do so. The elves are generally depicted as extremely fair-haired and fair-skinned." [22]

What Mott is describing there from European folklore could have come straight from the mouth of a modern abductee or researcher of the underground bases. The so-called greys of modern UFO legend appear to be the same as the beings known as the Galatur and Ushabtiu who abducted humans from underground in Sumerian and Egyptian myths, and the folklore of the Shetland Islands off the north of Scotland referred to the "little men" who abducted humans as "grey neighbours" and the greys. In the Americas you find the same legends and accounts of the underground people. They include humans, reptilians, reptilian humanoids, and various "monsters" and "demons". Their descriptions match those of other ancient cultures all over the world. Many Native American tribes, like the Hopi, claim to have lived within these underground cavern "cities" before coming to settle on the surface. In the Mayan epic, the Popol Vuh, two "semi-divine" (hybrid) brothers, Hunapuh and Xbalanque, enter the horrific underground world called Xibalba to battle a crocodile-headed monster and, as a result of their victory, the brothers brought an end to human sacrifice – the calling card of the reptilians to this day. These underground worlds are the origin of the belief in Hell being under the Earth. The poet, Dante (1265-1321), was an initiate of the Knights Templar. In his famous work, the Inferno, he is taken on a tour of the underworld. He says it consisted of ten levels where "sinners" are imprisoned and punished by horned demons and reptilian, bird-like giants called the harpies. The conditions and environment he describes in this "Hell" can be found in descriptions of these underground worlds and cavern communities everywhere. The accounts even include the idea of being imprisoned down there waiting for the day of judgement.

In Ireland and the Isle of Man, two major locations for Illuminati bloodlines and activity, much of their culture is based on fairy legends and "the little people" who live under the ground. Irish legends tell of the sexual relationships between the ancient Milesians and the Tuatha de Danaan, the Irish "underground gods" who fled into the Earth and settled there. St Patrick, who "removed the snakes from Ireland", is said to have seen one of these underground people, a "fairy woman", coming out of the cave of Cruachan. When St Patrick asks a Milesian about her, he replies: "She is of the Tuatha de Danaan who are unfading…and I am of the sons of Mil [human Irish], who are perishable and fade away." The usual tale of mortality and immortality. As Michael Mott reports, Daniel Bradley and other geneticists at the Trinity College in Dublin have discovered that the oldest "pure" racial bloodline in Europe continues to exist in the far west of Ireland. This, as I highlight in *The Biggest Secret*, is also the last bastion of an ancient Irish language called Gaelic, which is astonishingly similar to languages of North Africa, such as Libyan. Bradley told the Reuters news agency in March 2000 that the Irish came from a race that was different to other Europeans. He said: "When you look at this old genetic geography of Ireland what you find is that in the west (of Ireland) we are almost exclusively of one type of Y chromosome." They found that 98% of men with Gaelic names in western Ireland had this particular chromosome. If anyone is still in doubt that the legends of the "fairy" people and the "extraterrestrial" accounts of today are describing the same entities, Michael Mott summarises here the common attributes of the underground peoples of global folklore:

"They are mostly reptilian or reptilian humanoids or "fair" and Nordic; they are telepathic with superior mental powers; they can shape-shift and create illusions; they want to interbreed with humans and need human blood, flesh, and reproductive materials; they have advanced technology; they have the secret of immortality; they can fly, either by themselves or with their technology; they mostly have a malevolent agenda for humans; they cannot survive for long in direct sunlight; they have been banished from the surface world or are in hiding from surface people and/or the Sun; they want to keep their treasures, knowledge, and true identity a secret; they covertly manipulate events on the surface world; they have surface humans working for them through the priesthoods, cults, and secret societies; they have a putrid smell like "sulphur and brimstone".

The accounts are incredibly consistent over thousands of years. Mott writes:

"The reptilian aspect of some underworlders permeates folklore. One universal theme that recurs in the folktales of many, many cultures is that of the snake-husband or snake-wife, who can transform into a "human" or humanoid form and is invariably (of course) of royal blood among his or her own kind (talk about the ultimate pick-up line!). Often the snake or serpent-man exacts a promise of marriage, or the hand of an unborn human child in betrothal, consistent with the theme of the subterranean's interest in maintaining their own genetic diversity.

"A variant of this should be familiar to most readers of fairy tales, in the form of 'The Frog Prince'. The frog-prince is a Handsome Prince, but like the Japanese seducing dragon, he has a reptilian or amphibian form. The underworld link is complete, for frequently the frog lives in a deep well, from which he is discovered or rescued by the female protagonist. A possible connection is evident in the Scandinavian belief that some dwarves would 'turn into toads", if caught by the Sun, much like Mimoto's lover turned from a man into a 'dragon' when the same thing happened. Slovenia has its legends of fairies and 'little people', but Slovenian fairy tales are also permeated by the presence of the 'Snake Queen', a great, white, cave-dwelling creature who is part woman and part serpent. The serpentine-yet-human Nagas are still believed by devout Hindus and some Buddhists to dwell beneath India, Nepal, and Tibet." [23]

Denying the obvious

When you read and hear the horrendous accounts of the victims and witnesses of the grotesque reptilian agenda, ancient and modern, it is hard to comprehend how so many "researchers" and New Agers continue to believe that this "extraterrestrial" presence is good for humanity and a sign of positive change. Now, of course, not all "extraterrestrials" or interdimensionals are malevolent, but does that mean that we have to ignore the fact that some of them are? I have had "researchers" attack me who appear far more concerned with the effect of my work on the image of reptilians than they are with the horrors being perpetrated on abductees, mind-control victims, and the people of the world in general. Dr David Jacobs in his book, *The Threat*, picks up this point. He calls such people "the Positives":

"Often the New Age Positives band together into almost cult-like groups to defend themselves from their detractors – researchers and abductees who have come to different conclusions about the abduction phenomenon. The Positives reinforce one another's feelings and insulate themselves from the terror of their lives; they become angry when "less enlightened" abduction researchers question their interpretation." [24]

Certain researchers in England, Las Vegas, and the United States in general come immediately to mind. Dr Jacobs also names some of the "stars" of extraterrestrial research like John Hunter Gray, Dr Leo Sprinkle, Dr Richard Boylan, Joseph Nyman, and Harvard professor, Dr John Mack, among those who want to put a positive twist on the abductee reports:

"Both Boylan and Mack de-emphasize the effects of the standard abduction procedures. Boylan believes that gynaecological and urological procedures take place only with a very small number of abductees and he rarely focuses on them. And although Mack has found nearly the full range of alien physical, mental, and reproductive procedures, he only mentions them in passing while emphasizing what he finds to be spiritually uplifting elements. The benevolent 'spin' that the Positives (both abductees and researchers) put on the abduction phenomenon is puzzling, given the way most people describe their abductions: being unwillingly taken; being subjected to painful physical procedures (sometimes leaving permanent scars); enduring humiliating and abusive sexual episodes, including unwanted sexual intercourse; living with the fear and anxiety of wondering when they will be abducted again." [25]

James Bartley, the abductee and researcher of the reptilian connection, is rather more blunt in his appraisal of what he calls "the Muppets" – those who either refuse to see the malevolent nature of the reptilian agenda or actively seek to portray it in a positive light. He says the reason why so many abductees are hopelessly confused about this whole mess is because trigger mechanisms have been programmed into them to keep them from getting at the truth of their experiences. He says he has witnessed countless times how an abductee will immediately fall asleep the moment the lecturer begins talking about "fear-based" issues. But when he or she attends a lecture by a channeller or some other "light worker" saying positive things about the "aliens", the abductee is bright and attentive, and awake during the whole lecture. "Falling asleep is just one trigger mechanism," he says. Another is annoyance or anger at the "fear-based" lecturer or abductee. Likewise an overwhelming compulsion to get up and walk out, to get up and eat, to get up and smoke a cigarette, getting nauseous, a headache etc., etc. In an article challenging the methods of researcher and lecturer, Dr Richard Boylan, Bartley goes on:

"Boylan...[promotes]...the ludicrous notion that a woman abductee was merely suffering from spiritual retardation and was mentally incapable of understanding the 'benevolent' nature of the horrific and unwanted experimentation that was being conducted on her...We have worked with countless women who have suffered painful and bloody haemorrhages, sometimes lasting for days, after the 'benevolent ET' doctors had made an unwanted house call. What, the discerning human must ask, does profuse and painful bleeding have to do with 'spiritual' evolution? The New Age La-Dee-Dahs claim that there is no such thing as Evil or Demons, which makes [them] the butt of endless jokes by Witches, Warlocks and Satanists throughout the world because the latter derive their power from demonic entities.

"By constantly blaming 'the military' and the 'globalist industrialists', the reptilian propagandists condition the abductees into believing that **all** human institutions are bad and that the only hope one has to reach the... 'next level of consciousness, evolution, vibratory frequency' et al, is to look to the skies towards the same dark gods who are responsible for their current state of spiritual enslavement. Never mind that for the most part these 'Globalists and Militarists' are part of the same old fraternal orders, which worship the patriarchal serpent gods and in many cases are hosts for reptilian entities themselves. These hosts and their fellow travellers operate as a Fifth Column here on Earth to set the stage for the return of the Dark Reptilian Gods.

"The so-called UFO Research Community is awash with these 'Muppets'. Even I have to laugh at the irony of it: literal hosts for reptilian entities facilitating abductee support groups, lecturing at so-called 'UFO Conferences' and speaking on the Art Bell Show [the major "mysteries" radio show in the US]. This is so because of the long term genetic and soul matrix manipulation of the human race." [26]

How right he is and how fast the human race needs to wake up and grow up. The stories I have featured in this chapter are just a small selection of the reports and personal accounts describing reptilian experiences. If you want to see more, go to the Reptilian Archive on my website, read *The Biggest Secret*, or watch the Bridge of Love videos with Arizona Wilder, *Revelations Of A Mother Goddess*, and Credo Mutwa, *The Reptilian Agenda*, parts one and two. When you put these modern reports together with their mirrors in the ancient world, it constitutes a library of information that only the most imprisoned of minds could dismiss without further investigation. But, given the level of human conditioning, many still will. Especially the media.

SOURCES

1   David M. Jacobs, *The Threat: The Secret Agenda* (Simon and Schuster, New York, 1988), pp 131 and 132

2   James L. Walden, *The Ultimate Alien Agenda* (Llewellyn Publications, St Paul, Minnesota, 1998), p 11

3   Ibid, pp 141 to 153

4   Ibid, p 35

5   Ibid, pp 70 and 71

6   Ibid, p 93

7   Ibid, p 21

8   *http://www.reptilianagenda.com/exp/e100799d.html* There are other accounts of reptilian experiences here also

9   *http://www.reptilianagenda.com/exp/e090800a.html*

10   *http://www.reptilianagenda.com/exp/e020600b.html*

11   Alex Christopher speaking on KSEO Radio, USA, on April 26th 1996, transcript by the Leading Edge Research Group

12   *http://www.reptilianagenda.com/exp/e112299a.html*

13   *http://www.reptilianagenda.com/exp/e062600a.html*
     http://users2.50megs.com/reptile/menuexper.ht

14   *http://www.reptilianagenda.com/research/r100799e.html*

15   *http://www.reptilianagenda.com/exp/e100799b.html*

16   Quoted by the Leading Edge Research Group. See also:
     http://www.reptilianagenda.com/research/r100699d.html

17   See *http://www.angelfire.com/ut/branton* and *http://www.reptilianagenda.com/*

18   *http://www.reptilianagenda.com/exp/e101999b.html* and
     http://www.reptilianagenda.com/research/r100799i.html

19   "Aliens Under The Sea", London *Daily Mail*, November 11th 2000, pp 48 to 51

20   Ibid

21   *Caverns, Cauldrons, And Concealed Creatures*

22   Ibid

23   Ibid

24   *The Threat*, pp 217 and 218

25   Ibid, p 215

26   *http://www.reptilianagenda.com/research/r110699c.html*

CHAPTER 14

Calling the demons

Nothing would be what it is,
Because everything would be what it isn't.
And contrary-wise – what it is, it wouldn't be.
And what it wouldn't be, it would.
You see?

Lewis Carroll, Alice in Wonderland

So what's going on here? Unless people wish to enclose their minds in concrete, clearly something very strange is occurring on Planet Earth and has been doing so for many thousands of years.

There are so many questions and the more you know the more there is to know. But at this point in the journey it can be firmly stated that there is a considerable reptilian connection to ancient and modern control and manipulation of the human race. That is not to say *all* reptilians in all existence, just some of them. But then we need to ask about the *consciousness* that incarnates into the reptilian stream because in the end the decisions of action and behaviour are taken by consciousness. At that level the reptilian genetics, or insectoid, Nordic, and grey genetics, are only an outer shell that consciousness inhabits. So while we talk about the world being manipulated by reptilians, that is only one level of this. There is a consciousness that inhabits some reptilian forms because that genetics most suits the state of being of this consciousness. In other words, it operates through primal survival instincts rather than feelings and emotion. This state is reflected in reptilian genetics on the animalistic level and so the consciousness and the genetics are compatible. Then, through these reptilian bodies, this consciousness manipulates and possesses humanity. We are back to the Russian doll system again, one inside the other as we move down the frequencies. The manipulation of this world goes beyond the fourth density range and at least into the fifth. So who, or what, controls the reptilians?

Consciousness makes the decision, based on its state of being, of what form and bloodline to inhabit on the endless journey of evolution through experience. As with everything, our current state of being naturally attracts, or is attracted to, the physical form and experiences that are compatible with where we are coming from, mentally, emotionally, and spiritually. There is a vibrational synchronisation –

magnetism you might call it – between the frequency of the consciousness and the frequency represented by the DNA of the body. The base reptilian nature, as expressed through the reptilian genetics, includes the desire for top-down control, emotionless "cold-blooded" attitudes, an obsession with ritualistic behaviour, and so on. This reptilian DNA will naturally attract consciousness of like reality and desire. This consciousness is not "reptilian" in or of itself, it just takes a reptilian outer form. Consciousness is pure energy, an aspect of the infinite whole, the infinite "I". But it takes a reptilian genetic expression in the lower densities if this DNA is a match for its own vibrational state of being. As it evolves beyond those limitations of vision and perception, it begins to incarnate into other forms, or has no need for the lower densities at all. Some members of these Illuminati bloodlines, who are challenging the agenda from within, have confirmed these themes to me. One member of the "royal" Plantagenet bloodline (connected to the de Veres and the Houses of Anjou and Lorraine), told me:

> "We all begin as the smallest fragment of energy – barely a spark – and even before consciousness, we seek to unite with other sparks, like a moth seeking the light. At the point we realize we are separate, we attain consciousness, and continue to seek to unite with other consciousness. By this time, we are what I call light balls – our truest conscious nature. Just as in Darwin's evolution, we develop into more than just a light ball. But this does not happen over millions of years. Rather it happens in a single moment of clarity, a flash of consciousness. The vehicle for this transformative growth is reincarnation.

> "So those that people call the reptiles got to the reptile level of development and stopped. Some go on [and evolve beyond that]. Those who continue to take the reptile form do so because of the limitations of what they believe their options are – they're creating their own reality. Also, for those at that level, it isn't that they don't know. It is indeed their sheer pleasure in self-gratification and self-focused existence. For this reason, I do not like the term reptile because it implies they are something other than the rest of us (light balls), and that is, indeed, THEIR reality. So I prefer a term which reflects their state of consciousness, dino-brain." [1]

These points are soooo important in understanding the cosmic game and where the reptilian form fits in. The particular reptilian genetic stream I am highlighting in this book represents a lower level of development in the evolution of consciousness. It is the level at which fear dominates and there is no greater expression of fear than the need to control others and dictate their behaviour in relation to you. This reptilian stream also represents the need for consciousness to gratify the physical senses at the suppression of all else, including spiritual development and enlightenment. Consciousness in that state will be attracted to the reptilian genetics represented by the Illuminati bloodlines. If such consciousness gets stuck in this evolutionary groove and does not break this cycle of thought and behaviour, it will be doomed to incarnating into the same bloodstreams over and over because like attracts like. This is what has been happening. For this reason high consciousness has also been incarnating into these bloodlines through these thousands of years in an effort to rewire the DNA and resonate it to a higher vibrational state. Our attitudes and spiritual development change the DNA we are occupying with every thought and feeling, positive or negative. This could be the real meaning of the Biblical claim about the "sins" of the fathers being visited upon the children. Perhaps Princess Diana, who incarnated into a reptilian-hybrid bloodline (although more Nordic dominated in her case), was one of these souls who came to break these prison frequencies in the Illuminati DNA. In the same way, there are reptilian bloodlines that have moved beyond the base state of the Illuminati genetic codes and this reptilian DNA has evolved to a higher level of knowledge, understanding, and, therefore, frequency. Crucially, it has developed an emotional "warm blooded" nature, and the ability to feel and express love. Thus consciousness that mirrors this DNA frequency band is attracted to these bloodlines. These are the "good guy" Serpent People that are also described in the ancient texts, and there are many of them around today trying to help humanity – and the Illuminati reptilians – out of their mental, emotional, and spiritual prisons. Please keep this in mind when I talk of the reptilian connection to the Illuminati and the Satanists.

Food for the demons

One of the great difficulties that people have in grasping the enormity of what is happening is that they find it so hard to lift their imagination beyond the technology and range of possibility they see around them. It is the "that-is-not-possible-because-I-haven't-seen-it mentality. Shape-shifting is one example, and I understand this from the conditioned version of reality. Of course it sounds fantastic, but so many people have experienced this phenomenon all over the world over thousands of years to the present day that to dismiss it would be ludicrous. The idea of interdimensional travel is just some science fiction babble to most people and yet it is in understanding the interdimensional nature of Creation that so many of the answers lie. I do not dismiss for a moment the claims of physical reptilians and greys living within the planet in the underground bases and tunnel networks. That is clearly true from the explosion of ancient and modern accounts, and at the point of interface with surface humanity that is a vital aspect of this story. However, it is the interdimensional rather than the purely extraterrestrial and inner-terrestrial, which holds the key to unlocking the mysteries. The reptilian hybrid bloodlines have been created, in my view, for occupation by fourth, maybe also fifth, dimensional reptilian and other entities and it is they who are controlling the Illuminati. Indeed at the peak of the pyramid, they *are* the Illuminati. Satanic and secret society rituals are designed to create the means through which these mostly lower fourth-dimensional entities can possess the body of the initiate and also manifest directly in "physical" form. During the sacrifices the physical reptilians and hybrids consume the organs of the physical body, especially the heart, and drink the blood of the victim. At the same time, the lower fourth-dimensional "demons" or psychic vampires absorb the deeply negative energy generated by such horrors. The vibrational frequency of negative emotion, like fear and terror, resonates to the lower fourth-dimensional range or density and so those emotions generate energy for the fourth-dimensional reptilians and demonic entities. Energy = creative power, positive or negative. They are feeding off our emotions and they manipulate events in the world and our lives to trigger the desired emotional responses. Ancient Chinese philosophers claimed that humans were "Moon food" because their energy was being drained and absorbed by an extraterrestrial force that needed the energy to replenish itself. Researcher Alan Walton puts it like this:

"…the 'serpent race' will merely continue to do what it has always done with the 'human cattle' on this planet, which is to continue to feed on us like emotional, psychic and bioplasmic vampires and work to destroy our spiritual life and thus individuality until we are assimilated into their hive via psionic implants just as they have done with many other humans beyond this world, many within the underground military-industrial networks, and with many of the 'abductees' of recent years. And not only psychic assimilation, but also supernatural possession (by rep-oltergiest parasites) and also genetic assimilation as well…

"What if these 'wer-dracs', 'repti-poltergiests', 'demon-aliens', or whatever one might wish to call these serpentine sorcerers, had became adept over time at superficial molecular shape shifting as the indwelling 'poltergiest' or 'astral parasite' literally absorbed, consumed, devoured, or assimilated the reptilian 'host' from the inside out? What if in addition to this they were able to project some type of hypnotic or possibly laser-type holographic field around themselves so as to be able to intermingle with humans, undetected for what they really were?" [2]

This is precisely what they have done. There are so many reptilian "hosts" (possessed people) in positions of political, financial, media, and military power. They may look human, but behind their outward appearance they are not. The reason the Illuminati are so obsessed with bloodline is that the hybrid genetics were created to make these bodies more easily possessed by the lower fourth-dimensional entities because of the vibrational compatibility. It means that if you can put these bloodlines into positions of power, you are, in truth, putting these entities into power. This way they can control this physical world from their dimension while the human population think humans are governing them. The United States of America is not governed by Bill Clinton, George W. Bush, or any "president". Americans are governed by the reptilian entity that possesses the bodies we call Bill Clinton or George W. Bush. The John Carpenter movie, They Live, says it all, really. This is why two of Cathy O'Brien's mind controllers, Bill and Bob Bennett, told her they were "alien to this dimension – two beings from another plane". Remember that when Cathy saw people transform from physical humans to "lizard-like aliens", Bill Bennett said:

"Welcome to the second level of the underground. This is a mere mirror reflection of the first, an alien dimension. We are from a trans-dimensional plane that spans and encompasses all dimensions…I have taken you through my dimension as a means of establishing stronger holds on your mind than the Earth plane permits."[3]

Satanism is the serpent cult

The Illuminati, Satanism, and the serpent cult of the ancient texts are the same organisation. The most important hierarchy within the Illuminati is not that of politics, banking, or whatever. Your position is decided by the "purity" of your bloodline and the level at which you operate within the global network we call Satanism. In other words, the power of the "demons" that have taken possession of you during Satanic ritual. In this way, the other-dimensional hierarchy is reflected in the "human" hierarchy of the Illuminati. These demons fight among each other for power all the time and this is experienced within the Illuminati through their internal squabbles. The wars between these reptilian bloodlines over the years have been the wars between demonic entities for the right to be top dog, or demon, on Earth. This is also one origin of the ancient accounts of the great rivalry among the "gods". In ten years of full-time research I have met many former Satanists and the victims of Satanism and I will summarise the themes that have been repeated to me over and over around the world. The Satanic network is vast and if you have a fair circle of friends and acquaintances, you will know people who are Satanists. That's how widespread it is. Satanists are also very organised and, of course, extremely ruthless. They have code names known only to other members and they have among their number all the people they need to operate in secret and cover up anything that may go wrong. They are, therefore, very strong in the medical professions, police, the judiciary, coroners offices, politics, government administration, and so on. There is tremendous infighting within Satanism, as they battle for supremacy by seeking more and more powerful demonic entities. They hate each other as much as they hate humanity. In fact they just hate, period. Anyone weak is destroyed. Weakness is considered the ultimate "sin" in Satanism and so is defying the desires of the demons. The whole Satanic network is ruled by fear. Cult members are disciplined by having to watch their children tortured, beaten to death, or brutally raped. Others are sacrificed. Satanists are deluded into thinking that they control the demons when actually the demons are just using them as pawns. Incredible atrocities are committed by Satanists so controlled by the demons within them that they lose all emotions of love and compassion. Phillip Eugene de Rothschild, who claims he is an offspring of a French Rothschilds, says he is a direct descendant of a very old culture, "as old as Mankind itself". This culture, he says, worships "Satan as God" and is steeped in deep violence. He explains how he was exposed to every abuse, trauma, and "demonisation" imaginable. "This culture is unbelievably and ingeniously evil", he says. The trauma, both as a victim and perpetrator, was to sharpen his "dissociative potential" or Multiple Personality Disorder. He said that this dissociation was enforced by "victim and perpetrator, high-tech mind control programming in the US, often in government facilities and clinics, and at the Tavistock Institute in the UK". The Tavistock operation, as my previous books highlight, is a centre of the Illuminati's mind control network.

Human sacrifice is not confined to some barbaric period of ancient history. It is happening all around us and I don't care where you may live. Many sacrifices are babies produced by women called "breeders", who give birth in secret. Some are willing, but many are held captive. The babies are birthed by doctors and nurses who are part of the network. These children never appear on documentation and so they never officially exist and cannot officially go missing. Other sacrifices are people the Satanists have kidnapped, a cult member being punished, and even volunteers from the cult. It is common for Satanists, especially the most powerful ones, to die in rituals designed to transfer their power and demons to another person. When they die, their consciousness becomes the property of the demons, as ritually agreed when they become Satanists. The deal involves demonic power for the Satanists on Earth in return for their "soul" when they leave their body. This is where we get the term "selling your soul to the Devil". On other occasions the "soul" of the sacrifice will be transferred to a participant of the ritual. At the point of death, as many former Satanists have told me, the victim is fixed in an hypnotic stare – just like a snake – by the person who is going to absorb their life force and energy. This makes a vibrational, magnetic link, which draws the consciousness of the victim into the Satanist as it is released by death from the body. These grotesque rituals are taking place all the time and there are hundreds of thousands, at least, worldwide on the main ritual days of the year. The dead bodies, or what is left of them, are disposed of via cult members who work in crematoria or are buried in secret mass graves. I have also heard of "devil dogs" that are trained to eat the remains. Horrible isn't it, but if we don't face reality it is going to continue and expand. These guys are running our world for goodness sake.

Blood, the physical expression of the life force, is a key aspect of the rituals. Anyone who drinks blood and eats flesh absorbs the energy of that person and, in the case of drinking the blood of someone still alive, it makes a vibrational connection between the two people, which allows for psychic manipulation. Drinking human blood appears to be vital to reptilian entities to hold open DNA codes that maintain an outward "human" appearance. The reptilians also feed off an adrenaline that enters the bloodstream at times of extreme terror. The ritual is performed to increase this terror to its maximum at the time of death. This way the blood they drink is full of this desired adrenaline. The consuming of the heart is also at the centre of these sacrifice rituals and they have been performed in the same way for thousands of years going back to Atlantis and beyond under the control of the other-dimensional entities and serpent "gods". This ritual of cutting out and eating the human heart goes back as long as the bloodlines and can be found all over the world. The heart represents the very essence of who we are. The *Scottish Sunday Post* of January 2000 told the strange story of Alisdair Rosslyn Sinclair under the headline "Victim of Secret Holy Land Power Struggle?" He was a Scottish "tourist" who was named after Rosslyn Chapel, near Edinburgh, which was built by the Sinclair family, formerly the French St Clair family, which was involved in the formation of the Knights Templar. Alistair Rosslyn Sinclair was a direct descendent of this bloodline. He was originally from Arran, but apparently had been working as a musician in Amsterdam. He had researched his bloodline connections and had visited Rosslyn Chapel, an Illuminati "holy place", a number of times. In April 1998 he made an unexplained five-day trip to Israel and was arrested when he tried to leave the country. The authorities say he was arrested for having £3,500 worth of German currency concealed in a hidden compartment of his suitcase, but that is not illegal. They say that he later confessed to buying and selling drugs, but again why would he do that when there was no evidence? What happened next, however, has a very ominous ring. The police say Sinclair hanged himself with his shoelaces, a ludicrous claim for such a big man, and when his body arrived back in Scotland an autopsy revealed that…his *heart* was missing. The authorities say the heart was taken for closer examination, but they offer no credible reason why this was done or why the heart was "mislaid". The Israeli investigative author, Barry Chamish, claims that Alistair Sinclair was murdered as part of a much bigger conspiracy involving battles between ancient bloodlines and secret societies for control of Jerusalem. Chamish says that Alisdair Sinclair was killed because he became caught up in this clandestine war, and he points out that the removal of the heart is part of the Knights Templar tradition. The dying wish of the Scottish Templar king, Robert the Bruce, was for his heart be cut out and taken from Scotland to be buried in Jerusalem. But it is also an ancient ritual to eat the heart of your victim in such Satanic conflicts and this may well have happened in this case. The heart is so important to these sick people.

An old, old story

The Aztecs of Mexico were so obsessed with sacrificing to their serpent gods that they would kill thousands in a day. Wherever you find the worship of serpent gods, you find human sacrifice. The Mayan priesthood, the Nacoms and the Chacs, conducted ceremonies in which the victim was held down while his or her living heart was removed and offered to the gods. It was seen as the supreme offering and it still is by the Satanists today. What happened to Princess Diana's heart after she was ritually murdered on that ancient Merovingian ritual site for the Goddess Diana (Dana, Artemis) in Paris? Phillip Eugene de Rothschild also confirms that the Illuminati Satanists today are the modern version of the secret sects of Sumer, Babylon, and other ancient cultures. He says he was initiated into:

> "… the oldest, most pristine form of Satanism, the old Sumero-Akkadian-Babylonian mystery religion …Inherent in this culture is the presence and power of demonic spirits, and they became an integral part of my life and even my being. In a culture addicted to power, demonic spirits offered the ultimate power trip. If, in American culture, people are addicted to comfort, status, and prestige, in Satanic culture people are addicted to demonic power.

"Satanism has pervaded western civilization ...It has been growing for thousands of years, quietly weaving its way through the very fabric of the culture and the power structures of the nations in the West. It has adherents in all walks of life, in all incomes, and all social strata. It has exerted a profound influence on the intellectual life of the West for the past several hundred years ...Satanism has influenced politics, economics, art and music, through the spiritual-psychological process called dissociation, and dissociation is as old as human culture itself." [4]

Satanic rituals are also performed to connect with and often manifest other-dimensional demonic entities. Whenever these manifestations are described to me the pentagram or five-pointed star is a constant theme. Everything is energy and all symbols affect the vibrational frequency of energy. The five-pointed star within an occult ritual creates an interdimensional gateway or portal, I am told, which allows other dimensional entities to manifest. It is usually surrounded by a circle, which, in theory, creates a magnetic field or wall that prevents the demon from leaving that spot. Satanists are obsessed with demonic entities, but they are also terrified of them. The pentagram is a Satanic version of beam-me-up-Scotty, and is, therefore, the most important Satanic symbol because it allows their "masters of the universe" to appear to them. Now look at the pentagrams all around you, as on the US and other flags, and the logo of the European Union. Texaco is an Illuminati company and its logo is a pentagram within a circle with the T-square of Freemasonry in the middle. And the centre of a pentagram is a pentagon. This is why the headquarters of the Illuminati's US military is in a building called, and shaped like, a pentagon. When you begin to understand their codes and symbols, you can read them so clearly. For example, the Satanic sign for the "Devil", or their controlling force, is a particular hand signal. The two middle fingers are held down, usually by the thumb, and the two outer fingers point straight up like horns. I have seen many people in power make this sign after a speech or in acknowledgement. Go to the *picture section* and you will see three examples involving Bill Clinton during his first inauguration address in 1993 and George W. Bush during his year 2000 presidential election campaign. (See *The Biggest Secret* chapter, The Secret Language, and the Symbolism Archive on my website for more examples of Satanic symbolism all around us.) Satanists, like their ancient predecessors in the Mystery schools, use combinations of colour and sound to resonate the energy in the ritual to connect with the demonic dimensions. The sound involves humming, mantras, incantations, and specific words and phrases. The Illuminati is obsessed with the sound of words rather than their spelling for the same reason. Belial/Balliol is an example. The spelling doesn't matter, it is the sound, the vibration.

Former Satanists have described to me how demonic entities manifest in the rituals amid fire, smoke, and a blinding light. This explosion of electromagnetic energy, X-rays, gamma rays, and ultraviolet rays associated with interdimensional manifestation could be another reason why it was said to be dangerous or fatal to look directly at a "god". The effects of such fields are often found among "UFO" witnesses and abductees, who develop conditions like inflammation of the eyes.

Indeed the "foul smell" of "burning sulphur" associated with the appearance of reptilian and other "extraterrestrials" to abductees, is reported in exactly the same way by those who have seen these demonic manifestations at Satanic rituals. There is a connection here for sure and many, at least many, of the "extraterrestrials" are in fact "inter-dimensionals" moving into our frequency range and then leaving again. The descriptions of these "demons" often have a very familiar ring also – very tall, fiery red eyes, and reptilian in appearance with scales, fangs, and claws. Beings like that are commonly described, but demonic entities manifest in many forms. Some of the reptilians and blond-haired, blue-eyed "Nordics" could be the same entities in their other-dimensional forms. John A. Keel wrote in *Our Haunted Planet* about the knowledge of this phenomenon held by the ancients:

"Early investigators and thinkers soon realised they were dealing with magical beings who could imitate man and his works. Instead of being solid, physically stable, assemblages of cells and matter, these entities were apparently temporary manipulations of energy. So the word 'transmogrification' was used to describe them. These transmogrifications, according to the lore, could assume any form…from a wolf to a cat to a house, ship, or iridescent god of awesome proportions. They could appear clothed in rags or in gold crowns and expensive velvet robes. Worst of all, they had a penchant for playing all kinds of games with us, manipulating our fears and beliefs and even conning us into going to war against each other." [5]

A lot of New Age channellers and psychics, who think they are connecting with the "light" or "Ashtar Command" or something, are in fact connecting with these fourth-dimensional "demon" entities, which play them like a violin. The reports of demons appearing in a whoosh of fire, smoke, and light remind me of the stories of the genie in the bottle. The most famous, of course, is Aladdin and his lamp. The character of Aladdin, in fact, originated from the head of the goddess-worshipping terrorist group in Asia known as the Assassins, which interacted with the Knights Templar. He was also called the "Old Man of the Mountain".[6] Once again the Aladdin story with its genie appearing in a whoosh of smoke is awash with symbolism. Thanks to the rituals of the Illuminati Satanists, the interdimensional doorways are opened to allow the "genie", the reptilian or demon race in the lower fourth dimension, to be free to enter this one and cause utter mayhem. The most powerful entities can change frequencies at will, but most need the vibrational help provided by the rituals. This theme of demons manifesting in fire and smoke is common. Ancient and modern accounts of Satanism say the "Devil" materialises in a bonfire and steps forward to have sex with the women participants. I have heard many accounts of entities manifesting through the flames. Maybe the very vibration of fire itself creates an interdimensional gateway. A French book, published in the 1790s, called *La Secte Des Illumines*, included a description of the rituals of the Illuminati. They are a replica of Satanism and include once again the theme of fire:

"On the day of his initiation, the candidate was conducted through a long, dark passage into an immense hall draped with black …Ghostly forms moved through the hall, leaving behind them a foul odor …His clothes were removed and laid upon a funeral pyre. Then his pudena [genitals] were tied with string …Now five horrid and frightening figures, bloodstained and mumbling, approached him and threw themselves down in prayer. After an hour sounds of weeping were heard, the funeral pyre started to burn, and his clothes were consumed. From the flames of this fire a huge and almost transparent form arose, while the five prostrate figures went into terrible convulsions. Now came the voice of an invisible hierophant [priest] booming from somewhere below."[7]

John A. Keel points out that historical records say the priests claimed to have the ability to communicate with other-dimensional beings, and that the kings and emperors, including people like Julius Caesar and Napoleon, met with strange beings who materialised and dematerialised. The same goes with today's leaders who consult their other-dimensional demonic masters. Keel details the literature on secret societies that describes many materialisations of fearsome demons, which gave out orders and directed their followers to commit murder or political manipulation. Those who disobeyed would be killed by the entity or fellow members. "Thus," he wrote, "the ultraterrestrials are able to guide and control human events through evil men lusting for power."[8] Exactly. Keel goes on:

"…The startling truth, as carefully recorded by the ancient historians, is that ultraterrestrials have always been in direct contact with millions of individuals and that *they actually ruled directly over mankind for many years*. In recent centuries their influence has become more subtle, but it is always there."[9]

Only by understanding the nature of the infinite frequencies or densities of existence can we begin to see the plot. We are being controlled and manipulated on this planet from other dimensions or densities and have been for thousands of years, at least. The well known writer and researcher on "UFO" topics, Dr Jacques Vallee, asked the right questions when he said:

"Are we dealing…with a parallel universe, where there are human races living, and where we may go at our expense, never to return to the present? Are these races only semi-human, so that in order to maintain contact with us, they need crossbreeding with men and women of our planet? Is this the origin of the many tales and legends where genetics plays a great role: the symbolism of the Virgin in occultism and religion, the fairy tales involving human midwives and changelings, the sexual overtones of the flying saucer reports, the biblical stories of intermarriage between the Lord's angels and terrestrial women, whose offspring were giants? From that mysterious universe, have objects that can materialize and 'dematerialize' at will been projected? Are the UFOs 'windows' rather than 'objects'? There is nothing to support these assumptions, and yet, in view of the historical continuity of the phenomenon, alternatives are hard to find, unless we deny the reality of all the facts, as our peace of mind would indeed prefer."[10]

Well put, but I would contest the idea that there is nothing to support those assumptions. The evidence is overwhelming from where I am sitting. I have had so much confirmation from countless sources over the years of the involvement in human sacrifice ritual of some of the most famous names on the planet. They attend the rituals at the demand of their other-dimensional controllers and receive their orders to be carried out to the letter. They allow the demonic entities to possess their bodies in return for fame and fortune, which, by manipulating three-dimensional events and people from their fourth-dimensional level, these "demons" can usually provide. But such "riches" are only delivered if you serve their agenda. In the end you are just a body to them and you will be thrown to the wolves once you have served your purpose. These "contracts with Satan" are made by politicians, bankers, businessmen, and anyone who has a thirst for power so strong that they will literally hand over their destiny to demonic entities. Phillip Eugene de Rothschild told me how he attended these rituals from childhood with many people who are now world famous in politics, finance, and the media. Among them were Bill Clinton and Al Gore. He says of the bloodlines:

> "All people in the occult except for a very, very small group are fully human beings, with both X and Y chromosomes from human mothers and father. The facial changes you see come from their multiple personality disorder and the demonic spirits manifesting through them. The antichrist and the false prophet are not humans; they are true Nephilim with X chromosomes from human mothers but their Y chromosomes are from the 'angels'. ...These non-human humanoids are borne as a consequence of human idolatry with Satanic "angels", with a little help from the Illuminist medical researchers." [11]

Serpent worship

Phillip also says that all the top names he mentions, including the Rothschilds, etc., etc., worship the snake in their rituals – "old Satan himself", as he puts it. When they celebrated the old Babylonian rites, he said, they worshipped, handled, and venerated the snake and the deadlier the better. He said that all his "former brethren", including Clinton and Gore, have the worship of the snake in common. "It has always been so," he adds, "from the Babylonians, to the Egyptians, to the Mayans, the Incas, the Polynesians – the commonest thread of human idolatry is the snake and the dragon." The Satanic and secret society rituals are designed for reptilian/demonic possession to take place and suddenly, hey presto, the body of the target is now occupied by one of these fourth-dimensional entities. The movie, The Devil's Advocate, starring Al Pacino, portrays this very well as the "Devil's" consciousness field moved from body to body and took them over. People like Clinton, the Bushs, Kissinger, and the British royal family are just empty vessels occupied by these characters and that's why they act in such unspeakable ways.

Possession through sex

During sex the two energy fields merge, especially at orgasm, and this is a common way that these entities take possession of people. When a possessed person has sex with someone, it opens up the energy connection for his or her sexual partner to be possessed also. This is one reason why the Illuminati encourage a sexual free-for-all. There is nothing wrong with sex as such. In fact it is wonderful and we would not be here without it. But knowing the hidden agenda is vital to avoid some serious consequences. People have said that "extraterrestrials" that abduct them or appear in their bedrooms have forced them to have sex and I am sure that these "extraterrestrials" are at least mostly other-dimensional entities. It is also possible for fourth-dimensional "demonic" entities to possess a physical body and have sexual union with a human who may also be possessed by a similar entity. This is what happens in the Satanic rituals at the heart of Illuminati operations. The Roman Catholic and other "Christian" churches are fronts for widespread Satanic activity and child abuse and I was told by a man who has trained for the priesthood of his sexual experience of the reptilian-Satanic connection. He said he would never have believed he would be contacting me because my work appears, at first, to be so far from reality. But he had now seen that conditioned "reality" was very different to what was really going on. He said that he was subjected to a "very terrifying traumatic experience of…unbelievable nature". And yet, until his mind compartments began to break down, he had no memory of it. He said he was a seminarian studying to be a secular priest at a college in a monastery:

"On a break I went with two odd looking types (Hispanic/Oriental mix it seemed) to a town some distance away and, very briefly, I believe they were part of a Satanic group and they performed some ritual in which I was raped by a demon…[which seemed]…reptilian. (I have so much unconscious terror associated with this that I cannot recall at this time the details.) I actually suffered a wound to my anal area because this creature/demon had barbs or horns around the base of its penis. So when it raped me, it caused a wound that never healed. I was so embarrassed by it for years that I never had the nerve to have it looked at until the latter part of my military service, which determined that there was scar tissue around the wound. I later married and had an operation which removed the wound".[12]

The reptilians and other demonic entities are obsessed with sex because it allows them to possess the victim and to "vampire" their life force. Drugged and alcoholic states also open people to possession, as does fear and deep depression. These connect the person vibrationally to the demonic dimensions and so the Illuminati and their reptilian masters want people to take drugs and drink too much booze. Having sex with a demonically possessed person after consuming drugs or too much alcohol is like opening the front door to these guys and inviting them in. A lot of illness and death is caused by these demonic attacks and when we talk of battling with our dark side, it is often a battle with demonic possession or influence of some kind affecting behaviour. To survive if you are seeking to expose these horrors you need a very strong spirit and protection from spiritual forces that wish to set humanity free. To access that protection, you just need to ask. Forces of love do not impose themselves on people because that would be an invasion of free will. They have to be asked.

The possessed paedophiles

Understanding the nature of such possession can explain so many of the horrific events that pollute this planet. At last people are beginning, very slowly, to appreciate something of the scale of paedophilia and child abuse, although the False Memory Syndrome Foundation is trying desperately to keep the lid on. The scale is far greater than anyone can imagine, but at least it is coming more to light. Sex with children has been part of the Illuminati modus operandi from ancient times. Sexual and Satanic abuse of children are aspects of the same agenda. Sex creates an energy connection between the two parties, no matter who they are, and this allows the demonic entities in the perpetrator to take control of their victim. Trauma-based mind control involves demonic possession by other-dimensional entities, also. These, often reptilian, beings of the lower fourth dimension want to absorb the energy of children before puberty and orgasm because the energy is still "pure" and so of more use to them. They therefore possess people and stimulate within them the sexual desire for children. When the possessed person is having physical sex with a child, the fourth-dimensional entity is sucking out their energy and making the vibrational connection that allows the child to be controlled by the entity. Anal sex with children is also designed to create a reaction in the child called vaso-vagal shock. Pain and energy surges up the child's spinal chord and explodes in the brain, thus increasing the rate at which the mind "splits" into compartments or amnesic barriers. These energy vampires and mind controllers have been increasing their operations in the last few decades and so we have had a corresponding increase in paedophilia. This is also the reason why so many of the Illuminati bloodline like George Bush, Henry Kissinger, etc., etc., have sex with children. All over the world the stories of paedophiles and paedophile rings are coming to public attention, but they represent a mere fraction of the abuse that actually goes on. In *The Biggest Secret* I wrote about the abuse at children's homes in North Wales and after publication and years of fighting for justice by a handful of decent people, a government "inquiry" was forced to reveal the massive and systematic abuse of children at the homes for more than 30 years. However, as always, the big fish are protected by the system and the small fry are set up to take the consequences. This is why famous paedophiles and child abusers such as Bush, Ted Heath, and the UK businessman and politician, Lord McAlpine, are allowed to escape the law (see *The Biggest Secret* for the background to this and if you go to my website you will find a library of information exposing the paedophile activity of the elite). The reptilians and other non-human species have been abducting children for thousands of years on a staggering scale. There are endless ancient legends and stories which describe or symbolise these events, not least that of the Pied Piper of Hamelin. And it is still going on. Every year more than 2,000 children disappear in America alone every *day* and many end up with Satanic cults or in the underground bases. No wonder they are never found. The Satanist, Aleister Crowley, emphasised why human sacrifice is important to these sick minds and why children are so often the victims:

> "It was a theory of the ancient magicians that any living being is a storehouse of energy varying in quantity according to the size and health of the animal, and in quality according to its mental and moral character. At the death of this animal this energy is liberated suddenly. For the highest spiritual [sic] working one must accordingly choose that victim which contains the greatest and purest force. A male child of perfect innocence and high intelligence is the most satisfactory and suitable victim." [13]

The satanic mansions

Some of the most important centres for Satanic ritual are the often Gothic mansions and castles of the European royal families and aristocracy and their offshoots in the United States. I remember a visit to Hearst Castle in California, the vast mansion of the newspaper tycoon and high Illuminati initiate, Randolph Hearst, which is now open to the public during the day. It is one of the darkest places I have visited and still consumed by deeply unpleasant other dimensional entities. Goodness knows what must have gone on there during Hearst's tenure, and perhaps still does. Hearst Castle is full of original ancient artefacts from Egypt and elsewhere and lies in a major stronghold of Satanism between Los Angeles and San Francisco. I have felt the same vibes in Britain at places like Chatsworth House in Derbyshire, the ancestral home of the Dukes of Devonshire, and at Clivedon House, the former mansion of the Satanic Astor family. This theme was portayed by the Stanley Kubric film, Eyes Wide Shut, which stars Tom Cruise and Nicole Kidman, and explores the subject of Satanism among the elite. Kubric died immediately after the movie was finished. It features a Satanic cult involving the high and mighty of an American city who meet at a large Gothic mansion. Such places are located all over the world. In Belgium, for example, there is the Mothers of Darkness Castle where the British royal family and the Illuminati elite of Europe perform many of their major rituals, and there is Balmoral Castle in Scotland, where the British royal family spend their summer holidays.

The isle of light – and darkness

I live on the Isle of Wight, a few miles off the south coast of England, and it is a perfect example of the connection between the major vortex points and Satanism (*Figure 35*). The Illuminati Satanic network performs its most important rituals at the key vortex points on the global grid because their sickening ceremonies suppress the frequency of the Earth's energy field and therefore keep humanity in the same vibrational prison. It is also easier for an entity to manifest in these inter-dimensional vortexes. The Isle of Wight has always been a sacred place for those who know of the Earth's energy grid. The Druids had three centres for their elite

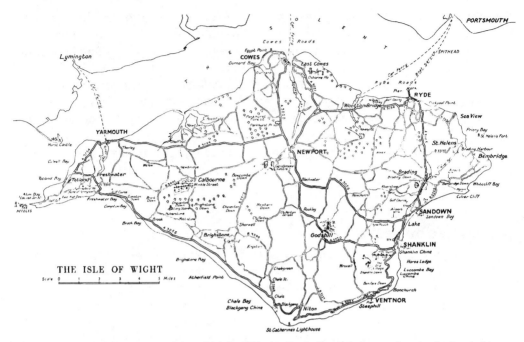

Figure 35: *The Isle of Wight, the "diamond isle", off England's south coast. A sacred centre for the druids and a massive location for Satanism today*

"Arch Druids" (hence Archbishop) in the British Isles. They were located on the "magical isles", the Isle of Man, the Isle of Anglesey in North Wales, and the Isle of Wight. Researcher Brian Desborough says that he has established that the first Christian church in Britain was on the Isle of Wight and not at Glastonbury as widely claimed. The Christian churches, especially the early ones, were located on the major vortex points as they replaced the "pagan" religion with their own. Today the Isle of Wight is a sacred place for Satanists because of its importance to the global energy grid. Author Mark Amaru Pinkham says that in ancient times it was called the Dragon Isle[14] and could be the "pivotal vortex" in the northern grid of the planet. Funnily enough, so many dinosaur bones have been found here that they have opened a dinosaur museum to exhibit them! Satanism is rampant on the island and involves famous names from the mainland British Isles as well as leading figures in island business, politics, police, the legal profession, and social services. There are two distinct faces to the Isle of Wight (also formerly known, apparently, as the Isle of "Light"). There is the one you see and the one you don't. The one you see is a stunning landscape and seascape, the beauty that attracted me here many years ago. But the one you don't see is very, very, dark indeed.

The island has a massive Freemasonic network, astonishingly so for a place with only 125,000 people, and I had many run-ins with them in the 1980s over environmental issues when the Masons were manipulating planning applications for building developments that were making some of them a fortune. But since my research into the manipulation of the world has advanced over a decade and more,

I realised that the Isle of Wight's dark secrets went very much deeper than that. It is one of the Satanic capitals of the UK and probably much further afield. At the same time, this beautiful island, which should be such a wonderful place to live, has, according to a local pressure group, the highest per capita rates of suicide and depression in the entire UK and that includes the neglected slum estates of the UK cities. Why? Because of the highly negative energy field the people live in. And this is caused by the rampant Satanic ritual at the vortex points, which resonate the island's energy field to the lower fourth-dimensional frequency. This is what the Illuminati are doing to the planet as a whole, creating and maintaining a vibrational prison that disconnects incarnate humanity from its higher levels of being. There are many centres for this Satanist-paedophile network on the Island, including a large house in the countryside where children are brought to parties for guests to rape. Other ritual centres include at *least* one yacht club and a seafront hotel. The chalk seam that runs from one side of the "diamond isle" to the other appears to be very important to the Satanists. Some years ago, a local community worker told the *News Of The World*, the UK's biggest selling Sunday newspaper, about the horrific Satanic rituals and sacrifice on the island and the involvement of Freemasonry, local politicians, council administrators, hotel owners, and other business people.[15] But nothing was done. It was just covered up. I have spoken to others who know what goes on and the story of the Isle of Wight is horrific, but the local media don't want to know.

Yet again, Ted Heath, the former Prime Minister who took the UK into the European Community, is among those named by victims who have suffered unbelievable abuse on the Island. Heath has been named to me by so many people who were abused and tortured by him as children. I have exposed him in *The Biggest Secret* and this book as a shape-shifting Satanist who tortures and sacrifices children. I am told that Heath is a regular guest at the secluded Priory Bay Hotel on the east of the Island and that former government minister Peter Mandelson also stays there, although I have not been able to confirm this at the time of publication. Mandelson is known to fellow MPs as "The Prince of Darkness" and has been forced to resign twice from government office over financial and misuse of power allegations. He has played a leading role for the Illuminati within Tony Blair's Labour Party. Both Heath and Mandelson are members of the Illuminati's Bilderberg Group, which I will highlight in a later chapter.

Co-incidentally, Tom Cruise and Nicole Kidman, stars of *Eyes Wide Shut*, have apparently been guests at the Priory Bay Hotel, according to a former worker, and Ernest Bevin, the British Foreign Secretary, was staying there when he wrote the speech proposing the establishment of a military alliance called the Western-European Union, now known as NATO. The British royal family also have great connections to the Isle of Wight. Queen Victoria and Albert, her high-level Freemasonic German husband, had a palace built on the island called Osborne House. The Satanist and Rothschild bloodline, Lord Mountbatten, was Governor of the Isle of Wight. Prince Charles is another visitor, as is Prince Philip, who comes publicly for Cowes Week, the elite's yachting bash. Many famous Satanists visit the island under the guise of coming to "sail". Interestingly, while writing this book, I received an invitation from the Rothschild Insurance group to attend a "financial conference" at…the Priory Bay Hotel. I would have gone to have a look, but circumstances took me elsewhere that week.

Singing for satan

The Isle of Wight is just one example of an immense global network of Satanic centres and cults involved in human sacrifice, blood drinking, and the summoning of other-dimensional demons. Most are unknown, but some, like the Church of Satan and the Temple of Set in the United States, have received mainstream publicity. The Church of Satan was founded on April 30th 1966 by Anton Szandor LaVey. April 30th through May Ist is one of the most important ritual dates in Satanism. LaVey's maternal grandmother came from Transylvania, legendary home of the blood-sucking vampire in what we call Romania. This is the region of Dracula, and many of the most important Illuminati bloodlines are connected with the area. LaVey, it is claimed, discovered Marilyn Monroe working in the strip clubs and used his contacts to make her a movie star. More like she was a multiple personality mind-slave. Hollywood (Holly-wood or Helle-wood, the sacred wood of the Druids) is awash with Satanists, as is the entertainment industry in general. Among LaVey's connections in entertainment and politics were President John F. Kennedy, Frank Sinatra, Sammy Davis Jr, Peter Lawford, and Jayne Mansfield. Sammy Davis Jr was an early member of the Church of Satan and the actress Jayne Mansfield, who died when she was beheaded in a "car crash" in 1967, was a high priestess (*see picture section*). Frank Sinatra was a handler and abuser of mind-controlled slaves and, as you can appreciate, Satanism and trauma-based mind control go hand in hand. One example of this was Michael Aquino. He worked with LaVey in the Church of Satan, but later broke away and formed his own Temple of Set. Aquino was a notorious mind programmer, named by Cathy O'Brien and many others, and a top man in the US Defense Intelligence Agency's Psychological Warfare Division. Aquino's wife, who worked with him, is called Lilith Sinclair. The name Lilith is a symbol of the reptilian bloodlines and one of the major strands of the Illuminati's genetic web is the Scottish Sinclair family, formerly the French St Clair bloodline. The St Clairs and the Black Madonna-worshipping, St Bernard, were fundamentally involved in the formation of the Knights Templar. The Sinclair chapel at Roslyn, near Edinburgh, is a shrine to the Illuminati and includes the image of the Green Man – the representation of Balder in the King Arthur stories. Lilith comes from Lilim or "children of Lilith", which relates to the symbolism of Set. Lilith Aquino founded the Lilith Grotto in LaVey's Church of Satan and was a member of its Council of Nine. The official Church of Satan website outlines its philosophy:

> "…we are the first above-ground organization in history openly dedicated to the acceptance of Man's true nature – that of a carnal beast, living in a cosmos which is permeated and motivated by the Dark Force which we call Satan. Over the course of

time, Man has called this Force by many names, and it has been reviled by those whose very nature causes them to be separate from this fountainhead of existence. They live in obsessive envy of we who exist by flowing naturally with the dread Prince of Darkness. It is for this reason that individuals who resonate [vibrate] with Satan have always been an alien elite, often outsiders in cultures whose masses pursue solace in an external deity. We Satanists are our own Gods, and we are the explorers of the Left-Hand Path. We do not bow down before the myths and fictions of the desiccated spiritual followers of the Right-Hand Path." [18]

No, they bow before the myths and fictions of other-dimensional entities. Unbelievable. And it is not a choice between the right-hand path and the left-hand path. There is another that goes straight ahead. The Temple of Set also denies it is involved in anything horrific. Its website assures us:

"Regretfully there still exist some individuals whose idea of 'Satanism' is largely a simple-minded synthesis of Christian propaganda and Hollywood horror movies [often made by Satanists!]. The Temple of Set enjoys the colorful legacy of the Black Arts, and we use many forms of historical Satanic imagery for our artistic stimulation and pleasure. But we have not found that any interest or activity which an enlightened, mature intellect would regard as undignified, sadistic, criminal, or depraved is desirable, much less essential to our work." [17]

Of course there is nothing undignified, sadistic, criminal, or depraved, about Michael Aquino, the inspiration of the Temple of Set, and his mind control and torture of men, women, and children; nor in being involved in the US military's Psychological Warfare Division. A former mind-controlled slave with an elite group called the San Diego Illuminati told me how she had worked closely with Aquino in the 1980s. "He was a cold, arrogant, ugly person in heart and spirit, enjoyed using people, had a weakness for young boys, and was a confirmed pedophiliac", the source told me. She said that Aquino had implemented "scientific experimentation" (mind control) at various military bases and at the estate of a Jonathan Meier, who, the source said, was the leading Illuminati "trainer" for new recruits in that part of America. Aquino also had an estate in Germany where he would take his leaders and the children he abused. The source, who was mind controlled to mind control others, said she visited there on several occasions.[18]

Hitler the demonic "host"

There is no better example of all the points I am making in this chapter than the Nazis in Germany, and no more obvious example of how the Illuminati bloodlines are possessed by demonic entities than Adolf Hitler. As you will see in *Appendix II*, Hitler was almost certainly a Rothschild bloodline. We talk of some people being magnetic and having a "magnetic personality", and that is exactly what they have. We are all generating magnetic energy. Some people transmit powerful magnetism and others less so. Negative energies are just as magnetic as positive. Those connected to, and therefore generating, the extreme negative vibration of the demonic entities will be very magnetic. You often hear highly negative people described as having a "fatal attraction". This is where the magnetism and charisma of Adolf Hitler came from. When he was standing on a public platform with that contorted face and crazed delivery, he was channelling the "reptilian" demonic consciousness and transmitting this vibration to the vast crowds. This affected the vibrational state of the people and turned them into equally crazed agents of hatred. It is the pied piper principle, using vibrational frequencies. As writer Alan Bullock said of Hitler:

"His power to bewitch an audience has been likened to the occult art of the African medicine man or the Asiatic shaman; others have compared it to the sensitivity of a medium, and the magnetism of a hypnotist." [19]

And Hermann Rauschning, an aide to Hitler, said in his book *Hitler Speaks*:

"One cannot help thinking of him as a medium. For most of the time, mediums are ordinary, insignificant people. Suddenly they are endowed with what seems to be supernatural powers, which set them apart from the rest of humanity. The medium is possessed. Once the crisis is passed, they fall back into mediocrity. It was in this way, beyond any doubt, that Hitler was possessed by forces outside of himself – almost demoniacal forces of which the individual man, Hitler, was only the temporary vehicle. The mixture of the banal and the supernatural created that insupportable duality of which one was conscious in his presence…it was like looking at a bizarre face whose expression seemed to reflect an unbalanced state of mind coupled with a disquieting impression of hidden powers." [20]

Hitler appeared to live in perpetual fear of the "supermen". Rauschning told how Hitler suffered from terrible nightmares and would wake in terror screaming about entities, who were invisible to all but himself. Hitler once said to his aide:

"What will the social order of the future be like? Comrade I will tell you. There will be a class of overlords, after them the rank and file of the party members in hierarchical order, and then the great mass of anonymous followers, servants and workers in perpetuity, and beneath them again all the conquered foreign races, the modern slaves. And over and above all these will reign a new and exalted nobility of whom I cannot speak…but of all these plans the militant members will know nothing. The new man is living amongst us now! He is here. Isn't that enough for you? I will tell you a secret. I have seen the new man. He is intrepid and cruel. I was afraid of him." [21]

This is the society planned by the reptilians and their reptile-Nordic (Aryan) "master race" if we allow their New World Order of global control to be introduced. Hitler's "secret chiefs" were demonic reptilians and others. The obsession with hierarchy and ritual outlined there are character traits of the reptilian brain, as we shall see. One of Hitler's heroes, the writer Houston Stewart Chamberlain, also fitted the description of demonic possession. He was an Englishman who married Eva, the daughter of another Hitler hero, the composer Richard Wagner. Chamberlain said that he felt himself to be taken over by demons and his anti-Jewish, pro-Aryan books were written in a trance or "fever". In his autobiography he said he did not recognise much of his writing as his own. Chamberlain became principal adviser to Kaiser Wilhelm (bloodline) and urged the king to go to war in 1914. Little more than 20 years later the forces that possessed Chamberlain also possessed Adolf Hitler as he triggered the second world war of the 20th century. Hitler's behaviour was extremely indicative of demonic possession, including his strange epileptic-like fits. Others close to Hitler said that the Fuhrer woke up in the night screaming and having convulsions. He would call for help and appeared to be half paralysed. He would gasp to the point of suffocation and often when fully conscious he would point to apparently empty space and scream: "He is here. There! In the corner."

After Hitler moved to Germany, he spent a lot of time in Bavaria, from whence the Bavarian Illuminati had sprung and he returned there after the First World War. That's the official line, anyway. Bavaria is a massive centre for the Illuminati. The following year he came across a tiny and rather pathetic political party called the German Workers Party. This was an offshoot of an esoteric secret society called the German Order, which was seriously nationalistic and anti-Jewish. Out of this Order came other similar societies, including the infamous Thule-Gesellschaft (Thule Society) and the Luminous Lodge or Vril Society. Hitler was a member of both. Thule comes from the name given by the Greeks and Romans to the frozen northern region of the Earth. They called this land Thule or Ultima Thule. Vril was the name given by the English writer and high Illuminati initiate, Lord Edward Bulwer-Lytton, to the force in the blood, which, he claimed, awakens people to their true power and potential to become supermen. For blood read DNA. Bulwer-Lytton was a British colonial minister heavily involved in imposing opium addiction on the Chinese. He was a close friend of the British Prime Minister, Benjamin Disraeli (an associate of the Rothschilds) and the writer, Charles Dickens. He was Grand Patron of the English Rosicrucian Society that included Illuminati agents Francis Bacon and John Dee among its earlier membership. He was also a Grand Master of the Scottish Rite of Freemasonry and the head of British Intelligence. One of his operatives was Helena Blavatsky, a contact told me, and Bulwer-Lytton is often referred to in her book, *Isis Unveiled*. He is best known for his work, *The Last Days Of Pompeii*, but his passion was the world of esoteric magic. So what is this Vril force in the blood that Bulwer-Lytton wrote about? It was known by the Hindus as the "serpent force" and relates to the genetic make-up of the body that allows shape-shifting and conscious interdimensional travel. The Vril force is, yet again, related to the reptile-human bloodlines.

Another big influence on Hitler was the Bulwer-Lytton novel *The Coming Race*, in which he wrote of an enormous civilisation inside the Earth, well ahead of our own. These underground supermen would, according to Bulwer-Lytton's novel, emerge on the surface one day and take control of the world. Many Nazis believed this. The themes of underground supermen or "hidden masters" can be found in most of the secret societies and in legends across the world, as we have seen. Certainly this was true of the Order of the Golden Dawn founded by Dr Wynn Westcott, a Freemason, and S.L. Mathers. They called their masters the "secret chiefs" and devised rituals to contact them. In the 1890s there were temples of the Order of the Golden Dawn in London, Edinburgh, Bradford, Weston-Super-Mare, and Paris, where Mathers made his home. One of their secret signs was the pointed arm salute that the Nazis would use when saying "Heil Hitler". Remnants of the Order of the Golden Dawn continue to this day, but the original version splintered after a row between the Mather faction and the Satanist, Aleister Crowley, which split the membership. Crowley then became involved with the Order of Oriental Templars or OTO. In 1933, the rocket expert, Willi Ley, fled from Germany and revealed the existence of the Vril Society and the Nazi's belief that they were to become the equals of the supermen in the bowels of the Earth by use of esoteric teachings and mind expansion. They believed this would re-awaken the Vril force sleeping in the blood. The initiates of the Vril Society included two men who would become famous Nazis, Heinrich Himmler and Hermann Goering. Vril members were convinced they were in alliance with mysterious esoteric lodges in Tibet and one of the so-called unknown supermen, who was referred to as the "King of Fear". Rudolf Hess, Hitler's deputy fuhrer until he made his ill-fated flight to England in 1941, was a dedicated occultist and a member, with Goering, of the Edelweiss Society. This was a sect that believed in the Nordic master race – the Nordic-reptilian hybrids I call the Aryans. Hess worshipped Hitler as the "Messiah", although how he could do this when the Fuhrer was hardly blond-haired and blue-eyed was not clear. The Nazis were manipulated by their demonic masters to instigate breeding programmes between the blond-haired, blue-eyed, Nordic bloodlines.

A founder of the Thule Society was Rudolf Glauer, an astrologer, who changed his name to the grand-sounding, Baron von Sebottendorff. His demands for a revolution against Jews and Marxists turned the Thule Society into a focus for the anti-Jew, anti-Marxist, German master-racers. Out of all this came the German Workers Party, which would become the Nazi Party. Another committed occultist and friend of Sebottendorff was highly significant. This was Dietrict Eckart, a heavy drinking, drug-taking writer, who believed he was here to pave the way for a dictator of Germany. He met Hitler in 1919 and decided he was the one, the Messiah he was looking for. It is Eckart who is credited with Hitler's advanced esoteric knowledge and the black magic rituals that plugged him so completely into the demonic reptilians. From now on, Hitler's power to attract support grew rapidly. Eckart wrote to a friend in 1923:

> "Follow Hitler! He will dance, but it is I who have called the tune. We have given him the means of communication with Them. Do not mourn for me; I shall have influenced history more than any other German." [22]

Other significant thinkers and groups that influenced the gathering Nazi philosophy were two German esoteric magicians, Guido von List and Lanz von Liebenfels. At the summer solstice, List used wine bottles on the ground to form the symbol of the Hermetic Cross, also known as the Hammer of Thor. It was the badge of power in the Order of the Golden Dawn and we know this symbol as the swastika, an ancient Sun symbol of the Atlanteans-Phoenicians. The original swastika was right-handed which, in esoteric terms, means light and creation, the positive. The Nazis reversed this to symbolise the left- hand path – black magic and destruction. Lanz von Liebenfels (real name Adolf Lanz) used the swastika on a flag that flew over his temple overlooking the Danube and for these two black magicians it symbolised the end of Christianity and the dawning of the age of blond-haired, blue-eyed Aryan supermen. They believed in the racial inferiority of those they called the dark forces, such as the Jews, Slavs, and Negros. Liebenfels recommended castration for these people. The two vons, List and Liebenfels, were to have a massive influence on Adolf Hitler. In 1932, with Hitler on the verge of power, von Liebenfels would write to a fellow believer:

> "Hitler is one of our pupils ...You will one day experience that he, and through him we, will one day be victorious and develop a movement that will make the world tremble." [23]

Heinrich Himmler, the head of the SS, was another dedicated occultist who was into all matters esoteric. He used this knowledge in the blackest of ways. Himmler was particularly interested in the rune stones. This is a system of divination in which stones, carrying symbols, are thrown or selected and the choice or combination read by an expert. It was Himmler who formed the notorious SS and, as with the swastika, he chose an esoteric symbol for his horrific organisation. This was the double S or "sig rune", which looks like two flashes of lightning. The SS was a virtually self-contained body and the epitome of all the esoteric knowledge in which the Nazis believed so passionately. Only those considered racially pure were allowed to join, and instruction in the esoteric arts, including the rune stones, was fundamental to their training. The SS was run and governed as a black magic secret society. Their rituals were taken from others, such as the Jesuits and the Knights Templar. The highest-ranking initiates were the 12 members of the Grand Council of Knights led by the 13th, their Grand Master Heinrich Himmler. Their black rituals were performed at the ancient castle of Wewelsberg in Westphalia. They celebrated the rituals of the Nordic pagans and the summer solstice. Here they worshipped Satan/Lucifer/Set, whichever name you prefer. Prince Bernhard of The Netherlands, a reptilian Habsburg and Merovingian bloodline, was a member of the SS. Bernhard was one of the founders of the Illuminati front, the Bilderberg Group, and is an extremely close friend of Prince Philip. The esoteric arts pervaded all that Hitler and the Nazis did, even down to the use of pendulums on maps to identify the positions of enemy troops. The mass rallies that Hitler used so effectively were designed with the knowledge of the human psyche and how it can be manipulated.

In the book, *Satan And Swastika*, Francis King says:

> "Hitler's public appearances, particularly those associated with the Nazi Party's Nuremberg Rallies, were excellent examples of this sort of magical ceremony. The fanfares, military marches, and Wagnerian music, all emphasised the idea of German military glory. The mass swastika banners in black, white, and red, filled the consciousness of the participants in the rallies with national socialist ideology. The ballet-like precision of the movement of the uniformed party members, all acting in unison, evoked from the unconscious the principles of war and violence, which the ancients symbolised as Mars. And the prime rituals of the rallies – Hitler clasping to other banners the 'blood banner' carried in the Munich Putsch of 1923 – was a quasi-magical ceremony designed to link up minds of living Nazis with the archetypal images symbolised by the dead national socialist heroes of the past.

> "The relio-magical aspects of the rallies were emphasised by the fact that their high points were reached after dusk and took place in a 'cathedral of light' – an open space surrounded by pillars of light coming from electric searchlights pointed upwards to the sky. If a modern ritual magician of the utmost expertise had designed the ritual intended to 'invoke Mars', he could not have come up with anything more effective than the ceremonies used at Nuremberg." [24]

And what applied then, applies now. The esoteric knowledge used by the Nazis for mass hypnosis on the German people is being used today to expand the global hypnosis within the human race. Symbols, words, colours, sounds, and techniques of which the public are not even aware are being used in the media and in advertising to hypnotise us. The propaganda ministry of Joseph Goebbels was based on the esoteric knowledge of the human psyche. He knew that people would believe anything if you tell them often enough and if you can engineer events which create the "something must be done" mentality in the public mind. He used colours, symbols and slogans to great effect. The slogans were used like mantras and were repeated over and over again, hypnotising the mass psyche. All alternative views and information were censored and the people were programmed to respond as desired. What is the difference between that and the constant drip, drip of inaccurate and biased information that is fed to us and our children by the media day after day? It may not have a swastika on it, but it is still mass hypnotism. It would seem to be a contradiction that Hitler sought to destroy secret societies like the Freemasons and to prevent the use of esoteric knowledge in German society, but it isn't. He knew as much as anyone of the power available to those with this knowledge and he wanted to keep that for himself. In truth, the Nazis were created and controlled by the secret society underground and ultimately by the demonic reptilians. They believed the Sumerian gods were the extraterrestrial master race. They launched expeditions to North Africa, Rennes-le-Chateau and Montsegur in Cathar country, and to Tibet where they believed the underground supermen were based. The Nazi connection with Tibet was confirmed when the Russians arrived in

Berlin at the end of the war to find many dead Buddhist monks who had been working with the Nazis.

The Nazis did not disappear in 1945, they just went underground or changed their name. The inner core of the Nazi secret society network was the Black Order, which continues today and is reported to be the innermost circle of the CIA. Allen Dulles, the first head of the CIA, was a Nazi supporter (see ...*And The Truth Shall Set You Free*) and he was a key force behind Project Paperclip that protected Nazis like Josef Mengele after the war and took them to America. At the same time, John Foster Dulles, Allen's brother, was the US Secretary of State. The Dulles family are cousins of the Rockefellers (bloodline in other words). Reinhard Gehlen, the man appointed by the Allen Dulles to set up the CIA network in Europe, was one of Hitler's SS chiefs. Gehlen said it was not so much "employment" as a "gentleman's agreement" with Dulles. Meanwhile, the Nazis considered expendable were sent to the Nuremberg show trials, which were designed to cover up what really happened (see ...*And The Truth Shall Set You Free* for the detailed story.)

The two "sides" in Ireland

What I have just described in relation to Hitler and the Nazis is the basic method of choosing and bringing to power the major political, economic, military, and media figures throughout the world. The decades of violence and civil war in Northern Ireland are not all that they seem. A contact called Jim Cairns has spent many years uncovering the scale of Satanism and child abuse in Northern Ireland and the Irish Republic (see his website at *http://www.esatclear.ie/~cairhaven*). More than that, he realised that the leaders of the two "opposing" terrorist groups, the Catholic IRA and the Protestant Paramilitary group, the UVF, were members of the *same* Satanic covens. This fits with the evidence I have found all over the world. Again and again opposing "sides" turn out to be the same side – the Illuminati – when you get near the top. Cairns had an attempt on his life in 1994 and fled Northern Ireland. He has made statements about his findings, but, of course, nothing has been done. He established that the Satanic network in Ireland operates behind the cover of the "Born Again" Christian movement. "I have no doubt that organisation is nothing more than a Satanist organisation involved in ritual murders," he said.[25]

Part of this story involves a Belfast boys' home called Kincora. This was the subject of a massive scandal in the 1980s when systematic abuse came to light going back at least 20 years. But, yet again, the big names involved were protected. The *New Covenant Times* said in its January/March issue of 1994 that the loyalist ("Protestant") paramilitaries supported an MI5 British Intelligence operation called "Tara", which had the intention of creating so much violence and tit-for-tat murder by both themselves and the IRA that the UK parliament would agree for Northern Ireland to be absorbed by the Irish Republic. Colin Wallace was a part-time soldier and public relations officer at the army headquarters in Northern Ireland. Later he was moved to another department controlled by MI5. It was here that he became aware of the Tara operation and the 20 years of child abuse at Kincora involving very big names. When Wallace demanded to be removed from the project, he was sent back to England and charged with a security offence and later unjustly jailed for murder. The journalist Paul Foot wrote a book called *Who Framed Colin Wallace?* (Macmillan, London, 1989). One victim of Satanism and mind control I have spoken with says she remembers vividly watching a very famous politician in Northern Ireland raping a little boy in a ritual in England and when it was over he produced a knife and cut the boy's throat. Is anyone still wondering how people can plant bombs in Northern Ireland that have killed and maimed thousands? These people do not feel the emotion we do in such circumstances. They are reptilian hybrids – on both "sides".

Jim Cairns said that a contact had told him that the children in the Kincora scandal were taken to Birr Castle in County Offally, Northern Ireland. This is the home of the bloodline Earls of Rosse. The 1st Earl of Rosse was a founder member of Ireland's Hellfire Club (El-fire), along with Colonel St Ledger of Grange Mellon, County Athy. At the same time that the Earl of Rosse was a Hellfire Club member in 1725, he was also the Grand Master of the Freemasons in Ireland. The present Earl of Rosse is the stepbrother of Lord Snowdon, the former husband of the Queen's sister, Princess Margaret, and she has visited Birr on many occasions. The Hellfire Club was founded on the estate at Wycombe, north of London, owned by the British government minister Sir Francis Dashwood, together with Benjamin Franklin, an Illuminati "founding father" of the United States. Dr Franklin, a "devout Christian", was also involved in the manipulation of Ireland. The Hellfire Club is a Satanic network based on human sacrifice ritual (see *The Biggest Secret*). Wherever you look in this story, Satanism appears every time because these rituals and sacrifices are vital to the continued reptilian control of the planet. Satanists operate in the pivotal positions to ensure the truth is covered up and, as Cairns says, the official number of Satanic ritual murders in Ireland, as with everywhere else, is a fraction of what is really happening:

> "... the figures conceal the much greater and hidden spread of Satanism throughout Ireland. The reality is, the powerful Satanic network in Ireland has been able to disguise many Satanic related crimes simply because it has infiltrated many of the essential state bodies, police, the press, judiciary, political institutions, the churches etc. I have no doubt that this is the case from the information which I have on audio tape from my cult sources. My 'Born Again' source tells me that top police, clergy, and politicians are Satanists." [26]

This is what you find all over the world. It is not through paranoia that people see Satanists or their puppets in the main positions of power. The very system makes it so because those who are not Satanists or under their control are overwhelmingly sifted out before they make it to the top jobs in the institutions that direct society. This is why the ratio of Satanists, blood drinkers, and human sacrificers, to people in power is so astonishingly high compared with the ratio in the rest of the population.

SOURCES

1   Correspondence with the author

2   *http://www.reptilianagenda.com/research/r100799c.html*

3   *Trance-Formation Of America*, p 174

4   Correspondence with the author

5   *Our Haunted Planet*, pp 96 and 97

6   *The Woman's Encyclopedia Of Myths And Secrets*, pp 16 and 17

7   *Our Haunted Planet*, p 168

8   Ibid, p 160

9   Ibid, p 144

10 See *Dimensions: A Casebook Of Alien Contact* (Ballantine Books, USA, 1988)

11 Correspondence with the author

12 Correspondence with the author

13 Aleister Crowley, *Magick Theory And Practice* (Dover, USA, 1929), pp 94 to 95

14 *The Return Of The Serpents Of Wisdom*, p 251

15 *News Of The World*, August 24th, 1997, pp 30 and 31

16 *http://www.churchofsatan.com/*

17 *http://www.xeper.org/*

18 Correspondence with the author

19 Alan Bullock, *Hitler, A Study In Tyranny* (Pelican Books, London, 1960)

20 Herman Rauschning, *Hitler Speaks* (London, 1939)

21 Ibid

22 Quoted by J.H. Brennan in *Occult Reich* (Futura, London, 1974) and Francis King in *Satan And Swastika* (Mayflower Books, London, 1976)

23 Ibid

24 *Satan And Swastika*

25 Correspondence with the author

26 Ibid

CHAPTER 15

Suffer little children

"It can't happen here" is number one on the list of famous last words.

David Crosby

In *The Biggest Secret,* I reveal in greater detail the scale of Satanic activity and its fundamental connection to the reptilians and the Illuminati. When you see what is happening in every community, especially to children, it defies belief.

Children are major targets because the reptilians prefer the "purity" of their blood and energy, and the most effective time to start trauma-based mind control is before the age of five or six. Changes take place in the blood at puberty and after the first sexual activity, which make it less useful from the reptilians' point of view. Many schools and pre-schools for small children across the world are fronts for Satanism and its offshoot, trauma-based mind control. Most of the children are suffering every day without their parent's knowledge, but they are also handed over to the cults quite willingly by their Satanic parents. Occasionally, the odd story gets into a newspaper, but this bears no resemblance to the staggering scale of the ritual abuse of children. The UK *Sunday Mirror* revealed the abuse of a woman they called Kate, who was then aged 34. She had been abused at a house on the outskirts of Dublin, Ireland, since she was three.

> "I still remember the first time it happened," she said. "It was evening time because it was dark outside and my mother made me dress up in my best clothes. I was excited because I thought I was going on an adventure. I was picked up by my aunt and uncle and taken to another house somewhere in Dublin.

> "I remember looking out at the city lights and feeling happy because I was out so late. But when I got to the house I became scared because everyone was dressed in dark gowns and hoods. I was stripped and made to lie down on a table in the living room. It was cold and I was absolutely terrified. So I started screaming and shouting for my mother." [1]

She was smeared with blood and assaulted again and again. She said the terror she felt was indescribable and she was in terrible pain. The table was surrounded by strangers in robes and hoods holding crucifixes, chalices and knives encrusted with jewels and they were "chanting in some strange language – it was just horrific". She was taken back home and she thought she was safe. Her mother hugged her, she said, but didn't say anything. She cleaned up the blood and treated the painful areas of her body. But the ordeal wasn't over. It had only just begun. A few nights later it happened again. "When I saw my mother bringing out my blue coat and best shoes I started screaming because I knew what would happen next," she said. Kate tried to speak to her parents about her abuse, but her father said she would be taken away if she said anything:

> "My uncle would knock at the door and then return to the car to my aunt to wait for my father to bring me out. Most times I'd be kicking and screaming and pleading with my parents not to send me away. But they said nothing. They just pulled me out to the car. Most times my father had to prise my fingers from the garden gate."

Kate said there were other children in the house where she was abused. Sometimes she was forced to watch while they suffered. She said she was constantly afraid and could hardly sleep. She hated going to Mass because every time she saw a crucifix, she'd have a panic attack. The enormous emotional debris of these experiences led her to a life of heavy drinking, drug taking, glue sniffing and a broken marriage because she could not bear anyone to touch her. "I hated myself, particularly when my body started developing during puberty. I wanted to look like a boy so I ate just enough to stop me from collapsing. I was six-and-a-half stone at my lowest point." Now this is not an isolated case. It is happening around you, in your neighbourhood now. That's the scale we are talking about. Rape Crisis Centres in Ireland were told so many "bizarre" tales of ritual abuse that a special helpline was created for them. Fiona Neary, the National Co-ordinator of the Rape Crisis Centres, said:

> "We could be talking about high levels of organised abuse which could almost be beyond the belief of many of the agencies tasked with dealing with this problem. Although it is unrecognised, ritual abuse does take place in Ireland and survivors of this type of abuse live here. Elaborate ritual, group activities, religious, magical or supernatural beliefs and practices may be used to terrify and silence children and to convince them of the absolute power of their abusers. The purpose of these rituals is to gain and maintain access to children in order to exploit them sexually. There is also evidence that some of the groups would exchange children to other groups abroad." [2]

It is a vast global network, fundamentally connected to the Illuminati and the reptilians and if you read the chapters, Satan's Children and Where Have All the Children Gone? in *The Biggest Secret* you'll see a stream of evidence to support this. The overwhelming majority of human sacrifice and other ritual abuse goes on unexposed and when it does come to light, the big names involved are protected, as with Kincora in Northern Ireland and the children's home scandal in North

Wales. One of the most famous cases was at the McMartin Day Care Centre in Los Angeles where 369 children said they had been sexually abused. The False Memory Syndrome Foundation has worked extremely hard to persuade people to dismiss the stories as fantasy. The children told of animals being slaughtered and other Satanic rituals. They described how they were buried, locked in the dark, and taken to different locations to be abused. These included a grocery store, church, cemetery, and a crematorium. The children said they were forced to drink blood and urine and they saw the eyes of a baby ripped out and its body incinerated. Others said that a rabbit was killed in front of them to show what would happen if they told their parents. The case was under investigation for four years, on trial for two and a half years, involved 124 witnesses, 50,000 pages of transcript, and cost almost $23,000 a day. But in the end the case fell apart and those responsible escaped with their freedom. Crucial to the children's stories was their description of a network of secret tunnels under the building, through which they said they were taken to be abused. It was claimed at the trial that there was no evidence that these tunnels existed. But five months after the files were closed on the McMartin case and the official cover-up completed, a team of trained investigators and excavators uncovered the tunnel system that connected to a vaulted room under the day care centre. They extended out to adjacent buildings where the children said they had been taken before they were driven to other locations. In 1991, an independent archaeologist also confirmed the existence of the tunnels and an alarm system inside the centre. In other words, the children had been telling the truth.

In Britain there have been, among many others, cases in Orkney, Nottingham, Rochdale, and Cleveland. Each time the social workers trying to expose Satanic abuse have been subjected to a blitz of condemnation by the mainstream media with the *Mail On Sunday* particularly vehement in its opposition. It went so far on one occasion as to describe the "spectre" of Satanism as "hysterical nonsense". Such remarks are so at odds with the worldwide evidence that they can only be the work of an uninformed idiot (quite possible) or someone who wishes the truth to remain undiscovered. As a result of such imbalanced coverage and, of course, the stunning nature of the children's evidence, most cases do not even come to trial. Even when they do very few lead to conviction. The public would rather accept the allegations are not true because they don't want to believe that such horrors are happening. Unfortunately they are, on a vast scale, and if you go into denial about it because you don't want to face the truth about your world, then you are helping to perpetuate this unspeakable treatment of children. As Caroline Lekiar of the National Association of Young People in Care, said:

> "I can understand people finding it difficult to believe, it's extraordinary, but yet, everything is showing that it is happening. Young kids are drawing the type of thing that doesn't come on TV. I have been dealing with this for the last two years, I have come across many cases of ritualistic abuse and a lot of it happens all over the place. People have really got to wake up."[3]

The Child Abuse Pyramid

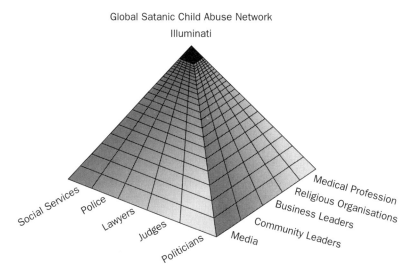

Global Satanic Child Abuse Network

Illuminati

Social Services
Police
Lawyers
Judges
Politicians
Media
Community Leaders
Business Leaders
Religious Organisations
Medical Profession

Figure 36: *The pyramid structure that allows widespread child abuse and Satanic ritual sacrifice to be covered up. The Illuminati place their operatives in key positions within social services, the police, judiciary, etc., to keep the lid on these global horrors*

Co-ordinated cover-ups

As I've said, Satanic ritual abuse is a global network, another pyramid of interconnecting groups, with the high and mighty of society among their number: top politicians, government officials, bankers, business leaders, policemen, lawyers, judges, doctors, coroners, publishers, editors and journalists. The Satanic network is structured with self-contained compartments, like the Freemasons, and remember what Jim Shaw, the former 33rd degree Mason, said:

> "The Mason swears to keep the secrets of another Mason, protecting him even if it requires withholding evidence of a crime. In some degrees treason and murder are excepted. In other, higher degrees, there are no exceptions to this promise to cover up the truth. The obligations, if the Masonic teachings are to be believed, may require a Mason to give false testimony, perjure himself, or (in the case of a judge) render a false verdict in order to protect a Mason." [4]

For Satanists the severe consequences of revealing secrets or refusing to carry out an order, are not threats, they are promises. The Illuminati and their Satanic networks place their people in the major positions of power in all the areas they need to control to prevent proper investigation or to ensure that any high-profile case that does get to court always fails (see *Figure 36*). You don't need to control all the policemen to stop an investigation. You just need to control the person who controls the policemen. You don't need to control every social worker, just the people who control the social workers. In other words, you only need to control the very few people who have the power to call off an investigation when necessary. These placemen and women are controlled by the same force and so the cover-up can be carefully co-ordinated through people who appear, to the outsider, to be unconnected – teachers, social workers, policemen, lawyers, judges, and media. The results of all this for the children involved are beyond the imagination of anyone who has not experienced the level of trauma they must suffer.

Zack's story

One unfolding story I have featured on my website is that of Zack. He is a little boy who attended a pre-school operated by a company called Kindercare at 100 Endeavor Way, Cary, North Carolina. Kindercare is the biggest pre-school organisation in the United States. Zack's experience contains all the elements of the constantly recurring reports of child abuse, both in what he says happened to him and the shocking lack of investigation by the authorities that are supposed to be protecting children. This story and all the quotes by his parents and grandmother are from direct correspondence and conversations with me.[4] Zack said that he was taken from the centre in Cary to a house where he was tied up and made to watch people sacrifice a little boy. He said that he and other children were made to drink the blood and eat the flesh of the dead child. He also said that they took his own blood. He had a small circular puncture on his elbow, which looked like a mole was growing there. He said this is where they put the "needle-knife" into him. He has also talked of large spiders he saw in movies on these occasions and of seeing "bad movies" all the time. The mother of another boy at the centre, a four year old called Tyler, said her son had asked her if it was all right for people "to eat each other". Zack talked about a "green" party at the school in which the children were given green food and juice. He said the children were given gifts at the party, but he was given 'poop'. When asked if anyone else got poop and he said: "No, only me – the other kids got cars and things like that." He said the sandwiches were all green with "yucky mustard" and "there was blood". Suzen, his grandmother, asked him what happened when he wouldn't eat it and he said: "We all went to sleep." He also said: "They put blood in the oatmeal at the school." Hearing his mother on the phone talking to someone about tunnels, he said he didn't like the tunnels at school. His grandmother, Suzen, asked him what was in the tunnels and he said: "There is blustering toys and I didn't want to play with them". She asked what the toys did and how he played with them. He said: "They blow everything around and make it cold. They like everything to be cold." Zack said that one of the people involved was called "Camelot" and he turned into a "dragon".

His parents told me that Zack, who was just five, began to talk about the Anunnaki and when he was asked what they were he said they were the "gods". He said that he learned about the Anunnaki at the "bad school". His grandmother, Suzen, asked him if he had ever heard the word "dingir" (she pronounced it ding-gear), a Mesopotamian name for the Anunnaki that translates as "The Righteous Ones of the Blazing Rockets". Pronouncing it ding-er, he said it was a bad word because the Dinger "eat people skin, people blood, and people bones". He added: "Their love goes away and they turn into vampires". She asked about the name "Enki" and he said: "that's a bad word". Then Enlil – "that's a fish word". This five year old then said: "They're brothers, aliens, and they're from Mars." Zack said he saw movies about it at school and they were going to destroy the world. The lizards looked like Darth Maul (in *Star Wars*) and also the "masks" they had at school, he told his grandmother. One day he saw a picture of France. He pointed to a place near the Alps called Gorda and Verona and said: "That's where the armies are saving people for the reptiles." Suzen asked him where he heard about reptiles and he said the people at the "mean school" told him they were reptiles. He said: "Aliens like to come here at Halloween and Easter. They like Easter." Suzen also realised that Zack pronounced words strangely as in fix-ed, try-ed, and spill-ed.

Zack first told his grandmother what had happened when she went to visit the family the week before Halloween in 1999. He later said that he did not tell his mum and dad because the "bad people" had said that his parents were involved in what was happening. This was untrue, but it is a technique often used to keep the children quiet. Another is to tell them that they will kill them and their parents if they talk. Zack said his teacher threatened to kill his parents as she chased him with a knife that she kept in her pocket. He was screaming for his mum and dad and she said: "They can't hear you. If you say anything to anyone I will cut your mom into pieces and burn your house down." As the children have seen people being killed in front of them they naturally believe this would happen. Suzen said Zack was visibly shaken and afraid to go to sleep. She and his parents, Margo and Johnny, wrote this off as fear of Halloween. But on November 5th, Zack's fifth birthday, he said that someone had "pulled my pants down at school and put their hand in my body." He said the hand had "icky stuff on it". Suzen, a court officer for child advocacy, felt there was much more to the situation than they had first thought. His father Johnny took him to a doctor and a paediatrician and both filed a report to social services. The mother of another child, Tyler, who had spoken of similar experiences, did the same. But the social services and police "investigations" were a disgrace.

The investigation that never was

Detective Hoya, the head of the Cary police child crisis unit, said that Zack's behaviour was "normal". One wonders what this guy would consider "abnormal". Suzen called every department of child services and every time was referred to another department. Finally the woman in children's mental health asked her what she wanted to happen. "I told her I wanted these activities to stop!" Suzen said. The woman's response was that no one would take this case and they were better off trying to do it themselves. Finally, a chance meeting at the police station with the new mayor focused the attention of the authorities. A detective was sent to interview the children and with him was the woman in charge of the pre-school section of social services. The detective, Stephan Lambert, seemed sincere and had a tape recorder running during the entire visit. When I spoke to him later he seemed to me to be a pawn in a game he didn't understand. Zack's father asked the woman from social services how she was going to help them and she said that she wasn't there to help them, Suzen recalled. She was just there to talk to the children. Suzen told her that she wanted to tape the interviews because they were not allowed to be in the same room. The woman refused. Suzen said:

> "She took Tyler into Zack's bedroom and started asking him questions about what happened. I listened outside the door and the detective taped the entire time. When Tyler said that…[a lady who still works at the Kindercare centre]…showed him her boobies and squirted him [she was post-natal], the social worker asked him if his mommy shows him her boobies. Being only five years old, his story got confused and the interview didn't last longer than a few minutes. When she asked for Zack, he refused to go near her or the policeman, even though the policeman seemed concerned and stated he thought 'something weird was going on'".

The police and social services appeared to have little interest in pursuing the case. During Zack's time at the Kindercare centre, he said they did something to him with his glasses. "Something so bad that he will only whisper when he mentions it," Suzen said. He has never told her what happened, except that they broke them by stomping on them in "poop". Staff at the centre told Margo, Zack's mother, that he broke them. Zack was given new glasses, but refused to wear them. He said that the "eye doctor" was mean and put something in his eyes that burned so bad that he cried. The original glasses were turned over to Detective Lambert for analysis for faecal matter. Months later he said the SBI (State Bureau of Investigation) and the SBI labs did not have the ability to test for faecal matter. The glasses were never tested to see if Zack's story was true and by the time they got the glasses back, his parents were told, the evidence would have been lost. Suzen also questioned a very nervous receptionist at Cary Police Department about why they had not received a complete copy of the police report. He said they never give out the investigation notes.

> "I told him that was ludicrous, I have seen many reports in my own experience! I said 'Shame on all of you! How can you sleep at night?!' Naturally he said he slept very well. I guess it's just the babies dreaming about depraved behaviour that can't sleep. Is Caligula still alive or what?"

I contacted the local police department in Cary and the case officer Stephan Lambert confirmed to me that an investigation into Zack's claims was going on. In fact, he said he couldn't speak to me because there was an investigation. Then when I said: "So you can confirm you are investigating," he said "No, I can't confirm that." Only when I pointed out the nonsensical contradiction in those two statements did he confirm that indeed he was investigating. He said I could fax him my questions and he would ask his "superiors" if he could answer them. I faxed the following questions. (1) Where is the tape recording of the first police visit to interview the children? (2) Why did you tell the parents on the second visit that you would arrest the three women named, thinking that [a centre employee] would turn

State's evidence, and then not do it? (3) Why for six weeks did you tell the parents you had to keep Zack's glasses because it was a State Bureau of Investigation (SBI) case, and then say the SBI does not have technology to detect faecal matter? (4) Why do you feel that hearing from two completely different children that they saw a pre-school teacher take off her clothes does not constitute enough to go on? (5) Why did the parents get an incomplete police report? Not even one word written by an investigator. (6) Have you sought to question other parents at the centre about any strange remarks by their children? The police to this day have refused to answer any of those questions, but staggeringly Detective Lambert told Zack's parents that he did not interview other parents at the centre!

Does Kinder-care?

I rang the Kindercare centre itself and was told by the new director that she had no idea that such allegations had been made. Given that there was a police investigation into them, albeit an excuse for one, that was an extraordinary statement. The director put the phone down on me when I asked other questions, but she did confirm that two employees (two of the three Zack had named in his story) had left the centre. I also contacted the corporate headquarters of Kindercare in Portland and they issued a short statement to me through a very nervous PR person called Kathy Vandenzanden, saying that the claims were "unsubstantiated". Of course, sitting in a corporate office on the other side of America, she would have known. I faxed them this list of questions: (1) What is Kindercare doing to investigate the claims of these children? (2) Why, after one boy mentioned two names at the centre as involved in his abuse, did those two people leave the centre's employment? (3) Why did [an employee I name] leave this Kindercare Centre? Where did she go? Is she still employed by you elsewhere? If so, where? (4) Why did the person the boy calls…[a name]…leave the centre after the boy told his story? What is this lady's full name? Where is she now? Is she still employed by Kindercare? (5) Why has a new director been appointed at this centre and why did she tell me on the phone that she knew nothing of these allegations? (6) Is it correct that Kindercare have refused to allow [an employee named by Zack who still works at the Cary centre] to take a polygraph lie detector test? Kindercare would not answer any of those questions. I received a letter threatening legal action against me if I did not remove all the information about Zack from my website. Instead I began to add massively to that section by investigating the background to the owners of Kindercare with my Webmaster, Lauren Savage. Well, well, well. What did we find?

Hiding in the Kravis

Kindercare began in Montgomery, Alabama, in 1969 and now has its corporate offices in Portland, Oregon. It employs 22,000 people at 1,149 centres in 39 states and has child care contracts with the Disney and Lego organisations. It turns out that Kindercare, the leading child-care organisation in the United States, is owned by the empire of Henry Kravis, a very close friend of George Bush, the reptilian shape-shifter, who is one of the world's most famous paedophiles and child killers.

Figures 37 and 38: *The ancient Egyptian symbol, the Eye of Ra, used by Kindercare in its publicity until this was pointed out on the David Icke website. But the Kindercare pyramid with the capstone missing remains in use*

Kravis is also closely connected with Henry Kissinger and the Rockefellers, both Illuminati to their core. Anyone this close to Bush must know of his paedophile activities, surely? Kravis was a member of the inner circle of the Republican Party around George Bush. Kravis' company, Kohlburg, Kravis, and Roberts, which owns Kindercare, made massive contributions to the Republican Party and the George Bush campaign for the Presidency. Kravis and Roberts also gave personally. One fundraiser at the Vista Hotel in Lower Manhattan, co-chaired by Kravis, raised $550,000 alone for the Bush fund. In all, their combined contributions to Bush's election fund totalled millions. In January 1990, a year after Bush's inauguration as President, Kravis was chairman of his Inaugural Anniversary Dinner. Kravis has also given considerable donations to the cause of Zionism and to celebrate Bob Dole's birthday. Kravis threw a $300,000 fundraising bash for Dole, the Republican Presidential candidate and lover of money for services rendered.

Illuminati everywhere

There is a network of Illuminati front organisations that have been increasingly exposed in recent years. Among them are the Bilderberg Group and the Council on Foreign Relations, and I will say more about this network in a later chapter. Henry Kravis, owner of Kindercare, is a member of the Council on Foreign Relations and has attended meetings of the Rothschild-Rockefeller-Kissinger-orchestrated Bilderberg Group. He was on the guest list at the Bilderberg bash at Turnberry in Scotland between May 14th-17th, 1998. His second wife, Marie-Josee Kravis, a senior fellow at the Illuminati-funded Hudson Institute, is also a Bilderberger and member of the Council on Foreign Relations. Her other connections include being a columnist on the Canadian Financial Post, a director of the Canadian Imperial Bank of Commerce, Ford Motor Company, Hasbro, Inc., Hollinger International, Inc. (headed by Bilderberger insider, Conrad Black), and The Seagram Company Ltd (a fiefdom of those major Illuminati operators, the Bronfmans). She has a number of published works on economics, including Lessons of the Mexican Peso Crisis (January 1996), published by the Council on Foreign Relations Press. The peso crisis was actually manufactured by a ring of major banks, headed by the Rockefellers' Chase Manhattan. This lady is just as connected as her husband. Quite a duo. Chase, Salomon Bros, BT Securities, and Smith Barney, who also contribute to the Council on Foreign Relations, appear to be involved in the financing of Kindercare. According to a Securities and Exchange Commission filing by Kindercare, Peat

Marwick are the company's accountants. Peat Marwick are Council on Foreign Relations contributors, as are Kindercare's other auditors, Delloite and Touche. Kohlberg, Kravis, and Roberts, or "KKR", as they are known, donate to the CFR, also. Why the interest by Bush's friend Ray Kravis in the education of pre-school children? They can surely make far more money in so many other ways. Maybe he just wants to help children, eh? Yes, that's probably it. Kindercare also used the Eye of Ra, an ancient Egyptian and Illuminati symbol, in its publicity material before I started to investigate this (*see Figure 37*). When I highlighted this on my website, Kindercare immediately removed the symbol! But they still have their version of the pyramid with the capstone missing (*Figure 38*). What on earth has the Eye of Ra got to do with pre-school education advertisements? And another question, what chance do a five-year-old boy like Zack and his family have of taking on a corporate giant like this and ensuring a just and open investigation of their case?

KKR – Koup, Kollapse it, and Run

KKR are based at 9 West 57th Street, Suite 4200, New York NY 10019. In 1997, they acquired approximately 85 per cent of Kindercare's stock. They moved its corporate headquarters to Portland, Oregon, after the takeover. David Johnson, the CEO of Red Lion Inns, a KKR company based in Portland, became the new CEO of Kindercare. They also replaced virtually the entire corporate staff. Kohlburg, Kravis, and Roberts are a New York "investment firm" specialising in leveraged buyouts, which are often hostile, and they use massive amounts of borrowed money. They often result in the dismemberment and/or bankruptcy of once solvent companies. KKR is Jerome Kohlburg Jr, Henry Kravis, and his cousin George Roberts. Its deals have included RJR Nabisco ($25 billion), Beatrice Foods ($6 billion), Safeway ($5 billion), and Owens-Illinois ($4 billion). Dealing continued in the 1990s with the Bank of New England, K-III Holdings (consumer magazines), and TW Holdings (Denny's and Hardee's restaurants). Other holdings include American Re-Insurance, Duracell, First Interstate, Fred Meyer, Stop & Shop, Union Texas Petroleum, and Walter Industries, according to Hoover's Handbook of American Business 1993. KKR has also acquired the publishing and media operation, PRIMEDIA (which has included magazines like *New Woman* and *Seventeen*); online mortgage lender Nexstar; Regal Cinemas, which have more than 4,100 screens at about 430 theatres in more than 30 states; and the controversial "in-schools" TV network, Channel One. Foreign subsidiaries picked up in the takeovers have included Del Monte Malaysia; Del Monte International in Panama; and Bandegua (Guatemala); the Philippine Packing Corp; Associated Biscuits Malaysia; and R.J. Reynolds Tobacco in Malaysia. Their financial backers included Metropolitan Life Insurance of New York, Prudential, Aetma, North West Mutual, Manufacturers Hanover Trust, Bankers Trust (a backer of Kindercare), and state pension funds in Oregon, Washington, Utah, Minnesota, Michigan, New York, Wisconsin, Illinois, Iowa, Massachusetts, and Montana.[6] I ask again. Why would a company like this want to run a pre-school operation? Put all this information together and there's a stench that defies fumigation.

Here's George again

John W. DeCamp, a former state senator for Nebraska, wrote a book called *The Franklin Cover Up: Child Abuse, Satanism, And Murder In Nebraska* (AWR Inc., Lincoln, Nebraska, 1992). In this, he details his knowledge of child abuse involving very famous names, including George Bush (father George). He was investigating a massive savings and loans fraud at the Franklin Credit Union involving a prominent republican called Laurence King, who sang the national anthem at the Republican Conventions of 1984 and 88. During these investigations, DeCamp discovered that King was also running a paedophile ring in Omaha, Nebraska, involving the chief of police, the owner of the local newspaper, and many other prominent people. In a video interview made in 1997, and now available through Hidden Mysteries at the David Icke website, he tells of a court case in which a young man was warned that if he told the truth about his abusers he would go to prison for 20 years. They had already done this with a young woman who was abused by the same prominent people. The man chose, hardly surprisingly, to keep quiet. DeCamp describes what happened when he approached the judge:

> "[I said] 'you know, I am so depressed. I love our system so much. I just...' The judge was well...he just kept saying over and over, 'I'm just a man, I'm not a god. I'm just a man, I'm not a god. I can only do with the things I'm given, the evidence.'

> "He was right, I suppose. I said, 'Everybody knows the truth. Everybody knows the truth. Every official, every judge, including you.' He said 'yeah' ...then he said something else. He said 'I can't change it but I can help you understand it. If you want to understand Franklin, if you want to understand the Franklin cover-up, you want to understand what really happened, go read Billy Budd. If you want to understand what happened in Franklin – you won't agree, you won't like it – go read Billy Budd.'

> "I said, 'Who the blazes is Billy Budd?'

> "He said 'Just go read it, you'll understand.'" [8]

DeCamp said the story of Billy Budd did help him to understand why a young abused woman went to prison; why 20 people he identified in his books were killed; and why things are as they are in Washington DC. *Billy Budd* was written by Herman Melville, the author of *Moby Dick*, and it is set in the "great" days of the British Navy when "Britannia" ruled the waves. Billy Budd is a teenage boy who finds himself in a squabble with a tough guy superior on a British ship. The superior dies in an accident, but Billy Budd is charged with his murder and faces a court martial. A series of witnesses testify that Billy is innocent and that the dead superior was probably one of the most vile people on Earth. But despite this evidence, the officers on the court martial decide that they can't find him innocent because it would break down the system of absolute control they believed was necessary to prevent a mutiny. And there you have it. Innocent people go to jail, guilty people go free, and untold numbers of abused children go unheard to keep the system of control in place by protecting the famous political, economic, media, and military names, who abuse, torture, and sacrifice children. They know that if the truth came out the people would mutiny. I've got news for them…the truth *is* coming out.

The experience of Zack has been suffered by millions of other children all over the world and it continues today. The trauma compartmentalises the minds of most them so they can't remember until much later in life or even not at all. Most of the rest are so terrified by the consequences of speaking about their experiences that they stay silent. That's why Zack is such a brave little boy. Those that do tell their story are faced with a system structured to suppress public exposure. The next time people want to close their minds to a child's "fantastic story" of ritual abuse, they should remember that.

SOURCES

1   *Sunday Mirror*, October 24, 1999

2   Ibid

3   Quoted by Andrew Boyd in *Blasphemous Rumours* (Fount Paperbacks, an imprint of Harper Collins, London, 1991), p 30

4   *The Deadly Deception*, p 149

5   See also ***http://www.davidicke.com/icke/index1a.html***

6   *Who Owns Whom 1990: Australia & Far East*, *Merchants Of Debt*, George Anders, *KKR And The Mortgaging Of American Business* (Basic Books, 1992); Sarah Bartlett, *The Money Machine: How KKR Manufactured Power And Profit* (Warner Books)

7   Aleister Crowley, *Magick Theory And Practice* (Dover, USA, 1929), pp 95 and 95

8   Full interview available through Hidden Mysteries at ***www.davidicke.com***

CHAPTER 16

"Spiritual" satanism and "christian" conmen

Nothing is easier to manipulate than genuineness that isn't streetwise.

David Icke

Christianity claims to oppose the force known as "Satan" and yet there are many themes of Satanic ritual within its beliefs and ceremonies. There are indications that the ritual of the Eucharist is a reflection of earlier rituals related to human sacrifice and blood drinking. There is the emphasis on symbolically eating the body of "Jesus" and drinking his blood as red wine. We might expect, therefore, that the Christian Church would be a front for Satanism and its blood and sacrifice rituals. That, it turns out, is precisely what it is.

Today the religions of the world remain a major tool of the Illuminati agenda. They maintain the climate of unquestioning, unthinking, ignorance, and their pseudo-morality provides a veil of hypocrisy, behind which the most sickening abuse of children can be hidden. Some of the most famous church "leaders" and evangelists on the planet are Illuminati operatives who use religion to manipulate and brain-wash their followers while engaging in Satanic rituals that beggar belief. That is not to say everyone is involved in these horrors, of course not. Most of the advocates of these religions would be as outraged as the rest of us if they realised what was going on. But religions are also compartmentalised pyramids that allow the knowing to manipulate the unknowing. Satanism and child abuse are an epidemic within religious institutions, and the wave of child abuse cases in the Roman Catholic Church and others are a tiny, tiny fraction of what is really happening. What better way to hide your Satanic rituals and networks than within a "Christian" church that condemns the work of "Satan"? What better way to hide your child sexual abuse than within a "Christian" church that worships "gentle Jesus"? And, with so many churches built on ancient pagan religious sites (energy vortexes and ley lines), the Satanists desire access to those "Christian" buildings for their rituals. This they can do if they control the church. Dr Loreda Fox is a Christian psychiatrist who has worked with many victims of Satanism and trauma-based mind control or Multiple Personality Disorder. She wrote in the *Spiritual And Clinical Dimensions Of Multiple Personality Disorder* (Books of Sangre de Cristo, Salida, Colorado, 1992):

"Some Satanists have invaded the church as it is the perfect cover for them. They masquerade as angels of light and gravitate towards positions of leadership in order to have more influence. Because much of what they say is sound doctrinally, they are rarely detected. Most survivors whom I have worked with had Satanist parents who were in high positions in churches; many were pastors." [1]

Billy Graham, the mind-controlled satanist

Note that she did not say *some* or even *many* of those Satanic parents were in high positions in the churches. She said *most*. The Illuminati deploys its agents, all of them under mind control of some variety, to lead their religious believers into the clutches of the Anunnaki agenda or "New World Order". One such man is the most famous evangelist in the world, the American Billy Graham, who is a 33rd degree Freemason and a practising Satanist. He joined the Freemasons some time around 1948. Graham is a friend of the shape-shifter, paedophile, and serial killer, George Bush, and they famously "prayed" together, according to Bush, the night he ordered the genocide in Iraq in 1991. That same year, Billy Graham said on his US radio show, *Embrace America 2000,* that the American people should support Bush's New World Order. Graham has also said that he thought UFOs could be the angels of God. Graham is close to Henry Kissinger, one of the most active manipulators for the Illuminati at operational level. Another friend was Allan Dulles, the Satanist Director of the CIA. Dulles helped to fund Adolf Hitler and founded the Illuminati's World Council of Churches. Dulles was also, significantly, one of the main architects of the infamous MKUltra mind control project. Agents of the Illuminati, like Graham, are all subjected to Multiple Personality Disorder programming. Through this, they are given cover personalities within a mind fractured into different compartments. The front compartment or "altar", the one that normally interacts with the daily world, may be of a church leader, a top politician, a doctor, and generally people who would never be suspected of being involved with the Illuminati's Satanic ritual network. "Oh, he'd never do that" is the response they are looking for if the truth ever threatens to come out. These programmes can give someone like Billy Graham a word-perfect grasp of Biblical doctrine, while his "back altars" or personalities take part in Satanic sacrifice ritual. This is why we should not view many of these people harshly. They, too, are victims of the other-dimensional entities, which inhabit their bodies and control their minds. David Berkowitz, the serial killer in New York known as the Son of Sam, said he was part of a Satanic group that had orchestrated the murders. In letters to a church minister, he revealed the kind of people involved in ritual human sacrifice:

"...Satanists (genuine ones) are peculiar people. They aren't ignorant peasants or semi-literate natives. Rather, their ranks are filled with doctors, lawyers, businessmen, and basically highly responsible citizens...they are not a careless group who are apt to make mistakes. But they are secretive and bonded together by a common need and desire to mete out havoc on society. It was Aleister Crowley who said: 'I want blasphemy, murder, rape, revolution, anything bad'."[2]

So there is nothing contradictory about Billy Graham being a Satanist and the world's most famous evangelist. Researcher Alan Walton writes: "These reptilian hybrids often lead a double life involving dual personalities, one which leads a "normal" life in the outer world, and one that is deeply involved with the underground alien society on a nocturnal basis."[3] He says this is especially true of what he calls "cocooned/hosted" individuals and "hybrids/abductees". Graham's bloodline goes back to Jakob Frank, the leader of a "Hebrew" Satanic cult called Sabbatianism and this later became known as Frankism. The Rothschilds were involved with Frankism (see ...*And The Truth Shall Set You Free*). Jakob Frank taught his followers to "convert" to another religion and to use that front to hide their Satanism. When Graham's ancestors first came over to America, they were from the Frank family. The American researcher Fritz Springmeier, himself a Christian, exposed Graham as a Satanist in his book *Be Wise As Serpents* in 1991. He expanded on this theme with the recovering mind control victim Cisco Wheeler in their book *The Illuminati Formula To Create An Undetectable Total Mind Controlled Slave* (Springmeier, SE Clackamas Road, Clackamas, Oregon, 97015, 1996).[4] Their sources included eyewitnesses and those who claim to have been abused by Graham. Among other sources was a member of the Illuminati's Council on Foreign Relations who is secretly against the New World Order; an operative with the US National Security Agency, who opposes the Illuminati; a high-level CIA administrator; Satanists and ex Satanists; a former 33rd degree Freemason; and various people who have worked with Billy Graham. On only two occasions, Springmeier and Wheeler say, were any of these people aware of what the others had told them. Phillip Eugene de Rothschild, who claims to have been conceived and brought up by Baron Philippe de Rothschild in France, says that he was given a front-altar personality as a pious Christian, which covered his Satanic programming. He was programmed ("dissociated") to infiltrate the Christian Church for the Rothschilds and the Illuminati network. In an Internet account of his life, he says:

"Like the hundreds of thousands of this occult family's other biological children, I had my place and function within this clan's attempt to control the world. My efforts and my family's efforts strove to have a member of the European nobility of the Habsburg family assume the pre-eminent position over humanity, a position called the Antichrist by Christianity. While others were seeded into government, academia, business, or entertainment, my place was within the Body of Christ. I was to be a focus for spiritual power and controller of a cult within this Church. In this Church have lived people who I have known all my life to be the controllers and power centers of both the Rothschild family's false prophet and the antichrist.

"Many dissociated Christians in the Body of Christ hold similar corporate spiritual, occult positions as part of the Satanic new world order. In my being I embodied the

Luciferian morning star within the Church. I represented the presence of all the other Satanists who were related to me in the morning star; their spirits were present in me in the Church. Constructed through ritual but empowered by legions of [demonic] spirits, I was a human and spiritual focus of corporate Satanic energy into the Body of Christ ...

" ...For the Rothschilds, and for Satan himself I am sure, this was the ultimate sadistic irony in using Christians to bring in the antichrist, but there is a certain demonic brilliance to it. By seeding the Body of Christ with his occult followers, Satan has been able to generate the spiritual and sociological forces that are required to bring in the false prophets and the antichrist's reign." [5]

Billy Graham is another such programmed front for Satanism in the "Christian Church". The trail to Graham was picked up in stages during general research into the Illuminati and you only have to look at the people behind him to realise that he is a pawn of the bloodlines. The newspaper tycoon William Randolph Hearst, a high-degree Illuminati initiate, funded his early "crusades". The Hearst mansion in California is furnished with hundreds of ancient Egyptian and other Near and Middle Eastern artefacts. Most of them are original and were shipped to the United States by Hearst at enormous expense. It was Hearst's support for Franklin Delano Roosevelt that won "FDR" the Democratic nomination and the presidency in 1933. Roosevelt, the wartime president, was one of the great Illuminati frontmen of the 20th century (see ...*And The Truth Shall Set You Free*). The Rockefellers, Witneys, and Vanderbilts, all Illuminati bloodline families, have funded other Graham "crusades". Ever wondered why Billy Graham has had such a close association with so many US presidents? According to the research of Springmeier and Wheeler, a high-ranking Scottish Rite Freemason and Mafia operative called David Hill lived for two years at Billy Graham's house. He was a friend of Graham's son, Franklin, they say. David Hill claims to have introduced Graham to the Mafia boss Joe Banana. Hill apparently turned against his former bosses and spent 18 hours over two days in a hotel room warning Graham about the Illuminati agenda. Springmeier and Wheeler report: "Billy Graham told David Hill at the end of their two days of talking in this eastern US hotel room that he was 'a captive of that [New World Order]'." They add: "Billy Graham has the choice of continuing his job for them, or being destroyed. Since they created who he is, they can destroy him. And he knows it." [6] David Hill was murdered when he had completed a manuscript exposing the Illuminati plans, they say. In March 2001, Springmeier and his wife Patricia were raided by the FBI and the Bureau of Alcohol, Tobacco and Firearms, the agencies involved in the mass murder at Waco. Springmeier's research was taken together with money and other items. A breathtakingly biased and distorted news story followed. Usual technique.

Springmeier and Wheeler say that when Graham's crusade went to Portland, Oregon, where they live, his staff was able to contact many recovering victims of trauma-based mind control and Satanic ritual abuse. How could they do that?

They were invited to a meeting with Graham. At this meeting, some of the victims say, Graham used a series of classic trigger words and phrases to re-establish their programming. Graham has surrounded himself with Freemasons, including William M. Watson, the Director of Graham's Evangelistic Association and a chairman of the Illuminati's Occidental Petroleum Corporation; and David M. McConnel, another director of Graham's "Association", and US ambassador to the United Nations (1968-69). The latter is an important Illuminati post also held by the Illuminati's George Bush and Madeleine Albright. Graham has supported the "ministries" of Robert Schuller, Norman Vincent Peale, and Oral Roberts, all 33rd degree Freemasons, according to Springmeier and Wheeler. Phillip Eugene de Rothschild told me the following about Oral Roberts and his son Richard Roberts from his own direct experience in the Satanic network of the Illuminati:

> "Oral Roberts succeeded in hijacking contemporary American Christianity to worship a different Jesus under the power of a different holy spirit. Oral has been (and still most probably is, despite his retirement) an occult priest of the old Sumero-Akkadian mystery religion. Satanism in its most pristine form. Mr Roberts was my occult spiritual mentor and indoctrinator. He has been the closest of friends to my Rothschild family and to Prince Philip... Mr Richard Roberts is a corrupt tele-evangelist from Tulsa, Oklahoma. Richard is now actively enlarging the occult spiritual legacy of his father. Mr Roberts is an occult sorcerer par excellence who is empowering the apostasy of contemporary American and Western Christianity." [7]

The evangelists Robert Schuller and Norman Vincent Peale offer a similar story. Schuller, like Graham, is sexually served by women from the Illuminati mind control programmes. Peale, a good friend of Graham, is a 6th-degree Illuminati through the Pilgrim Society, another strand in the web. By far the largest number of "new converts" from Graham's New York Crusade have been handed to Peale's church. Oral Roberts has been seen by Springmeier and Wheeler sources taking part in Satanism and mind control. The Charismatic Movement is an Illuminati creation. Graham helped to launch the Oral Roberts University in Tulsa, Oklahoma. The Southern Baptists, of whom Graham is a member, are Illuminati controlled, through the Freemasons. Jesse Jackson, another Illuminati "preacher" and friend of Graham, is a Prince Hall Freemason, the order for black people. What a monumental fraud this guy Jackson is, but then he's not alone. The 33rd degree of the Scottish Rite of Freemasonry is an honorary degree and can only be attained at the behest of those who control the 33rd degree from its supreme headquarters in the serpent-decorated temple in Washington. Jim Shaw, who was initiated there, said in *The Deadly Deception* that he saw some very famous faces at the ceremony:

> "There were some extremely prominent men there that day, including a Scandinavian king [King Gustav of Sweden is Illuminati and, of course, bloodline], two former

presidents of the United States, *an internationally prominent evangelist, two other internationally prominent clergymen*, and a very high official of the federal government, the one who actually presented me with the certificate of the 33rd degree."[8] (*My emphasis*).

They hail from Yale

Another famous Illuminati face within the "Christian" movement is Pat Robertson, the American television evangelist and close friend of the Bush family. Robertson is yet another product of Yale University, the home of the infamous Skull and Bones Society. Bill and Hillary Clinton graduated from Yale in 1973, Gerald Ford, a Yale Law School graduate, became President of the United States in 1974 after the Watergate scandal removed Nixon, and George Bush senior and junior are both Yale men who were initiated into the Skull and Bones Society. Interestingly, according to a History Channel documentary in February 2001, son Bush's Skull and Bones name was "Temporary"! In its windowless mausoleum across the road from the Yale campus, the Skull and Bones initiates take part in their blood rituals. These involve drinking from a human skull (see *...And The Truth Shall Set You Free* and *The Biggest Secret*). Jim Shaw reveals that the initiation into the 33rd degree of the Scottish Rite of Freemasonry includes drinking wine from a human skull. The Knights Templar, out of which Freemasonry sprang to a large extent, were accused at the time of the purge in 1307 of using skulls in their rituals, and indeed they used to fly the skull and bones flag on their ships. Pat Robertson's father, Senator A.Willis Robertson, helped to block the Congressional investigation into the banking and currency practices of the Illuminati's Federal Reserve Bank. Pat Robertson wrote in his book, *The New World Order*, that his father was Chairman of the House Banking and Currency Committee, and went on to chair its equivalent in the Senate. He said his father had:

> "...the hearty support of the banking committee [and] as I write this I am looking at a lovely sterling silver tray given him by the American Bankers Association at their annual meeting in San Francisco, October 25th, 1966. My father was also a colleague in the Senate of Prescott Bush, the father of George Bush."[9]

Robertson boasts in the book about his "distinguished heritage that goes back from colonial days to the nobility of England". Oh, I am surprised. His father's buddy, Prescott Bush (Yale, Skull and Bones), was one of the funders of Adolf Hitler via the Harriman Empire. A Harriman company, the United Banking Corporation (UBC) interfaced with the steel and banking network of Fritz Thyssen, who was acknowledged at the Nuremberg Trials as a major financial supporter of the Nazi war machine. It was through the UBC, headed by Prescott Bush, that vast sums were channelled from the American Illuminati bloodlines to fund Hitler's military expansion (see *...And The Truth Shall Set You Free*). No wonder Robertson lent his support for the "election" of President George W. Bush, or "Shrub" in 2000.

Figure 39: *The logo of Pat Robertson's Christian Broadcasting Network*

Figure 40: *The lion, white horse, and dove, of the Trinity Broadcasting Network*

Robertson claims to be a born-again evangelical Christian. He founded the Christian Broadcasting Network (CBN) in 1961 and is the host of its stunningly tedious daily talk show, The 700 Club. The Christian Broadcasting Network has received funding from Illuminati families and has their classic lighted torch symbol as its logo (*Figure 39*). The other major US Christian channel, the Trinity Broadcasting Network (TBN), has a lion and a white horse on its logo – both ancient symbols for the Sun – and the dove symbolic of the Illuminati goddess (*Figure 40*). If you are in America give TBN a watch. It is an experience you will never forget, nor will your eyes believe what they are seeing. Robertson was a candidate for the Republican presidential nomination in 1988 and a year later founded the Christian Coalition political pressure group. He was born in Lexington, Virginia in 1930, studied at the New York Theological Seminary, and was ordained into the Illuminati-controlled Southern Baptist Church in 1961. A 'Bible conservative', he says he believes in 'traditional values'. In 1981 he started the Freedom Council to recruit evangelical Christians for political action. He supported the then President George Bush in his re-election race in 1992 and Robertson's "Christian Coalition" or "The Religious Right" were massively involved in the Bush camp. Confidential documents obtained by CNN showed that Robertson hand-picked more than 30 Bush campaign leaders, and the Bush campaign had advance information on the printing and distribution of 40 million Christian Coalition voter guides favourable to Bush. In turn, he raised money for the Christian Coalition.[10] How ironic this is when you consider that George Bush is a paedophile, child killer, drug runner, mass murderer, and Satanist. How does that square with the alleged "Christian" beliefs of Robertson and his gang? But then there is far more to the "Religious Right" than religion. If, indeed, at its top level, there is *any* religion at all that would pass for Christianity. It's all a scam and I urge Christians to investigate who dictates their religion, just as I urge Jewish people to look at how they are manipulated mercilessly by their self-appointed leaders at B'nai B'rith, the Anti-Defamation League, the British Board of Jewish Deputies, and Bronfman-fronts like the Canadian Jewish Congress and the World Jewish Congress. These organisations that control the "Christian" and "Judaic" con men are themselves controlled by the *same* force.

As I was completing this book, George W. Bush nominated Senator John Ashcroft to be his top law officer as Attorney General. Ashcroft is another member of the Religious Right who appears to have emerged from the same do-what-I say-not-what-I-do-mould that spawned Pat Robertson. He describes himself as a Christian conservative who doesn't smoke, drink, or dance. He is against abortion because it takes a human life created by God and yet supports the death penalty. Go work that one out. Ashcroft's big claim to fame is his war on drugs and addictive substances and he demands the death penalty for some such offences. At the same time he has taken $44,500 dollars from beer companies since 1993, including $20,000 from St. Louis-based Anheuser-Busch. He has also been lauded by the booze industry in a video tribute produced by the Beer Institute of America. When Mother Jones magazine questioned this contradiction, Ashcroft said: "It's a product that is in demand. And when it's used responsibly, it's like other products." Oh, right, and the fact that it makes you money makes no difference, of course. Ashcroft also accepted money from the tobacco industry for his 1994 Senate race and said of tobacco that people should be free to make bad choices. Unless Ashcroft decides otherwise, that is. He is another Robertson-type clone who will typify the Bush administration – a far-right hypocrite with a selective "morality" that changes by the sentence to meet the needs of the moment.

Support the poor and needy...er, Pat Robertson

Pat Robertson, this man of Christian compassion, uses the viewers of his television station to support his business interests or rather "the poor and needy". He operates a massive media and business empire and it mixes very nicely thank you with his Christian "Ministry". One of his notorious business arrangements was in the Congo, formerly Zaire, which is now being ravaged yet again by an Illuminati war. Robertson's business there involved his friend, the vicious and criminal dictator, the late Mobuto Sese Seko. Mobuto raped his country's finances and placed billions of dollars in sequestered accounts in Switzerland and elsewhere. It was said that Mobuto could have solved Zaire's financial nightmare just by writing a personal cheque. Robertson tried to sell Mobuto as a bastion of Christian anti-communism who was maintaining the line against Marxist guerrillas in Africa in support of US interests. The two were close friends and on one occasion Mobuto wined and dined Robertson on his personal yacht during a business trip. Robertson set up the African Development Company to mine diamonds and this was also given lumber concessions by the Zaire Government – by Mobutu in other words. This is where Robertson's 700 Club, operated by his Christian Broadcasting Network, came in so handy. The members and other viewers were told that they were contributing money to "Operation Blessing" to help the needy in Africa. The needy, it seems, being better known as Pat Robertson, if what employees of this operation say is correct. Pilots for Operation Blessing told reporters that apart from a limited number of flights to transport medical supplies, most of their time in the air was spent ferrying mining equipment and other materials required for Robertson's African Development Company. One airman, Robert Hinkle, told the *Virginia-Pilot* newspaper:

"We got over there and we had 'Operation Blessing' painted on the tails of the airplanes but we were doing no humanitarian relief at all. We were just supplying the miners and flying the dredges from Kinshasa out to Tshikapa [the operations base for the African Development Company].

"We hauled medical supplies one time," added Hinkle. "It might have been 500 pounds at the most..." [11]

State officials in Virginia have refused to comment on the findings of an investigation into Robertson's charity and his diamond mine venture. The Virginia Office of Consumer Affairs has been "investigating" allegations of impropriety since June 1997 when a state senator first raised the issue of tax exemptions for Robertson, and possible consumer fraud. According to the *Virginia-Pilot* newspaper edition of October 1, 1998, State Attorney General Mark Earley refused to disclose any information or findings. Robertson contributed $35,000 to Earley's election campaign – the largest donation from a single individual. Would you take moral lectures from Pat Robertson? Would you buy a used Bible from him? No, nor even a new one. But millions do. Robertson has since condemned Mobutu in an attempt to distance himself from the scandal.

Many people don't realise that the Family television channel was created by Pat Robertson's International Family Entertainment (IFE). Robertson wanted, he said, a family values channel, which did not pander to the lower moral instincts of sex and violence. He then sold the Family Channel along with IFE to...Rupert Murdoch's News Corporation for nearly $1.7 billion! It made multi-millions for Robertson. His Christian Broadcasting Network held 3.8 million shares of International Family Entertainment (IFE). Robertson said that $136.1 million from the stock sale would be used to fund a global evangelism programme. CBN will also get an additional $109.3 million from a trust set up by Robertson using IFE stock. That money will become available in 2010. In addition, Robertson's Regent University sold its 4.2 million shares of IFE stock for $147 million. Robertson said the money would go into his school's endowment fund. [12] These are just a few of the headlines exposing the background of the man who seeks to tell Americans how to live their lives and who should govern them. The leader of the moral majority? Bullshit. Christianity and religion in general were created to deceive at their very foundation and they have been used for deception ever since. The guys who reach the top are those who know that the whole basis of the "faith" is nonsense. To them it is a money game and a means to support the agenda of their Illuminati masters.

The Church of Jesus Christ of Latter Day Hybrids

Wherever you look at the top of these religions you find either con men or Satanists, often both, and those who are simply too manipulated to see what is going on around them. The religious con men have a simple philosophy: I'll say what I need to say and be what I need to be to get what I want. In my experience so far, the most obvious Satanic church is that of the Mormons, or the Church of Jesus Christ of

Latter Day Saints, based in Salt Lake City, Utah. Cathy O'Brien in *Trance-Formation Of America* says the Mormon operation in Salt Lake City is a major centre for Illuminati trauma-based mind control. The Mormons were an Illuminati creation, as I mentioned earlier, and its founders were all high-level Freemasons and Merovingian bloodline. The Rothschilds supplied their funding. Joseph Smith founded the Mormons after an "angel" called Moroni appeared to him in 1823, as I outlined earlier. The Book of Mormon claims to be an account of how the "lost tribes of Israel" came to America. But there were no "lost tribes", as the Samaritan people confirmed. Joseph Smith also claims in his fairy tale that Jesus visited America to see the civilisation his chosen people had created. Smith became an Entered Apprentice Freemason on March 15th, 1842, and the next day was made a Master Mason. According to Freemasonic rules there should be at least a 30-day gap, but the Grand Master of the Illinois Lodge, Abraham Jonas, waived this. In his work, *History Of The Church*, Joseph Smith confirms he was a Freemason and notes that on March 15th 1842: "…I received the first degree in Free Masonry in the Nauvoo Lodge, assembled in my general business office." The next day he records "I was with the Masonic Lodge and rose to the sublime degree"(Master Mason). Dr Reed Durham, a president of the Mormon History Association, said:

> "There is absolutely no question in my mind that the Mormon ceremony which came to be known as the Endowment, introduced by Joseph Smith to Mormon Masons, had an immediate inspiration from Masonry. It is also obvious that the Nauvoo Temple architecture was in part, at least, masonically influenced. Indeed, it appears that there was an intentional attempt to utilize Masonic symbols and motifs…" [13]

If anyone is in any doubt that Mormonism is Freemasonry under another name, they should compare the Masonic oaths with those of the Mormons. Here is just one example: In the Mormon ceremony it says: "We and each of us do covenant and promise that we will not reveal the secrets of this, the Second Token of the Aaronic Priesthood, with its accompanying name, sign, grip, or penalty. Should we do so, we agree to have our breasts cut open and our hearts and vitals torn from our bodies and given to the birds of the air and the beasts of the field." The Masonic ritual says: "I …most solemnly and sincerely promise and swear…that I will not give the degree of a Fellow Craft Mason to anyone of an inferior degree, nor to any other being in the known world…binding myself under no less penalty than to have my left breast torn open and my heart and vitals taken from thence…to become a prey to the wild beasts of the field, and vulture of the air…". Joseph Smith's "Mormon" Endowment Ceremony was simply rituals from Freemasonry's Blue Lodge Degrees. Even their *underwear* is the same. On Mormon underwear a carpenter's square covers the right breast and over the left is a Freemasonic compass. There is an opening at the navel to symbolise the disembowelling penalty for disclosing Mormon secrets. They are told that their underwear will be their "shield and protection", especially the Masonic symbols, and they can only use their worn-out underwear for other purposes if they cut or burn out the areas depicting the Masonic square and compass. These instructions are straight from occult or ritual magic. Jim Shaw, the former 33rd degree Freemason, describes yet another Freemasonic connection to the Mormons:

> "A recommendation for acceptance is called a 'recommend' in the Lodge, as is the case with Mormons seeking admission to the secret rituals of the Mormon Temple. Much of the Mormon Temple ritual is the same as the Masonic Ritual, having been borrowed from it by Smith." [14]

The Mormon buildings are adorned with Illuminati symbols. The inverted pentagram, the most obvious of Satanic symbols, can be found on the Temple at Salt Lake City, on the Mormon museum nearby, and on other Mormon properties. The pentagram is used in rituals to summon demons in Satanism and, in its inverted form, is said to be the sign of "Satan", the Goat of Mendes, or Baphoment. This is the deity some of the Knights Templar were accused of worshipping when they were purged in France in 1307. Wherever you find an Illuminati Satanic operation, the symbols of the Sun and Moon will be prominently displayed. The Mormon Nauvoo temple included 30 2.5-ton stones depicting the radiant Sun and 30 moonstones before the building was destroyed. Smith said the Sunstone symbolised the Mormon's "Celestial Kingdom" – another steal from Freemasonry. Sunstones, Moonstones, Saturn stones, star stones, Earth stones, and a depiction of Ursa Major, are all to be found on the Salt Lake Temple. So, too, is the Illuminati's all-seeing eye, one of their most obvious symbols. The Mormons use the symbol of the beehive, a symbol of the Merovingian bloodline. This is hardly surprising with the two Smiths and Brigham Young from that genetic stream. The beehive is further symbolic of the ancient Goddess Artemis, also known as Diana. The Salt Lake Temple is built with granite, a rock that has been used throughout the ages for temples on Earth power centres and for esoteric initiation. When I spoke in Salt Lake City, near the Temple, I came across the fascinating book by William J. Schnoebelen called *Mormonism's Temple Of Doom* (Triple J Pub., Idaho Falls: 1987). Schnoebelen was initiated into the Wicca pagan religion, then into Freemasonry, before going through the Mormon initiation in the Salt Lake Temple. He shows in great detail that all three initiations were the same. They have the same oaths, secret handshakes, and garb. We are looking at one face hidden by many masks. Joseph Smith even used the Freemason's code for distress in his dying words. When a Freemason is in trouble he says: "O Lord, my God! Is there no help for the widow's son?" Smith's dying words included: "Oh Lord, my God, is there no help for the widow's son!" He also gave the Freemasonic sign of distress. Joseph Smith carried a dove medallion given to him by an English Masonic lodge and the dove is Illuminati symbolism for Queen Semiramis (El), the female deity in their Babylonian trinity and for the Dragon queens. Today the Mormons, as an important branch of the Illuminati, have a strong influence in Washington. Congressman Orrin Hatch, an elder (El-der) of the Mormon Church, is one of their representatives, but there are many others.

The rank-and-file Mormons who knock on your door or stop you in the street with their scrubbed faces and their smart clothes have no idea about any of this. When I visited Salt Lake City in 1999, two lovely Mormon girls gave me a tour of the temple site. One was from Thailand, the other from Hong Kong. They had been working day and night back home to earn the money to pay for their flight to America and all their expenses for the "privilege" of serving the church in this way. They told me what the hierarchy told them to tell all the visitors, and they repeated their script without question. I told them a few facts about the "Jesus" story and they said they had no idea this information existed. I asked them if there was any significance in the fact that the founders of the Mormon Church were Freemasons. They looked at each other in bewilderment and eventually one said "What are Freemasons?" This is the way the few control the many. Then there is the strange story of the toad, which Smith said appeared when he went to find the plates on which the Mormon religion was founded. Smith worked from time to time for the family of Benjamin Saunders. In an interview in September 1884, which is still in the Mormon library archives, Saunders says that Smith described how he saw a toad-like amphibian transform into a man. Saunders said:

> "I heard Joe tell my mother and sister how he procured the plates. He said he was directed by an angel to where it was. He went in the night to get the plates. When he took the plates there was something down near the box that looked something like a toad that rose up into a man which forbid him to take the plates. ...He told his story just as earnestly as anyone could. He seemed to believe all he said." [15]

In 1833, Willard Chase corroborated the story in an affidavit: "He saw in the box something like a toad, which soon assumed the appearance of a man, and struck him on the side of his head." Given the evidence available to expose the Mormon Church for what it really is, one may think that its followers must have also been struck on the side of the head by a blow of some considerable power. But so many people find blind faith a source of such comfort that they will defend their belief to the death, even though they, themselves, are victims of it. You can find more detail about the real Mormon Church in the Religious Archives at *www.davidicke.com*, and elsewhere on the Internet. There is a Mormon expose site run by two former Mormons, Jerald and Sandra Tanner, at www.utlm.org. Sandra Tanner is the great, great, granddaughter of Brigham Young.

Mormon satanism

So the Mormon religion was founded by Freemasons, uses Freemasonic, Illuminati, and ancient rituals and symbols, and is big into blood atonement and terrible vengeance for revealing the secrets. It has all the signs of being a front for Satanism and so it is. I have received many testimonies from the victims of Mormon Satanism and mind control and the following story is indicative of all of them. It comes from a woman who was brought up in the Mormon faith in Utah. She told me that "most of the early faithful were from the Merovingian bloodline, which is Illuminati" and that the abuse of children was handed down through the generations to create robotic-slaves of trauma-based mind control. "They helped each other by abusing each others' children and traumatising them to split their minds," she said. It is interesting how many "faiths" encourage, even demand, that people marry within their "church". As researchers of trauma-based mind control have established, the Illuminati are looking for families with a history of child abuse and trauma because each new generation of these bloodlines becomes more open to mind control as their DNA is reprogrammed by the experiences. To have family networks of abused children is to have a breeding ground for those who are more open to mind control than the rest of the population. If you ensure that these family networks are of the Anunnaki bloodline, you have hit the jackpot. You have people who are both very open to mind control and, through their genetics, it is easier for the fourth-dimension entities to "possess" their bodies. The Mormon Church, of course, is obsessed with genetics and bloodlines and its massive genealogical data banks are used by the Illuminati to keep records of who has the reptilian bloodline and who does not. Researcher Alan Walton writes:

> "My genealogical line intersects with the ancestry of the English royal family, and from what I understand many of the hybrid lines have ended up in the neo-Masonic lodge known as the Mormon/LDS church, which serves as a cover for many of the old reptilian blood lines... possibly the reason why LDS prefer large families, i.e. to 'breed' out the normal human genetic lines to be replaced by reptilian/hybrid lines? I am familiar with many, many Mormon cultured hybrid abductees who are also MPD [Multiple Personality Disorder]. However I have also found that there is tremendous pressure placed on these people especially in Utah (one of the major underground nesting areas for both reptilians and hybrids) NOT to discuss their abductions, even though the Mormon church officially does teach in the existence of extraterrestrial civilizations. There are, however, even more full-blooded reptilian and hybrid blood lines who reside permanently in the underground society, and who are sold-out Satanic worshipping, blood-festing, shape shifters." [16]

I will call my Mormon informant Jane, because, like most of the people who tell their stories, they are concerned for the consequences.[17] This is especially true when they have seen at close hand what these guys will do. She said the first Mormon ritual she attended was in Bountiful, Utah, wearing the dress her mother had made for her fourth birthday. A woman beat her with branches from a tree and she was told: "See, Jesus doesn't love you and he is not going to save you." This is straight from the manual of trauma-based mind control. Jane said the beating was so intense that she left her body and was watching herself being hit. This often happens in these circumstances and it is the mind "dissociating" (splitting, withdrawing and distancing itself) from the trauma. People of certain bloodlines with family histories of child abuse dissociate easily, and each time they do so another compartment is created in their mind. The woman who beat her was the one who welcomed the children at the Sunday school. When Jane saw her the next Sunday, she did not recognise her because the trauma had been compartmentalised. But she reacted by kicking and screaming, although she did not know why at the time. Since her memories have begun to return, as they have for many such victims, she recalled vividly being placed in a cedar chest and the lid secured. She was left in there until she lost consciousness and when she was revived she was told that Jesus didn't love her and that Satan had come to save her. This happened several times and was designed, obviously, to turn her allegiance to Satanism. She also has memories of nearly drowning many times. She says she was belittled, beaten, and starved. Her father would eat in front of her and her brother while they went hungry. Her mother was treated the same. All this is classic mind control technique. When people go for long periods without food and are mentally, emotionally, and physically exhausted, they are more open to suggestion. After world wars, for example, the global population is most open to suggestion because they are mentally, emotionally, and, at least many, physically exhausted. When Jane's family moved to Murray, Utah, her school sent her to a social worker once a week and he sexually abused her. She was told she would be in big trouble if she revealed the secret. As we've seen, children are often told that they or their loved ones, including their animals, will be slaughtered if they ever tell anyone. They are also drugged and made to perform sacrifices on other children. This is videoed and played back to them in a non-drugged state. They are told that if they don't do as they are told the police will be shown the video and they will be locked in prison. Jane remembers at least two occasions when her parents held her down and gave her a shot of something from a syringe, and the sexual abuse of her and her brother was incessant:

> "I was sodomized so badly during those years that I developed fissures in my rectum three different times. It never occurred to me to tell my mother because the programming to keep the secret was so in place. ...I just suffered in silence. I also remember this man using my mother for sex and she has no memory of it at all." [18]

She says she was taken to the most secret Mormon rites at the Salt Lake Temple at the age of 20. Instead of entering the temple through the front door, she was taken through a tunnel under the street. I was sent some material just after my visit to Salt Lake City, which was claimed to come from a military source. It described how the Mormon temple is on top of a reptilian underground base that could be accessed from the temple itself. Many ancient pyramids, temples, mounds, and other earthworks also had entrances to underground reptilian cities. Jane was taken through a tunnel to a place called the Pink Room. There she saw several of the Mormon leaders dressed in black worshipping Lucifer in a ritual called True Order of Prayer. This is a ritual form of the ceremony the regular Mormons go through with all the signs, tokens, and penalties. She said she saw one Mormon leader, a President Benson, tied to a chair and gagged when he refused to watch the sacrifice. When he still refused to participate, she says he was put in a white bag, like a laundry bag, and they all beat him. Jane also experienced the unexplainable disappearance of foetuses she was carrying:

"I would be fine and three or five months pregnant with not a sign of anything wrong and then I would not be able to feel my baby by feeling my abdomen or feel it move and I would not be pregnant. One time I was very far-gone, but I don't know how far, maybe seven months, and the baby disappeared and I was kept drugged for six weeks. When I came out of being drugged I felt my stomach and there was no baby.

"A couple of years ago I remembered delivering that baby in a room...I was attended by two men that I don't know and one said he was the father of the baby. After he was born, they held him up for me to see and I never saw him again and have never known what happened to him. I also remember having four babies removed from my body and them being sacrificed while I was tied to a cross shaped stone alter. Everyone had on black robes and hoods and we were underground in a cave or something. I also remember seeing two monsters fighting furiously dripping blood and fighting about what they were eating. They were reptilian and looked something like the dinosaurs that a teacher at school used to show us. I don't know what they were eating. I keep thinking that my mind wants to heal and I have to face that they ate my baby, but for now I can't handle it so I think of it as just a nightmare. I can't get the furiousness of them eating out of my mind. It is so horrific." [19]

I'm afraid that eating the baby is exactly what they were doing. The scene that Jane describes under the Salt Lake City Temple is the same as that described by Arizona Wilder at the rituals conducted for the British royal family at places like Balmoral Castle. When we read all those ancient stories of sacrifices to the "gods", including the thousands sacrificed by the Aztecs of Central America alone, we are looking at literal sacrifices to literal "gods". Jane said: "The blood that they crave is like a homeopathic formula for our feelings and thoughts to be transmitted to them." She said that she would see the greys and tall beings with black robes. Her children and daughter in law would also see them, she said. "[What] was so weird is that we could feel them around, but not always see them. They seemed to delight in showing themselves to me separately when I was alone." Her daughter-in-law became pregnant with twins who disappeared before birth and she became an alcoholic, and committed suicide because of her experiences. Jane became pregnant again and, in May 1992, shortly after hearing strange, but familiar, "whooshing" noises in the house, she started to haemorrhage. She was rushed to hospital where only the placenta was found:

"The baby had gone and the cord was sheared off like somebody cut off a piece of liver, but that part had not bled, only where the placenta was tearing away from the uterus. The sac was entirely missing also. I was very upset and knew what had happened, but of course could not discuss it with the medical personnel. I now think that the first noises that I heard were beings coming to harvest the baby, but I was not asleep or controlled by the sound in the usual way. They must have gotten it later because when the placenta came out the baby had been extracted earlier." [20]

In October 1992, the month her husband died of cancer, she says she was lying on her bed with only a robe on when a light came through the window and burned a hole in her abdomen about the size of a pencil all the way into the organs. "It was probably the height of the uterus but to the right side a little bit." This caused a serious infection, she said, and she has since had huge burns on her abdomen. She recalls that the doctor asked how she got the burn and she could only tell him that it was there when she woke up. "I just told him he couldn't handle the rest of the story. He could not figure it out, but wanted me to have skin grafts and I told him no. He made the appointment and kept pestering me to go which I refused. I got it healed up after several weeks and it is smooth, but still quite red. The second time that it happened it was at least the size of a hand spread out." I have been told stories along the same lines by mind control and Satanic ritual victims in many religions because they are ultimately one religion, the Illuminati. Staggeringly, in the circumstances, Jane has shown enormous determination to recover her compartmentalised mind and, as this continues, more memories of what happened flood back into her consciousness reality. She has been helped, she said, by a deep faith in Jesus. I find that many recovering mind slaves hold on to a strong belief in Jesus and this appears to be part of their programming. It's the double bind. They use Jesus as the opposing polarity to "Satan" and play these off against each other in the victim's mind. So whichever aspect of the programming they access, they are connected to an Illuminati deity.

Jehovah's mind control cult

The Jehovah's Witnesses, or Watchtower Society, is another Illuminati religion used for mind control and a front for Satanism. It systematically disconnects its members from non-members in the way of all mind-control cults. The Jehovah's Witnesses are a replica of the Mormons, even down to the Freemasonic founders, like Charles Taze Russell. It's amazing how everything fits together in the world of the Illuminati if you are prepared to dig deep enough. The people and organisations that attack and abuse each other in public, or appear to be in competition, turn out over and over to be different masks on the same face. We are told the Mormons and the Jehovah's Witnesses are different organisations that stand for different "beliefs" and the followers of both would be aghast at the thought that they could be connected in any way. But the mass of unthinking followers in any religion are merely the fodder and the screen behind which the real business goes on.

Charles Taze Russell was from the Illuminati's Russell bloodline, which also founded the infamous Skull and Bones Society at Yale University. Russell was a Satanist, a paedophile according to his wife, and a friend of the Rothschilds. Indeed it was the Rothschilds who funded the Jehovah's Witness operation into existence, along with other Illuminati bankers. They enjoyed "contributions" from organisations like the Rothschild-controlled B'nai B'rith, which also helped the Mormons. This was proved in a court of law in Switzerland in 1922, according to researcher, Fritz Springmeier. One of the key people involved in these contributions was Frank Goldman who later became President of B'nai B'rith. Why would an organisation set up (in theory) to help Jewish people and promote the Jewish faith, be funding the Jehovah's Witnesses? I think the name Rothschild answers the question. Charles Taze Russell was a high-degree Freemason and Knights Templar. He promoted Zionism, another Rothschild creation, on behalf of his friends and backers.[21] Russell's family was formerly known as Roessel and went to Scotland from Germany. Both are massive occult centres. Germany is where the Rothschilds emerged and Scotland is one of the key areas of the world for Illuminati bloodlines.[22]

From the start, Charles Russell used his new Watchtower Society, based at Bethel, Brooklyn, New York, as a front for black magic, or Enochian magic as his brand of Satanism was called. He put the flying Sun disk on the front of his books, an ancient Illuminati symbol going back to Egypt and Babylon. *The Watchtower* magazine has always been a mass of subliminal and less subliminal occult symbolism and the very name, Watchtower, is part of Illuminati and Freemasonic legend and code. To them watchtowers are areas of the "magical universe", the unseen realms. Russell was buried under a pyramid in the United States after, according to some researchers, he was ritually killed on Halloween 1917. As I've said, these leading Satanists of the Illuminati are ritually killed when their time comes, so their occult power can be passed on. The Jehovah's Witness organisation is named over and over by survivors of trauma-based mind control for being involved, like the Mormon Church, in unspeakable mind control projects. The Mormons and the Jehovah's Witnesses are the same organisation at the top level where the El-ders of the Mormons and the Watchtower Society operate a very different agenda to the one revealed to their followers.

Jehovah's Witnesses are told to believe in and welcome Armageddon because that's the day the world will be destroyed and only they will avoid the holocaust. We billions of non-believers will perish. But I am quite looking forward to that when I think of what the world would be like with Jehovah's Witnesses in charge. The Jehovah prophets have predicted this Armageddon over and over since their religion was created, but as each date has passed, another date has been announced to replace it. Witnesses and their children are separated from society and only the minimum necessary contact with non-believers is encouraged. This isolates them from other information and visions of reality, and families are broken up by disconnecting Witnesses from non-Witnesses. While this isolation from mainstream society goes on, they attend meetings three times each week to be brainwashed with the religion's dogma, hatred, and fear. Look at these examples from their own publications:

"Is it proper for a Christian witness of Jehovah to have business relationships with one who has been disfellowshipped? Generally speaking, it would be desirable for us to have no contact with disfellowshipped persons, either in business or in social and spiritual ways."
(*The Watchtower*, December 1st 1952, p 735)

"In the case of the disfellowshipped relative who does not live in the same house, contact with him is also kept to what is absolutely necessary. As with secular employment, this contact is limited and even curtailed completely if at all possible." (*The Watchtower*, July 15th 1963, p 443)

"In faithfulness to God, none in the congregation should greet such persons when meeting them in public, nor should they welcome these into their homes." (*Organization*, 1972 ed. p 172)

As always with mind-control cults, which all religions are in the end, there is the pressure not to think or question:

"Avoid independent thinking! How is such independent thinking manifested? A common way is by questioning the council that is provided by God's visible organization." (*The Watchtower*, January 15th 1983, p 22)

"Fight Against Independent Thinking! Yet there are some who point out that the organization has had to make adjustments before, and so they argue: that shows that we have to make up our own mind on what we believe. This is independent thinking. Why is it the danger? Such thinking is an evidence of pride." (*The Watchtower*, January 15th 1983, p 27)

And then there is the call for Witnesses to hate in the name of their god. Very appropriate given the hateful nature of the Biblical Jehovah:

"In order to hate what is bad a Christian must hate the person with whom the badness is inseparably linked." (*The Watchtower*, July 15th 1961, p 420)

"We must hate in the truest sense, which is to regard extreme and active aversion, to consider as loathsome, odious, filthy, to detest. Surely any haters of God are not fit to live on his beautiful Earth. What do you do with anything loathsome or repugnant that you detest and abhor? The answer is simple. You get away from it or remove from your presence. You do not want to have anything at all to do with it. This must be exactly our attitude toward the haters of Jehovah." (*The Watchtower*, October 1st 1952, p 599)

I have met many people who have seen their families destroyed by the Jehovah's Witnesses and their mental dictatorship. Children will not talk to their parents, brothers and sisters (and vice versa) because they believe them to be evil for not worshipping Jehovah. When people leave the organisation, no matter how much they may have served its cause, they are treated like lepers and their children who remain in the religion, are told to hate them and refuse to speak

with them. The former Witness who sent those *Watchtower* quotes to my
website, wrote:

> "I was a Jehovah Witness for 37 years. I disassociated myself from the organization
> due to the extreme control and manipulation of the people. Because I choose not to
> be a Jehovah Witness I am ostracized and shunned. I am not allowed to see my
> relatives that are still trapped in a hard and cold and unforgiving religion. I am not
> allowed to see my nieces and nephews. The shunning laws are breaking up many
> families, causing many divorces, also driving people to suicide." [23]

But then what does the Watchtower leadership care? The organisation is not
there to serve the interests of its members. It is there, and always has been, to serve
the Illuminati. Witnesses are discouraged from listening to popular music,
celebrating festivals and holidays with non-witnesses, and urged to read the Bible
every day. The way they should interpret that Bible, however, is laid down by the
hierarchy in Brooklyn, New York (one of the Illuminati's global centres). They are
told to take everything literally and so when Acts 15:29 speaks of the need to
"abstain from blood", the Jehovah's Witnesses refuse blood transfusions even if it
means their child will die. What greater level of mind control can you have than
that? Hebrews 10:25 says: "Do not forsake the gathering of yourselves together"
and this is used to pressure people to attend Kingdom Hall meetings five times a
week. Not only the minds, but the clothing and hairstyles of the Witnesses are
monitored. Every area of their lives is dictated, including the movies and television
programmes they should and should not watch; celebrating birthdays; lotteries;
relationships after divorce; inter-racial marriage; drinking tea and coffee; wearing
cosmetics and jewellery; national anthems; contraception methods; oral sex in
marriage, and masturbation. The latter is forbidden, but then just allowing yourself
to take this crap would qualify you for the title of "wanker", surely? While all
Witnesses may not submit to all of these impositions to begin with, the repetition
defeats them in the end with the power of the group submerging the individual.
Serious rebellion is "counselled" and the threat made of "disfellowship". Some
have been thrown out for documenting the provable errors in Watchtower literature
and history. No questioning or rebellion against the leadership is tolerated, and
Witnesses are pressured to inform on each other. This creates the nowhere-to-run,
no-where-to-hide, mentality that is always used in mind control operations. The
micro-chip and the explosion of spy cameras are designed to have the same effect
on the collective mind. Doing anything "wrong" becomes so difficult to keep
private and the consequences of it become so harsh that in the end the most
determined of rebels can be worn down and battered into conforming. Encouraging
Witnesses to "confess their sins" to an El-der opens the way for unlimited
blackmail. Nor is the privacy of these confessions maintained, as former Witnesses
have confirmed. They are kept in a constant state of fear and unworthiness, another
foundation of mind control programmes. If you want to give your mind and your
life away, join the Mormons and Jehovah's Witnesses. In fact, join any religion.

If you look through the Religious Archives on my website, you will see the scale of Satanism and child abuse in the churches of all denominations. Protestant, Catholic, Mormon, Jehovah's Witnesses, Pentecostal, all of them. And they are a fraction of the cases that are known, let alone the far greater number that go unreported. What is even more sickening is the way such crimes against children and others are covered up to protect the "good name" of the church. Not only are the stories on which the churches are founded a blatant fabrication, they do not even follow the more positive aspects of those faiths. The most senior Roman Catholic in Britain, the Archbishop of Westminster, has been exposed for allowing a known paedophile to continue working as a priest. The church secretly paid compensation to two of his victims to keep them quiet and they never informed the police. The priest, Father Michael Hill, was sheltered from public exposure by Archbishop Murphy-O'Connor and appointed as chaplain to Gatwick Airport. There he abused a youngster who missed his flight and went to the airport chapel for comfort. Hill was jailed for five years in 1997. One of his many victims, then aged nine, told BBC radio: "He used to come in to me, kneel next to my bed and start reading me stories about Jesus…you know, the Lord…and he used to put his hand under the cover and down my pyjama bottoms. I used to hate it, you know, my worst nightmare." Archbishop Murphy-O'Connor, a man officially appointed by the Pope, was warned in 1983 that Hill was a child abuser, but continued to support him. The Archbishop says the church takes child protection very seriously. Oh really? I think priest protection and own-skin protection is a rather higher priority.

The new age, old age, religion

You would not think, on the face of it, that Christianity would have anything in common with the so-called "New Age", but it has. The New Age claims to have rejected the official religions to pursue a "personal" and "direct" connection with what we call "God". In fact, while I have much in common with the metaphysical basis of much "New Age" thought, that's where the connection ends. The "New Age" is just the latest Illuminati religion created to seize the minds of those who cannot be imprisoned by official religion or what we bravely call "science". Understanding the metaphysical nature of multi-density, multi-dimensional life, is far too close to the truth. Something must be done. So vast swathes of the New Age is populated by those in the ultimate illusion: those who are convinced they are thinking and feeling for themselves when they have simply given their minds away to another master. It could be a "channelled" entity from another density, "Ashtar Command" (an Illuminati-created myth of some extraterrestrial "saviours"), or the apparently endless stream of gurus and "Living Gods on Earth". I have seen many over the years on videos and at conferences of various kinds. The audience are in awe of these people and yet at least the majority, are either multi-personality programmed operatives for the Illuminati or consciously conning their followers. There is no difference between these New Age heroes and the television "Christian" evangelists who fleece and mislead the watching millions. The times I have heard these New Age saviours saying that some entity or other had said this or that had happened or was happening when it was provably not true. One guy told his fawning audience that he and his team had changed the vibration of the vehicle pollution in Phoenix, Arizona, and so dramatically reduced the fumes. This claim was greeted with wild applause. So when I drove through Phoenix later that same day, the fume cloud hanging over city and the pollution I breathed in must have been a figment of my imagination.

Sigh Baa, Baa

I can offer no greater example of the New Age conmen and the millions who hand over their minds to them, than Sai Baba. This guy is a guru figure worshipped as a "Living God on Earth" by vast numbers of people worldwide and at all levels of society. He operates from his "Ashram" in Puttaparthi, India. Thousands go there and just sit in vacant awe at this man in the long orange frock. I attended an event once in England in which the audience was asked to sing a song of worship to Sai Baba by a woman almost overcome with emotion for this "god". But do you know who Sai Baba really is? A paedophile, con man, thief and almost certainly worse. Don't take my word for it. Ask people who have worked closely with him for 20 years and more. Long-time Baba devotees, Faye and David Bailey, have massively exposed him as a colossal fraud from their own experiences and by collating evidence from countless others who have seen that Baba is a manufactured myth. The accounts of his sexual abuse of children, teenagers, and adult men, are enormous, and he is described as a thoroughly vicious piece of work. He is famous for producing "vibhuti", an ash substance, and "valuable" watches, rings, and trinkets "out of nowhere", by manifesting them from another dimension. The Baileys, and the stream of testimonies they have compiled, proved that the "vibhuti" was manufactured in tablets from roasted cow dung and kept hidden between Baba's third and fourth fingers until required to "manifest". The "valuable" jewellery turned out to be worthless trinkets purchased in the local village and elsewhere. Baba "materialised" a ring for David Bailey, which, the living god told him, was of great commercial value. When he took it to a jeweller in southern India for repair, the man in the shop immediately recognised it as a "Sai Baba ring". He said that the stone was a valueless zircon and underneath he would find a piece of silver paper to make the zircon glitter. When the stone was removed, there indeed was the silver paper and the jeweller said that the rings were made especially for Baba to "manifest". The Baileys also document how Baba has conned people and the local community out of tens of millions of dollars and how he is implicated in a number of murders. This is the man to whom millions have conceded their minds, left their families, and married others purely on Baba's say so. For the full details of Baba's child abuse and con trickery, contact Faye and David Bailey, read their quarterly newsletter, *The Findings*,[24] and see the Religious Archives on my website.

Religion and much of its New Age mirror is a cesspit of lies, corruption, hypocrisy, and iniquity. By that I don't mean everyone who goes to church, follows a faith, or operates within New Age circles. Hundreds of millions of genuine people are involved in the old religions and the New Age. I mean those who control these Illuminati fronts and use them as a veil for the very behaviour and abuse they claim to oppose. But they say there is one born every minute and, with religion, it must be every ten seconds. These guys can only manipulate religion so effortlessly because there seems to be an endless supply of people desperate to give their minds away. When the Baileys began to expose Sai Baba, a couple of his devotees phoned to say that they knew that what was being exposed was true. But, the couple said, "…he is God and God can do anything he likes". There are still Christians being injured and even killed who handle snakes. They do this because it says in Mark's Gospel, Chapter 16, Verse 17: "They shall take up serpents." Dewey Chafin, quoted in the American People Magazine, said: "See, I handle serpents because it's in the Bible, like a commandment. And I drink strychnine because the Bible says it won't hurt me. Now, either every word in that Bible is right or it's wrong."

And a few people can't control the world? It's a doddle.

SOURCES

1   Dr. Loreda Fox, *The Spiritual And Clinical Dimensions Of Multiple Personality Disorder* (Books of Sangre de Cristo, Salida, Colorado), p 196

2   Written in letters to a church minister and quoted in Blasphemous Rumours

3   See ***http://www.angelfire.com/ut/branton*** and ***http://www.reptilianagenda.com/***

4   *The Illuminati Formula*, pp 126 to 150. For more about Billy Graham read Springmeier and Wheeler's book, or *The Biggest Secret*, or go to the Religious Archives on my website, ***www.davidicke.com***. You will also find Graham material at ***http://www.deceptioninthechurch.com/polls.html*** and ***http://www.geocities.com/CapitolHill/8988/billy.htm***

5   Correspondence with the author

6   *The Illuminati Formula*, p 133

7   Correspondence with the author

8   *The Deadly Deception*, pp 104 and 105

9   Writing in his book *The New World Order*. See ***http://www.davidicke.com/icke/index1a.html***

10 ***http://www.davidicke.com/icke/index1a.html***

11 ***http://www.davidicke.com/icke/index1a.html***

12 ***http://www.davidicke.com/icke/index1a.html***

13   David C. Martin, *Mormon Miscellaneous*, October, 1975, pp 11 to 16

14   *The Deadly Deception*, p 29

15   Mormon library archives

16   See ***http://www.angelfire.com/ut/branton*** and ***http://www.reptilianagenda.com/***

17   "Jane's" experiences were detailed in correspondence with the author

18   Ibid

19   Ibid

20   Ibid

21   See *Bloodlines Of The Illuminati*, pp 313 to 364

22   Ibid

23   Correspondence with the author

24   ***http://www.saibabaguru.com***

CHAPTER 17

Serving the dragon: the future

Tell a lie loud enough and long enough and people will believe it.

Adolf Hitler

The Sumer Empire was the start, or rather *re*-start, of the Anunnaki takeover of Planet Earth, and the period we are living through today is designed to see its completion. If we take a deep breath and refocus our eyes, the human predicament could hardly be clearer. For the few to control the many, decisions affecting the many must be made by the few. This demands the constant centralisation of power over all aspects of life. And if you wish to control the entire planet, as the Anunnaki-Illuminati do, the major decisions must be made at a global level. Now look at what has been happening throughout these thousands of years since the last cataclysm. First there was Sumer – a centralised empire controlled by the same bloodlines. When that dismantled amid the squabbles of the "gods", this empire collapsed into its individual parts and, for a time, decision-making was decentralised. But the Anunnaki covert empire, which then began, has manipulated the world once more to the brink global dictatorship. In fact, in most areas of our lives, that is already the case. As the bloodlines and their influence expanded, especially from the Near and Middle East, tribes have been brought together into nations; the nations are being brought together into power blocs like the European Union; and the final stage, which we are now seeing unfold, is to bring the power blocs together under a world government, central bank, currency, and army. Game, set, and match to the shape-shifters – unless we awake from our hypnotic state. All this is not by accident, but by coldly calculated design and the structure they are planning to introduce can be seen in *Figure 41 (overleaf)*. Without it, the centralised control of the world by the Anunnaki would not be possible. Try controlling from the centre if the key decisions affecting countries and communities are being made by those who actually live there and care for the freedom of their fellow citizens. You would have such a potential diversity of decision-making and, therefore, decisions, that you could not guide the world in the direction that suits your agenda. The co-ordination would not be possible to make all the individual parts decide the same thing. But if you create a structure in which global policy in politics, business, finance, media, and military is decided by world bodies, all controlled by the same force, you can dictate to the entire human race while calling it "democratic freedom".

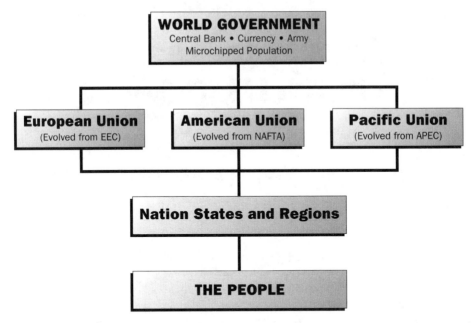

Figure 41: *The global fascist structure the Illuminati have been working towards for so long. We can see the world moving in this direction every day*

The more you centralise, the more power you have over people and events, and so the more you can centralise. This is one reason why the pace of the agenda has quickened, especially in the last 150 years, and is continuing to do so. Gathering the tribes together into nations took the longest time, but once that was achieved everything became so much easier. The takeover of the Native American lands by the Europeans was a wonderful example of how a vast culture of diverse tribes and decision-making was fused into a centrally controlled nation, the United States. This was achieved in a relatively short time because by then the Illuminati had built a power base within the nations of Europe, particularly, in this example, Britain and France. Under the tribal system, it was impossible for the Illuminati to centrally control the Native Americans. But under the US Federal Government, it is child's play to dictate centrally to a nation of some 260 million people today. I am not suggesting that we need to go back to living in tee-pees or caves, or operating in tribes. It is the level at which decisions are made that I am highlighting here. You can have a modern society and still have diversity of decision-making. The Illuminati are desperate for you to believe that this is impossible, and that the more we advance technologically the more we must centralise everything. This is not true; they just want you to believe that so they can justify their agenda.

The European fascist dictatorship

The Illuminati global web is now a maze of interconnected secret and semi-secret groups who are manipulating to the same end: the centralisation of power in all areas of our lives. It is these groups that have been responsible for the emergence of

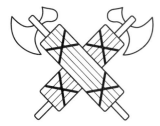

Figure 42: The fasciae is a symbol of the Roman Empire, from which we get the term, fascism. It symbolises individuality (people, countries) being tied together and ruled from above by the symbolic axe head – the Illuminati

Figures 43 and 44: Here we see the symbol of fascism used in the logo of the US secret society, the Knights of Columbus, and on the state seal of Colorado

the centralised fascist state called the European Union. Its structure is a mirror of the very symbol, the fasciae, from which the word fascism came. The fasciae is a symbol from the Roman Empire. It is a bundle of rods tied together with an axe head at the top symbolising the destruction of diversity and the imposition of top-down dictatorship (*Figure 42*). This symbol is used by many secret societies, like the Knights of Columbus in the United States (*Figure 43*), and can also be found in the US Congress Building and on the seal of the State of Colorado (*Figure 44*). The rods are the countries of Europe and the axe is the centralised dictatorship that now controls them. The European Union is classic fascism and this is precisely the governing structure they want for the world. The "EU" is a 100% Illuminati creation, manipulated into being by covert operators and a network of organisations co-ordinated by a secret society called the Round Table. This was first headed by the infamous Illuminati operative Cecil Rhodes, who left money to fund so-called "Rhodes Scholarships", which continue to finance the expenses and education of Illuminati-selected students from around the world to attend Oxford University. Here they are schooled to become Illuminati agents and, if they agree to serve their masters, they go back to their countries and later enter significant positions of power. Bill Clinton is an excellent example of a Rhodes Scholar and so is the former Australian Prime Minister Bob Hawke. The Rhodes Scholarship network connects with the Round Table and the rest of the web, and Oxford University is the centre of the Illuminati manipulation of global "education". It is no coincidence that an area near the present Oxford University was the site of one of the earliest Druid initiation schools founded in Britain.

The round table network

In *…And The Truth Shall Set You Free,* I have documented in detail how the European Union was founded by Illuminati placemen like Jean Monnet, Count Richard N. Coudenhove-Kalergi, Joseph Retinger, and others. They were the public face for the forces manipulating the creation of the centralised European dictatorship we see today. Retinger, a Polish "socialist", was also involved with Prince Bernhard of The

Netherlands, in the formation of the Bilderberg Group. This is an Illuminati operation funded by the Rockefellers and the Rothschilds. It was officially named after the Bilderberg Hotel in The Netherlands where its first official meeting took place in May 1954, but Bil can have many connotations. "Bil", for instance, was another name for "Thor", the first king of Sumer, according to the Edda, and Bil also relates to Bel, the ancient Sun God. Bil-der-berg actually translates, apparently, as "Bil or Bel of the Mountain". The Bilderberg Group is co-ordinated by lovers of humanity like David Rockefeller and Henry Kissinger. Prince Bernhard, a German Habsburg and former Nazi SS officer, married into the Dutch royal family, the Merovingian House of Orange. This is the same bloodline as William of Orange who played such a pivotal role for the Illuminati when he sat on the British throne, signed the charter to create the Bank of England, and started conflicts in Ireland that continue to this day. The House of Orange connects into the Orange Order, a "protestant" secret society involved in the conflict in Northern Ireland. The Orange Order, in turn, connects into the Freemasons, the Knights Templar, and so on. Bernhard is a close associate of Prince Philip and they operate that Illuminati front, the Worldwide Fund for Nature, which is exposed at length in *The Biggest Secret*. What a coincidence that all the key players behind the formation and subsequent centralisation of the European Union have been attendees of the Bilderberg Group, which has pursued a policy for the centralised control of Europe since it was officially created in 1954! The very official suggestion to form the Bilderberg Group came from Joseph Retinger, one of the founders of the European Community, now Union, and Prince Bernhard. The present chairman of the Bilderberg Group is the Viscount Etienne Davignon, another bloodline placeman with the perfect career record. He was vice-chairman of the European Commission in the 1980s, and Chairman of Societe Generale De Belgique – the massive banking and utility conglomerate in Belgium. He is also chairman of the Illuminati front, the European Round Table of Industrialists. This formulates policy for the European Commission, which then dictates to the European Union. Davignon is a founder member and president of AMUE, the Association for the Monetary Union of Europe, as well as being a member of David Rockefeller's Trilateral Commission, the European Institute in Washington, and a director of Anglo-American mining. European monetary union is a progression to the world currency. In his position as Industry Commissioner in the 1980s, Davignon was instrumental in turning European institutions from supporting small business to supporting big business. He did this by getting European industrialists, through his European Round Table of Industrialists, to draft European policy. This anti-democratic practice continues to this day. No wonder the Bilderberg elite chose this guy to replace Lord Carrington, the Rothschild bloodline, who was the Secretary-General of NATO before becoming Bilderberg chairman in 1991.

The Bilderberg Group (Bil) is part of a network of organisations, which are all masks on the same Illuminati face. They are controlled by the same people and have different roles to play in advancing the agenda of global centralisation. The others are the Royal Institute of International Affairs in London (RIIA), the Council on

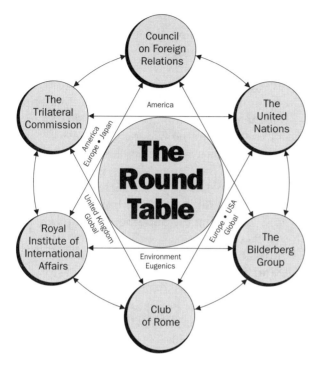

Figure 45: *The Round Table network. Different masks on the same face*

Foreign Relations (CFR) in the United States, and the Trilateral Commission (TC), which operates in the United States, Europe, and the Far East. From this point I will indicate members and attendees of these groups by using those abbreviations after their names. They are satellite organisations orbiting their central core, the secret society called the Round Table (*see Figure 45*). It was elite members of the Round Table in Britain and the United States who manipulated the First World War and wrote the "Balfour Declaration" in 1917 in which the British Government officially announced its support for a Jewish homeland in Palestine (see *...And The Truth Shall Set You Free* for the background detail). The Balfour Declaration was a letter sent by Lord Balfour, the Foreign Secretary and elite member of the Round Table, to Lord Lionel Walter Rothschild, who was funding the Round Table. The Rothschilds have controlled Israel since its foundation and funded the terrorist groups that bombed it into existence. This, by the way, is not a condemnation of Jewish people living in Israel, just a comment on the merciless way they and others have been manipulated by forces they have no idea exist.

The Bilderberg Group and the other strands of the Round Table network have among their number the top people in global politics, business, banking, media, military, "education", almost every aspect of human life. It is their job to co-ordinate the same policy through apparently unconnected countries, political parties, military commands, newspapers and media, business and financial organisations. These people are compartmentalised, as with all Illuminati operations, and there are basically three levels: **1** the inner core who know the big picture, and these are Anunnaki shape-shifters; **2** the regular attendees who know most of the picture, and they will be Anunnaki shape-shifters lower down the hierarchy; **3** those who are invited to a Bilderberg meeting because the Illuminati require a certain course of action from them at a particular time. Many of these will not be Anunnaki bloodlines, just manipulated stooges, who have their egos massaged and are made to think they have "arrived" on the world stage by such an invitation to rub shoulders with the "big boys". These guys will know little, often nothing, of the

Illuminati agenda. I have been talking and writing about the Bilderberg Group for more than 11 years and older researchers have been doing so for a lot longer. Those few journalists who even bothered to listen have dismissed this information as a crazy "conspiracy theory", but even some of those are now having to think again, purely by the weight of evidence. However, much as I welcome the increased attention focused on the Bilderberg Group and its network, I would stress that this is not *the* conspiracy, as many believe. It is merely one compartment of it. I have met Bilderberg researchers who have a padlocked mind to the wider conspiracy of which that is only a small part. The Bilderberg Group is not even close to being the centre of the conspiracy. It is an interface between the Illuminati and global politics, banking, business, etc., that's all. It is controlled by far more elite secret societies that dictate its actions and policy. Even the Round Table is not the top of the pyramid, only another strand in the web. Discovering the Bilderberg Group is to see one entrance to the labyrinth, not to locate its core.

I can give you a feel for how the manipulation works by listing some of the Bilderberg attendees. The Secretary-General of NATO, the head of the biggest military force in the world, is appointed by the Bilderberg Group, a private organisation that 99.9999% of the human race has never heard of. Take the last six Secretary-Generals alone, Joseph Luns, Lord Carrington, Willy Claes, Manfred Woener, Javier Solana, and George Robertson. All are Bilderbergers. How many people know that? Exactly. And how many know that James Wolfensohn, the President of the World Bank (and Rothschild partner), and heads of the World Trade Organization like Peter D. Sutherland and Renato Ruggerio, are Bilderbergers? Or US President Bill Clinton, UK Prime Minister, Tony Blair, the German Chancellor Gerhard Schroeder, and his predecessors, Kohl, Brant, and Schmidt? Or previous British prime ministers, Margaret Thatcher, James Callaghan, Harold Wilson, Ted Heath, and Sir Alec Douglas Hume, a former Bilderberg chairman? Hardly anyone knows this, including most members of their own parties! It was shape-shifter Ted Heath who signed the UK into the European "Community" in 1972 and government documents recently released under Britain's "30-year rule", have shown that Heath knew from the start that this would lead to a centralised European state. It was Douglas Hurd, Heath's close associate, who signed us further into the web with the Maastricht Agreement in February 1992, which turned a "free trade area" into political union. Since then the centralisation of power has continued to advance with the single European currency, the Euro, and now they are talking of a full-blown United States of Europe that will make nation states mere administrators of European law. They virtually are now. That has been Illuminati policy going back almost a thousand years to the founding of the Knights Templar. They wanted a United States of Europe even then.

I said way back in the 1990s that the Labour Party's Tony Blair (Bil) would be brought to power in Britain to take us further towards the single European currency and destroy British sovereignty. That is precisely what he is doing and unless British people wake up – and fast – this is going to happen. Among the prominent "opposition" Conservatives supporting Tony Blair (Bil) in the policy of taking the

UK into the Euro are Ted Heath (Bil), Kenneth Clarke (Bil), and Lord Howe (Bil). Because the Illuminati bloodlines are in the positions of power all over the world, they can activate apparently unconnected people in support of the Illuminati agenda. Thus we have the heads of Japanese corporations with factories in the UK threatening to close them if the UK does not join the single European currency. Tony Blair is delighted with these statements, of course, because they make his job easier. The manipulation of fear is the greatest weapon the reptilians have. Everything is based on this, and that's the idea behind the warnings from Japanese corporations. The Illuminati plan is to create American and Pacific Unions based on the same structure we have in Europe. One would encompass the whole of the Americas and the other would control the Asia-Australia region. The Illuminati are preparing to use the same method they employed in Europe by evolving these political unions out of the "free trade areas" called the North American Free Trade Agreement or NAFTA, and the Asia Pacific Economic Co-operation or APEC. Presidents father George, Bill Clinton, and now "boy" George, have all called for an Americas-wide extension of NAFTA. I said years ago that the Canadian currency would be artificially depressed to encourage the Canadian public to replace their currency with the US dollar as part of this political and economic union of the Americas. That "debate" has now begun as the value of the Canadian dollar has collapsed. You don't have to be a prophet to predict the future; an understanding of the Illuminati and their plans is quite sufficient.

The following are among the main foundations of their agenda. Some are already happening and others are in the process of being manipulated to happen. While I was writing this book in December 2000, it was agreed that the European Union would expand to include a dozen more countries and that many more decisions would be made by majority voting. In other words, countries would lose further rights to say "no" to a policy agreed by the European Union centralised state. Tony Blair made much of the fact that he refused to agree to majority voting on tax and social security decisions and this allowed him to paint it as a "victory" for Britain's national sovereignty. In fact, that was a smokescreen behind which the Illuminati plan for a European dictatorship could advance still further.

The world government

The United Nations was a vital achievement for the Illuminati. They tried and failed with their League of Nations after the First World War and so they engineered the Second World War to batter nations into agreeing to a global "forum" to replace, in Winston Churchill's phrase, "war, war" with "jaw, jaw." But as the Illuminati well knew, as did the committee of the Council on Foreign Relations that wrote the charter, the UN was only a stalking horse for a fully-fledged world government. It is the same ruse played out to evolve the European Union out of the European "Common Market". The plan has always been to create so many "problems" in the world that the only answer to them is perceived to be a global government to "sort out the mess" (problem-reaction-solution). What the public has not been told – until now – is that those pressing for the world government are the same people who are creating the problems to justify it. Another scam is to persuade us that a world government would be the way to bring all people together as one humanity, caring and sharing, and recognising we are all one family. Very nice sentiment on the face of it, but from the Illuminati point of view, that is their worst nightmare. They want humanity to be divided and ruled not united and free. They use terms like the "Global Village", "Global Commons", "Global Neighbourhood" and "One World" to manipulate people into missing the fundamental difference between "One World" (coming together in mutual support and co-operation) and a global centralised fascist dictatorship. Wasn't the United Nations supposed to achieve all the goals they are claiming for the world government? It's like the carrot and the donkey. They sell you a solution that involves centralisation and when that doesn't work (on purpose) they sell you another solution that involves more centralisation. The Illuminati, as my other books document, controlled the people who created the United Nations and they have controlled those who have administered its policy to this day. Even its headquarters in New York is built on land donated by the Rockefeller family, who also donated the land for the headquarters of the League of Nations. The UN building was previously the site of a slaughterhouse. With the Illuminati obsessed with blood sacrifice and symbolism, that is no coincidence.

The world central bank and currency

Money, together with fear, are the main weapons of human control. When you follow the bloodlines through history there are a number of themes that constantly recur: human sacrifice and blood rituals, war and conflict, and the system of lending people "money" that doesn't exist and charging interest on it. When you go into a bank and agree a "loan" they don't print a single new note, mint a single new coin, or move an ounce of precious metal a single inch. They simply type into your account the amount they have agreed to "loan". They have created "money" out of nothing and it has cost them nothing to do it. But from that moment you start paying them interest on that "money" which has never and will never exist. They call this "credit". The same force, the Illuminati, which created the banking system and controls all the banks, also created the political system and controls all the major governments. This has allowed these governments to pass banking laws that allow their banks to lend at least, and it is *at least*, ten times what they have on deposit. In truth, it is far more than that. Every time you put a pound or dollar in a bank, you are giving them the right to lend ten pounds or dollars they do not have. This system of so-called "fiat" money and "fractional reserve lending", means that banks can create money out of thin air whenever they choose. The deluge of debt, with which people, businesses, and governments constantly battle, is this same fresh-air "money". Personal debt, national debt, "Third World" debt – all of it. None of this really exists, except as figures on a computer screen. Think about the suffering, poverty, and death that these crushing debts cause every day and yet they are just figures on a screen written by a clerk in a bank. Nothing more. Imagine how the world would change if money was created interest free? They tell you that this can't be done because that's what they want you to believe. Of course it can. Both

President Kennedy and President Lincoln began to issue interest-free money. What else do these two men have in common?

Governments could create their own interest-free money and remove instantly the need to pay fantastic sums in interest to the private banks. Isn't that simple common sense? Then why does no government or major opposition party ever suggest it? Answer: (a) the Illuminati who control the banks control the governments and the hierarchies of the major political parties; and (b) most of the lower politicians in these parties are stunningly uninformed about the money system. I have even had to explain how money is created to professional "economists" before now. I kid you not. I met a retired bank manager in England some years ago and it was only in the last months before his retirement that it dawned on him that all the money he had been lending for the bank throughout his career was just an illusion. It had never actually existed. In the United States the trillions of dollars of government debt, serviced by the sweat and toil of the people, is "owed" to the US "central bank", the Federal Reserve. This was launched in 1913 by agents for the Rothschild, Rockefeller, and J.P. Morgan banking families (see ...*And The Truth Shall Set You Free*) and, ever since, the US government has borrowed its "money" from the "Fed". The head of the Federal Reserve is currently the Illuminati Satanist Alan Greenspan (Bil, TC, CFR), who took over from Paul A. Volker (Bil, TC, CFR). You get the picture. Greenspan attends the rituals at Bohemian Grove and, according to Phillip Eugene de Rothschild, is high up in the Illuminati ritual hierarchy. The "Fed" decides the interest rates in the US, a fact that has a fundamental effect on the world economy because of the interdependency the Illuminati have built into their system. It makes centralised control so much easier if you have key power centres where the decisions have a global effect, and frontmen like Greenspan ensure that one individual holds such power. It is worth noting that the first policy change made by the UK government of Tony Blair (Bil) was the announcement by his Chancellor of the Exchequer, Gordon Brown (Bil), that interest rates would no longer be set by the elected government, but by the Illuminati's Rothschild-controlled Bank of England, run by its governor, Eddie George (Bil).

Americans believe that because the word "Federal" appears in the title that the Federal Reserve is part of their Federal Government. This is not true. The Federal Reserve is neither federal nor has any reserve. It is a cartel of private banks controlled from Europe, i.e. the Rothschilds and the Illuminati. It has not produced audited accounts since it was formed in 1913 and yet this is the source of the national debt in the United States. This is how it works. When the government wants to borrow money it issues a government "bond" or "IOU" to the bank, say for a billion dollars. The bank then prints a billion dollars or simply creates it on a screen and this costs the "Fed" nothing because it pays the negligible cost of a few thousand dollars with more fresh-air "money". From that moment the US taxpayer begins to pay the privately-owned "Fed" interest on a billion dollars. More than that, the government's IOU, now in the Fed's hands, is counted as an *asset* of the bank and so it can now lend ten times its "value" (in this case ten billion dollars) and charge interest on that, too. This is happening in every country in the world!

When you go into a bank and sign over "collateral" for a loan, the same scam is played. Your house, land, or business is counted as an asset of the bank and they can lend ten times its estimated value to other customers. When you take out a loan you are borrowing your *own* wealth and paying the bank for the privilege. Also, the banks have a system known as "bank trades," which allows them infinite potential for loan "capital". If, even by these ludicrous banking laws, a bank does not have enough on deposit to make a certain loan, it "borrows" money from another source. That source only has to put money on deposit at the bank for a short period – a month, even a few days – and during that time the bank can legally make a loan of ten times the figure the outside source has deposited. Once the loan has been made, the source gets its money returned, plus a massive interest payment for its trouble. There is no need for anyone to be hungry or in poverty in this world. This is purposely engineered through the system of "money" and debt created by the Illuminati. The central banks are part of one network, the same as the oil companies, and they are all controlled by the Illuminati bloodlines. The Bank of International Settlements in Basle, Switzerland, and the International Banking Commission, are the bodies that co-ordinate the policies of the apparently unconnected central banks. See ...*And The Truth Shall Set You Free* and *The Biggest Secret* for the fine detail and sources of what you are reading in this chapter.

The public does not have a clue where money comes from. They just have some vague idea that the "government" prints it or something. In truth, all except a fraction of the "money" in the world comes into circulation through the private banks making "loans" of non-existent "credit". So "money" comes into "existence" as a debt from the very start because "money" is brought into circulation by the banks issuing a loan or "credit". In this way, the banks (ultimately controlled by the same people) have complete control over how much "money" is in circulation. And the money in circulation decides if we have an economic boom or depression. People suddenly deciding they don't want to work, buy things, or have a home, is not the cause of economic depressions. They happen when there are not enough units of exchange ("money") in circulation to generate the economic activity that provides the necessary employment and income. Who controls how much "money" is in circulation? The Illuminati banks do. The following is a summary of how the "economic cycle" has been played out for centuries.

First you make lots of loans at low interest rates to encourage people to borrow money from you. This increases dramatically the amount of money in circulation and so makes more available for people to spend. This stimulates an increase in demand for, and production of, products and that creates more jobs. We have a "boom". It is an interesting fact that people tend to get into more debt during a boom because they are so confident financially that they borrow more money to buy a bigger car, bigger house, and better holidays. Companies borrow more from the banks to buy new machinery to meet the increased "demand". The stock markets explode and people invest more of their money in this global casino, even taking out loans to do so. Then, when this "boom" reaches the optimum point for the sting to be most effective, the banks, under central co-ordination, begin to take money out of circulation. They push up interest rates through their Federal Reserve, Bank of England, and other central banks. Suddenly a lot of money that had been circulating and buying products is withdrawn to pay the higher rates to the banks, and banks change their policy to ensure that they make fewer new loans. Eventually, more "money" is coming out of circulation than is going in and there is not enough money in circulation to buy all the products and services available. People begin to lose their jobs. These job losses increase the rate of economic depression because those people no longer have the money to purchase what they did before. With no other jobs available, the unemployed lose their homes, their families go hungry, and businesses go bust. These homes and businesses were bought with "loans" of fresh-air "money" from the banks. In doing so, the borrowers agreed that the banks were entitled to those homes and businesses if they did not keep up the payments. The depression, created by the banks, now gives the banks the right to confiscate all that real wealth – houses, land, business property and assets – in exchange for loaning nothing more than figures on a screen. In short, the banks make lots of loans in stage one and then withdraw so much money from circulation that there is not enough to pay them back. This ensures that they can legally steal the real wealth of the people. This is what smart-suited, and mostly thoroughly ignorant, "economics correspondents" on the television news call the "natural economic cycle". There is nothing natural about it. The whole thing is a scam. The fishing line is cast in stage one, the "boom", and then reeled in during stage two, the "depression". This cycle of manipulation has been played out for hundreds and even thousands of years, back to the banking operation of the Knights Templar and to Babylon and beyond. This is the cycle that has sucked the real wealth of the world into the hands of the tiny few and it still goes on.

Now the Illuminati are planning to complete their financial control of the human race with a world central bank and one global electronic currency. This bank would make all the major financial decisions affecting every country. The currency would eventually bring an end to physical "cash" and all other currencies. While I was writing this book, a UK paper called Metro reported on December 20th 2000 that Singapore was moving to a cashless society by 2008. In an article "Beginning of End for Cash", the paper revealed that Singapore (a British-controlled Illuminati "country") was phasing in "e-money" and would insist that everyone used it. Financial transactions would be made using money stored on computer chips, it said, and cash will be a thing of the past as money changed hands electronically using digital pulses transferred through mobile phones, hand-held computers and even watches. This is just the phase before they bring in micro-chip implants for everyone. Under the Singapore scheme, shoppers will be able to point a mobile phone at an item to register the price. The phone would check the shopper's bank balance on the Internet and deduct the money from the account if it was told to buy the item. The Singapore's government said this will save a small fortune on labour, security and transportation costs involved in making and moving notes and coins. Low Siang Kok (so have I), currency director at Singapore's Board of Commissioners of Currency, said: "The physical notes and coins will be a thing of the past. There's no point in fighting technology. If you want to give your kids pocket money, you pass it to them by phone. They can use it for bus fares, in the school cafeteria, or whatever." He then listed all the merits of the cashless society that I have long predicted they would use to sell it to the people – safer than cash and credit cards etc. etc.

Mayer Amschel Rothschild, the founder of the Rothschild banking dynasty, said: "Give me control of a nation's currency and I care not who makes the laws." This has been attributed to another Rothschild also. The fewer currencies there are, the more control you can have over the money system. This is why the Euro has been introduced within the European Union and the pressure is mounting for Canada to take the US dollar. These are stepping-stones to the world currency. Under the Euro, for example, a group of unelected bankers at the European Central Bank in Frankfurt (where the Rothschild banking dynasty began) have control over the interest rates and financial policy for the whole of Europe. Anyone ever questioned that? Or even bothered to find out in the first place? The next stage is to create the World Central Bank in which Illuminati bankers would set interest rates and financial policy for every country on the planet. The world currency will be electronic because this will make control of the people so easy. At the moment if you hand over electronic money, a credit card, and the computer will not accept it, you can still pay with cash. What happens when there is no cash and that computer says no to your credit card or your micro-chip, which is designed to replace it? You will have no other way of purchasing and whoever programmes that computer to accept or not accept your card or chip will control what, where, and whether you purchase anything. Also, whenever you buy a product of any kind, the place, time, item, and cost will be recorded. That's the idea, and the amount of physical money in circulation is already a fraction compared with electronic pulses on computer screens. Even this ratio is falling all the time.

Money-tree policy

One other point on money. The Illuminati control the banks, big business, and governments, and, therefore, they take pretty much all the money we spend or save. Some 80% of the cost of fuel in the UK is government taxation and the oil companies say we can't blame them for the cost because they only take a small part of the pump price. Well, actually, this is not true. The Illuminati own all the oil companies and take an enormous profit from their slice of the price. As I was writing this book, BP-Amoco announced it was making around £3,306 a *second* in profits. But, of course, it could never get away with charging for itself what the governments take in tax. So government taxation allows the Illuminati to rob the population of far more money and, as they control government policy through their placemen and agents, that taxation is overwhelmingly used to advance their agenda. According to Phil Schneider, who helped to build underground bases in the United States, the "Black Budget" for Illuminati projects takes 25% of the gross national product of the United States and (speaking in 1995) he revealed that it consumed $1.25 trillion every two years. The same situation applies to the tax on alcohol. The Illuminati, through bloodline families like the Bronfmans in Canada, control liquor producers and distributors. Liquor is also heavily taxed and the same applies here as with fuel. In the UK we have a sales tax called VAT or Value Added Tax. People buy products from Illuminati businesses and pay extra in taxation for the privilege. This tax goes to the government to fund the agenda. OK, don't buy so much and keep your money in the bank. If you do, you will be giving the Illuminati the right to lend and charge interest on ten times and more what you put on deposit. Give your money to cancer research and you will be giving it to the Illuminati drug cartel that has no intention of finding a cure for cancer. Give it to the Worldwide Fund for Nature and you will be giving it to another Illuminati front that is using environmental concerns for its own ends. Has humanity been stitched up or what? As Henry Ford said: "It is well enough that the people of the nation do not understand our banking and monetary system, for if they did, I believe there would be a revolution before tomorrow morning."

"Free trade" is stealing the planet

The Anunnaki-Illuminati have worked ceaselessly to make all countries dependent on the world financial and trade system, which they created and control. Once again it is far more difficult for the few to dictate to the many if the many operate in economic units (countries) that can decide their own financial and trade policy. So the Illuminati first created the GATT "free trade" agreement to stop nation states from defending their economies from the importation of goods that are destroying local jobs. Their placemen in government signed the agreements, which were negotiated by Illuminati agents like Peter D. Sutherland of Ireland, the Bilderberger head of GATT. He later became head of the World Trade Organization in the Illuminati stronghold of Switzerland. This replaced GATT and now has extensive powers to impose enormous fines on nations who do not follow its rules. By the way, Switzerland is never attacked in wars because that's the country through which the Illuminati finance the wars! History is so simple when you can see behind the veil. Sutherland was replaced at the World Trade Organization by the Italian, Renato Reggerio, another Bilderberger, and went on to become joint head of one of the major Illuminati companies, British Petroleum or BP-Amoco. He took over from the previous BP chief, Sir David Simon, who joined Tony Blair's government as his "Minister for Trade and Competitiveness in Europe" with the brief of taking the UK into the Euro and the United States of Europe. The end of trade borders in Europe under the Common Market removed more control by individual countries over their economy, and the same with the North American Free Trade Agreement between the US, Canada, and Mexico, negotiated by the paedophile George Bush (TC, CFR), and that rapist of mind-controlled women, Brian Mulroney, who was then the Canadian Prime Minister. I am sure they thought "free" trade was for the good of humanity.

The powers of the World Trade Organization ensure that poor "Third World" countries cannot use their land to feed their people first, nor keep out imports that are causing hunger and poverty by destroying local employment. If you have ever travelled in Africa you will know that the idea that this continent cannot feed itself is utterly ludicrous. It could feed much of the world. People are hungry because food-growing land is not being used to fill empty bellies, but to grow cash crops for the Illuminati-owned transnational corporations or to fight Illuminati-engineered wars. A book I wrote many years ago, *It Doesn't Have To Be Like This*, documents examples of this cash-crop scandal. The transnationals pay little or no tax to these countries and by owning the land at the expense of the people, they can pay poverty wages to the workers who have no other form of employment and no chance of self-sufficiency. The Illuminati transnationals are leeches sucking these countries dry of money, opportunity, and resources. They are, in short, purveyors of genocide. But then they are owned by the Illuminati bloodlines who think nothing of sacrificing a child and drinking its blood, so what are they going to care about the plight of the people they abuse economically? The Anunnaki view humans in the same way that most humans view cattle.

When the European countries "withdrew" from their colonies across the world and granted them "independence", they only did so on the surface, as I outlined earlier. Physical occupation by foreign armies was replaced by financial occupation by the banks, and the plan is to go back to physical occupation through the transnationals and the United Nations. The Illuminati bloodlines and secret societies continued to control most of the "independent" African, Asian, and South and Central American leaders. Indeed, by controlling the system, the Illuminati have controlled them all, even the few who are not directly in their pocket. It was these leaders who made the agreements to hand over the food-growing land to the transnationals. They told their people they would be able to import food they could be growing themselves with the "money" the country received for exporting resources and commodities. But the price of those commodities is decided in the commodity markets in Europe and America. With the Illuminati dictating the price of commodities sold by "Third World" countries, they could bring them to their knees whenever they chose. The puppet-leaders are rarely affected because they are well paid for serving the dragon. Ask the mass murderer Robert Mugabe in Zimbabwe. The Illuminati's greatest coup on the developing nations was the creation of "Third World" debt. I detail this story in *...And The Truth Shall Set You Free*, but, briefly, the Illuminati told the dictators in the Arab oil countries that they would vastly increase the price of oil on the understanding that the Arabs deposit the profits from this fantastic wind fall in specified Illuminati banks. The Arab dictators agreed. Illuminati operatives then got together at the Bilderberg meeting in May 1973 held at a Swedish island called Saltsjoebaden, owned by the Wallenberg bloodline banking family. Here they agreed the details of the colossal hike in the price of oil. The next stage was to manufacture an excuse to do so and, five months later, Henry Kissinger, a Bilderberg executive, manipulated the Yom Kippur War between Egypt and Israel. In 1973 he was the US Secretary of State and National Security Advisor. Kissinger's United States and the "West" supported the Israelis during the war with Egypt, and this gave the Arab leaders a reason to retaliate economically. Right on pre-arranged cue, the Arab oil dictators feigned their disgust at western support for Israel and used it as an excuse to "punish" the West by increasing the price of oil to levels that brought the world economy to its knees. You know when newsreaders say that the "OPEC" countries are discussing the price of oil? Well, actually, they're not: the Illuminati are deciding the price of oil because they control the OPEC leaders and all the oil companies.

With these unimaginable amounts of money flowing from the Arab dictators into their banks, the Illuminati threw their next card. They went to all the "Third World" countries and offered them enormous loans at low interest rates to "boost" their economies and "industrialise". The spin was that the Illuminati banks didn't want these loans repaid for reasons I will come to. They knew that the money would largely be wasted by their placemen and, anyway, they had insured against repayment by their next move. Enter Margaret Thatcher (Bil), the "Iron Lady", who was, in fact, one of the most controlled and manipulated leaders of the 20th century. The strings around her were pulled by her foreign secretary and Rothschild bloodline, Lord Carrington. He is Henry Kissinger's close associate, a former chairman of the Bilderberg Group, and the UK foreign secretary who engineered the Falklands War and handed power to the dictator Robert Mugabe in the former Rhodesia, now Zimbabwe. And these are the least of this man's crimes against humanity. If that's not true, Lord Carrington, then do please sue me and let's get the truth about you and your mates exposed in a public court. Margaret Thatcher introduced "her" vicious economic policy known as "Thatcherism" after her election in 1979. Her victory was ensured by the demolition of the previous Labour Government caused by the Illuminati-created "Winter of Discontent" in which they activated their agents within the British trades union movement to call an explosion of strikes. At one point rubbish was piled up in the streets and even the dead could not be buried. (The Illuminati were also behind the squabbles, scandals, and strife within the Conservative Government just before the election in 1995, which brought the Labour leader Tony Blair to power with a landslide victory.) A year after Thatcherism was launched in the UK, exactly the same policies were introduced in the United States under the name "Reaganomics" with the election of the puppet president Ronald Reagan and his controller, the vice-president George Bush. Thatcherism and Reaganomics imposed economic conditions that brought tremendous rises in interest rates.

Now we complete the circle. The "Third World" countries, which accepted those enormous loans at low interest rates, were now faced with such an increase in their repayments that they would never be able to repay the interest, let alone the principle. The term "Third World debt" was born. The cost in human misery defies belief and in came those Illuminati creations, the International Monetary Fund (IMF) and the World Bank (currently headed by the Rothschild partner and Bilderberger, James Wolfensohn). They told these debt-ridden, poverty-stricken, countries that they had to cut subsidies for food and health care and "restructure" their economies in line with the instructions of the IMF and World Bank. If they did not, they would get no further "help". By now these countries could not revert to self-sufficiency because the Illuminati transnationals controlled much of the food-growing land and they were faced with both world trade restrictions and debt repayments. What happened? People starved and are still starving, and any leader who seeks to challenge the Illuminati immediately finds his country involved in a war. But the Illuminati were still not finished. Why would they not want these countries to repay their loans? For the same reason they don't want many people in the industrial countries to repay their loans. They want their land and resources and the control that debt ensures. Now "debt-relief" policies are being implemented in which these poor countries hand over rights to their land and resources *forever* in return for the "forgiveness" of debt. A debt that only exists as figures on a computer disk. You may note that governments are "forgiving" Third World debt without demanding a return because they are lending taxpayers' money. No problem, there'll be more. But the banks are selling the "debt" for land and resources, in other words the Illuminati bloodlines are.

The same technique is involved in the "debt-for-nature-swaps" in which poor countries are "forgiven" debt if they hand over large tracts of their land to the United Nations and environmental agencies to "save the planet". How ironic that the greatest destroyers of the ecology are the very policies of the IMF, World Bank, and Illuminati banks that devastate "Third World" countries and force the people to destroy their own environment, including the rainforests, just to survive. And how strange that while Illuminati banks and transnationals pursue policies that are devastating the environment, it is the same Illuminati families, like the Rockefellers, who finance and front reports saying that the planet is dying and we must "save her". Strange, too, that many environmental pressure groups are Illuminati agencies, not least The Worldwide Fund For Nature. This is headed by Prince Philip and long-time Bilderberg chairman, Prince Bernhard of The Netherlands. It was Bernhard who chaired the meeting in Sweden that agreed to hike the price of oil with its catastrophic environmental consequences. But, in fact, none of this is strange at all. "Saving the environment" suits the Illuminati perfectly because it involves the imposition of centralised global laws and the acquisition of land on a stupendous scale by the United Nations and other agencies of the Illuminati in the name of "environmental protection". Look at how many invading armies that cause genocide in places like Rwanda and Burundi, are sheltered in the nature and wildlife parks along the borders and invade through those lands. *The Biggest Secret* has the detailed background.

The system has been set up so that he who controls the money controls the world, and the Illuminati bloodlines control the money. But there is so much good news here, too. It means that all these so-called unsolvable problems like poverty, debt, and war, are not a "natural" occurrence. They are made to happen because it makes humanity easier to control and manipulate. There is enough on this planet to give abundance to everyone, don't let them kid you otherwise. For some to be well fed it is not necessary for others to go hungry. So why is there so much poverty amid such potential abundance? By controlling the creation and flow of money, the land, and resources, the Illuminati limit choice and create dependency – on them. Their World Central Bank and currency are designed to impose that control even more fiercely. Their equation is simple:

Scarcity = dependency = control. Abundance = choice = freedom.

The world army

I have been writing for many years, along with other researchers, about the plan for a World Army. In earlier books, I said there would eventually be an amalgamation of the United Nations Peacekeeping Force and NATO, with NATO the senior partner. I also wrote that we should expect more conflicts to be engineered in which NATO was used to intervene and "save the people". This would set the precedent and change the status quo until NATO became, step-by-step, a world police force. This process is now well under way and the wars in the Gulf, Bosnia, and Kosovo are all part of that. An organisation called Kissinger Associates is always heavily involved in manipulating such conflicts. Henry Kissinger, the Illuminati's roving manipulator, controls the company, of course. One of the founding directors was his buddy, Lord Carrington, chairman of the Bilderberg Group for nearly ten years and a secretary-general of NATO. There is no better example of the hidden hand than the common connections between the major "peace negotiators" during the war in Bosnia.

The peace negotiators appointed by the European Union in Bosnia were: Lord Carrington (chairman of the Bilderberg Group, president of the Royal Institute of International Affairs, Trilateral Commission member, and Kissinger Associates); he was followed by Lord David Owen (Bil, TC); and then came the former Swedish Prime Minister, Carl Bildt (Bil). The United Nations-appointed peace negotiators were: Cyrus Vance (Bil, TC, CFR) and Thorvald Stoltenberg of Norway (Bil, TC). Stolenberg's son became Prime Minister of Norway. When they failed to achieve peace, along came an "independent peace negotiator", Jimmy Carter (first Trilateral Commission President of the United States and Council on Foreign Relations member). By now the public and political clamour for "something must be done" had been focused by the horrendous television pictures coming out of Bosnia, and the Illuminati could play their sting in this classic problem-reaction-solution scenario. Along came Bill Clinton's special envoy, Richard Holbrooke (Bil, TC, CFR) to negotiate the Dayton Agreement that installed a 60,000-strong NATO world army in Bosnia. This was the biggest multi-national force assembled since the Second World War. Holbrooke answered to US Secretary of State Warren Christopher (TC, CFR) and Defence Secretary William Perry (Bil). Their boss, at least officially, was President Bill Clinton (Bil, TC, CFR). The first head of the NATO world army in Bosnia was Admiral Leighton Smith (CFR) and the head of the civilian operation was Carl Bildt (Bil). The media won't tell you any of this because most journalists think investigative reporting is reading the morning papers and the official press releases. And the Illuminati control the newspapers through subordinates like the "owner" of the *Washington Post*, Katherine Graham (Bil, TC, CFR) and the Canadian, Conrad Black, an inner-core member of the Bilderberg Group, who heads the Hollinger media empire. This includes the London *Daily Telegraph*, the *Jerusalem Post*, and has owned some 70% of newspapers in Canada. Members of these organisations control all three television networks in the United States, NBC, ABC, and CBS. They also control the *Los Angeles Times*, *New York Times*, *Wall Street Journal*, and the empires of Rupert Murdoch, Time-Warner, including CNN, and the major media operations throughout the world. Even four out of five local newspapers in the UK are now owned by the big media cartels.

The main aim of the Bosnian war was to advance the NATO role of world police force. When the conflict began the UN peacekeepers were always sent to such trouble spots. But the Illuminati wanted to change that and while those terrible pictures of death and suffering were bombarding the public mind around the world, a media campaign was waged to condemn the UN operation in Bosnia as ineffective and next to useless. This was the excuse to bring in NATO forces and in doing so the Illuminati agenda moved forward significantly. When the Kosovo conflict was manipulated, there was no talk of sending UN soldiers because the status quo had been flipped by what happened in Bosnia. From the start the world looked to NATO to intervene in Kosovo and, as a result of their grotesque bombing campaign, they extended their control of that region. People have said to me that they could not understand the need for a world army because there would be no one to fight! Yes there would – the people. The world government would control the world army. Its job would be to implement the laws and decisions of the world government, should any country rebel and refuse to comply. We are talking global fascism here and the structures are being introduced before our eyes to impose that. The Illuminati know there is a chance that if US troops were asked to abuse and murder US citizens that many would rebel and perhaps mutiny. So they are covertly locating foreign troops in the United States under the guise of the United Nations while sending vast numbers of American troops abroad. The same with other countries, too.

The mental, emotional, and physical onslaught

If you want to control a population you must suppress their desire or ability to think for themselves and see what is going on around them. This is done through the manipulation of the mind and emotions, and with drugs, vaccines, and food additives. It is vital that we realise that those who control the drug companies are the same as those who control the food giants – and the "health agencies", media, governments, banks, corporations, and all the rest. Millions of people are dying every year of diseases like cancer and AIDS who could be returned to health if they were allowed to choose from all the treatments available and not be confined to the primitive scalpel and drug. I have sat in treatment rooms, for example, and watched people cured, sometimes in 15 minutes, of complaints for which their doctors have either offered major and expensive surgery or no hope at all. This includes a woman who was so ill with lung cancer she had to be driven to the treatment centre because she did not have the strength to drive a car. After one treatment she was driving herself. Eventually, as her treatment and improvement continued, she went back to the doctors, who had said there was nothing they could do. Their new tests showed that she was cancer free. This "treatment" is no miracle because there are no miracles, only the natural laws and forces of creation at work. It is our knowledge of how to harness these forces that has been suppressed and people ignorantly follow what the "experts" tell them is possible. One healer I know used to be a conventional surgeon until he saw the truth of what was going on and how knowledge was being kept from us all. This includes doctors. The Illuminati has structured the training of the medical profession to turn out people who advance their version of "truth". You only pass your medical exams if you conform to this official "truth" and you only keep your job if you continue to do so throughout your career. It is the same with scientists, teachers, government officials, the whole lot.

The manipulation of medicine

There is far more to the human entity than a physical body. That is the least of what we are. It is the genetic spacesuit through which our eternal consciousness, the thinking, feeling us experiences this frequency range we call the physical world. The brain is the computer, the switching station, which connects our immortal mind to our mortal body. We don't think *from* the brain, we think *through* the brain. People with brain damage do not have damaged minds; they have a damaged computer, which cannot transmit the messages of the mind to the physical level of experience. The mind is an energy field working through the brain, not the brain itself. Our emotions are another energy field and these different levels of being are connected through a series of vortexes known as "chakras", a Sanskrit word meaning "wheels of light". In this way, stress in our emotional energy field, which manifests as an imbalanced vibration, is passed down the levels through the chakras. What is the first thing that happens when we get stressed and emotional? We stop thinking straight. This is the imbalanced emotional vibration disrupting the clarity and balance of the mental energy field. If the stress is serious enough, and goes on for long enough, the imbalanced vibration begins to affect the physical body. This vibrational imbalance interacts with the body cells to cause chemical changes and this is what we call "disease", or dis-ease as it really is. It is only at this point that the medical profession gets interested, when the vibrational imbalance affects the physical. They either prescribe a drug to try to reverse the chemical changes or take the person for surgery to cut away the result of the chemical changes. This is what we call "advanced" medicine! They treat the symptom and not the cause because they do not understand what the human entity really is. They see, and therefore treat, only the physical body. That is what the Illuminati system trains them to do and insists they do not deviate from.

True healers treat and remove the energy imbalances that are causing the physical effect. They do this by using their own bodies to "channel" energy from the infinite supply all around them through their hands to the patient. There are many other forms of vibrational and energy healing, also. Acupuncture needles balance the energy flows around the body, while crystal therapy and homeopathy are using the vibrations of crystals and plants to balance the patient's energy field. Of course there are charlatans in these alternative methods, too, but on nowhere near the scale of those in the drug cartels and medical authorities. When the cause is removed, its physical consequences disappear and this is reported as a "miracle cure", but, like I say, it is nothing of the kind. I have experienced some of these "miracles" myself. The physical body has an energy blueprint known to healers as the "etheric body" and when this is damaged or imbalanced it manifests as physical dis-ease. You might imagine the etheric body standing by a pool and its reflection in the water as the physical body. When the etheric changes its state or form in any way, the same happens to the physical. So if you keep the etheric level in good shape, the physical will do the same. While I was writing this book, I bashed my toe and after ten days it was getting worse, not better. It was extremely painful to walk. A healer did some "hands on" healing, channelling energy to repair the damage to the etheric level. Within half an hour my toe was feeling better and within two days it was back to normal.

I have met healers who have worked on some famous people in the Far East and these are the healing methods the Illuminati use. They don't want us to know about such treatments and so they ridicule them, call them "quackery", or condemn them as evil, while secretly using them for their own benefit. Most of the "quackery" goes on every day in the official hospitals and doctors' surgeries and the evil is in the billions of people who suffer and die when they could be cured if these suppressed healing methods were in widespread use. This is not to condemn all doctors, only the system which imprisons them. Why do you think so many of the most prominent Illuminati like David Rockefeller and Henry Kissinger are able to jet around the world like 40 year olds when they are both in their 70s? By using the drugs that the Rockefeller pharmaceutical empire turns out for the rest of us? You must be joking. These people know they are causing the death and suffering of billions by their actions, but they don't give a shit, just as most humans don't give a shit about the plight of cattle. Their "medicine" is not designed to make us well in the true sense. Its prime aim is to suppress and dim our thinking processes, and make us subservient to authority. It's like sedating a cow or a sheep so they can be controlled more easily and won't run away when they see the slaughterhouse. Most of the medical profession have no idea this is so. They are just the fodder. They have to use the methods dictated from above if they wish to keep their jobs. When Guylaine Lanctot, a wonderful lady and professional doctor in Canada, began to expose the manipulation of the drug cartel and its agents in medical administration, she was struck off. See her excellent book, *The Medical Mafia* (Here's The Key, Inc, Canada, 1995), available through Bridge of Love and my website. She also shows why the suppressed and ridiculed "alternatives" are more effective than the treatments she was trained to administer. We are multi-dimensional beings and exist on all frequencies and dimensions of creation. We can access the infinite ocean of consciousness or stay imprisoned in our little droplet, disconnected from the true enormity of who and what we are. If you were the Anunnaki-Illuminati where would you want humanity to be – stuck in the droplet or sailing on the ocean? One way they do this is by feeding us drugs and chemicals that suppress brain function, clarity of thought, and the ability to connect powerfully with our higher levels of being, or "sixth sense" of psychic awareness and intuition. This is the real reason behind all the drugs, vaccines, and food additives we daily consume. I will give you some examples of this war on the human brain and immune system, but really the list is simply endless.

Aspartame[1]

One of the weapons is aspartame, an Illuminati creation that suppresses the intellect. It is now used in thousands of foodstuffs and almost every soft drink. And who are the biggest consumers of soft drinks? Children. They want to get the kids as early as possible and turn them into unthinking, unquestioning, clones for life. Aspartame is an "artificial sweetener" and marketed as an alternative to the negative effects of sugar – which the Illuminati also control! It is known under trade names like NutraSweet, Equal, and Spoonful. Aspartame, which is 200 times sweeter than sugar, was introduced in 1981 and has been the subject of 75% of the complaints reported to the Adverse Reaction Monitoring system of the US Food and Drug Administration (FDA). These complaints have included headaches, dizziness, attention difficulties, memory loss, slurred speech, and vision problems. Such symptoms are now known as "aspartame disease", just as the affects of the preservative Monosodium Glutamate are called the Glutamate Syndrome. John W. Olney, MD of the Washington University Medical School in St Louis, believes there may be a link between aspartame and brain tumours. In an article published in the Journal of Neuropathology and Experimental Neurology, he says that animal studies reveal high levels of brain tumours in aspartame-fed rats. Dr Olney adds that aspartame has mutagenic (cancer-causing) potential according to studies, and a sharp rise in malignant brain tumours coincides with the increased use of aspartame. Even the US Navy and Air Force published articles in Navy Physiology and Flying Safety warning that:

> "Several researchers have found aspartame can increase the frequency of seizures, or lower the stimulation necessary to induce them. This means a pilot who drinks diet sodas is more susceptible to flicker vertigo, or to flicker-induced epileptic activity. It also means that all pilots are potential victims of sudden memory loss, dizziness during instrument flight, and gradual loss of vision." [2]

And aspartame is no longer confined to diet drinks. It changes brain chemistry and lowers the threshold for seizures, causes mood disorders and other problems of the nervous system. It is also addictive. Hence people often find it difficult to stop consuming the soft drinks that contain aspartame. Symptoms of multiple sclerosis, chronic fatigue, rheumatoid arthritis, depression and other mood disorders have vanished in many patients after they stopped aspartame consumption. Ten per cent of this legalised poison breaks down after ingestion into methanol, a nervous system toxin also known as free methyl alcohol or wood alcohol. This is extremely harmful to the optic nerve. It is the main ingredient of "moonshine" liquor made during Prohibition and this was notorious for causing blindness. Methanol is rapidly released into the bloodstream, where it can become the neurotoxin and cancer-causing formaldehyde and formic acid, the poison in ant stings. Fancy a soda?

The Food and Drug Administration (FDA) in America, like its equivalent in other countries, is an Illuminati front to block products that are good for humanity and to push through, without proper testing, those that suit the agenda. This happened with aspartame. First the FDA approved its use on the basis of ridiculous data and then had to withdraw that permission in the face of studies showing that it caused seizures and brain tumours in animals. But the FDA restored approval in 1981, despite the unanimous opposition of a Public Board of Inquiry, which had reviewed the scientific data and recommended a delay. Dr Ralph G. Walton, a Professor of Psychiatry at North Eastern Ohio University College of Medicine, reviewed all the studies on aspartame and found 166 with relevance for human safety. All of the 74 studies funded by the aspartame industry gave it the all clear, but 92% of those independently funded revealed safety problems. Which ones would you believe?

The reason this poison was approved against all the evidence is simple corruption. A commissioner of the Food and Drug Administration, an acting commissioner, six other operatives, and two attorneys assigned to prosecute NutraSweet for submitting fraudulent tests, left the organisation to work for... NutraSweet, a trade name for aspartame. One genuine scientist working for the FDA wrote to a US senator: "It's like a script for Abbott and Costello. It works like this: 'Approve our poison, and when you stop being a bureaucrat we'll make you a plutocrat! After it's licensed we'll pay off the American Dietetics, the American Diabetes Association, the American Medical Association and anyone we need who's for sale'." Coca-Cola knew of the dangers of aspartame because, as a member of the National Soft Drink Association, it opposed the approval by the Food and Drug Administration. Its objections were published in the Congressional Record of July 5th, 1985. It said that aspartame was inherently unstable and breaks down in the can, decomposing into formaldehyde, methyl alcohol, formic acid, diketopiperazine and other toxins. So what is aspartame now doing in Diet Coke, the sales of which soared when it was added because it is so addictive? And "Diet" Coke is not "diet" at all. People who drink it get fatter, as with all aspartame products, because it increases the craving for carbohydrates by suppressing the production of seratonin. We are living amid a gigantic confidence trick. By the way, the Monsanto Corporation of St Louis, Missouri, owned NutraSweet and another aspartame product, Equal. This is an Illuminati company to its fingertips and the promoter of genetically modified food, another part of the Illuminati assault on the human mind and body. It is using the same methods to win approval for genetically modified food as it did for aspartame. Members of the Working Group on Bio-Safety connected to the Convention on Biological Diversity in Cartagena, Colombia, make recommendations on the use of genetically modified food. The members include:

Linda J. Fisher, Vice President of Government and Public Affairs for Monsanto and formerly with the US Environmental Protection Agency; Dr. Michael A. Friedman, Senior Vice-President for Clinical Affairs at G.D. Searle & Co., a pharmaceutical division of Monsanto, formerly with the US Food and Drug Administration; Marcia Hale, Director of International Government Affairs for Monsanto, formerly assistant to the President of the United States; Michael (Mickey) Kantor, director of Monsanto, former Secretary of the US Department of Commerce; Josh King, director of global communication in the Washington, DC office of Monsanto, former director of production for White House events; William D. Ruckelshaus, director of Monsanto, former chief administrator of the United States Environmental Protection Agency; Michael Taylor, head of the Washington, DC office of Monsanto Corporation, former legal advisor to the Food and Drug Administration; Lidia Watrud, former microbial biotechnology researcher at Monsanto, now with the United States Environmental Protection Agency's Environmental Effects Laboratory; Jack Watson, staff lawyer with Monsanto in Washington, former chief of staff to the President of the United States, Jimmy Carter. Others include representatives from Dupont (major Illuminati bloodline) and Dow Chemicals (Illuminati). Their representative is Clayton K. Yeutter, former Secretary of the U.S. Department of Agriculture, former US Trade Representative, who led the US team in negotiating the US-Canada Free Trade Agreement and helped to launch the Uruguay Round of the GATT negotiations. He is now a director of Mycogen Corporation, whose majority owner is Dow Agro-Sciences, a wholly owned subsidiary of the Dow Chemical Company. I am sure their recommendations will be devoid of any bias whatsoever, or my name isn't Charlie Shufflebottom.

Prozac[3]

The story of Prozac, produced by the George Bush drug company, Eli Lilly, is the same tale of Illuminati corruption to impose a mind suppressant on the population. In 1982, David Dunner of the University of Washington began to accept more than $1.4 million from Lilly for research and seminars. Some of this "research" was for conducting a clinical trial with 100 people for Prozac. At the same time he was a member of the Food and Drug Administration's Psychopharmacologic Drugs Advisory Committee, responsible for reviewing new drug applications for the FDA. Dunner was asked if he had any conflict of interest with Eli Lilly when he began to assess Prozac for the FDA, but he replied: "No pending commitments at the present time." The FDA accepted this and yet Dunner had already given five seminars sponsored by Prozac producer Eli Lilly before this date. The seminars were about "depressive disorders"- the target market for Prozac. Dunner also failed to disclose that he had agreed to two further seminars for Lilly arranged to take place after Prozac was approved. According to the public record, Lilly's test on Prozac showed it was little more effective than a useless placebo and an FDA statistician suggested to Lilly that the test results be evaluated differently to indicate a more favourable result. This they did. An FDA safety review established that Lilly failed to report psychotic episodes during Prozac's testing, but there was no reprimand. By 1987, two months before the FDA approved Prozac, 27 people had died in controlled clinical trials. 15 were suicides, six by overdose, four by gunshot and two by drowning. Prozac was directly connected to all of them. Twelve other people in the trials died, but the cause was not directly related to Prozac. In 1991 the FDA executive, Paul Leber, said he noted "the large number of reports of all kinds on Prozac" (more than 15,000). But Leber pressured personnel in charge of the agency's adverse reporting system to discount these reports as "of limited value". The number had reached 28,600 by 1992 with another 1,700 deaths. Yet the Commissioner of the FDA, David Kessler, has said that: "Although the FDA receives many adverse event reports, these probably represent only a fraction of the serious adverse events encountered by providers. Only about one percent of the serious events are reported to the FDA, according to one study." On that basis there were really around 2,860,000 adverse reactions to Prozac by 1992 alone. What will it be by now? The number is almost unimaginable. But they are introducing a form of Prozac for children and it is widely used among victims of mind control. I understand that Thomas Hamilton, the killer of the children at Dunblane in Scotland, was taking Prozac, and Eric Harris, one of the teenagers in the Columbine High School shooting, was reported to be taking the drug Luvox, which is given the same classification as Prozac. The main active ingredient in Prozac was found in the blood of Henry Paul, the driver of the car when Princess Diana was murdered. Prozac is just one of a long list of drugs designed to have the same effect.

Ritalin

Ritalin is another mind-altering drug that is targeted at children and can seriously affect their behaviour. It has been connected to many acts of violence. A 1995 report by the Drug Enforcement Agency warned that Ritalin "shares many of the pharmacological effects of … cocaine". In fact, the US government classifies Ritalin in the same category as cocaine and heroin. Dennis H. Clarke, the chairman of the Executive Advisory Board, Citizens Commission On Human Rights International, said: "The use of Ritalin on children has no purpose other than to slow them down, shut them up, and make it more difficult for them to move around." He says it is an easy way out for parents and teachers to give them a drug. Clarke highlights the findings of the Diagnostic and Statistical Manual of Mental Disorders, Third Revised Edition, published by the American Psychiatric Association. He says this supports his claims of the dangers of Ritalin for children. He says that all the critical information about Ritalin has been removed in the more recent edition and this confirms, he says, that the industry is involved in a cover-up. The industry says the removal was simply "an error". Clarke suggests that children who take Ritalin in elementary school are often switched to Prozac and other drugs as they get older. The effects of Ritalin can continue long after the prescription is stopped, Clarke warns. Dr Ann Blake Tracy, Director of the International Coalition for Drug Awareness, supports this view. She points out that adults who use these drugs are far more likely to commit violent crimes. Dr Tracy comes from Utah, home of the Mormon Church, where the use of Ritalin and Prozac is reported to be three times greater than the rest of the country per head of population. She said Utah's rate of murders and suicides has increased by a similar amount.[4] Dennis H. Clarke says that the high number of incidents involving violent children and the increase in child suicide, can be attributed to an ever-increasing number of children who are

given drugs to control their behaviour. Clarke gave an example of a youngster
involved in the Jonesboro killings in Arkansas:

> "We do know, for example, that the 13-year-old in Jonesboro was being treated.
> Apparently they were saying he had been sexually abused as a child. They were saying
> he was now a sexual abuser. He had a hyperactivity type label put on him as well – or
> 'attention deficit disorder.' So we had several different things working with him. There
> is no chance under the Sun, Moon, or stars that this kid was not on drugs." [5]

Clarke says that when a violent event happens, the pharmaceutical "crash
teams" go to work to keep things quiet. Teams of psychiatrists are sent to the
locations and quickly ensure that medical records are kept sealed, doctors are
convinced to keep quiet, and victims are bought off to stop the case going to court.
"It's all being covered up, and it's deliberate. There are billions and billions of
dollars at stake here," he said. David M. Bresnahan, a contributing editor for
WorldNetDaily.com says he was told by an elementary school teacher in Utah that
she routinely makes recommendations for children in her classes to be given
Ritalin.[6] She said 11 of the 29 children in her first-grade class are now taking the
drug in school each day. Dennis Clarke predicts that the future will see even more
violent children, unless the connection between Ritalin and violent acts is openly
accepted. Clarke says that the general public, health officials, and parents are not
recognising the extent of a pandemic that is already sweeping the nation. Even the
CIBA Pharmaceutical Company says in a product information release:

> "Warning: sufficient data on the safety and efficacy of long-term use of Ritalin in
> children are not yet available." [7]

Unbelievable. They are handing out Ritalin like sweets to ever gathering
numbers of children and they admit they have no idea of the long-term effects!
This warning is only there to head off lawsuits later when the long and short term
effects are accepted. Herbert S. Okun, a member of the International Drug Control
Board for the United Nations, told a news conference that his board is very
concerned that methylphenidate (Ritalin) is massively over prescribed in the
United States. He said there are *330 million* doses of Ritalin taken each day in the
US, compared with 65 million for the rest of the world. Our children are being
systematically drugged and the teachers and parents are watching it happen, often
encouraging it. The main targets are the kids with active minds and those who act
differently to the norm.

Fluoride. Come on, drink up

Fluoride is another major intellect suppressant that is being added to drinking
water supplies and toothpaste. Sodium fluoride is a common ingredient in rat and
cockroach poisons, anaesthetics, hypnotics, psychiatric drugs, and military nerve
gas. It is one of the basic ingredients in Prozac and the Sarin nerve gas used in the

attack in the Japanese subway system. Independent scientific evidence has claimed that fluoride causes various mental disturbances and makes people *stupid, docile, and subservient*. This is besides shortening life spans and damaging bone structure. The first use of fluoridated drinking water was in the Nazi prison camps in Germany, thanks to the Illuminati's notorious pharmaceutical giant, I.G. Farben. This was the company that ran camps like Auschwitz and it still exists as its constituent parts like Bayer. Does anyone think the Nazis did this because they were concerned for the teeth of the inmates? This mass medication of water supplies with sodium fluoride was to sterilise the prisoners and force them into quiet submission. Charles Perkins, a chemist, wrote the following to the Lee Foundation for Nutritional Research, Milwaukee, Wisconsin, on October 2nd 1954:

> "...In the 1930's, Hitler and the German Nazis envisioned a world to be dominated and controlled by a Nazi philosophy of pan-Germanism. The German chemists worked out a very ingenious and far-reaching plan of mass-control, which was submitted to and adopted by the German General Staff. This plan was to control the population in any given area through mass medication of drinking water supplies. By this method they could control the population in whole areas, reduce population by water medication that would produce sterility in women, and so on. In this scheme of mass-control, sodium fluoride occupied a prominent place." [8]

Charles Perkins said that repeated doses of infinitesimal amounts of fluoride will in time reduce an individual's power to resist domination, by slowly poisoning and "narcotising" a certain area of the brain, thus making him submissive to the will of those who wish to govern him. He called it a "convenient light lobotomy". The real reason behind water fluoridation is not to benefit children's teeth, he said. If this was the real reason there are many ways in which it could be done that are much easier, cheaper, and far more effective, he points out. The real purpose behind water fluoridation was to reduce the resistance of the masses to domination and control and loss of liberty. Perkins said that when the Nazis under Hitler decided to go into Poland, both the German General Staff and the Russian General Staff exchanged scientific and military ideas, plans, and personnel, and the scheme of mass control through water medication was seized upon by the Russian Communists because it fitted ideally into their plan to "communise" the world:

> "I was told of this entire scheme by a German chemist who was an official of the great I.G. Farben chemical industries and was also prominent in the Nazi movement at the time. I say this with all the earnestness and sincerity of a scientist who has spent nearly 20 years' research into the chemistry, biochemistry, physiology and pathology of fluorine – any person who drinks artificially-fluorinated water for a period of one year or more will never again be the same person mentally or physically." [9]

That is the very reason the Illuminati has been expanding the consumption of fluoride ever since and what better way to suppress the minds of the population than through the public drinking water supplies? When we drink anything made from fluoridated water, including beer and soft drinks, we are being slowly and consistently drugged. Fluoride is a by-product of the aluminium industry and the scam to add it to public drinking water came from the Mellon family in the United States, which controls the aluminium cartel called ALCOA. The Mellons are big-time bloodline, close friends of the British royal family, and dictators of US policy through the Illuminati network. Industrial fluorines are major polluters of rivers and streams, poisoning land, fish, and animals. It was costing the aluminium industry a fortune to deal with them, but the Mellon family manipulated a situation in which this poisonous waste product became an enormous source of income and human control. In 1944, Oscar Ewing was employed by ALCOA at an annual salary of $750,000. Imagine what that would be today! But within months he left to become head of the US Government's Federal Security Agency and began a campaign to add sodium fluoride to public drinking water. The Mellons now sell it for use in drinking water and toothpaste at a *20,000%* mark-up. Fluoride goes into drinking water at approximately one part-per-million, but we only drink $1/2$ of one percent of the water supply. The rest goes down the drain as a free hazardous-waste disposal for the chemical industry. And we pay for that. But the main reason, as always, is not money. It is control. A former mind controller with the Illuminati told me of the Mellons' deep involvement with the Illuminati and Satanism. She said that to her knowledge the Mellon National Bank in Pittsburgh, Pennsylvania is an Illuminati operation that launders money for them. Would you trust such a family to put chemicals in drinking water and toothpaste because they want to keep your teeth healthy? Not that fluoride does.

We have a Member of Parliament here on the Isle of Wight where I live in England called Peter Brand, who is pressing for fluoride to be added to our drinking water because it is "good for children's teeth". This man is a professional doctor and the "health" spokesman for the Liberal Democratic Party. In fact, he doesn't know his arse from his elbow and provides yet another example of how doctors are so deeply uninformed. But because they are doctors, many people think that they must know it all. Dr Hardy Limeback, BSc, PhD in Biochemistry, head of the Department of Preventive Dentistry for the University of Toronto, and president of the Canadian Association for Dental Research, was once Canada's leading promoter of fluoride in water supplies. But then suddenly he announced he had changed his mind. He said: "Children under three should never use fluoridated toothpaste or drink fluoridated water. And baby formula must never be made up using Toronto tap water. Never."[10] A study at the University of Toronto revealed that people in cities that fluoridate their water have double the fluoride in their hip bones compared with non-fluoridated areas, and they discovered that flouride was changing the "basic architecture of human bones". There is a debilitating condition called skeletal fluorosis caused by the accumulation of fluoride in the bones, making them weak and brittle. The earliest symptoms are mottled and brittle teeth, and Dr Limeback said that in Canada they were spending more money treating dental fluorosis than treating cavities. But hold on. At least putting this poison in the water and toothpaste is keeping teeth healthy and preventing cavities, yes? Er…no.

As Limeback points out, they have been putting fluoride in the Toronto drinking water for 36 years while Vancouver has never been fluoridated. Get this: the population of Vancouver has lower cavity rates than Toronto! He said that cavity rates are low all across the industrialised world – including Europe, which is so far 98% fluoride free. This was due, he said, to improved standards of living, less refined sugar, regular dental check-ups, flossing and frequent brushing. There were now fewer than two cavities per child in Canada. He said that those who continue to promote fluoride are working with data that is 50 years old and questionable at best. "The dentists have absolutely no training in toxicity," he said. "Your well-intentioned dentist is simply following 50 years of misinformation from public health and the dental association. Me, too. Unfortunately, we were wrong." And not only are we drinking the poisonous sodium fluoride, we are getting all the other crap from the aluminium industry, too. Limeback said:

> "But certainly the crowning blow was the realization that we have been dumping contaminated fluoride into water reservoirs for half a century. The vast majority of all fluoride additives come from Tampa Bay, Florida, smokestack scrubbers. The additives are a toxic by-product of the super-phosphate fertilizer industry.

> "Tragically, that means we're not just dumping toxic fluoride into our drinking water. We're also exposing innocent, unsuspecting people to deadly elements of lead, arsenic and radium, all of them carcinogenic. Because of the cumulative properties of toxins, the detrimental effects on human health are catastrophic." [11]

Alzheimer's disease has been linked to aluminium and to aspartame. In an address to students at the University of Toronto Department of Dentistry, Dr Limeback told them that he had unintentionally mis-led his colleagues and students. For the past 15 years, he had refused to study the toxicology information that is readily available to anyone. "Poisoning our children was the furthest thing from my mind," he said. "The truth was a bitter pill to swallow, but swallow it I did." Yet even though the biggest supporter of fluoride has now condemned its use, the Illuminati-controlled Canadian and American Dental Associations and public "health" agencies, together with those in the UK and worldwide, continue to tell the people that fluoridation is good for them. This is just one example of "the bigger the lie, the more will believe it". Illuminati placemen in the positions of medical administration and "scientific research" tell the doctors and dentists what is "truth" and what they should believe. They tell this to their patients and the media, who simply take the official line and repeat it like parrots. Because hardly anyone does any research of their own, dentists, doctors, "journalists", or public, it becomes an accepted "fact" that fluoride in drinking water and toothpaste is good for teeth and not harmful. That same scenario is repeated in relation to every subject every day and, as a result, the human population lives in its own little fairyland. This manufactured illusion is so entrenched in the human psyche that when the truth does come out, most people laugh in its face. There need to be massive class action lawsuits against the authorities by those who have already had their health devastated by fluoride, Prozac, and aspartame. This is already happening in Canada over the use of mercury, another poison and intellect suppressant, in tooth fillings. And there you have that phrase again which is constantly repeated when the adverse effects of drugs, food additives, and other chemicals in our diet are listed: intellect suppressant. With the truth about fluoride now being more widely circulated, suddenly "new research" has conveniently revealed that it is good for stopping brittle bones and reduces the risks of fractures. This has been used to apply yet more pressure for the expansion of fluoride in drinking water. Fluoride is not there to protect teeth. That's just an excuse. It is there to suppress the intellect of the population so they don't think, question, or rebel.

Vaccinations[12]

It is the same story with vaccines. This is a highly efficient way of pumping mind-suppressing drugs and immune system destroyers into billions of people while they think you are trying to help them. Whole generations of children worldwide are contaminated in this way every year while the figures show that the claims made for the benefits of vaccination are utter baloney. Dr Guylaine Lanctot exposes the reality of vaccinations in her book, *The Medical Mafia*. She says that repeated vaccination exhausts the immune system and opens people to all sorts of diseases the body's defences would normally repel. As so many studies have shown, the diseases the vaccines were supposed to protect us against were in free-fall *before* the vaccine was introduced. Ian Sinclair, an Australian researcher, has documented the lies behind vaccination in a series of books and articles, including *Health: The Only Immunity*.[13] He says that he discovered the following.

- Graphical and statistical evidence showing that more than 90% of the decline in death rates from infectious disease occurred *before* vaccination commenced. All medical journals acknowledged this decline was caused by improved sanitation, hygiene, better nutrition, and living standards. In other words, vaccination was not responsible for wiping out infectious disease as medical authorities claim.
- A tuberculosis vaccine trial in India involving more than 260,000 Indians resulted in more cases of TB among the vaccinated than the unvaccinated. But this vaccine is still being given to Australian children and others around the world.
- The cost of the whooping cough vaccine leaped from 11 cents in 1982 to $11.40 in 1987 because of the $8.00 a shot the company was putting aside to pay for legal and damages costs for the brain-damaged and dead victims of the vaccine.
- Millions of children in "Third World" countries were still dying from measles, tuberculosis, diphtheria, tetanus, polio etc., despite being fully vaccinated.

The consequences of vaccines for health, both short and long term, are appalling. But they serve the Illuminati perfectly in both the health and mental effects for the population they wish to control and the profits they accumulate. Again, think pyramid. Those at the top, the Anunnaki bloodlines, created and control the World Health Organization at the United Nations. This supports in its statements the agenda of the Illuminati and their drug companies. The World Health Organization announces there is going to be an epidemic of something or other and the Illuminati agents in government start a mass vaccination against this alleged "danger" via the medical profession. The Illuminati drug companies then sell them the vaccines. This happened with measles vaccinations in the UK in the 1990s. The mass vaccination programmes in the "Third World" are funded and administered through the Illuminati's World Bank, World Heath Organization, and other UN agencies. This allows them to target certain peoples in their campaign of genocide. Dr Lanctot writes in *The Medical Mafia*:

> "Vaccination decimates populations. Drastically in Third World countries. Chronically in industrialized countries. In this regard, Robert McNamara [Bil, TC, CFR], the former President of the World Bank, former Secretary of State in the United States, who ordered massive bombing of Vietnam, and a member of the Expanded Program on Immunization, made some very interesting remarks. As reported by a French publication, j''ai tout compris', he was quoted as stating: 'One must take draconian measures of demographic reduction against the will of the populations. Reducing the birth rate has proved to be impossible or insufficient. One must therefore increase the mortality rate. How? By natural means. Famine and sickness (translation from French).'"[14]

"Draconian methods" = methods employed by the Draco. Dr Lanctot says that vaccination enables the selected populations to be decimated. It allows "targeted genocide" and permits the killing of people from a certain race, group, or country, while leaving others untouched. All can be done in the name of health and well being, she says. Diseases have been dispersed among "Third World" populations through vaccination and water supplies. Dr Gotlieb, a cancerologist, told a hearing investigating the CIA that he dispersed a large quantity of viruses into the Congo River in Zaire in 1960 to contaminate the water used for drinking by local people. Dr Gotlieb went on to become head of the National Cancer Institute to further his campaign to "fight disease". Cancer research organisations, to which people give millions of pounds through charity fundraising worldwide, are more Illuminati fronts to stop the discovery of a cure those on the inside already know exists. If you give money to them, you are giving it to the Illuminati, although the genuine people shaking their collection tins in the street are not aware of this.

The AIDS scam[15]
AIDS is another of the diseases causing untold misery and suffering, which the Illuminati artificially introduced through vaccination. The biggest smokescreen to this is the claim that HIV causes AIDS. Doctors, media, and public accept this as unquestioned truth. Nonsense. The fact that large numbers of AIDS victims are not

HIV-positive is proof alone that all AIDS cases are not HIV related. HIV is actually a weak virus and it has been labelled the all-encompassing villain to hide the real causes of shattered immune systems. What a coincidence that "wonder drugs" to treat people with HIV, like the Rockefeller cartel's infamous AZT, have a rather significant side effect: they destroy...the immune system! No, it's true. AZT was a chemotherapy drug for cancer and was found to be so toxic it had to be withdrawn. When you see the effects of chemotherapy drugs that are still in use, how toxic must AZT really be? Chemotherapy drugs have a simple role. They kill cells. Not just cancer cells. All cells. The question is will they kill all the cancer cells before they kill enough healthy cells to kill the patient? This is why chemotherapy patients get so ill and even if the cancer is eliminated they have a permanently damaged immune system because the drug also kills the white cells that protect us against disease. When Illuminati agents whipped up the anger of homosexuals to demand that a treatment be found for HIV, a Rockefeller company took AZT back off the shelf as a "wonder drug". Its "wonder" was that it increased the creation of white blood cells, the body's immune system that HIV is supposed to destroy. What they didn't tell you was that this initial increase in white cells was because AZT was so poisonous, the body's defence mechanism jumped into action when it was administered and produced all the white cells it could to ward off the invader. However, AZT then went to war on these white blood cells, thus destroying the immune system, and the patients die of "AIDS". No, they don't. They die of the treatment. Also, when you die of the so-called "AIDS diseases" and you are HIV-positive, the diagnosis is recorded as "AIDS". If someone dies of those same diseases and they are not HIV-positive, the cause of death is recorded as whatever the disease was that killed them. In this way, it is built into the very death records that only those with HIV die of AIDS. This is a lie, but it suits the Illuminati. For the truth about AIDS and HIV, see the brilliant book by Christine Maggiore, *What If Everything You Thought You Knew About AIDS Was Wrong* (Health Education AIDS Liaison, Los Angeles Chapter, 1996). It is available through my website and Bridge of Love. Christine was alerted to the lies and deceit when she had a positive HIV test, followed by negative ones, followed by positive ones. The whole AIDS network, the drug companies and the AIDS charities, are Illuminati controlled or manipulated and it has created a multi-billion-dollar industry through which both drug companies and charities massively benefit. Christine Maggiore realised how much the charities care about what is really happening when she took her documented and extensive research to them and was quickly shown the door.

So where did AIDS come from? A disease very similar to AIDS, called the Kalaazar, killed 60,000 in the south of Sudan. It destroys the immune system and the victims die of other diseases. Africa has been a major target of disease by injection because the Illuminati want complete control of that continent with its fantastic natural wealth, and it has long embarked on a campaign of genocide against the black African peoples. In 1988, the Ambassador of Senegal announced that AIDS had ravaged his country and whole villages were being decimated. A few years earlier, scientific and medical teams arranged through the World Health Organization had come to vaccinate the people against hepatitis B. A vaccine for hepatitis B was also tested on homosexuals in New York in 1978 and two years later in San Francisco, Los Angeles, Denver, Chicago, and St Louis, in a programme by the World Health Organization and the National Institute of Health. The "AIDS epidemic" began among the homosexual communities of those very cities in 1981. Dr Lanctot reveals:

> "There are reports of collaboration between these two organizations in 1970 to study the consequences of certain viruses and bacteria introduced to children during vaccination campaigns. In 1972...[they focussed]...on the viruses which provoked a drop in the immune mechanism. Wolf Szmuness directed the anti-hepatitis B experiments undertaken in New York. He had very close links with the Blood Center where he had his laboratory, the National Institute of Health, the National Cancer Institute, the Food and Drug Administration, the World Health Organisation, and the Schools of Public Health of Cornell, Yale, and Harvard [all Illuminati controlled]. In 1994 a vast vaccination campaign against hepatitis B was undertaken in Canada. It is useless, dangerous and costly. And what for? Is there a hidden agenda? I was there in 1993. It troubled me to see that it was aimed at a whole generation (1 to 20 years), in only one province (Quebec). Since when do viruses respect borders, and especially provincial ones at that?" [16]

Dr Lanctot established that there was no hepatitis B epidemic, nor any risk of one. She said that three different vaccines were administered, each in a designated area. Certain nurses were selected and trained to administer a special vaccine; all children were entered into a computerised data bank; the pressure to vaccinate the children was enormous and schools were turned into clinics. Those who did not want to be vaccinated were pointed out and treated as social outcasts (exactly the same happened in the UK with the measles vaccine programme in the 1990s). Nurses chased down parents at home who did not want their children vaccinated (ditto). Dr Lanctot knew one mother who did not want her child vaccinated. A nurse came to the house and made her think it was compulsory. The mother gave in and the child is now physically and mentally handicapped. In 1986, without explanation or permission from the parents, the hepatitis B vaccine was given to Native American children in Alaska. Several died and many became ill because of what appears to have been a virus called RSV (Rous Sarcoma Virus) in the vaccine. Native North American tribes have been the targets for many "vaccination programmes" because the Illuminati want their lands and resources and to complete the genocide they began when the Europeans came. To this end, as I know from my own research, they have infiltrated the tribal elders and control the agencies responsible for "Indian affairs" which answer to the Federal Government. Dr. Lanctot tells how she met a group of Native women to talk about health and the subject of vaccinations came up. The group's nurse told her that the federal government had given her complete freedom in the management of their health, but with one strict condition: every vaccination had to be scrupulously applied to all. "The silence was deafening. We all understood," Dr Lanctot recalls. [17]

Death by doctor

Doctors in the United States are now statistically more dangerous than guns. Every year there are around 120,000 deaths caused by doctor errors, an average of 0.171, per doctor. There are 1,500 deaths by guns, an average of 0.000181 per gun owner. We have an outcry from many people for guns to be banned, fuelled by Illuminati propaganda, and yet a doctor is, according to these figures, 9,000 times more likely to kill you.[18] Hundreds of thousands of people are in hospitals right now because of the effects of the drugs that were supposed to make them well.[19] The UK National Audit Office also highlighted the astonishing dangers presented by "modern" medicine. They show that some 100,000 patients acquire infections in UK hospitals every year, resulting in 5,000 deaths and making a "substantial contribution" to another 15,000 fatalities. These figures also confirm a report in the London *Daily Express*, which claimed a massive cover-up by hospitals of the dangers patients face in their care and the scale of the annual death toll. The fact that the cause of death is a hospital-acquired infection is being hidden from patients' families and not mentioned on the death certificate.

One of the other problems highlighted is that of the so-called "super-bugs", which have mutated an immunity to many antibiotics because doctors have been prescribing them like confetti for so long – another Illuminati plan to destroy the effectiveness of the human immune system. As a result, they no longer kill the bugs. Such an outcome has long been predicted by "alternative" healers and others who could see the obvious. It is staggering to consider the attacks by the medical profession on "alternative" healing methods when figures prove that the dangers of being treated by the Illuminati-controlled medical establishment are infinitely greater. These alternatives to the drug cartel and the medical establishment have to fight for their very existence against Illuminati-initiated laws to legislate them into oblivion. Even our right to take food supplements and natural alternatives to drugs is being threatened by the Codex committee, an offshoot of the World Health Organization. Public campaigns are already being fought to protect the basic human right of deciding what does or does not go into our bodies. If we don't have control of our own bodies, what freedoms are left? But that's where we are going. In the UK we pay multi-billions in our taxation to fund the National Heath Service or the Human Debris Processing Unit, as I call it. But even though it is funded with the public's money, the public cannot decide on the methods of treatment they have. Alternative methods are suppressed in favour of the scalpel and the drug.

Food supplements are being taken to overcome the loss of nutrients we once used to get from our food. The emergence of chemical farming after the Second World War, which is destroying the soil and adding lethal poisons to the food, was another Illuminati operation. When this change in food production methods was being introduced in the UK, the man behind it was Lord Victor Rothschild, friend and "adviser" (dictator) to shape-shifter, Ted Heath, as the head of the Heath's policy unit, the Central Policy Review Staff. Victor Rothschild was one of the great Illuminati manipulators of the 20th century (see *...And The Truth Shall Set You Free*). The Illuminati own the transnationals that make the poisons sprayed on our food –

and most of the farming land on which it is grown. They are now destroying the natural crop varieties and patenting their own replacements. These only grow if farmers use their "fertilisers" and the poisons they manufacture. It is against the law for poor farmers to use patented seeds unless they are bought from the transnationals (Illuminati) at the prices they demand. Destroying the natural varieties is being done to ensure that these farmers have no alternative, but to do so. This is all co-ordinated in line with the agenda for the mental, emotional, and physical control of the human race by the Anunnaki bloodlines. All these manipulations are part of one manipulation, the Illuminati agenda.

Micro-chipped population

The most important goal of the Illuminati is a micro-chipped population. Their aim is to have every person on the planet micro-chipped and every child micro-chipped at birth. This is no science fiction fantasy. It is already happening. Of course, they won't come out and be honest about it because they know that many people will resist (well, some, anyway). They are doing it by stepping-stones to obscure what the real game is. They began with the micro-chipping of animals, first voluntarily and now often by law, and the same method is being used on humans. In 1997 a friend introduced me to a man in America. He had asked to meet me because he was a scientist working against his will on CIA secret projects that the run-of-the-mill politicians have no idea are going on. When I asked him why he used his genius to advance the agenda, he opened his shirt and on his chest was a see-through "sachet", similar to those used for shampoo. The CIA calls them "patches". Inside I could see an orangey-golden liquid. He said that he joined the CIA in the belief that he was serving his country, but he soon realised that they did not want his knowledge to help humanity. The idea was to control them. When he began to rebel against the misuse of his work, he left home one morning and remembers nothing else until he woke up on a medical-type table. When he began to focus, he noticed the "patch" on his chest. They have manipulated his body to need the drug the patch contains and it has to be replaced every 72 hours. If he doesn't do what he is told, they don't replace the patch and he begins to die a long and painful death. Large numbers of brilliant scientists, who could be setting the world free from poverty and hunger, are in the same situation.

This man told me about the micro-chipping agenda and much else besides. He arranged to meet me to expose what was being planned for the human race because he had no idea how long they would allow him to live. When these scientists have served their purpose, the patch is no longer replaced and they die painfully, taking with them the knowledge of what is going on. First he said that the cure for cancer has been known for decades, but they would not release this to the public because they did not want people to survive and were making far more money drugging the dying and treating the symptoms than they ever would curing the disease. He said the technology existed to create abundant growth in deserts without water by stimulating the energy fields of the plants. At its optimum, it was like watching a time-lapse photograph, so fast did they grow, he said. This would eliminate hunger by itself if it were made available. But this same technology was, instead, used to kill thousands of people in a mass murder that he witnessed. The CIA (an Illuminati agency) had gathered a vast multitude together in Ethiopia during the famine. He was in a plane that he thought was flying over the area to cast a vibrational field across the land to stimulate plant growth. When he came to the front of the plane to see what was happening, he saw thousands of people lying dead. They had been killed by the power of the magnetic field because the CIA was testing his technology as a weapon that could kill people, but not damage property. He also said that the technology to give us all the power and warmth we need without pollution or utility bills – free energy – has been known for decades. I know this from people I have met who are producing these systems, but they can't get them into production because the Illuminati control the patent offices, the money, and the major companies required to mass-produce them. Imagine a piece of kit in your home giving you warmth and power every day forever without cost. Again this technology uses the pool of unseen vibrating energy all around us and turns it into usable power. All this technology would be ours today if it were not suppressed by the Illuminati.

But it was when he turned to micro-chips that the CIA scientist became most animated. He confirmed that the Illuminati plan was to micro-chip everybody. On one level it was to tag us and keep a constant track of where we are and what we are doing, he said. But the main reason was to manipulate at will our mental and emotional processes. He said that people should not only think about the messages going from the chip to the computer. Far more important were the messages from the computer to the embodied chip. He said people had no comprehension of the level of technology in the Illuminati secret projects. Once people were chipped, he said, the computer could make them docile or aggressive, sexually aroused or sexually suppressed, and close down their minds to a point where they were like zombies. From where I am looking, I think it's already begun! He asked me to urge people to resist the micro-chip at all costs because once we concede to that we would be nothing more than machines controlled by the "aliens" he confirmed were behind the whole thing. We need a global campaign of "SAY NO TO THE CHIP" and we need it NOW! The chip is in almost every piece of technology and is embedded in newer cars. This can externally immobilise the engine from satellite, as well as tracking every journey. As I predicted in my books of many years ago, it is already being suggested that people should be chipped to make the world more efficient. Professor Kevin Warwick of Reading University in England has been used to promote the use of the human micro-chip. He was implanted with a chip amid enormous publicity and has introduced us all to the benefits of controlling electronic devices at a distance. Wow. The latest I heard was that he and his wife, Irena, were going to be implanted with another chip which would connect their nervous systems to data processors, batteries, and radio transmitters. Apparently their teenage daughter, Madeleine, was asked to join the exercise, but said "No way". There is at least *one* thinking member of the family, then. "This is the next step of merging man and machine," said Professor Warwick, "We will be able to have communications between two nervous systems across the Net." Well glory be.

He is being funded, according to the London *Daily Mail*, to the tune of some half a million pounds by major US Internet firms. Professor Warwick admits that he and his wife could suffer permanent physical damage to their arms, but added that he hoped "there will be no mental damage". One wonders how they would tell.

We are now seeing people chipped with their medical records and other personal details. The plan is to sell the chip as a way to stop people being mugged for their money because their financial details would be on a chip under their skin. Preventing credit card fraud is another excuse. They will also promote the micro-chipping of children by claiming that they could never be lost again because the chip could always locate them. The more children that go missing or are murdered and the more they promote the danger of paedophiles in the community, the more likely parents are to be frightened into micro-chipping their kids. Of course, the greatest abusers and murderers of children are the very Illuminati who are promoting the chip. Problem-reaction-solution. A guy called David Adair, who has worked on high-tech projects with NASA, has been on the New Age lecture circuit in America for years extolling the benefits of micro-chipping our children. I cannot believe that someone with his insider knowledge of secret technology would be unaware of what that would really mean in terms of tagging and mind control. Implants have been found in people who claim to have been abducted by "aliens", and how many people are already micro-chipped without their knowledge? The CIA scientist told me in 1997 that micro-chips in the secret projects were now so small they could be injected through a hypodermic needle during mass vaccination programmes. Some years later, a picture appeared in a British newspaper of an ant holding a micro-chip in its pincers and that's only the size they allow us to see. You will find that shot in the *picture section*. Chipping people so they can "talk" to their personal computers and the Internet is another approach. The London *Sunday Times* reported:

> "The next computer you buy may be the last one you will need. In future, scientists want to insert electronic chips into our heads so we can plug directly into the information superhighway. British researchers are among international teams working on an implant to translate human thought into computer language. In a generation, one group says, people with a peppercorn-sized chip in the back of the neck will be able to talk to machines." [20]

What they don't tell you is that the machines will be able to talk to them, too. In *...And The Truth Shall Set You Free*, I tell the story of Dr Carl W. Sanders, a highly acclaimed electronics engineer in the UK, who was developing a micro-chip implant to help spinal injury patients. He said that his project was hi-jacked by the one-world brigade and he attended 17 meetings with them in places like Brussels and Luxemburg. He told *Nexus* Magazine:

> "I was at one meeting where it was discussed: "How can you control a people if you can't identify them?" People like Henry Kissinger and CIA folk attended these meetings. It was discussed: "How do you make people aware of the need for

something like this chip?" All of a sudden the idea came: "Let's make them aware of lost children, etc. This was discussed in meetings almost like people were cattle. The CIA came up with the idea of putting pictures of lost children on milk cartons (which they did). Since the chip is now accepted, you don't see those pictures anymore do you? It's served its purpose." [21]

Dr Sanders said they want the chip to contain the name and picture of the person, an international (world government) social security number, fingerprint identification, physical description, family and medical history, address, occupation, income tax information, and criminal record. People will be told that if they are chipped, they will have no need for passports or any other personal paperwork and enough apparent benefits will be thrown in to persuade a comatose population unaware of the game to agree to, literally, give their minds away. Or their brain function, anyway. Micro-chipping will begin as a voluntary programme, with people encouraged to enjoy the convenience of being the clone of a computer. Then it will be made compulsory. The more missing children, terrorist bombs, mass shootings, and other horrors the Illuminati can engineer, the more the compulsory micro-chip will be "justified" and accepted by the sheeple. Those refusing the chip will be said to have "something to hide" (the old trick), or not care about the missing children or those killed and maimed in the bombings and shootings. The "threat" of terrorists with nuclear devices in suitcases will also get a mention, it usually does. The global computer network to which these chips will answer is already in place underground at many locations. One is in Brussels, Belgium, a major Illuminati centre, and the location of NATO and the European Union. Another is at Cheyenne Mountain in the United States.

While I was writing this chapter, a company called Applied Digital Solutions announced the launch of a human micro-chip it calls Digital Angel. Angel = reptilians. It is a human implant designed to monitor the wearer's physiology, like pulse and body temperature, and their location. The company claims it is the first operational human chip that can be linked to the global positioning satellite tracking systems. It will allow your every move anywhere on the planet to be tracked from satellite. It is also designed to connect with the Internet and to become a user-identity device for the web. It is described as a "dime-sized" implant, inserted just under the skin. The chip will be powered "electromechanically" through the movement of muscles and it can be activated by the wearer or the monitoring technology. It has, according to the official statements, been developed by Dr Peter Zhou and his research team and has progressed "ahead of schedule". The Illuminati agenda is not dependent on the necessary technology becoming available by accident. It is developed well in advance and is introduced in line with the planned timescale. At that point we are told the technology has just been discovered when in fact it has been waiting in the wings for years. The tax-exempt foundations, like the Rockefeller Foundation, give vast sums to scientific research, but, as a US Congressional Committee established in the 1950s, they do not lose control of how the money is spent and insist that the research serves the needs of the global agenda. The Illuminati-controlled Princeton University was involved in the development of this micro-chip along with the New Jersey Institute of Technology. Dr Peter Zhou is the chief scientist at *DigitalAngel.net* Inc., a wholly owned subsidary of Applied Digital. He stresses, of course, the benefits for people becoming human robots connected to a satellite. He said he was excited about his chip's ability to save lives by monitoring medical conditions and giving an exact location to rescue services. I predicted many years ago that this would be one of the ways they would sell the chip to the people when the time came for its introduction. He said that the implant would become as popular as cell phones and vaccines (one of which fries your brain and the other suppresses your intellect and undermines your immune system). Dr Zhou then delivered some of the most chilling sentences I have ever read:

> "Digital Angel will be a connection from yourself to the electronic world. It will be your guardian, protector. It will bring good things to you. We will be a hybrid of electronic intelligence and our own soul." [22]

Just read those words again, especially the last sentence. This is what we conspiracy "theorists" have been predicting for all these years and now it is here. I heard that the introduction of this particular chip design may now be in some doubt, but it gives you an excellent idea of what is planned. And it is not only the chip. Just look around you today and see all the methods of control and surveillance. You cannot walk through a town or city without moving from one camera to another. Go into a shop or take money from a wall machine, drive a car, catch a train or plane, and you are being watched. This unbelievable scale of surveillance has been introduced little by little by the Illuminati until you wake up one morning and realise that George Orwell's "Big Brother" is not just coming – he's here. All the examples I have given in this chapter, and they are only a tiny few, are each part of the *same* agenda. I cannot stress that enough. Seeing how all these strands are connected is the key to lifting the veil. There are pressure groups fighting and uncovering the facts about environmental destruction, poisoned food, vaccinations, the drug cartel, oil cartel, transnational corporations of every kind, corruption in government, the banking scam, Third World debt, manipulation of wars, poverty, cancer, AIDS, child abuse, Satanic ritual sacrifice, media suppression, assassinations, erosion of freedoms, high taxation, and a whole list of others. But what we need to see for the mist to clear is that these are *all* part of *one* agenda working to *one* aim. All the scams are *one* scam. We can go on opposing these individual strands for a hundred lifetimes, but we will never make any fundamental change until we stop focusing on the symptoms and start homing in on the cause of them all: the Anunnaki bloodlines and their plan for a global fascist state. Whenever something that has remained hidden is close to becoming physical reality, there must always be a time when it hits the surface and can be seen. This is the period we are now living in. We are seeing massive global groups and empires fusing with other massive global groups and empires in banking, business, and media, while the concentration of political power continues apace through the European Union, "free-trade areas," the United Nations. The same people have long controlled all these aspects of our society, but now we can see they do as they move the final pieces into place for the global fascist state or "New World Order".

Losing their cover?

One theme of many insiders and former insiders who have talked to me, is that the reptilian shape-shifters are finding it more and more difficult to hold their "human" form. Maybe this is why so many more people seem to be seeing the shape-shifters these days. The explanation I am given is that the vibrational frequency of the planet is changing as it completes a vast cycle and enters a new one. Some have called this new cycle the "Age of Aquarius" as the Earth moves through the area of the heavens dubbed "Pisces", which it entered around 2,000 years ago, and into a "new age" of Aquarius. It is almost like passing through a curriculum at a school with the different energy combinations affecting the Earth, offering different eras and experiences for those who choose to be here at the time. The Maya peoples in the Yucatan, Mexico, left records of their measurement of "time" and their small, medium, and great cycles, of the Earth's evolution. One of their great cycles, which apparently began in 3113BC, is due to be completed in 2012. Other researchers of these ancient measurements of "time" suggest that much longer cycles than this are also ending in this same period. The base resonant frequency of the planet, known as Schumann Cavity Resonance, was discovered in 1899 and remained pretty constant until the mid-1980s when it began to quicken rapidly. This has continued to increase and one effect of these higher vibrations is that "time" appears to be passing much faster. Some researchers, psychics, and "mystics" suggest that our frequency is getting closer every day to the fourth-dimensional range. This would be another explanation for why people are seeing shape-shifters more often and why the reptilians know that the day is fast approaching when they will not be able to hide their real nature any longer. I am told that the sacrificial rituals and blood drinking increased dramatically from the mid-1980s as the vibrational change forced them to work harder to hold human form.

It is no coincidence that this period coincides with the completion of their centralised global state with its world army, micro-chipped population, and fierce structure of globally centralised top-down control of all weapons, finance, media, and government. They know that we are going to see them in the next few years as they really are. Another role of the micro-chip could well be to close down that area of the brain that would allow us to see them. We are clearly being prepared for the great unveiling, especially the children, by the explosion of reptilian imagery and themes in the mass media. The movies and television are awash with dinosaurs and "good guy" reptilian characters in children's cartoons. The US television series called V in the 1980s, now a Warner Video, produced a most accurate potential scenario, I believe. It told the story of a world controlled by reptilian extraterrestrials, which hid their true nature within an apparently human form. These extraterrestrials were called the "Visitors" and were given control of all the positions of power by appearing to have humanity's interests at heart. They would announce that they were making available to humans this or that serum to cure this or that "incurable" disease. They also worked with compliant humans who were well rewarded for doing what they were told. One resistance group had realised that the "Visitors" were not human, but reptilian, and the movie shows how a few human rebels, helped by some sympathetic reptilians, exposed the truth and killed the "Visitors" by releasing a disease that only affected them. There was, naturally, poetic licence in the movie, but the basic theme was extremely accurate and whoever came up with the plot must know what is going on. I emphasise again here that not all reptilians wish to control the planet and treat humans like cattle. I am talking of one significant faction. But if we don't focus on that faction and its agenda, we are going to deeply regret not doing so. One victim of Illuminati mind control, who claims to have seen the reptilians in underground bases and other locations, said:

> "Considering that the Dracos and Greys, in general, lack any sense of spiritual integrity, and are rather controlled for the most part by their predatory instincts, all efforts to negotiate with them are forever doomed to fail, just as if one were to try to 'negotiate' with a cancer tumour. For in every single case that I am aware of, the Dracos and Greys have historically, and without exception, violated every one of their so-called 'treaties' with the human race, and in fact have consistently used these treaties as weapons of infiltration and conquest." [23]

It is a widely held view in the UFO research community that leading world governments, particularly the United States, have entered into "treaties" of mutual benefit with the reptilians and greys in return for technological knowledge, but these "agreements" have been used to further establish their control. If these reports of such treaties are correct, they only tell part of the story. It depends which level in the hierarchy you are dealing with. For thousands of years, the top Anunnaki bloodlines have been knowingly working to the reptilian agenda. These guys did not just arrive in the 1950s and start doing secret deals with governments. They have been here all along. If there were "treaties" agreed around that time it was with those levels of government that do not have the big picture of what is happening. I have heard it suggested many times, also, that an "alien" invasion force is heading for this planet, but we should be very careful here, I think. What better way to justify a global fascist state, or giving power to the reptilians, than to sell the idea that we must join forces to meet a threat from beyond. A Swiss delegate apparently wrote down the words of Henry Kissinger at the 1992 Bilderberg meeting in Evian-Les-Bains in France:

> "Today, America would be outraged if UN troops entered Los Angeles to restore order; tomorrow they will be grateful. This is especially true if they were told that there was an outside threat from beyond, whether real or promulgated, that threatened our very existence. It is then that all peoples of the world will plead with world leaders to deliver them from this evil. The one thing every man fears is the unknown. When

presented with this scenario, individual rights will be willingly relinquished for the guarantee of their well being granted to them by their world government."

What an irony it would be if the reptilians that have been here for hundreds of thousands of years, were wheeled out as our "saviours" from an "alien invasion". But anything is possible given the stunning compliance of the human mind, even without the micro-chip. Many of the most important elements of the reptilian agenda are very close and if we are going to restore true freedom to this planet, and dismantle the Anunnaki web, a vast number of people have got to wake up and grow up very quickly.

SOURCES

1   You will find the background to aspartame in the Medical Archives of the David Icke website and specific articles related to this section can be found at:
http://www.davidicke.net/medicalarchives/badmed/asparaddict.html
http://www.davidicke.net/medicalarchives/badmed/lowdownaspartame.html
http://www.davidicke.net/medicalarchives/cover/whoswho.html
www.dorway.com

2   *http://www.davidicke.net/medicalarchives/badmed/lowdownaspartame.html*

3   More background to Prozac is in the Medical Archives of the David Icke Website. Articles specific to this section are:
http://www.davidicke.net/medicalarchives/badmed/prozac.html
http://www.davidicke.net/medicalarchives/badmed/prozactruth.html
http://www.davidicke.net/medicalarchives/badmed/navyprozac.html

4   They Are Doping Our Kids: *http://www.illuminati-news.com/doping_kids.htm*

5   How Psychiatry Is Making Drug Addicts Out Of America's School Children:
http://www.wealth4freedom.com/truth/Ritalin.html

6   They Are Doping Our Kids: *http://www.illuminati-news.com/doping_kids.htm*

7   Ibid

8   *http://www.davidicke.net/medicalarchives/badmed/stupidflouride.html*

9   Ibid

10   *http://www.davidicke.net/medicalarchives/badmed/flouride2.html*

11   Ibid

12   There is considerable background to vaccinations in the Medical Archives at the David Icke website and those specific to this section are:
http://www.davidicke.net/medicalarchives/badmed/vaccinemafia.html
http://www.davidicke.net/medicalarchives/badmed/forcedvaccine.html
http://www.davidicke.net/medicalarchives/badmed/vaccinemafia.html
http://www.davidicke.net/medicalarchives/badmed/vaccineautism.html

13 Ian Sinclair, *Health: The Only Immunity* (published by Ian Sinclair and available from 5 Ivy
    Street, Ryde, New South Wales, Australia, 2112)

14 See also *http://www.davidicke.net/medicalarchives/badmed/vaccinemafia.html* and
    http://www.davidicke.com/icke/articles/lanctot.html

15 There is a long list of articles on AIDS in the Medical Archives of the David Icke Website

16 See *The Medical Mafia* and
    http://www.davidicke.net/medicalarchives/badmed/vaccinemafia.html

17 Ibid

18 *http://www.davidicke.net/medicalarchives/badmed/doctorguns.html*

19 *http://www.davidicke.net/medicalarchives/badmed/5000die.html*

20 London *Sunday Times* reported: on April 16th, 1995

21 *Nexus* Magazine, summer 1994

22 *http://www.davidicke.net/newsroom/global/090800a.html*

23 *http://www.reptilianagenda.com/exp/e020900a.html*

CHAPTER 18

the Matrix

The Matrix is everywhere. It is all around us. Even now, in this very room. You can see it when you look out your window or when you turn on your television. You can feel it when you go to work, when you go to church, when you pay your taxes. It is the world that has been pulled over your eyes to blind you from the truth.

Morpheus in the movie, *The Matrix*

We think we live in a "world". In fact we live in a frequency range. That's all it is. We are trapped in a frequency range and therefore trapped in an illusion. This is what the well-known movie calls the Matrix.

The "world" we see around us is merely the tiny fraction of multi-dimensional infinity that our physical senses of sight, hearing, touch, smell, and taste can access. The physical world we perceive is like a radio station and our physical senses are tuned to its frequency. So that is all we see. But all around us are the other frequencies or densities of infinite creation – the ones that "science" has denied exist. They are all around us on frequencies beyond the range of our physical senses. These are the frequencies that can be seen and heard by animals, like cats, when they react to apparently "empty" space, and dogs when they hear sounds far higher than we can. Newborn babies also react to "empty" space until their senses are imprisoned by conditioning. These are the frequencies accessed by true psychics – the oracles of the ancient world – who can raise their vibration to tune into these unseen realms. The Italian physicist Giuliana Conforto in her brilliant book *LUH, Man's Cosmic Game* (Edizioni Noesis, 1998) puts it like this:

> "…a good 90% of total calculated mass is in fact dark and unobservable, while only 10% is observable by means of the infinite rainbow, which is light. The visible universe we do observe, with its billions of stars and galaxies, is in turn only a narrow perspective of this already scanty 10%. …Inside every physical body there is an invisible, but far more massive reality (90%), a non-observable substance, that can be felt and experienced as emotions, intuitions, and feelings."[1]

It is within the realms of this unseen "dark matter" that other-dimensional entities like the reptilians operate. Giuliana Conforto also points out that in some galaxies, this dark matter, unseen by the human eye, is 100 times the mass we can observe. We can see from our frequency range just 1% of what exists in such galaxies![2] When we open our minds and expand our own frequency range of perception, so we will "discover" more planets and stars. The atom is said to be the foundation of physical matter and yet all but a fraction of the space within an atom is, to the human eye, "empty". A "physical atom" from which all physical forms are made, consists of a nucleus with electrons orbiting around it like a mini solar system. Dr Douglas Baker said in his book, *The Opening Of The Third Eye* (Aquarian Press, Wellingborough, England, 1977): "If we expanded the hydrogen atom to the size of a cathedral, its electron would perhaps be the size of a nickel!"[3] The overwhelming majority of the "space" within an atom is "dark matter" operating on frequencies we can't see and it is the same with our solar system and the entire dense physical universe. If only "science" were led by Giuliana Conforto's way of thinking, instead of the concrete minds of academia, we would already live in a world of infinitely greater awareness of who we are and the nature of life. But look at her figures there and apply them to the "scientific" denials of intelligent life beyond this planet. We are asked to believe that life as we know it has only evolved on this one physical planet among the billions of planets and stars in this visible universe, which is, itself, only a fraction of visible "light", which is in turn only 10% of total mass? What a joke. God save us from official "science". And, of course, all this is only by current calculations. That fraction of 10% of total mass that we can see might turn out to be an extremely optimistic view.

The kingdom of heaven is within you

All around you now, and sharing the same space as your body, are all the radio and television frequencies broadcasting to your area. You can't see them and they are not aware of each other because they are vibrating to such different frequencies that they pass through each other and your body without anyone noticing. The only time they "interfere" with each other is when they are very close on the frequency band. When you turn on your radio, the frequency you have accessed is passing through the windows and walls of your house to reach the radio receiver because the walls and broadcast frequencies are so far apart on the density scale. This is how "ghosts" and "extraterrestrials" can apparently walk through walls and why some people see them and others don't. It depends whether your mind is tuning to their frequency or not. These other-dimensional entities, including the reptilians, are all around us sharing the same space. You can sometimes feel them when the vibes in a room change and you sense an icy chill or, with positive entities, a feeling of great love in the atmosphere around you. They are so close to our frequency range, but just outside it. Credo Mutwa talks of the vibrational "blind spot" that people have which prevents them from seeing these entities and I think this is manufactured externally in some way, probably through a frequency broadcast from below ground that shuts off part of our DNA's multi-dimensional potential. The DNA is a transmitter and receiver of vibrational information and can therefore be reprogrammed by vibrational and electromagnetic fields. Nikola Tesla, whose genius was responsible for much of today's electrical system, understood that other frequencies existed, but the most profound parts of his work were suppressed. He once said:

> "We cannot even with positive assurance assert that some of them [other dimensional entities] might not be present here in our world in the very midst of us, for their constitution and life manifestations may be such that we are unable to perceive them." [4]

As I said earlier, when you move the radio dial and tune to another station you can no longer hear the first station because you have moved the dial out of its range and so now you are hearing another. But the first station has not disappeared, it goes on broadcasting. It's just that you can't hear it anymore. If you choose to retune your dial again, there it will be. It is the same with Creation. We are like droplets of water in an ocean of infinite energy taking infinite forms. This ocean of energy manifests as different densities or frequencies and at this moment we are tuned to this one, the "physical world". But all the other frequencies are around us and interpenetrating us while we perceive only the density that our physical senses can see, touch, hear, smell, and taste – the Matrix. As physicist, Giuliana Conforto, put it: "The fact that we are not able to observe [it] doesn't mean it doesn't exist, rather that human perception is severely limited." The late and great Bill Hicks, the brilliant and highly intelligent American comedian, encapsulated these truths magnificently. He said:

> "Matter is merely energy condensed to a slow vibration. We are all one consciousness experiencing itself subjectively. There's no such thing as death, life is just a dream, and we are the imagination of ourselves." [5]

Look at the findings of Albert Einstein, the most famous scientist of the 20th century. His E=MC2 shows that matter is just a form of energy and that energy cannot be destroyed, only transformed into another state. It's official, our consciousness, which is energy, is indestructible. We live forever. The truth is in front of our eyes. Purely by changing the temperature (frequency), ice becomes water and water becomes steam and steam "disappears". That simple temperature change turns "solid" ice into invisible vapour because different temperatures represent different frequencies. It is all the same energy, but in a very different state. Our bodies consist of many different sub-frequencies within the dense physical range. Look at X-rays. They are tuned to frequencies that match our bone structure and so they do not portray the outer flesh, which is vibrating to a different frequency. X-rays don't show the walls of buildings, just the rods of iron within them for the same reason. Look at the world from the X-ray frequency and it looks very different than it does from ours. How an object or person appears depends purely on the frequency from which you are observing. The human aura, as technology has shown, is a mass of different colours (frequencies) that change as our thoughts and emotions (frequencies) change. The X-ray is just one example of frequencies that science has confirmed exist, but we can't see. Ultraviolet, gamma-rays, infra-red, radio waves, etc., are some of the others. But had you suggested to a conventional scientist that any of those existed before they were officially discovered and he would almost certainly have called you ridiculous or dangerous. Every scientific "norm" since the dawn of the "scientific age" has been proved with time to be either flawed, not the full picture, or, often, unbelievably inaccurate and patently ludicrous. Yet generation after generation society clings to the "scientific" norms of its day until its knuckles turn white and its hair turns grey. "Science" goes on judging possibility by the apparent "laws" of this frequency range and yet scientists know that 90% of the mass of existence, what they call "dark matter", is not subject to these laws like gravity and those of the electromagnetic field. If we take the laws of physics as they may apply to one frequency and judge what is possible in other frequencies on the same basis, we will be in ignorance forever. What applies to one, does not apply to another.

There is no spoon

The key point in Bill Hick's superb encapsulation of hidden truth is: We are the imagination of ourselves. Our lives, our physical experience, are a manifestation of our thoughts. We are what we think we are. Our imagination of self and the world around us becomes our physical experience. You think you are ordinary? You will be "ordinary". You think you are powerless? You will be powerless. You think the best things in life happen to others? So they will. Everything is created by thought – our thoughts. In this dense, treacle-like, frequency range we live in, the time between the thought and its physical manifestation can appear to take a long time, but thought is still the creator. For instance, look around you now wherever you are. The buildings, furniture, and all the trinkets and utensils, are provably created by thought. Unless someone had *thought* to design them and *thought* to make them they could not exist. Without the thought there can be no physical creation. In other realms, where the energy is far less dense, the thought and its manifestation are simultaneous. The thought becomes manifest in an instant. All this means that we live in a world of illusion because the world is a reflection, a mirror, of human thought. What we think the world is, it will be. Or at least that will be our perception of what it is. In the movie, *The Matrix*, a little boy is bending spoons at will. But he says that the real truth is: "There is no spoon…it is not the spoon that bends, it is only yourself." What is real? Real is merely what you *believe* is real. As the Morpheus character in *The Matrix* says: "Real is just electrical signals interpreted by your brain." For goodness sake, we don't even see objects, only the light they are reflecting. Close the curtains and turn off the light. What can you see? Nothing. And if you can see anything it is only because some light source is reflecting from whatever you can see. The term "dark matter" refers to that which does not reflect light in our frequency range and therefore we cannot see it. We don't see anything, except reflected light. Even then the object enters our eyes upside down and has to be flipped over by the brain so we perceive it the right way up! And we don't even "hear" sound as such. Our ears convert pressure passing through the atmosphere into a series of waves and our brain transforms these waves into a perceived "sound". This is what televisions and radios do. The broadcasts don't travel through the air as pictures and sounds. Can you imagine episodes of Friends or Frasier flying over the rooftops? Or hearing all the radio shows on every station simultaneously wherever we went? Of course not. It doesn't work that way. The programmes are sent as broadcast waves, and television and radio technology decodes them into pictures and sound.

Welcome to my world

We each live in our own personal universe and when people come into our space they are entering our unique world of reality. There are areas where our universes agree and connect. Most people, for example, agree that the road outside your door and the cars driving past really exist. But apart from these basics, our universes can be very different. In my universe, to chase a fox with horses and hounds and tear it to pieces is an abomination. But to other universes, it's fine to do that. In my universe, a few people are controlling the planet through a network of secret societies working through all "sides". But in most other human universes these "sides" are completely unconnected and the world has an infinite diversity of decision-making and ownership. In my universe, some of the most famous people on the planet are torturing and sacrificing children. But most other human universes cannot conceive that such horrors could be taking place and so in their universes, they don't. Our minds observe the visible, physical world, and what we make of it becomes our reality, our personal universe. Because I see the world and events in very different terms to most people, there are far fewer points of agreement and connection between my universe and those of the mass of the people. For this reason, I am considered strange, extreme, or a "nutter". But that is only those people's *perception* of me from the perspective of their own universe. It's not what really is, only what they believe it is. It's a self-generated illusion.

You can prove over and over that the physical world is controlled by the non-physical mind. A stage illusionist can convince millions of minds that he has performed a "miracle" when it is just sleight of hand. There is one trick in which a girl is tied up and placed in a large box. The lid is shut tight and, after a roll of drums, the magician opens the box to find that the woman has disappeared. What she has done is hide in the box's false bottom giving the appearance that it is empty. The magician then moves to an identical box on the other side of the stage. When he opens it the woman miraculously reappears to wild applause. The minds of the audience have been convinced that somehow the woman has been transported from one box to the other. This, therefore, becomes their reality, part of their universe. But you know what really happens? The magician uses identical twins wearing identical clothes. It's that simple to delude the mind. I sat next to a guy on a television programme who ripped up the front page of the morning paper, crumpled the pieces together in his hands, and then opened it out in its original state. I was no more than two feet away. He ripped that paper to pieces. I saw him. But of course he didn't. He just convinced everyone that he did and once a mind is convinced of something it becomes that person's physical reality. A stage hypnotist can manipulate a member of the audience into believing that dog pooh is a prime piece of steak or that the woman next to him is naked or that he is anything from a donkey to a racing driver. The Illuminati are simply applying these techniques on a mass scale because they know how it all works – that's the knowledge they have worked so incessantly to keep from us.

Creating our own reality

We are not our physical bodies. That is merely one level of us for a short time while we experience this frequency range. The body is a holographic projection that allows our consciousness to interact with the dense physical realm. Plato said, quite rightly, that all bodies are only the shadows of true reality. Every particle of a hologram contains a picture of the entire image. This is why every cell of the body contains the information needed to create an entire body. A hologram is an illusion. It is not 3-D, but it looks 3-D. Same with the body. "Conventional" medicine concentrates purely on the holographic image and ignores the multi-frequency forces like thought and emotion that can harmonise or destabilise that image. Thus, official medicine has its entire focus on the symptom and not the cause of physical dis-ease, disharmony. We are certainly more than our bodies. We are, in truth, all that exists, has existed, and ever will exist. I am you, you are me, I am everything and everything is me. We are not only *part* of that infinite energy from which everything manifests, we *are* that energy. All of it, all of us. In the end there is no "me" or "we", just one infinite "I". Look out at the world. Look at the explosion of planets and stars in the night sky. All of it is you and that's only the fraction of you that your physical senses can see. We are all one energy, all each other. The divisions between us are an illusion and conflicts between us are conflicts and illusions within ourselves. The outer conflict is the expression of the inner conflict and those who come into our space, positive or negative, are outer projections of our own inner state of being. In this way, those who hate themselves and have no self-esteem attract, vibrationally, into their lives, their universe, people who will punish them. They don't know they are doing this, it's all played out in the subconscious mind. Look at how many women who are beaten violently by their partner end up with a new partner who also beats them violently. I have known women who changed partners four or five times and every one knocked the living shit out of them. Until the inner self changes, its outer manifestation cannot change. All the answers are within, not without. That's why the Illuminati encourage and manipulate us to look outside of ourselves for answers. They know that this way we will never find them. They want us to believe that the answers lie in the physical world, the "mirror", when that is just a reflection of what we are projecting from within. Thus, we see solutions in new laws and new powers for the police and authority when that is only papering over the cracks and diverting us from the real problem – the state and attitudes of the inner self, our consciousness. The Illuminati are delighted with this because they know that nothing fundamental will ever change until we go to the source of all experience – inside ourselves. They want us to believe that we can change the movie by focusing on the screen when the only way to change the movie is to change what is being *projected* on the screen. One simple example: if we loved each other, there would be no conflict in the world. Because we don't, there is. It's just a choice and those choices become manifest on the news and in our lives every day.

The reptilian brain

The more you understand about the reptilian mind the easier it is to see the Anunnaki-Illuminati at work in our society across the centuries. They have distinct character traits and they are seeking to make humans the same. These reptilian characteristics and their connection to the human brain are fundamental to the perpetuation of the illusions I call the Matrix. For those who, understandably, find even the idea of a reptilian race to be unimaginable, never mind the shape-shifting, I repeat the words of cosmologist Carl Sagan: "There are more potential combinations of DNA [physical forms] than there are atoms in the universe." Far from it being impossible for such a race to emerge, it would be more surprising if it had not. Studies have suggested that if the dinosaurs had survived, and some may have done so within the Earth, they would have evolved a reptilian humanoid form by now. Dale Russell, the senior palaeontologist at North Carolina University, was asked by the US space agency NASA to produce a report on what extraterrestrial life might look like. He evolved the Troodon dinosaur in line with genetic changes over millions of years and created a model of a being he called a dino-sauroid. It was a reptilian humanoid and identical to those that abductees and others have claimed to see. There is so much more to know about the dinosaurs. After all, their existence was only discovered by scientists in the 1880s. Credo Mutwa and others say that reptilians originated on this planet and were driven off before returning to claim what they believe is rightfully theirs. Maybe, maybe not. We only have their word for that and their word does not seem to be worth a lot. But this planet certainly has an enormous reptilian history. While I was writing this book, it was revealed that the fossil of a reptile that walked on two legs had been found in a German quarry in rock estimated to be at least 300 million years old. The find demolished previous scientific belief on reptilian evolution. Dinosaurs were not, as believed, the first reptiles to run on two legs. This newly-discovered biped, Eudibamus cursoris, was a reptile unrelated to the later dinosaurs. The Eudibamus skeletal structure suggests that it could run swiftly, probably standing up on its toes, with its forelimbs swinging in a pendulum-fashion. This is similar to the posture adopted by running humans, say the US, Canadian and German scientists. Researcher Alan Walton has compiled a large amount of background to the reptilian presence on Earth. He says:

> "Aside from reports and even photos of human footprints found fossilized *inside of* dinosaurian prints, suggesting a common existence – I discovered some interesting biological facts concerning 'reptilians'. It seems that biologists agree that snakes ultimately mutated from lizards, and lizards from the larger 'thunder lizards' or dinosaurs of ancient times. And what was the earliest dinosaur discovered? Well the

two contenders are the Eoraptor (which gave rise to the very cunning and dexterous Veloci-raptors as depicted in the Jurassic Park movies) and a similar saurian biped which walked upright like a man, about the size of a human being, and with hands that were ideal for grabbing and ripping flesh, the herrerasaurus: both were meat-eaters, however there are enough differences and similarities between Eoraptor and Herrerasaurus to suggest that they had a common ancestor a 'few branches down' the saurian tree."[6]

The most ancient part of the brain is known by scientists as the R-complex or "reptilian brain" (*Figure 46*). It is the most obvious remnant of our reptilian genetic history, apart from those who are still born with tails. This reptilian brain or R-complex is vital to understanding the ways that the Illuminati manipulate human thinking and perception. Most people have no idea of the reptilian heritage of the human body and its influence on our behaviour. Scientists say that the R-complex represents a core of the nervous system and originates from a "mammal-like reptile" that was once found all over the world in the Triassic period (205-240 million years ago). It is believed this was an evolutionary link between the dinosaurs and the mammals. There may be other explanations, too! All mammals have this reptilian part of the brain. Now look at the character traits of the reptilian brain as agreed by scientists. I quote here from a fascinating Internet article by Skip Largent:

"At least five human behaviours originate in the reptilian brain …Without defining them, I shall simply say that in human activities they find expression in: obsessive-compulsive behaviour; personal day-to-day rituals and superstitious acts; slavish conformance to old ways of doing things; ceremonial re-enactments; obeisance to precedent, as in legal, religious, cultural, and other matters…and all manner of deceptions."[7]

Add other traits of the R-complex such as "territoriality" (this is mine, get out); aggression; and the idea that might-is-right, winner-takes-all. Put that little lot together and you have the very attitudes of the Illuminati. Racism comes from the reptilian brain also and aggressive, violent sex, which the Illuminati bloodlines indulge in big time – ask US Presidents "father" George Bush and Gerald Ford, Vice President Dick Cheney, and the list of other famous Illuminati names I expose in my books. Can it really be a coincidence that the Illuminati manifest the classic traits of the reptilian brain while, at the same time, the evidence suggests that they are reptilian bloodlines? Cosmologist Carl Sagan, who knew far more than he was telling, wrote a book, *The Dragons Of Eden* (Ballantine Books, New York, 1977), to highlight the reptilian influences on humanity. He said: "…It does no good whatsoever to ignore the reptilian component of human nature, particularly our ritualistic and hierarchical behaviour. On the contrary, the model may help us understand what human beings are all about." Other areas of the human brain balance the extremes of the reptilian characteristics in most people, but they can still be seen, for example, in those who live their lives as a daily ritual, such as going to

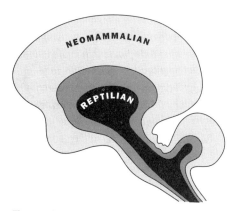

Figure 46: *The reptilian brain or "R-complex" is an ancient part of the human brain. From here we get the character traits of cold-blooded behaviour, the desire for top-down hierarchy, and an obsession with ritual. These are balanced by other parts of the brain in humans, but not in the full-blown reptilians, which manipulate this planet*

the same supermarket at the same time every week and having the same meals on the same days. Those with the most dominant reptilian traits, the Illuminati bloodlines, would, it seems obvious, express more of those characteristics associated with the reptilian brain and so you have the reptilian bloodlines of the Illuminati utterly obsessed with ritual. Equally obviously, the reptilians understand the R-complex better than anyone and how it can be manipulated. Predictably, therefore, it is through the reptilian part of the brain that humanity is most controlled and directed.

The human brain is in two parts or hemispheres, the right brain and the left-brain, connected by a mass of nerve fibres. The left side is the rational, logical, and "intellectual". It works closely with the physical senses and can be summed up by can I touch it, see it, hear it, smell it, or taste it? OK, it must exist. It communicates through spoken words and written language. The right brain is where we manifest imagination, intuition, instincts, dream-states, the sub-conscious. It is the artist, musician, creative inspiration. It communicates through images and symbols, not words. This right side is closely related to the R-complex. Reptilians communicate through imagery and symbols – just like the Illuminati secret society network as widely detailed in *The Biggest Secret* and on my website. They have an entire secret language based on symbols. This brings us to the most effective form of human conditioning by the Illuminati – movies and television. As Skip Largent says:

"All movies and television are a projection of the reptilian brain. How so? Movies and television (video games etc.) are all undeniably dreamlike, not only in their presentation of symbolic-reality, but also in that humans experiencing movies, etc., have the same brain wave patterns as when they are dreaming. And guess where dreaming originates in your head? In the reptilian brain (although other parts of our brain are involved) …The "language" of the reptilian brain is visual imagery. All communications transferred by reptiles are done so by visual symbolic representations, each having specific meaning." [8]

And this is precisely what the Illuminati do. So how does this relate to human control? The movie and television industries are not only owned and directed by the Illuminati – they created them. They understand how visual images can be used to condition the population. In normal circumstances, the reptilian-dominated right brain receives images through the eyes or the imagination, and the left brain decodes those images into thoughts, words, and conclusions. The Illuminati-Anunnaki have intervened in this process, however, to control the human mind. Their aim is to disconnect the functions of these two distinct parts of the brain so we can be manipulated through the right brain while only being conscious of the left. They plant images into the right brain (the dream-state, the non-conscious) using symbolism, subliminal imagery, and pictures, while often telling the left brain how it should interpret those images. This is done through "education", "science", and the media. The television news is a classic. The right brain is shown pictures of thousands of refugees pouring across the border out of Kosovo while the reporter's voice-over tells the left brain how to interpret those pictures: i.e. the refugees were fleeing Serbian atrocities. This explanation increased public support for NATO bombing of the Serbs. What later emerged, of course, is that many of those refugees were actually fleeing the effects of the NATO bombing. Same images, but a very different story or interpretation. It is the same with newspaper pictures in which the caption interprets the image for the reader's left brain. Often what the caption says is not the true background to what the reader is seeing. What is happening all the time is that the left-brain is being told by external sources how to decode right brain images. What we need to do urgently is regain control of our left brains and decide for ourselves what our right brain images mean. That requires breaking away from the herd, thinking for ourselves, and questioning all that we see and hear. That includes what you are reading in this book. If it doesn't make sense, walk away.

You will find that words like imagination, imagine, dream, and such like are used constantly in advertising. They know that if they can use trigger words that encourage a right brain, non-conscious, day dream state, they can access your mind with imagery and then tell your left brain how to decode it into conscious language – "I want that car"; "I think the police should be given more powers to stop crime"; "I need to take Viagra to be a proper man again"; "We need a world government to solve our problems". Television and movies are producing a fantasy world of make-believe to open up the unconscious right brain and allow the Illuminati a secret access through that to the conscious mind. Children are most at risk from this and they are being bombarded with fantasy images to this end. In early childhood, the mental state is controlled almost exclusively by the reptilian brain and the purveyors of children's "entertainment" like Disney exploit this knowledge. Disney is a major Illuminati operation. Music is used in the same way. There is nothing wrong with music in itself, and the same with fantasy and dream-states, so long as we are doing our own decoding. As with everything, it is the way this is manipulated that I am talking about. And who controls the music industry? The same people who control Hollywood and the global media in general – the Illuminati. The biggest music operation in the world, for instance, is Universal Music, controlled by the Bronfmans of Canada, which also controls Universal Studios. The Bronfmans were a gangster family during prohibition and later owners of one of the biggest liquor operations on the planet, Seagrams. The Bronfmans control a stream of other media organisations including such deeply intellectual, mind-expanding, programmes as *The Jerry Springer Show*. Universal Music is the force behind the Satanic "shock rocker" Marilyn Manson. The Illuminati control the music industry and it is widely used for subconscious and vibrational conditioning. A former employee of the music corporation, EMI, told me how they had "supervisors" who ensured that only the "right" artists the "right" music were signed and promoted. The Bronfmans are a reptilian bloodline and very close to the Rothschilds. It is the Bronfmans, through various front organisations and stooges, particularly operating out of their headquarters in eastern Canada, who are seeking to stop me speaking all over the world. In accordance with the Illuminati method of controlling all sides in a debate or conflict, two of the most vociferous critics of Edgar Bronfman Junior, the head of Universal Pictures, are former Bush and Reagan cabinet minister, Bill Bennett, the shape-shifting child abuser exposed by Cathy O'Brien, and Joseph Lieberman, the vice-presidential running mate of blood drinker and shape-shifter, Al Gore. This pair say that Universal Studios encourage people to be immoral! Is there no shame?

Manufacturing illusions

Through the reptilian brain, the Anunnaki-Illuminati manipulate our perception of reality. This frequency range or physical world is controlled and manipulated from outside, from another frequency range or density, which I have called the fourth dimension. As in the movie, *The Matrix*, the "agents" of this force come into this world to delude and manipulate us – like the other-dimensional Men in Black. They do it through direct manifestation, aided by the Satanic rituals, or by occupying and possessing the bloodlines that most resonate with them – the Illuminati bloodlines. Some of these "agents" appear to be capable of "miraculous" feats. But they are not miraculous at all. It is just that they are using a knowledge of physics and energy that is systematically kept from us. They know that this world is not solid, only that it appears to be. Everything from a breath of air to a drop of rain, to a mountain or a ten-ton truck is vibrating energy. Look at anything under a microscope, no matter how dense and "solid" it may seem to be, and you will see that it is just vibrating energy. The slower it vibrates, the more solid it looks, the faster it vibrates the more ethereal and transparent it appears until its speed moves beyond our physical senses and it "disappears". Look at a simple spoked cartwheel. When it is turning slowly the spokes looks very solid. But when it is travelling at speed the spokes are just a blur and no longer "solid" at all. In fact they can even give the illusion of going backwards while the cart is going forwards. Optical illusions are just simple expressions of the Great Illusion. I have been writing for ten years that the speed of light, 186,000 miles per second, is not the fastest speed possible. It is only an outer limit of our frequency range, after which anything travelling above that speed enters another range, another density and we cease to perceive it. This is how UFOs and extraterrestrials appear and "disappear", and how demonic entities manifest and de-manifest at Satanic rituals. They switch frequencies. As John A. Keel points out, the colour changes seen in interdimensional materialisations are often described in "UFO" sightings as the "objects" scan the electromagnetic spectrum. "UFOs often appear as a purplish blob and then descend the visible scale until they turn red," he wrote "at which point they sometimes solidify into seemingly material objects."

We exist on all dimensions and densities in the Great Infinity. At our core we are pure love, what some people call the spark or flame of God within all of us. At that level of our infinite self, we are vibrating at incredible speed. There is no form. We are pure energy. We just are. Everything just is. We are all one. We are consciously everything that has ever, does, or will ever exist. These is no time, no location. We are all time, all places, all thought and feeling. We interpenetrate all existence. We are the infinite and the ultimate. And that is everybody, no matter what you may be doing at the moment in this Great Illusion. But to experience all the densities on our endless journey of experience, that spark, that pure love, has to surround itself with an outer shell that resonates with the frequency range it wishes to experience. Without that, it could not interact with that "world" because it would be too far away on the dial. If my consciousness did not surround itself with a physical body on the same frequency range as this "world" I could not tap the keys of this computer. My consciousness would pass straight through them. For this reason, our inner spark of pure love has taken on a vast number of outer "bodies" to interact with and experience all densities down the scale. We are, therefore, like a series of Russian dolls, one inside the other, all vibrating at different speeds. And all, except that spark of love that interpenetrates all existence, are illusions of varying degrees. The dense physical body, the outer of all the shells, is therefore part of the greatest illusion because it not only has its own personal illusions, it encompasses all the others, too.

The nearest "bodies" to the dense physical are the etheric, astral, mental and emotional. They are all vibrating at higher speeds than our physical senses and so we can't see them, although psychic people can when they access those frequencies. We feel them, however, as good and bad "vibes". The etheric is a mirror image of the physical, but less dense, and the lower levels of the astral frequency range (lower fourth dimension) appear to be the realms from which the Illuminati demons, reptilians, and other malevolent "extraterrestrials" largely operate. The "lower astral" is the traditional home of malevolent entities in esoteric thought. Abductees have reported that when they looked at their bodies during an extraterrestrial experience they looked different to normal and, as we saw earlier, the American, Jim Walden, said that his body looked like those of the "aliens" who abducted him. Walden felt that this was another dimension of him, which inhabited his human form. He believed from his experiences that the "aliens" could transcend time, transform matter, manipulate human thought and behaviour, and create "distracting illusions to satisfy the needs of our simple human minds".[9] He concluded that they could move between dimensions and that they were less "extraterrestrial" and more "interdimensional". I think that is correct. The demonic entities and the malevolent faction of the reptilians are overwhelmingly astral beings that can move between densities, thus appearing human one minute and then shape-shifting into something else the next. They are like those agents in *The Matrix* movie. But, also like those agents, they are still stuck in an illusion themselves. It might be less of an illusion than humans because they know of other dimensions and so on, but they are still stuck in their astral illusion as humans are stuck in the physical one. *The Matrix* character, Morpheus, says of the agents:

> "I have seen an agent punch through a concrete wall; men have emptied entire clips [of bullets] on them and hit nothing but air. Yet their strength and their speed are still based on rules. Because of that, they will never be as strong or as fast as you can be."

That is why the Illuminati and their other-density masters have worked so hard to suppress our minds. They know that we are potentially far more powerful than they are if only we can free ourselves of their mind control. Their aim, in effect, is to keep us in a bigger illusion than their own. It is like the short sighted manipulating the blind. Within every human is a genius waiting to manifest. I never cease to be amazed at the levels of excellence that humans achieve in the whole range of professions and talents. Find someone at the top of his or her craft and you will be in awe at their brilliance. And this is despite all the manipulation and suppression of our potential. Just think what we could achieve when this control is dismantled. The climax in *The Matrix* movie is when the initiate, Neo, ceases to see the world as a series of "solid" people and buildings and instead sees everything and everyone as a flow of fast moving numbers and codes – vibrational frequencies. Once he reaches this point of awareness and multi-dimensional connection, he is able to brush aside the previously unbeatable agents of human servitude because he can operate outside of their rules and limitations. Symbolically he has expanded the point of his awareness beyond the astral realms to much higher levels of himself. Higher levels than his controllers can access. Once he achieved that, he becomes as powerful to the agents as they were to him when he was still in the physical illusion and they were in the astral one. How do we get out of this mess? We open up to who we really are and let go of who the system tells us we are. The whole Illuminati plan has been designed to keep us trapped in the physical illusion and therefore ensure that we can be controlled and manipulated by their astral illusion. This is why, among so many other things, they have done the following:

● Systematically destroyed or kept hidden as much ancient knowledge as possible because it contained the understanding of who we are and the true nature of life.
● Hi-jacked all the major investigations and searches for ancient hidden knowledge and artefacts across the world to ensure that nothing is found that tells the truth of our nature and origins and, if anything significant is found, it is never made public nor its true importance understood.
● Created religions to seize the minds of the populace, fill them with a sense of limitation and inferiority, and portray esoteric knowledge as "evil".
● Established "science" to recognise only the physical, deny the existence of other frequencies of life, and suppress the knowledge of our multi-dimensional selves. This is done by rewarding those who repeat the party line and destroying the reputations of those who do not.

- Introduced the media to assault our minds with the reality the Illuminati wish us to have; and to attack, ridicule, condemn, and destroy anyone who threatens to expose the scam and the illusion on which it depends.
- Bombarded us with an orgy of physical stimuli and materialism in which success is judged by what you own rather than what you are.
- Focused the world and communication on all that is physical – money, winning the lottery, possessions, and promoting an obsession with sex as a physical rather than a spiritual experience. Sex based on lust alone holds down our frequency because it is a purely physical act. Sex based on love increases our frequency because it reconnects us with our spark of pure love.
- Isolated male and female energy, so creating the duality and preventing the fusion of male and female energy within us all that would create a third, potentially high-vibrational force, and set us free of this vibrational prison, the Matrix.
- Filled our food, drink, medicines, vaccines, water, air, and electromagnetic environment, with chemicals and frequencies designed to suppress our ability to experience our multi-dimensional selves and to block the channels through which our higher levels can communicate with the physical.
- Manipulated our DNA directly and through other means to dim this higher-dimensional connection. The genetic code agenda that is sold to us so positively as a way of preventing disease has a far more sinister background and motivation.
- Held highly malevolent Satanic rituals at the planet's major vortex points to hold down the frequency of the entire global energy field – the field that we operate within. In this way, our own energy field can be vibrationally suppressed by living within such a low vibrational environment.
- Created wars and conflicts at all levels of global society and ensured financial dependency and insolvency to keep us in low vibrational emotional states like fear, guilt, anger, resentment, and frustration.

The vibrational prison

This manipulation, together with the physical illusion, means that we access only a fraction of our potential consciousness. We are literally in a vibrational prison, disconnected by all these methods from the multi-dimensional ocean that we really are. These astral entities work to maintain and expand this situation and thus maintain and expand their control of the billions entrapped in the illusion. At the same time, the low-vibration emotional energy that the illusion causes us to generate is vibrating to the lower astral frequency range. This means that a cycle is created in which the astral manipulators use their energy to set up physical events; these events cause emotional reactions that generate emotional energy; this pours into the astral dimension; and the astral entities recycle it back to continue and increase the cycle still further. In *The Matrix*, it is said that we live in a computer-generated dream world built to keep us under control and to use humans like a battery. Symbolically that is correct. The only ones who can break the cycle are ourselves by ceasing to fall for the illusion and so generating the emotional energy the reptilians and others demand. Morpheus tells his initiate, Neo, in *The Matrix*:

"...you are a slave Neo. Like everyone else you were born into bondage. Born into a prison that you cannot smell or taste or touch – a prison for your mind. Unfortunately, no one can be told what the Matrix is – you have to see it for yourself ...I'm trying to free your mind, Neo. But I can only show you the door. You're the one that has to walk through it."

Or, as the aerospace scientist Dr Gordon Allen said in his book, *Enigma Fantastique*, after a lifetime of study:

"The purpose today is identical to the purpose in the times of the magician-scientists of ancient times, the purpose of the controlling priesthood of the Egyptians, the Caesars, the Roman Catholic Church, the Inquisition. The ecclesiastic control of the various ruling families had for its purpose the rule of the people in their material bodies on this Earth-plane ...A nation is said by Eastern philosophers to lie under certain occult (or secret) controls. Nations who go to war on the Earth-plane reflect certain wars in Heaven." [10]

I think there is validity in the myths and legends that consciousness became trapped in this dense physical frequency range and, as its own frequency fell, it could not get out. We are talking maybe of millions, even billions, of years ago when this began. The Fall of Man was a vibrational fall, perhaps. I certainly would not rule out for a moment that at least the early stages of what is known as Lemuria/Atlantis, were fourth-dimensional, not third-dimensional phenomena, and they might still exist in fourth-dimensional reality. The fourth-dimensional range is very close to this one and it could well be that events unfolded in which these far ancient societies, or aspects of them, became denser and denser until they fell vibrationally into three-dimensional reality. Once here, the temptations and limitations of such dense vibrations with all the physical sensations available became like an addiction to the consciousness that experienced it. The Italian physicist Giuliana Conforto writes in *LUH, Man's Cosmic Game*:

"The human body is made of physical matter, the solid state of the substance, that is cosmic Thought, Information. The many parallel universes are therefore different modes of thinking or software: either rigid, dual, typical of the solid state, or more fluid and thus tuned to cosmic oneness. 'Falling' in temperature from a hotter parallel universe, the human body underwent a phrase transition that solidified the substance and stiffened its modes of thinking. If it is so, we can understand why it may be possible for the human body to 'rise' again, as many hermetic traditions suggest too." [11]

There are those who believe that when our physical body dies, our consciousness returns to some wonderful heavenly realm. Personally, I don't accept that this happens as a matter of course. Death is no cure for ignorance and when we leave this world as the physical body dies, we gravitate to where our consciousness is focused. It's our vibrational state that decides where we can go. In other words, *we* do. If we are the embodiment of pure love, we will peel off our outer shells, the Russian dolls, and our consciousness becomes that spark of pure love that permeates all existence. If we are still seriously stuck in the illusion, which the vast majority of people are, we will perhaps get no higher than the astral realms because our vibrational state will hold us there. When Satanists do deals with demonic entities and sign contracts in blood with them, it is a vibrational contract. In return for demonic manipulation to give them power and all that they want in this world, the Satanist agrees that their demons should own them when they leave this physical realm. When they leave the body, Satanists move the tiny vibrational distance into the lower astral or fourth dimension, that's all. The more souls (energy) of that malevolent nature these demonic entities can pack into their frequency range, the more powerful the vibrational prison that surrounds or interpenetrates the third dimension. Those who are not Satanists, but still firmly controlled by the illusion, will leave the physical and move to higher levels of the astral frequency range and experience another illusion. I am personally convinced that most people on Earth are trapped in a cycle of reincarnating between the astral illusion and the physical illusion and back again. In the end people can become so detached vibrationally from their higher dimensions that they are virtually operating as a completely separate fragment or "lost soul". That's the situation the lower fourth-dimensional entities have worked so vociferously to create. Consciousness incarnates from higher realms to try to expose the scam and the illusion that underpins it, but many of these people also get trapped in the illusion and forget why they came. It's a tough school, this one, because the vibrations are slow and therefore the energy is dense. But when we can focus our consciousness and reality in the higher realms while occupying a physical body, we ground that higher-dimensional consciousness (energy) in this density and raise both awareness of the illusion and the frequency of the Earth's vibrational field. When we have reached that higher state, we are *in* this world, but not *of* it.

So what does all this mean? We are in a low vibrational prison – the Matrix – and living a daily illusion. It is the illusion that holds the whole show together, and the Illuminati have set up the media, science, education, religion, medicine, finance, and business, the whole grotesque system, to assault our conscious and subconscious minds with messages designed to programme the illusion deeper and deeper into our sense of reality. If we buy that, and all but a few people do, we will never get out and break free. The bottom line of all bottom lines of the Illuminati agenda is the manipulation of humanity's imagination of itself. Without that, the rest of their agenda becomes impossible. I will make some suggestions in the final two chapters about how we can get the hell out of here, but our choice is very clear: to *exist* in the Great Illusion or to *live* in the Great Infinity.

Put another way: do we want the prison or the paradise? If it's the paradise, we have some work to do.

SOURCES

1   Giuliana Conforto, *Man's Cosmic Game* (Edizioni Noesis, 1998), pp 11 and 12

2   Ibid, p 44

3   Dr. Douglas Baker, *The Opening Of The Third Eye* (Aquarian Press, Wellingborough, England, 1977), p 13

4   Quoted in *Our Haunted Planet*, p 179

5   Bill used this line in many of his stage performances and videos

6   See ***http://www.angelfire.com/ut/branton*** and ***http://www.reptilianagenda.com/***

7   ***http://www.telepath.com/skipsil/trirept.html***

8   Ibid

9   *The Ultimate Alien Agenda*, p 65

10   Quoted in *Our Haunted Planet*, pp 170 and 171

11   *Man's Cosmic Game*, p 24

CHAPTER 19

the gatekeepers

"The Matrix is a system, Neo, and that system is our enemy. When you are inside, you look around, what do you see? Businessmen, teachers, lawyers, carpenters, the very minds of the people we are trying to save. But until we do, these people are part of that system and that makes them our enemies. You have to understand most of these people are not ready to be unplugged. And many are so…hopelessly dependent on the system that they will fight to protect it."

Morpheus in *The Matrix*.

That is a profound quote and a brilliant summary of the dilemma we face. I don't see Matrix-plugged people as my personal enemies because once we see this as a conflict or war between "us" and "them" we are confirming just how "plugged" we are. "Us versus them" is Matrix thinking, a Matrix perception. This should not be viewed as some kind of "fight" because what you fight, you become.

But Matrix-minded people are the enemies of freedom that's for sure. Enemies of their own freedom and the freedom of all who exist in the Great Illusion. They are the gatekeepers of the Matrix, daily suppressing the thoughts, desires, people, and information that could set us – and them – free. Of course, the conscious agents of the Illuminati are placed in the positions of economic, business, media, political, legal, and military power to hold this mental and emotional sheep-pen together. But they could not do this alone. They have to manipulate humanity to suppress itself. Humanity is like the security guard. He often doesn't know what he is guarding or why he is doing it. He is an automaton, just doing whatever he is told to the letter and never for a moment considering the possibility that he should think for himself and interpret a situation on its merits. It is black and white, no shades of grey. Rules is rules, mate. Every "plugged" person is an enemy, or potential enemy, of freedom, but some are more arrogantly enthusiastic about it, or, in other words, more profoundly entrapped by the illusion than others. If we are going to break out of this vibrational prison cell we all need to resign immediately from our role as agents of the thought police. For us to be free, we must set everyone else free. To cease to be a sheep, we must cease to be a sheepdog. How simple that is, yet how difficult it seems to be for humans in their present hypnotic state. But we can only stop being a sheep dog when we realise that we *are* a sheep dog and we are so blind to our own desire for control over other people's lives and thoughts. Ask anyone if they believe in freedom and all except a tiny minority will say "Yes". Its not something that people like to be seen to be against. Not good street cred. So we all believe in freedom by reflex action, but do we live it by everyday action? You have got to be kidding. If we did, this book, and all my others, would have no reason to be published. We would already be free and reconnected to multi-dimensional paradise.

Who are the gatekeepers of the Matrix? Who are the prison warders, the border guards of the Great Illusion? *We are.*

The gatekeeper parents, partners, and priests

We want our children to live in a free world, right? Then why don't we even allow them to live in a free home? Intergenerational conditioning by parents of their children is one of the greatest of all gatekeeping activities. If the parent is a Christian, Muslim, voter for this political party or that, a racist, a sexist, working class, middle class, upper class, whatever, that is the conditioning they overwhelmingly insist on imposing upon their offspring. The child is conditioned to be a reflection of the parent and the pressure to be like them can be enormous. The very idea that a vehement Christian or Muslim, or Jew, or Hindu, would respect their child's right from birth to reach their own conclusions without pressure to conform to their parents' beliefs, would be utterly abhorrent to such people. Indeed most could not begin to comprehend such a level of mental and emotional respect for their child's uniqueness, and freedom of thought and expression. As I said at the start of the book, I debated at the Oxford Union with the former Chief Rabbi of Great Britain and he could not see the difference between information and indoctrination. "How can I do the best for my children," he said, or words to that effect, "If I do not bring them up to believe what is right?" No, Rabbi, what *you* believe is right. That's not informing them of your view; it is indoctrinating your beliefs while suppressing and discrediting all alternative versions of reality. It's mind control. Priests, rabbis, bishops, popes, and all the rest of the long-frock brigade are professional gatekeepers working for those who control the Matrix. Yet most of them are so mesmerised by the Matrix themselves, they have no idea that this is so. It is the same with the vast majority of parents.

It goes further. Parents, conditioned by *their* parents, who were conditioned by *theirs*, and so on, often decide what is best for their children even after they leave the nest. I met a guy once in his 60s who was still being destroyed inside by the guilt that he did not achieve what his father wanted for him. Well bollocks to the father, I say. If he is such a parental dictator and emotional manipulator, he deserves to be friggin' disappointed. Do him good. But how many of us don't do what we really want to do in our lives because we fear what our parents will say or because we don't want to disappoint them? Stuff that. They either respect our right to be who we are and express who we are or they can go on their way. Their choice. This is so important to breaking free of the web of fear, guilt, and the need for approval that dominates so many child-parent relationships and continues long after the child becomes an adult. They are not our parents, in truth, anyway, except according to Matrix reality. They are the ones who seeded our physical form and with whom we spent our formative years. They are close by genetics in this physical realm, but they may not be at all close when it comes to vibrational connection. Many are, but they don't have to be. An obsession with doing nothing to upset our parents or the people around us is the Matrix mentality, a key part of the prison that keeps us in line.

It is the same with our wives or husbands, partners, and children. Observe your own situation. How many people around you, people you love and care for, are suppressing what you want to do with your life because you are concerned by the way it will make them feel? It is a mental and emotional Alcatraz. It can turn a relationship into a prison sentence, and a marriage and family into a prison cell. Don't get me wrong here. I am not talking about being violent because you fancy it, or making their lives miserable for the sake of it. No, no. I mean to express what you are, say what you think, live your uniqueness, without suppressing yourself because those around you will not like or understand the real you. It means to stop living what *they* think you should be; the blueprint for what *they* want you to be; and start being the you that you really *are*. If they can't handle that, that's their problem and they should find someone else who will suit them better. And if they can't, and insist that you suppress the real you to suit them, they are unpaid, unaware gatekeepers for the Matrix.

But it goes both ways this. Everyone, or almost everyone, is concerned about their own freedom, but what about the freedom of others? How many times a day do you impose your will, your reality, on those around you? I spoke at some financial conferences that were designed to promote "freedom". All you had to do was stand on the stage and talk about freedom and you were sure of wild applause. But most of those clapping their hands, and the organisations that promoted the conferences, did not want freedom at all. It's the last thing they wanted. They couldn't handle freedom. Most didn't know what it was and those who had some idea were horrified at its implications. The organisers were terrified that I would use the "E" word, extraterrestrials. Even the "F" word would have been less life-threatening to them. They couldn't care less if the extraterrestrial information was true or not. They couldn't care less if *anything* I said was true or not. So long as it didn't upset the audience, which the organisations were using and manipulating mercilessly to make their fortune, that was OK. So long as the people liked what they heard, who gave a shit if it was true? Once I began to question in my books the existence of Jesus, sections of the audience who had previously given me a standing ovation for exposing the conspiracy, began to demand that I be removed from the speakers list. My crime? Expressing a different view to theirs. I am sure many of them are still attending, still being manipulated, and still giving standing ovations to the kind of freedom they really want – the freedom to hear someone support their own beliefs and the freedom to suppress anyone else who has a different view. In fact, that is the "freedom" that most people want. I observed another financial group based in Arizona, and heard them talk about freedom from the system, freedom of expression, and all the usual stuff they think will pull people into their web. They said the organisation was created to promote freedom when it was merely created to make as much money as possible. Fine, if that's your thing, but be honest about it and don't bullshit me with tearful, carefully rehearsed, garbage about how you are doing it to free the people. Free your overdraft, more like. Funnily enough, it turned out to be one of the most dictatorial, vicious, unscrupulous, manipulating organisations you could ever see and awash with monumental purveyors of bullshit. Both of these "financial" operations and most of their audience are gatekeepers masquerading as promoters of freedom and that, perhaps, makes them the most deluded of all.

The greatest gift we can give our children is the freedom to think for themselves, even if, outrage of outrage, we don't agree with what they believe; to encourage them to question, read, and come to their own conclusions; to respect their right to be different without feeling the need to impose our beliefs because we know best. Of course, it has to be pointed out when their behaviour is unfairly and unpleasantly affecting others, but that's not what I mean here. I mean to encourage them to free their minds and be open to all possibilities. Far too many parents are more concerned with what their neighbours, friends, and the teachers will think of their children, rather than what the children think of themselves and the world. We need to set the children free to think the officially unthinkable and question at every turn the officially unquestionable. If we can't set our children free, we fall on our arses at the very first step on the road to global freedom.

In our personal relationships, we need to set each other free of the blueprints for what a relationship must be. We are imprisoned by blueprints and expectations, and who creates the blueprints? The system, the Matrix, does. Once we have an expectation and a mental design for what constitutes "love", a relationship, or anything at all, we are imprisoned by that thought form. It becomes the focus from which everything is judged. If the relationship takes another expression we are disappointed; it might be perfect for our personal growth and evolution, but it is outside the blueprint, so it can't be right. "You don't kiss me and hold my hand like the couple across the street. " Well that's probably because I am not the couple across the street, I am me. Ironically, blueprint relationships are usually the most fragile and superficial because they are often based on image and posturing rather than substance. Relationships are everything. The relationships between planets and stars, water and air, hot and cold, thought and energy, are constantly creating and changing the world around us. Relationships are literally what makes creation possible and human relationships are an expression of this. It is the main way that we learn and grow, but if blueprint rules are laid down on how relationships should be and the direction they must go, we are immediately building barriers to all other potential experience and, therefore, greater understanding. The flow of life leads us to what we need to experience and who with, and the flow comes from within ourselves. Once we lay down the way it must be, or else, we are challenging that flow, which may have other plans for us. This creates a battle between the inner flow and the outer, conscious, blueprint demands, and there is always only one winner in such conflicts. I love to be hugged and held and operating in harmonious situations, but there is so much more for relationships to offer than the classic blueprints and often the experiences they present to us are not very nice. But if the love is truly there between two people they can survive and grow enormously from those challenges because whatever happens nothing will break that bond. True love is not conscious, it is beyond the bounds of the conscious mind. It is also beyond words. I think we have lost touch with what love really is. Instead we often create an illusion of love and confuse it with purely third-dimensional blueprinting. Among the New Age mentality, hugging people is part of the persona, the blueprint, the mental and emotional uniform to show that you are a "loving person". But I have seen many in the New Age hugging people as a public show while saying how much they hate their guts once they have gone. I have known many relationships of the "kissy, kissy, my little cherub" variety, which, on the surface, have been perfect matches. "Oh what a wonderful couple, they are so in love, it's obvious, isn't it?" Yet at the first sign of a problem between them, the relationship falls apart because it is built on sand. They can't handle it once the blueprint is breached and you also find, talking to them after the break-up, that their lovey-dovey-go-through-the-motions relationship was a cover for the lack of a deep inner connection that nothing could destroy. I have heard that two people in a relationship should never say goodbye on any occasion without saying "I love you". Really? Just say it now: "I love you." See how easy it is? You don't have to mean it, you don't have to feel it, you just have to say it. How many people say those words every day, just to get what they want? And how many don't follow that blueprint, yet feel an enormous love for another person and show it in other ways? I saw a quote once that said: "Just because I don't love you the way you want me to doesn't mean that I don't love you with everything I have." The need to hear "I love you" all the time or experience constant public shows of affection can say more about that person's own insecurity than a statement about another's love for them. If you had to make a choice, would you rather have a blueprint relationship that collapses when the going gets tough or one of real substance in which you know your partner will be in the trench with you, no matter what, even if they don't say "I love you" every five minutes? Sometimes you can have both, and that's great if that's what you want, but there are other infinite expressions of love that don't come with a set of rules and regulations.

I was married to Linda for 29 years and although we are no longer husband and wife, we are still very close on a deep level, far beyond the nonsensical idea that to be officially "together" you have to sign a piece of headed notepaper. We will remain so forever because our mutual and deeply painful experiences since 1991 have exploded all blueprints and expectations into tiny fragments. She knows I will always be there when needed, no matter what, no matter where, and vice-versa. If it had been a blueprint relationship it would have been over in an instant ten years ago. But it wasn't and it isn't, and that is why it has endured and grown, even though the form it takes may have changed. The experiences we have endured, shared, and overcome have made us stronger, wiser, more enlightened people. And, most importantly, more individual people, expressing a far greater inner strength and sense of confidence and respect for who we are. This has been the whole evolutionary reason for what we have experienced: to make us emotionally stronger and free as our own unique selves without the need to have anyone alongside as an emotional crutch. I leaned on Linda emotionally for a long time. I don't now. She leaned on me. She doesn't now. We are all being challenged to become whole people and we attract the relationships that help us to do that. Such relationships rarely follow the conditioned blueprints. It's funny how we utter sparkling truths without realising in our every-day words and phrases. Like when we talk of our partners as "our other half". That's what they are for most people, or as much of the "other half" as they can find, anyway. In most relationships, the partner expresses an energy that we have not accessed within ourselves. This is why opposites can so powerfully attract. The male is balanced by the female, who in turn is balanced by the male, or again, by as much as they can manage. We are accessing such a fraction of ourselves that we need a partner to make the balance and form some kind of "whole" – our other half.

I wrote earlier about how, when two polarities, male and female, are fused together it creates a third force of fantastic creative potential that can take us vibrationally out of Matrix mode. For this reason, the Illuminati have worked furiously over thousands of years to keep male and female apart and maintain the duality. Most relationships do not create the necessary vibrational "wholeness" and fusion to trigger the third force in all its magnificence. So relationships as we know them today are not a problem to those in control. In fact, male-female relationships as they are currently perceived are a wonderful tool of the Matrix. Even two halves becoming one is not the ultimate goal on our Freedom Road – it is the one becoming one. It is believed by some that the ideal "spiritual" partnership is two polarities becoming one whole with male and female creating the third force when two compatible people come together. I went along with that for a while, but not any more. It is only half the story. Two halves becoming one still leaves the two individuals concerned as less than whole people. We are everything. Just because we live in male bodies doesn't mean we don't have as much potential female energy within us as a woman. At the level of consciousness, we are both male and female. Just because we live in female bodies doesn't mean we don't have as much potential male energy within us as a man. But our conditioned roles within the Matrix are designed to pressure the consciousness in a male body to suppress its female aspect – "macho man, big boys don't cry" – and the consciousness in a female body to suppress its male aspect – "little girls play with dolls and big girls look after the kitchen".

What we are being challenged to do here is for all of us to access all of us. Therefore to become balanced "wholes" within ourselves without the need to find an external "other half". The third force then manifests within all of us, and relationships are the interaction of two whole people and not two halves seeking external balance. Those relationships are based on the mutual respect of each partner for the other's wholeness and individuality. If they don't fulfil the blueprint then fine because whole people do not want a relationship with a blueprint. They want to be with another vibrant, whole, individual, unique, expression of all that is. And if they don't kiss you at the door or say "I love you" every time they leave your presence then who gives a shit because that is them being them. It doesn't mean they don't love you in their own unique way. Blueprints are such a foundation of the Matrix and without them one of its key structures would collapse. Relationships as they are currently perceived, desired, and demanded, serve the Matrix magnificently because they suppress what is necessary for the partners to reach wholeness within themselves. Once whatever they need to express or experience on that journey starts to affect their partner in ways they don't like, the pressure is applied, internally and externally, to suppress that experience and stay in the prison cell. If this attitude does not stop, the Matrix will continue to hold together for as long as the attitude prevails. It will always produce the gatekeeper relationship in which each partner keeps the other in mental and emotional servitude while calling it love and the ideal relationship.

There is another aspect to this crazy little thing called love. People talk about love all the time, but what is it, what does it mean? "Love is never having to say you're sorry" is one definition I have heard. Yet others think that not saying sorry is a really undesirable trait. So one person's definition of love is another's definition of being unloving. Which one is right? It depends on your blueprint and the perspective from which you are observing. There is a different definition of love for almost everyone on the planet and that's because love is indefinable. It just is and expresses itself in infinite ways, most of which we are not aware of in the Great Illusion. And something else we need to ask: which level of the person is expressing the love in a relationship? This physical aspect of us is only a holographic projection into this frequency range by the higher levels of who we are. Our physical level is the experiencer and the giver of experience. It is not who we are. We are all that exists. Do we want a relationship with a holographic image according to a conditioned blueprint? Or one with the multi-dimensional consciousness of our partner, which will always provide the experience – the love – that is necessary to open our hearts and minds to the true magnitude of who we are? We might not like the experience, but from realms beyond this world, it is given with love because it is what we need to set us free of the illusion. Do we want the comfortable, predictable, commitment of the cul-de-sac? Or the unpredictable, no guarantees, roller-coaster-ride, the long and winding road that leads us to multi-dimensional freedom? Those two standpoints will judge a relationship and "love" in very different ways, and from very different wavelengths and universes. When a partner, parent, child, whoever, gives us an experience we don't like, and does not fulfil our blueprint of someone who loves us, we can get caught in the Matrix big time. How do we grow and evolve? Through experience. All experience, the good and the bad, the pleasant and the unpleasant. In fact, we grow far more profoundly from the challenges than the easy rides. So who loves us most on a higher level, where it really matters? Those who present the challenges from which we grow and evolve, or those who fulfil our blueprints for an ideal relationship, look after us, take care of us, and shield us from responsibility and challenge? Mmmm. Topsy-turvy world, isn't it? Nothing is what it seems.

Gatekeeper teachers

It is crucial to the Illuminati agenda that their gatekeepers serve the cause in complete ignorance of what they are doing. There is no greater example of this than the "professional" classes like teachers, journalists, doctors, psychiatrists, politicians, scientists, bank staff, and so on. There are exceptions, of course there are, with the great and often brave people in these professions who know the score and try to do what they can within the walls imposed by the system. What I am talking about here, however, is the general rule within which the exceptions have to operate. The emergence of the "education" system has been hailed as a great step forward in human society. But, like the Internet, it is a two-edged sword and the edge marked indoctrination is far sharper than the one marked enlightenment. Yes, "education" means that children can learn how to read, write, and understand numbers to an extent. That's a good thing on a basic level. But the "education" system is a manipulator's dream. If you wanted to turn out adults who thought as you wanted them to think and saw the world in a way that suited your plans, what would be the ideal situation for you? It would be to take them as small children, three and four years of age, and have control of what they are taught for at least five days a week throughout their childhood and often into their 20s. You could not ask for a better structure of indoctrination than that. And that's what they have. As Albert Einstein said: "The only thing that interferes with my learning is my education." We don't have education. We have the indoctrination of a belief system – the belief system of the Matrix. Teachers are the gatekeepers of the developing mind, telling children what is reality, what is history, what is true and false. And these teachers, overwhelmingly, have no idea that this is what they do.

Look at how a teacher is produced. First they have to do very well in exams in their own school and university life. Put more bluntly, they have to be sponges for the system's version of truth and reality, and be able to express that accurately on an exam paper. Then they go off to teacher training college and they learn how to indoctrinate their pupils with the same "truth" and "reality" that has been programmed into them. Incidentally, you also have to be a good sponge at school and university and pass the system's examination of your conditioning, before you qualify to go on to learn how to be a doctor, scientist, journalist, and, more often than not, politician. Those who are good at passing the system's exams are merely confirming their level of indoctrination and it is a mental prison cell that stays intact in most people for their entire physical life. Children and young people who do their own research, think for themselves, question, and offer a different reality to the indoctrinated "norm", do not pass their exams and are called "a disruptive influence in the classroom". Oh you mean they ask difficult questions? Right, gotcha. Much of what young people are taught about politics, history, banking, business, science, and all the rest, is provable baloney. But it's what the Illuminati want you to believe and that's all that matters. Teachers work to something called a curriculum, a word meaning, in the Icke dictionary of terminological translation: "The version of reality we want the masses to believe." This is decided by the top of the "educational" pyramid and dictated to all below. Either the teachers follow the curriculum or they consider their other career options. This is the way that all of these "professional" classes are kept in line and any rebels are weeded out. Teachers teach what they are told to teach, or else; journalists write within the bounds dictated by the editor, or else; the editor edits within the bounds dictated by the owner, or else; scientists give a version of reality and possibility within the boundaries of official "science", or else. Doctors treat patients within the strict, scalpel or drug, dictates of the medical establishment, or else. So it goes on wherever you look. The few at the top dictate and the rest do what they are told to do. It is the same with the teacher-pupil relationship as we come further down this pyramid. Children find out very early on that life is a lot simpler if you don't question what you hear and just accept it.

I instinctively knew from an early age that schools were the places where the clones of tomorrow were honed and produced. I was, therefore, a rebel from the start. I have never passed a major school exam in my life (and never taken one), never went to college or university, and have done all my learning in my time and on my terms. Teachers are crucial gatekeepers for the Illuminati, not least because, in my experience, the vast majority are so stunningly uninformed about the wider world. Most only know what they are conditioned to know. Well-informed teachers, journalists, scientists, doctors, and politicians, are the last thing the Matrix wants. Being informed of what is really going on is not a good career move. Those teachers who are informed and do understand that the system is an indoctrination machine, will tell you the consequences for trying to challenge it. The "education" system is a well-oiled conveyor belt that sucks in virgin minds at one end and turns out programmed adults at the other. There are some who survive with their thinking processes still intact, but very few. For the rest their only hope is to spend their adult lives de-programming themselves from the indoctrination that "educated" them. In the USA, and other parts of the world come to that, parents who are already indoctrinating their children at home, are working a second or third job, saving, and going without, to ensure that their children get a good indoctrination at college and university. The wheels go round and round as everyone plays their part in indoctrinating everyone else and keeping them in the pen. It is so brilliantly done that they genuinely believe they are doing their best for their children.

Gatekeeper police and soldiers

Police, the military, government officials, and "civil servants" are at the front line in the imposition of Illuminati policy on the global population. What I am about to describe is "democracy", a word that has become interchangeable with "freedom" in the newspeak of Illuminati propaganda. I wonder if you think this sounds like freedom: first you elect a government by voting once every four or five years and choosing between two or more masks on the same Illuminati face. These governments then do almost whatever they like in their period in office and there's nothing that can be done within the "law" to remove them until another farcical election is upon us in which we can, if we want "change", elect another Illuminati mask. Governments pass laws in which you have had no say and, because of their majority in Parliament or Congress among the voting fodder that pass for "politicians", they can get virtually any legislation into "law". Once that happens, yet more fodder-people – gatekeepers – appear on the scene. We call them police and soldiers. Theirs is not to reason why, theirs is just to do or die. You are not paid to think, just to implement the law and follow orders. We pay for the use of your body and your trigger finger, not your brain, soldier. Now FIRE! YES, SIR! If it were not so tragic, it would be hilarious. Little boys playing soldiers at the expense of other people's lives.

Hey, soldier, you left a pile of bodies there in a country you only arrived in yesterday. What did they do to you?

"They're the enemy, Sir."

Have you ever spoken to them?

"Of course not, Sir."

Never considered that they are just like you, with families and children, and aspirations to build a better life in the face of the bloody dictator your army has been flown in to defend?

"No, Sir."

Ever read anything about this country you're in?

"No, Sir."

Then how do you know they're your enemy?

"My commanding officer told me, Sir."

And who told him?

"His commanding officer, Sir."

And who's the chief commanding officer at the top of this heap?

"The President, Sir."

And who commands the President?

"The people, Sir, this is a democracy."

How many of "the people" just told you to kill that pile of bodies?

"Well, one, Sir."

And who was that?

"My commanding officer, Sir."

And who told him?

(See above).

The training in the military is pure, classic, mind control. It is designed to break the spirit of a recruit to the point where he will do, by reflex action, whatever he is told to do, whenever and wherever, he is told to do it. The more elite the regiment, the more profound is the mind control. The training for the elite of the British military like the SAS and the Parachute Regiment, or the Delta Forces or Green Berets in the United States, is designed to produce robotic psychopaths because that is the mentality most suited to requirements. Thinking in the military is another bad career move. It is these clones of someone else's commands that are used to implement the decisions, often on innocent people, of the Illuminati networks operating within global politics, the United Nations, and NATO. They are perhaps the nearest thing to zombies that you could imagine. That is not to say that out of uniform there are not intelligent, thinking, people among them. There are. But once the military garb is upon their person, their programming locks in and the gatekeepers take their positions at the checkpoint. If soldiers, and others in uniform, refused to follow orders without asking for justification, the Illuminati could not survive. Then the dog would wag the tail, instead of, at present, the other way around.

The police are the same. It is not that we don't need the police in today's society, it is that we need them to think for themselves and assess situations on their merits, and not implement the law to the letter no matter what. There are some who try to do that, but the system constantly discourages them, as it does with teachers who tell their pupils to think and question. Many world police forces have "quotas" to maintain every month and so we have the pathetic situation in which more drivers are ticketed for speeding at the start of the month to get them off to a good start and at the end of the month when they are trying to complete their quota. It's called justice. We need the police to ask themselves if a course of action is fair in the circumstances, even if the law insists that rules are rules. Otherwise they are just robots to another's command. Thinking for yourself is called "insubordination". You see this on a minor level when cars are ticketed for illegal parking even though they are not causing a problem and there are reasons why they were there. We have reached the point now where parking a car in an "illegal" area for two minutes can cost you £50 and, if it is clamped, far more than that. To some, the cost of being unclamped is a week's wages that should be putting food in their family's bellies instead of in the pockets of vicious "security" firms who win the clamping contracts. The more they clamp, the more they collect. This is another of the system's little tricks. You make sure that those who serve you and implement your agenda benefit financially from doing so. In this way, you divide and rule the population by setting enforcer and victim at war with each other and making the enforcer benefit from the victim's plight. Why is it that dictators always ensure that their army is well looked after? The explosion of laws and regulations and of signs all round us telling to do and don't, are designed to bombard our minds with a constant flow of orders and commands. This programmes the subconscious into weary submission to following orders and opens people to react robotically to another's instructions. If you drive into your town or city, park the car, and walk through the streets, you will be astonished at how many times you are instructed what to do.

People like soldiers, police, wheel clampers, and government officials all glean their power over others from the "law". This "law", they know, will back them every time, even though to implement it in certain circumstances may be insane. That's the point you see. The "law" has become the god of society. Laws are passed by "elected" dictatorships, implemented by unthinking yes-men, and defended by the general population who are conditioned to "respect the law" and be "a law-abiding citizen". What more obvious prison can we live in than to see laws passed in which the people have had no say, and those same people to believe that, even though the law is ludicrous or fascist, they must respect it? People should only respect the law when the law respects the people. The "law" is just a piece of paper that results from a group of mostly uninformed or corrupt politicians voting for its introduction. *That's all it is*. If the Suffragettes had respected the law that denied women the vote in Britain and had they not protested and chained themselves to official buildings (against the law) women would not have won the right to vote when they did. Had the peoples of Serbia and the countries of Eastern Europe respected their laws they would still live in open dictatorships. The very people who say we must respect the law would jump for joy if the Chinese people broke their laws and overthrew the Communist regime. What hypocrisy. What self-delusion. The only difference between the Chinese dictatorship and the "democratic" dictatorships at the level of "law" is that one is an open dictatorship and the other masquerades as freedom. The police and the military are front-line gatekeepers and, like traffic wardens and cops, wheel clampers, security guards, and all the other uniformed enforcers, they are the most obvious examples of the masses policing themselves. They think they administer the law when the law administers them. They do not answer to what is right and just in given circumstances, they answer to their masters who introduce the "law" and, in truth, the masters of their masters, the Illuminati.

Gatekeeper "scientists"

The foundations of "science" were created by the Francis Bacon-inspired Royal Society in London. This "science" claims that we come from oblivion, have a short physical "life", and then return to oblivion. Even by its own official history the Royal Society was created by Freemasons – people like the Illuminati agent,

Benjamin Franklin. Another inspiration was Isaac Newton, a Grand Master of that
elite Illuminati secret society, the Priory of Sion, which manipulates on behalf of the
Merovingian bloodline. Newton, like the founders of the Royal Society, knew that
much of what official "science" tells us to be true is utter garbage. But that was the
idea, to sell us a lie to keep us from the truth. It is far easier to control people if they
believe they are cosmic accidents, who come into existence merely by chemical
reactions and then go back to oblivion at death. It is much harder to control those
who are aware of their multi-dimensional infinity. Also, what better way to hide the
fact that we are controlled from another density than to have people believe there
are no other densities? The scientist, like the law, has become a "god", who is given
free reign to pontificate about the great questions because he is a scientist and
therefore he should know. Modern scientists are mostly babes-in-arms when it
comes to understanding the nature of life and existence, and yet they arrogantly
insist that only they know best. Worse, anyone inside or outside of their closed
order who questions their norms is subjected to hate campaigns of ridicule and
vilification. Virtually every major scientific breakthrough, including the Earth being
a sphere, was first greeted with laugher, anger, or denial, by the "scientists" of the
day. Science is a fascist club in which all members must stay in line or have their
funding and reputation destroyed. When Immanuel Velikovsky published his
books on the devastation he said was caused by the Venus "walk-about", he was
castigated beyond belief because he dared to question the norm of conditioned
"scientific" orthodoxy. The leading "experts" bombarded his publishers with letters
full of bile and vitriol saying they would boycott the company if they did not
withdraw Velikovsky's book. As the company was a publisher of official "scientific"
textbooks, it once again put bucks before backbone and the rights were passed to
another publisher. The assistant editor who suggested publishing Velikovsky's book
was sacked. All this happened because a different view to the scientific norm was
presented for people to see. John A. Keel wrote:

> "In retrospect many of the anti-Velikovsky critiques read like the work of deranged
> lunatics who had not even bothered to read the book they were attempting to
> criticise. They were against the book simply because it propounded ideas that were
> contrary to the accepted theories of the day ...Above all they resented the fact that
> the book was very well written (most scientists are miserable writers)."[1]

Alfred Wegener, a German meteorologist, died in 1930 after 15 years of ridicule,
slander, and contempt from his peers and colleagues. His crime? Suggesting that
the Earth once consisted of two landmasses, which split and drifted apart over vast
periods of time to form the continents. He supported this proposal with much
evidence, but because he was challenging the official "norm" he paid with an
onslaught of character assassination. We call his theory today "Continental Drift".[2]
The theme of what he said was correct! As Max Planck said: "A new scientific truth
does not triumph by convincing its opponents and making them see the light, but
rather because its opponents eventually die, and a new generation grows up that is

familiar with it." What passes for science is a sick joke. Most of its efforts are not aimed at answering the big questions of existence because there is little money or sponsorship in that. Science is geared to finding a new drug or industrial technique that will generate a fortune for its funders. It's a money-making machine and not inspired by an open-minded spirit of discovery. As a Congressional Committee established as far back as the 1950s, those funders of "scientific" research in US universities, the tax-exempt foundations like the Rockefeller Foundation, were dictating what the outcome of that research would be before it had even started!! Without such an agreement, the funding was not handed over (see ...*And The Truth Shall Set You Free*). This policy is to suppress an undesired outcome because, in Carl Sagan's words: "All inquiries carry with them some element of risk. There is no guarantee that the universe will conform to our predispositions." The whole "scientific" system is structured to suppress knowledge, not advance it, because the Illuminati is desperate for us to remain in ignorance of who we are and the nature of life. If enough people knew the truth, their game would be up.

Scientists, and their offshoot, the medical profession, are some of the most concrete-minded of the gatekeepers. They are also some of the most important because they suppress the nature of multi-dimensional existence and that is guaranteed to keep us in the Matrix. They are feted as experts and yet they are, like so many teachers, journalists, and politicians, astonishingly uninformed. Their whole structure is designed to keep them compartmentalised in their "speciality" so they are partial masters of one trade and jack of none. Only when we connect the dots can we begin to see the picture, but most scientists spend their entire careers specialising on one dot. In the UK, one of the most infamous gatekeepers in my experience is one Dr Susan Blackmore, who is constantly wheeled out by the media to dismiss any claims of the "paranormal". The more that people experience such phenomena, the more ludicrous Dr Blackmore's "explanations" become. But, of course, because she is an "academic" with a title she is seen as more credible than the people actually having the experience. In the New Scientist magazine of November 4th 2000, she was again given the freedom to rubbish all other scientists who say the mind and brain are not the same thing. The arrogance with which her padlocked mind dismisses anything outside the official "scientific" norm is a wonder to behold. We, the people, are the only ones who can break this stranglehold on true science. We need to stop being impressed by titles and letters after someone's name and focus purely on the evidence. We are encouraged to believe that a scientist must know better than a "layman" by definition. He's a scientist, isn't he? The track record of scientists talking complete cobblers is simply enormous and goes back to the very start of the "scientific method". While I was writing this book, an official report in the UK exposed how government "scientists" and "experts" had misled the British public for years about the so-called mad cow disease being transmitted to humans through eating beef. The scientists said it could not be passed to humans and so safety measures were not taken when any idiot could see that the chances were high that it could. I remember saying so on a

BBC farming programme in 1989 when I was a spokesman for the British Green Party. But the scientists knew best and people are still dying today as a result. Was it a layman or woman who came up with Thalidomide that led to so many fundamentally deformed babies? No, it was scientists who said it was perfectly safe. It would take a library to list all of the horrors that have resulted from these "experts" we call "scientists". But the masses go on believing them without question and, until we stop, the Matrix will remain unexposed to the vast majority. The motto of the new and true science should be the words of Albert Schweitzer: "…those who sincerely seek the truth should not fear the outcome".

Gatekeeper censors

Censorship is the life force of the Matrix. If you can stop the free flow of information you are already well on the way to global control. If I emphasise one thing and suppress the opposing view, I am going to get large numbers of people to make imbalanced and inaccurate conclusions about a person, event, or possibility. It is that simple. So if you are a censor, you are a gatekeeper, a prison warder for the Matrix. All censors are, by definition, arrogant beyond belief because they are saying that their view should be emphasised at the expense of another. They believe they have the right to decide what others shall and shall not have the freedom to hear. I can speak from experience because there have been endless attempts to censor my work. The closer I have gotten to the truth the more determined those attempts have become, especially since I began to speak and write about reptilian hybrid bloodlines. There have been attempts to close down my website, *www.davidicke.com*, and to stop me speaking at public meetings and in the media. If what I am saying is so crazy and wrong, why the obsession with denying me a platform?

I'll give some examples of how fragile our freedoms really are. The attempts to silence me started in the mid-1990s when I began to publish detailed accounts of the conspiracy in books like *…And The Truth Shall You Free*, since updated many times. On to the scene came a couple of naïve and immature young "journalists" called John Murray and Matthew Kalman. They had decided, on no evidence because the opposite is true, that I am "anti-Semitic". Their whole case was that I quoted in a previous book, *The Robots' Rebellion*, from the Protocols of the Elders of Zion, which, I suggest, were planted by the Illuminati to blame it all on the Jews and for other reasons. What the Protocols do, however, is reveal in detail the techniques that have been provably used to advance the Illuminati agenda these past 100 years and more. It mattered not to Kalman and Murray that I called them the Illuminati Protocols, nor that I had emphasised in the book, and later ones, that this is *not* a Jewish plot. It mattered neither that the first edition of *…And The Truth Shall Set You Free* was funded into existence by a Jewish friend of mine. The vast majority of Jewish people have been victims of the Illuminati, not the perpetrators. But mention a few Jewish people, like Kissinger, the Rothschilds, and the Bronfmans, among the 95% I have named over the years who are not Jewish, and you become "anti-Semitic". This has long been the prime and most effective tool used by the

Rothschilds and the Bronfmans to stop research into their activities, and its effectiveness has allowed them to continue unexposed with the manipulation and abuse of Jewish communities as much as anyone. Some brave Jewish people are trying to make these points also. Norman Finkelstein, whose own parents suffered in the Nazi concentration camps, has published a brilliant and explosive book called *The Holocaust Industry* (Verso Books, July 2000), which reveals how the Jewish elite have mercilessly exploited the Holocaust for their own financial ends while denying the true victims their just compensation. There are some quotes from this book in *Appendix III*. Kalman and Murray, who appeared to think they were Woodward and Bernstein on the *Washington Post* exposing Watergate, had decided what I was and that's all that mattered to them. Don't let the truth spoil a good story, especially when there is money and kudos in it. Suddenly articles began to appear in national newspapers saying that I was an anti-Semite (which in fact really means anti-Arab!). What no one was told was that all of these stories were either written by, or the "information" supplied by, the same disastrous duo, Matthew Kalman and John Murray. Their writings led to my events being banned by venues, so people could not hear how their lives were being manipulated, wars created, their freedoms removed, and staggering numbers of children tortured, abused, and ritually murdered. Well done chaps, great job.

This was in the mid-1990s and I had demonstrations by the Anti-Nazi League at some of my events. My children have always been brought up to see racism of any kind as silly and ridiculous. My daughter Kerry supported the Anti-Nazi League and wore their badge all the time. She threw it in the bin in outrage at what they were saying about the father she knew found all racism obnoxious. Friends went outside to the protesters to ask them if any of them had read my books. They had not. Had they ever heard me speak? They had not. So why were they there? Because of what they had read in the papers and what they had been told by those who ran the Anti-Nazi League (see the earlier section about the soldier and the commanding officer, because there is no difference). They were just a bunch of mindless pawns in a game they did not begin to understand, and they were so full of their own sense of self-purity, they never considered that they were behaving exactly like the Nazi fascists who systematically wrecked the public meetings of those in Germany who were trying to warn of the consequences of Hitler getting to power. A policeman who attended one of my meetings because of the demonstrations said that he had policed the infamous and violent confrontations between the fascist National Front Party and the Anti-Nazi League in the UK in the 1970s. He said that it had been impossible to tell the two "sides" apart because their attitude and behaviour had been precisely the same. Exactly. They are opposames. Just because people call themselves anti-fascist does not mean they do not express fascist behaviour. They are just not bright enough to see it. As a result they become an army of self-indulgent censors, gatekeepers for the Illuminati, and fascists who talk of stopping fascism. When the protestors were invited free of charge to come in and hear my talk and see for themselves, they refused. In doing so, they denied their right to be taken seriously. The same happened at Swansea

University, but then universities are the home of mind control and mental conditioning, the breeding ground of what I call the "Robot Radicals". The London School of Economics is a prime example.

Kalman and Murray have long since left the scene. They suddenly went very quiet. Maybe they realised they had been massively duped into duping others. Maybe the story got old and the fees from the newspapers ran out. Who knows and who cares? However, their nonsense was now in print thanks to newspapers like The *Sunday Times, Guardian, Independent*, and the London *Evening Standard*, all run by highly intelligent people, you'll understand. Once in print, even if the sources themselves may no longer believe it, the articles can be used to further censor what people can hear. Enter stage right, far right from where I am sitting, one Richard Warman. Never heard of him? You are not alone. No one seemed to have heard of him until he decided to dedicate his life to preventing me speaking and anyone having the opportunity to hear me anywhere in the world. No, you didn't mis-read that. This man, by the way, works for the Canadian Green Party, which condemns the censorship of freedom of speech! Just like David Taylor of the British Green Party who also sought to have my events banned. The stench of hypocrisy fills the air. Richard Warman is an official of the otherwise insignificant Ontario Green Party working out of Ottawa and Toronto, one of the global centres of the Illuminati and one of its key bloodlines, the Bronfmans. This is the gangster family behind Universal Music, Universal Studios, the liquor giant, Seagrams, and the force behind promoters of peace and love like the Satanic "rock star", Marilyn Manson. Warman has worked closely in his campaign of vilification and censorship against me with the Canadian Jewish Congress or CJC. This was formed and funded by the very same Bronfmans. Just a coincidence, nothing to worry about. Warman wrote triumphantly after denying my freedom of speech in Ontario in 1999:

"Now that the dust has settled over the recent attempted speaking tour by British hatemonger David Icke, I would like to offer a word of thanks on behalf of the Green Party of Ontario to all those with whom we worked to oppose this individual's message of division and intolerance. Our concern with David Icke stems not only from the need for solidarity with the Jewish and other communities whom he attacks, but also because Icke attempts to gain credence for his beliefs from his prior association with the British Green Party, without ever mentioning that they have disowned Icke and condemned his writings in no uncertain terms. The level of success that was achieved in informing the public and venues of the true nature of David Icke's paranoid conspiracy theories was due in large part to the tireless efforts of Rubin Friedman and Karen Mock of the B'nai B'rith League for Human Rights [Rothschilds], Daniel Fine and Bernie Farber of the Canadian Jewish Congress [Bronfmans], and Stacia Benovitch of Vaad Ha'lr, Ottawa. It was extremely encouraging to note that, apart from Hart House Theatre, every venue that was contacted made the decision that they were not willing to be a platform for David Icke or his followers. Most impressive was the Bronson Centre in Ottawa and the Order of Grey Nuns who run it. In a remarkable display of common sense, they always try to find out a little more about anyone who approaches them to rent space, and after a minimum inquiry on their own, they quickly decided they weren't interested in having Icke as a guest in their facility." [3]

This is a classic of its kind and typical of the thrust of the disinformation that has caused venues around the world to cancel my meetings. Note that he says that one venue cancelled after a "minimum inquiry" of its own. Normally it is no inquiry at all and my freedom of expression and the freedom of the audiences to listen is denied purely on this guy's say-so. He says the decision to cancel by the Order of Grey Nuns was impressive. But, of course, like all disinformers, he fails to mention that they did not cancel because they said I was anti-Semitic. They did so because I was questioning the literal existence of "Jesus". He also fails to mention that the Canadian Jewish Congress was founded and funded by the Bronfman family or that B'nai Brith was founded and funded by the Rothschilds. It is the same with the Anti-Defamation League. They were created by the Rothschilds to use the label "hatemonger" and "anti-Semite" to prevent legitimate research into their grotesque activities. You have read this book. Many will have read previous ones. Where am I a hatemonger? Where do I condemn the Jewish people? I don't, and Warman knows that I don't, but then that's not the point is it? And what are Warman and Farber (the Bronfmans) seeking to do in this campaign of personal abuse? To get as many people as possible to *hate* me. So who are the real hatemongers here? But the funniest part of all is the claim that I am trying to "gain credence" by emphasising my links with the British Green Party. Mr Warman, when you are trying to gain credence, the last thing you do is emphasise any connections to the British Green Party, never mind your own.

The bile circulated by Warman and Farber (the Bronfmans) led to me being stopped by both customs and immigration at Ottawa Airport and kept there until two o'clock in the morning. Every item in my luggage was searched (glad I brought those dirty socks) and every piece of paper was read in pursuit of "hate material". They found nothing and in the end the officer-pawn involved could see it was all a set-up. But I still could not leave because some immigration technicality was then found to hold me still longer. I was brought back the following lunchtime, the day of my talk. They kept me there for hours and then asked me what time my talk was due to end that day. I said four o'clock. They let me go at four o'clock. More men and women in uniform, more gatekeepers of their own freedoms. They treated me like a criminal, as if all the propaganda by Warman and Farber (the Bronfmans) was true. In other words they were mind controlled by a preconceived idea, planted by someone else. There is nothing more powerful than the preconceived idea because once that is implanted all you see is evidence to support your preconception. The power of that thought form so often unconsciously filters out information that would show that your original perception was wrong.

Richard Warman's abuse of my character devastated my meeting in Ottawa, where the venue had to be changed again and again in the last 48 hours, and the one at Windsor, Ontario, was cancelled. Together with the Bronfmans' Canadian Jewish

Congress and its vitriolic spokesman, Bernie Farber, and others, Warman organised a demonstration outside my talk at the Hart House Theatre at Toronto University, which they had failed miserably to stop. A friend of mine, who was married to a Jewish man for many years, went outside to the demonstrators and asked them how they knew I was anti-Semitic. It was the usual tale. "Someone" (Warman and Farber) had told them, they said. Had they read my books? No. Had they heard me speak? No. Would they be going inside to hear me now? No. Why? Because he is anti-Semitic! The only reason the Toronto talk went ahead was because the head of the university refused to bow to pressure from Warman and Farber to block my freedom of speech. He was a brave man because the pressure was enormous. Soon afterwards, he left the university by "mutual consent". As a result of the lies directed at me, the head of the Canadian Police Hate Crimes Unit was in the audience. We shook hands afterwards and he had no problem with my talk whatsoever. Warman and Farber (the Bronfmans) never mention that. As I walked off the stage I was greeted by two agents of Canadian Immigration, who threatened me with immediate arrest if I did not agree to see an officer the next morning. When I did so, I was banned from speaking at any more events. Ask a Canadian if he or she lives in a free country and most will say enthusiastically that they do. I was told that a teacher who had hosted a meeting for me lost his job as a result of this character assassination and, although this turned out not to be correct, many people have had their reputations attacked for their association with me. The campaign continued when Warman flew across Canada (who paid?) to gather support for a campaign to have my event in Vancouver banned in the spring of 2000. Only a few mindless people were interested, but they still managed, thanks to "Farber's" (the Bronfmans') influence in Toronto, to have the major Canadian book chain, Chapters, cancel a book signing; have invitations to appear on radio withdrawn; and "organised" a rabble dressed as reptiles to rush into a book signing at an independent bookshop and throw pies at me. Isn't it good to know that our freedoms are being protected by those with this scale of intellect and maturity?

And while all this was unfolding, the children went on being abused, tortured, and sacrificed, and the wars and other horrors went on being manipulated, as Mr Warman and Mr Farber worked so ferociously to stop it being exposed. They have made their priorities very clear.

The Vancouver event, attended by 1,200 people, only survived because it was at an independent theatre. Any connection to a council, government, or major chain and it would have been pulled like so many before and since. Warman sat through my talk and in those more than six hours, he saw at first hand that I do not speak about a Jewish plot at all and never even mention the word "Jewish" because there is no need, except to emphasise what a travesty of the truth Warman is seeking to purvey. This talk can be seen on a video called *From Prison To Paradise* and you can see for yourself that what I am saying here is true. If Warman had simply been stupid and mis-guided, this is where it would have ended. But it didn't. That was the point when Richard Warman's true motives became clear in my opinion. This guy had an agenda and, given what small fry he is in Canada, it must, I believe, be someone else's agenda. To this very day he and Farber have refused to meet me face to face or debate with me on the radio, though the opportunity has been there. Warman, from his home in eastern Canada, now seeks to prevent me speaking anywhere on the planet and if anyone wants to know how easy it is to control the world, they should look at how easy it is to stop freedom of speech without moving from your desk. All he does is check on my website where I am speaking and waits until a few days before the event to ensure that there is not enough time to find another venue. He then either rings the venue or sends them a package claiming I am anti-Semitic and will be blaming Jews for a global conspiracy, something he knows from his own experience is not true. Ironically he quotes the articles in British newspapers written or inspired by Kalman and Murray all those years ago. Perhaps most sickening of all, he includes the fact that I am exposing famous people as abusers and sacrificers of children as a reason why venues should not let me speak. A few tell him where he can place a large object and they stand up for freedom of speech. Depressingly, many just pull the meeting on the basis of what he says. Just by doing this, in the course of writing this book, Warman has, from eastern Canada, caused my events at London's Blackheath Concert Rooms, Stourbridge Town Hall, and the Burlington Hotel in central Birmingham to be cancelled because the venues banned my talk. That's how easy it is. The venues refuse to discuss the situation and could not care less about the inconvenience and the cost, not least to the audience, and they could care even less about the freedom of human expression. So long as it does not affect theirs, they don't give a damn. They do not have the intellect to understand that in banning my freedom of speech they are undermining that freedom for everyone by setting the precedent that it's OK to deny a person's right to express views that don't suit you (even if you don't know what they are!).

It has gotten so ludicrous that I was almost banned from speaking down the road from where I live on the Isle of Wight in a theatre where I have appeared several times with no problem over many years. If I had not challenged the council on local radio, they would have pulled the event, I am sure. The council even sent a "monitor" to my talk with legal advice on hand and the authority to stop the event if I overstepped their mark. Not naming people who abuse and sacrifice children appears far more important to them than the plight of the kids themselves. The monitor told the local newspaper that there was not a single moment when I said anything that concerned her in any way. This is what the Canadian Police Hate Crimes Unit said, who were set up specifically to make "Anti-Semitism" a criminal offence. So that should be the end of it, you may think, but no. When the Burlington Hotel in Birmingham had the Warman treatment three weeks later they pulled the meeting and refused to even speak to me and explain. They were given the chance to speak to the council monitor on the Isle of Wight to see that what Warman was claiming from thousands of miles away was nonsense. But the Burlington Hotel did not want to know. I understand that after pressure they did contact the City Varieties Theatre in Leeds where I had spoken so successfully just two weeks earlier. But even though the Burlington was told that there were no problems whatsoever in Leeds, they banned me all the same. They sent a very short fax, signed by a Sarah Small, the conference sales manager. My talk had been cancelled, she informed me, because they thought it would damage the reputation of the hotel. It could not possibly do any more damage to your "reputation", Ms Small, than the outrageous behaviour of you and your colleagues. Paul, the organiser of those British events, had worked his socks off to make them a success. He did it because he believed that the freedom of all of us is under fundamental threat. But it was all for nothing because the combination of one phone call or package from Richard Warman thousands of miles away and pathetic venue managers in the UK is all takes to deny this most basic of freedoms.

Everyone concerned with these events is a gatekeeper for the Matrix. There are so few on this planet who are not. People like Richard Warman and Bernie Farber (the Bronfmans) know they are, that's the difference. Either that or their brain cell count must be dangerously low or their capacity for self-delusion dangerously high. But equally responsible are those Green Party members in Canada and worldwide who have been informed of what he is doing in their name and yet just sit on their hands and let him go on unchallenged. Those who stay silent and allow the bullies to prevail are also gatekeepers by their inaction. I was a spokesman for the British Green Party for a couple of years in the 1980s and it, and its equivalent around the world, is the global headquarters of Navel Contemplators Anonymous. That's why Warman can use it to front his attempts to have me silenced, including his bid to have my Internet site taken down. This caused us to move quickly to another server to keep the information available. It was yet more time and effort used to overcome his attempts at censorship that could have been exposing what is happening to so many people, not least to children. Apparently, Mr.Warman was outraged that his activities were being exposed on the website and that his official Green Party office numbers and e-mail addresses were published so that people whose freedom he had denied could let him know what they thought. Richard Warman, gatekeeper to the Matrix, would be a legitimate dictionary definition for the word "hypocrisy". You will find the contact numbers for the Canadian Green Party on the website. At the same time Warman was having my events banned, the leader of the US Green Party, Ralph Nader, was condemning the "censorship" that saw him denied a place in the televised presidential debates between Bush and Gore. Warman summed up his attitude to freedom when he told a journalist of equal intelligence in the British *Independent On Sunday*:

> "He has taken all the conspiracy theories that ever existed and melded them together to create an even greater conspiracy of his own. His writings may be the work of a madman, or of a genuine racist. Either way they are very dangerous. There is an unpleasant anti-Semitic undertone in his work [I thought I was a "hatemonger" openly condemning Jewish people] that must be brought to public attention. If he's unstable then so are his followers, who hang on his every word. What benefit can there be in allowing him to speak?"

If someone had spoken those words in the middle of the last century while wearing a Nazi uniform, no one would have been surprised. If the speaker in Warman's opinion is unstable, so, by definition, must be everyone who listens. Now that is truly terrifying and truly, truly, dangerous. Think of the implications of that statement. The Soviet Union's psychiatric hospitals were filled with perfectly sane dissidents of that fascist/Communist system because the very same attitudes expressed there by Mr Warman were used to justify their imprisonment. And even more sinister: "What benefit can there be in allowing him to speak?" The arrogance of that question beggars belief. No fascist in Nazi Germany, no Communist in China or the Soviet Union, could ever have said it better. But I still respect his right to express his view. As Voltaire said: "I may disagree with what you have to say, but I shall defend, to the death, your right to say it." Pity that Mr Warman does not feel the same about others. Green Party members of the world, this man claims to speak for you. How long are you going to sit there in silence? While you do so, you are responsible for everything this man does and says in your name. How many more venue owners are going to have their decisions made by such a fundamental enemy of freedom? The "journalist" who wrote that *Independent On Sunday* article, one Jason Cowley, just let those quotes pass without comment while calling my work "extreme", "dark", and "dotty". If more dark and extreme words have ever been spoken than those, then I haven't heard them.

But in one way, Richard Warman, this misguided holographic image, provides a service to those who care about their freedoms. His behaviour has shown how fragile those freedoms are and, indeed, what an illusion they are. The idea that we live in a free world is self-delusion on a monumental scale. People in Manchester, England, think they live in a free city and yet it has proved impossible to find any venue there that will accept a booking for my talk. The people of Brighton, on England's south coast, think they live in a free city and yet I have not been able to speak there for many years because venues are threatened with mass protests by the "anti-fascists" who tell them that they will not be able to guarantee the safety of the audience. The Brighton Art School lied to me when they said the police had ordered them to pull my meeting there. The police had done nothing of the kind. It was just an excuse because it is easier that way when your backbone is made of jelly. When we booked an alternative venue at Crawley, north of Brighton, the council asked to see a video of what I was going to say. They watched it and confirmed there was no problem; 24 hours before the talk, they cancelled because an anonymous caller had indicated the possibility of violence against the audience if I was allowed to speak. The caller was an "anti-fascist", by the way. Another gatekeeper, another sheepdog in the bewildered herd.

Censorship of the Internet is next on the Illuminati agenda. The Internet is an Illuminati creation and only exists because of military technology. It has been sold as a means of allowing the free flow of global information, but that is only the cover. The real reason is that it allows for the easiest possible surveillance of personal communications through e-mails, and the websites visited by individuals give the authorities the opportunity to build a personality and knowledge profile of everyone. It's about control. Slowly, and now less than slowly, the benefits of the Internet, the free flow of views and information, are being targeted and the most prominent advocates are... the Bronfmans! You are going to see an onslaught against Internet freedom, just as Richard Warman and his string-pullers targeted my own site. Censors never admit to being so. It's not good for the image, especially if you publish articles calling for freedom of speech like the Green Party. They will always find a way of justifying why they are defending freedom rather than destroying it. But when the same criteria are applied to them, they scream like a three-year-old. Self-delusion is the very mind-state of the Matrix. Welcome to the Matrix, Mr Warman.

Gatekeeper "journalists"

The media is the force that holds the whole Matrix together. That's why the Illuminati own it. Without the minute by minute flow of Matrix propaganda through the global media, the power of the illusion would be nothing like as fundamental as it is. You don't have to control every journalist to dictate what the public will or will not hear. If journalists were open-minded, thinking, intelligent, people who care about freedom, there would not be a problem. But most of them aren't and those who are aware and try to tell some real truths soon realise what a prison of expression they work in. I was a journalist for years and I know how uninformed they are about the world outside the morning papers or the TV news. I have seen them at work from the other side since I began to communicate this information and it is a stunning experience to view at close hand the intellect that stands between what is happening in the world and what the people are told is happening. And I am talking about top television correspondents as well as the propaganda fodder on the large and small newspapers. There are basically two types of personality who reach the top in journalism, and politics come to that: (a) The few who know what is really going on and support that agenda; and (b) the rest, the majority, who do not understand what is happening in the world. The British Prime Minister Tony Blair and his deputy, John Prescott, are perfect examples of both kinds and journalists are precisely the same. And yet these are the people who tell us every day what to think about people and events. As the old saying goes: "You cannot bribe or twist the great British journalist, but seeing what they will do unbribed, there's no reason to."

Journalists in general are, like most politicians, some of the most uninformed people on the planet. They are slaves to the Illuminati "norms", the mental and emotional sheep-pen. Once the norms are set of what is right and wrong, good and bad, possible or impossible, the media report the world from that perspective. They are clones of the Matrix. A few centuries ago today's media would have ridiculed and condemned as dangerous anyone who said that the Earth was not flat. Why? For no other reason than the "norm", the accepted "truth" of the official establishment system, was that the Earth was indeed flat. Because the "journalists" report everything from the perspective of the "norms" in every generation, it means that anything that is different is always dubbed either dangerous or dotty. Or, in my case, both. They don't do any research into whether that which is different is actually true. They assume it must be wrong simply because it is so different. And, of course, they have the ultimate self-delusion of believing that because they are "journalists" they would know about it if it were true. Ask a journalist about the

Bilderberg Group and see his or her eyes glaze over. "Bilder-what?" I have tried it over and over across the world and I have yet to find one, *one*, who has heard of it. But at the same time they dismiss conspiracy information as a dotty and paranoid "theory". Now if you were the Illuminati wishing to keep people in ignorance, is not this the very mentality you would want to have working for your media? Of course it is, and that's why we have it.

I could give you many specific examples of this, but one experience I had while writing this book can serve as an example of them all. I was called by a guy named Jason Cowley, who writes for the *Independent On Sunday*. "Independent", by the way, is newspeak for anything but. You call a paper "Independent" in the same way that violent dictators who rule with their army call their countries "democratic fronts". It attempts to obscure the reality. The *"Independent"* newspaper group is owned by an Illuminati frontman called Tony O'Reilly, who also owns a list of media operations around the world, including the main newspaper group in South Africa. O'Reilly, who loves to show off his connections to people like Henry Kissinger, is a close friend of Robert Mugabe, the corrupt and vicious dictator in Zimbabwe. Yep, what a perfect man to own the *"Independent"* newspaper. Anyway, this chap Cowley calls me and says he's coming to my talk in the Isle of Wight I mentioned earlier. My first impressions were not good. He had no interest in what I was saying and changed the subject whenever I got into any substance. He said he wanted to write a "philosophical piece". Now this, in journalistic-speak, means: "I have got in my head the theme of what I will write, my preconceived idea, and I am not going to let anything get in the way of that." Like the facts. I have had so much shit written about and thrown at me over the years by those of Jason Cowley's mentality, and I knew that he was preparing to throw some more. These days I can see them a mile off because they're such transparent people. I said to a friend: "I think this *Independent* guy is a monumental prat and I know what he is coming to do." Cowley also told me that he was "coming with an open mind", and that's always a red flag to me. I wish I had a dollar for every journalist I have met with a concrete mind who assured me that he or she was coming with an open one. So along he came. He was actually planning to arrive at the talk some three hours after the start and then write his article about what I was saying! It was only when I pointed out how ludicrous and unacceptable this was, that he agreed to try to get there earlier. This is simply confirmed clearly that my first impression had been correct. He didn't give a damn what I was saying, he had the article and its theme in his head already. Most of them do. Even then he spent long periods of the day outside the theatre and so could not hear the evidence I was presenting. What an insult to his readers and what contempt he must have for them to behave in that way.

Throughout the day, members of the audience were telling my family that Cowley had been asking them silly and leading questions and it was obvious to them that he had come to do a demolition job. Meanwhile he thought he was hiding his intentions really well! You have got to laugh. In fact, in the end people were laughing at him, as he flitted around in and out of the theatre making his intentions so obvious while thinking no one would notice. He spoke to me for around

40 minutes about my own mental state (I'm different, so I must be mad) and an amazing experience that happened to me in Peru in 1991 (none of which he quoted). I was not asked a single question about the conspiracy. From all this "research" by Jason Cowley, one of the least intelligent "journalists" I have met in my own experience, the following was published as fact: "Icke's vision has darkened as it has become more delusional and paranoid, and there is much that is sinister, as well as dotty, in his vast conspiracy theory."[4] This was written by a man who doesn't know what I am saying because he couldn't be bothered to find out. He ended by concluding that perhaps the biggest secret is that there is no secret and that there was no unified field encompassing everything. Some brilliant and open-minded real scientists would be very surprised to hear that, but who can doubt the all-knowing, non-researching, Mr Cowley or the journalistic herd in which he operates? The problem with my ideas, he said, was that they were based on no sacred texts or a belief in a single deity. He had just attended a talk (or rather not) in which I said all that exists is one infinite consciousness. He quoted G.K. Chesterton in support of his view of my "problem": "When a man stops believing in God, he doesn't then believe in nothing, he believes in everything, in anything." So if you don't believe in an official version of God, you are not to be taken seriously.

So how much research had Cowley done to see if what I am saying is true? None. Just like all the rest. And he would have written all that he did had he turned up, as he intended, three hours into my talk. Had he read my books? No. This, ladies and gentlemen of the Matrix, is the mentality that keeps the people enslaved in the illusion because he is not the exception, he is the rule all over the world. The blind leading the blind and the bland leading the bland. I spoke in the talk about famous people sacrificing and abusing children, people like Ted Heath. What did Cowley write about even the *theme* of massive ritual murder and abuse? *Nothing*. What research did he do into it afterwards to see if it was true? *None*. What did he say about all the detailed connections I made in the talk that showed, for instance, that members of the same organisations, like the Bilderberg Group, were named as all the major peace negotiators in the Bosnian conflict? *Nothing*. What did he report about any specific detailed information I gave that day? *Nothing*. All this specific information and detail was dismissed as me having a conspiracy theory for everything. That was it. Mr Cowley, like 95% of his fellow "journalists", is not intelligent enough to realise that he is a gatekeeper of other people's minds, as well as his own. But, like I say, he's the norm, not the exception. I don't think that Mr Cowley and his like would know *how* to be an exception. They live in the world dictated by norms and then confirm and perpetuate them for other people.

I met a "journalist" on the British *Observer* newspaper in 1997 while in the United States, by the name of Taylor, I think it was. I told him about the mind control projects and the widespread child murder and abuse involving people like George Bush and others. He called it the "story of the century". I offered to put him in touch with victims and those involved directly who could tell him more. I gave him my number to call me for their names and contact addresses. He never called. He just went away and the following Sunday wrote an article that took the piss.

And all the time the children go on being sacrificed, tortured, and abused in Satanic ritual and mind control projects. If you saw life in a typical newspaper or radio and television newsroom, it would blow your mind. They take reports that come up constantly on the teleprinter from the global (Illuminati) news agencies and just publish them or broadcast them as if they were true. These news agencies have correspondents in every country and when a major event happens there, the report of that one journalist is sent all around the world to every major news organisation. If that one journalist gets it wrong, or has an agenda, every newspaper, radio, and television news bulletin, gets it wrong or communicates the desired spin. Every hour on radio stations across this planet, newsreaders are ripping pre-written news bulletins from the teleprinter and reading them as truth. In the BBC in the UK, this process is actually known as "rip n' read". The person reading that "news" has no idea who wrote it or from what source it came, never mind if it is accurate. The listeners hear this "news" and it affects their view of life, people, and the world. That's why we have to question everything we are told through such sources. Just listen to any television news report and invariably the journalist will have taken the official version of the event and put this in his or her own words. We now have the policy of the newsreader interviewing a reporter about people and events instead of the people directly involved.

"We go over to our correspondent John Reynolds at the scene. John, what's going on?"

"Well Michael, terrorists, believed to be from the Middle East, appear to have planted the bomb." (Official sources have told him that terrorists believed to be from the Middle East planted the bomb.)

"I understand that police and the security agencies are focusing their investigation on a terrorist group connected to Libya, Iraq, Iran, etc., etc." (Official sources have told him they are focusing their investigation on such a group. It doesn't matter if they are or not, he reports what they say.)

"It appears that the bomb was planted as a protest over UN policy in the Middle East and the Prime Minister says that the policy must continue because they cannot give in to terrorism. New security laws are to be rushed through parliament to protect the public from further attacks." (All this has come from official sources and the reporter has no idea if it is true or not. The way it is worded: (a) supports the continuance of a UN policy; and (b) equates new laws that will remove freedoms with the need to protect the public.)

The reporter is not trying to dupe people or give false information. But he gets his information from official sources and so he becomes a mouthpiece for the official version of events. This happens every day. He is not an independent observer and reporter, he is little more than a public relations man for the official version that they want the public to believe. When a BBC reporter called Peter Snow tried to report the Falklands War impartially, and used phrases like the British Government claims or says, rather than accepting its accuracy without question, he was catastigated by the government and the *rest of the media* for being anti-British! The men and women of the global media, with a few very honourable exceptions, are some of the key gatekeepers for the Matrix and some of the most deluded of the Matrix mentality.

One journalist wrote an appalling article indicating that I was anti-Semitic and talking paranoid nonsense about a conspiracy. He apparently even made a call to a television programme that led to my appearance being cancelled. Years later he contacted me to say he no longer believed that I was anti-Semitic and had seen enough in his own experience since to see that there was definitely an investigation to be done into a global conspiracy. At least he had the guts to change his mind and he will not be the last as the evidence becomes more and more obvious. When it does, the Cowleys, Taylors, Warmans, and Farbers will have all those abused children to answer to. I trust they will have a good excuse prepared for looking the other way and ridiculing the evidence of this abuse while doing no research to see if it is true. Or, in the case of Warman and Farber, vociferously seeking to suppress exposure of the children's plight. In so many ways, the global media is the Matrix and the global journalistic herd are its, largely unknowing, propaganda machine.

Gatekeeper people

We are all gatekeepers to an extent because the illusion is so powerful. It is just a matter of degree. Among the major gatekeeper professions and mentalities I have highlighted here, there are many decent, caring, people who are intelligent within the Matrix version of intelligence. It's the intelligence of the inmate who is street-wise about his prison, who can duck and weave and play the game successfully within its confines and rules. What this intelligence cannot see, however, are the prison walls. It thinks it's free. It's not intelligence that we need to break out of here. It's wisdom. I have been emphasising in this chapter how the closed minds and Matrix conditioning of the gatekeeper professions and mentality lead them to stand on guard at the gates to mental, emotional, and spiritual freedom. Their professions make them especially effective gatekeepers, but in truth everyone is. Everyone, that is, who seeks to impose their reality on others by suppression, ridicule, and misrepresentation of another view; or by parental, peer, and partner pressure to conform to someone else's reality. Partners gatekeep their partners; parents gatekeep their children; children gatekeep each other; neighbours gatekeep neighbours; priests gatekeep their believers; journalists gatekeep the masses. As a friend of mine, Michael Roll, once said:

> "You are born to loving parents and they tell you that 2 + 2 = 5; you go to school and teachers tell you that 2 + 2 = 5; you go to university and professors with letters after their name tell you 2 + 2 = 5; the media constantly confirms that 2 + 2 = 5 because that's the 'norm' they slavishly serve and promote; and all the people around you believe the same because they have been through the same system that you have.

In those circumstances, and that's what we face every day, is it any wonder that billions of people go through an entire physical lifetime believing that 2 + 2 = 5?"

It is an excellent point. The answer goes on equalling four, it's just that people don't know that and most can't be bothered to find out. If we want to be free, it is time that we did.

SOURCES

1   *Our Haunted Planet*, p 79

2   Ibid, pp 69 and 70

3   This communication was dated January 13, 2000

4   Jason Cowley, "The Icke Files", *Independent On Sunday, The Sunday Review*, October 1st, 2000, pp 6 to 9

CHAPTER 20

It's just a ride

We are not humans on a spiritual journey. We are spiritual beings on a human journey.

Stephen Covey

We are all faced with a series of great opportunities brilliantly disguised as impossible situations.

Charles Swindoll

OK, let's put all this into a greater perspective. I have been talking throughout this book about the multi-dimensional nature of existence. That makes it hard, indeed impossible, to give the true picture of what is happening in our world, our frequency range.

I mean, what is true? Once you enter the realms of multi-dimensional reality, you see that there is no ultimate truth, except that we are all the same energy expressing itself in infinite ways. After that we are pretty much through with "truth". Everything else is not so much truth, but our perspective of what we see. Or think we see. What is true in my universe will not necessarily be true in yours. What you have been reading is my universe, my reality, at this point. Or, rather, *one* of my realities. We are imprisoned by the belief that if one thing is "true" the opposite can't be true. But it can, and it is. It's just that they come from different perspectives of the same event. For instance, if the world is not perfect, how, at the same time, can it also be perfect? But it can and it is. When you look at the world from the Matrix perspective, it is far from perfect, whatever perfect is. We see untold suffering, abuse, conflict, and sadness. So the reality that the world is not perfect is valid and supportable. But how can we evolve and grow into greater knowledge, wisdom, and understanding unless we face the consequences of our actions? We can't. If a child had no consequences of his or her behaviour, they would not change the behaviour and make different choices. What Creation does magnificently is to put the consequences of our choices, or more accurately the *intent* behind those choices, in front of our faces. This imperfect world is the consequence of human choices, the choice of those who wish to control and destroy, and the choice of those who sit back and let them do it, or close their minds to what is happening because they think it is easier that way. So in terms of our evolutionary journey, Creation is presenting the consequences of our action and inaction and, in doing so, it makes the world we live in absolutely perfect because we are experiencing what we need to experience. Two apparent opposites, but both are true. Life is a paradox, but then again, it's not, because these are not paradoxes, they are different perspectives. They are not contradictions, they are comprehensions.

I have been told from time to time that I am contradictory in what I say and do. But I'm not. That is just those people's perspective. And if you judge a multi-dimensional being from one perspective, you are going to see apparent contradictions. As we judge what a person says or does, do we ever ask which level, therefore perspective, those words and actions are coming from? No, we see one person and make judgements as if they are one person. But we are many "people". If I am reacting or seeing something in that moment from the view of my Matrix-level holographic "physical" image, I am going to see things a certain way. But, in another moment of reflection when I open up the connection to my higher levels of being, I will see the same events and experiences in a very different light. That's not contradiction, it is the comprehension of the level that is observing. If you watch one of my talks you will see me moving realities as I go along, always culminating in the ultimate reality that we are all one and that one is love. So I have written this book from one perspective of reality and it offers, I would submit, an accurate *theme* of what is happening in that reality. But it's not the only one, and I see this same theme and story from many other realities. At the highest reality I have accessed thus far, it's all just a game. A cosmic game called evolution, a game called love.

The Matrix is like a cinema screen and we are the cast in the picture. Or, as "Shakespeare" put it, all the world's a stage and we are the players. If the reptilians and other astral manipulators did not exist, we would have to invent them. In fact we probably have. They are other levels of ourselves putting ourselves in our face. They are a level of our own infinite self, one of our realities, that we are being challenged to face and transform. If we hate them, we hate ourselves. They are our shadow, that part of ourselves that we do not want to face, acknowledge, or admit to. While our shadow self is hidden from us, the reptilians will stay hidden and continue to covertly control. As we acknowledge it, so they will emerge and we will see what is going on. One is a reflection of the other. The more we deny our shadow side, the more the consequences will be placed before us because that's the way the game works. The longer we stay in denial, the more powerful and challenging the consequences become. That is our choice. See it now or see it later. Because we *are* going to see it. The question is how extreme must be the consequences before we do? In this movie, The Great Illusion, we play our parts in mutual service to the cosmic game. If Richard Warman did not determine to silence me and suppress my information, I would not have the challenge to overcome that frustration and grow from it. If Richard Warman did not have me, he would not face the consequences of his actions and learn from the experiences that Creation will present to him. If journalists like Jason Cowley did not misrepresent me and my work, I would not have the major challenge to disconnect from Matrix reactions and, again, feel the frustration at what is written. Nor would I be given such a wonderful opportunity to see how journalists defend and underpin the Matrix mentality. If Cowley did not have me, as the evidence emerges to show the validity of what he dismisses and ridicules, he would not have the opportunity to see what a prison he lives in and perpetuates for others. If we did not have the Illuminati, we could not experience the consequences of what happens when you give your mind away to someone else's reality and insist that everyone else does the same. If the Illuminati did not have the human race, they could not face the coming consequences of seeking to impose their will on others. We are all providing experiences for each other. In fact, we are providing them for ourselves because we are everything. There is no us and no them and no "we". There is only one infinite "I". *We* are the reptilians and the "demons" and, at the same time, we are those they manipulate because we are all the same "I".

So what I have presented here is one level of the Cosmic Game – the point where the game interacts with dense physical reality. It is not the *whole* story, only *part* of it. The challenge of the game is to see that it's a game. Once we do that and see through the illusion, we hit the jackpot, the doorway opens, and we get out of here. We can still be *in* it physically, but we are no longer *of* it. The experiences my life have set before me since 1991 particularly, often extreme and played out in the public eye in Britain, have not yet freed me from the Matrix. But they have made me free-er than ever before. And I'll get there. I have yet to meet anyone who is fully free of the illusion because we look it in the face every minute of our lives. I have met many who think they are, but they are just caught in another facet of the illusion. They are entrapped by the illusion that they are free of the illusion while continuing to be controlled by it. The more I disentangle my lower mind from the Matrix, the crazier and more extreme people think I am. But I'm not crazy and extreme. That is only the perception of those mesmerised by the Matrix and if only they could step back and observe the world they believe is "normal" and "sane", they would see just how extreme and crazy *that* is.

In my experience, and that's all I can speak from, the first step to freedom is to realise that we live an illusion. Without that, the Matrix always wins. Doing this is not easy when everything seems so "real". Our senses deceive us and confuse us because they are accessing such a tiny fraction of all that is. If our radio and television could only tune to CNN or the BBC we would get a very narrow band of reality. It would be a desperately limited and biased vision of life and possibility. There would be so much that we would never know about. Our physical senses disinform us in the same way, unless we balance that by opening ourselves to our higher frequencies of perception and intuition that can recognise an illusion when they see one. So the foundation of freedom from the Matrix mentality is to know that we live in a dream world created by our own minds and those who condition them. More and more, I look at the physical world and see it as vibrating energy. The numbers and codes in the Matrix movie is a good way to visualise it. I find that this constantly re-confirms to me that I live in a virtual reality computer game and what we see is whatever we think we see or are told we see. It keeps me on my

guard against falling for the Matrix mentality. When you perceive those who
harass you and situations that challenge you as merely vibrating numbers and
codes, it takes the sting from the experience and your emotional response because
you can see it's not real. You know you are like the guy in the computer game
dodging the bullets fired by a spotty-faced 15-year-old sitting in his bedroom hour
after hour. If you get hit, the game just starts again. No one's really dead. They just
play dead and then continue their eternity. We live forever. We are the players in
the game and we are those controlling the game and observing the game. We *are*
the game. As Bill Hicks said of life:

> "It's like a ride in an amusement park and when you go on it you think it's real,
> because that's how powerful our minds are. The ride goes up and down, round and
> round, it has thrills and chills, and it's very brightly coloured and it's very loud. And
> it's fun for a while. Some have been on the ride a long time and they begin to
> question: Is this real, or is this just a ride? And others have remembered and they
> come back to us and they say: Hey, don't be afraid ever, because this is just a ride.
> And we kill those people.

> "Shut him up, I've got a lot invested in this ride, shut him up. Look at my furrows of
> worry, my big bank account, and my family. This has to be real. It's just a ride, but we
> always kill those good guys who try to tell us that and let the demons run amok. But
> it doesn't matter because it's just a ride and we can change it anytime we want. No
> job, no savings money, just a choice right now between fear and love."[1]

And that's all it is. Fear in all its infinite expressions like guilt and resentment
and a desire for revenge, is the low-vibrational emotion that holds us in the pen, the
Great Illusion. Love, in its purest sense, is our highest vibrational state and one that
connects us with the highest level of all that is. All that we are. That transformation
of perspective, from fear to love, vibrates us out of the Matrix mentality and we step
out of the game and out of the illusion that it's all "real". If you observe parts of this
book, particularly the chapter, The Gatekeepers, you will feel my Matrix level, my
holographic image, screaming inside with frustration at the way we control and
imprison each other. That's one reality and a valid one from that point of
observation. But when I open my heart to the love vibration and open my mind to
acknowledge the illusion, the frustration dissolves because it's just a game, just a
ride, just a movie of our own making. We can make it a nice picture or a horror film.
That's our choice. It is, always was, and will always be.

So I love you Richard Warman; I love you Bernie Farber; I love you Jason
Cowley; I love you George Bush, Queen of England, Queen Mother, Prince Philip,
Henry Kissinger, David Rockefeller, Edgar Bronfman, Rothschild dynasty, Lord
Carrington, Al Gore, Ted Heath, Tony Blair, Peter Mandelson, Billy Graham, and all
the others named in my books. If I don't love you, I don't love myself, because I am
you and you are me. We are different aspects of the same infinite whole. No, we *are*
the infinite whole.

A time to choose

The game is reaching a crucial stage in terms of choice. We can take the left hand path and live in a Matrix controlled by the lower astral consciousness – a global fascist state in which the illusion will be imposed by the law and the jackboot. That, from the viewpoint of eternity, is of little consequence because there will be other chances to make different decisions and make other movies. The game never ends, it just changes as we change. But do you really want to have the experience of living in a fascist global state with your freedom of expression and choice denied in its most basic form? If you do then just sit on your arse and watch it happen because it will. It *is* happening. What Richard Warman and Bernie Farber (the Bronfmans) are trying to do to me will be written into the law of the land. Such laws are already being introduced. If we don't want that, we need to make another choice and make it now. We can take the straight-on path and walk the Freedom Road. If that's our choice, there are some fundamental changes to make. First, we free ourselves from the illusion and the reactions and responses of the Matrix mentality. Unless we start to free ourselves, how can we hope to free the world around us, which is merely an outward manifestation of the inner self? We live in an *external* prison while thinking we are free because we live in an *internal* prison while thinking we are free. The prison without is a reflection of the prison within. Change ourselves and we change the world. Look in the mirror. Try changing the image you see without changing the image it is reflecting. You can't, of course you can't, but the human race has been trying to do that for thousands of years and that's why it has never worked. I have written before of the three crucial elements that I believe are the key to unlocking the gates and the portals to multi-dimensional freedom.

1   We let go of the fear of what other people think of us and start living and expressing our own uniqueness of lifestyle, view, and reality. When we do this we step out of the herd and if enough of us do it, there is no herd.

2   We allow everyone else the freedom and respect to express their uniqueness without the fear of ridicule and condemnation for the crime of being different. When we do that we cease to be a sheepdog keeping the herd in line.

3   No one seeks to impose their beliefs or reality on anyone else, so always respecting the freedom of others to make different choices. This is the balance point that stops one person's free will imposing itself on another.

These three steps would trigger a transformation of such magnitude that they would turn this prison into a paradise. And all three, as they relate to us, we have the power to introduce right now. This book may have said much about bloodlines and the history and techniques of human servitude. It may have highlighted at some length the reptilian genetic connection to all this. That's important because people need to know what is going on at that level of reality. But what this book has really been about is humanity freeing itself from the Great Illusion. If I had to choose one thought that people would remember from these pages, one thought that would transform this world more than any other, it would be this:

It's just a game. It's just a ride. And we can change it anytime we want. The truth is not out there. It is within you. And that truth is love.

SOURCE

1 Bill Hicks ended many of his performances with these words.

APPENDIX I

The Illuminati bloodline

These are just some of the stunning bloodline connections between those who ruled the people thousands of years ago and those who still rule them today. The Merovingian-Windsor-Bush bloodline and its offshoots includes a long list of pharaohs in ancient Egypt, including Ramses II (1295-1228 BC), who is considered to be the greatest pharaoh of all. He was his country's master architect (sacred geometry) and his name can be found on almost every ancient shrine. The gold mines of Nubia made him rich beyond the imagination. The bloodline also includes the Anunnaki-human hybrids who ruled Sumer, Babylon, Greece, and Troy, and which, today, rule the world. In turn, they go back to Atlantis and Lemuria. One common link in this bloodline is Philip of Macedonia (382-336BC), who married Olympias. Their son was Alexander the Great (356-323BC), a tyrant and "Son of the Serpent" who plundered that key region of Greece, Persia, Syria, Phoenicia, Egypt, Babylon, the former lands of Sumer, and across into India before dying in Babylon at the age of 33. During his rule of Egypt he founded the city of Alexandria, "City of the Serpent's Son", later one the greatest centres for esoteric knowledge in the ancient world. Alexander was taught by the Greek philosopher, Aristotle, who had been taught by Plato, who had been taught by Socrates. The bloodline and the hidden advanced knowledge have always gone together.

This key bloodline comes down through the most famous Egyptian queen, Cleopatra (60-30BC), who married the most famous Roman Emperor, Julius Caesar, and bore him a son, who became Ptolemy XIV. She also bore twins with Mark Anthony, who has his own connections to this line and its many offshoots; the bloodline also connects to Herod the Great, the "Herod" of the Jesus stories, and continues to the Roman Piso family who, some claim, wrote the Gospel stories and invented the mythical figure called Jesus; the same bloodline includes Constantine the Great, the Roman Emperor who, in AD325, turned Christianity into the religion we know today, and King Ferdinand of Spain and Queen Isabella of Castile, the sponsors of Christopher Columbus, who instigated the horrific Spanish Inquisition (1478-1834) in which people were tortured and burned at the stake for in any way questioning the basis of the religion their various ancestors had created. More than that, the most used version of the Bible was commissioned and sponsored by another strand in the same bloodline, King James Ist of England. The line of James, according to the genealogy sources listed below, can be traced back to 1550BC and beyond, and includes many Egyptian pharaohs, including Ramses II.

The bloodline moved into France and northern Europe through the Franks and Meroveus or Merovee, who gave his name to the Merovingian bloodline, and it continues with the rest of the Merovingian clan like Clovis and the Dagoberts who connect into the elite secret society, the Priory of Sion and the Rennes-le-Chateau "mystery" in the Languedoc region of southern France. From the Merovingians, this bloodline's connections to the present day include: Charlemagne (742-814), who ruled as Emperor of the West in the Holy Roman Empire; a stream of French kings, including Robert II, Philip I, II and III, and Louis I, II, VI, VII, VIII, VIIII, XIII, IX, XV, and XVI. The latter married Marie Antoinette of this same bloodline and both were executed in the French Revolution. But they produced the son who became Daniel Payseur, who, as *The Biggest Secret* explains, was taken to the United States where he became the secret force behind the Morgan and Carnegie empires, and owned vast amounts of real estate, banking, and industrial holdings.

This bloodline also connects to the de Medici family that supported Christopher Columbus and produced Catherine de Medici, the Queen of France who died in 1589. Her doctor was Nostradamus. It includes Rene d'Anjou, Duke of Lorraine, and the House of Lorraine employed Nostradamus and Christopher Columbus. The bloodline relatives of the de Medicis and the House of Lorraine, Queen Isabella of Castile and King Ferdinand of Aragon, were sponsors of Columbus when he "discovered" the Americas. This bloodline also includes the Habsburgs, the most powerful family in Europe under the Holy Roman Empire; Geoffrey Plantagenet and the Plantagenet royal dynasty in England; King John, who signed the Magna Carta; King Henry I, II, and III, who were extremely close to the Knights Templar, as was King John; Mary Stuart and the Stuart Dynasty, including King James Ist of England, sponsor of the King James Version of the Bible; King George I, II, and III; Edward I, II, and III, Queen Victoria; Edward VII; George V and VI; Queen Elizabeth II; Prince Charles and Elizabeth's other offspring, Anne, Andrew and Edward; Princes William and Harry from Charles' "marriage" to Princess Diana; US presidents, George Washington, John Adams, John Quincy Adams, Thomas Jefferson, Franklin Delano Roosevelt, and George Bush are all strands of this bloodline; it was passed on to the new U.S. President, George W. Bush, and his brother, Jeb Bush, the Governor of Florida. It also includes Bush's opponent at the 2000 election, the blood drinker Al Gore. In fact if you go deeply enough into the genealogical research you will find that *all* the presidents are from this line. Genealogical sources, like the New England Historical Genealogical Society and *Burke's Peerage*, have shown that 33 of the 42 presidents to Clinton are related to Charlemagne and 19 are related to England's Edward III, both of whom are of this bloodline. A spokesman for *Burke's Peerage*, the bible of royal and aristocratic genealogy based in London, has said that every presidential election since and including George Washington in 1789 has been won by the candidate with the most royal genes. Now we can see how and why. United States presidents are not chosen by ballot, they are chosen by blood. This same bloodline also includes key Scottish families like the Lords of Galloway and the Comyns; Marie-Louise of Austria, who married Napoleon Bonaparte; Kaiser Wilhelm II, King of Germany at the time of the

First World War; and Maximilian, the Habsburg Emperor of Mexico, who died in 1867. On and on it goes, into country after country. This bloodline connects into every surviving royal family in Europe, including King Juan Carlos of Spain and the Dutch, Swedish, and Danish royal lines.

And this is just *one* of the reptilian bloodlines and just *some* of its offshoots. There are others that connect with these names and span the same period and beyond to thousands of years BC. There are so many genealogical links between these bloodlines that the same connections can be made via other routes, too. The Piso Homepage genealogy is the most up to date in their research so far. Other genealogical sources include the New England Historical Genealogy Society, *Burke's Peerage*, and a genealogist in the United States, who has been studying and charting the bloodlines of the elite families for 26 years. He wishes to remain anonymous for obvious reasons.

Detailed family trees of the above are available on the Internet at Piso Homepage and on *www.davidicke.com*

Hitler was a Rothschild?

Official history is merely a veil to hide the truth of what really happened. When the veil is lifted, again and again we see that not only is the official version not true, it is often 100% wrong.

Take the Rothschilds. This bloodline was formerly known, among other names, as the Bauers, one of the most notorious black occult bloodlines of Middle-Ages Germany. It became known as Rothschild (red-shield or rotes-schild in German) in the 18th century when Mayer Amschel Rothschild founded a financial dynasty in Frankfurt, working in league with the Illuminati House of Hesse and others. They took their name from the red "shield", or hexagram/Star of David on the front of their house in Frankfurt. The Star of David or Seal of Solomon is an ancient esoteric symbol and only became associated with Jewish people after the Rothschilds adopted it for themselves. It has absolutely no connection to "David" or "Solomon", as Jewish historical sources confirm. The Rothschilds are one of the top Illuminati bloodlines on the planet and they are shape-shifting reptilians. Guy de Rothschild of the French House heads this bloodline dynasty today. He is one of the most grotesque exponents of trauma-based mind control, indeed the top man according to many of those who have suffered mercilessly under his torture. Guy de Rothschild has been personally responsible for the torture and death of millions of children and adults, either directly or through those he controls. He conducts Satanic rituals, as all these bloodlines have always done, and goodness knows how many human sacrifices he has been involved in. If what I am saying is wrong, Guy de Rothschild, then take me to court and let's reveal the evidence. You are a multi-billionaire and you control the courts and the media. By comparison, I have next to nothing. I should, therefore, be a pushover. So come on, Mr Rothschild, let's have you. Let's take these claims into the public arena and have you and me in the witness box. Make my day.

Already I can hear the clamour gathering to condemn me as "anti-Semitic" because the Rothschilds claim to be "Jewish". Organisations like the Anti-Defamation League and B'nai B'rith have made strenuous efforts to label me in this way for exposing the Rothschilds and to stop me speaking in public. How funny then that both organisations were created by, and continue to be bankrolled by, the Rothschilds. B'nai B'rith means, appropriately, "Sons of the Alliance" and was established by the Rothschilds in 1843 as an intelligence arm, and to defame and destroy legitimate researchers with the label "anti- Semitic." Many of their speakers openly supported slavery during the American Civil War and today they seek to condemn some black leaders as "anti-Semitic" or "racist". Every year, the Anti-

Defamation League awards its "Torch of Liberty" (the classic Illuminati symbol) to the person it believes has served their cause the most. One year they gave it to Morris Dalitz, an intimate of the notorious Meyer Lansky crime syndicate that terrorised America. Perfect choice.

So who was Hitler?

Of course, the strength of feeling that fans the flames of condemnation against anyone dubbed "anti-Semitic" today is the sickening persecution of Jewish people by the Nazis of Adolf Hitler. To expose or question the actions of the Rothschilds or any other Jewish person or organisation is to be called a "Nazi". How strange then, that as I have documented in... *And The Truth Shall Set You Free* and *The Biggest Secret*, along with endless other researchers and scholars, Adolf Hitler and the Nazis were created and funded by...the Rothschilds. It was they who arranged for Hitler to come to power through the Illuminati secret societies in Germany like the Thule Society and the Vril Society, which they created through their German networks; it was the Rothschilds who funded Hitler through the Bank of England and other British and American sources like their Kuhn, Loeb bank, which also funded the Russian Revolution. The very heart of Hitler's war machine was the chemical giant I.G. Farben. Its American arm was controlled by the Rothschilds through their lackeys the Warburgs. Paul Warburg, who manipulated into existence the privately owned "central bank" of America, the Federal Reserve, in 1913, was on the board of American I.G. Indeed Hitler's I.G. Farben, which ran the slave labour camp at Auschwitz, was, in reality, a division of Standard Oil, officially owned by the Rockefellers, but in truth the Rockefeller empire was funded into existence by...the Rothschilds, among others. See ...*And The Truth Shall Set You Free* and *The Biggest Secret* for the detailed background of this and other aspects of this story. The Rothschilds also owned the German news agencies during both world wars and thus controlled the flow of "information" to Germans and the outside world. Incidentally, when Allied troops entered Germany they found that the I.G. Farben factories, the very core of Hitler's war operation, had not been hit by the mass bombing and neither had Ford factories – another supporter of Hitler. Other factories nearby had been demolished by bombing raids.

So the force behind Adolf Hitler, on behalf of the Illuminati, was the House of Rothschild, this "Jewish" bloodline that claims to support and protect the Jewish faith and people. In fact they use and sickeningly *abuse* the Jewish people for their own horrific ends. The Rothschilds, like the Illuminati in general, treat the mass of the Jewish people with utter contempt. They are, like the rest of the global population, just cattle to be used to advance the agenda of global control and mastery by a network of interbreeding bloodlines, impregnated with a reptilian genetic code, and known to researchers as the Illuminati. Indeed, the Illuminati are so utterly obsessed with bloodline, because of this reptilian genetic code, that there was no way that someone like Hitler would come to power in those vital circumstances for the Illuminati, unless he was of the reptilian bloodline. But hold on. Hitler couldn't be the same bloodline as, say, the Rothschilds because, as we all know, the Rothschilds are defenders of Jewish people and Hitler slaughtered them, along with communists and gypsies and others who opposed him or whom he wished to eliminate. The Rothschilds are Jewish, they'd never do that.

Oh really.

Not only was Hitler supported by the Rothschilds, a book by a psychoanalyst, Walter Langer, called The Mind of Hitler, suggests that he could have *been* a Rothschild. This revelation fits like a glove with the actions of the Rothschilds and other Illuminati bloodlines in Germany who brought Hitler to the fore as dictator of that nation. He was also supported by the British royal family, the House of Windsor (in fact the German House of Saxe-Coburg-Gotha), and these included the British royal "war hero" Lord Mountbatten, a Rothschild and a Satanist. The fundamental connections between the British "royals" and the nazis have yet to come out – but they will. Indeed, as this book headed for the printers I spoke with a researcher who connects Hitler fundamentally to the British Royal family. Their royal relatives in Germany, who you would never have thought would normally support an apparent guy from the street like Hitler, were among his most enthusiastic supporters. But, of course, they knew who he *really* was. Langer writes:

"Adolf's father, Alois Hitler, was the illegitimate son of Maria Anna Schicklgruber. It was generally supposed that the father of Alois Hitler (Schicklgruber) was Johann Georg Hiedler. There are some people who seriously doubt that Johann Georg Hiedler was the father of Alois...[an Austrian document was] prepared that proved Maria Anna Schicklgruber was living in Vienna at the time she conceived. At that time she was employed as a servant in the home of Baron Rothschild. As soon as the family discovered her pregnancy she was sent back home...where Alois was born."

Langer's information came from the high-level Gestapo officer, Hansjurgen Koehler, and was published in 1940 under the title "Inside the Gestapo". Koehler writes about the investigations into Hitler's background carried out by the Austrian Chancellor, Dolfuss, in the family files of Hitler. Koehler actually viewed a copy of the Dolfuss documents, he says, which were given to him by Heydrich, the overlord of the Nazi Secret Service. The file, he wrote, "caused such havoc as no file in the world ever caused before" (*Inside The Gestapo*, p 143). He also revealed that:

"...The second bundle in the blue file contained the documents collected by Dolfuss. The small statured, but big-hearted Austrian Chancellor must have known by such a personal file he might be able to check Hitler. ...His task was not difficult; as ruler of Austria he could easily find out about the personal data and family of Adolf Hitler, who had been born on Austrian soil ...Through the original birth certificates, police registration cards, protocols, etc., all contained in the original file, the Austrian Chancellor succeeded in piecing together the disjointed parts of the puzzle, creating a more or less logical entity...

"A little servant girl… [Hitler's grandmother]…came to Vienna and became a domestic servant, mostly working for rather rich families. But she was unlucky; having been seduced, she was about to bear a child. She went home to her village for her confinement. …Where was the little maid serving in Vienna? This was not a very difficult problem. Very early Vienna had instituted the system of compulsory police registration. Both servants and the employers were exposed to heavy fines if they neglected this duty. Chancellor Dolfuss managed to discover the registration card. The little, innocent maid had been a servant at the…Rothschild mansion …and Hitler's unknown grandfather must be probably looked for in this magnificent house. The Dolfuss file stopped at this statement."

Was Hitler's determination to take over Austria anything to do with his desire to destroy records of his lineage? A correspondent to my website who has extensively researched this subject writes:

"It appears to me that Hitler knew about his connection long before his Chancellorship. Like his father before him, when the going got rough, the Hitlers went to Vienna. Hitler's father left his home village at an early age to seek his fortune in Vienna. When Hitler was orphaned, after his mother died in December of 1907, he left for Vienna not long after the funeral. There he seemed to drop out of sight for ten months! What happened during this ten-month stay in Vienna is a complete mystery on which history sheds no light. It makes sense, now that it has become established that Hitler was a Rothschild, that he and his cousins were getting acquainted, and his potential for future family endeavours was being sized up."

The Rothschilds and the Illuminati produce many offspring out of wedlock in their secret breeding programmes and these children are brought up under other names with other parents. Phillip Eugene de Rothschild, who claims to be one of these offspring, says that the Rothschild family has produced hundreds of thousands of unofficial children to be placed in positions of power under different names. I know that sounds a fantastic figure, but much of this is done through Illuminati sperm banks and artificial impregnation. Like Bill Clinton, who is almost certainly a Rockefeller, these "ordinary kids from ordinary backgrounds" go on to be extraordinarily successful in their chosen field. Hitler, too, would have produced unofficial children to maintain his strand of the bloodline and there will obviously be people of his bloodline alive today. So which Rothschild was the grandfather of Hitler? Alois, Hitler's father, was born in 1837 in the period when Salomon Mayer was the only Rothschild who lived at the Vienna mansion. Even his wife did not live there because their marriage was so bad she stayed in Frankfurt. Their son, Anselm Salomon, spent most of his working life in Paris and Frankfurt away from Vienna and his father. So Salomon Mayer Rothschild, living alone at the Vienna mansion where Hitler's grandmother worked, is the prime, most obvious candidate. And Hermann von Goldschmidt, the son of Salomon Mayer's senior clerk, wrote a book, published in 1917, which said of Salomon: "…by the 1840s he had developed a somewhat reckless enthusiasm for young girls"…and…"He had a lecherous passion for very young girls, his adventures with whom had to be hushed up by the police."

Hitler's grandmother was a young girl working under the same roof and would obviously have been a target of Salomon's desire. And this same girl became pregnant while working there. Her grandson became the Chancellor of Germany, funded by the Rothschilds, and he started the Second World War that was so vital to the Rothschild-Illuminati agenda. The Illuminati are obsessed with putting their bloodlines into power on all "sides" in a conflict, and the Rothschilds are one of their most important bloodlines. And it is all a coincidence? This accumulation of evidence points to a clear theme: *Hitler was a Rothschild!*

The state of Rothschild

The Second World War was incredibly productive for the Illuminati agenda of global control. It led to an explosion of globally centralised institutions, like the United Nations and the European Community, now Union, and many others in finance, business, and the military. Precisely what they wanted. It also put countries under an enormous burden of debt on loans provided to all sides by…the Rothschilds and the Illuminati. The Rothschilds had long had a plan to create a personal fiefdom for themselves and the Illuminati in Palestine, and that plan involved manipulating Jewish people to settle the area as their "homeland". Charles Taze Russell, of the Illuminati-reptilian Russell bloodline, was the man who founded the Watchtower Society, better known as the Jehovah's Witnesses. He was a Satanist, a paedophile according to his wife, and most certainly Illuminati. His new "religion" (mind control cult) was funded by the Rothschilds and he was a friend of theirs, just like the founders of the Mormons who were also Rothschild-funded through Kuhn, Loeb and Company. Russell and the Mormon founders were all Freemasons and Merovingian bloodline. In 1880, Charles Taze Russell, this friend of the Rothschilds, predicted that the Jews would return to their homeland. It was about the only prediction Russell ever got right. Why? Because he knew that was the plan. He wrote to the Rothschilds praising their efforts to establish a Jewish homeland in Palestine.

Then, in 1917, came the famous Balfour Declaration, when the British Foreign Minister Lord Balfour stated on behalf of his government that they supported the creation of a Jewish homeland in Palestine. Now when you hear that phrase, the Balfour Declaration, you get the feeling that it was some kind of statement or public announcement. But not so. The Balfour Declaration was a letter from Lord Balfour to…Lord Lionel Walter Rothschild. Researchers say that the letter was in fact written by Lord Rothschild and his employee, the banker Alfred Milner. Now get this. One of the most important secret societies of the 20th century is called the Round Table. It is based in Britain with branches across the world. It is the Round Table that ultimately orchestrates the network of the Bilderberg Group, Council on Foreign Relations, Trilateral Commission and the Royal Institute of International Affairs. How fascinating then, that Lord Balfour was an inner- circle member of the Round Table, Alfred Milner was the Round Table's official leader after the death of

Cecil Rhodes, and the Round Table was funded by...Lord Lionel Walter Rothschild. These were the very three people involved in the Balfour Declaration of 1917. Two years later, in 1919, came the Versailles Peace Conference near Paris when the elite of the Round Table from Britain and the United States, people like Alfred Milner, Edward Mandel House, and Bernard Baruch, were appointed to represent their countries at the meetings that decided how the world would be changed as a result of the war these same people had created. They decided to impose impossible reparations payments on Germany, so ensuring the collapse of the post-war Weimar Republic amid unbelievable economic collapse. This created the very circumstances that brought the "Rothschild", Hitler, to power. It was while in Paris that these members of the Illuminati Round Table met at the Hotel Majestic to begin the process of creating the Bilderberg-CFR-RIIA-TC network. They also decided at Versailles that they now all supported the creation of a Jewish homeland in Palestine. As I show in my books, *every one* of these people was either a Rothschild bloodline or was controlled by that family. The American President Woodrow Wilson, was "advised" at Versailles by Colonel House and Bernard Baruch, both Rothschild clones and leaders of the Round Table in the United States; the British Prime Minister, Lloyd George, was "advised" by Alfred Milner, the Rothschild employee and Round Table leader, and Sir Phillip Sassoon, a direct descendant of Mayer Amschel Rothschild, the founder of the dynasty; the French leader, Georges Clemenceau, was "advised" by his Minister for the Interior, Georges Mandel, whose real name was Jeroboam Rothschild. Who do you think was making the decisions here? But it went further. Also in the American delegation were the Dulles brothers, John Foster Dulles, who would become US Secretary of State, and Allen Dulles, who would become first head of the new CIA after the Second World War. The Dulles brothers were bloodline and would later be supporters of Hitler. They were employed by the Rothschilds at Kuhn, Loeb and Company, and were also involved in the assassination of John F. Kennedy. Allen Dulles served on the Warren Commission that "investigated" the assassination. The American delegation at Versailles was represented by the Rothschild-controlled Paul Warburg of Kuhn, Loeb and the American branch of I.G. Farben, while the German delegation included his brother, Max Warburg, who would become Hitler's banker! Their host in France during the "peace" conference was...Baron Edmond de Rothschild, the leading force at the time pressing for the creation of a Jewish homeland in Israel. See ...*And The Truth Shall Set You Free* for the fine detail.

The Rothschilds have always been the true force behind the Zionist Movement. Zionism is in fact Sionism. Sion = the Sun, hence the name of the elite secret society behind the Merovingian bloodline, the Priory of Sion. Contrary to most people's understanding, Zionism is not the Jewish people. Many Jews are not Zionists and many non-Jews are. Zionism is a political movement, not a race. To say Zionism is the Jewish people is like saying the Democratic Party is the American people. Jewish people who oppose Zionism, however, have been given a very hard time. Now, having manipulated their puppet-governments to support their plan for a personal fiefdom in the Middle East, the Rothschilds began the process of settling

Jewish people in Palestine. As always they treated their own with contempt. Enter once again Baron Edmond de Rothschild, the "Father of Israel", who died in 1934, the man who hosted the Versailles "peace" delegations. Edmond was from the French House, like Guy de Rothschild and Baron Philippe de Rothschild. Edmond, in fact, began to settle Jews in Palestine as far back as the 1880s (when Charles Taze Russell was making his prediction). He financed Russian Jews to establish settlements in Palestine, but it was nothing to do with their freedom or birthright, it was to advance the Rothschild-Illuminati agenda. Edmond financed the creation of farms and factories, and ran the whole operation with a rod of iron. The Jewish farmers were told what to grow and they soon found out who was in charge if they questioned his orders. In 1901, these Jewish people complained to Rothschild about this dictatorship over their settlement or "Yishuv". They asked him:

"...if you wish to save the Yishuv, first take your hands from it, and...for once permit the colonists to have the possibility of correcting for themselves whatever needs correcting..."

Baron Rothschild replied:

"I created the Yishuv, I alone. Therefore no men, neither colonists nor organisations, have the right to interfere in my plans..."

In one sentence, you have the true attitude of the Rothschilds to Jewish people, and indeed, the human population in general. The Rothschilds are not Jews, they are a bloodline with a reptilian genetic code, who hide behind the Jewish people and use them as a screen and a means to an end. According to Simon Schama's book, *Two Rothschilds And The Land Of Israel* (Collins, London, 1978), the Rothschilds acquired 80% of the land of Israel. Edmond de Rothschild worked closely with Theodore Herzl, who just happened to be the founder of Zionism, the political movement created to ensure a "Jewish" homeland in Palestine. Rothschild was also the power behind Chaim Weizmann, another leader of Zionism. As Rothschild told Weizmann:

"Without me Zionism would not have succeeded, but without Zionism my work would have been stuck to death."

So now with the Rothschilds increasing their financing of Jewish settlements in Palestine, and with their agents in governments officially supporting their plans for a Rothschild, sorry, Jewish homeland, they needed a catalyst that would demolish Arab protests at the take-over of their country. That catalyst was the horrific treatment of Jews in Germany and the countries they conquered by the Rothschild-funded Nazis and one of their own, a Rothschild called Adolf Hitler. The wave of revulsion at the Nazi concentration camps gave vital and, in the end, crucial impetus to the Rothschild agenda. It was they who funded the Jewish terrorist operations like the Stern Gang and Irgun, which committed mayhem and murder to bring the State of Rothschild (Israel) into being in 1948. These terrorist groups, who slaughtered Jewish people with equal enthusiasm, were led by the very people who later rose to lead the new Israel...people like Menachem Begin, David Ben-Gurion, Yitzhak Rabin, and Yitzhak Shamir. It was these Rothschild-controlled Zionist gangs that murdered the international mediator Count Bernadotte on September 17, 1948, apparently because he had been intending to present a new partition resolution to the United Nations. And the Rothschilds were not satisfied with causing the unimaginable suffering of Jewish people under the Nazis, they also stole their wealth when the war was over, just as they stole the Russian wealth during the revolution they had financed.

In early 1998, during a speaking tour of South Africa, I met Winnie Mandela when she came to my talk in Johannesburg and later I had a personal meeting with P.W. Botha, the apartheid President of South Africa during the 1980s. The invitation came out of the blue when I was speaking a few miles from his retirement home. We spoke for an hour and a half about the manipulation of South Africa and it was not long before names like Henry Kissinger, Lord Carrington, and the Rothschilds came up. "I had some strange dealings with the English Rothschilds in Cape Town when I was president," he said, and he went on to tell me a story that sums up the Rothschilds so perfectly. He said they had asked for a meeting with him and his foreign minister, the Illuminati operative Pik Botha. At that meeting, he said, the Rothschilds told him there was massive wealth in Swiss bank accounts that once belonged to German Jews and it was available for investment in South Africa if they could agree an interest rate. This is the very wealth, stolen from German Jews who suffered under the Nazis, which has come to light amid great scandal in recent years. The Rothschilds have been making a fortune from it since the war! Botha told me that he refused to accept the money, but Pik Botha left the meeting with the Rothschilds and he could not be sure that they did not come to some arrangement.

Breathtaking. But the world is not what we think it is. To this day the Rothschilds continue to control the State of Israel, which has their family symbol on its flag. It is they who use that country and its people, Jew and Arab, to maintain the conflict. This involves civil war within its borders and with surrounding Arab countries that has allowed the Illuminati-Rothschilds to control their so-called "Arc of Crisis" in the Middle East through divide, rule, and conquer. It has allowed them, not least, to control the oil-producing countries since the war when the oil really came on line.

Please Jewish people of Israel and the world, look at this. You are being played off against non-Jewish peoples and vice versa. You and all of us who care about our children and the freedom of the world must unite and focus on the force that is manipulating all races. Fear of each other, and divide and rule have always been the basic tools of dictators. And I say this to Arab people: never, never, never, do the Rothschilds and the Illuminati control only one side in a conflict. If they did they could not be sure of the outcome and that's not the way they play the game. So we know who controls the Jewish leadership in Israel – the Rothschilds. Who, therefore, controls Yasser Arafat? The same people, I would suggest, who controlled Menachim Begin of Israel and President Anwar Sadat of Egypt during the "peace agreement" brokered by the Rockefeller-controlled Jimmy Carter administration.

What is done is done and the people of Israel-Palestine need to work together in harmony and mutual respect. There is no other way, except for more deaths, suffering, and conflict – exactly what the Rothschilds and the Illuminati desire. They have horrendous plans for Israel in which all sides will suffer, not least their plans for a major event at the Temple Mount mosque. Come on peoples of Israel and the world. No matter what your race, colour, or religious belief. The freedom of all of us is at stake here and why we divide along manufactured and irrelevant racial and religious fault-lines that freedom is doomed.

APPENDIX III

The Jewish voice of reason

The truth about the grotesque exploitation of the true victims of the Nazi concentration camps is magnificently exposed by a brave and defiant Jewish man, whose parents genuinely suffered in the camps.

Norman Finkelstein, in his explosive book *The Holocaust Industry* (Verso Books, July 2000, and available through my website), reveals how: the Holocaust has been exploited to extort cash; that most "survivors" are bogus; and that too much money is spent commemorating the Nazi genocide. He has said what many non-Jewish researchers have been trying to say for so long. But they have immediately been dubbed "anti-Semitic" and face campaigns to have their public meetings cancelled or their books banned. I have not been denying, never have, that there was widespread and unimaginable suffering by Jewish people (and gypsies and communists) in Nazi Germany. My point has been that the Jewish hierarchy, which claims to be the voice of every Jewish person on the planet, has sickeningly exploited that suffering to serve the agenda of their Illuminati controllers, like the Rothschilds and the Canadian gangster family, the Bronfmans. To expose the exploitation of the mass of Jewish people by the few is, according to the agents of that hierarchy and the non-Jewish juveniles who serve them, to be "anti-Semitic".

Well Norman Finkelstein cannot be accused of that because he is Jewish and his parents suffered under the Nazis. But, naturally, he has been dubbed a "self-hater", a label applied to any Jew who seeks to expose the scam. Here are some quotes from Norman Finkelstein's *The Holocaust Industry*. Finkelstein is a star.

> "'If everyone who claims to be a survivor is one', my mother used to exclaim, 'who did Hitler kill?'"

On the Simon Wiesenthal Centre:

> "The centre is renowned for its 'Dachau-meets-Disneyland' museum exhibits and the successful use of sensationalist scare tactics for fund-raising."

> "I sometimes think that American Jewry 'discovering' the Nazi Holocaust was worse than its having been forgotten."

> "I do care about the memory of my family's persecution. The current policies of the Holocaust industry to extort money from Europe in the name of 'needy

Holocaust victims' has shrunk the moral stature of their martyrdom to that of a Monte Carlo Casino."

"The Holocaust only emerged in American life after Israel's victory in the 1967 six day war against its Arab neighbours. [Since then]…too many public and private resources have been invested in memorialising the Nazi genocide. Most of the output is worthless, a tribute not to Jewish suffering, but to Jewish aggrandisement."

"The Holocaust has proved to be an indispensable ideological weapon. Through its deployment, one of the world's most formidable military powers, with an horrendous human rights record, has cast itself as a 'victim' state, and the most successful ethnic group in the U.S. has likewise acquired victim status. Considerable dividends accrue from this specious victim hood – in particular, immunity to criticism, however justified."

(See Canadian Jewish Congress (Bronfman family), B'nai B'rith (Rothschilds) , Anti-Defamation League (Rothschilds), World Jewish Congress (Bronfmans), British Board of Jewish Deputies, ad infinitum, underpinned by mindless, unquestioning sycophants like the Canadian and British Green parties, the Anti-Nazi League, Searchlight, also ad infinitum.)

"As the rendering of the Holocaust assumed ever more absurd forms, my mother used to quote (with intentional irony) Henry Ford: 'All history is bunk'. The tales of 'Holocaust survivors' – all concentration camp inmates, all heroes of the resistance – were a special source of wry amusement in my home."

"[The Holocaust]…has been used to justify criminal policies of the Israeli State and US support for those policies."

"The time is long past to open our hearts to the rest of humanity's sufferings. This was the main lesson my mother imparted. I never once heard her say: 'Do not compare.' My mother always compared. In the face of the sufferings of African-Americans, Vietnamese and Palestinians, my mother's credo always was: 'We are all Holocaust victims.'"

"The Israeli prime minister's office recently put the 'number of living Holocaust survivors' at nearly half a million. The main motive behind this inflationary figure is not hard to find. It is difficult to press massive new claims for reparations if only a handful of Holocaust survivors are still alive."

Talking of the way the $60 billion paid in compensation by Germany to Holocaust victims has been stolen by the Holocaust Industry hierarchy and make-believe victims, Norman Finkelstein says:

"When Germans or the Swiss refuse to pay compensation, the heavens cannot contain the righteous indignation of organised American Jewry. But when Jewish elites rob Jewish survivors, no ethical issues arise: it's just about money."

"Others involved in the reparations process have also done well. The reported annual salary of Saul Kagan, long-time executive-secretary of the claims conference, is $105,000. Kagan rings up in 12 days what my mother received for suffering six years of Nazi persecution."

"In recent years, the Holocaust industry has become an outright extortion racket. Purporting to represent all of world Jewry, living and dead, it is laying claim to Holocaust-era Jewish assets throughout Europe."

"Meanwhile, the Holocaust industry forced Switzerland into a settlement because time was allegedly of the essence: 'Needy Holocaust survivors are dying every day.' Once the Swiss signed away the money, however, the urgency miraculously passed. More than a year after the settlement was reached, there was still no distribution plan. By the time the money is finally divvied out, all the 'needy Holocaust survivors' will probably be dead. ...After lawyers' fees have been paid (total attorney demands for the case run to $15 million) the Swiss monies will flow into the coffers of 'worthy' Jewish organisations."

On Elie Wiesel, Nobel laureate and Holocaust survivor:

"Elie Wiesel's performance as official interpreter of the Holocaust is not happenstance. Plainly he did not come to this position on account of his humanitarian commitments or literary talents. Rather, Wiesel plays this leading role because he unerringly articulates the dogmas of, and accordingly sustains the interests underpinning, the Holocaust."

On Deborah Lipstacht, the Holocaust scholar who won a libel case brought by historian, David Irving:

"To document widespread Holocaust denial, Lipstacht cites a handful of crank publications. Her piece de resistance comes from Arthur Butz, a non entity who teaches electrical engineering."

On David Irving:

"Irving, notorious as an admirer of Hitler and sympathetic to German National Socialism, has nevertheless made an indispensable contribution to our knowledge of World War II."

"The Holocaust industry has always been bankrupt. What remains is to openly declare it so. The time is long past to put it out of business. The noblest gesture for those who perished is to preserve their memoirs, learn from their suffering, and let them, finally, rest in peace."

Bibliography

Acharya S: *The Christ Conspiracy, The Greatest Story Ever Sold* (Adventures Unlimited, Kempton, Illinois, 1999).

Allen D.S. and Delair J.B.: *The Day The Earth Nearly Died* (Gateway Books, Bath, 1995).

Baigent, Michael, Leigh, Richard, and Lincoln, Henry: *Holy Blood, Holy Grail* (Corgi Books, London, 1983).

Baker, Dr. Douglas: *The Opening Of The Third Eye* (Aquarian Press, Wellingborough, England, 1977).

Boulay, R.A.: *Flying Serpents And Dragons, The Story Of Mankind's Reptilian Past*, new revised edition (The Book Tree, P.O. Box, 724, Escondido, California, 92033, 1997).

Boyd, Andrew: *Blasphemous Rumours* (Fount Paperbacks, an imprint of HarperCollins, London, 1991).

Bramley, William: *The Gods Of Eden* (Avon Books, New York, 1993).

Bullock, Alan: *Hitler, A Study In Tyranny* (Pelican Books, London, 1960).

Christopher, Alex: *Pandora's Box*, Volumes 1 and 2 (Pandora's Box, 2663, Valleydale Road, Suite 126, Birmingham, Alabama, 35224).

Churchward, Albert: *The Origin And Evolution Of Religion* (Kessinger Publishing Company, 1997).

Churchward, Colonel James: *The Lost Continent Of Mu; The Children Of Mu; The Sacred Symbols Of Mu; The Cosmic Forces Of Mu, books one and two* (All available through the David Icke website).

Conforto, Giuliana: *LUH, Man's Cosmic Game* (Edizioni Noesis, 1998).

Crowley, Aleister: *Magick In Theory And Practice* (Dover, USA, 1929).

Deane, Reverend John Bathhurst: The Worship of the Serpent (J.G. and F. Rivington, London, 1833).

DeCamp, John W.: *The Franklin Cover Up: Child Abuse, Satanism, And Murder In Nebraska* (AWR Inc., Lincoln, Nebraska, 1992).

DeMeo, Professor James: *Saharasia: The 4000 BCE Origins Of Child Abuse, Sex-Repression, Warfare And Social Violence, In The Deserts Of The Old World* (Natural Energy Works, USA, 1998).

Dickhoff, Robert E: *Agharta* (Health Research, PO Box 850, Pomeroy, WA, USA 99347Health Research, U.S.A., 1996).

Doane, T.W.: *Bible Myths And Their Parallels In Other Religions* (Health Research, first published 1882).

Dujardin, Edouard: *Ancient History Of The God, Jesus* (Watts and Co., 1938).

Emery, Professor W.B.: *Archaic Egypt* (Penguin Books, UK, 1961).

Findlay, Arthur: *The Curse Of Ignorance, A History Of Mankind* (Headquarters Publishing Company, London, first published, 1947).

Finkelstein, Norman: *The Holocaust Industry* (Verso Books, July 2000).

Fix, Wm R.: *Pyramid Odyssey* (Jonathan James Books, Toronto, Canada, 1978).

Flem-Ath, Rand, and Colin Wilson: *Atlantis Blueprint: Unlocking The Mystery Of A Long-Lost Civilisation* (Little Brown, London, 2000).

Foot, Paul: *Who Framed Colin Wallace?* (Macmillan, London, 1989).

Fox, Dr. Loreda: *The Spiritual And Clinical Dimensions Of Multiple Personality Disorder* (Books of Sangre de Cristo, Salida, Colorado, 1992).

Frawley, David: *Gods, Sages And Kings: Vedic Secrets Of Ancient Civilization* (Passage Press, Salt Lake City, Utah, 1991).

Gardner, Sir Laurence: *Bloodline Of The Holy Grail* (Element Books, Shaftesbury, Dorset, 1996).

Gordon, Professor Cyrus: *The Common Background Of Greek And Hebrew Civilisation* (W.W. Norton and Company, New York, 1965).

Graves, Robert: *The White Goddess* (Octagon Books, New York, 1972).

Hall, Manly P.: *America's Assignment With Destiny, The Adepts In The Western Tradition* (Philosophical Research Society, Los Angeles, 1979), part five.

Hall, Manly P.: *The Secret Teachings Of All Ages* (The Philosophical Research Society, Los Angeles, California, the Golden Jubilee Edition, 1988).

Hansen, Lucille Taylor: *The Ancient Atlantic* (Amherst Press, Amherst, Wisconsin, 1969).

Harrison, Jane, Themis: *A Study Of The Social Origins Of Greek Religion* (Peter Smith Publishing, Glouster, Massachusetts, 1974).

Hoagland, Richard: *Monuments On Mars* (North Atlantic Books, California, USA, 1996).

Horn, Dr Arthur David: *Humanity's Extraterrestrial Origins* (A. and L. Horn, PO Box 1632, Mount Shasta, California 96067, 1994).

Jacobs, David M.: *The Threat: The Secret Agenda* (Simon and Schuster, New York, 1988).

Jackson, John: *Christianity Before Christ* (American Atheists, 1985).

Keel, John A.: *The Mothmen Prophecies* (Signet Books, New York, 1976).

Keel, John A.: *Our Haunted Planet* (Fawcett Publications, USA, 1971).

King, Francis: *Satan And Swastika* (Mayflower Books, London, 1976).

Koestler, Arthur: *The Thirteenth Tribe – The Khazar Empire And Its Heritage* (Hutchinson, London, 1976).

Lanctot, Guylaine: *The Medical Mafia* (Here's The Key, Inc, Canada, 1995).

Leedom, Tim C. (editor): *The Book Your Church Doesn't Want You To Read* (Kendall/Hunt Publishing, Iowa, USA, 1993. Available from the Truthseeker Company, PO Box 2872, San Diego, California 92112).

Maggiore, Christine: *What If Everything You Thought You Knew About AIDS Was Wrong* (Health Education AIDS Liaison, Los Angeles Chapter, 1996).

Mott, Wm. Michael: *Caverns, Cauldrons, And Concealed Creatures* (Hidden Mysteries, Texas, 2000). Available direct through the David Icke website.

O'Brien, Cathy, and Phillips, Mark: *Trance-Formation Of America* (Reality Marketing Inc., Las Vegas, Nevada, USA, 1995).

Oldham, C.F.: *The Sun And The Serpent: A Contribution To The History Of Serpent Worship* (London, 1905). Based on papers read before the Royal Asiatic Society in 1901.

Pinkham, Mark Amaru: *The Return Of The Serpents Of Wisdom* (Adventures Unlimited, Illinois, USA, 1997).

Rollins: *Ancient History*, edited by Edward Farr (Hurst & Co., New York, Vol.2, circa 1907).

Roney-Dougal, Serena: *Where Science And Magic Meet* (Element Books, Shaftesbury, 1991).

Rauschning, Herman: *Hitler Speaks* (London, 1939).

Sagan, Carl: *The Dragons Of Eden* (Ballantine Books, New York, 1977).

Schnoebelen, William J.: Mormonism's Temple of Doom (Triple J Pub., Idaho Falls, Idaho Falls: 1987).

Shaw, Jim: *The Deadly Deception* (Huntington House Inc, Lafayette, Louisiana, 1988).

Sinclair, Ian, Health: *The Only Immunity* (published by Ian Sinclair and available from 5 Ivy Street, Ryde, New South Wales, Australia, 2112).

Springmeier, Fritz, and Wheeler, Cisco: *The Illuminati Formula To Create An Undetectable Total Mind Controlled Slave* (Springmeier, SE Clackamas Road, Clackamas, Oregon, 97015, 1996).

Springmeier, Fritz: *The Illuminati Bloodlines* (Ambassador House, Westminster, Colorado, 1999).

Temple, Robert: *The Sirius Mystery* (Destiny Books, Vermont, USA, 1998).

Trench, Brinsley Le Pour: *The Sky People* (Award Books, New York, 1970).

Velikovsky, Immanuel: *Ages in Chaos* (Doubleday & Co., New York, 1952).

Velikovsky, Immanuel: *Earth in Upheaval* (Dell Publishing Co., New York, 1955).

Velikovsky, Immanuel: *Worlds in Collision* (Pocket Books Simon & Schuster, New York, 1950).

Waddell, L.A.: *Egyptian Civilisation, Its Sumerian Origin And Real Chronology* (available from Hidden Mysteries through the David Icke website).

Waddell, L.A.: *The Phoenician Origin Of Britons, Scots, And Anglo Saxons* (Christian Book Club, California, 1924).

Waddell, L.A.: *The British Edda* (Christian Book Club, California, 1929).

Waddell, L.A.: *Makers Of Civilisation* (Luzac and Company, 1929).

Walker, Barbara: *The Woman's Dictionary Of Symbols And Sacred Objects* (Harper-Collins, 1988).

Walker, Barbara G.: *The Woman's Encyclopaedia Of Myths And Secrets* (Harper Collins, San Francisco, 1983).

Walden, James L.: *The Ultimate Alien Agenda* (Llewellyn Publications, St Paul, Minnesota, 1998).

Wheless, Joseph: *Forgery In Christianity* (Health Research, 1990).

Most of these books are available through bookends at:
www.davidicke.com

The special section for books in this bibliography is:
http://www.bridgeoflove.com/bookstore/matrix/

Index

Other work by
David Icke

THE BIGGEST SECRET $25.00   £15.00

More than 500 pages of documented, sourced, detail that exposes the forces that really run the world and manipulate our lives. He reveals how the same interconnecting bloodlines have been in control for thousands of years. Includes the background to the ritual murder of Diana, Princess of Wales, and the devastating background to the origins of Christianity. A highly acclaimed book that broke new ground in conspiracy research.

FROM PRISON TO PARADISE – video $59.95   £32.00

A six hour, profusely illustrated presentation on three videocassettes recorded in front of 1,200 people at the Vogue Theatre, Vancouver, Canada. It will make you laugh, it may even make you cry, but for sure it will blow your mind as endless threads and strands throughout history and the modern world are connected together to reveal the hidden hand, the hidden web, that has controlled the planet for thousands of years.

...AND THE TRUTH SHALL SET YOU FREE $21.95   £12.95

Icke exposes in more than 500 pages the interconnecting web that controls the world today. This book focuses on the last 200 years and particularly on what is happening around us today. Another highly acclaimed book, which has been constantly updated. A classic in its field.

I AM ME • I AM FREE $19.95   £10.50

Icke's book of solutions. With humour and powerful insight, he shines a light on the mental and emotional prisons we build for ourselves...prisons that disconnect us from our true and infinite potential to control our own destiny. A getaway car for the human psyche. A censored sticker is available for the faint-hearted!

LIFTING THE VEIL $10.00   £6.95

Compiled from interviews with an American journalist. An excellent summary of Icke's work and perfect for those new to these subjects. This title is available from Bridge of Love UK and the Truthseeker Company, San Diego, USA.

IT DOESN'T HAVE TO BE LIKE THIS   £4.99

One of the early David Icke books in which he highlights the way we, through the economic and political system, are destroying the planet's ability to be a haven of life. Available from Bridge of Love UK.

TURNING OF THE TIDE – video $19.95   £12.00

A two-hour presentation, funny and informative, and the best way to introduce your family and friends to Icke's unique style and information.

SPEAKING OUT – video $24.95   £15.00

A two-hour interview with David Icke.

THE FREEDOM ROAD – video $50.00

Another triple video by David Icke in which he presents the story of global manipulation. What has happened? What is happening? What will happen? All are revealed in this eye-opening, heart-opening, mind-opening video package. Not available in UK.

David Icke's earlier books are published by Gateway. See back page for contact addresses where all these books and tapes are available.

The Reptilian Agenda

Stunning confirmation of *The Biggest Secret* from Credo Mutwa

David Icke has produced
video packages totalling more than six hours,
with the Zulu Sanusi (shaman) Credo Mutwa, who David describes
as a genius and the most knowledgable man he has ever met.

The Reptilian Agenda, part one • (3 hours 30 minutes)

Credo Mutwa reveals a stream of astonishing and unique knowledge that, up to now, has only been available at the highest level of initiation in the African shamanistic stream. But, Credo says, the world must know the truth. He tells of how a reptilian extraterrestrial race has controlled the planet for thousands of years. Fantastic confirmation of *The Biggest Secret* and *Children Of The Matrix*.

The Reptilian Agenda, part two • (2 hours 45 minutes)

Credo takes the story on from ancient times and explains how the reptilians have taken over the world and what we can do about it.

Both are available from Bridge of Love USA, UK, Australia and Africa.
See back page for contact addresses.

The Arizona Wilder interview

Revelations
of a
Mother Goddess

Arizona Wilder conducted human sacrifice rituals for some of the most famous people on Earth, including the British Royal Family. In this three-hour video with David Icke, she talks at length about her experiences in an interview that is utterly devastating for the Elite that control the world.

This astonishing video is available for **$24.95** in the United States or **£15** (plus **£1.50** p&p) in the UK.

See back page for contact addresses.

Other books available from Bridge of Love...

The Medical Mafia

The superb expose of the medical system by Canadian doctor, Guylaine Lanctot, who also shows how and why 'alternative' methods are far more effective. Highly recommended.

Trance Formation Of America

The staggering story of Cathy O'Brien, the mind controlled slave of the US Government for some 25 years. Read this one sitting down. A stream of the world's most famous political names are revealed as they really are.
Written by Cathy O'Brien and Mark Phillips.

What If Everything You Knew About AIDS Was Wrong?

HIV does NOT cause Aids, as Christine Maggiore's outstanding book confirms. Concisely written and devastating to the Aids scam and the Aids industry.

E.T. 101 by Mission Control & Zoev Jho

Extremely funny and yet very profound. It is a "guide book" for those currently on Earth who have come to make the changes necessary to remove this planet from servitude. It cuts the bullshit and offers some excellent advice.

The Last Waltz

Jacqueline Maria Longstaff encompasses the work of David Icke into her own spiritual vision. Funny and very thought provoking. She describes the book as "the enlightened consciousness embracing the collective shadow".

For details of prices and a catalogue of all Bridge of Love books, tapes and videos, please send a self addressed, stamped envelope to one of the contact addresses on the back page.

Bookends

The online bookstore for conspiracy and spiritual information. We already have a substantial book list and it is growing every week.

David Icke's books and tapes and most of those listed in the bibliography, are available via Bookends at *www.davidicke.com*

Bookends also includes the Hidden Mysteries bookstore with its excellent list of rare and unique books on the subjects discussed in *Children Of The Matrix*. Hidden Mysteries can also be contacted via:

Hidden Mysteries
P.O. Box 950
Yoakum, Texas 77995
361-293-7698

info@hiddenmysteries.com
http://www.hiddenmysteries.com

www.davidicke.com

One of the world's most visited websites on conspiracy material. More than 600,000 "hits" in its first year and visitors have doubled and more in the second year. Page hits are running at *half a million* a week – and growing all the time.

3,500 webpages of detailed information on all the subjects covered in this book – and more. The site is updated with current information every day and includes the award-winning *Reptilian Archives*, a library of ancient and modern information, and personal experiences of the reptilian connection.

Many attempts have been made to close down *davidicke.com* and hack into the system to disrupt this site. But we're still here. See for yourself the information they are trying to block.

Bring David Icke to your city or conference

If you would like David Icke to speak at your conference or public meeting, contact Royal Adams in the United States, **tel: 636-458-7824** or **fax: 636-458-7823**

For British and European inquires, contact Bridge of Love, **tel/fax: 01983 566002**

Can you help?

If you have any information you think will help David Icke in his research, please write to, or email, him at one of the addresses on the back page.

Please source the information wherever you can and it will be held in the strictest confidence.

To order David Icke's books and tapes, contact one of the following:

UK　　　　　**Bridge of Love Publications UK**
　　　　　　　PO Box 43
　　　　　　　Ryde
　　　　　　　Isle of Wight
　　　　　　　PO33 2YL　　　tel/fax:　**01983 566002**
　　　　　　　England　　　　email:　　**dicke75150@aol.com**

USA　　　　**Bridge of Love Publications USA**
　　　　　　　c/o Bookworld
　　　　　　　1933 Whitfield Park Loop
　　　　　　　Sarasota　　　　tel:　　　**636 458 7824**
　　　　　　　Florida 34243　fax:　　　**636 458 7823**
　　　　　　　USA　　　　　　email:　　**bridgeloveUSA@aol.com**
　　　　　　　　　　　　　　　order number:　**1-800-444-2524**

AUSTRALIA　**Bridge of Love Publications**
　　　　　　　PO Box 5155
　　　　　　　Daisy Hill　　　tel:　　　**61 7 3209 7902**
　　　　　　　Queensland 4127　fax:　　**61 7 3209 9906**
　　　　　　　Australia　　　freecall:　**1 800 099 902**

Visit the David Icke website:

www.davidicke.com

to order directly via the Internet